Frances Fyfield is a criminal lawyer, a profession that has inspired and informed her novels, though not exclusively. She is widely translated, winner of the Crime Writer's Association Silver Dagger and the Prix de Litterature Policière in France. Several of her books have been televised. She lives in London and in Deal.

D1080593

FRANCES FYFIELD OMNIBUS

Seeking Sanctuary

The Nature of the Beast

Frances Fyfield

sphere

SPHERE

This omnibus edition first published in Great Britain in 2007 by Sphere
Copyright © Frances Fyfield 2007

Previously published separately:
Seeking Sanctuary first published in Great Britain in 2003 by Little, Brown
Paperback edition published by Time Warner Paperbacks in 2004
Copyright © Frances Fyfield 2003
The Nature of the Beast first published in Great Britain in 2001
by Little, Brown
Paperback edition published by Time Warner Paperbacks in 2002
Copyright © Frances Fyfield 2001

The moral right of the author has been asserted.

A CIP catalogue record for this book is available from the British Library.

ISBN: 978-0-7515-4009-3

Papers used by Sphere are natural, recyclable products made from
wood grown in sustainable forests and certified in accordance with
the rules of the Forest Stewardship Council.

Printed and bound in Great Britain by Clays Ltd, St Ives plc
Paper supplied by Hellefoss AS, Norway

Sphere
An imprint of
Little, Brown Book Group
Brettenham House
Lancaster Place
London WC2E 7EN

A Member of the Hachette Livre Group of Companies

www.littlebrown.co.uk

Seeking Sanctuary

For Donna Leon

PROLOGUE

(Documents in the possession of K. McQ., E. Smith and one other, viz, one draft will and one final version, for dispersal as and when necessary.)

Document 1

DRAFT WILL

Dear Smith, I'm returning the draft will, with explanatory notes. I wish to die very soon, so get on with it, I can't stand it any more. If I die and someone comes for me, I'd rather it was Satan than God.

THIS IS THE LAST WILL AND TESTAMENT of me, Theodore Calvert. *(With bugger all to show for myself except a house, a friend and an obscene amount of money. Everything else is lost.)*

1. I hereby revoke all other wills and testamentary dispositions made by me, prior to the date of this, my last will. *(Fifteen, at the last count.)*

2. I appoint E. Smith, solicitor, to be the executor and trustee of this my will, with power to appoint an additional executor and trustee if he thinks fit.

3. I wish to be cremated. *(I mean, burned to a crisp after death, without prayers of any kind, and my ashes thrown in the face of the nearest priest to show my contempt.)*

3

4. The said E. Smith, or any executor or trustee whosoever he shall appoint, engaged in a legal capacity, shall be paid all usual professional charges for work or business done in proving my will or in the execution of or in connection with the trust thereof, including work or business of a professional nature which a trustee could do personally. (Blah, blah, blah.)

5. I leave the following specific bequests:

To Kay McQuaid, the sum of £20,000 per annum, as long as she is resident in my house. (Is that enough? She never did me a bad turn, did she? Or did she? Only person I trust, anyway.)

6. SUBJECT TO AND AFTER PAYMENT of my just debts, funeral and testamentary expenses, I GIVE, DEVISE AND BEQUEATH all my real and personal estate whatsoever and wheresoever not otherwise disposed of by this my will, inclusive of anything I might stand to inherit, unto my trustees upon trust to sell, call in and convert the same into money, with power to postpone the sale, calling and conversion thereof as long as they shall in their absolute discretion think fit. (Blah, blah, blah.) My trustees shall hold the net proceeds of sale, calling and conversion upon trust for a period of two years after my death, paying any existing standing orders specified in the addendum to this my will, in the meantime. (Blah.)

7. I GIVE, DEVISE AND BEQUEATH the proceeds of the said trust fund to my two daughters, to be shared between them equally ON CONDITION THAT for the aforesaid period of two years, they remain free of SIN. (No, I do not mean they should obey the ten commandments and all that crap of the catechism of their mother's ghastly church. I mean

4

real SIN. I want them to <u>blaspheme</u>, dance on graves, do sloth, gluttony and wildness, but you said I couldn't make it a condition. Conditions have to be negative. I wish them to be <u>rude</u> and <u>rebellious</u> and even <u>disgusting</u>. I don't believe in SIN, but I want them to know what the avoidance of it involves. I wish them ANYTHING but their mother's destructive piety.)

For the purposes of this my will, SIN is hereby defined as INCEST, CRUELTY and TREACHERY. The commission of the sin will be self-evident. (Your advice to limit it. This is not a random selection. I can't think of anything worse than the categories I've described, except murder, and all these involve murder of the soul. These are the sins of which I was accused, always <u>in the name of God</u>, by my wife, and the only ones I have never committed. Gettit?)

8. IN THE EVENT of either of my daughters being discovered to have been in the commission of any of the aforesaid variations of SIN, the bequest to them fails and the residue of my estate shall pass to Jack McQuaid, absolutely. (Why? You idiot, why? Because it might, just might, redeem him, and if not, it may as well go to the devil as anywhere else.)

Signed by the said THEODORE CALVERT as his last will in the presence of us both present at the same time who in his presence and in the presence of each other have hereunto subscribed our names as witnesses.

(Don't ask why, Smith. I am going away into that dark night and shall be gone for a long time. Grief kills me. Just do as I ask, for Godsakes.

5

I don't mean for GOD'S SAKE. NOTHING is for God's sake. I HATE GOD, I hate God ... I hate that Christ and all his shoddy saints. I hate the level to which my daughters are reduced. I hate the God of my wife, a perverted, obsessive Christian who raised my children steeped in holiness, cocooned and stole them from me, taught them to hate me, and I hate the Church, which moulded her madness and fear of the devil. And taught me, thereby, what hell is like. It is losing the recognition of your own flesh and blood and having them revile you. It is the knowledge of hatred and impotence and heartbreak, being useless and watching your children wasting their lives. It is being eaten alive with love and regret. Hell is HERE.

Send this back quickly. I want to die.

Document 2

FINAL VERSION

This is the Last Will and Testament of me, Theodore Calvert.

1. I hereby revoke all other wills and testamentary dispositions made by me.

2. I hereby appoint E. Smith, solicitor, to be the executor and trustee of this my will, with power to appoint an additional executor and trustee if he thinks fit.

3. I wish to be cremated.

4. The said E. Smith, or any executor or trustee whosoever he shall appoint, engaged in a legal capacity, shall be

paid all usual professional charges for work or business done in proving my will or in the execution of or in connection with the trust thereof, including work or business of a professional nature which a trustee could do personally.

5. I leave the following specific bequest: To Kay McQuaid, the sum of £20,000 and the residency of my house for two years.

6. SUBJECT TO AND AFTER PAYMENT of my just debts, funeral and testamentary expenses, I GIVE, DEVISE AND BEQUEATH all my real and personal estate whatsoever and wheresoever not otherwise disposed of by this my will, inclusive of anything I might stand to inherit, unto my trustees upon trust to sell, call in and convert the same into money, with power to postpone the sale, calling in and conversion thereof as long as they shall in their absolute discretion think fit. My trustees shall hold the net proceeds of sale, calling in and conversion upon trust for a period of two years after my death, paying any existing standing orders during the meantime.

7. I GIVE, DEVISE AND BEQUEATH the proceeds of the said trust fund to my two daughters to be shared between them, equally, ON CONDITION THAT for the aforesaid period of two years, they shall both remain free of SIN. For the purpose of this my will, SIN is hereby defined as INCEST, CRUELTY AND TREACHERY. The commission of the sin will be self-evident.

8. IN THE EVENT of either of my daughters being discovered to have been in the commission of any of the aforesaid variations of SIN, the bequest to them shall fail and the residue of my estate shall pass to Jack McQuaid, on sufficient proof of his identity, absolutely.

Signed by the said THEODORE CALVERT as his last will, in the presence of us both present at the same time, who in his presence and in the presence of each other have hereunto subscribed our names as witnesses.

[signature]

WITNESSES:

[witness signature and address]

[witness signature and address]

CHAPTER ONE

Honour the Lord your God

The convent chapel was as warm as a hospital ward. The climate inside was humid with a series of scents, wilting flowers, disinfectant, damp overcoats, starch from the bright, white chasuble of the Bishop, the odour of sanctity from his hat and the overpowering, choking smell of incense. The receiving of the Eucharist followed a sermon lacking either real conviction or sincerity. Anna Calvert watched the row of nuns waiting to receive the Sacrament before resuming their places on the opposite side of the aisle from where she sat, and blew her nose.

The oldest of the Sisters had died; granted she had died at an age and condition that made death appropriate, a release from discomfort bravely borne and the final stage on a long, narrow pathway to heaven, but it still marked the final breath of a good heart. They were celebrating the death of a woman whose achievements and profound influence the Bishop chose not to mention, and Anna wondered why. It was an occasion for praise, but he seemed to have difficulty in remembering names and elected instead to deliver a homily on the state of the Catholic Church, peppered with dire messages along the lines of how we must all, even the deceased, atone for our sins.

Anna blew her nose again and eased the damp collar of her blouse from the back of her neck to relieve her own sense of puzzlement. Why was it so airless? The window behind the altar curved gracefully towards the ceiling in as perfect a peak as the Bishop's hat, shaped to reach out to heaven, and the trees, visible through the glass, making it seem as if they were in a forest of birches. She looked sideways towards her younger sister, Therese, who sat on the other side of the aisle next to the other nuns, looking ridiculously young in their elderly company. Therese, who was also looking towards her with equal anxiety, twiddled her fingers in a minute, secret signal of reassurance and rolled her eyes. Anna ducked her head to hide a smile of relief. Maybe there were some advantages in such a dry, impersonal service that inhibited tears.

What did the Bishop mean by *sins*? Sister Jude had been able to define malice, because she was fond of definitions, and she may have made mistakes, but *sin* was something quite unknown to her, unless humour and irreverence counted, which, judging from the style and content of this miserable, artificial ritual, they did. Good taste and emotion were also notable for their absence. Sister Jude was the aunt of Anna's late mother, but also a tutor, friend and inspiration, mentor and sufficiently grand, substitute grandmother. She had been a teacher in the real world: she had been a piece of wonder. She had provided stability and wisdom to this small community of Sisters. And, although she might have quarrelled frequently with her great-niece, the only inconsiderate thing she had done was to die when she was still needed, like everyone else had done. Overwhelmed by loss, Anna reminded herself that the act of dying had not been wilful, to use one of Jude's words. It had merely been a question of everything else but the mind wearing out.

The old Sisters stood in a row, heads bowed, hands clasped in the attitude of servants, looking like a set of tearless statues. It was a drab occasion, Anna thought with a spurt of despair; dry and drab. No weeping or wailing, the only gnashing of teeth her own. Formulaic, taped music, dull prayers intoned dully, no sense of occasion or grief. Service number 52, as bland and impersonal as breakfast cereal, peculiarly loveless and as such, an aid to self-control.

The heat exaggerated the scent of the lilies she had provided, left overnight in the chapel along with the body in the coffin and now almost dead, while tiny Sister Jude, her most consistent if critical friend, despite a difference of fifty years, began to putrefy. There had been no substance in those bones and no sin, either. The drone of prayer failed to do justice either to the dead or to the unspoilable dimensions of the chapel. For the sake of the living, Anna swallowed the thistle of tears.

They crowded out from the soft light inside and spilled, politely, through the building and out into the road at the front, single file through the narrow door. Therese joined her. She tucked a stray strand of Anna's hair behind her ear and Anna did the same for her, before they linked elbows tightly as they walked to the funeral cars. The rough material of Therese's long-sleeved tunic felt warm against Anna's skin. She squeezed her arm gratefully and felt the pressure returned. The cemetery was miles away. They sat in one of three sumptuous vehicles, which looked suitable for the carriage of a visiting pope, and watched the rain form into glistening drops against the windows. Admiring

11

glances were cast at the two blonde girls, so indisputably sisters, sitting calmly with their fingers interlaced, intensely proud of one another. They united to put at ease the two ex-pupils and a relative of the deceased from the unknown side of the family they had never met, all conscientious Catholics complimenting the service and applauding the presence of the Bishop.

The route out to the suburbs and beyond was long and ugly, a last tedious journey in search of the appropriate cemetery for the exclusive use of those of the faith.

'She might have preferred a field,' Anna murmured to Therese.

'She'd have loved this upholstery,' Therese said, both of them suppressing a sudden desire to giggle, which seemed to go with the occasion. The funeral cortège passed the wire fencing surrounding an industrial complex and then the cars wound uphill to the cemetery with its view of the wire fences beneath and the grey sky beyond. Anna did not want her to be buried here. It seemed the final indignity to be interred among everlasting flowers on graves to the mumble of prayers by rote in that condescending idiom, which had begun to enrage her.

The words at the graveside were as neutral as those indoors and there was a rule that governed funerals, dictating that it should always rain and that all persons present should behave with a shifty stiffness as if under suspicion themselves. They gathered round the hole in the ground as the coffin was lowered and water sprinkled upon it from a plastic bottle by the deputy substituted for the Bishop, who had already gone on to another appointment. He intoned the prayers in the manner of one practising fast elocution by reading the telephone directory, and Anna had the urge to fling her piece of earth over the crowd instead of letting it drop on the casket where the other pieces of earth landed with small, thumping sounds as if they were pelting the dead. Shoulder to shoulder with Therese, anger and indignation began to fill her head like a mushroom cloud, until she thought she would explode with it. Therese leant against her.

Then the contemporaries of Sister Jude, four of the very oldest Sisters, Matilda, Agnes, Joseph and Margaret, with gowns and veils flapping in the wet breeze, suddenly stepped forward in unison. With one accord, led by Margaret, they began to sing.

Salve, Regina, mater misericordia,
Vita, dulcedo, et spes nostra salve,
Ad te clamamus, exules filii hevae.

Hail, Holy Queen, mother of mercy, hail our life, our sweetness and our hope . . . Thin, reedy, elderly voices of peculiar, wistful beauty. They huddled together, feet planted uncertainly in the muddy earth excavated from the grave, the plainchant wavering, the notes as clear as the chiming of bells, the sound of it spontaneous and pure. Lumpen women, singing to the greater glory of God, with lungs and hearts and soul. *O clemens, O pia, O dulcis Virgo Maria* . . .

For a moment, Anna knew them.

They both wept, she and Therese, in each other's arms, with their feet rooted into damp grass, weeping as if it would never end. Weeping in loss and bewilderment, while Anna also wept with sheer frustration, because from beyond her grave, Sister Jude had done it again. Set the hound of heaven upon her *again*: she could hear the beast baying and Jude's light recitation of her favourite poem,

13

echoing behind the singing. *I fled Him, down the nights and down the days; I fled Him down the arches of the years; I hid from Him . . .* The sound died on the air. The noise of distant traffic intruded, subduing the slighter sounds of flourished handkerchiefs, shuffling feet and grief.

'You remember that poem she liked so much?' Anna mumbled to Therese. 'Say you do.'

'Course I do,' Therese said, into her ear. 'Yes, I do.'

From those strong feet that followed, followed after . . .
They beat – and a Voice beat
More instant than the feet –
'All things betrayest thee, who betrayest Me.'

Therese's hand on her shoulder moved to stroke the back of her neck, reluctant to let her go.

'Just keep saying it, Anna. Say it again and again. It's a good one. Will you be all right?'

'Yes. We have to be, don't we?'

'We should be used to it by now. Us dear little orphans. Poor little us.'

Anna smiled slightly at that, dashed at the tears on her face with a fist, leaving a red mark on her cheek. The mocking of any suggestion of self-pity was a running joke between them.

'Hey, sis, less of the *little*. I suppose you're going back with the old crows?'

'I must. Sister Joseph is beside herself . . . you understand?'

'Course I do. Don't worry.'

'You won't come in for lunch?'

'You know I won't. Take care, love.'

Anna did understand. Therese was her real sister, but

14

the Sisters were her family now, as they had been for over a year, and all the same the priorities hurt like a blister. So much that she found she was murmuring that wretched poem with imperfect memory as the car to which she was directed filled and the occupants shrank away from her. A pretty *little* girl who muttered words to herself and manufactured an inane grin.

'Sorry,' she gabbled with manic cheerfulness. 'I was trying to remember her favourite poem. About God chasing a soul all over the world . . . She made me learn it off by heart. Do you know it? And isn't the Bishop a SILLY OLD FART?'

A parishioner patted her hand, in pretended understanding. After all, the dear deceased had never distinguished in life between the mad and the sane, and it was better to follow that good example than be shocked. The sun broke through and the group of four eased themselves into platitudes as they drove back, with Anna hunched in the corner, disturbingly silent. She slipped out of the car without farewells as it came to a halt beside the narrow door, ran to the end of the road and disappeared, knowing with a flush of humiliation how they would see her now. A strange, spoiled child, they said. How old was she? Twenty-two, apparently, looking fifteen. Such a small girl. A little touched in the head, maybe.

She went left and left again, on to the main road. Left again, past the walls of the convent, which looked like any other walls, up the road on the left and into the block of flats where she lived. The more direct route into the convent would have been through the back door into their garden, which she passed on the way, but nobody ever used that. The door was embedded into the wall and almost obscured with ivy. Once inside her apartment block in the next-door building, she ran up the five flights to her own, took off her tidy clothes, put on T-shirt and shorts and went up to the roof.

The route to the roof was via a retractable stepladder from her attic living room, out through a dormer window not intended as an exit, on to a flat surface flanked by a parapet that went two thirds of the way round. Anna had told Sister Jude that this was the true kingdom of heaven. A small walkway surrounding a raised roof, housing a ventilation shaft and other furniture such as an open tank covered with wire. Heaven, if anywhere, was above the height of the trees, with sufficient space to lie in the lead-lined gunwales and catch the sun.

From the back, with her elbows propped on the parapet, she could see the convent garden. Straight into it, or as straight as it could be in the late reaches of summer, before the foliage began to go. It was ironic that in wintertime, when the human movement in this garden was minimal, she had the greatest chance to spy, whereas in summer, when there was far more to watch, she was forced to see it in tantalising glimpses down through the trees. There were the smaller trees at this end, wavering things, beastly sycamores, the weed of trees, but loved by birds. The ivy covered the inside walls; there were numerous shrubs and overflowing berberis and blackcurrant bushes. Still, she could see the paths in the wilderness, and Edmund, the gardener, sitting on a bench by his shed in the clearing at the end, getting his breath. Edmund was always getting his breath. Through the trees, she could see how his belly flowed to his thighs and the empty barrow by his side was in danger of capsizing. A youth came and joined him, lifted him gently by the arm and took him into the shade.

Anna frowned, forgetting the grief for a full minute.

The sight of this youth made her heart skip a beat. She had seen him before, several times, but she did not know who he was and she needed to know who everyone was because it was part of her mission to look after Therese and make sure she was safe. He had yellow hair before the trees obscured him and he had become, insidiously, part of the landscape. They should get a tree surgeon to those trees – there were too many sycamores, they starved the ground upon which they grew – but not even Sister Barbara would hire a tree surgeon to perform on the day of a funeral, because those days became a Sabbath and anyway, all surgeons cost money. Breeze stirred the trees, which were shabby in late summer; the same breeze stirred Anna's long hair. Restlessly, she prowled round the small domain of the roof space, holding on to the parapet with one hand. It was chest height; she could not have fallen over, but she always held it as she moved.

On the south side of the roof space, she could look down into the road, which was a fine contrast with the peace of the overgrown garden. It was a single carriageway road with a small row of shops, café, the Oppo Bar, the delicatessen, florist and upmarket grocery with newspapers, luxury shops, to complement the residents with money in a pleasant part of London. Plenty to watch from up here, from the emptying Oppo Bar at night, to the greengrocer unloading in the morning, with the satisfaction of bad-tempered traffic jams around parked cars at rush hour. It was early afternoon quiet. Anna returned to the garden side, sat with her back to the parapet wall with a view of nothing but her own feet. Out of the breeze, the heat warmed her; she kicked off her shoes and cried a little more.

It was as well Therese had not come straight out into the

17

garden, but then she never did. Her flesh and blood sister, not her sister in Jesus bloody Christ, but the dear one who had once been called by another name and was now called Therese. If she had seen her, she might have shouted down at her, *Are you really all right? Are you sure?* and only been heard as a distant shout, enough to give away the game and reveal the very act of watching. Therese, we are too young to be bereaved, like this. We have no one left. What did we do to deserve it? Where are you, *sister* Therese? Doing God's will in the kitchen? Oh, you stupid, beautiful drudge.

The convent drawing room was heavy with the scent of flowers removed from the chapel. Father Goodwin held his teacup awkwardly and reflected briefly on the fact that in all the years he had been coming here, he had never yet managed to explain to them how he preferred instant coffee in a mug and a seat by a kitchen table, to the faded glories and polish smell of this receiving room. Rooms like this were peculiar to convents; he never encountered them anywhere else. A room saved for best, like an old-fashioned parlour and referred to as such, used only on high days and holidays, cleaned within an inch of its life in the meantime and furnished with a couple of solid sideboards, circa 1930, too heavy to shift, too ugly to be saleable. At least, he noted with approval, there was the underlying smell of tobacco and the pile of plastic stacking chairs in the corner, which indicated it had once been used far more than it was currently, before Barbara arrived as a relatively recent Sister Superior. It had justified its spacious existence with meetings of Alcoholics Anonymous once a week, the Mothers' Guild and other charities, which Barbara had decided simply did not pay. He thought he

18

might prefer the company of the Alcoholics to that of Sister Barbara and then he reminded himself of his Christian conscience. She was a good woman and if she was also insensitive, that was forgivable. She was trying to preserve the unpreservable and the vulnerable, and there was a certain virtue in it. She was also a woman of genuine conscience, a listener, capable of changing her mind. Sometimes she was limited by lack of imagination. What else could he expect? He drained the teacup with loud appreciation and thought first of what a hypocrite that made him and then, wistfully, of what he was missing on television. Arsenal *v.* Tottenham. The Races. That was what he had planned for the afternoon before he caught the train.

'It was a good send-off, Father. The family were very pleased. I wished you'd have been there.'

'So do I. But you wanted the Bishop and I had another dying soul. Dermot Murray, did you ever know him?'

He did not say that he had been glad of the intervention of duty. Sister Jude had been an obdurate friend and her demise made him sick to the heart. Barbara did not know Dermot Murray and she did not care. She crossed herself quickly.

'A very good send-off. Even with her loss, little Therese excelled herself with the lunch, they ate it all. I don't know how she manages with that foul-mouthed girl alongside. Who must be a trial to her. She's so conscientious, so *mature*, for twenty-one.' She leaned forward, confidentially. 'And do you know what, Father? The contributions were tremendous. We're actually in profit. The undertaker always does me a good deal. We might branch out into doing funerals, professionally, even weddings, perhaps. We're committed to Sunday Mass, of course. The chapel,

19

as the Bishop says, is a resource. Should I have taken the money from the relatives? Still, they should be grateful we've kept Sister Jude for all these years.'

He did not suggest that such gratitude was inappropriate. Jude's pension had kept her; a good pension after forty years' teaching, pocketed by the Order in return for hospice care. She was not a charity case. She had been an investment. This was not a diplomatic suggestion, simply one that crossed his mind. He had been fond of Sister Jude, an intellectual of the most pragmatic kind, a lover of gossip and laughter and the keeper of secrets. Through her, he understood this institution better than he might have done if his only source of information was the Principal, whom he faced across the teacups. The strain of the day and the week before was beginning to tell on her. Barbara was in charge of a dying institution, but it did not make her immune to the personal force of death. Everyone had loved Jude, although some, like Barbara, had also been afraid of her.

'Father, I can't stand it. I wonder if God put me upon earth to tolerate a set of mostly elderly eccentrics gathered under the same roof, for a terrible number of different reasons. As well as bad language from the staff.'

'Yes, he did.'

'And do I have to tolerate the council tax and that greasy estate agent writing to me every day, telling me how much the place is worth?'

'Yes, you do.'

'And do I have to put up with the Bishop's bursar phoning on a weekly basis, suggesting the place must be commercially viable, pull its weight, or otherwise it goes on the market and the Sisters out to grass?'

'Yes, you do.'

'And do I have to live in a building that is falling apart in all directions because we can't pay anyone to get anything mended? And do I have to live with that wilderness of garden and the old goat of a gardener who's fit for nothing any more?'

'Yes.' His breath became shorter and he was dreaming of football. Dreaming of another kind of *YES*, the roar from the terraces on his television screen, which would leave him punching the air, incoherent with pleasure.

'And do I, and the rest of us, have to put up with that vicious little minx coming in and out as she pleases, simply because her sister Therese is one of us and she herself lives so near? Do I have to do it, now her aunty's dead? The minx, the silly—'

'*YES!*' he shouted. 'YES! Especially, YES.'

She was stunned into silence, put down her own teacup with extreme caution and quietness before she remembered to close her mouth. 'Why?'

He paused. 'Because she is shunned by heaven and poised for hell. You, we, cannot take responsibility for pushing her in either direction. You *must* let her in. Whenever she wants.'

There was a fly buzzing at the window, unlamented. He longed to swat it at the same time as feeling grateful for the distraction of the noise. The game would be half over by now, even allowing for histrionics and injuries. Sister Barbara adjusted the folds of her skirt, disturbed, unconvinced, disappointed with everything, even the fly. He remembered diplomacy.

'Anna could be very useful to you. And besides, they stand to inherit a great deal of money,' he added, hating himself.

'Who told you that?' she asked sharply.

'Sister Jude did. Of course, she was a great friend to the

21

whole family, before the girls were . . . ill. And before their mother, poor soul, lost her reason.' He was choosing his words carefully.

'Oh Lord, I knew Isabel Calvert, too,' she said, decisively. 'We were at the same school for a while. She was very devout, even then, poor woman. A lesson to us all. Marries a rich man that much older and what does she get? A swine who abandons her with two sick children. It just shows you the dangers of not marrying a Catholic. Did Jude also tell you he'd abused the girls?' She leaned forward confidentially. '*Sexually*, I mean.'

'She did tell me that suggestion had been made,' he said delicately. The fly continued its futile racket. 'I understand it to have been her opinion that the abusive parent, if either, was the mother.'

'Absolute nonsense,' Barbara stated. 'Everyone knows the woman was a saint.'

They glared at one another. Christopher Goodwin knew he could not win an argument based on hearsay. He shrugged and smiled, prepared himself to move. Once he got home, he could take off the dog collar. Although he felt as naked without it as Barbara probably would without her uniform, there were days when it was an affliction. Someone must have opened a window to let in the fly: he wished they did it more often.

'Well,' he said, rising, 'the Calvert family brought you the only young novice the Order has attracted in years. There must be something in that. Novices are as rare as hens' teeth, are they not?'

She nodded in reluctant agreement. 'Surely. Therese is a blessing. It's Anna who's the curse.'

'These things are sent to try us,' he murmured, hating the cliché. 'And even a curse can be useful.'

22

He patted her shoulder in the manner of a senior uncle, although she was older than he, marvelling as he did so at the fact that she, the most decisive and competent of women, was always slightly deferential to men. They all were, with the exception of the late Jude, and he was never sure if it was ingrained, or if it was mocking, or if it was the result of a constant need for the foil of masculine opinion. A man could get away with murder in a convent. They were vulnerable to their own deference.

'The boy Edmund has been bringing with him to help is an exceptional worker,' Barbara said, rising and changing the subject while moving to the door in one fluid movement. 'Would he take over on Edmund's wages, do you think?'

'You can't sack Edmund, Sister, you simply can't.'

'I'm *sick* of putting up with lazy second best for the sake of charity, but I suppose you're right. A pity: the boy's a good Catholic.'

Knowing this was the ultimate character reference, Father Goodwin held his peace.

'We'll talk about it at the meeting tomorrow, shall we? Anna said she would come and take the notes. You know how good she is at that, as well as with the suggestions, computer literate, too. She's a breath of air, Sister.'

'Yes, I suppose so.'

They parted beyond the door, she to answer the phone, which shrilled in the near distance of her office, he to make his way to the front door. He was fond of this particular corridor, although always preferring it on the way out to the way in. The floor was flagged with black and white stone, diamond shaped, and the walls were panelled with warm wood, reminiscent of the graciously clumsy house it had been and where the relics of the former beauty now remained solely in the corridor, the refectory and the chapel. It had been bequeathed to the Order in the last century by a holy spinster, who had run her family house as a primary school for the poor of the area. The nuns were to continue her good work and reside in her house for ever. But the school was long closed; the place was a home for those in the Order either in transit or too old for further use, while outside its walls, the poor of the parish were thin on the ground.

Sister Agnes was waiting in her seat by the door, where she sat for most of the day in her small cubby hole, occupying a hard seat, reading in the poor light from the leaded panes of the window next to her head and never looking at ease, even when she was asleep. Why, for Lord's sake, did she not have a better chair? He looked at her fondly as she struggled to her feet and opened the door he could easily have opened for himself. She was dimpled and pink-cheeked and plump and breathless, with the smile of an angel. He always wanted to hug her and plant a big smacking kiss on her papery cheek, and he never did.

So, he argued to himself as he walked quickly down the street in the evening sun, feeling as he always did after interviews with Barbara as if he had been let out of school, the place does have a purpose after all. It is to keep women like Agnes, who could no longer live in any other way, safe and free from harm, locked inside a goldmine. It crossed his mind to visit Anna Calvert, but God help him, he was charged with so much to tell her, he did not have the strength and he did not want to ring her doorbell praying she would be out at work. Besides, she would be back inside the chapel later, saying her own version of prayers; she would not be able to resist that. The child haunted the chapel. God would help her. Father Christopher Goodwin changed his mind about going home at all, and went for the train. The Lord was also served by partaking of the pleasures of friendship and any man had to pace himself, even a priest.

Such a *deceitful* door, Anna thought, a door that gives no indication of what lies behind it. It was flush with the wall and the pavement, with a spiteful lintel above it, so that rain dripped directly on to the head of a waiting visitor on rainy days. The fabric of the door was wooden and cracked with something churchlike about its unvarnished, faded contours and the discreet mullioned window, about the size of a tile, set at eye level. The bell was on the side, high in the wall, so that she had to reach to ring it. A normal height person would not have to stand so close to the door to demand entry in this way, but Anna did. She was so small she could shop in the children's department: it was as if her height had failed to grow into the maturity of her figure. She reached for the bell, almost pressing herself to the wood, and then stood back, quickly. The door had a way of taking a person by surprise. Agnes lurked behind it, hardly ever bothering to look through the window, the worst, most indiscriminate doorkeeper they could have chosen, but there was no choice because this was her self-appointed task and she was not to be separated from it. The bell rang; she answered it. If she operated by anything, it was smell rather than sight. She would let in the devil, even without sheep's clothing, and when she saw it was Anna, turned away in disappointment, holding the door open politely nevertheless. Anna was hardly a novelty and not even a sinner, although in Agnes's eyes, sin was the privilege of men.

'I'm sorry for your loss, Anna. Did you want Therese?'

25

she asked in her quavering voice. 'It's six o'clock, you know. She may be resting before supper.'

'No. Thank you.'

The 'thank you' sounded hollow. Anna strode down the black and white corridor, which always, somehow, pleased her. The tiles were worn to a dull sheen in the centre, the black sharper at the edges near the panelled walls. The geometric pattern invited a game of hopscotch, the way she had played when she came here first as a reluctant child visitor, only slightly fascinated by the prospect of visiting someone described as an aunt, but very old, dressed in a bonnet and looking like a bat. Sulky, dragged by her mother to see her mother's Aunt Jude. Therese trailing behind and hiding resentment with better success than her elder sibling because she was instantly charmed by the place and she was, in any event, instinctively charming herself. Anna had remained churlish until she was told, yes, she could hopscotch on those black and white tiles and go into the garden and shout if she liked. A little noise would do the place good, Jude said, which puzzled her in retrospect since there had been a small Montessori school for fifteen girls held in a single classroom to the side of the corridor in those days. A long time ago. Sixteen years.

The chapel looked spare without a coffin and the profusion of flowers, a large enough room to seat fifty with ease and in the current state of emptiness smaller, cooler, sweeter than ever. There was a traditional altar against the back wall, and a long, narrow table in front for the preparation of Communion. Dominating the whole, elegant room, the crucifix hung centre stage across the tall window, which arched to the ceiling, letting in a strong, colourless light that beat against the Cross, so that it cast a shadow from the window to the door and the figure of the crucifix

26

was blurred and featureless. Anna crossed herself with the automatic gesture of one who had learned how at the same time she had learned speech, nodding at the figure.

'OK, Jesus? Is your dad in tonight?'

The silence was profound. She crossed her arms. Behind the face of the Son, there was always that of the Father. Preferably, a round-faced paterfamilias, like an old Italian restaurateur.

'Oh, stop messing about. You heard me.'

The birch trees in full leaf flicked against the curved window. The small windows, set high on each side of it, shone like jewels. There was a draught from one of those, opened with a pole to clear the incense and mercifully forgotten. Christ drooped on his cross. Anna nodded, satisfied by the sounds of the trees.

'OK, you're in tonight. Where the hell were you this morning, Lord?'

The crucifix did not answer. She sat, cross-legged, in the centre of the aisle. There was a low rail separating her from the area of the altar, not intended as a barrier between officiating priest and congregation, but a simple necessity for those who could only kneel with a little support. Some of the nuns insisted upon kneeling to take Communion; those in tune with modern traditions stood. Easier for the priest if they knelt, especially if the priest was like Father Goodwin, permanently stooped although nimble enough when he raced down the road away from the place. Still, he beat the shit out of that Bishop.

'You definitely weren't here this morning, Lord. The whole thing was perfectly, bloody godless.'

The silence was incomplete. She could hear the tall birch trees breathing through the high window behind the altar. It was the window that lent the place distinction, curving the full height of the high wall in the shape of an upturned boat, with the leaded panes in the shape of elongated diamonds, smoky glass, slightly blue with no other colours, giving the place a bright but subdued glow, even when the sun hit hardest. Framed in pale oak, the window seemed as if it was leaning in towards her, as if she was sitting in the shelter of the boat; it embraced. The crucifix was made of the same pale wood as the surround of the window. She could see it more clearly from the aisle as she sat in the shadow of it. The figure lounging uncomfortably upon it, with well-muscled arms, elongated torso and, to Anna's mind, greasy, outmoded hair in an unbecoming shade of brown, looked as if he might have been in an Armani suit, or at least, if lain flat, slightly contorted on a deckchair. The face had the look of a hangover, a slack mouth, and half-closed eyes. Refined puzzlement was the most prominent impression and for a murdered man in a cumbersome loincloth, he was remarkably clean and free of blood, far more an effete Italian than a chunky carpenter.

When Anna spoke to God, or as like as not, hectored him, she spoke to the God who had inspired the window, rather than this depiction of his son *in extremis*, but her eyes still strayed to the vague face of the crucifix.

'You know what?' she said. 'You can't make up your mind if you want them to be sorry for you or fancy you.'

She was jeering without shouting. Even in the worst throes of anger, contempt and frustration, she could not shout in the chapel. In the street, she could yell, she could raise two fingers and bawl at strangers, but in here she could not shout although she often longed to do so. In here, a shout would become little more than a whisper. There was still the lingering smell of the incense, an aftertaste from the earlier service despite the open window.

'I cannot understand,' Anna said, 'why, if you really live in this place, with all this light, you let them coop you up without air. Then let them fill the place with smells. You've no control, Lord, you really haven't.'

She removed herself from the middle of the aisle and sat on one of the chairs. They had rush-covered seats, which tickled the back of her knees. The neglect of human comfort infuriated her. Even God did not demand it.

'I have come, dear Lord, to announce my *evil* intentions. Do you hear me?'

The sun was passing over the window. Once, she had believed that the shafts of sunlight that shone from behind clouds signalled the presence of angels and it was the angels who finally blew away the clouds. Sometime later in the history of her imagination, the shafts of sunshine became a kind of heavenly semaphore between saints.

'Dear Lord, I am going out to intoxicate myself and possibly fornicate. In other words, get off my face and maybe find a shag.'

The wind made a soothing noise in the birches. Again as a child, she had thought that the sound of the wind in the trees was the sound of God, breathing. Because God, she had been told, made everything and she could not imagine a silent Creator. A God who had made the world would surely signal the fact by making as much row as possible. All natural sounds belonged to God; only the sounds of cars and aeroplanes and machinery belonged to man.

'Did you hear me?'

Get drunk and have a shag? Which commandment did that offend?

'All right, then. I could strangle Agnes on the way. That would make it worse, wouldn't it?'

Yes.

Anna spread her hands in despair.

'Damn you, how can you do this to us? Oh, I don't mean me in particular, but them. Why are you letting this place go to hell and why have you trapped her in it? You're the one who seduces virgins like my bloody sister, and you aren't even good-looking. You *bastard*! You *fucking fraud*!'

This time her voice did reach shouting pitch. Almost. As she regretted it, mumbling an apology, she heard the sound of the door behind her. Anna did not move, sat waiting for the footsteps to come towards her, light steps in soft shoes. Therese always wore soft shoes. A figure, taller than her own, sat beside her. Out of the corner of her downturned eyes, Anna could see that she held an old missal, which she placed quietly on the seat to her right. Therese always carried something.

'Anna, stop it.'

Anna breathed deeply and let her hands uncurl in her lap. 'Stop what, little sister? I was only praying.'

'Yes, I heard you. You're sad and it always makes you cross. You weren't praying, you were denouncing. Why should Jesus listen to you if you call him a bastard?'

'But that's what he was. Exactly. A bastard, born on the run.'

'Even less reason to abuse him.'

Therese was angry, Anna could tell. She was satisfied. Her gentle, soft-voiced sister vibrated with a fury which would be as it always was, short-lived, ready at the faintest hint to turn itself into forgiveness, understanding or supplication, not necessarily in that order, but with an inevitable, infuriating progress. Even angry, she was full of grace, sitting with her back as straight as a pole, knees

30

together, heels raised off the floor, feet arched like a delicate dancer about to practise.

'Grace is a virtue, virtue is a grace . . .' Anna chanted.

'And Grace is a naughty girl who would not wash her face,' Therese finished. 'But then, there is always amazing grace, how sweet the sound.'

There was an awkward silence for a full minute apart from the murmuring of the trees outside and Therese's soft breathing. Then she touched Anna's bare arm. Anna flinched, until Therese's hand wrapped itself around hers and stayed there.

'Oh, Anna, love, why do you do it? Why do you beat yourself up?'

'And how do you manage to recover so quickly, you cold-hearted niece?'

'Because I had to prepare the food. That was the best I could give. Jude loved food, you know that.'

'God's drudge, that's what you are.'

'So you say, but it's my choice.'

'It's a waste of your life. Cooking food for old women. A con trick, a waste of life.'

'And yours, I suppose, is that much better?'

'I'm free.'

'If you say so.'

There was a contrast in the colour of their skin. Therese's slender forearm emerged from the same plain blue blouse she always wore indoors, an arm as white as milk while Anna's was berry brown. Therese's lack of pigment seemed to her to be a sign of captivity: prisoners looked like that. The anger surfaced again; she struggled to control it.

'I wonder if it was always going to turn out this way. Pre-ordained, if you excuse the expression.'

31

'God's will? I really don't know. All I know is that I am usually perfectly happy and I would dearly wish the same for you.'

'Oh, shuttit. Do you know what you sound like?'

Therese continued to hold her hand firmly. 'Listen, lovey, you can question me as much as you want, but you mustn't worry the others. You can't suggest to women of their age that their lives, lived in faith, are nothing but a sham. It isn't fair. It achieves nothing but pain.'

'What did I say? I merely suggested to bloody Barbara that without the shackles of the Sisterhood, Sister Jude might have been something special. A force in the real world.'

'She *was* a force, you idiot. And without the shackles, she might have been nothing at all. Lost without trace. And so might I.'

'You'd always have me. You always have. I'd hold you up.'

'You aren't enough. No human being is.'

There was a wariness in her voice that suggested a conversation often repeated, if not in the same words, at least with similar themes. Therese lifted the missal from the seat beside her and placed it in Anna's lap.

'The relatives went to her room, to choose whatever they wanted. I got there first.'

'Jude had nothing to leave.'

'She had books and tapes. I took her old missal, for you.'

Anna touched it. It was very old, bursting with holy pictures and notes, held together with an elastic band. It repelled her, slightly. She did not want it and yet knew it was hers.

'Do you want me to go away?' she asked humbly. 'Am I just a nuisance?'

32

'No, of course not. We would all miss you. You should only go when you're ready.'

'Not without you.'

Therese sighed. 'And you tell me *you're* free.'

She detached her hand, gently but finally, pulled Anna's hair and brushed past her bare knees in the calf-length skirt which looked, like her blouse, a well-worn piece of second-hand clothing and smelled, faintly, of the kitchen. She genuflected to the altar, made the sign of the cross and left in her soft shoes. There was a slight draught as the door closed quietly. The room was darker without her. Anna felt thwarted, drummed her feet on the floor. Small feet. The noise was swallowed in the space, but still comforting.

'So you see, Lord,' Anna addressed the trees and the darkening sky of the huge window, 'you see how she trusts me? She leaves me here, knowing I won't wreck the place. Well, don't bank on it. You've wrecked more lives than you've ever saved. Anyway, they can do that all by themselves. You *BASTARD*!'

In the darkening light of the room, the vibrant colours of the Stations of the Cross shone from the walls. The supercilious agony on the face of the crucified Christ remained immobile, along with the pristine white folds of his modest loincloth. She wanted to cut the wire that held the crucifix to the ceiling, watch it fall and break into pieces. She wanted the walls to come tumbling down, like Jericho: she sat still, gripping the seat of the chair and willing it to happen.

Then there was the pistol shot.

One of the large panes of glass in the main window shattered. The glass imploded into the air: a shower of glistening hail caught the light as it cascaded to the floor in

33

silvery fragments, tinkling and colliding, rolling away in a lethal dust until the silence resumed. Anna scrambled from the seat, grabbed the missal and ran for the door. There she stood and looked back. Half of the broken pane remained in the frame, with sharp, jagged edges. The sound of the trees was louder. *Nigh, nigh, draws the chase, With unperturbed pace, Deliberate speed, majestic instancy . . .*

She ran down the black and white corridor and out of the building. Agnes's chair was empty; no one heard. Anna went on running.

In another garden, the jackdaw fell to earth. Kay McQuaid picked up a housebrick to finish it off. Full of fleas.

Got you, by God, you bastard.

CHAPTER TWO

Thou shalt not make to thyself any graven image

The magpie had fallen to earth in a shower of debris. It was no longer the jet black of springtime. Edmund saw the matt dullness of the feathers and the curled feet as he picked it up carefully in a cloth, feeling the warmth of it through the flannel, holding it gingerly in case it should horrify him with a sudden movement, the throb of a heart-beat or the opening of a single eye, but it was dead enough; would have been dead as it fell, dead when the branches of the tree through which it descended caught at its wings and delayed the fall, until it landed in a flurry of feathers and pale green leaves. Edmund wept. Carrying the burden respectfully, arms extended so that it should not be close to his own body, he stumbled from the birch trees along the path towards the bottom of the garden, tears blurring his unsteady progress. Tears and shame. The path was uneven crazy paving. At the end, by the statue, he stumbled. The dead bird fell out of his hands as he collapsed in the attitude of a penitent, falling against the knees of Sister Matilda, who sat calmly on the stone bench, which in turn rested against the ankles of the statue of Michael the Archangel, leader of the angels of God, predominant in the

35

fight against Lucifer. She was telling the rosary from the beads hung at her waist – *Hail Mary, full of Grace, The Lord is with thee, Blessed art thou among women . . .* – beneath the statue of the saintly hero, half-covered in green moss. It had been a damp summer. Edmund's stumbling fall was cushioned by the folds of Matilda's habit, bunched round her knees.

'There, there,' she murmured. 'He'll not have tears before bedtime, you know. Sit down, Edmund, dear.'

Edmund rose, groaning and weeping, sat on the stone bench beside her, muttering the latter half of the prayer he had heard her begin, the sound of it a balm to his spirit. *Holy Mary, Mother of God, Pray for us sinners, Now and at the hour of our death. Holy Mary . . .* It sounded like mumbled swearing. The dead magpie was at his feet. Averting his eyes, he pushed it further away with his foot and looked towards it briefly as he dropped the white cloth, intending to cover the body. The beak of the bird protruded, sleek and dead. Edmund's shoulders heaved with sobs.

'What have I done? What have I done?'

He leaned forward and buried his head in his hands in palms that smelt of death. If he looked, he would see the bird already crawling with maggots, or that was what his eyes would imagine. Matilda placed her ample hand on the broad of his back and rubbed gently. Then she leant forward and hugged him, her arms round his shoulders and her bosom pressed into his spine. He could feel the warmth of her, but it could not yet calm him.

'I heard the blackbird this morning,' he sobbed. 'It was *singing*, singing like it did in April. As if there was a dawn for it. As if it was the end of the world. A blackbird! Singing in September!'

She waited for him. Ever since she had forsaken the

chapel for the garden, hours in his company had informed her of the power of the blackbird's song, how its voice rose and fell, the fount of all music in the dawn choruses of the year. How the jubilant song of it celebrated broods of babies, nests and warmth, and how the nurturing of their life in this garden, alongside his other friends, had been the crowning glory of all the years of Edmund's tenure. Some of it she could hear; some of it she could not with her inconsistent deafness. There was an ongoing family of great tits which fed from his hand, but the blackbirds were the triumph. There were families and visitors, foragers and predators. She withdrew from the hugging of him and resumed a slow, rhythmical rubbing of his back.

'But they don't *sing*, this time of year, do they? I mean, they *call*, but they don't sing. Do they? They've finished singing, you told me.'

'Blackie *sang*, I tell you. He sang the way he sings with a brood in the nest. He *sang*. And then the magpie drove him away.'

Again, she waited, rubbing his back with the one hand, caressing the feet of St Michael with the other. St Michael should have smooth feet, covered in skin-deep gold leaf, warm to the touch. These feet were pock-marked with moss and decay, rough and cold to the touch. Leaning forward, she saw the dead magpie. It was bigger than it looked when it strutted on a branch, smaller than it seemed on the wing. Ugly brute, the noisy bully of the garden, entirely without charm to her mind.

'So, I said . . . I said . . . I said I wished he were dead,' Edmund sobbed. 'Because he's a tyrant. He drives the others away and he eats their young. Most of the year here and I thought he would go. God knows, I've tried to make him uncomfortable. But when the blackbird sang and he drove it away, Oh Lord, I hated him. But kill him? God forgive me.'

'St Michael would forgive you,' she said. 'He would have throttled the horrid thing at birth.'

She turned and looked up at the statue. The feet of the Archangel Michael rested comfortably on a fat stone serpent, which he had clearly overpowered with the spear embedded in the form of it, his hands still holding the shaft, his face upturned to the sky. St Michael occupied the right-hand side of God in heaven. He had led the good angels in the battle against the devil and *he* knew that ultimately, enemies must be killed. Edmund was not like that. To Edmund, the life of a bird was sacrosanct, even a vulture. The sobbing resumed.

'But I only said I *wished* it were dead. I watched it fly and *wished* it. If it had stayed, making that noise, driving the others away before the weather turns cold, they won't come back and nest. I wanted it to go. I didn't mean to kill it.'

Matilda marvelled at the power of prayer, and did not feel a shadow of Edmund's guilt. He had spoken with such vitriol on the subject of the magpie from February right through to July and with greater passion when the other birds, the blackbirds and the great tits, had been brooding in their well-established nests and he had spent a fortune on cheese and nuts to augment the food supply, feeding the magpie too, to keep it quiet. Then it had left. The return had been a bitter blow. She had prayed for the demise of the bully of the garden, and her wish had been granted. The downside of the wish was turning Edmund into a murderer. She wondered how he thought he had killed it. With a catapult, like David did Goliath? Hardly. She smiled and shook her head.

There was no doubt about the ownership of this garden and to whom it was dedicated. It had become designed, cultivated and entirely orchestrated as a reserve for birds. Matilda was always puzzled that no one else in the convent appeared to notice this. It was a secret she shared with Edmund and St Michael and would have loved to share with Sister Joseph, if Joseph were not so transfixed with misery and so irritated by Matilda's intermittent deafness. Everyone else simply accepted the garden as being increasingly impenetrable, blaming Edmund's infirmities and in the case of Barbara, her own indifference to anything that happened beyond the inner walls.

The uncontrolled ivy that covered the back wall unchecked was encouraged to proliferate because certain birds liked it for nesting. The low branches of the newer sycamores were perfect perches for fledglings, who would be in danger if they slept on the ground. The ivy hid Edmund's nesting boxes beloved of the great tit, and the virginia creeper camouflaged the holes in the wall, which he had enlarged in the hope of attracting home the house sparrows and the robin redbreast family, which had sojourned, quarrelsomely, two years before. The blackcurrants were solely for blackbirds. The oversized, ugly garden shed, which was supposed to house Edmund's gardening tools, was bare of anything much except fork, spade, hammer, nails, knives and twine, plus his seat and a sack of grain. Matilda did not know what he had done to deter the London pigeons, but it would never have been poison. She suspected it had been the effective use of a water pistol.

Edmund kept the area nearest the convent building at the back of the chapel neatish and tidyish, with a single flowerbed. Down this end, he let the shrubs encroach, encouraged two small, gloomy holly trees, which were good for winter berries and supporting mistletoe. The over-weening cotoneaster, which crept across the path around the bend from St Michael, had an orange fruit the birds adored. Edmund was a gardener who could not prune.

Matilda withdrew her hand from his back, suddenly disturbed. She held on to her rosary, tightly. The warm wooden beads were a constant comfort. She had learned to slip it in her pocket when she came down this end of the garden, in case the clicking sound of it should alarm the birds.

'Edmund, dear, how did the poor brute die? It didn't just fall from the sky because you wanted it dead, did it?'

Or because I prayed to St Michael for exactly such an event, she thought, and her mind wandered. Really, Edmund was as intractable as her dear Sister Joseph: they would neither of them accept affection and forgiveness, as if they could never believe they deserved it. Dear St Michael, so much more accessible than God. Such a nice young man. She had created a whole personality for him, as well as a wardrobe. St Michael was a deferential, charming lieutenant with perfect manners and he was the only one, standing on the right side of God, who could tell God jokes. She relied upon that now, to hide a distinct feeling of misgiving. She leant further towards Edmund to hear his reply, although her deafness was confined to distant sounds and she was grateful for the cocoon it made. Matilda wanted nothing more than human voices and birdsong to intrude upon her consciousness, and only the sounds of her favourite people and favourite feathered friends, at that. There were voices she liked and those from which she shrank. She liked Edmund's burr; she liked little Sister Therese's youthful voice; she liked the shriller, more definable voice of that wicked sister of hers, the one who was probably named after St Ann, the mother of Mary, as boring a saint as any. Much better to be named after an angel, like Michael.

'How did it die?'

'I don't know,' Edmund mumbled. 'I wanted it to.'

'So did I, but *how*?'

'He fell out of the sky. The chapel window broke.'

'Oh, dear.'

She knew in an instant. The boy had done it. She thought she had heard him, but perhaps she was wrong. That glorious, blond-haired boy, who had slunk around Edmund for the last two weeks with the solicitousness of a doting grandson. She had seen him, sliding past earlier as she sat there, where she so often sat, treating her as if she was dumb and blind as well as partially deaf. An old woman held no interest for a boy, and when he did speak, she did not like his voice.

'*You* didn't kill it,' she protested. 'He did. The boy. The one who's got you by the balls. He did. He's got an air rifle. I saw it.'

'No. Francis would never do that.'

'He just did.'

'No, he's gone home, hours ago. He never did. He loves the birds, does Francis.'

She closed her eyes and considered Lucifer the Serpent, who was once, in her imagination, a quite magnificent brunette youth with a pushy torso, slim hips and great big forgive-me eyes. Francis bore a passing resemblance to that Lucifer. It was an impression she could not quite shake off, despite wanting to like him if only for his name. St Francis was the patron saint of birds, and a boy with his name must be good, surely part of the reason Edmund adored him, even granting the fact that Edmund was an

41

old, celibate homosexual, by no means beyond the demons of desire that Francis had awoken. He had no idea that Matilda knew what he had scarcely guessed himself. The crying had stopped.

'Francis would never do such a thing,' he said firmly. 'Even if he thought it was what I wanted. Either it was done through prayer, or someone else did it. And now I'd better bury that bird.'

She nodded, and slapped his back, heartily. If that was going to be the version of events, so be it. She was not going to add her two pennyworth or tell tales.

'When you've done that,' she said, 'do you think you could give St Michael a wash? Get rid of the moss on his feet?' And the bird shit, left by the magpie, which had been the final insult.

Edmund leant his dusty hand on her knee to lever himself upright. 'Good idea.'

By the time he had gone, it was almost dark. Matilda had the fleeting thought that perhaps the young fledgling magpie sons reared in this garden might come back on some vengeful mission to look for their brother, but she dismissed the thought. The birds slept early and for now it was peaceful silence. As she moved up the path towards the beech trees and the clear ground, she paused to wave. She always knew when someone was watching.

Yes, it had been a sin to pray for the death of a living thing. Perhaps it was also a sin to ignore God in favour of saints. She never could pray, except to an image. And she wished that Sister Joseph, whom she loved and had loved for years, would accept her own virtues and forget the rest.

Seventy miles away, Kay McQuaid flung the dead jackdaw on to the compost heap at the bottom of the garden, wiped her hands on her trousers and walked back to the patio. It was a short, unencumbered walk across a close-cropped lawn with a circular flowerbed in the centre, containing purple dahlias and not much else. There were neat shrubs around the edges of the walls, flowerpots on the patio, which was the same size as the lawn and the most important feature of the garden. A modest sized garden, encroached upon and thoroughly tamed by a conservatory and a patio and the ruthless application of insecticide. Low maintenance was the key. Too much shade was provided at certain times of day by the low tree that flourished next door. It was the best a tree could do so near the sea, but if it had not been preserved by the family next door, Kay would have been over there with an axe long since. Anything that diminished the sporadic sunshine of an English summer was forbidden. The bloody jackdaw had come from that bloody tree.

The sound of the sea at the front of the house was a soothing background murmur, punctuated with the shrill cry of a seagull.

'Cheers,' she said to her companion, raising the glass she had left on the table.

'If it had been a pheasant,' he said, referring to the dead bird, 'you could cook it.'

She shook her head. 'You might. I doubt if I'll cook anything ever again. Have the peanuts.'

'You could grow vegetables instead of lawn. Eat them fresh.'

She yawned. 'Oh yeah? I got too much tension already, this time of year. I put the sunbed out, lie down, cloud comes over. I get up, take it in. Then I take it out again, then I take it in, and then I go and look at brochures for where else to go. I haven't got any time to cook, God help me. Anyway, thanks for coming all this way. It's always good to see you.'

'It's an easy journey. A break for me. You know I love coming here. How did the bird die?'

'It came in the window, dirty beast, looking for my rings. I threw a plate at it, managed a hit. Not enough to kill it, mind. It was poorly to start with. Something it ate. Might have had a heart attack. They feed the wretched things next door. Then they come and shit on the patio.'

Father Goodwin looked around the neat area. There was a water feature consisting of a stone pond, guarded by a gnome with a fishing rod and bright red and green garments. The patio floor was grey brick, designed, he thought in his ignorance of such things, for the embellishment of a few minimalist pots with monochrome evergreens, the sort he had seen in magazines. He read the style sections, mainly for the food, if there was time after the sports pages. Easy to tell what Kay had added. Orange and yellow geraniums, pink daisies and all of the seven dwarves. He eyed the one sitting to the side of the water feature, which he otherwise liked for the soothing sound of it.

'Now, Father, what's the matter? You wouldn't be here if there was anything good on the telly. No, there never is tonight, is there? And stop looking at Droopy like that. He won't hurt you. He's a helluva lot friendlier than those horrible things you had in the presbytery. I always did hate that one of the Sacred Heart, the one in the glass case. The one of Himself with the heart on the front of his robe? Pickled Jesus, I used to call it. Well, we Catholics grew up with those things. Perhaps that's why I like the gnomes. I must miss that kind of furniture. Are you sure you don't want a drink? Yes, you do. Help yourself.'

He went indoors, past the Pogenpohl kitchen with the

air of clean disuse, through to the lounge beyond, as different from the nuns' parlour as anything he could imagine, making him pause to wonder what it might have looked like before Kay's relatively recent tenure as the sole occupant had stamped her definitive mark on it. Plain and functional, he guessed, without the addition of throws in vibrant colours, a huge TV-video console and a drinks cart, in the form of a wheelbarrow drawn by a toy donkey, full of highly coloured bottles of everything ranging from Tequila to Southern Comfort, through Slivovic to Martini, gifts and mementos from foreign travels, largely undrunk. There was banana liqueur from the Canaries, Metaxa brandy from Greece and something suspect from Turkey. Father Goodwin seized upon a bottle of Jameson's, noting that only the bottle of Tanqueray gin bore the sign of fingerprints. That was Kay's tipple, treated with care. The shininess of the display was admirable. You can give a cleaning lady new tastes, he thought, but you can't stop her cleaning.

In the fireplace, there was a large gold statue of Buddha with a well-polished stomach, which she may have put there simply to annoy him. He found a glass in the kitchen and sloshed a liberal dose of Irish whiskey for himself. Kay, sitting on her sunbed, nursed her long gin and tonic with the still melting ice and a cocktail stirrer with an umbrella on the top.

She was as brown as well-tanned leather. You didn't need a hot summer to get brown, she had told him: you simply needed time to sit in the sun whenever it came out. Especially if you'd done a bit of Tenerife in the spring. Brown skin suited her alarming choice of clothes. She was small and round and early fortics, several years younger than himself, her face as sweetly wrinkled as a walnut shell,

45

with dark brown eyes at odds with springy, bleached hair, turned even lighter by the occasional bursts of sun. He had adored her, in his understated way, ever since she had crashed into the presbytery, a skinny girl, cursing to high heaven at the time, along the lines of how she didn't want preaching, she wanted a bloody job. Kay had got her bloody job: no one else wanted it even then, on those wages. After two weeks of reasonable cooking and cleaning, she produced the hitherto unmentioned illegitimate son. He watched her now, surreptitiously. Not much changed.

'Are we all caught up with the news?' she asked, brightly.

She had lasted five years in the presbytery before finding the plum job with the Calverts, with plentiful, colourful rows in the meantime. Food had been thrown, he forgot why. Holy water under the bridge, she said, later. But the plum job with the Calverts had turned into the job from hell until they divorced, and Kay ended up as housekeeper to Mr Calvert, in his separate house, by the sea. This very house, which bore some resemblance to the way it was when he had been alive in it.

Kay and Christopher Goodwin had always stayed friends, usually by short letters, for which he thanked every saint in the universe. He drank his whiskey and thought, God was good, and this was compensation enough for the guilt of evading his duty and missing the match.

There were several compensations for missing the match. Mrs Katherine McQuaid, being drunk enough with the sun and the gin to speak freely, was a bonus for a wretched day. He put a touch more gin in her glass. Yes, the news of the old parish had been thoroughly covered, right up to the last funeral. She always wanted to know every detail of the Calvert girls.

'Oh, give us a good shot, will you ever, Christopher? Then I'll be able to pray to God for better weather and someone to supply me with drugs.'

'You want for nothing, Kay. You've landed on your feet. Not even your son bothers you.'

'No, he's to make his own way and not sponge off me. But what do you mean, I've landed on my feet? None of this is permanent, although God knows, I've earned it. This is Cinderella stuff. The pumpkin'll be arriving any minute. So don't you be telling me to get off my arse and do good works.'

'Would I? Didn't he leave you enough for ever?'

'Theodore? No, he bloody did not. I can live in this house for now, but his lawyer can repossess it whenever he wants. Enough money to last a year more with a few holidays thrown in. He wasn't *giving* me anything permanent. He just wanted me to go on housekeeping and he made it worth my while.'

'Isn't that rather cruel?'

'He could be cruel, for sure, but what's so cruel about it? A taste of the good life's better than no taste at all.'

'Isn't that what he gave his wife, too?'

'Now, you look here, *Christopher*, don't you join in maligning the dead. The trouble with you is that you're a fool for women. You're so soft on them, you always believe they're right.'

He knew this was unjust, but she was at least partially accurate. He was soft on women because he simply liked them best.

'I'm not maligning him, Kay. But doesn't a man's choice of wife reflect upon himself? You said he wasn't happy with the girl he had here. Can't have been all their fault.'

She adjusted herself on the sunbed, prepared to be

47

angry, without quite having the energy. It was getting cold out here, but not cold enough to justify going into the conservatory. She tucked the folds of her capacious purple robe round her ankles. He wasn't sure what you would call a garment like that.

'Look, he left his wife because she wouldn't let him near his own children. You don't stay with a woman who gives you the evil eye and treats you as if you were the devil. The only other girlfriend was that one he caught on the rebound, greedy little cow. You never could tell if she was feeling his prick or his wallet or both at the same time.'

He laughed, the moment for argument over, which he regretted, slightly.

'And he was very good to Jack.'

'Yes, he was too, but I'm not going to talk about Jack.'

Kay's virtues included her passion for argument, which allowed him to indulge himself. There was nowhere else he could have an argument and no one he could argue with: he was the peacemaker, the listener, and that was his role. But with Kay, he could manufacture a quarrel just for the hell of it: they could have a shouting match and then forget all about it, no offence taken. The fact that he disagreed with her on most subjects helped, as did the way she flaunted her heresies, and she wanted pastoral care like she wanted a hole in the head. What a relief. Even the torture once provided by her physical presence was a dim, almost comfortable memory, but despite all the ease of this friendship, there were questions he never dared ask. Such as exactly what relationship Kay had had with the rich employer who had elevated her status to that of housekeeper, rather than cleaner, and endowed her so eccentrically. Nor had he ever asked her who was the father of her son. That would have been impertinent.

'Remind me of how fairy godfather Calvert made his money?'

Kay winked at him. 'Nothing fairy about him, Christopher. He made it wanking, sorry, banking.'

She only ever called him Christopher when she was two gins down. Christopher was such a pansyish name, and besides, that particular saint, as she never failed to remind him, had been knocked off the saintly calendar thirty years ago. Christopher, for whom a million medals had been forged, was no longer a proper saint for universal intercession. It seemed like the story of Father Goodwin's life.

'I like the golden Buddha,' he said from the increasing comfort of his chair.

'Oh, that?' she said, waving a brown hand with crimson nails. 'Thought I might become a Buddhist. They're ever so friendly.'

She struggled upright, the better to explain as he choked on his drink. The jumpsuit gaped to reveal a thoroughly upholstered, flower-patterned bikini, which somehow reminded him of an apron.

'Oh, for God's sake,' she said, crossly, 'I was only teasing, but I do sometimes think. I miss *religion*, God help me.'

'Buddhists tend not to drink,' he told her, gently. 'And you wouldn't be allowed to swat a fly, let alone kill a bird. Can I bring Anna Calvert to see you?'

She sat bolt upright, startled. 'Why? Why the hell should I see her?'

'Because Sister Jude died. And apart from me and my scanty knowledge, you're the only one left who knew her parents, properly.'

'So that gives me a duty, does it? Bollocks. No, I shan't see her. I've had it up to here with sodding duty. But you can take me to bed if you like.'

49

He laughed and shook his head. It was an old joke, as old as sin. 'I wished you'd told me as soon as Theodore went and drowned,' he said. 'I could have helped.'

She shuddered, violently. 'No,' she said, 'you couldn't. I wouldn't want anyone else to see that poor, bloated body on the beach. So near home, too. It was horrible. And besides, he would turn in his grave if he thought you were standing over his corpse, saying prayers.'

Two in the morning, and Anna was walking home. No drinking, no shagging, just shift work at the taxi place. Therese would have been right not to fear for her soul tonight since all she had done was listen to voices.

It was wrong to be so fearless of the dark, but it was a fear she had never learned and the lack of it made her indifferent to being followed at night. Girls being followed was a fact of life. She could run far faster than any thief and, besides, had nothing to steal in her shoulder pack, except, tonight, the missal she had placed in there without being quite aware she had done so. Placed it on the table at work alongside the sandwich and put it back in the bag to go home, unopened.

The footsteps tailed away as she neared her own flat. Probably the one who followed tonight was one of the homeless who parked themselves at the back door of the convent, encouraged by the rumour of Christian charity. They had banged on the door last winter in the middle of the night, persisting until the ivy had grown down to shield the exit and announce its permanent disuse. The garden door was a false signal to the one or two who gathered in the hope that it would open and benefits would arrive.

She was ashamed of herself because she should have told Sister Barbara about the pistol shot breaking the window, but she had run away instead. When the footsteps behind her trailed away into silence, long before she drew level to the back door on the way to her own, she saw that the ivy had been clipped, neatly trimmed to frame the wood. She stopped and looked.

Once inside, she went upstairs and on to the roof to gaze down into the garden where there was nothing to see. Looking up she could see the stars, imagine the souls in the firmament. Sister Jude and her darling mother. Her father would surely be in hell.

Tucked in bed, she took the elastic band from the missal and let it fall open. It was stuffed with holy pictures, memoriam cards, decorative bookmarks with saintly depictions and messages scrawled on the back. Not so much a book of prayer, but one of memorabilia. Anna stuffed back the notes, letters, cards, pictures, as alienated by the sentimental reproductions as she was by the texture of the old leather and the tissue-thin pages, which stuck to her fingers. Still, it looked like a holy book rather than anything else, and that would do. Maybe it would provoke Ravi to talk to her, since he always had one himself. It would be a strange way to attract attention.

Still sleepless, warm with the indigestible anger that had hounded the day, she picked up the notebook which always remained by her bed and, propped by pillows, wrote in it, in pursuit of an old habit started by her father and encouraged by her mother, when she and Therese were confined to bed and told to record their symptoms, the better to diagnose the strange sickness afflicting them. Sometimes the notebook filled those distressing minutes when sleep was as vital as it was impossible and there was nothing else to do. When TV bored her, music failed to console and the radio was just another voice.

My name is Anna Calvert. (She always began this way.)

A benefactor pays my rent. I am a lucky girl.

I want anything but guidance.

I have read lots of books.

I would like not to be a freak. I miss Aunt Jude.

I wish I had never been baptised; it leaves a big black hole in my brain.

My father was a giant.

I am not fully formed.

Her eyelids began to feel heavy and the pen faltered.

There are four whole years of my life missing.

Four whole years, and I can never get them back.

Then she scribbled, *Therese is safe! Ravi smiled at me! The old man phoned again! Can't be bad!*

And everyone else is DEAD.

Then she slept.

CHAPTER THREE

I am the Lord thy God

Therese saw that they were lined up by the refectory door, like a waiting tribe, with Sister Joseph at the head of the queue. Today was the feast day of St Joseph, not the more famous St Joseph of Nazareth, husband of Mary and father to Jesus, but another Joseph altogether, an obscure man of Aragon, who founded a religious congregation for the education of the poor. Sister Joseph had taken the name when she entered the Order and although it was better than her own, it could never be as good as a martyr, like Agnes. The taste in her mouth was sour.

Her feast day was going to be, if not ignored, at least diminished by more important events, such as the breaking of the chapel window, discovered last evening by Barbara on her last round of the building, the funeral of Sister Jude the day before and the consequent emptying of the larder. Her own grief and her participation in the singing did not count. She looked at the others with irritation. Helpless ninnies. Sister Bernadette had twisted her ankle and moved with a crutch and obvious heroism. Matilda, the dearest, kindest friend she had rebuffed, was waiting to eat everything available. Joseph tried to despise her. Margaret was sniffing with her usual incessancy, while Sister Joan, named for a warrior and really a mouse, sparkled with anticipation of her pathetic weekly excursion to the market. Therese, the postulant, finished off the laying out of breakfast with her usual serene efficiency, smiling as if they were all new-found friends. Silly creature. Joseph's own room was draughty from the broken window catch; the door to this room would not shut from warping; the place was falling apart. Joseph's feast day would be forgotten. She eyed the array of sensible cereals, already cold toast, jams and milk with the contempt she might otherwise have shown to humanity. The one thing she wanted was a drink.

She was going to be ignored, when she was surely now the highest in the pecking order when it came to deserving respect for her achievements. She had followed the example of her saint, had worked in the missions, knew about the world, heat, dust, starvation and the devil of alcoholic addiction. Dear God, she wanted a drink. Plus a touch of respect for her age and someone to notice it was *her* day. And an end to the guilt she felt about hurting Matilda.

'Happy feast day, Sister,' Therese murmured, helping Joseph with the milk jug. Trust that bright-eyed girl to notice that her hands were shaking. Joseph grunted a non-committal response and went to her usual seat at the table. A single rose, glistening with dew from the garden, lay across her place and she had the grace to feel momentarily ashamed. Matilda would have done that. Matilda never forgot. The coffee looked weak. There was the usual twittering of conversation. Barbara tapped a spoon against her cup and stood at the head of the table. The murmuring ceased.

Not a pretty bunch, Barbara was thinking as she waited for silence. A community of thirty, once, shrunk to fifteen, with the inevitable prospect of further wastage through old age and death, although they were not dying off fast enough by certain standards. Clingers to the wreckage. Only the Irish had existing relatives, excluding Agnes, although Agnes waited at the door every day in the hope that one would arrive. The family of Christ and the Blessed Virgin were not a substitute for the ties of blood, whatever vows they had taken, and as for what they actually, individually believed, Barbara neither knew nor minded. It was bad enough keeping them fed and the fabric of their shelter from further decay.

'Sisters,' she began, knowing the need to be brief. Food was of paramount importance. 'Sisters, a word, please. I think you all know there was an unfortunate accident with the chapel window being blown in by the wind last night, so there may be an extra bit of activity around the place while we work out how to get it fixed. There'll be a team of useless, expensive men, I daresay,' she added bitterly. 'That's all. For what we are about to receive, may the Lord make us truly thankful, Amen.'

'Amen.'

Each made the sign of the Cross with different degrees of absent-mindedness. Conversation began again, interspersed with the noise of cutlery. Therese took her place at the foot of the table and ate her chewy toast. From where Barbara sat at the opposite end, she looked like a little princess, small and golden and pink, doing nothing to make herself shine the way she did. It was simply youth, with nothing bleached out of her strong hair or the healthy, luminous complexion with which no other skin compared. Eight of the Sisters still wore the veil, the oldest ones who would have felt indecently undressed without the uniform they had worn for a lifetime and thus wore it still. Among the others, dressed either in the charcoal calf-length tunic or ordinary clothes of their own choice, style was difficult to detect, although here and there, there was a hint of vanity. A bright blue hairslide for Sister Joan, bought from her beloved market, and a blouse with a bow for Monica, who was given her clothes by a niece. Otherwise, they seemed to exist in various shades of grey. Barbara looked down at her plate, thought of the budget and how, if selling a soul to the devil was worth hard cash, she might do it. She was slow to notice that silence had fallen, a silence of curious wonder.

At the door of the refectory stood the boy, Francis. He was standing awkwardly, like an old-fashioned servant anxious not to command attention, but needing it, and like Therese, he did nothing to attract the eye, although all eyes strayed towards him until eating stopped and the silence was total. He was not a complete stranger; the minority who ever went more than one or two steps into the garden knew who he was, just as they all knew Edmund, but it took a year for a face to be familiar. The decision to take him on had been hers alone, because he was free, and even she scarcely knew him. That was just after the last monthly meeting where her decisions could be discussed democratically if ever a quorum bothered to attend. Really, both she and they preferred dictatorship. The boy had simply arrived at least a couple of weeks before and, up until now, he had never come indoors. He was a creature of the garden and the garden had a life of its own. Agnes, for one, found the sheer size of it frightening and sat now, halfway up the table, with her mouth open in a smile of recognition. Matilda, always hungry, chewed methodically and thought he looked like St Michael today, clad for fighting. Joseph, with her wider education, thought he looked like the God Pan.

There was nothing pagan about bare arms and bare knees on a boy wearing shorts and a vest on a humid morning. Loose working clothes suited his slender physique, which was in itself a lesson in anatomy. His broad shoulders and sculpted arms looked as if they had been carved out of oak to illustrate the perfect function of interconnecting sinew. Long, baggy shorts, so large they might have belonged to another man entirely, revealed brown, grubby knees and athletic calves. He stood, shyly, flexing his hands by his sides, nodding awkwardly towards the head of the table, and his knuckles, like his knees, were convincingly dirty. He looked fit to run away; a boy with work-stained knees, inhabiting the body of a man, held together with a belt round his middle, his head crowned by golden curls as if he had stepped from a medieval painting. When Barbara got up and hustled him out into the kitchen, conversation resumed behind them. The tips of his ears grew red, as if he knew he was being discussed.

'You're welcome, Francis,' Barbara said tartly, unfazed by his beauty, but rattled by the sudden silence it had caused. 'But we like to take our breakfast in private. What is it?'

'Oh, sorry. I didn't know what else to do but try to find you, soonest. Edmund tells me you're going to call in the glaziers and all to do the window. It'll cost a bomb, Sister, really it will, and . . .'

He stuck his hands in his pockets and bowed his head. The golden curls danced. There was a single gold ring in one ear, and she noticed, with relief, a small crucifix suspended from a gold chain round his neck.

'And?'

'I could do it, Sister. I promise I could, only he won't believe me. It's only the one pane, God love us. For the

57

price of hiring a ladder and buying the glass, I could do it, easy. To be honest, I was desperate to stop you before you spent the money. If they charge you fifty, they charge you a hundred.'

She did a mental review of the quotations she had solicited in the last hour, from any emergency firm who happened to be awake. He was right, if inaccurate on the downside of what they quoted to do any job involving ladders and height. Nothing was done for charity, not any more.

'Are you sure?'

'Sure I'm sure. I'm older than I look, Sister, worked all my life. I can do anything.'

He nodded vigorously. When he raised his head, she caught the full blast of brilliant, turquoise eyes, before he lowered them again, to stare at his own feet, clad in boots, without socks. The calves were marked with scratches. He looked competent, from this close distance, definitely more of a man than a boy and quite outstandingly endearing.

'What else can you do?'

'Oh, for sure, Sister, anything. Basic plumbing, electrics, washing machines, woodwork, changing plugs, mending fuses, painting, filling holes, changing carpets, shifting things, dealing with damp . . . all that. No good with cars or gas cookers, but most things else. I want to be a gardener, though, but isn't that a waste if there's nothing to do in a garden and you have a window to mend? If you see what I mean.'

It was a rushed and breathless delivery, a race to provide information and, to her ears, oddly touching in its eager boastfulness. It had ever been the dream of her life to find an able-bodied man desperate to work.

'You really can do all those things?'

He nodded.

'Why didn't Edmund tell us?'

He shook his head and scuffed his feet. 'I don't know. He thinks he needs me more. But I don't think he does. It's coming on colder, Sister, the garden can wait.'

Barbara felt as if a cloud had been lifted as she marched him back into the refectory, guided him back to her place at the head of the table and banged again with her spoon against her cup. Undrunk tea slopped on the table and the prospect of money saved made her clumsily cheerful.

'Sisters! A word, please. Francis here is going to fix the window, OK? And if there's any one of you needs something else fixing in their own room, or knows of something needing fixing anywhere else, will you please raise your hand?'

There was a pause, before arms were raised in an almost universal salute. White hands, pink hands, one gnarled brown hand with a missing finger.

'I also do errands,' Francis whispered to Barbara, audibly.

Sister Joseph raised her hand, last. Agnes gazed at him, mesmerised. Therese kept her eyes fixed on the surface of the table and her hands in her lap. She did not want to look at the boy she had glimpsed before. Instead she looked at Kim, staring at him from the door of the kitchen. Kim would like that.

Later, to the sound of distant hammering, she and Kim stacked the dishwasher, which was a vintage model with settings of sheer simplicity and so far indestructible. There was a butler sink for the equally indestructible pans and a gas cooking range of industrial size, installed in the days when there had been more to feed and more money to go round, a sound investment. The kitchen surfaces were chipped, but that was merely cosmetic. Nothing prevented Therese from preparing the delicate food for invalids which was her speciality. One day, God willing, said Barbara, she would turn those skills into qualifications and make herself employable. She had no ambition to do anything else. Kim was the dogsbody who came in daily for the morning, Monday to Friday, foraging for cash to feed two children. Kim liked it here because it was so quiet, but for the exclusive benefit of Therese, her language was deliberately and provocatively filthy.

'By yie! He's shaggable, in't he?'

'Who?'

'That lad, Francis, isn't it? Shaggable, I said. Phaw! I'd like to gerra hold of him! Have you been hiding him, or what?'

'No. He's never come in before. Edmund comes for tea.'

'Yeah, I bet. Well, you better get that Francis to come for tea when I'm around. I could teach him a thing or two. My old man's not bad in the sack, mind, but it does a girl good to have a change. Someone who'd take it a bit slower, for a start, though if I'm in the mood for a shag, I don't care how long. Usually takes him the same time it takes to boil a kettle.'

'Does it?' Therese asked. 'Why does it take so long?'

'Shagging?' Kim asked incredulously.

'No, boiling a bloody kettle.'

Kim cackled. This kid was smart, for a virgin. Dead easy to shock and dead good at fighting back.

'So, what do you know about shagging, then?' Kim said.

'You could put it on the back of a postage stamp.'

She was busying herself about the sink and Kim, looking at the deftness of her movements as well as the pink blush of her face, wondered how the two personalities she

60

had could be reconciled to one another. Therese was sexy and impossible to understand.

'How fucking old are you, Therese? Don't you think you should have given it a try before saying you'd never do it?'

'Twenty-one.'

'Twenty-one, never been shagged, and a bloody nun. You're every bloke's wet dream, you are. Bloody disgrace.'

'So you tell me. Can't say I miss it. Look where it's got you. Two kids and no money.'

'Yeah, right. Funny, you're not like your sister, then. She gets around, I reckon. Shaggable, both of you.'

'I know. I worry about her, and she worries about me. Daft, isn't it?'

Kim crashed the last plate into place. 'I should like someone to explain to me,' she said, 'well, I'd like *you* to explain to me, why someone like you who's got looks and brains *and* tits should want to keep it all under wraps. You could get rich and lucky with looks like yours. You wouldn't even need to shag for it. Beats me. Oh, *Treesa*, lay off, will you?'

Therese was doing her catwalk, parading past the cooker with the exaggerated pelvic thrust of a model, hands on undulating hips, head thrown back and her wide mouth pursed in a kiss. She flung herself into a chair, lounged against the back, ran her hands through her hair, crossed her legs, ran her hands down the sides of her body, hitched up her skirt to show her knees and then lowered one eyelid in a vampish wink. Kim screamed with laughter.

'Yeah, just like that. Oh, you slay me, you do. Christ, I'd kill for legs like yours.'

The distant hammering resumed. The dishwasher rumbled.

'But you aren't going to get away with it, *Sister*. You never answer a question, you. Come on, you've been a holy nun for a year, you've got a bloody lifetime of answering questions, so you might as well start with me. Why the fuck are you doing it? *Why?*'

Therese sat up straight, adjusted her skirt and straightened her face. An expressive face, designed for laughter, although at other times, as blank as an empty page.

'Oh, Kim, you're as bad as Anna. I never thought it would be so difficult to understand or, at least, respect. There isn't a choice, not for me. I dreamed of a life like this, I dreamed of it, when other girls would dream of men and money and Lord knows what. I'm not giving anything up. Nothing I want, anyway.' She drummed her fingers on the table, seeking the right words and knowing that none would do. 'Don't you see? If you dedicate your life to God, then it means that every single thing you do has value.'

'Yeah, right.'

'It means every single thing has a purpose. I might hate scrubbing pans, but if I offer it to God, it has a purpose. It has a value. And I myself have a purpose. I have a straight line to follow. Everything I do is for the greater glory of God, and that makes me joyful. It's so simple, Kim. It means I can endure anything and I don't need approval from anyone, even though I'm only human and I want to be liked. It means I don't need to be loved . . .'

'Approval? Where do you get all your long words? And don't tell me you don't need to be loved. Everyone does. Except your bloody sister.'

'I *am* loved, Kim. I'm loved by a father and a brother, whose guidance I can trust with absolute conviction, which is more than most people could ever say. And I got my faith and my vocation from my mother.'

The fridge door slammed. 'Blimey, I got two beltings a week from mine. Did she also teach you to cook?'

'Nutrition and contemplation. Also singing.'

'But nothing about shagging?'

'Come on, Kim, what mother ever teaches her daughter that? She got us books, she made us read, she made us learn and she taught us to pray . . . Even Anna can't shake that.'

'I can't get my kids to sit still.'

Therese laughed, scratched her head. Three golden hairs fell on to the table and she brushed them away. However she got her hair to gleam like that with that rotten, cheap shampoo they all used in their crappy bathrooms, Kim never knew. It was a greater mystery than the whole of religious life.

'I don't know how she managed. But we were very ill, you know, Anna and I. We didn't leave the house for four years. That's when we learned to pray.'

She jumped up from the table with the spring of a dancer, flourished a duster from out of her pocket and flicked it round Kim's head. Kim giggled and wrenched it away.

'Go and find Mr Shaggable, Kim,' Therese said. 'Stop him tempting Sister Agnes into mortal sin, and be nice to Joseph. It's her feast day and she's feeling her age.'

'She's a miserable old cow.'

'No, she's not. She's seventy-five, forgotten more than she remembers and I think she has a drink problem. Don't you women of the world notice anything?'

It was a big, overbright world that morning. On balance, when it came to the shift work she did (Anna called it shifty work), she preferred to work at night. Up on the rooftop at eight o'clock in the morning, the view into the convent garden was as misty as if someone had lit a fire. There was a fog about the place, an early, misplaced, rogue sense of autumn, as if the mist, which belonged in a field, had been dumped in the wrong place in the middle of the wrong town and lingered there, looking uncomfortable. It was as if it knew it did not belong, but could not find another place to go. Edmund was visible in the unravelling threads of fog, unconscious of it, although from the height of her roof, Anna could see his confusion as he moved away from his over-large shed, which also seemed out of place. He was looking for something he could not find. His bumbling progress was mesmerising to her tired eyes; he looked like a lazy bumblebee. The sun promised to shine and she did not want to move. She watched him get down on to his knees to retrieve something from under a bush, and watched him again while he picked himself up without damage. Maybe he was praying. He carried something cupped in his palms towards the statue of St Michael, where Matilda so often sat in summer, but never this early in the morning. Edmund's bent posture foretold the imminence of autumn. In May, she had seen him out there at dawn, standing as still and upright as a soldier, mesmerised by the music of the dawn chorus, and she knew his secret; he had never queried her presence and she loved him for that. Anna looked out for the Golden Boy and could not see him at all. It was time to go to work.

Compucabs' office was a mile away. A brisk walk, a bus ride, a run, sometimes a combination. She worked five shifts a week, three nights, two days, eight hours a time among the employees, who were all treated with suspicion until they had turned up regularly for months on end and worked their unsociable hours. Payment was per shift and there was no payment for absentees. Each of them was a mouthpiece at the end of a phone, connecting someone who wanted a taxi to someone who was driving it. That simple. Anna entered a big, open-plan office with fifty people clamped like cars into their tiny, individual stations, each with a headphone, mouthpiece and screen. The seat at her station was still warm from the last incumbent and the phone rang immediately. Somehow the missal had crept back into her knapsack. She put it on the desk, hoping someone would notice, unable to get over her unreasonable expectation that the first call of each shift would be personal. Someone out of the blue would know she was there and would call to say hello.

'Hello, Compucabs, how can I help you?'

Which was, she thought, a foolish greeting. There was only one form of help they could offer and it came in the form of a taxi. They were either phoning to ask for one, or phoning to complain that the one they had ordered had failed to arrive, and it was only in the latter kind of conversation that she had to employ charm. Otherwise tact was sufficient, even in emergencies.

'Can I have your account number, please? And the account name? Same name for the passenger? Do you want him to come to the door?'

Anna liked the fact that it was all so repetitive. She was hired for being a voice, which spoke first to a customer, then to a driver, while her fingers typed the details on to the screen, flying across the keyboard, faster than she could read.

'Paddington Station, you said? Shall I give you the job number?'

Conversations with the drivers were equally brief and she had trained herself out of any show of annoyance to become a valued veteran after eighteen months. There was nothing else she felt fit to do. Few lasted as long, although some seemed to have been there for ever. Stop-gap job, well-paid, no questions asked. Inside this room, with its buzz of repetitive words, she felt she had gained approval, and that however simple the routine was, she had mastered it entirely and won respect. The whole place reminded her of a well-disciplined school classroom where no child teased another.

They were friends. They chatted in a scruffy, smoke-filled restroom at the back during teabreaks, where the opaque fog of nicotine was sometimes undercut by the smell of dope when Jon was there and he thought no one would notice, although they all noticed and no one cared. You could be a serial killer, a turbanned sheikh, an ancient tart or a shepherd from Outer Mongolia and no one would care. Ravi read his battered scripture book and drank nothing but water, saying little, other than into his mouthpiece, but he smiled at her, exclusively. Anna always wanted to talk to Ravi and sensed that he might have liked to talk to her, from the way he eyed her from beneath his fierce black eyebrows, but so far it was confined to pleasantries and a shy, mutual awareness. Instead she talked to Jon the smoker, and Sylla, the Chinese girl, who always brought some knitting, fashioning in between calls a succession of tiny white garments for babies that she was always willing to describe and Anna to admire. She and Ravi were the only ones who always carried a book. Perhaps that gave them something in common. Maybe Sister Jude's missal, another book of prayer, would finally break the ice. Amid the frenetic activity in the open-plan room with the muted buzz of voices, it was a peaceful, intimate place without scope for rivalry or rows. They could only be as good as one another, they were all paid exactly the same and there was a sense of camaraderie at night.

Which was one of the reasons why she preferred the night shift, especially in summer when it left the day free to sleep in the sun on the roof. She found it easier to sleep in the day; the night was crowded with images, while after-noon siestas were sound, sound sleep. Anna did not relish sleep and the dreadful waste of time it was, did not even like her own bed and knew it was because Therese and she had spent so much time lying down a whole, separate life-time ago: a great, yawning hole, which left them incomplete, gullible, untouchable, out of sync with the rest of the world, alien to their contemporaries and only at home with strangers. Warped, somehow. At least, she was.

The day slid by quickly.

'Good afternoon, Compucabs, how can I help you?'

'I want a taxi.' It was him, again.

She smiled. 'Well, you've come to the right place, sir. What was the account number?'

'Haven't got one.'

'Might take a little longer in that case. Have you ever thought of opening an account with us, sir?'

Account holders had priority. They had to pay for the journey as soon as it was booked, even if they changed their minds. Drivers preferred them: payment was guaran-teed; less chance of a drunk en route to an unpleasant destination at the far end of a back alley.

'I don't want an account, I want a taxi. I *think* I want a taxi.'

'Right you are. From where?'

She knew from the voices when the use of 'sir' or 'madam' was going to soothe. She could pick up the nuances of anxiety, inebriation, arrogance, loneliness. She knew that a twenty-four-hour number prominently displayed in the London telephone directory attracted the lonely and the cranks, and there was training on the subject too, drummed into them from day one. Get rid of them, quick; the lonely were losers, they did not have cash. Get them off the line; time is money. But Anna could not resist the voices. She was a sucker for voices.

'Do I need a taxi?' the voice asked. An old voice, full of tiredness and indecision. A voice as old as Sister Jude's and so reminiscent of it, she was suddenly moved. Probably an old man, staring at a page in the directory, wondering why he had picked up the phone at all. Nothing like the brash, confident voices, bellowing into mobiles, wanting transport now, now, now.

'Are you going somewhere nice?' Anna asked pleasantly. 'Only you might be a bit late for lunch.'

It was the slow time of the day, one forty-five, when half of the population were either eating or thinking of it. She had a sudden yearning to be one of those people, sitting in a restaurant, eating whatever she liked and the only person in the group who could translate the menu. The telephone line crackled with silence. A sigh.

'I never go anywhere.'

'Why not? It's a lovely day out there. At least it was. Is it raining yet? The forecast was for rain, wasn't it?'

'No, it isn't raining yet. Yes, I'll do that. Yes, I'll go out.'

'Will you be wanting a taxi, then, sir?'

'Whatever for? I'll walk.'

'Have a very nice day. 'Bye.'

A variation on his last conversation, poor old thing. Anna had taken calls from people who dreamed of getting out of the house, and used the calling of a taxi to fulfil an unfulfillable wish. Called it then cancelled it, because they

68

knew they could not move. Businessmen called taxis in the middle of meetings as a way of encouraging the meeting to end, dreaming of getting away. This old gent, whom she visualised with grey hair to go with his somehow artificially refined voice, was merely muddled and she hoped he lived in comfort with someone to tie his shoelaces before he went out. The spookiest callers were in the middle of the night shift, one, two or three in the morning, lonely or drunk or drugged, forgetful of where they were and unable to quote either a meeting place or a destination, and even when they irritated her, she could sometimes smell their fear, prised information out of them with infinite patience and hated it when she had to leave them on the side of the road. They haunted the rest of the shift. At least the lonely callers, who simply wanted to talk, phoned from indoors.

Ravi passed by her station on his way and placed a paper cup of water in front of her, pausing only to smile. So much went into a smile. It occurred to her to wonder if they were the only two in the room who ever thought about God and she had worked out that he must think about God, for him to carry his prayerbook with him, refusing to part with it except when he went to the lavatory and left it by his phone. Maybe she should look at his prayerbook, find a clue in it as to how to conduct daily life better than she did. Maybe other people's scriptures were better than the ones she abhorred. She knew when people were sad, or tired or hungry, but she was otherwise ignorant. The sense of it overwhelmed her. She was twenty-two and she felt like a stupid baby.

In the slack hours, right up to a fortnight before, Anna would phone Sister Jude. Sister Jude had the dispensation of a phone by her bed, purely for receiving calls, never for the expense of making them. Anna would phone and tell her jokes, infantile communications to punctuate Jude's insomnia, instead of the urgent requests for information she had wanted to make. Instead of asking, *What was my mother really like? Do you know where my money comes from? Why, if you believe in God, are you so frightened to die?* she would say, Hi, Jude, it's me. Have you heard the one about the Catholic priest on the aeroplane just about to make a forced landing? Well, anyway, the stewardess asks him to do something religious to comfort the passengers. So he says, yes, I'll just organise a collection . . . And they had never had the final conversation. And Anna was suddenly, unspeakably angry with her for dying, severing that last link with what she was and what she was to become. And setting the hound of heaven upon her. She pushed back the wheeled chair and left the big room.

Outside, the rain fell in a soft drizzle. She stood in the shelter of the porch and smoked a cigarette. Now what had brought that on? A lonely old voice on a phone? The memory of the day before? The pistol shot through the chapel window? She wiped her nose on her sleeve, remembering being told, *Don't do that*. Once she was in the open air, the need to weep had turned itself into a runny nose. There were dripping trees in this quiet street. No one would have guessed the function of the building, which looked like a meeting hall without windows, dwarfed by larger buildings, not ugly but nondescript.

Ten minutes max, that was all that was allowed before the reprimand followed, in accordance with the strict regime in there, although not slavery and all the restrictions seemed perfectly fair in Anna's inexperienced estimation. Work and you were paid; don't work and you got the sack. There was nothing complicated about that. She had only had one other job with which to compare it and that had been in a shop. They had liked her there, too, because she could pick up the complications of the till quicker than anyone else, but when it came to customer relations, she was less successful. Telling someone that if they didn't like the goods they didn't have to buy them and why didn't they just fuck off was not what you did. It was the faces that frightened her, not the voices. With voices she was fine: she could afford patience. Five minutes gone. Anna sighed. Time to go back.

And then Ravi was standing beside her in the rain, his battered copy of whatever it was stuffed into the top pocket of his shirt and his brown eyes squinting at her with concern. He seemed breathless, as if he had been running, and stood with his hands on his hips as if that would help to get the breath back.

'Wassa matter? You all right?' He sounded gruff and aggressive, more challenging than comforting. From this close, she could smell what she thought might have been cloves. There was oil in his hair, which made it shine. His sudden appearance and the abruptness of his surprisingly deep voice made her defensive.

'Course I'm all right, you made me jump. Go away.'

He did not move, stared at her so intently she could not meet his eyes. She never met anyone's eyes, except, in these last weeks, the washed-out eyes of Sister Jude and now and then, those pale green eyes of Father Goodwin, yearning to explain. Clove oil: she remembered it was an inefficient antidote for toothache, a sharp and pleasant smell when removed from those associations.

'You aren't all right.'

There are very few people who deserve for you to be rude to them, a sentence flashing through her mind like a neon sign from the many sayings of Sister Jude, delivered in one

71

of her memorably mild, generalised remonstrances, such as, *Treat people as you would like to be treated.* Strange how the epithets of an old woman had come to predominate, even to be ignored. Anna smiled apologetically, thought of a shortcut to an explanation in a form anyone might understand.

'Nah, sorry. Only my aunt died, you see. Bit upset, that's all.'

He nodded gravely, sat on the step beside her. 'Walk you home later?' he asked.

Again, the voice startled her with its depth, while the words sounded like the sort of invitation a ten-year-old might risk at school before they knew the tyranny of teasing, and that was what they would look like too if he did walk her home, two little kids walking home hand in hand down a tree-lined avenue, like something from a dimly remembered advert for Start Rite shoes. And then, a more uncomfortable thought: how did he know that she walked home, or that home was within walking distance? Was he psychic, was he guessing, or was he the one who followed her? She decided, in a fraction of a second, that it did not matter if he was, might even be nice, but she still spoke sharply.

'No, thanks.' The thanks sounded lame, the rejection immediate. He shrugged, in that 'No offence taken' kind of way a teenager might think they had perfected to hide wounded pride, but that was only a guess. He was almost as small as she was, at least when they were sitting down.

'Can I tell you something?' he said, ignoring the knock-back. 'There is always something you can do when you're sad. You can always pray. I find it works best. For me.'

This advice suddenly seemed hysterically funny. Anna threw back her head and laughed loudly.

'Does it work?'

'What do you mean, work? You have brought your book of prayer with you yesterday and today. I noticed.'

She took a deep breath. 'I meant does it *work*? As in getting you what you want. Do you get what you ask for after you've prayed for it?'

He shook his head, puzzled. 'We do not pray to ask for *things*. We pray for guidance.'

'Yeah, right,' she said sharply. 'Like those Muslims bombing New York. Guide this plane for me, God. Let's take out a few thousand. Must have been one helluva powerful prayer.'

She heard his sharp intake of breath, listened to it exhale in a patient sigh.

'Why should a Muslim understand a terrorist murderer any more than a Christian understands an IRA bomber? I am Hindu, by the way. You and I are the freaks who carry prayerbooks. And I was worried about you.'

It was a surreal conversation to be having on the steps of Compucabs telephone exchange.

'Yeah, well. Right. We'd better get back to work.'

'Walk you home?' he repeated.

'All right,' she said. 'That'd be nice.'

CHAPTER FOUR

This wasn't nice. It wasn't nice at all.

'Father! It's you! I'm sent to collect you for the meeting. So you wouldn't be late. I'm to give you a lift.'

On that evening, Christopher Goodwin would rather have walked through the valley of death. His heart sank as he stood at the door, looking down at the squashed face of Sister Margaret, who wore her veil halfway down her forehead like a helmet, forcing her eyebrows into a frown which was at odds with her smile. Her control of the red Volkswagen made it a death trap. His TV muttered in the background with the soothing noises of a cricket commentary. He was refreshed, if troubled, by his day away and Barbara was perfectly right, he *had* forgotten the nuns' meeting and his tedious role of de facto chairman. All he could remember was that he could no more refuse the lift for the mere half mile than he could otherwise have turned off the television when Beckham was about to score a goal, and wasn't it marvellous, the way that the obligation of manners and the desire not to cause even minor offence could make a man risk his own life without a word of protest. Such was the priesthood.

She winked at him. 'C'mon, now, Father. It's your last chance in this vehicle. Barbara says we have to sell the car and that's a topic for this evening as well. What a shame.'

He got into the passenger seat and fumbled for the belt with a fixed smile on his face. Sister Margaret never bothered with hers, or with locking the car doors when she left it parked, so that it was a doubtful act of mercy that the beast had never been stolen. She made the sign of the Cross, sang out a prayer as she gunned the engine and the car lurched off the kerb with a screaming clutch. At the first junction, he closed his eyes, waiting for her to slow down and indicate, listening to her loud humming, which was the only sound above the protests of the wrong gears. She consigned each journey to Jesus and relied entirely on His protection, a faith so far rewarded, apart from the time she had taken Edmund to hospital with his stroke scare and he had fainted in the back. Sister Margaret knew that Jesus and Mary would see her through traffic lights of any colour and five-point turns on any highway, as long as she began with a prayer and did not stop. They arrived within five terrible minutes. He opened his eyes as the car hit the kerb and he was hauling himself out like an animal escaping captivity before he remembered the seat belt. So much for dignity. He could have murdered them both. The relentless good nature and blithe optimism worn on the sleeves of the likes of Margaret this afternoon was so intensely irritating that he wanted to scream, or bark, while on another day it might infect him with a broad smile and an awful tendency towards platitudes, such as, *Have a nice day, It'll be all right on the night, Don't worry about anything*, phrases that were no use to any troubled mind. He hardly noticed the black and white tiles of the passageway as Margaret spirited him through, only hoped that someone would come along and crush the damn car before there was any chance that he would be prevailed upon to get in it again, especially after dark. And it was that time of the year when darkness began to make itself felt earlier and earlier and the idle, polite talk would be of an Indian summer to compensate for the disappointments of the real summer passing and the sky broody with rain.

He could imagine who would be at the meeting, and hoped it included Anna, to add some substance and enliven the usual dull proceedings. They were pseudo democratic, these ill-attended meetings, invented by Barbara and frequented only by those who either were too humble to make suggestions or might otherwise be asleep. He did not know why Barbara convened them or why he, as Chaplain, should have to attend with the usual smattering of volunteers not clever enough to find alternative duties. Damn, damn, damn.

When he entered the parlour, he was late and cross, and found, dear God and all the saints, it was full to bursting. Anna sat at a table in the corner, looking suspiciously demure and tiny, facing a laptop, ready to take official minutes. She really did look useful like that and he was touched that Barbara had found her something to do.

'Ah, here you are, Father,' Barbara said, beaming. 'And here we all are,' she added irrelevantly. 'Including Anna, who *insists* upon being helpful. She can work that machine that Monica's niece gave us, which is more than I can. Now we're hoping to keep this brief and be finished in time for supper. I've two motions to put before the meeting. The first is that we sell the car—'

'But we need the car, Sister.' The voice of Agnes rose, quavering. 'Shopping and emergencies and—'

'It costs about three thousand a year to keep the car,'

76

Barbara said firmly. 'More, if you take into account all the repairs.' She looked at Margaret, kindly. Divine protection had saved lives inside that car, but had not preserved the bodywork from her driving or the wing mirrors and windows from the attention of vandals. 'Margaret is our only driver until Therese has a chance to learn, and even that'll cost money.'

'If I could make a suggestion,' Anna said, raising her hand. They looked at her in alarm, ready to tolerate until she opened her mouth. Today, the laptop gave her a role and the proceedings a more official status. For once, Barbara was pleased with her, although she never liked to admit they needed help.

'Yes?'

'You could do the bulk shopping on-line,' she tapped the screen of the computer, 'and have it delivered, all the heavy goods anyway. That would save leg-work. And you could get a taxi account, so that whenever you needed one, you just phone. You'd have to go mad on taxis to spend anything like three thousand a year, even if you all use them.'

'Excellent idea,' Father Goodwin said. 'A money saver *and* you'd have the money from the car itself to play with.'

'That's not the way it works,' Barbara said. 'There's no money to *play* with.'

He rebuked himself.

'And who would do the ordering of the stuff off the computer, which I suppose is what you mean by *on-line*,' Barbara went on. 'It was good to be given that thing, but nobody knows how to use it.'

'I do,' Anna said mildly. 'Therese does and somebody else could learn.'

'I bet you Francis knows how,' said a voice from the

77

side. Father Goodwin turned to look at poor Sister Joseph. She was always 'poor' Sister Joseph in his mind because, of all them, she was the only one who struck him as profoundly unhappy, on a different scale to the others with their various moods disciplined into an even state, while her misery was permanent and unconsolable, although he had tried more than once to define it and been turned away. In Joseph, he sensed a person who was not a natural celibate or even a believer; like himself, someone who had to fight for her state of grace.

'Francis could do it,' she repeated. 'Francis can do everything.'

He realised, with a shock of surprise, that she was drunk. Badly inebriated rather than falling-off-the-chair drunk, her voice slurred and her face mottled. No one else appeared to notice and, as he watched, Joseph clamped her mouth shut, crossed her arms and sat straighter, aware of the danger of saying anything more. The hubbub that followed her contribution deflected attention and brought them round nicely to what they were all desperately anxious to discuss. Francis. Father Goodwin was puzzled, a frequent state and not always alarming. Francis, ah yes, the garden boy.

'Can we sell the car and everything else, but keep Francis?' Agnes asked, breathlessly. 'That boy is a marvel. He's mended my curtain rail and the hinge on the door . . .'

'He mended the chapel window . . . no time at all . . .'

'He changed the washer and stopped the tap leaking . . .'

'He changed the sash cord . . .'

'He put those shelves straight . . .'

'And he *sings*, Father, he sings. Like an angel.'

'What does he sing?' Father Goodwin asked, still seeking clues, bewildered by the chorus. It seemed that he and

Anna were the only ones in the room who needed them. The others were vying in the giving of praise.

'He sings hymns, Father. Beautifully. "Praise to the Lord, the Almighty, the King of all nations" and "I know this my Redeemer lives" . . .'

'And how he works. Like a wee slave.'

He scanned the faces, alive with enthusiasm, and succumbed to the slow realisation that in the course of a day, this boy Francis had been elevated to the level of a saint, into that dizzy realm of sanctified indispensability, which he himself had never occupied. A talented lad with a screwdriver and a bag of nails. It annoyed him. Only Matilda sat silent, counting the beads of her rosary, slower to believe in miracles.

'Sisters,' Barbara said, 'Francis is a temporary worker, brought in by Edmund. We cannot possibly afford to keep them both. And we cannot let Edmund go.'

She looked at the priest for confirmation. He nodded.

'Besides,' she added, 'he's a young man and he wouldn't stay for long. They never do.'

'He said he would stay as long as we needed,' Agnes said.

There was a silence, in which the priest detected disappointment rather than mutiny and wished that excitement came to them more naturally than resignation. He glanced at Joseph and wondered how the hell she had got hold of the drink or who had given it to her. Matilda gazed sadly in the same direction. Joseph kept her eyes on the ground.

'But he'll be here for a few days?' someone asked, hopefully.

'Yes. Not tomorrow. He's away to see his mother. A good boy.'

Again, that chorus of approval.

'You should get about five thousand for the car,' Anna said, flatly. 'I looked up the prices and Father Goodwin could announce it in church. It'll go by the end of the day, for cash.'

Something had been accomplished. The buzz was satisfying.

Over the heads, Anna looked at Father Goodwin and smiled. A real smile, not the usual perfunctory thing, warm enough to have a temporary effect on the acute feeling of unease that had suddenly engulfed him even as he tried to fathom the source of it in the bustle of departures. It was his own, self-taught custom, which owed less to religious discipline than to necessity, that he should control the uncertainties of his temper by asking himself why, at any given time, should he feel as he did. Am I hurt to have another man praised to the skies and my presence ignored? Am I upset by that dreadful car journey? Is my blood sugar low? Am I an old man who hates change, even for the better, or am I worried by the fact that I must soon have this serious conversation with Anna and I dread it? Or has it occurred to me that the only person who could have fed poor Joseph with her own poison would be this gardening boy, because Barbara scarcely lets her out?

The meeting broke, as inconclusively as always. There was a drift towards supper. He was invited and refused; they had no time for him really. He walked through and into the garden, looking for Anna, hoping she had gone. Or maybe to find some trace of the miracle worker, Francis. The garden soothed him. It was exactly as a garden should be, with a small area of scarcely tamed ground leading on to a labyrinth, a total contrast to Kay's garden. It was, he thought, a garden to the greater glory of God, because, like the Garden of Eden, it might well contain a serpent or two and of itself it revealed to man his own inadequacy in the face of nature. At least it did if the man in control was Edmund.

> The kiss of the sun for pardon
> The song of the birds for mirth,
> One is nearer God's heart in a garden
> Than anywhere else on earth.

Surely there was a tune to go with that? He began to hum. Halfway between the beginning and the end of this garden, from the point when he met that hideous statue of St Michael, only dignified in his own eyes by the amount of lichen obscuring the details of the figure, he realised that a person in search of hygienised nature in the middle of a city might be better off in the park. Indeed, that was where most of the Sisters tended to go, and with the park so near, perhaps the garden really was a waste. There was always the suspicion that Edmund let it run riot in order to deter intruders, to make life uncomfortable, since he was an awkward bugger, who might also be a breeder of rare spiders for all he knew. There was a sort of nurture going on here, which was difficult to detect. The path was swept, the bindweed under control and the shrubs were healthy. There was an interesting variety of plants of what Father Goodwin would have called the jungle variety, based only on his reading of the style sections of magazines where he so often looked and admired, the better to be able to hold informed conversations with the increasingly rich end of his parish when he visited their houses. He sighed as he pushed aside the fronds of a fern, disliking the feel of it while acknowledging that it was handsome in a savage kind of way. Whatever had happened to lawns and roses? The sigh was on account of his inability to stop his thoughts hopping about like so many baby frogs – or more like errant toads, he told himself, because down near the bottom of this garden, he was remembering that it had shocked him to realise he preferred to visit the houses and apartments of the rich, not only for the many pleasures of looking at their arrangements, but because it was usually easier on the spirit. If the rich were in spiritual need, he was rarely the only source to which they looked. They looked also towards doctors and psychiatrists and new age gurus, or they cured themselves, while the poor of the parish sometimes reached towards him like drowning men and he the only one to save them from hell. The only one who could fill in a form, contact a relative, claim housing benefit and tell them how to get legal aid and avoid deportation, or evict a violent husband, while he, so often, would have to shake his head and say, I cannot do all that. I cannot keep you alive. It is the lot of a priest in a secular society to have responsibility without the power to influence events, let alone pull strings down at the Department of Social Security. Or the Inland Revenue or the Police or the Bailiff. He paused and fished in his pockets.

Difficult to explain to a mother that he could not get her child off the street and into school and that all he could do was invite her to pray, be optimistic and resign herself to fate, because fate was the will of God, and belief would help, it would, honestly. He could only put her in touch with others in the same boat and mitigate the isolation. Nor could he tell the man that he was not going to die in hospital without his children around him although he had been called purely for the purpose of denial. He did not want the communicants who believed his every platitude, and on balance, was it so bad to prefer the rich? He had been a priest for a long time, become afraid of being considered indispensable, nervous of his inabilities in the face of raw need. It was simply that it was refreshing to be asked his advice by those who had other options, rather than being the one who was asked to throw the rope to the drowning man, while knowing that not only was the rope frayed, but it would not reach. Fewer and fewer of them called for a priest and he was ashamed of himself for being grateful.

He stopped by the fern, beyond what he called the St Michael Bend, and lit a cigarette. Five a day only, usually reserved for that blissful time when he sat in front of the television and listened to the roar of a crowd. If football had replaced religion as the opiate of the masses, he could not criticise since it certainly worked with him. God forgave everything, surely, even a priest who liked looking at the decor of handsome houses and gossiping about them more than he liked the insides of impoverished flats, and enjoyed spectator sports better than anything. At least he had no envy in him. He just liked the looking, was all, just as he enjoyed the sight of a beautiful woman. He was, he supposed, running out of emotional steam, wanted to be useful, but no longer wanted to be furious with pity. Compassion ate you alive. Someone was calling his name.

'Is that you, Father?'

Even being called Father irritated him. He had a *name*, for God's sake. He was nobody's *father*, more was the pity, and he particularly disliked being called Father by men older than himself. Like Edmund, who had the same shape and reminded him of his own wrong turnings. But it wasn't so bad to be hailed by Edmund, who had never, so far, demanded spiritual solace, thank God, and seemed devoid of day-to-day problems, apart from his health. Edmund would want one of his cigarettes and was welcome, even though he should not, since the man had had one stroke at least. Not a big one, but a warning and not bad enough to prevent him from racing back to his garden, Christopher remembered, although, looking at it now, it was difficult to see quite what it was that made him feel so necessary. Edmund was wonderfully slow moving. Whatever had provoked the stroke was not his excitable temperament, but probably an unfortunate genetic disposition together with an acquired addiction for booze and fags and a tendency towards tears, as well as all those wrong choices a single life makes.

He was crying now. A big, sad, clumsy man, sitting on the dirty bench, which would always be in the shade on the brightest day, and after a summer of plentiful, if inconsistent good weather, he was still pale, with the sagging abdomen Father Goodwin somehow associated with the celibate and hated to see in himself. Approaching, he disposed himself towards sympathy and fumbled again in his trouser pocket for the cigarettes. He should carry more than his own ration: they were far more effective consolation for those so inclined than anything else, and he could hardly refuse to offer one when he had one lit himself. Without the cigarette, Edmund might not have known he was there. Oh, dear, how tiresome it was to have to manufacture sympathy instead of having it available in an endless, free supply. And to have those hopping thoughts interfere to remind him that while Edmund was a good soul, he was also a very plain man for whom washing was not a priority. It was easier to help clean, healthy people. A true saint would not notice the difference, but Christopher was not a saint, and he did.

'What ails you, Edmund?' he asked, heartily, sitting beside him and patting his thigh with his left hand, determined not to relinquish the cigarette. Then he looked down at Edmund's big feet, preparing himself to meet his eyes, and he could see exactly what was making the man cry. Within a yard were four bird corpses, blackbirds, he guessed without knowing one from another, although a closer glance showed them to be different sizes, and, it followed, different breeds. The cigarette dropped from his fingers and he brushed it away.

'Will you bless them, Father?' Edmund asked, calmly. 'Before I bury them?'

'They can have the full rites.'

He improvised. 'In your mercy, Lord, dispel the darkness of their night. Let their household so sleep in peace, that at the dawn of a new day, they may, with joy, awaken in your name. Through Christ our Lord, Amen.' This did not seem adequate. The priest moved to the corpses, made the sign of the Cross over each in turn, intoning softly, 'Upon you no evil shall fall, no plague approach where you dwell. For you He has commanded his angels, to keep you in all His ways. Amen.'

Edmund blew his nose. 'Thank you, Father.'

Christopher Goodwin sat down again and produced the cigarettes. Maybe it was disrespectful to smoke in the presence of death but Edmund would be the judge of that. He took a cigarette from the miserable packet of ten and Father Goodwin had an irrelevant memory of a grieving son who, when it came to the time to toss the clod of earth on to the coffin, had absent-mindedly thrown in a fag end instead. It was still grief.

'Were they killed by a cat?' he asked. Edmund began to shake. It looked as if he might weep again. He looked at the cigarette burning in his fingers and took a shuddering draw on it instead.

'They were . . . they were . . . murdered.'

'Surely not.'

'She was right,' he murmured. 'Matilda was right . . . She told me this morning he was a wicked boy and he shot the magpie and he poisoned these. What am I to think, Father? I loved him.'

'Loved who, Edmund?'

The cigarette was finished during this halting speech, which contained more pauses than words. They were as many words as Edmund could manage. He seemed, finally, to sense Father's inadequacy and pity him for it.

'Never mind, Father. The wicked get punished, don't they?'

'Not always in this life, Edmund, but often enough. Are you all right now? Shall I help you with the burial?'

'He's careful. He killed the females so the big boys won't come back to nest,' Edmund said.

'Who did?'

'Never mind,' Edmund repeated. 'I'd better get on. And so'd you, I expect.'

'Can I send someone to you?'

'No, thank you. Matilda will be out after supper. She says her prayers out here, you know.'

'Does she?'

'Thanks for the cigarette, Father. I owe you.'

The sense of unease had come back in full force, along with that familiar sense of being redundant. Feeling insensitive and unkind, Christopher Goodwin left.

It was half past six, the ridiculously early hour at which the Sisters sat down to a meal which he would have called tea and they, in their wisdom, called supper. Cold meats and salads at this time of year, augmented by soups and things on toast when the weather grew brisk. Some ate like troopers, others like sparrows, and the virtually bed-ridden group, which had included Sister Jude, ate nursery food in solitude. These he was supposed to visit on a weekly basis at least, depending on their state of health, which meant that up until now, he had stayed five minutes with Pauline and Dympna (who, as befitted one with the name of the patron saint of mental illness, was away with the fairies), and as many hours as he could spare with Sister Jude, who was never asleep and always lucid. He missed her and it reminded him that he was too frail for further effort this evening, too much on his mind even before Edmund and his dead birds. He detoured to the chapel. Snatched items from the meeting had lodged in his memory, something about the window being broken and mended in a miraculous way, leaving a residue of curiosity which, when he was as tired as he felt today, remained the only emotion he could sustain.

It looked the same as ever, the same as it had been when he said Mass here the Sunday before and less adorned than it had been when he had seen it with Jude's body lying in state amid the floral tributes she would have enjoyed better if she had received them when she was alive. There was no sign that any window had been broken: the room remained quiet and serene, mercifully free from the excessive and lurid statuary that marred so many a Holy Roman Church. Really, he was becoming so intolerant, reaching a state in life when mere opinion became so callused it turned into a prejudice. Maybe that joyful anarchist Kay was right and it was time to look for another religion. One without recrimination, prospects of hell and promises of heaven; one entirely without decorative gold leaf. One actually shared by the majority of the population. A life without duty and the burden of secrets.

Ahead of him, nearest the altar, was Anna, sitting, not kneeling mind, but still in an attitude of thought. The sight of her was obscurely disappointing. It should have gladdened his heart but had the reverse effect. He slunk down the black and white corridor, feeling like a criminal for the second time in ten minutes, past the refectory and the sound of talking, out of the front door, which was for once unguarded by Agnes. He felt like Judas.

Christopher: named for a famous saint and yet there was no benevolence about him today, no blessing from that saint as he strode down the road, so relieved not to be in the car that he walked like an athlete in training, thinking of the legend of his name and how he would tell it. That saint was a big man, a giant who wished to serve only the strongest and most magnificent of kings. Now, one great king and the promises of the devil had tempted him into service, but their demands were so puerile they disappointed him, and he defected into the life of a hermit, settled by the side of a dangerous river, where his self-appointed task was to carry travellers across, in a humble but useful employment for his physique, until one dark and stormy night, while he was carrying a mere baby across the torrent, the child became heavier and heavier, until he stumbled and sweated and almost fell, in despair of his own strength. Ah, said the child, I am Jesus, the king you have always been seeking, you are carrying the weight of the whole world.

My dear Anna, Father Goodwin, née Christopher, told her in mental communication, which lasted him until he turned into the park, that is what it is to have this belief. It

88

is a tyranny as well as a blessing. Please do not succumb, or at least, not yet. Let the hound of heaven bite at your heels for a long time before you turn and feed it.

It was a park of peculiar beauty, his frequent solace. As an added incentive for him to walk further, it surrounded a football ground for children to practise and he loved to watch them. Tiny schoolboys, kicking the shit out of the thing, sometimes indistinguishable in mud, playing in all weathers with no audience, no cries from a crowd, only exhortations from coaches and parents, and a burning desire to win in an orchestrated riot of energy. He never watched for long, in case anyone should assume that a dog-collared, cheap-suited man must be either a halfwit or a paedophile, although no one had ever thought so, as far as he knew. Paedophiles didn't chat to parents and yell themselves hoarse as he was inclined to do, but still, he left before the end. There was always a point in a game where he knew who would win, but it was a shame to miss the individual act of courage, the verve of the one who could play in the team and play without it.

He could write her a letter, rehearsed it in his head. *Dear Anna, Please continue being a pagan. Do not assume the mantle of a creed. Make your own rules. You have had the most appalling examples to follow, although you don't know it yet. Your mother, the saint . . . Ah well. Leave us, make a life without rules. Just make one. Do not kneel to anyone or anything. Never, ever kneel.*

And then he thought, what about all the other letters Anna must have received and Sister Jude alluded to? Letters regarding deaths, her mother's and her father's. What would she want with an old fool adding his own?

Inside the chapel, she did not kneel. She never knelt, she

89

simply conversed, in the manner Sister Jude had suggested, without the suggestion ever becoming an order. The window was mended without a trace of the destruction she had seen, as if it had never happened, truly a miracle.

'He walked me home, Lord, but I left him on the corner for the last bit. I don't want him to know where I live, although he might know already. Christ almighty, is he serious or is he *serious*? Anyway, I might have been late for the meeting if I hadn't run. I'm sure you approve.'

She eased her shoes off her feet. They were all still at supper and much more animated than usual, so that would last longer and leave her in peace. Her feet smelled slightly from a long day in trainers, but the Lord would have to put up with that. This wasn't the climate for going about barefoot, or wearing a long cotton robe like a disciple.

'Trust me to find another God freak,' she continued, twiddling her toes. 'With a hole in the brain, but maybe that's what you intended. Anyway, I'm sure you'll be delighted to know I've signed all these silly billies up for a taxi account. Told bloody Barbara I could get her a discount, and as you know that's always a draw. 'S'what Catholics have in common, always after a discount. Poor cow. I can't get her a discount, of course, but that isn't the point. How do you feel about lies?'

Black and white tiles in the corridor. Black lies are bad, white lies are fair.

'You know the trouble with you?' Anna said. 'You're looking such a pillock. Time to change the garments and upgrade. Get yourself an image. Make them speak Latin or something, get back a bit of that old mystique that everyone can sing along with. *Credo in Unum Deum*, get it chanted on a single note by absolute wallies in pink cassocks, that'll get them in. Evening classes. You'll get all the anoraks who can't otherwise string a tune. Plenty of those.'

She rested her bare feet on the chairback in front, tilting it towards her, the better to examine her toes. Fine little feet, which did not, at the moment, seem admirable. Too small for further use and uselessly perfect, apart from the grime between the toes.

'I tell you what, Lord. You were my best fucking mate when I was a kid, and then you buggered off and left me. And I could quite see why, because you were never there at all. Big-time illusion. Why didn't you make us well? Why have I got that priest on my back trying to tell me why we were cooped up for so long and my father left? Does he think I don't know? Well, I do know. Simple. He was too bad and she was too good.'

She put her feet back into shoes. It was getting cold and she did not want to lose her sense of jubilation. She leant towards the window, stared at the mended pane, willing it to do it again, wanting the sound of the smash, sitting back with her feet warm, wanting to be home and knowing it was near.

'You know what he said, Lordy? He said, aren't you small, and why are you so small? I said, you aren't so tall, either, you're half the size of my father and what's it got to do with you if I never grew? He's called Ravi. He's a Hindu. And do you know what he said to me? He said that all Gods are good Gods and all religions teach harmony. Why didn't anyone tell me that when I was ten? Anyway, I kidded him about it. Aren't we a sad pair? I told him. Two people of our age, walking down roads on a nice afternoon, talking about God. I mean, how sad can you get?'

She considered her feet and turned her face to the window.

'Anyway, I thought I'd let you know that for all the bad stuff Allah's supposed to have inspired, I think I like the sound of him better than you. And if I took up with Mohammed, I could still have Jesus and the Archangel Michael. But it looks like I'd better look at the Hindu first.'

She bent down and retied her shoelaces.

'Speaking of which,' she addressed the window behind the crucifix, 'I don't know what you did with that guardian angel of mine. Aren't we all supposed to have one? Muslims have two, you know. I'd be no good as a Hindu. No point thinking about it, I'm too impure. And I haven't got the option of honouring my father and my mother, have I? He left us and she's dead. That shocked Ravi. He said Hindus wouldn't do that. Do what, I said, die? Completely fucking pathetic, he is, when he should have been saying your place or mine if he knew what he was dealing with, just so I could say I never fuck in my place.'

Silence.

She yawned and rose.

'Night-night, Lord. Take care of Therese, even if you do a lousy job.' Then she sat down again. 'Look, OK. I'm beginning to see something about my sister. If this is where she thinks she belongs, she'd better stay. If this is where she gets happiness, she's got to have it. And that means I do anything, I mean anything, to keep this place afloat. Understood?'

She went slowly down the black and white corridor. Agnes was by the door. Agnes loved to be touched and hugged, so on an impulse, remembering with gratitude her voice, singing so unaffectedly by Sister Jude's grave, Anna patted her on her plump shoulder and found her own hand gripped and squeezed hard.

'Night, Aggie. You should do some more singing.'

'Goodnight, dear. I'm a very happy woman today. Do you know why?' She pulled Anna down to whisper in her ear. 'My son came to find me.'

Ah well, they all talked in code, sometimes. God made everyone batty, not necessarily bad.

Back inside her own flat, Anna went up to the roof. The sky was clear in one of those perfect evenings that made her feel cheated of the day until she remembered the rain, and Ravi. The trees by the chapel window shimmered as the shadows deepened. At the rear of the garden, she could make out the figure of Edmund, sitting. Too cold for an old man to sit out as if he had no home; it was late for him to be there, but that was his choice and Matilda would be somewhere around until darkness fell completely. How well she knew their routines in the garden, although not what any one of them really thought, believed, needed, and she was suddenly humbled. If Ravi the Hindu paid respect to other, alien creeds, then so should she.

Down below, among the silent shrubs, she thought she saw a flash of gold. A moving head, standing by Edmund's side and just as suddenly obscured. There would be a full moon tonight and Anna was too tired to watch for it; she would wait for the new moon and wish on that. Her whole small body vibrated with a massive, satisfying yawn. It was so peaceful out there and she had made her mark today, spoken out and someone had listened. She knew, for once, what it was like not to be angry. Maybe God lived on the moon and that was his face.

'Matilda? Are you there? Help me, please . . .'

'It isn't Matilda.'

'In the name of God, help me. Oh, you bastard boy. You killed them.'

'And I shall kill all the others. The thrush and the sparrow. Destroy all the nests. You can die as soon as you like, old man.'

'Help me . . .'

Darkness fell early.

Autumn began with a scowl on the face of the moon.

CHAPTER FIVE

Thou shalt not steal

It might be the last hot morning of the year.

Dear Mrs McQuaid

Re: The estate of Theodore Calvert
Thank you for yours of the 8th Inst.
    This is to confirm that your tenure of the house remains secure for at least the next six months, from today's date. As I know you will understand, Mr Calvert's investments were of the global variety and it will take some considerable time to convert the same into cash and assess the tax situation . . . Please apply to the signatory should you require funds for the maintenance of the house . . .

So that was all right then.

It was only in the unholy light of a milky morning that Kay liked the sea with the kind of emotion that was anywhere near genuine affection. She was fond of it when it was calm enough to look like something out of a travel brochure advertising long days in the sun somewhere else entirely, where the language, the food and the climate were so different it was surprising that the human beings had the same shape. The house was one road back from the front itself, sheltered from storms. She could hear the sea from there without being able to see it.

Today, it was warm, inviting and friendly, without much of a hint of the mysterious, which she did not like, and even less of a hint of power, which she liked even less. On a morning like this, it looked like a great big bath, with some strange jacuzzi effect going on underneath the surface. Clad in her ankle-length dressing gown of pale lilac towelling, shower cap and plastic shoes, Kay walked gingerly across the shallow incline of the shingle, shed the robe and waded into the water. Up to the chest in three steps, four strokes left and four right without ever taking her sunglasses off, that was enough, and emerged triumphant. The days when she might have stayed in longer and offered up the pain as a penance for her sins were long gone. The water was pleasantly bracing rather than cold, but there was no point getting chilly. Chilliness was uncomfortable.

Theodore Calvert, her employer, went swimming until well into winter, but then he always had something to prove. Either he was proving his virility, or he must have been a closet Catholic. What was it the Jesuits said? Give me a boy before he is eight and he is mine for ever? Even if he railed against that religion for as long as she knew him, Kay theorised that he might have been got at as a boy and that was what had given him that awful mindset, which she was still doing her best to eradicate in herself, namely the strange belief that discomfort equalled virtue and, by the same token, luxury bordered on sinfulness.

The problem about the open sky, mirrored in the

endless stretch of invigorating water, was that it drew her towards it and made her think, even when breakfast was more what she had in mind. The lulling noise of the quiet waves, so welcoming to her feet, was the voice of conscience. The sea was calm enough for a prophet to walk upon it. She looked at her toes through the opaque material of the plastic shoes and tried to concentrate on the fact that it was time for a pedicure, let the towelling robe soak the salty moisture from her skin as she sat comfortably on the warm shingle, telling herself she would be better off in the garden with a less awe-inspiring view, but she could not move. Theo Calvert had loved the sea and regarded it as a kind of playground, while, most of the time, she thought of it as cold, wet and inconvenient. After he had left his wife, he had moved to the coast because that was where he had always wanted to live. He had bought a house big enough for his daughters, but of course they had never arrived, not even for a visit. Theo had been a fool to expect any such thing. Also a fool to battle for custody of children who were not only ill but easily old enough to make up their own minds. His lawyers had told him he was mad. He was the one who had left the matrimonial home, was more of the grandfatherly age and bellowed that all his daughters needed was plenty of fresh air and an introduction to sex. His daughters had told a judge that they hated him and Theo had cursed and invoked the devil and thrown himself into the sea for early morning swims in the bitter cold. If she had told him then that he was mortifying his flesh to distract his thoughts, he would not have believed her.

Theodore Calvert claimed that he did not understand any of that. The religion of his wife, which informed her motherly self-sacrifice, was anathema to him, and the sea would be his undoing. It made him brood. Kay dragged herself back into the present world by fishing in her pocket for cigarettes. Too much oxygen was bad for the body. She must look a rare sight, walking from the big house up the side road and sitting on the beach dressed like this, but who cared? The place had its fair share of eccentrics, of which she was among the youngest. It was a seaside resort that had always attracted the elderly, close enough to London for an easy train ride, far enough away to be remote. Why the hell he had chosen it, God knows. He said he wanted a big sky, room to breathe. She lay back on the shingle so that she did not have to look at the sea. Definitely the voice of conscience.

Why the hell had she accompanied him all those years ago? She could have stayed in London and got another job, although not on those wages. Calvert was ludicrously generous, one of the reasons why she had stayed with the damn family as long as she had. Stayed, and been indispensable long after she had sussed what Mrs Calvert was like. It took one Roman Catholic, however lapsed, to recognise the symptoms of a terrible holiness in another. A tiny creature, Mrs Calvert, with huge eyes and an elegant gentleness in everything she did. Beautiful manners, soft, solicitous voice, the quiet movements of a convent-educated girl who had never kicked over the traces, although her dress sense was not anything she could have learned in a nunnery. She made you feel like a carthorse, but she was a lady, and it would have been a lady Theodore had wanted. Kay stuffed the cigarettes back into her pocket, suddenly sick at the thought of one, pushed her sunglasses up on her forehead and down again. The sunlight on the water was so bright it was an accusation to her eyes.

Look, she told herself, it's easy. She had followed Theodore to his rich retreat by the sea because she would never repeat such wages for the relatively easy work, and because of her son. Also, to be fair, because she could not bear to see those girls so sick or watch what Mrs Calvert was doing or be anywhere near it, but mostly because of Jack, or was it? A better life for rebellious Jack. That was it. Bring Jack with you, Theodore had said, he'll only get into trouble if you don't. Kay got to her feet and turned her back on the water. No, she had done it to spite that dreadful woman who had begged her to stay, she had done it out of solidarity with him and to please herself, the way she usually did. Oh, for God's sake, woman, you did what you thought was best and you still do.

Only, for someone raised as a Catholic, 'best' was never enough. What was it with them, she raged at herself, walking faster and faster on the way home, suddenly self-conscious about the shower cap, that made them such miseries? Not *them*, YOU. Hadn't she dumped the whole Catholic, nun-ridden Irish girlhood before she'd so much as looked at a boy? Didn't she poke fun at it? Didn't she take the fear of hell and drown it good and proper? She was thrown out and threw it out, been throwing it out ever since. What Christopher Goodwin had disturbed in his visit the day before last was an entirely irreligious, natural conscience, the sort that lived in the sea and shone light in her eyes like a torch, with a delayed effect, along with his plea that she should meet Anna Calvert and tell her what her father had been like, so that the child had a chance to form an honest picture of her past. In order to construct a future, Christopher had said. Excuse me, I'm on holiday, she said. I don't owe anything, I just do as I'm told.

She squelched to the back door without seeing a soul. A quiet place, sometimes too quiet. What had she ever done that was so wrong? She had not really encouraged old

Theodore to give up fighting for his daughters and love her own Jack instead. No, that was *not* the way it was. That was not what she had intended, but that was what had happened. She had wanted so much better for sulky Jack. She had never meant Theo to treat him as a son. She was breathing heavily, the shoes rubbed. Definitely the last swim of the year. Her body tingled and her head felt light. She touched the key to the house, held round her neck on a piece of string.

Nor had she meant it to filter back to Isabel Calvert that Theodore lived with his housekeeper as a convenient tart and preferred her boy to his own flesh and blood. Now that would have added to Mrs Calvert's saintly martyrdom no end. And it was not true. Theo adored his daughters. He had their movements monitored, although there was little enough to report when they never left the house. He also had his wife hounded by every official agency under the sun and Kay supposed that, in the end, he won. Mrs Calvert was forced to relinquish her hold on her invalids. The children were, in a manner of speaking, freed, with liberty to hate him even more for what he had done, but it was certainly true that he had been fond of Jack.

Kay unlocked the back door and padded upstairs to the master bedroom, which faced the main road. Theo's room, which she used as a dressing room, sitting on the balcony to get the late afternoon sun and watch the world go by, such as there was. It was the main thoroughfare into the town and nicely removed from it. She remembered that the regatta would be passing in the early evening and the thought cheered her. As soon as the bath was so full that the foam began to creep over the rim, she wallowed into it with a grateful sigh, a brown face emerging from white bubbles. Once she was immobilised, she began to think that the bath was a bad idea. It was not the sea that played havoc with conscience; it was the act of immersion in any old water. Some horrible throwback to baptism. She sank beneath the foam. The fact that she was a natural born liar was not a new realisation, or even a shameful one. It came from a lifetime's practice of telling people what they wanted to hear.

Anna Calvert had been a kid who loved sunshine. When Kay had been deputed to take that ten-year-old to the park, they both ignored the command to have a nice, healthy walk and sat on the grass instead, with their tops off and their skirts tucked into their knickers. Therese would have been younger, giggling like mad at the mention of a word like knickers, hopping around them like a plump pigeon. Nice, easy girls, then. The scene played before her eyes. Then she remembered the day when she had tried to introduce them to her son by bringing him along to say hello. Eighteen months older than Anna, he might have seemed glamorous to them, but there were not to be any dirty little boys in Mrs Calvert's house. Kay blew water out of her nose and reached for the bath plug. Surely they all could have played together? Maybe those girls would have civilised him. Crap. Nothing could have done that. Jack was streets ahead. He was eleven going on fifty and he never saw them again, except in photos, which Theo had in every room of this house. Kay finished the towelling dry (big, fluffy, indestructible towels she had persuaded Theo to buy), and felt conscience recede. It was soluble in soapy water, wiped away by moisturiser. Funny, the way she bothered about her skin and her appearance when her life was so isolated. Self-love was what it was, in deference to those advertisements that said, pamper yourself because you're worth it, and it was more to do with the sheer joy of idleness than attracting men, although there were always a few fellows hopping round like seagulls, making equally silly noises. Sod that. She did not really want the mess or the sheer effort of a man, and however much she might tease poor Christopher on his monthly visits, she only did it because he was a priest. If she was ever offered a night of passion, or a tumbler of Drambuie, she knew which she would choose. OK, she was a liar and she was lazy and she was sometimes a flirt, and that was fine. The only real question was what to wear.

A door downstairs slammed. Kay heard it, even with her head muffled in a towel, and she froze. Had she left the back door open, the fool that she was, while she was lying in her bath waiting to be drowned? She ran into the bedroom, naked as a beast, clung to the doorframe for comfort. The wind must have taken the patio door and slammed it shut, that would be what it was. She was not a housekeeper for nothing; she was paranoid about security. She knew she had left no doors open, and there was not the slightest breeze. Kay listened, waiting for the sound of footsteps, of breathing, a cough. Waited two whole minutes, getting cold. Nothing, until she heard the reassuring sound of a car passing in the road. Pulling on her gown, she tiptoed to the top of the stairs and sniffed the air. All she could smell was the familiar emptiness of the house, free from anything but the lingering scent of bubble bath. She must stop behaving like this, reacting so dramatically to sudden sounds. It was an old house; it had a language of its own. Let other silly women become neurotic about living alone; she loved it and she was not going to be one of them. Kay thumped down the corridor to her own room at the back, reminding herself it was the regatta today, so she

102

would enter into the spirit of the town's annual celebration and wear something just a bit festive. Sex was too much trouble for words, but she did like to be admired, and the balcony of Theo's room was a ringside seat for the carnival parade.

She had made her own room pretty as a picture. Pastel wallpaper with a flowered border, toning colours on the deep flounce of her bed, frilled net curtains of snowy white beneath the pale velvet of the heavier drapes, which she pulled at night. A series of flower prints on the walls and a dressing table with the legs hidden by lace. She made her bed and realigned the decorative cushions as soon as she got out of it in the morning, so that whenever she came back into the room, it would look as she liked to see it, as sweet as it was orderly. Not now.

The differences were small, but significant. One of the pictures was crooked, as if someone had brushed by. There was a bottom-shaped indentation on the bed. The top drawer of the chest was half-open. She felt sick, made herself breathe slowly. Someone had been here and she thought she knew who it was. He had been, he was gone and he would be back.

Just a kid looking for money.

For letters, for papers, for something.

For her.

Like before.

Today was the afternoon shift. Anna could have slept far longer if the blind in her attic room blocked out the light. She lay where she was, torn between curling herself back into sleep and the compulsion to find the source of the light and bask in it. Summer was ending, the heat of the sun was rationed, wasting it was tantamount to a sin and

103

getting up, putting on shorts and T-shirt to climb on to the roof, was almost a duty. She hauled up a sleeping bag and a cup of coffee. Sleep could be resumed in the sun. It was a grumpy pleasure. First, she examined the view. A ritualistic prowl around the small space of the roof, as if she were a sentry patrolling the ramparts of a castle.

The road at the front was fully awake. The newsagent was open, water was being sloshed over the pavement in front of the bar, two people waited at the bus stop. The sound of cars was pleasant from this distance. Leaning over, she could see a figure emerge from the main entrance of the block and walk away purposefully. What other people did all day was a subject of intense curiosity. They were all trained for life in ways she was not and it was better not to make comparisons, but few of them were as free as she was. Looking down at the bustle of the street below, she wondered how she would ever explain to Ravi how or why it was her rent was paid until the end of the year by some blood money arrangement set up by her father before he drowned and how she had no choice but to accept it because she could not possibly live anywhere else. She had to be close to Therese. It was a lovely day, and that, for the moment, was all that mattered. Anna yawned, clasped her hands above her head, and stretched as far as she could, rotating her hips, unknotting sleepy joints and enjoying the sensation. She would do the exercises later. The bathroom towel rail served as a barre and the bedroom as a gymnasium. All she needed was a floor. She had to be strong for the day when Therese would need her again.

With looser limbs, she moved round to the other side of the roof and looked down into the convent garden. The trees were turning autumn coloured; soon there would be bare branches rattling against the chapel windows with their own music and there would be the carpet of leaves, which she had seen the year before and which Edmund would be slow to clear. When it was done, and the leaves were dry, he would pick a grey day and take the risk of lighting a delicious fire, forbidden in a smoke-free zone, and all the more exciting. She recalled from last year, in her first autumn here, her delight in the pure smoke, which rose and drifted away across her roof. What harm in burning leaves, instead of piling them into bags for someone else to do? She would offer to help this year, unless this Francis, whom she had nicknamed the Golden Boy, was all he needed. She must meet this boy, whom the nuns had so taken to heart. They could make money out of their garden; there were innumerable things they must do if they were going to survive. Edmund would have to help. She peered over the wall. Why there he was, sitting on his bench, looking comfortable and remote from this height. She was tempted to call out to him, but he would never hear, and besides, no one inside the convent walls knew that she watched and no one must know. They tolerated her, but she was always on probation. Barbara was beginning to find her useful, but if anyone knew she watched like an amateur spy, she would be banished, with Therese's blessing, and that would be unbearable. Anna ducked back in case Edmund looked up, as if he ever would, he who never seemed to lift his eyes higher than the walls. Then she looked again.

He was sitting so still, in the same place he sat in the spring of the year to listen to the dawn chorus of his birds. He sat in the same immobile way she had seen the night before, with a slight difference in attitude, so his body twisted sideways, uncomfortably, the way a person might sit in order to have a conversation with someone who stood behind them. One hand appeared to grip the back of the bench. It was not natural to sit like that when alone, especially not for a weighty man like himself, who always adjusted his stance to accommodate his bulk. It came to her, in a slow, dark realisation, that he had sat there all night. Entirely against the rules. Everyone other than the Sisters went home before supper, via the front door.

She scrambled down the ladder, paused only for shoes, raced down the stairs, out of the block and round to the convent door. Left, left and left again, bumping into two pedestrians without having enough breath to say sorry. She stabbed at the bell at the side of the door, waited and stabbed at it again. She looked at her watch. Christ, it was scarcely breakfast time in there, they might all be in chapel or asleep. It occurred to her, even in the rising panic, which made her heart race, that she did not *know* what they did in there in the majority of time when she was absent; she did not even know what her beloved sister did with each of her waking hours, only that she disapproved of it with all the fury of a rabid dog. Where was Agnes? Where was anyone? What was the fucking point of being at fucking prayer when you should be answering the door? Who do you think you are?

The door was flung open, with none of Agnes's creeping, smiling reticence, which always gave the impression she had slid three or four bolts and removed a chain to get that far and, however welcoming, would replace all the armoury as soon as you left. To Anna's discomfiture, it was Barbara, all bossy briskness and twinkling, interrogative eyes behind her glasses, looking as if she had slept well enough to slap down the nonsense of the day with a firm hand. The likes of Anna could be consumed before

106

breakfast. To Anna's further alarm, she smiled. Perhaps this was her best time of day.

'Ah, Anna, my dear. How nice to know you young things are up and about at a decent hour. Although scarcely dressed, I see. I wanted to have a chat, as it happened. Come in.'

She followed, meekly. Another time, the tart reference to shorts and T-shirt would have made her furious, but she was suddenly aware of the quandary she was in. She wanted to shout, *There is something the matter with Edmund*, but yelling any such thing would be too much of a revelation to Sister gimlet eyes, who would be sure to say, *How do you know?* And then she would have to say, *I can see him from my rooftop*, and Barbara would say, *You what?* She was dumbstruck, followed in the draught of Sister Barbara's voluminous tunic, which hung from her big bosom as if supported on balloons, until they were both in the passage with the black and white tiles.

'Come into the parlour, dear. We've things to discuss. I've decided I haven't been entirely fair to you and you had such *good* ideas at the meeting yesterday, entirely in accord with my own. Of course we have to get rid of the car. The idea of a taxi account is brilliant. Are you sure about the discount? But what I chiefly wanted to explain to you, dear, is what Therese does here, because I've got an awful feeling you might not know.

'For a start, this is a liberal, secular order. She does not have to wear a hairshirt, she does not have to sing Matins, Lauds, Prime, Sext or even Vespers, although she is exhorted to pray, in a formal fashion, and we do still have the Angelus, because we like it. A lovely prayer, I think. I just wanted to reassure you, as her nearest and dearest, that she isn't in for a life of flogging and she can go whenever she wants, but I'm sure dear Sister Jude reassured you of that. Things have changed since your mother was a child. Not always for the better, but there it is. I still prefer the Latin, myself. So much more poetic.'

It was a virtual torrent of words from someone who was indeed at their best first thing in the morning, after her restless nights had digested facts and advice and spat them out as priorities. Anna found herself thinking, She's a kind old tart, telling me useful information, and dear Lord why didn't I realise that before instead of being so frightened of her, while still mightily frightened.

'Father Goodwin told me you were awfully sensible, and I must admit, I was slow to comprehend. But you are, my dear, you are admirable. Full of good *initiatives*. Was there something you wanted? Breakfast will be in a minute. You're welcome.'

Just in time, she remembered the vernacular of their relentless courtesy, which, in the past, made her itch.

'You're kind, Sister. It was just that . . . just that . . . I heard on the news about a bomb, oh not real, just one of those scares. Wanted to check you knew about it. I don't know what you know, if you see what I mean. It's very warm, Sister. Do you think we could go into the garden?'

'Jolly good idea. Don't use it enough.'

There were French doors from the parlour out on to the terrace part of the garden. Barbara flung them open with the same potentially destructive aplomb she used on the front door, impatient but efficient with all the clumsy locks that surrounded them.

'Such a nuisance,' she announced as she struggled with the grille. 'But we have to keep people out, you know, especially these days. As soon as anyone knows the existence of a convent, they're outside the doors wanting food and everything. Which we want to give as far as we can, but not if they abuse us. There's beggars and beggars.'

The door was open. That was what a convent was like, Anna thought, door upon door, upon door. The garden was like an escape to another planet. Barbara went on talking.

'We've got to make use of space. My dear, that's a buzz word, or do I mean *phrase*, years old. Now, if you have any ideas of what to do about this, I'd be grateful to hear, in fact I'm all ears.'

She had big ears, Anna noticed, clamped to the side of her thick, close-cropped grey hair like a pair of horns. They went with her bosom.

'Perhaps we could walk down to the end,' Anna suggested. 'Get the measure of it.'

'Good idea. Brave the bugs and walk the estate, such as it is? Yes!'

They found Edmund on his bench, by his shed, a short walk only impeded by the brushing away of branches.

Barbara saw him first and called out merrily, 'Edmund, dear, so soon? What a fine day it is!'

Anna wanted to catch hold of her sleeve and hold her back, but Barbara ploughed forward, delighted at the thought of lazy old Edmund being so soon for work, not wondering yet about who had let him in. A fly crawled on his forehead; another hovered around his open mouth, from which a line of dried saliva crept down to his chin. It was his tolerance of the flies that signified his death. Barbara waved them away, touched his cold hand without saying a word. She withdrew her own, quickly, as if she had been stung, then, shielding the body from Anna's gaze, she deftly closed Edmund's ghastly eyes and made the sign of the Cross. She was perfectly calm; she had closed the eyes of the dead more often than she could count, but never in these circumstances and she did not know quite what to do.

'I'm afraid he's dead. Must have been a stroke.' It was an inadequate remark, but that was all she could say, although she wanted to bite back the words as soon as they were spoken. She was expecting screams, but Anna was not to be protected. She had moved behind the bench and looked down at him. This was an obscenity, Barbara thought, suddenly angrier with Edmund than she had ever been. No girl of her age should witness death. Anna surprised her.

'You'll be needing to phone for the doctor and Father Goodwin. I'll stay with him, shall I?'

'Are you sure?'

'Yes. We can't just leave him, can we?'

'No. I'll send Therese.'

'Don't—'

'She'll be the only one dressed.'

She was gone, running up the garden with enough noise to make the birds rise from the trees. Anna registered the sound of their tuneless alarm as she sat on the bench beside Edmund's body. She could not touch him, confined herself to waving the flies away from his face and standing guard against the nameless enemy, which had already struck. And praying. *Kyrie eleison*, Lord, have mercy. In the silence that followed the chatter of the birds, she wished she had told Barbara to fetch Matilda, because Matilda was Edmund's friend, but that, too, would have begged an awkward question, even if it was one delayed until Barbara had time to reflect. The guilt was as acute as pain; she had seen Edmund sitting here yesterday; she could have intervened, knocked on the door. She tried to concentrate on Edmund himself, maybe speed his soul to a painless heaven and

110

deny her own revulsion at this defunct bundle of oddly sweet-smelling flesh. She had not seen the corpse of her mother, nor had she seen Sister Jude; she had reeled from the impact of death, but of bodies, she knew nothing. The curiosity about it was greater than the shock.

On the bench, beside Edmund's clenched fist, was a small, gold crucifix on a broken chain. She picked it up and examined it. Cheap, but durable, easy to mend. She supposed it was his in the same moment she hid it inside her shoe. Thinking that if there was any memento of Edmund, it should go to Matilda, and Barbara could not be trusted to do that.

There were light footsteps coming back down the garden. Therese appeared, carrying a blanket.

'Go away!' Anna yelled.

Therese paused, came forward with the blanket. 'Don't be silly.'

With soothing sounds, she tucked it round Edmund's form. Anna stood up to make room. They hugged, fiercely.

'Come away, Anna, do. You're cold. He was a good man, gone to a better life.'

The pious platitude made her blood boil.

'Oh, for *Chrissakes* . . . Can't you do better than that?'

'Be quiet, Anna.'

They stood with their arms around each other, Therese tugging her hair as if that would keep her warm, making Anna wonder, with the unexpected objectivity that follows shock, which of them was designed to protect the other and wondering all the more, because she had always thought the role was hers.

Kay felt protective about this house. Nothing else had been disturbed, not Theo's desk, nothing. Kay was sure she would notice and knew at the same time that maybe she would not. It was vanity on the part of a zealous house-keeper to think she would detect any other fingerprint than her own, when in reality, a burglar could cover his tracks if he was careful and refrained from the obvious such as eating the food. No marks on the clean bottles of the drinks trolley, but then, not even burglars fancied liqueurs before breakfast.

By late morning, after another bath, she was trying to make herself laugh, as well as tell herself that the burglar, with his minimal interference, was a complete stranger. A big old house with no man in it was bound to be a draw. Envy was what it was. There were several possible culprits, but none with a key. Crap. She knew the neighbours in a polite and cooperative way, which had been forged when Theo had been carried home drunk by the man of the house on the left. There existed between herself and the house on the right an adequate relationship founded by her never refusing to return a football or complaining about children's noise, even if she did try to clip their tree. They kept her house keys in case of emergencies and she kept theirs. Kids . . . that explained it all. Like the very first time she had an illicit visitor, soon after Theo departed life.

She was reluctant to change the keys. They had been the same keys ever since she came here. By mid-afternoon, she told herself it was not serious and all would be well. Little, bitty, pathetic attempts at theft were not important, a fact confirmed when she went back to her bedroom and had a sudden vision of little Anna Calvert, caught in the act of stealing. Frozen, she had been, that titchy ten-year-old, about to filch her mother's earrings as Kay barged in with the Hoover, the little mite so mesmerised by making her selection, trying them on and stuffing the favourite bits in her pockets, that she would not have heard an elephant, let alone the anonymous cleaning lady lugging a machine and wondering how soon she could get this done and have a smoke. Bashing the Hoover against the door and catching Anna, facing the mirror, her small face as pale as a ghost, the mouth a gash of her mother's lipstick and guilt oozing out of every pore, as if, at that age, she was even capable of sweat. The conscience of a child was so variable and so brave. It had the same capability of an adult in lust, with self-delusion to the fore, suppressing the native knowledge of what was wrong and what was going to be a heap of trouble, until the two came together in a moment of shameful truth. Kay had caught Anna at just such a moment and knew when she did so that the actions of the child would be treated as if they were serious sins. So, aware of Mrs Calvert in the kitchen, she had simply gone into the bathroom and handed Anna a sheet of loo paper to wipe her lips and then, over the sound of the Hoover, mouthed, *Put them back.* The child had emptied her pockets, stuffed jewellery back where it belonged, cast Kay a beseeching glance and run from the room after interpreting Kay's *and wash your face* with a desperate nod. This little vignette of memory cheered Kay no end. If she had found the little shit who had got into Theo's house this morning, she knew she would have done something along the same lines. Attempted theft was not the worst of crimes. Besides, the sun was out, and she could lie in the sheltered patio for an hour, and that made everything bearable and believable, all by itself. The day passed.

No, she owed that child nothing.

The light would be going by half past seven. The carnival parade was due about seven. Funny old town, this, she thought with affection. Everyone else has their sodding parades earlier. She got a drink, turned on every light in the house in case she had to come back indoors into darkness, stuck her amazingly sensible casserole, which had displaced another hour of the day in the making, into the oven, and settled herself on the balcony in Theo's stargazing chair. It was rusted from the salt, but the cover was as clean as her hair and the air was warm. There was a thumping of drums in the distance. The carnival parade would be unsophisticated, amateur, a bit trashy, a dying but lively tradition, but it would be fine. On the second gin and tonic, sipped to forestall the inevitable delay, Kay reflected to herself that she was easy to please. You could take the girl out of her small town, but you could never take the small town out of the girl.

And yet, when the parade began, rumbling into view from the distance on its final leg of the loop around the town, where it had begun and got stalled an hour before it reached her, she felt as lonely as all hell. So what, it was simply one of those days when cheerful things were depressing and somebody's story about having breast cancer would be positively cheering. She lived here, without belonging, without certainty, with a past she chose to ignore, obligations, loyalties and a future that depended on promises. The first float came level with the window and the mood passed.

Such an effort they made, such things they revealed. The parade was headed by a Scottish band, swinging along as if they meant it. A man with a leopardskin cloak to cushion the strap of the enormous drum strapped over his belly, with legs like tree trunks, socks like a footballer and a hat down over his brow. Another man, equally large, with a wailing bagpipe and a red face, the last of his lament drowned by the stereo sound of the float behind, booming out *Yeah, yeah!* something to herald the arrival of three carnival queens dressed like bridesmaids with the maquillage of forty-year-olds plastered on teenage faces above corseted, bosom-uplifting frocks with nothing to uplift. Kay frowned in disapproval. They waved in a sketchy fashion to the hangers-on walking alongside; they were tired. Not as fatigued as the boys on the Boy Scouts' float that followed theirs. Five cub scouts huddled around a large leader, recognisable as Mrs Smith, an enormous woman dressed in feathers who otherwise worked in the fish shop. Another band, girls this time and far more alert, followed by the Kitty's Tea Room float, featuring jolly women sitting around a huge papier mâché teapot, sipping wine from china teacups and pretending to eat cake. No one could eat cake for an hour. They were nicely merry and Kay raised her glass to them. More carnival queens, poor little ducks in their gooseflesh-revealing evening gowns. There was a loud float for a disco, a small float for Julian's Kidney Appeal towards which she threw money, a nice float for a dancing school, which included sweet little tots with plenty of energy left to boogie to the music, followed by the rugby club float, with a whole lot of men dressed like apes, benignly drunk, firing water pistols at the accompanying crowd, who fired back, followed by another set of those wretched carnival queens. A crowd of camp followers followed either side of each performance. A tired wee show, with too much booming for her taste. Singing was always better. The last three floats belonged to the churches.

The town had three at the last count. Episcopalian, Methodist and Catholic, where she had, contrary to every other instinct, made Jack go, with his talisman of a necklace, and it was as if, in their annual advertisement, they competed in a vain attempt to draw followers. The first two had the best hymns, belting out 'When the Saints Come Marching In' and promising real joy in the delivery, even though their voices were hoarse. The flatbed lorry on which they travelled had no followers and nobody collecting money in buckets, the way the others did. The third float, for St Augustine's Holy Romans, singing 'Abide With Me' faster than usual, almost in ragtime, also had the figure of the devil dancing like a dervish, whirling and writhing in his lizard-like costume of scales and tail, his headdress of horns already gone with the effort of lying down every few minutes in a mimic of surrender, while one of the hymn singers, dressed as an angel, poked him with a long-handled, obviously plastic fork as he lay down, before springing up and doing the whole business all over again. As they passed her balcony, the devil got up and bowed. And then he spat. A magnificent spitting unnoticed in the split second it took for the spittle to land at the edge of the balcony, on her feet. A posse of three fat policemen followed behind, encouraging the tail end of the parade to turn the corner.

That was Jack.

Her bastard, Jack, whatever he called himself now.

A policeman on a motorbike looked up at her and smiled in admiration.

She smiled back, frozen with terror.

Wishing she could pray.

CHAPTER SIX

Honour the Sabbath Day

It was at the next Sunday Mass, six days later, when the convent chapel was open to the public, that Anna first saw the Golden Boy at close quarters. There was something peculiarly striking about him, quite apart from the obvious fact of good looks. What it was did not strike her immediately, but somewhere near the end of the recitation of the Creed, when the rest of the congregation were mumbling in unison . . . *we acknowledge one baptism for the remission of sins. We look for the resurrection of the dead and the life of the world to come* . . . while she was keeping her own mouth firmly shut, sneaking a glimpse at the crucifix and the trees beyond the windows so that she could keep herself from fidgeting and try not to show how much she was there on sufferance. For the reasons that it would please Therese, make a gesture of respect for Edmund, who would be the subject of prayers, maybe afford an opportunity not available in the last few days to give his crucifix to Matilda and because it was convenient for her meeting Father Goodwin immediately afterwards. An appointment for counselling, no doubt, heavily and clumsily described as an invitation to lunch. He had been hovering ever since the death of Sister Jude.

The priest was resplendent in a chasuble of peculiar beauty, which did not suit an old boy who would look better in jeans, as he led the congregation in the undramatic translation of the Creed, which he probably thought was infinitely better in Latin. She concentrated on the back of the head of the Golden Boy and worked out what it was about him that struck such a chord.

He could have been the model for a painting of St Sebastian, the soldier martyr, pinned against a tree and shot to death with arrows, only Sebastian had dark hair. He could have been a saint or an angel, that was it, Michael the Archangel, with an expression of suffering. It meant that he simply looked as if he belonged, he could almost have stepped down from the walls of a church in Florence, straight out of a fresco. Even in a shabby suit too large for him, he could equally have been one of the figures from the Stations of the Cross, which mimicked the same style of haughty faces and plentiful hair. Anna looked at the ground. She had made a concession to the occasion, as well as to the rest of the day. Proper shoes, little red pumps, and a long skirt, which almost reached her ankles. Father Goodwin turned to face them all. Cynically, she considered that full attendance at this particular Sunday Mass might be explained by the extreme brevity of his sermons.

Which would consist of kind words for Edmund, plus a homily on the nature of impermanence for a man buried two days before and not, it had to be said, extravagantly mourned. Anna felt she was the only one to notice, not because she had really known him, but because she had seen him and it came on top of another death. For the community as a whole, it seemed to be a bit of a relief, but then if death was merely a rite of passage to heaven, they could take it as a mere blip in infinity. She tried to imagine

118

Edmund's lumbering form suddenly transformed into a lithe body fluttering about with wings, like the birds in the garden, and stifled a smile. It was funny and it helped to suppress the notion that Edmund's dying was a blessing to the dear Sisters, because now they could have Francis, instead. She hoped in his early morning Mass at the parish church, Father Goodwin had remembered to mention that the convent car was for sale.

In the early stage of the Mass, there was the rite of penance. *I confess to Almighty God, to you, my brothers and sisters, that I have sinned through my own fault, my own fault, my most grievous fault* . . . She could no more say that aloud either, than she could fly over the moon. Sin was an inexplicable concept in her interpretation of the catechism, because it seemed to have so little to do with the causing of harm, and surely a sin demanding penance and forgiveness should at least have done that. When she, as a newly emancipated twenty-year-old, had hunted down a couple of men a week until she had systematically rid herself of her virginity, simply to find out what it was like and prove that she could, there didn't seem to be any harm to anyone. It had been a curiously impersonal exercise and she could not see how it qualified as sin. All she had done was read a couple of books about it, then went out and did it, because that's what everyone did and it was easy if you weren't fussy and got drunk first. Lord, she addressed the window, You're a repressive old git. Let me know what sin is before I do worse to find out. That was the difference between her and Therese. Same upbringing, same shackles of love and faith, but in her case it was like an inoculation that did not take, leaving this incomplete, contemptuous disbelief. Perhaps it was simply the difference between good and bad.

Her gaze drifted back to the Golden Boy, examining his profile during the moment in the service when they all turned round and shook each other's hands in one of those poxy little rituals she particularly disliked. A saintly face, rather mournfully handsome and sensual, making her shiver as she remembered the couplings of her experimental months without shame, but a sense of wasted time. None of them had looked like him. He was entirely at home in here, but still exotic.

Ite missa est . . . The Mass is ended. The insoluble mystery of the Son of God becoming man, dying horribly, rising nobly and making his flesh available with each consecration of the host. Bloody barbaric. How could Therese believe it? She lingered at the end, hoping for a word, but the chapel was slow to empty and the Lord was never available in a crowd. Sister Barbara was standing by the exit, defying anyone to ignore the wooden collection box fixed to the wall. There were no children today.

She met Father Goodwin by the front door, flanked by Agnes, who looked radiantly happy and ready for the lunch that would follow and was better than average on Sundays in case there were guests. Anna hated the way they kept the best for everyone else and the worst for themselves. Christopher Goodwin, freed from vestments, looked like a tired horse at the starting gate, wanting to run but fatigued at the thought of the effort. It had taken her a long time to realise that she frightened him and now she realised he wanted to get away from all this smiling goodness as much as she did. She crooked her arm through his, and led him out. In accord, they scuttled down the street, liberated, almost at ease.

'I got paid, yesterday,' she said. 'So I'm buying, OK?'

'Oh no, you mustn't . . . I thought . . . McDonald's,' he

said, delighting in the contact, pressing her arm against his side, embarrassed about his budget for this, or any occasion.

'Is that as far as your pocket money stretches?' she asked. 'I thought we might go for curry and beer.'

The mention of pocket money riled him for a second, but that passed before they turned the corner. It was one of his embarrassments, to live on an allowance that never quite stretched and made him more than slightly dependent on the charity of others, not for dull necessities, but certainly for luxuries. He would never, ever be able to reciprocate the hospitality he received, and that irked him, particularly in the company of a young woman who needed a father figure in his estimation, preferably one who could say that the price of a meal was not a problem, unless it was inside his own, self-catering kitchen, where he produced for himself an endless succession of things on toast. Tasty things on toast, to be fair, and infinitely better than the ruthless convent meals to which he was so automatically invited. Toast and butter never failed. He could compromise on things on top in order to buy a beer to go with an important match on the telly. Two cans for a Cup Final, although that was always tempting fate. Someone was bound to interrupt. The thought of curry and beer made him weak with pleasure he did not want to reveal. This was a serious occasion, although she was so skittish, she seemed to have no comprehension.

'Lead on!' he commanded, feeling a berk. He was desperately hungry: Sundays always did that.

'I forget how young you are,' he said, relinquishing her arm because she was going faster. 'You won't have had the regime I was born to. If you went to Mass on Sunday, you had to fast from midnight on Saturday, which was all well and fine if you took your Communion early in the day, not otherwise. A good rule, I think. I've always kept it. I could eat a horse.'

'So could I,' she said fervently. 'We'll ask for it.'

Thanks be to God, he told himself. So far so good. Let her take charge.

'So how much do you earn at the taxi place, that you're taking an old man out for his food when it should be the other way round?'

'Enough,' she said.

The Standard Tandoori was everything it should have been, dark, dismal and almost deserted, with tables in booths that reminded him of an old confessional. She lit up a cigarette, offering one, too, which he thought it prudent to refuse and then changed his mind, to hell with it. Who was trying to make an impression on whom? He had known this child, spoken to her on and off, for over a dozen years, yet he did not know her at all. It was difficult to know how to get on with her, especially when he knew so much about her from other sources, Sister Jude and Kay, to be precise, their information overlaid with his memory of what Anna had been like as a young teenager, which was pretty, pugnacious and sweet.

'I'll order for us, shall I?' she asked.

He was touched to see that there was enough of that child left in her to enjoy her current superiority. He did not know where to start with this menu and it gave her an advantage. She was on familiar territory; he was not.

'Of course,' he said humbly. 'Unless you're meaning to poison me.'

She laughed at that, and reeled off a list of orders to a hovering waiter, who wrote nothing down and went away.

'So how are you keeping?'

'I'm fine. I thought this curry was a good idea though. Indian food might get me in the mood. I'm off to visit a temple this afternoon.'

'A temple?'

'As in a Hindu temple,' she said, watching the waiter pouring the beer into his glass.

'Ah yes,' he said, recognising this as some sort of challenge. 'Would that be the one in Neasden, or the one in Watford? They vary a great deal, you know. Each has a different character. I find the Hindu tolerance of diversity quite amazing. I wish we had it.'

He did not know if she expected him to question her about why the hell she might be venturing into the buildings of some pagan faith and pour scorn on the idea, but she simply nodded, satisfied with the response. The food arrived with indecent speed and they began to eat, with quiet and intense enjoyment. Looking at her eat was a pleasure. She was like a delicate little cat, making sure not to miss a morsel.

'Lord, I don't know where you put it,' he said, confidence restored along with his blood sugar. 'And now will you tell me how you really are? Just humour an old friend, will you? I want nothing, but I need to know. And if you're telling me that you're about to embrace another faith and run off with a Hindu, let me be the first to congratulate you. I've scarcely had the chance to tell you how sorry I am about Sister Jude.'

She sat back, relaxed, no aggression at all. How hard it was to cross the age gap, and convince someone almost three decades younger than yourself that you actually had something in common, such as normal human emotions. Then he remembered Anna was different, had always been at home with her elders, entirely undeterred from

123

argument by the age factor, and had, as Sister Jude had told him, an extraordinary range of sympathy for someone of her age. Don't condescend to her.

'Yes,' she said, slowly. 'I'm sorry for the conversations we might have had, and all the things she might have told me. Selfish. We had excellent conversations, but a lot of the time I raged at her about Therese. Blamed her for influencing Therese into the Order. She told me she had tried to stop her and I told her she was a liar. I should have known better. Therese is as stubborn as a mule and does what she wants, always has, and Jude couldn't lie. She was bloody economical with the truth, though. She held out on me, she always did. We could joke with each other, but she still held out on me. So now I have to think about what she said. Examine the innuendoes.' She laughed. 'I think most of this happens in my sleep. The thinking, I mean. I can't do it consciously, it has to happen when I'm not aware. Isn't that a contradiction in terms?'

'Like children, growing in their sleep.'

'Not that much in my case.' She leaned forward, eyes on the last piece of thick naan bread, tearing a piece off the corner.

He hesitated. 'You know, I'm a bit puzzled about basic information when it comes to you and Therese,' he said. 'Slightly at sea on some of the details. I was parish priest when you lived in the big house on Somertown Road, when you got ill the first time. Lord, it's less than a mile from here, but it seems so far. Your mother was devout, very helpful in the parish, but I was not, er, *encouraged*, to visit.'

'That would be my father. The sod.'

He did not correct her. 'I don't think I was paying sufficient attention. It's easy to assume, you see, that a family as

124

well off as yours can take care of its own needs, spiritual and otherwise. Then I was away for almost two years. I had . . . a nervous breakdown.'

'Did you? I never knew.'

'Well, we Catholics don't talk about embarrassing things like that. Especially mental affliction, it's a terrible sign of weakness.'

'Why did you have the breakdown?'

Don't condescend to her. 'Ah well, that's difficult to explain, but I think it was because of a slow-burning realisation that I shouldn't be a priest, that I should be something else, and I got better when I realised that I had no choice, because it was what I was fit for and even if I was a square peg in a round hole, there was no better way for me to serve God. But we aren't talking about myself.'

'I'd rather you did.'

'Another time I should like to as well. Very much, but not now. When did you and Therese become ill? You were only a nipper.'

'I'm still a nipper,' she said, bitterly. 'But I was too old to count as one.'

Apparently unbidden, two large glasses of sweet lassi arrived. He eyed his with suspicion, drank cautiously and was surprised to find how much he liked it, despite a general aversion to things that tasted as if they were good for him. He was staggered with relief that she was in the mood for talking. Something nice must have happened to her.

'It started with me. I got some bad viral infection, might have been pneumonia. Thought it was the wrath of God for experimenting with drink and getting sick as a dog at the age of fourteen, or whenever it was. I just didn't get better, for months. It was like having flu all the time. Then Therese succumbed and I suppose, basically, we took to

125

our beds. ME was the diagnosis, after lots of proddings and tests. We both stopped school, of course. Mum waited on us hand and foot, like a slave, bought us books so we could understand our own symptoms, chivied us along and it just went on like that. We were ferried off to hospital several times, but Mum got us out. She was wonderful.'

She swallowed, not liking this recall, wanting to hurry it up. Someone cleared the plates. Christopher could feel the spicy food, eaten too fast, percolating in his stomach.

'Friends from school used to come for the first year, but that stopped. We must have been incredibly boring, even on the good days when Therese could manage cooking lessons and I could read, which was all I could do, all I did do, most of the time. We were terrified of germs. Mum had the theory that if we lived in a germ-free zone, our own natural resources would make us better, only they didn't. Only prayers could do it. One year went into two, three . . . four. That's it, really.'

'And your father?'

'He was a bastard. Didn't believe in this ME mumbo-jumbo. Ranted and raved and kept on trying to put us in a car and take us to the seaside, which he thought was the cure for all ills, even when I could scarcely get down the stairs. Shelled out a fortune for doctors without ideas, had rows. In between work, of course. He was a workaholic to save himself being an alcoholic. Bastard. Then, about two years into it, he went, just like that.'

'Well, he had to work to earn the money,' Christopher said, choosing his words carefully. 'Did he just *go*, or could it have been, do you think, that your mother *locked* him out?'

She looked at him with cold fury. Such amazing eyes, she had. He almost winced.

'Forgive me,' he went on. 'Simply an idea, something she might have done if she thought he was interfering with your treatment. Preventing your development by his attitude. That was the time when I was off the planet myself, so to speak.'

'Climbing walls,' she said, smiling. 'I know that one. You might have been like us, wishing the illness was because of some big, dramatic car smash with plenty of wounds and broken bones to show. A noble sort of illness. Something to boast about, instead of mere paralysis.'

'Yes,' he said, delighted by her understanding. '*Yes*, yes. I wished I'd been mugged.'

She signalled for coffee by sticking one finger up in the air in a gesture that looked rude, but had the desired effect, without offence. Meals in restaurants involved a different language.

'And I don't see how he could be locked out when it was his house. He just went with Kay, the cleaning lady. We stayed where we were, only more peacefully, just drifting in and out of one long doze. Then someone came and took Mum away. We were dumped in a nursing home and we got stronger. My mother, well . . . my mother died. I think my father and the effort of looking after us must have driven her mad. It can't have been suicide, she was a Catholic, she would never have done that. Pneumonia, like us. Then we went into that hostel, you know, the one near the station, which was . . . terrible. We were middle-class freaks. I spent my whole time stopping us getting beaten up. Then the flat I have now. Some arrangement through Sister Jude, she would never explain that, either. My father wanted to see us then. It was too late and we said no. He might as well have killed her. We came back into the real world, clinging to each other. Then we were told he had

127

drowned. Therese joined the Order. My mother had always wanted that. Are you thoroughly up to date?'

Five years, he calculated, of abnormal life. Of missed education, of bonding with peers, of everything crucial to development. He felt unspeakably angry. She continued, airily, as if it were not painful.

'At least my father paid for things, even if he never came near, and he pays my rent. If he's going to leave us any money, I don't want mine. That's quite enough of that.'

She folded her arms and leant across the table. 'Now tell me, Father, what do you think of the Golden Boy?'

He shook himself back into the present, stirred his coffee, the colour of treacle and almost as thick, laced with a small carton of cream, which splashed on his cassock as he struggled to undo it. He crushed the carton in his fist and accepted the change of subject. It was her party.

'Francis? That's a good description for him. I don't know. He's charming in speech and wonderful with the old ladies. Perhaps a bit too good to be true.'

'You don't like him.'

'On brief acquaintance, no. But I mustn't say so, because my feelings are probably inspired by an overpowering envy of his good looks, his physique and the fact he could get any woman he wanted. He's all I could be if I shed twenty kilos, rather more years, and won the lottery. Of course I don't like him.'

Her laughter made him feel part of the human race, glad to be in it. She was still laughing when she paid the bill and they were outside the darkness of the place, where the sun hit like a hammer blow. Christopher knew he was being dismissed and did not mind. They had made a racing start. It had been far more productive than he could have dreamed.

'Well, maybe next week, if you're free, I can do the buying.' Yes, for sure, for the sake of his male pride, even if he had to starve all week and raid the poor box.

'Great, you're on.'

'And do me a favour, will you? Once you've been to this temple, go back to the chapel. There's nothing wrong with making comparisons.'

She planted a swift kiss on his cheek and ran off up the road. He stood in the sunshine, touching the spot and feeling blessed.

Until he remembered the four years and regretted the little lies he had told, such as not knowing the bulk of what she had told him, although his knowledge was second-hand. He had known the history, only wanted to hear it from her. And he was wondering if it could ever be the duty of a priest to tell a woman that her mother, the saint, had been a warped power freak and that Anna bore a greater resemblance to her dead father.

There was nothing cathartic about confession. In Catholic terms, it was a Sacrament. At least once a year, the sinner, and they were all sinners, must go to the priest and confess his sins, honestly, omitting none of them and begging for forgiveness. In return for this humiliating exercise, he would receive a penance, a blessing and official, divine absolution, which was the same thing, in Anna's opinion, as a licence to go out and do it all again, confident of another reprieve. To whom did a priest confess? she wondered as she made her way to Compucabs to meet Ravi. She supposed he must confess to another priest, which would be terrible. Another priest would know exactly the shorthand most penitents used to skate over the description of their sins to minimise the shame of them, like a patient going to a doctor and lying about his symptoms in order to receive a more positive diagnosis. She only thought of this as she wondered what Christopher Goodwin did with the burdens of his soul, because she could recognise him as a man who carried a whole sackful of them, and the knowledge of that was oddly comforting. He was *nice* in his old way, even though, like all the others of that generation, he told such dreadful lies. It seemed, in the space of a week, as if she was being offered *friendship* wherever she turned and it was a novelty.

Ravi was standing outside the nondescript building, standing by a black cab, and her heart lifted. She had an absurd desire to thank him for being alive and having this ridiculous effect on her of making her feel giddy, like a vodka on an empty stomach, and all he had ever done was chat and walk her halfway home. *Is he courting you?* Sister Jude would have asked, and she would have laughed at the expression and denied it. *Don't be silly*, she would have said. *He's just someone who has helped me through a very bad week, and yeah, I like him so much, it hurts.*

'Hello,' he said, with a strange little bow to hide a very wide smile. 'I've got us a taxi.'

She noticed he was wearing a suit of dark blue and a white shirt, which made his brown skin glow like velvet, and she was pleased she had made an effort with her own appearance, so that the pair of them were distinguishable from the two workaday people who sat and manned telephones. And a taxi, my word. It was one thing to order them up for other people to take, another thing to ride in one. He ushered her inside. The suit was just right on him. If he had put a tie on as well, he would have looked a prat. They set off like royalty.

'So, how are you?' he asked, rather formally. 'Did you enjoy your lunch?'

She had told him about that. She had told him a lot of things in the last few days, although one of the things that distinguished their early relationship as far as she was concerned was that they so often talked about things outside themselves. Walking around and in the park was all they had ever done, but he was the only person she had ever known who could comment on the beauty of the trees or the sky or the shape of a house without any hint of self-consciousness. And of course, they talked about God – she jeeringly, he patiently – and they talked about food. What an odd way to carry on, but infinitely preferable to any other company. She was not much good with her contemporaries, never knew what to say.

'Did you have a good shift?'

He was conscientious, she knew that, so a difficult shift would affect his mood. Ravi wanted to do whatever he did perfectly. It was only a temporary job before he went back to college, but it still mattered.

'Ah, yes. Before I forget, a man phoned for you.'

'A man?'

'Yes, an old man. Wasn't sure whether he wanted a taxi or not. He said he wanted to speak to the girl with the nice voice who knew what he wanted, so I knew that must be you.'

'Ah, that one. I wonder if he ever goes anywhere. One of these days, I'm going to get his number and find out where he lives. Probably Outer Mongolia.'

'I hope you won't find this strange,' Ravi said, changing tack. 'Going to a temple. Perhaps there is something else you would rather do.'

'No,' she said, 'absolutely nothing.'

This was not strictly true; his suggestion that this would be the way to spend what was their first formal outing

131

together had come as a bit of a surprise, but why not? She was odd, she knew that, so she may as well be odder with another eccentric who looked like he did and was the same height as herself. And then there was this taxi. If the expense of the taxi and the quality of the suit were all for the sake of arriving at his bally temple in style, rather than for her benefit, that didn't matter much either. She loved taxis. Old boxy London cabs, new rounded ones with wheelchair ramps, yellow ones plastered with advertisements; they would always be associated in her mind with childhood treats. They were the first things she had noticed when she swam back into the world, taxis, a slightly different shape from the ones she remembered. Speeding along in spacious comfort, without ever having to think of directions, with all the time to watch, that was luxury. If only everyone of her small acquaintance knew how easy she was to please.

The temple rose from the depth of indifferent streets, which were dwarfed not so much by the height of it, but by the style. It reminded her of a huge white wedding cake, topped with flags and viewed today with the perfect backdrop of a vivid blue sky. On the first glance, it looked as if designed for celebrations, wild parties, raves and spectacular firework displays. A millionaire's folly, devoted to decadence. Ravi was telling her all about the vast quantities of marble involved, the tons of Burmese teak, the years of workmanship, but she was not listening. The taxi dropped them near a vast, low entrance, which seemed humble by comparison. He led her in, holding her arm solicitously, as if she were his grandmother, his anxiety surprising her into the realisation that above everything else, he desperately wanted her to like this place. He was ushering her forward as if showing her his own home. It was warm inside, with the kind of warmth that would tolerate the wearing of either a coat, or the silk garments of the women in the foyer, like so many butterflies. He showed her where to leave shoes and they proceeded through the hall. The floor, even where wood gave way to carpet and then to stone, was pleasantly warm on her bare feet.

There was no problem about liking or respecting. The problem was not to be overwhelmed by the colours of the carpet design and the massive doors into the vaulted hall of the shrines, where the marble ceiling was sectioned into individual areas, each different from the others. She listened, without comprehension, to Ravi's low-voiced explanations. The room of the shrines has three doors, he was explaining; you have seen only the one. They stood in front of the statue of Ganesh, the Elephant God, sitting behind glass, brilliantly illuminated to show his crown, his small, wise eyes, his decorated trunk curled down over his rounded stomach, one of his two sets of hands raised, the other resting on his robed thighs. The one visible foot was plump, with painted nails and bracelets. He looked like a God who lived well and bore the complexities of his appearance with cheerful dignity.

'We begin with Ganaparti when we come to pray,' Ravi said. 'He is the God who preserves health and prosperity. And next to him is Hanuman, the Monkey God, the warrior, who will protect the individual and his possessions from all evil. Here we pray about our daily concerns, pay our respects and make our requests. It frees us up to consider our souls when we pray to the other Gods.'

The Monkey God was as endearing as Ganesh, equally ornamental, but more aggressive and the brilliance of his apparel almost blinding. They moved into the main area of shrines, which smelled uncloyingly sweet, the floor still mysteriously and pleasantly warm. A variety of people in uniformly clean clothes moved around and either bowed to the deities, prostrated themselves, knelt or stood with a complete lack of self-consciousness in a private, public worship which seemed as natural as breathing. There was nothing furtive about this piety. He was explaining the Gods, Krishna and Radha, but they resembled, to her, nothing more than highly dressed dolls. They were brought food, washed and dressed daily, he told her, which, hiding her own reaction to the worshipping of graven images, she found endearing. Even more endearing was Ravi, standing before an image of Swaminarayan and telling her it was his favourite.

'Are you allowed favourites?' she asked.

'Of course. You respect all the Gods and there may come new Gods, but you will always prefer the one who suits you best.'

'Ah.' That was a revelation. 'I think my favourite is Ganesh.'

He smiled at her, bursting with pride. 'The choice of many,' he said. 'Come, I shall show you what might be more familiar.'

He was sensitive to her bewilderment and she was grateful for it. The more familiar aspect of the place came back into view as they went down the stairs away from the shrines. By the entrance was an open shop, selling pictures, books, music tapes and trinkets, which looked for all the world like rosary beads. Throughout the whole building, not at all discordant with anything else, there were collection boxes inviting donations. She turned to him, grinning mischievously, only now aware that this was a place of sublime happiness and she was allowed to tease him. She pointed at the largest collection box of all.

134

'This is familiar,' she said. 'This makes me feel at home. This tells me I'm in church.'

'The Gods and money,' Ravi said, gravely, 'have always gone hand in hand. Poverty is bad for everything.'

Poverty, chastity and obedience. With every will in the world and with all due deference to the will higher and greater than her own, Therese could not love Sundays. It was not that the world outside beckoned, but that the world inside was so still. For all the fuss of the preparation for Mass, the additional morning prayer, it was still a designated day of rest, where the afternoon and evening were an anticlimax. A day for meditation, but she found that meditation was better when interspersed with work. No one knew better how the devil breeds mischief for idle hands. She had not joined the Order lightly, or because it was already familiar; she had joined it to *work*, for the greater glory of God. The vows she would make at the end of her probation did not frighten her. *Poverty* did not mean starvation: it meant owning nothing of her own, and she rejoiced in the freedom of that. As for *chastity*, she could see nothing negative about it. A free body, divorced from its own urges and restraints, had more to offer the pure service of God and humanity, and if she was honest, it was humanity she wished to serve. She wanted people to be happy, fulfilled, cured, imbued with love and well-fed, and she did not see how she could ever do that under the yoke of some man like her father, and how could she ever fall for a man, when God had called first? Others could serve both God and man; she could not see it as an option, and besides, she had no real curiosity about the longings of the flesh. It was enough to be strong and healthy, to feel energy and sound bones. *Obedience* made sense. She knew so little, she must wait to be guided, how could she do otherwise? She would have to be guided until she could form her own judgements and she did not believe that this prevented her from asking questions, but she was coming to understand, all the same, it was obedience that was the problem.

Not obedience to discipline, adherence to the strict routine of the days, but to the dictates of others, whatever the impulse in the other direction. Following rules that did not seem necessary. She must look for guidance, and the guidance for this lonely afternoon was to read the words of St Therese of Lisieux and her contemplations of the God of love, which ranged from the obtuse to simple tips for coping with the vicissitudes of religious life. Therese turned the page. St Therese had been a contemplative of remarkable youth and holiness, who advocated the turning of daily irritations into acts of patience and forbearance which, if offered to God, would aid the world and bring Him closer. She described in the *Little Way*, from which her namesake read, how, when she was engaged in the laundry of her convent, she was always stood alongside another, clumsy nun, who constantly splashed her with dirty water. Rather than draw back and express annoyance, this Therese learned to welcome the irritation, suffered it and offered it in expiation for the sins of the world. Which might be easier if the water was warm, and the irritation unintentional. There was an apposite proverb lingering somewhere. *The patient man is better than the valiant, and he who rules his own spirit is better than he who takes cities.* None of it was making sense. Therese decided it would be better to go to the chapel. God and his guidance were everywhere: she had plenty of experience of being confined to a room, but to go to read in a room entirely dedicated to worship must be an improvement. She had so much to learn. She had no belief in an entitlement to happiness every moment of the day; she had known this would be hard, but no one could quite know when and where it would be most difficult.

Therese wished she had been as dedicated a reader as her sister. It was Anna who should be in here in these idle hours, with her thumb stuck in her mouth, content to read and digest like a cat who slept on its food. In this institution, where the elderly were prevalent, the rule of Sunday afternoon was slumber. There was no Kim, no noise. There was simply Barbara's instruction to watch over them all and report anything untoward. This was the test of obedience.

She reached the chapel and found it chilly and empty. The glory of the place at this time of year was early evening when the sun hit, while her kitchen, at the other end, was favoured in the morning. There was nobody there, apart from Joseph, slumped in a chair. Therese was on the one hand pleased to see her, and on the other dismayed. It was not company she wanted, but another form of solitude. If she were to follow the lessons of St Therese of Lisieux, she would sit beside Joseph, listen to her breathing and let it interfere with her already muddled thinking, which was telling her that she really did not like her chosen saint at all and found the self-sacrifice that had once inspired her puzzling and repugnant. She sat apart, and after one, pregnant minute, realised that Joseph was snoring rather than slumbering, maintaining her balance on the rush-seated chair as a result of a miraculous accident. She had heard this stertorous breathing when her father had drunk too much and lain down in uncomfortable places, such as kitchen, landing, study, although her memories of that were confused. It had been a phase of his, not permanent, but etched on memory. She had never known, for as long as it had lasted, when he was sick or merely pretending, only that when he was like that, he was unreliable, not available for questions or games, and Anna was the only one who could chivy him out of it and make him move. Joseph turned in her sleep and collapsed to the floor, noisily. She lay awkwardly, with her left arm doubled beneath her, her bare head with her scratchy hair hitting the floor with a mild thud.

Therese knelt beside her and tapped her shoulder. Then she shook it, so that the head remained still and the torso moved, slightly, as if she were pushing a dummy. Then the eyes opened and the mouth moved. She thought she heard the words 'You silly little cow,' before the eyes closed again and she made an automatic movement to cross her arms across her chest for warmth. The skin of her wrist, mottled with liver spots, felt cold to the touch. Therese shook her again.

This time she came wide awake and ready to fight. She levered herself off the floor and spat words and fury – 'Leave me alone, bugger, bugger, bugger . . .' – levered herself half upright and began to cry. Sitting there, sluggishly gathering her old limbs until she sat cross-legged with one hand supporting her and the other over her face with the tears coursing between her fingers. She stank. Of disinfectant and white spirit, like new paint, overlaid with bile and despair. The prevalent smell was soap. The smell of Therese's father had been whisky, with the same overtones of desperation. At a point in her life, it had filled her dreams, and become part of his monstrous identity. How often had it happened? Once? Twice?

'Who got you the drink, Sister?'

Therese found herself sounding like Barbara.

'The devil.'

'And what form did he take, Sister?'

She was becoming an inquisitor, sharper with every note, more furious as the weeping went on. *Poverty* meant no money for indulgences, *chastity* meant freedom from cravings, *obedience* meant adherence to a rule of conduct. Joseph was an appalling example, a disgrace; she was too disgusting to touch. And yet, she was also a crying, mortified woman, stinking with shame on a Sunday afternoon, pitiful and frightened in the place she had come either to be forgiven, or to hide.

'Who got it for you, Sister?'

'Francis.'

She thought of obedience and the way Sister Barbara would be angry. The anger of that woman was excoriating. Barbara would make Joseph squirm, but the rule of obedience demanded Barbara be told everything. Therese glanced around, expecting her any minute, then tugged Joseph to her feet. Humiliation was best not shared.

'Better get to bed, then, hadn't we? C'mon, c'mon, quick as you can. It's all right, it's all right, come on, this way.'

Joseph was thin, but heavy. Her arm laid across Therese's shoulders was the weight of lead and the route to her room was long. The smell of her, particularly in her tiny, enclosed room, was nauseating. She lay on her bed with her arms crossed again while Therese made sure the water was in reach. With gritted teeth, she removed her shoes, brushed her hair and forced the window open. Joseph gripped her wrist so hard, she was sure it would leave a bruise. Patience: slowly the bony hand released its hold and Joseph fell asleep. Therese turned her head on one side. It all seemed to take a long time.

There were three empty cans of Diamond White in a

polythene bag. She padded them out with a newspaper she found under the bed and took them away. The Angelus bell went at six o'clock. Halfway down the black and white corridor, Therese met Sister Barbara, cannoning in the other direction. They both paused, briefly.

'*Bendicamus Domino,*' Barbara said, distractedly.

'*Deo Gratias.*'

'You look pale, child. Go and rest.'

'I'm fine, Sister.'

'Have you seen Joseph? I couldn't find her anywhere.'

'She was praying in the chapel, Sister, just now, and then she went to rest. You must have missed her.'

'Now why didn't I think of that?'

She sped on, humming. Therese watched her go, half tempted to go after her. Whatever she had just done, it was not obedience. The walls of the black and white corridor seemed to close in on her. Disobedient. Could actions that were entirely instinctive also be disobedient? She fled through the parlour and out into the garden, relieved to find the door unbarred. It was a purposeless flight. The still warm air of early evening cured nothing. She wanted to find Francis and throttle him. How dare he? He could come and go as he pleased, he could work through the heart of the place, whistling and everyone smiling on him, but what he had done was treachery. Restlessly, she moved down the path, reluctantly and only because there was nowhere else to go. The garden was not a place she had ever enjoyed, not even as an aid to meditation, and after seeing Edmund dead in it, she liked it less. She only liked Edmund's shed at the very end, because it reminded her of one they had in the garden at home. His bench had become identified with a corpse, and Francis would not be here on a Sunday. Sunday was the day of rest. Rounding the bend in the path, she almost stumbled across Matilda, sitting at the feet of the statue of St Michael, arms resting on her knees, staring at the ground. Sitting in the middle of the pathway, enjoying a patch of sun and busy in the act of washing, was a large ginger cat. It was a handsome beast, with an undomesticated air, apparently immune from the desire for human contact, indifferent to Matilda and unmoved by the sound of Therese's soft footsteps. There was a chorus of alarm from the birds in the trees, strident and unmusical. There were no animals in this institution. For a moment, the cat distracted her and Therese regarded it with delight. It was such a pretty, powerful and graceful thing, she wanted to pick it up and hold it, stroke that fine fur. The cat finished its self-ministration, stretched and walked away without a backward glance. Oh, for such confidence. It made her want to laugh in admiration. Look at the thing, a trespasser and bold as brass. Then Matilda was by her side, clutching at her arm, in the same spot, with the same insistence as Joseph.

'Therese, oh Therese . . . a cat! How could he?'

'It's a lovely cat, Sister. What's wrong with it?'

Her arm was sore. She did not want to be touched and pulled and could not resist the urge to shake Matilda off, pull herself free of another old hand of surprising strength. She did not want the breath of another old body, standing too close and looking crestfallen and beseeching, staring at her, wanting something she could not give or understand. St Therese of Lisieux would have embraced her. Matilda stepped back and felt for her rosary.

'Yes,' she said, 'it's a pretty cat. Edmund would have hated it, but I can't expect you to understand, you're too young. Therese, my dear, when your sister comes next, will you ask her to come and see me? It's very important.'

'Yes, of course, Sister. Does it matter what time?' She was trying to overcome the effects of her own rudeness by putting warmth into her voice.

'Thank you and no, it doesn't matter what time.' She shivered. 'And now I think we had better go in.'

She spoke it like an order. This time, Therese was obedient.

CHAPTER SEVEN

Thou shalt not covet thy neighbour's goods

Sunday: the day of rest, without there ever being any rest for the wicked. Kay had so few yearnings of the flesh she should have been a nun, provided she could have been an unusually pampered kind, with access to long immersions in water, facials, sunbathing, pedicures and the general stroking of self, none of which was any substitute for her present, intense desire to be hugged. Embraced into oblivion. Kidnapped, taken away into a deep warm forest and hidden in a cave. She had been sitting in Theo's study during the day and wishing he was there. There had been something of the grizzly bear about Theo. He could snarl, he could prowl, he could hug and he could fight. Sitting at the back of the church and hating herself for being there, Kay wished he was alongside, threatening to bomb the priest and whispering heretical remarks in her ear. Theo would have observed the congregation and told her how that woman over there needed a hairdresser more than she needed God. If he were here, where he would not be seen dead, he would mock her for this blatant backsliding, this superstitious slinking into church in the silly hope it might do something for her.

Kay argued with Theo in her mind, telling him she was here for a purpose and the reason behind the purpose was all his fault. She was not here for forgiveness or enlightenment, and it had taken her five days to find the strength. A little Dutch courage helped, as well as the pall of boredom that hung over Sundays. She entered a bland church, brick-built Edwardian in a side street, surrounded by suburban houses in a similar style, east facing on the dark side of the road, so that it was never light or warm. It had been stripped of idolatrous ornamentation in the happy clappy days of the seventies, when a few tambourines and guitars had been the essential ingredients of feelgood services. The original personality of the place had never recovered. The wooden pews had made way for a shrinking number of seats, drawn close to the altar in an attempt at cosiness. The priest did his best, but he was a dual-purpose priest, who also taught at the school on the edge of town and campaigned for converts to his community with a zeal not quite marked by results, but characterised by hope and a distant memory of the Ireland of his birth. He still thought that a club serving lemonade and playing music until the ungodly hour of nine at night would keep the youth of the town from drugs, and believed that a float in the carnival parade would have them flocking to the doors.

In that sense, he was right. Kay was here because of the parade after all, although she was clearly in advance of a flock. She sat dumbly through an amorphous service she did not recognise; an amalgam of a Church of England evensong without singing and the Catholic service of benediction without pomp. Things had changed since she had last attended, apart from the predictable sprinkling of old devotees, chatting in the backlog of departure, waiting to say hello and goodbye to the priest who would be wanting to lock the door and go home.

Kay did not want to speak to the wretched priest; well, yes, she did and no, she didn't, because it was information from the likes of him she both needed and dreaded. He was youngish, prematurely old, held together with a thin, vibrating enthusiasm, a stud in one ear and fashionable glasses on the end of his nose. A little oik from Connemara. Someone pulled at the sleeve of her coat.

It was her second-best mackintosh with a silvery sheen and she resented it being touched by any sticky fingers not her own. Facing her was Mrs Boyle, teacher from the school where Kay had forced Jack to go and where, against all the odds, he had done surprisingly well.

Probably, this was because of the likes of Mrs Boyle, a slab of no-nonsense woman who looked like a dour Presbyterian, but taught English and drama and knew that negotiating with teenagers was a waste of time. She ruled by terror, slaps on the legs and threats of exclusion from the school play. Kay remembered Jack coming home, surprisingly upset about such severities, and her own response, which was to say, *It must have been your fault. You're a bad boy, always were.*

'Ah, Mrs McQuaid.'

She was one of those women who never, ever forgot how to put a name to a face, and when she did, you would know the world was about to end. A classroom voice, which, even reduced to the respectful levels of church, still resonated like a stage whisper. 'I'm so pleased to see you. And wasn't it nice to see young Jack in the week?'

Kay thought she might faint. She felt her face was suffused with the single gin consumed before she set out. Nodded.

'Such a happy chance. Called in to see us, sweet boy, just as we were getting the carnival thing ready, and one of our stars went down with the flu. Wasn't it good of your boy, stepping into the breach like a good 'un? Played the devil to perfection! You must have been so pleased to see him.'

'Yes.'

She was not about to confess to Mrs Boyle that her son could travel the distance to what had once been his home town from the age of fifteen to eighteen, without coming to see her at all. And a complete stranger for the four years since, to her own, enormous relief.

'Doing so well, isn't he, but fancy changing his name. Says he never liked being called Jack. Too much like Jack the Lad, ha ha! He said he'd gone for being called Francis, on account of the fact that there wasn't a St Jack, and Francis suited a gardener. Bless.'

'Francis,' Kay echoed. A *gardener*? Him? She rallied and put on her chattering face.

'Well, Francis was always his second name. I think he sort of grew into it. I expect kids do that all the time, now. I mean, change their names if they don't like what they've been given.'

'They do what they want.' The queue for departure shuffled forward, impeded by an earnest man who was bending the ear of the priest in urgent tones. 'And he's far from a child now. That hair! I ask you! How old will he be?'

A note of cunning, in that bossy, Scottish voice, sensing her hesitation, waiting to pounce and exploit her ignorance of her own son.

Kay knew the game, tapped Mrs Boyle's handbag, confidentially. 'You should have seen the colour it was before. Terrible.'

'Well, I thought it suited him. Whoever would have

146

thought he'd knuckle down to be training for a gardener, with a job in a convent, of all places, with looks like that? But he is in London, I suppose. That makes it different.'

'A *convent*?'

She recovered herself quickly, before her voice rose to a squeak. The thin priest had got rid of the fat man and the desultory queue shuffled forward. Kay pretended to search her pockets for coins, acknowledging the presence of the inevitable collection box. Things did not change that much. You had to pay to come in from the cold, even if it was colder within. She made herself smile widely at Mrs Boyle.

'He must always have liked you, Mrs Boyle, to tell you that. A secret, I thought. A boy like that, working in a convent, it's hardly *cool*, is it?'

'Well, I suppose it's all comparative. Better than staying in this backwater. Half his old girlfriends have babies already.'

Mrs Boyle smiled, knowingly. She was so sharp, she could cut herself. Kay was remembering everything she hated about church services, which included all those bitches, lurking with their poisonous information network. She was the next in line for that runt of a priest, knew his handshake would be as wet as fresh cod, took it, dropped it and ran. Mrs Boyle was one of those who could distinguish gin on the breath from the night before, let alone the hour, and she herself was in desperate need of sea air. She had got exactly the confirmation she had been dreading. It seemed a long way home, and although she was wearing the right shoes for the short taxi drive it had taken her to get there, they were wrong for the way back. Silly shoes, with kitten heels, under her bright red trousers. No wonder Mrs Boyle had stared at her feet. Kay tottered through the back streets, into the main street and on to the front. At the very end of a humid day, with darkness threatening, a mist had formed, blurring the horizon. It gave her the privacy to scream. Standing there, like a lunatic, making animal sounds. *Aaarrgh*, beating her chest with her fists, like some mad penitent, the *aaarrgh* turning to *shiit, bugger, dammmn*, without providing either satisfaction or relief. A man walking a dog stopped to stare at her. She found to her horror that she crossed herself automatically before she hurried on. *Francis? A gardener in a convent?* There was more than one convent in London, there were probably dozens, but she only knew of the one and was willing to bet that he did too. Big, bold Jack, who thought everything should be his for the taking, still never departed far from the places he knew best. He would stick to where he knew, that parish of his wretched, screaming babyhood where she had no idea what to do with him. A place of terrible loneliness for her, until things had improved, and there were moments, if only moments, when she stopped wishing he had never been born. Jack would have gone back to home territories when he was cast out of Theo's house, and that is where he would have remained. She had written to him, at a Post Office address, the last letter telling him of Theo's demise, but there had never been replies. Jack always had friends and places to stay. Strange, older friends, shifty men with whom he took refuge when he was still a child, acquaintances from whom she had dragged him away when they moved with Theo. He had seemed to blossom in this new, smaller school, his city streetwise aura making him king of the class. And what had her illogical insistence on a Catholic school done for him? Only given him enough religious knowledge to be able to fool anyone naive that he was a Roman Catholic Christian, if that would help him get a job. He liked the hymns. *A gardener?* A quick learner, with enough knowledge of pruning and such in this back yard to pass muster, but a proper gardener? Maybe a leopard can change spots, and Jack, *she must remember to call him Francis*, had found a vocation. A helluva strange one for a boy who only seemed to like nasty films, power tools and sex. The sky grew darker; she looked at her watch and could scarcely see the dial. It always seemed to get darker sooner on Sundays and probably that was her fault, too. She had hated the Church and all it stood for, added her voice to Theo's chorus of derision, but she used it whenever she needed it for herself or her son and that might be why a Sunday would always seem like a day without joy.

She determined not to break into a run along the quiet seashore. It would ruin her shoes and add to the fear, so she walked smartly until the road bent away from the sea and turned into her own with the good houses and the street lights responding to the premature darkness by casting little pools of light every fifteen yards. There were cars in driveways, life conducted indoors, a child's tricycle of the kind she could never have afforded for Jack lying abandoned on a doorstep. In his youth Jack, no, *Francis*, would have pinched that and sold it. Theo's house stood solid and comfortable.

She always had to remind herself that it was Theo's house, not hers. Ignoring the fine front door as usual, she went round the back. If *Francis* had found his way in again, she would have to face him, but *Francis* was a long way away, being a *gardener*. In the same convent as that little Calvert girl. Before she put the key in the lock, Kay screamed again, *Shiit!* and then entered, calmly.

The golden Buddha glowed in the living room, providing no more comfort than church, but the donkey drinks cart was reassuringly full. She patted the Buddha, which was really there because it felt so nice to touch and she liked to talk to it sometimes and ask it what it would like to drink. The habit of talking to statues was probably ingrained from infancy. Gin in hand, feeling mightily better after the second scream, she went to Theo's study.

All his assorted, unsent letters and the several drafts of that wretched will. Letters to his daughters, returned to sender, unopened, until he had stopped writing to them, preserving the returned letters and their envelopes in date order. A few letters to Francis (she was learning to think of him as that) also returned, but not unread. She wondered if it was more insulting to have a letter read, spat upon and returned than it was to have it sent back without even the effort of opening it, decided the former was worse. *My dear boy,* Theo had written to Jack, *I wish you all the luck in the world, but it's better you don't come back. I don't want what you have to offer . . . Cheque enclosed, which I hope you will find useful. Please write to your mother.* The cheques were kept, only the letters themselves derisorily returned. Talk about biting the hand that fed.

She sat back in Theo's chair, the gin refusing to remove the gnarled knot of worry, which settled in her gut like an ulcer and made everything taste foul. Admitting to herself that darling Francis could have got into this house with his old keys any time he wanted, time after time, months ago even, and she would not have noticed, or at least not after the drink or two she invariably needed before she could bring herself to look at this stuff. She was trying to concentrate. If Francis was gardening in the convent of the old parish, he wouldn't be let near the nuns, and dear old Father Goodwin, who said he was there more often than he liked, would have rumbled him by now. Relief coursed through her veins, and the gin tasted better, until she thought, would he, though? How long since Christopher had seen her boy in the flesh? Years, and my, how they grew and disguised themselves. The blond hair on the devil in the parade had even fooled her, for a second. She choked on the drink, sat back in the chair, with watering eyes. Francis, a gardener? What a joke. Why, everyone knew what Francis was going to be. A tart. 'A *tart*,' she yelled at the wall. 'A tart.'

She thought of him let loose in a convent and screamed with shrill laughter. A piece of corruption among the lily-white nuns, serve them right. Then she stopped laughing and began to shake. Stuffed her fingers into her mouth and continued shaking, swallowing flakes of her own rose-pink nail varnish as she chewed and considered the phenomenon of her own creation. Francis, Jack, a creature of the devil and his own illusions, the product of a rape.

She leant over Theo's desk and stuffed the documents back into their neat folders. He who sups with the devil requires a long spoon, Theo said, or was that Christopher? Her hand hovered over the phone. She withdrew it quickly, slapped her own wrist.

She would do what she had always done. Tell lies by silence. Do nothing, look capable. Now, which of the drafts of Theo's will had her bastard read?

Sundays had a blight. It was too late to gain entry to the convent by the time Anna got back. Not late by the standards of the outside world, only late because it was dark and they had been walking in the park for far too long. At least, she had. Ravi had suddenly turned into a Dracula, needing to be home as soon as it was dark, just at the point when she would have preferred him to kiss her, and then it all turned on its head, just like a Sunday.

'I have to go home. My parents expect me and they worry.'

She was suddenly, excruciatingly, breathtakingly furious.

'How old are you, Ravi? Twenty-two? Do you still get pocket money?'

She had thought the afternoon would extend into evening, that they had all the time in the world, and the disappointment was bitter, but she was beginning to understand that every hour of his day was accounted for in work and duty, with so few gaps it was a miracle he had ever had the time to walk her home. He could add an hour or two to each of his shifts, and get away with it, but no more. He did not say as much, but she sort of guessed, and although she did not realise it, envied him the omnipresence of demanding parents. She tried to swallow both her pride and her curiosity and failed.

'Do your mother and father get on?'

'Yes, of course. They irritate each other, sometimes, but they talk, and they love us. Fed us, taught us, tolerated us, were there when we breathed our first, so we must be there for them.'

'Whenever they want?'

'Yes.'

'And they come before everyone else?'

'Yes. Here,' he said, handing her a tiny statue of Ganesh. 'You said you liked him. I bought it for you.'

It was no compensation. It came from his pocket and was stuffed into hers, a small, plaster statue of a sturdy elephant man with too many limbs, a gift of kindness and one that failed to placate, although there was nothing to be angry about, no promise made, or broken. That bit was by the duck pond, where the birds muttered and nestled down with families, chirping and burping as the last of the year's fledglings tried to stay close while Mummy and Daddy drove them away into independence. Her envy was so acute, she was glad when he had to go. Even though she said, *Fine, go then, just fucking well bugger off. I've gone to your temple and then you've got no more time. Just bugger off, you wanker.* All of it rage and frustration in the dying embers of a lovely day. Because she was being left. Rootless, parentless, without direction, fucking deserted, everything else forgotten. She sat by the pond in the growing dark, traversed the football ground at a fast, furious pace, wished she was going to work, wished every living, chirping thing would belt up and when she got to the gates of the fucking park, found them shut. Measured them with her eye, ran at them from ten yards away, clambered over the top. Easy. Pain in her chest, easy; running home easier still. Wanker. She stopped in a pub and had two double vodkas, quickly, left when someone tried to talk.

On the way home, still cantering, she ran past the convent door and knew it was too late to go in. Agnes might still be sitting in her porch, but after the dot of nine o'clock she was under orders not to answer until she had fetched Barbara to see whoever it was. Barbara might have mellowed towards her, but she was still not going to let Anna inside so late, even if Anna said she wanted to pray. Nor would she be allowed entry to say goodnight to Therese.

There was an overpowering desire to see Therese. Her sister was a physical presence she missed all the time. She skittered past, left and left again, unready to go home, passing the door at the back, and pausing beside it to draw breath. Stuck with the unpleasant realisation that she had probably shouted at Ravi only because he had better things to do with his evening than spend it with her, and he had

153

left her with all this energy and nowhere to go. That was a lie; there were plenty of places to go and drink away the energy, let everyone know that she knew how to have a good time. Bars and clubs by the dozen, just beginning to warm up for the night, and none of them places where she wanted to be. If she could not have the chapel, she wanted the forbidden territory of the park or the silence of that garden for a quiet shouting match with God. She was shut out from everywhere. Knowing she was behaving like a spoiled child, she kicked the door. Winced and then looked at it more closely.

It still looked peculiarly naked without the curtain of ivy, which had almost covered it and was now shaggily trimmed so that a couple of branches hung like tendrils around the frame, escaping from the dense foliage that covered the whole wall. The handle was still so rusted, it looked as if it had not been used in several lifetimes, but there were marks in the woodwork on the door, as if someone with heavy boots had kicked, hard and repeatedly. They were futile dents in an obdurately solid door, but they were ugly, angry marks. Anna stared at them in the street light. A car passed, booming with music; on the other side of the road, the houses were softly lit. No one would notice. She thought of Edmund, dying in the garden while she had slept, and the desire to get inside became overpowering. It was simply not enough to spy from the rooftop.

She went to the middle of the road, zipped her purse into the pocket of her jacket and measured the distance. Ran and leapt for the ivy. Found herself spreadeagled against the wall with her feet scrabbling for hold and her hands seizing fistfuls of branches. The sinews of the ivy held her up. She was a lightweight. Her small feet slithered among the leaves and found purchase. In the distance she could hear another car and the sound of it had the effect of adrenaline. After that it was easy. In another second, before the car headlights passed, she was astride the top of the wall, looking down into the other side, feeling exhilarated but foolish. What the hell did she think she was doing? Below her was a further mass of ivy; getting down the other side and up again was well within her powers. Anna enjoyed sitting on top of the wall; it crossed her mind to stay there, triumphantly, and wave. Not such a high wall after all, a mere fifteen feet, strange that no one had tried this route before, but why should anyone bother? A small amount of street light penetrated far enough into the garden to show the contours of Edmund's shed and his bench. Otherwise the darkness was intense. The door of the shed was open and the bench was unoccupied. That was a relief. She had been afraid she would find someone sitting there, listening for the quiet birds. Looking up, she could see the outlines of her block with the small back windows of the apartments. She was, after all, very close to home and slithered down the other side, noisily.

The walls of the garden blocked sound from the road and created the effect of a tunnel. The shrubbery was less dense than it appeared from her high view, when the foliage seemed to cover most of the garden in a carpet of various greens with scarcely a hint of the walkways. On ground level, the grey stone of the path was almost luminous. Anna had scarcely ever been in the garden, except the other day, when the dead presence of Edmund on the bench had blinded her to anything else. Her sense of its geography was skewed by her own perspective: down here, in the dark to which her eyes were slowly adjusting, it seemed bigger and easier to penetrate, although the distance between where she stood and the high window of the chapel seemed further than she could have imagined. The top end of the garden and this were separate worlds, and the world on the outside different again. Without any particular purpose, but drawn as always to the chapel, she began to walk up the winding path, arms outstretched to feel her way, as if she was playing Blindman's Buff, trying to define the different scents she could smell. Something like juniper, walnut, the mossy smell of soil, a whiff of lavender, the oily scent of evergreens and the sharp, ammonia smell of urine. Something brushed against her legs, slinking into the bushes to the left, emerging again, spitting with a guttural hiss, which sounded as loud as a shout. A cat without colour; she could only guess at the size. Its eyes glared like beacons before it disappeared with an angry flourish. Anna's heartbeat slowed back down to almost normal. Her foot encountered something slimy on the path. Up until then, she had been feeling apologetic to the cat, until she scraped the slime from the bottom of her shoe with the realisation that whatever it was was bloody and fleshy and as likely as not the indigestible portion of a feral meal. She could visualise, without seeing, the uneaten gizzard of a blackbird, shook herself and stepped forward, gingerly, angry with the cat, knowing it should not be here. It was the trespasser, not herself. It should be trapped and taken away from a place that was a sanctuary for birds. At a bend in the path, she could smell blackcurrant, something with the scent of pepper, gooseberry and rust. Her outstretched hand encountered mossy stone. She touched it, felt the damp hem of the robe of St Michael, with big, cold feet, and with that came the realisation that this was all stupid and infantile, because she had no more place here and even less purpose than the cat. Anna turned to retrace

156

her steps, walking away from the light of the windows and back towards the wall. There was a sudden change in the smells, a sensation of warmth.

There were no footsteps, there was simply a presence, cannoning into her from behind, sending her stumbling to the ground. She broke the fall with her hands, felt the bones in her wrists jarring against stone. He had hit her with the full force of his body, launching out of space, like a heat-seeking missile, *wham* into her shoulders. She twisted as she fell, resisting some of the force, and was slithering out of his grasp in a frantic crawling away towards the bushes, like the cat. Slower than the cat, easier to pursue, clumsy as a cripple. There were big paws, grasping at her ankles, then her thighs as she crawled ineffectually until he pressed her into the ground of the grey path, and she felt he would bite her in the neck. Her feet drummed against the ground; she lay, pinned beneath him, his torso coming to rest against her back like a dead man, while her legs thrashed and his hand circled her throat and as they lay, breathless, groin to buttock, she could feel his prick against the curve of her buttocks, rigid as a stick. She struggled with every ounce of strength and as he began to release her, screamed every obscenity she knew, so loud that the birds flew out of the trees with a *caw! caw! caw!* of outrage and the ground-floor lights of the building flickered awake. *You fucking cunt bastard shitface leggo of me bastard.*

'Scream away,' he whispered into her ear. 'Love it. That'll get them running.'

He pulled her up against himself, raising them both so that he seemed to have her in his lap in a willing embrace. As the lights from inside grew visible, they were suddenly partially outlined, her silhouette drawn against his,

157

extremities entwined, legs and bodies fixed in an unholy glow. He lifted her to her feet, held her in his arms briefly and dropped her unceremoniously on to the path. Then he placed his foot on her waist, so great a foot, bigger than St Michael's, it could have crushed her spleen unless he held it there, neatly balanced, like some big game hunter posing for a photo with the newly killed prey he did not want to damage. Leaning over her gently with the lights coming closer, he took hold of her right, curled fist and held it against his face.

'Go on, my lovely, Go on.'

She clawed at him, vainly, scratching him harmlessly down the left cheek. He took her open hand, fastened his own around her knuckles and dragged the imprisoned fingers with their long nails down the other side of his face.

'Good girl,' he murmured, hauling her to her feet, pinning her arms behind her, linking his own through her crooked elbows, bending her forward. Her shoulder blades seemed to scrape together and she began to cough with a ghastly, chest-clearing throttle, like an old man fetching up phlegm. He yanked her upright with the same deceptive gentility, hair hanging over her face, until she found herself staring through it at the waist of Sister Barbara's dressing gown, and saw her large feet lit by a torch. She could see the glimpses of another uniform, up to the neck and down to the ankles, with cloth slippers resembling boots, on which Anna kept her eyes fastened, listening to the angry voice of fear.

'Francis, what is this?'

Barbara was trying to exert control, but the voice, even with the muted resonance of plainchant attached, sounded shrill in the silence, descending to a *tut, tut, tut* as she squinted at the tableau they made. There was large, manly

158

Francis, pillar of the Establishment, with blood beginning to seep from the scratches on his face, holding a captive as sweetly as a trainer might hold a potentially fierce dog, with one hand on her bent neck, the other pinning her arms.

'Are you all right?' Francis addressed the back of Anna's neck. 'I'll let you go if you behave.' He was speaking unnecessarily loudly.

'What's going on?' Barbara yelled.

'Shhh. Wait a minute, Sister. I'll just get her to sit.'

Propelled by sheer weight, Anna sat at the feet of Michael, Archangel, where the stray light from the parlour, augmented by Barbara's torch, almost penetrated. The voices of Francis and Barbara seemed to come from another planet. Hers was sharp.

'What are you doing here, Francis? We don't pay you for Sundays.'

He took a deep breath and stood calmly in the light of her torch, which wavered at the end of her wrist. Someone hovered behind him. Anna raised her head and gazed into the limpid eyes of Sister Matilda, who was standing to one side gazing at her, with one finger pressed against her own lips, the instruction for silence. Anna scarcely needed any such advice; she could hardly speak, but she refrained from trying. Of all of them, Matilda was a favourite, the one she trusted simply because she was the most visible, the one who came into the garden most often as a gentle and undemanding presence, just visible from the roof and therefore the most familiar, and she had forgotten to give her Edmund's crucifix. It lay in her pocket, ready for morning Mass, with Ganesh alongside. Matilda was fully dressed, as if the veil was something she never shed, even in sleep.

'Oh, do get out of the way, Matilda.' The light from Barbara's torch swung into Anna's face and down over her body. Her dress was filthy. Barbara gasped, swung the beam back towards Francis, where it lingered on the scratches, oozing blood. He reached his hand towards Anna, then let it drop to his side.

'Are you all right?' he asked softly. 'I didn't mean to hurt you.'

The torchlight wavered back to her face. Matilda had disappeared into the background. In a gesture of extraordinary childishness, which she would remember afterwards with greater embarrassment than anything else, Anna stuck her tongue out and pulled a face. It was a stupid, unsympathetic thing to do, acting as an admission of guilt, and if there was any chance that Barbara was going to side with her, she lost it in that moment of puerile rebellion. The voice of Francis continued.

'I know I shouldn't be here, Sister,' he was saying to Barbara, apologetically. 'But I was passing on my way home and I saw someone climbing over the wall. There was no time to phone you, which would have been the most sensible thing. So I came in after her. I thought it was a kid. I didn't realise it was someone you knew. Someone I saw in chapel this morning.'

Apology and certainty oozed from him and Anna was suddenly furious all over again, for being so small. His voice was so quiet and confident and masculine, it could cut a swathe through all their female voices and command instant attention. If she spoke now, she would sound as silly as a parrot. A man could always do that, with the same ease he had knocked her over. The grit on the dress felt like ash as she clutched at the fabric to cover her knees, automatically trying to hide the grazes. She could almost have believed his voice herself, apart from knowing what a noise it made to scramble down the ivy and knowing that she

160

would have heard him long before he could ever have surprised her. He had been there, waiting. She opened her mouth to protest, closed it again. Nausea threatened. Barbara's sympathy, if it had ever been there for the taking, was waning so fast words would not help, although when Anna thought about it later, she would wonder what she could have said. *I had two vodkas and fancied climbing a wall for a chat to God. Wanted to tell him he would look better if he grew a long nose.* Yeah, great. There was nothing to say. The last realisation before he overpowered her had been the right one. She had no business here. She began to shiver. Barbara was listening to him.

'I thought it was a kid,' he was repeating. 'And . . .' He hesitated. 'I thought it was the same kid I saw last week, hanging round on the day the chapel window was broken. I thought it was the same kid, with a catapult, maybe even an air gun. I couldn't take the risk of it happening again.'

'You bastard,' she hissed. 'You bloody liar.'

'Be *quiet*!'

He turned to Barbara beseechingly. 'On that evening, Sister, I walked on by, because it was still light and I didn't want to interfere. I was always sorry about that, which is why I didn't tonight. I didn't think, I just reacted. I haven't hurt her, have I? I'm so sorry. I only asked her who she was and she leapt at me like a cat. Is she a friend of yours?'

The torchlight wavered between them with increasing agitation, finally focusing on Francis's ravaged and beautiful features. Not so much ravaged as scratched, the marks enhancing the planes of his cheekbones and making him look like . . . a martyr. That instant familiarity of the holy picture face, glimpsed in the chapel that morning, as if it had been transferred from the sanitised but tortured face of an apostle on the Stations of the Cross.

'No,' she shouted. 'I didn't break the fucking window. I came in the front door that night, you great turd, I was *in* the sodding chapel . . .'

She was twisting the skirt of her dress in her fist. The statue of Ganesh that Ravi had given her fell out of the pocket with a suspicious clunk; she scooped it up and pushed it back, feeling and looking like a burglar caught in the act. Sneaking in some subversive idol, hiding an implement of harm. No one investigated it, but the noise and the flurry of movement was incriminating. The gold crucifix on the broken chain remained glowing on the ground. She watched, disbelieving her own eyes, as Francis scooped it up in one smooth, surreptitious movement.

'That's mine,' he said. 'You poor little girl, was that all you wanted?'

Barbara sighed. 'Oh Anna, how could you? I thought you had stopped hating us.'

'I don't . . . I didn't . . .'

'What is it you want?'

Barbara's voice was low. In the torchlight, she looked like an elderly lioness leaning over prey, still willing to explain why she was about to eat it. Anna lost the last of her dignity and credibility by being sick. It took her entirely by surprise. Vomit splashed over Barbara's sensible slippers and she could not hide a *yeugh* of disgust. It could have been deliberate, like the silly, insulting face with the tongue out.

'Perhaps we should call the police,' Francis murmured. Looking at her own feet in the torchlight made Barbara suddenly decisive. Decision making was her strong point.

'No, Francis dear. That is simply not appropriate. We'll all go inside.' She was directing her decisions and the explanations for them entirely towards him, as if no one else was present, relying on him to carry Anna with them as she used one foot to wipe the muck on the other. Rancid smells, far removed from those of the garden, assailed their nostrils. Anna felt entirely despicable.

'Anna here has a relative in the community,' Barbara was saying to Francis. 'It would not be kind to her sister to involve anyone else. Besides, she's a little touched in the head. Come along.'

Silent Matilda led the way up the path, through the open door of the parlour and into the bright light of the room. Prodded by Francis, Anna followed. On the far side of the parlour, Matilda disappeared into the other regions of the building, melting away like a ghost. Barbara had no intention of lingering either. They did not pause among the ugly chairs, but followed her down the black and white corridor to the front door, watched her struggle with the bolts and keys until the door was open. She made an expansive, sweeping motion with one hand, as if brushing rubbish out into the street.

'Off you go, Anna. And I don't think you'd better come back. Now, Francis, I'm sure I can trust you to see this child to her door. The morning is soon enough for a discussion.'

She stood back to let them through, commanding obedience in the very rigidity of her posture, so that without a word of the furious protest that fizzed in her throat, Anna passed by and began to walk away. *Don't come back*. The words ringing in her ears blotting out pain, eradicating anything else, including fear of the man who fell into step behind her and Barbara's casual cruelty in sending her away *with him*. The enormity of that struck her after fifteen steps. Barbara had thrown her out into the city night with an enemy for company. A lying, creeping, dangerous *bastard*. She began to run, only to find her legs were made of jelly. He caught her at the corner, grabbed her elbow.

'I'm to see you home,' he said, mildly. 'Pretty little things shouldn't be out after dark, all on their own.'

'You sod.'

Traffic passed in the road. A couple walked on the opposite pavement, reassuringly normal, a reminder that it was not even near the middle of the night, scarcely bedtime for those who lived normally. He put his arm through hers, holding her close to his side, mimicking the couple in their affectionate stroll. They walked stiffly for a few more steps. She had the sensation that he knew exactly where she was going; just as he had known her identity long before the bizarre introduction of Sister Barbara. *Anna here has a relative in the community.* The things Anna holds most dear are inside those walls. She pulled herself free of him.

'I'm the king of the castle, you're the dirty rascal,' he taunted. 'But you're even prettier than your sister. I wouldn't know which to have first.'

He pulled her towards him by the hair and ignoring the sour taste of her mouth, kissed her. Then pushed her away from him, so that she nearly stumbled again. She heard him laugh as he turned and left.

'You heard what she said,' he shouted after her. 'Don't come back. No one will let you in.'

And those were the only words that echoed.

164

CHAPTER EIGHT

Therese was wide awake.

She had sensed the disturbances of the early part of the night, rather than heard. She kept to her room in obedience to the general rule made for the good and the peace of them all.

Hers was on the first floor, at an angle of the building facing the roof of the opposite house, with a limited view of the road. The other Sisters on this floor included the habit-wearing seniors of the sorority, which long ago she and Anna described as penguins. Most had a TV or radio, and although the rule of respecting personal privacy was not written in stone, it was followed out of preference. Each room was sparse without being spartan, equipped with a washbasin; there was an amicable sharing of one bathroom and two lavatories and an unspoken agreement of silence at night. None of the rooms had a mirror.

Therese had heard the swish of Matilda's robes down the linoleum corridor as she began to contemplate sleep, guessed who it was by the footsteps, which she knew by heart. Matilda stayed awake late and when Agnes sometimes wept at night, it was Matilda who went to her. There would be brief, soft murmurings, followed by silence, occasions when Therese realised that she could never quite share their thoughts or their preoccupations, because she did not know what they were. They might share a set of circumstances and a code of behaviour, but they were old and she was young.

Sister Joseph's room was immediately above Therese's on the next floor, with an empty room on either side, an unplanned isolation occurring by accident after one Sister had moved to another convent and Sister Jude had died, leaving Joseph almost exclusive use of the bathroom on that floor, which suited such an assiduous washer who insisted upon doing her own laundry instead of putting it in a laundry bag for Sunday night collection like all the others. The old partition walls were solid enough to deaden most sound, except cries, the loudest of snores and the most persistent of coughs, which Therese could hear now as a long night moved towards dawn.

The sound of it vexed her beyond endurance and she blamed it for her inability to pray. By the weak light of her reading lamp, she had read again the advice of St Therese of Lisieux on how to turn an irritating noise into a sacrifice. *I set myself to listen attentively as though it were delightful music, and my meditation was passed in offering this music to Our Lord.*

Therese found this exercise impossible and so she tried the comforting, formulaic prayer of the rosary, skipping the beginning, going on to the Lord's Prayer, followed by ten, whispered Hail Marys, while she tried to keep her mind fixed on the Joyful Mysteries of the Annunciation of the Conception of Jesus and His Nativity, her mind slipping constantly into the present. There were spells of blissful silence between the distant coughing; in each pause, she would hold her breath and pray it had finished. Then it started again.

Therese gritted her teeth and thought about faces instead, which put the origin of the cough into perspective. Poor Joseph. Surely, when you were as *old* as Joseph, you had got life sorted. She lay back in her bed and stared at the ceiling, seeing, in colour, Joseph's mottled face in the stark white of the paint, finding that her contemplation of that face lessened her irritation with the owner of it, realising, not for the first time, that she was merely a practical person without the makings of a mystic. She was better at doing than thinking: she would never be able to make her mind transcend the interruption of sound, or the memory of a face.

It had never really occurred to her before seeing Joseph in the chapel that a person with their profound and all-encompassing belief in God could be *lonely*. They could be unhappy, from time to time, yes; troubled by events, and personal inadequacies, beset by challenges, often ashamed, but never *lonely*. It was impossible to comprehend, because it was the very essence of her belief that God and his saints never slept, that they never failed to listen and always forgave. God was a father, tied by an umbilical cord to all his children. Forgiveness was natural; His face was never turned away from an apology. Saints did not sulk and take umbrage like parents even if you disappointed them; they were constant companions, friends and family for life and beyond. So how could anyone be lonely, even if they were sad? Repentance for failures always equalled forgiveness.

And yet that was what Joseph had been; gut-churningly, utterly lonely, beyond the reach of any intercession, beyond asking. The thought of that frightened Therese because she could not see how it could happen. The coughing resumed. This time it was more pitiful than irritating. If

167

Joseph did not seek help, it was not for her to interfere, other than to tell her superiors and let them, in their wisdom, find solutions. To act otherwise was to compound yesterday's disobedience.

And then, other favourite words swam into mind. *Love is patient; love is kind and envies no one. Love is never boastful or conceited, nor rude, never selfish, not quick to take offence. Love keeps no score of wrongs . . . I may speak in tongues of men or angels, but if I am without love, I am a sounding gong or a clanging cymbal . . .*

Therese buttoned her heavy nightgown up to the neck, slipped out of her room, down the corridor towards the stairs. Light framed Matilda's door, but if she was awake, she would not hear. Therese had not needed to learn the art of quiet movement; she had seemed to know it in advance of living here, could not remember ever making a noise. The door of Joseph's room was also framed in light. She was relieved about that; at least she was not saving electricity by sharing her misery with the dark. Therese knocked softly and entered without invitation. There was a fusty smell to the room, although the small window was open wide, and Joseph was hunched over the washbasin. She turned a baleful glare on her visitor and began to splash water on her face. The front of her white nightgown was splattered with blood.

Therese swallowed. The splatters of blood were brilliantly red against the white of the old gown, which Joseph would have cleaned herself. She finished washing her face. The vomiting spasm had passed and her skin was as pale as plaster. Therese stood awkwardly, staring at her as she wiped her face dry. Joseph smiled. There was always something sardonic about Joseph's smile, as if she had to force it into operation.

'Hello, little Therese. Come to help again? Could you reach me my other nightgown – from the cupboard, there. If I don't soak this one, it'll stain.'

Therese did as she was told. There was a folded nightgown, identical to the one Joseph wore, on the top shelf of the tiny wardrobe, which was otherwise occupied by nothing but a coat, a blouse and a pair of shoes. She reached down the gown and stood holding it until Joseph snatched it from her hands.

'Turn round, child.'

Therese turned her face to the door, heard the rustle of cotton as Joseph pulled the soiled dress over her head, and replaced it with the clean one. Only in the event of illness were the Sisters ever on such intimate terms as this. Therese knew she could cope with a dead body, but she had a horror of seeing Joseph naked.

'There, that's better. You can turn round now.'

Therese turned. Joseph bent to collect the nightdress crumpled at her feet, groaning as she did so.

'Here, let me—'

'*No!*'

She watched as Joseph began to rinse the bodice of the gown in the washbasin, which was too small to accommodate it. Everything in the room was small. Therese felt she fitted into her own, identical space as neatly as if it had been made for her, but could imagine that Joseph, tall, gaunt, clumsy and twice her weight, would bruise herself in the restricted space as she prepared for bed. She watched, mesmerised by the pink water, as Joseph rinsed. Cleanliness is next to godliness, but it seemed strange in someone who was content to poison her own body, to say nothing of her own mind. Perhaps the washing was a secret penance; maybe it had a purpose. Joseph began to shiver.

'Get into bed, Sister. I'll finish that.'

Joseph lurched the two steps to the bed, which also seemed too small for her. The window was alongside, curtains drawn back, showing a shiny new catch, which kept it propped open. For Therese, obedience from someone so much older was a disturbing novelty. She wrung moisture from the nightgown and spread it over the basin. Then she took the cushion from the single chair and placed it behind Joseph's head to supplement the single pillow.

'Thank you, child. You're very kind. May your reward be on earth, rather than in heaven.'

Therese sat on the edge of the bed, gingerly. 'What's the matter with you?' she asked bluntly. She had been considering the wisdom of asking, Do you want me to call Barbara, the doctor, anyone? but she knew the answer would be no.

'Cirrhosis, dear. Acquired in the service of Jesus, in foreign parts.'

Therese understood. The medical dictionary had once been a Bible for herself and Anna as they looked up their own symptoms without ever finding any real answers. They began with A and went on to Z. Mother had encouraged it.

'So drink could kill you.'

'*Will* kill me, with a bit of luck.'

'Is that why you want it?'

Joseph fiddled with the neck of the gown. The brown liver spots on her hands were like extra large, misshapen freckles.

'Possibly. Mostly I want it because I want it, and life is completely meaningless, dull and futile without it. Not worth having. Don't worry your head, child. You couldn't possibly understand.'

'No, Sister, I don't understand. I can't—'

'Sister Jude understood,' Joseph went on. 'But then Jude understood everything, that old fraud.'

'Fraud?'

'Such a liar, that woman. I never knew one half as good at keeping opinions to herself, which is the same as lying. No one's interested in my opinions, she would say. I write them on the back of holy pictures to keep them short and stuff them in my missal, she said.'

'And what do you do with yours, Sister?' Therese asked, trying to lighten the tone.

'Swallow them whole and cough them up.' She laughed drily. She was beginning to become sleepy; it softened the lines of her face.

'You seem to have forgotten to ask God to help you.'

Joseph's eyes shot wide open. She was terrifyingly amused. 'Oh, Him? My dear, we parted company a long time ago. No more transmissions. Over and out. Neither giving or receiving. The radio bust. Knock, knock, nobody home. I told him, God, you're so *boring*. He left.'

If Joseph had spat or peed, Therese could not have been more shocked. She struggled with the very idea of believing that God the Father would simply go away, like her own parent had done, leaving behind a great big space. She knew such a prospect would make sense to Anna, or someone like Kim, who had never crossed that barrier or felt that *presence*, like a pair of enfolding arms, but for an old woman who was a lifetime servant of the Lord, it seemed an obscene admission of negligence. One who knew God could never send Him away; He would not allow it. It was impossible to lose something that was essentially yours and as much a part of you as the blood in your veins. The martyrs had preferred to die rather than take that risk; so, she thought, would she.

'Inconceivable, you think? Faith might be a gift, Therese, but don't bank on it being permanent. It can leave you just like that, or you leave it. And once it's gone, you can't nurture it back into life, whatever St bloody Therese says. Once you start to realise the possibility that man made God for his own convenience, rather than the other way round, you've got Him on the run. Let in the light of logic and He goes to ground. As unreliable as anything else synthetic and man-made.'

She laughed again, humourlessly. Therese kept her gaze fixed on the bedspread, to avoid scrutiny and the pounding of her own heart.

'How many of us have real belief, Therese? How many of us *here*? We, the quintessential believers? What do you imagine we think about? Agnes dreams of the bastard son who was taken from her. She sees him in every young man she encounters, although he'd be old himself, now. Barbara thinks of the Lord as an occupational hazard. Poor Father Goodwin continues with what tattered remnants of faith he has left. My dear Matilda, to whom I dare not speak in case I spread corruption . . . Matilda spends all day chatting to St Michael, who probably resembles someone she once saw in a film. He is, after all, the patron saint of policemen and other fascists. It isn't worship, it's idolatrous hero worship. Everyone has their own God. We make the one that suits us.'

Therese wanted to scream at her to stop. It wasn't true, any of it. It was the drink talking, even if Joseph was sickly sober. Drink made people mad: it made Anna nasty, her father pathetic, it was the stuff of devilment. Tomorrow, she was going to get Francis, tell him what he had done . . . For the moment, she was angrily calm.

'If you don't believe, Sister, and you feel God has deserted you, why do you stay?'

'Don't be naive, child. Where would I go? With *what* would I go? No, the Church has had the best of me, it can have the worst.'

She pulled the blankets up over her chin, so that all Anna could see was her haunting, blazing eyes.

'I'm sorry, child. I'm being grotesquely unkind. Loneliness should not be contagious. You'd better go for your beauty sleep. I'd rather you didn't tell Barbara about the coughing. She has enough to do. It wouldn't be *charitable* to either of us.'

Therese nodded, aware that it was a promise. Joseph closed her eyes. On the other side of the door, with the first hint of daylight beginning to creep along the floor from the long window at the end, Therese paused. Instead of going straight back to her room, she went to the one next to Joseph's which Sister Jude had occupied. It was clean, but not entirely cleared. Each of the Order and Jude's relatives had taken from her shelves whatever they had wished, either to remember her by, or because they liked it. The selection had been small. Poetry, prose, a minimum of religion, the maximum of music for her Walkman, which had gone, the radio, which was gone, leaving a few literary souvenirs. Therese found herself searching for the spot where the missal had been, remembered how she had taken it for Anna, because it was Anna Jude loved. Anna who did what Jude liked best, argued, raised the devil, asked questions and demanded answers, making Jude test herself, age against youth, so that they lost their tempers with one another. Therese would never have dared to do that, any more than she would have wanted to do it. She hated confrontation. She had thought obedience was natural. Jude had never respected her for that. Her sainted aunt had a preference for sinners, did not believe what her own

173

mother had taught her by example, *Be good, sweet maid. And let who will be clever.*

It was Jude who advised her against following her vocation; Jude who said no child should ever do a thing because her mother wished it. But that was not why she had done it. Nor had she entered the Order because she thought it would be easy. She had done it because it felt entirely natural and she had been confident it would always feel like that. On her way back to her own room, grateful for the dawn, she found herself feeling envious of Anna. Wanted a touch of that anger, as well as a touch of the street wisdom, which would teach her what to do with Francis, who by the simple act of supplying Joseph with her own poison had made her imagine that she had lost her faith. Faith could be spat upon and scorned, but never lost. What rubbish. She would find Francis and tell him not to do this and then everything would be all right. She would appeal to the better nature every soul had. Stripping off her own nightgown, pulling on her day clothes and washing her own face before she clipped back her hair, she encountered the sneaky, unknown thought that she would prefer a better, less scratchy nightdress than this, and if she were ever to die, which seemed a remote possibility, she would also prefer to have more than a single pair of shoes.

Kim came in early. 'Only thing that bastard ever does,' she grumbled, 'is give the little sods breakfast and take them to school. Bastard. I'd rather be here than round our place. It's a madhouse. Hey, Treesa, are you awake? How long have you been sitting there? You gonna talk to me or what? Otherwise, I might as well stay home.'

The kitchen was beautifully empty; a place waiting to spring into life. Being in it cheered Therese immeasurably. It was her favourite place; there was nothing wrong with being Mary rather than Martha and she desperately needed to laugh. So, sighing dramatically, she launched into the familiar Monday morning routine she and Kim had perfected.

'I'm a bit weary, to be honest. Shagged out, as a matter of fact, Kim. Weekends in here get so *wild*. Clubbing Saturday night. Vodka and ketchup, ever tried it? Lethal. Sunday morning, ended up God knows where with the Sisters, sobering up and hanging out with the priests. Back up here for a line of coke and bacon sandwiches. You know how it is. Tiring.'

'That's better! Thought you were dead. So who got luvverly Francis, then? No luck?'

'No, we took a vote. We decided he preferred blokes.'

'You don't say! Makes sense, though, doesn't it? Such a pretty boy.'

'What makes sense? Nuns on coke, or what?'

'Francis, being gay. Name like that, hair like that, you know. Shame, innit? What a bloody waste. Oh, forget it. He's still shaggable.'

Overwhelmed by a sudden sense of her own ignorance, Therese sat down. She could never play this game for very long.

'How do you know if a man's gay?'

Kim was decanting milk into a jug. The kettle was coming to the boil. Everything was cheerful and soon there would be food on the table. Therese was ravenously hungry.

'Gay men? You don't know. Only they're often too good-looking for their own good and they sometimes wear their willies on the outside. They like perfume, wash more than ordinary. That's one sign, anyway. Oh, and they know how to be nice to women. Come to think of it, that would suit

175

Francis down to a T. Gay chaps know how to get on with girls. I mean they talk to us, which is more than the other buggers do.'

'Ah.'

'Shame none of you scored. Do you want coffee for your hangover?'

'Yes, please.'

'I think you ought to stay indoors more, Treesa. Have an early night for a change. Get Francis to tuck you in. If he's gay, he'll be safe as houses, even if you throw your knickers at him. Which reminds me. We've got to do the laundry today. Get it started before breakfast.'

The laundry bags, collected from the Sisters' rooms each week, stood in the scullery off the kitchen, which housed the boiler, a hanging rail and a large, noisy washing machine.

'I think we ought to get Francis in to look at that washer, Treesa. Give you a chance to get to know him, like everyone else. You just smile at him and scuttle away. You haven't talked to him yet, have you?'

'No, but I want to.'

'Get you, you cheeky sod! Why's that then?'

'I want to ask him not to run errands for Sister Joseph.'

'Oh, he does, does he? Well, I can hardly blame him for that. She's very persuasive. She was always asking me and it was hard to say no. Sweet youth like Francis hasn't got a chance. She'll tell him he was doing her a kindness.'

Therese sat, rooted to the chair. How very, very little she knew. As little about their bodies as their souls. How much they conspired to protect her.

'I don't understand where she gets the money.'

'She's got some of her own. And I can tell it isn't you polishes the collection box by the chapel. Someone gets the bottom off and robs a bit every week before anyone counts. Easy. Are you all right, Treesa?'

She was not all right; she was reeling with shock all over again. Poor Joseph really was a soul damned to eternity, or at least in the eyes of Sister Barbara. She sipped the coffee and wished it had more taste.

'Laundry,' she said.

Dealing with the personal laundry of a dozen women bore no resemblance to the tasks described by St Therese of Lisieux in her cold convent cellar, battling with dirty water and filthy suds. It was merely a simple job of sorting the contents of the laundry bags into two piles with the rough division of delicate and hardy. Most of it was hardy, but the process of sorting always felt like prying to Therese. Each Sister placed her underwear into the bag in which she would receive it back. There were a vast number of handkerchiefs, which seemed to be essential. Therese hated the handkerchiefs, while Kim always either laughed or tut tutted over the rest. There were Agnes's flannelette bloomers, worn winter and summer, Barbara's monstrous, indestructible bras, the sometimes more holey than godly vests preferred by the others, the schoolgirl sensible stuff used by the youngest, including Therese, and not a trace of lace anywhere. Except on the handkerchiefs, those items most often given to the Sisters by relatives for lack of anything else appropriate. Embroidered hankies, colourful hankies, linen and silk hankies. Matilda went through a dozen a week. They formed the bulk of her laundry. Nestled down among them at the bottom of her bag was a knife.

Not a particularly sinister-looking knife, but lethal all the same. A fruit knife with a rope-strapped handle and a short blade which looked as if it had been honed to dangerous, surgical sharpness on a stone. If Therese had not been so timid in extracting the handkerchiefs, the pointed blade would have nicked her fingers. She put it on top of the washing machine and both of them looked at it. A laundry bag was a good hiding place, but why was she keeping a knife? Such a sharp knife.

Barbara's voice rang out from the kitchen. '*Bendicamus Domino!*'

'*Deo Gratias,*' Therese murmured, slipping the knife into the pocket of her tunic while Kim carried on as if nothing had happened. Secrecy was becoming second nature.

Kim grabbed the last garment, which she had been waving round her head like a flag, stuffed it inside and slammed the door of the washing machine. Barbara hove into view, filling the door of the utility room with her feet, as if she was about to flow inside and all around them, like lava. Her normal demeanour was one of relentless cheerfulness, overseen by those scrutinising eyes, which seemed to take in every detail, while smiling throughout. The smile was missing today. She looked indefatigable, but tired. It was Kim's daily complaint that she hated the woman, which Therese had long since translated as a benign kind of fear and a hearty dislike of being bossed about. For Therese, Barbara was in another sphere. She was the first adult human being she could remember as having taken her seriously and she was afraid of her in an awesome way. Barbara was the embodiment of all higher authority, the representative of the Order she obeyed and the person who knew the answers to everything. But in that one moment, with Barbara's feet and Barbara's bosom swelling into the small space, she could only think of the bosom and the monstrous brassiere Kim had just stuffed into the circular mouth of the washing machine.

The item, lying within sight in the machine, resembled part of a comical suit of armour. Therese looked at it as if she had never seen it before. Barbara's posture was part of her authority. She wore her bosom high, so that it preceded her, like a woman carrying a box, and only the two of them here knew the superstructure that lay behind.

'Good, good. You're at work.'

She was a trifle agitated, but the solid bosom trembled not a bit. Two white bras she had, wire and cotton, grey straps and six hooks and eyes. When she was agitated, she forgot to keep her voice down and she had not remembered to brush her hair.

'Always, Sister,' Kim said demurely.

'Terrific,' Barbara said. 'Keep it up. Keep your pecker up! Therese, a word with you after breakfast, please.'

She swept away, and as soon as her squeaky shoes were out of hearing they both began to giggle, nervously.

'What does she know about peckers?' Kim said.

'Probably more than me,' Therese said, unsure of what she meant. In Kim's laughter, somehow the knife was forgotten. Being late with the breakfast had all the makings of a sin. Despite her hunger she would not eat the breakfast, in reparation for the laughter, which felt, if not sinful, something close to it.

There was a hierarchy of sins. There were the sins committed on a daily basis – evasions, dishonesties, the failures to remember holy things. Therese had learned her catechism the way other children learned to count, but the definitions of what made a sin mortal and what made it venial were more difficult. There was no straight line between the two. The venial was the daily sin, easily expunged; the mortal was the sin that divorced the soul from God. If a person died with such an unrepented sin

179

scarring their soul, they would never be reunited in the next life with the God who had made them. The thought was enough to strike terror: it was the threat of permanent expulsion from everything that could provide happiness or safety, but all the same, she was never sure what kind of a sin it could be. A sin that slaps God in the face, Jude had defined it. A really serious sin. Your conscience will tell you when it is yours, even if the reactions of others do not make it clear, because you will despise yourself and know that your Father waits for you to acknowledge what you have done and make amends. You will feel it in your bones. But what kind of sin is it? she had asked. Is there a list? No, no list, apart from the ten commandments and the catechism.

All that Therese knew as she moved round the dining room table, delivering milk and juice, finally standing with her head bowed during the prayer, was that she felt in a state of sin, unable to join in with the words, *For what we are about to receive, may the Lord make us truly thankful.* The hunger had gone and she formed her bread into small pellets to avoid eating it, knowing that here, wasting food was regarded as far worse than eating too much of it. She should have sat next to Matilda, who would have eaten it for her. But what is my sin? she was asking herself, furiously, as the pellets of bread stuck in her throat. I have listened to Joseph's heresy and slander, and I have helped her to hide her own sins. I have laughed at Barbara and disobeyed her, in spirit at least. Is that enough to make me feel so bad that my sin is mortal? Forgive me, Lord. She looked at the face of Matilda watching her anxiously from halfway down the table and found herself suspicious of the glance. Matilda's knife was in her pocket; Matilda wanted to see Anna; they were keeping secrets. Agnes, supposedly the mother of a child, sat staring towards the door, as if expecting a vision. Joseph was serene. She waited until the last as Therese was stacking plates and the others had filed away, came up behind her and touched her on the shoulder.

'Therese, my dear, I must apologise for troubling you. It was selfish of me.' She hesitated, but it was not the hesitation of conscience. She looked surprisingly decisive and fresh, a woman capable of self-reinvention, looking at Therese closely but kindly, as if trying to ascertain if Therese could remember a fraction of what she had said. That was how Therese's newly suspicious mind interpreted it.

'It was no trouble, Sister. The less said, the soonest mended.'

She was becoming like the rest of them, resorting to well-worn clichés.

Joseph nodded. 'But there is one thing I wanted to say, child. I mentioned Sister Jude's missal. Don't look at it. She put her opinions of your mother in there.'

She departed as Matilda sidled back, smiling, dipping her head in greeting to Joseph's departing back and resting her hand on Therese's shoulder. In her heightened state of nervous awareness, Therese had the unbidden impression that the two women wanted to behave differently.

'Therese, lovey, you won't forget to tell Anna to come and see me, will you? As soon as Barbara has the sense to let her back.'

Therese was confused. 'Of course, Sister, but I never know when she's going to appear.'

'No, but if she ever does . . . She will, soon, won't she? It's very important that I see her.'

It could not be soon enough. Therese was swept away

by a longing to see her flesh-and-blood sister. Hear her voice, even if it mocked. Confess her miseries to someone who did not rely on God for an answer, and for once, be touched by the flesh of someone who was not old. Old flesh, old smells, old, old . . . old sins.

Barbara's office, with her bedroom behind it, was next to the parlour, off the black and white corridor. Agnes had already taken up residence by the front door. The day and the week was beginning like every other week for the last year, but without the same optimism that buoyed her being and without the comforting sense of it being *right*. The three younger Sisters, who never spoke to her, like new postgraduates to a student in her first term, had departed in their usual quiet flurry of activity to their teaching jobs. Without quite realising it, Therese had formed a settled dislike of them, because they were so importantly useful. They were allowed to be exhausted in the evening and they had more to say to their elders, who had followed similar careers, than they ever would have to say to her. It was Martha and Mary all over again. As she stood back, dutifully, to let them pass, she saw Agnes open the door to the outside world, chirruping farewells like a squirrel. The door was halfway closed, Agnes being as efficient at closing as she was at opening, leaving Therese with the sour thought that she should have been a lift attendant, *oh, what was the matter with her today?* when Agnes leapt forward to open it wide. Seen in profile, her smile was one of sheer adoration, the sort reserved for spiritual ecstasy, as she opened her arms. Francis stepped into the hall, picked her up in a hug and swung her round as if she were weightless. Agnes had lost the knack of screaming, but she made, instead, small squealing noises of protesting pleasure. He was so strong, he could measure the swing he made with

182

her bulky body held at her belted waist, so that her feet only left the ground by a couple of inches and she had no cause for alarm before she found herself back with both shoes on the floor, guided towards her accustomed seat with a deft kiss planted on her left cheek.

'How's my boy?' she crooned.

'Never better, Mother. Gotta go, work to do.'

'Of course, son, of course.'

The light was bad in the vicinity of the front door once it was closed, and Agnes's eyesight was even worse. She was content with her embrace, patted him on the arm and shooed him on, not noticing the details of his face. The black and white corridor was the route to the garden as well as everything else. He turned into it and collided with Therese, lightly, she moving and he moving faster, a glancing contact between her shoulder and his elbow, enough to stop him and make him recoil.

'I'm so sorry, I beg your pardon,' both of them speaking in chorus, before she stood back, yet again, to let him pass. She was sick of standing back; soon she would fall over herself. She knew who he was and that she disapproved of him, and kept her eyes to the black and white floor. Strange, that in so small a place, she had been able to avoid the conversation with him that everyone else had so enthusiastically enjoyed in the last ten days, to find she needed it now. Everyone else had come to know and love him. There was no mistaking Francis. He was a foot taller than anyone else and smelled of man.

'Francis? I'm Therese. We haven't met. Can I talk to you later?'

It came out in a stutter. She had no social graces appropriate to men: she could only be silly, or silent, or gruff. She did not quite know what to do when he offered his hand, except take it, shake it and feel the fact that it was twice the size of her own and like dry sandpaper encircling her own, callused palm. He shook her hand vigorously, holding her arm by the elbow with his other hand as he did so, steadying her.

'Very pleased to meet you, Therese. Sure, I'm in the garden today. Or somewhere. Wherever Barbara lets me go.'

Which was everywhere, she thought, remembering the new window catch in Joseph's room as he relinquished the hand and the arm. She had the sensation of the grin and the eyes without really seeing either, rubbed her hand down the side of her tunic and heard him stride away, as softly as the rest of them, in indefinable shoes, which made no sound. She touched her right palm with her left and relived the feeling of his handshake. It had been so spontaneous and undemanding, not like the grasp of the old. There was no time for thinking about it. Their dual motion, the moving handshake, had brought her to Barbara's door. She would tell Barbara everything. She would confess.

You are even prettier than your sister. Anna clambered up to the roof and gazed down into the convent garden, seeking him out. It was a cold morning: summer had ceased the rearguard action against autumn and it seemed as if, overnight, the last of the leaves had gone from the deciduous trees, leaving them stripped bare. If she knew how, she could shoot him dead from here and she wished she did know how. She tried to imagine what it was like not to feel in disgrace. It felt like a state of sin, and she wished she could not recall the stupid act of putting out her tongue. She tried to be nonchalant about being dismissed from the Garden of Eden and told herself there were others.

184

Facile. The garden was empty and her mouth was dry with a sense of dread, the half-formed knowledge of something she had to do. So much confusing rubbish floating round in her sore head, the prospect of going to work and immersing herself in that other world beckoned attractively. She wanted to forget the place she watched, and everyone in it, as well as her own wretched stupidity. What was the worst thing she had done? Put out her tongue? Scratched his face? Encountered evil and run away? Torn herself from its grasp.

The breeze was strong, gusting in the night and tearing at the leaves. She settled herself down in the gully behind the parapet out of the wind. If she could not berate Therese's God in the chapel ever again, she would have to do it here. She took the little statue of Ganesh out of her pocket and put it down beside her, trying to find defiance, but it was difficult.

'Well, a fat lot of good you were,' she said, clutching her knees to her chest. 'I know you didn't have the power, but I still say you should have stopped me climbing over the wall, but there you go. If I hadn't climbed over the wall, I wouldn't know what was going on.'

She could feel the grazes on her knees through the stiff fabric of her jeans. Punishment.

'I'm sorry, Elephant God, but I really can't talk to you. Nothing personal. You're just far too nice. I want an ugly, vengeful sort of God. A brute. I want someone to shout at.'

She adjusted herself for comfort, looked at her feet. Boot weather today, all the better for kicking shit. Shit, shit, shit. She stood up stiffly, and with folded arms regarded the sky. There were scudding clouds, grey and greyer, no inspiration. Down in the garden, she could see the stripped trees and the figure of Matilda, aimlessly waving. Without

Edmund, it seemed as if she was calling down the birds to eat. Anna ducked back behind the wall.

'Look here, Lord, I don't know what it is, but you seem hell bent on destruction.'

She closed her eyes and imagined the chapel crucifix, with its weary face and artistic blood. The image was fuzzy and pale. Anna rubbed her eyes, furiously. All she could feel was the repellent sensation of Golden Boy's kiss, the confirmation of utter humiliation. Tried to remember when she had ever felt so claustrophobically powerless inside the embrace of someone who wished her harm. Without any prompting, she remembered struggling in the arms of her mother.

There were two hours before the start of her shift. Just enough time to find Father Goodwin, if she ran on her jelly legs. She wanted to ask him something in particular – *did Edmund wear a little crucifix, I can't remember* – but when she arrived at his door, there was no reply. God and his officials were always out.

Therese came back to the kitchen about eleven. She had detoured via the chapel, stayed there a long time. Kim had unloaded the laundry into the dryer and was bagging rubbish for the Tuesday collection. Somewhere in her sorting, she had found six cans of Diamond White and an empty vodka bottle.

'Bugger me, Treesa. No wonder you're so pale. You weren't fucking joking, were you?'

186

CHAPTER NINE

'Weren't you a little harsh?' Father Goodwin asked.

He remembered that St Barbara was the patron saint of gunners: a virtuous virgin imprisoned sometime in the third century AD and then executed by her father in some bloody fashion for espousing the Christian faith. But as soon as he murdered her, he was himself struck by lightning and reduced to ashes, leaving his daughter's legend to be symbolised as a tower of strength. All that fitted the current image, although he was finding it hard to reconcile this bosomy Barbara with the beautiful girl of the story, as well as finding it easy to imagine why the parent of the original saint had wanted to kill her.

They had removed themselves from the office to which he had been summoned peremptorily for the interview with Therese, and into the parlour with the view of the first part of the garden. The paved area he could see through the French windows was cleaner and tidier than he recalled, so much so that it was faintly reminiscent of the immaculately manicured patio where Kay McQuaid lived. This time last year, he was sure that all he could see was a mess of dead leaves and leggy plants long past their best. Now he could see black bin-liner bags ready for removal, a colourful array of busy lizzies in the pot nearest the window, and Francis, stage left, tidying an already clean and empty border. In less than a fortnight, he had made a revolution. The dead and the dying souvenirs of summer had been ruthlessly removed.

'We've loads of bulbs for a good show in the spring,' Barbara said, chattily, evading the issue.

'Isn't it a little early yet to plant bulbs?' Father Goodwin asked.

'Francis says not. Bulbs are so cheap. We shall have three dozen daffodils for a matter of pennies.'

'But no birds.'

'Why not?'

'No Edmund to encourage them. And there's a cat.'

'Has Francis provided a cat? How clever of him. We had mice in the place last winter. I never thought of a cat. You were saying, Father?'

'I was saying, weren't you a little harsh on Therese?'

She reached for the coffee pot and filled his cup. He was unsure if the taste was blander than the tea and decided he would not take bets on it. Later, in the afternoon, he would be visiting the sick, namely a virtually speechless old man equipped with a huge television. They would join in pastoral care by the silent watching of old football replays. The prospect beckoned sweetly.

'I didn't mean to sound harsh, Father. Should I apologise?'

He remembered, reluctantly, Barbara's good points, including her occasional bouts of humility.

'What you told her will have made her very unhappy.'

'Oh, come now, Father, I only told her that her sister was a disgrace and we didn't want her coming in here ever again.'

'You told her Anna was a thieving little savage with aspirations to burglary and assault, and also the person who broke the window. You told her all that on what seemed to me to be the scantiest of evidence—'

'But Francis told me. He was *hurt*.'

'*Yes*, Francis *said* and has the wounds to prove it, but tell me, Sister, does any of this accord with the Anna Calvert you know? The one who makes helpful suggestions, supplies useful outside knowledge, and was so kind when Edmund died? An orphan of considerable bravery. A young woman with no elders of her own. Dead mother, dead father, and then Sister Jude? Surely she's allowed to be a little unhinged.'

Barbara was breathing like a horse at the end of a race.

'Not on our premises, she isn't. I can't take responsibility for her, I simply can't. We're stretched to the limit as it is. We haven't either the financial or spiritual resources to deal with a window-breaking heathen who wants to undermine us. Of course, it's terrible she's had to face so much death, but I can't shoulder that, either. She *hurt* Francis, how could she? Poor, dear Francis, so good to us. And we all lose people sooner or later and their father was no loss at all.'

He spluttered over the coffee, temper rising, thought of a perfect goal, soaring high and down into the net and the elated roar of a crowd.

'How do you know? They hadn't seen him for years, but it doesn't mean it didn't matter. The point is that *there is no one left*, for either of them. You can't ban Anna from Therese, because Anna's all she's got.'

'Anna annoys her and Therese has *us*,' Barbara said, defensively.

It seemed imprudent to say, *It isn't enough.*

189

'Well, you can't forbid Anna from Sunday Mass. It's open to the public and if you do, I can't possibly say it for you.'

'There are other priests,' she said, loftily.

He found he was biting his tongue to the point of pain.

'I believe,' he said, 'that the business of Theodore Calvert's estate remains unsettled . . .'

She shifted uncomfortably.

'Well, yes and no. I've meant to discuss it with you ever since Sister Jude died, but it's been so *busy*. I get regular letters from a dry lawyer who speaks gobbledygook. He tells me that there is an ongoing argument about something or other. At first he wrote that the will was complex, and then he says there must be investigation into blood relatives, in case the will is invalid, which won't make any difference, because under the rules of intestacy, his daughters inherited anyway, but he has to look for forebears, or something. Only a matter of time, he keeps saying.'

'You get the letters?'

'Yes. I don't censor incoming mail for everyone, if that's what you think. Therese asked me to do it for her, and some of the others do as well. They want bad news to be filtered and they want complicated news to be decoded. What I mean is that they'd rather hear about illness in the family from me than read it before breakfast.'

'But you never hide anything from them?'

She cleared her throat and considered the question. She *wants* to be truthful, Christopher realised with a start of surprise. She just can't quite do it.

'No, of course not. But I do ration, we all have to do that. If Matilda was stricken with pneumonia, I might decide that the time was not right to tell her that her brother had died. And if ever it happened that Agnes's

190

so-called son demanded to see her again, I might not tell her at all.'

'Ah.'

'I can't discuss it with her because I'm not supposed to know. There's a lot of it about, Father,' she said kindly, in deference to his ignorance of things sexual, 'just as there was forty years ago.'

He was silent, thinking of Agnes waiting at the door, day in, day out. Of the cruelties of youth and how Barbara's decision might endorse them: of a disgraced girl from rural Ireland being taken in by a convent, to sit by the door ever since. Of Barbara as the buffer zone between herself and her Sisters, and how she did, at least, take decisions and stick to them, rather than use his own evasive techniques, and he humbly supposed there was a degree of moral courage in that. He held his hands steady in his lap, almost sorry that his temper was under control.

'Did Therese ever get a copy of her father's will?'

'She handed it to me, unread. A will and a draft will, which seems to be there by mistake. I'm afraid I kept it from her. It was obscene. I shall let the lawyer sort it out.'

'You kept it from her?' He found his voice was rising again.

'As I was *asked* to do.'

She sat, elbows on the knees spread beneath her long tunic, leaning forward for emphasis. She was plain and wholesome, he thought dispassionately, the most unfeminine creature he had ever known. Was it wrong to prefer a woman who smelled of perfume and cared for her skin?

'Where Therese entered the Order, eighteen months ago, it was just before they'd been told, by Calvert's fancy woman, I believe, that he had drowned. Therese was no stranger to us, as you recall, she brought with her all her

191

worldly goods. Including a pile of correspondence addressed to Anna and herself. They were all with the same lawyer's frank and none of them were opened. I don't know if that was a joint decision, or if Therese kept them from Anna when they shared that flat. They are ridiculously protective of each other. I've no doubt Therese kept house . . . she's the responsible one. She told me that neither of them had any interest in their father . . . why should they respond to letters from the grave when he had never responded to the letters they wrote to him when they were ill? So the lawyer writes to me. Oh, come, Father, you know very well that I didn't just sit on them when Sister Jude was alive. She agreed with me that the will was obscure but obscene. She saw all the correspondence and very likely showed it to you.'

There was a hint of something, a kind of jealousy. Barbara was suspicious of clever people conversing with one another. It was bound to be subversive.

'No. She discussed the situation with me in broad terms, not the letters or the will itself.'

'Oh Lord, the pedantry of priests. Isn't it better for them not to know that their father was as mad as a snake?'

'And their mother . . .'

'Died of a broken heart when she was parted from them. A saint.'

'Oh yes, I'd forgotten.'

He rose, stiff in the limbs and suddenly cold. The parlour was never really warm, not even in summer. He tried to imagine the empty fireplace full of logs and cheerful flames, and found it a leap of imagination too far. Perhaps the wonderful Francis could sweep the chimney and provide cheap fuel: all he would have to do was cut down the trees in the garden. Father Goodwin moved to the windows and looked out over the clean patio towards the forest of shrubs beyond the bend in the path. Francis had disappeared. Christopher had a vision of a golden serpent slinking back into obscurity and the clarity of the image shocked him.

'Shall I apologise to Therese?' Barbara asked, humbly.

'I can't advise you on that, Sister. You are the one in loco parentis. But I do think you should reconsider about Anna.'

'No.'

'In which case, I think you should give me copies of the letters and that wretched will. You might have the right to withhold such things from your postulant, but not from her sister, who is not, as you say, your responsibility.'

She nodded, patently relieved. 'I'll get the copies for you.'

And that, he thought to himself, as she fetched a bulky envelope of papers, was what you call an Own Goal. The final confirmation of an uncomfortable commitment to interfere in other lives. As he took the parcel and turned to leave, he saw Francis entering through the French windows and heard Barbara greet him with anxious affection.

'Ah, you poor *pet* . . .'

The boy was welcome to the remainder of the coffee and the sympathy of his adoring employer. He had more power here than Father Goodwin had ever had and the priest was ashamed of his own petulance.

The nondescript premises of Compucabs looked as safe as any prison. All Anna wanted was a longer shift than six hours, ten until four with no time to think. From her knapsack, she took the little statue of Ganesh and put it next to the paper cup of coffee she had brought in with her. It would have been kind to bring one for Ravi, but, as she remembered, he drank neither tea nor coffee, only water. The presence of Ganesh by the telephone would be her conciliatory gesture for all that infantile, childish foot-stamping of the distant afternoon before, which sneaked in around the edges of bigger anxieties and made her blush.

She had distracted herself on the way here, pushing back the essential, indigestible weight of panicky worry, by trying to think up an alternative place to pray. Not praying as in pathetic rosary bead praying, or kissing the ground, but praying as in thinking and arguing with a logical force, and that, she had realised on the rooftop this morning, definitely required a designated place. That was what places of worship were *for*. She wanted a place where she could shout inside her own head and ask, *What are you going to do about my sister?* She wanted a place where she could hear some reassuring voice come back and say, *It is all your imagination that she is locked inside strong walls with a virus that has already affected all her brethren. She is not in danger. She is really stronger than you and all the more strong with a barrage of saints and angels to protect her.* Of course.

As she walked, not jogging today in her autumn jeans, because her legs were wooden, she was remembering the grander churches they had frequented as children on the high days of her mother's religion. Wherever they went, they had found a church, entered it and exited quickly if the church was not one of Rome. It was as if her mother was drawn to them all, regardless of denomination, purely for the purposes of comparison, so that she could say, see? Ours are so much better. Cathedrals in Coventry, Ely and Canterbury had all been spurned. She had promised them Chartres and Palma, although it had never happened. She mourned the fact that they lived in the wrong country for the best examples of Roman Catholic cathedrals and they had to make do with Westminster, where they had gone sometimes, like tourists to a palace. There had been an Easter service there where Therese had sneezed at the incense and Anna, prodded by her father, had giggled.

The other item in the rucksack was the missal, carried around for no good reason but the comfort granted by its weight. Anna surveyed the room, looking for Ravi's sleek black head and listening to the buzz of conversation. He looked up and smiled at her, stuck up his thumb in a brief salute and carried on talking into his mouthpiece. The smile was like a blessing. Everyone knew that Ravi was incapable of smiling to order. She was forgiven. He found it impossible to pretend. Unlike herself, who made an effort to smile, because she knew a smile helped to offset the sullen and ferocious impression she so often created. The smile of a person so insecure, she had practised it earnestly and used it not necessarily to express pleasure but to please. Somewhere in the sick years, she had lost the art of smiling and had made an effort to reacquire it, in shops, the hall, the bedroom or bathroom, wherever there was a mirror. She could be a smile counsellor now, with all that practice, and smiled at the thought, for a brief moment, laughing at herself for no longer ever knowing when she smiled or scowled. Maybe concentrate on being ridiculous; she could turn it into a whole way of life, wear scarlet and feathers and furs and hats, or nothing at all . . . She waved at Ravi and the room, wiggled her hips in the way she and Therese had done as they aped magazine models in the invalid years and sat down to imagined applause. Her phone buzzed as she donned the headpiece.

'Good morning, Compucabs.'

There was a whole second of hesitation, then a deep voice.

'I asked for you yesterday and you weren't there. I was so worried, I nearly, oh never mind what I nearly did, dear, dear, dear . . .'

'Account number, sir?'

'I'm not sure, must be about here somewhere . . .'

She recognised the voice of her caller and knew, for once, she was smiling for real. He was a waste of space, but he made her smile.

'Bit early for worrying about where to go for lunch, sir. No need to book early, it isn't Christmas yet.'

'No, it isn't. Are you all right?'

'Never finer, how about you?'

'I was worried about you. Tried you yesterday.'

'I have days off, Sundays, you know how it is.'

Another sigh. 'Bloody Sundays. Why are they always awful? They just go on so long . . .'

'You're so right,' she said ruefully. They go on long enough for unsmiling people to commit acts of inexplicable folly.

'You know what Sundays are?' He was shouting into the phone. 'The dog days of the year. Did you go to church?'

She thought of the temple, touched the little statue of Ganesh with her spare hand. Ganesh did not mind looking silly; perhaps he was one of her Gods, after all.

'Yes, I did, in a manner of speaking. Now what about that taxi?'

'I wanted to ask you to come to lunch.'

'I'm working today, sir, another time, perhaps.'

He hesitated again. 'What church did you go to?'

'Well, I tried the Catholics first and then the Hindus.

196

They're a lot more fun, but they still have collection boxes.'

There was a soft chuckle and the line went dead. He did that sometimes, her elderly gentleman caller with the strained voice and the manners of confusion. Anna waited for the phone to ring again. Today of all days, it failed her. The silence of it was reproachful. Half an hour passed. Ravi might have smiled but he did not come close. In the surrounding buzz, it was as if she were contagious. It was warm and she was overpoweringly tired. To pass the time, she began reading the messages scrawled on the backs of the holy pictures in the missal. Then she closed the book, folded her hands over the soft leather of the volume and used them to cushion her head. There was no alternative to thinking, after all.

Someone was shaking her awake, supervisors standing over her, jiggling her left shoulder, making her yelp. She was in the middle of a dream where she was being touched and kissed. Hugged by Therese, who had grown a whole foot taller.

'Steady on, girl. What do you think you're doing, coming here to kip? You've got your set turned off. What do you think we pay you for?'

It was more puzzled than censorious: concern for a good worker.

'Sorry.'

'Wouldn't have noticed, only everyone else is busy. And this parcel came for you. Your birthday or something? Or was that yesterday and you're sleeping it off? You look bloody rough. Go home, why don't you?'

'I don't want—'

'You don't want to let us down, right?'

She did not want to go home. She saw Ravi, standing by the supervisor, and loathed the way he looked at her, with all that genuine concern, making her feel like a sick cat.

'Just come back tomorrow, love, when you feel better. Do you need a taxi?'

The irony of that almost made her laugh, but not quite. Ravi put the missal and the statue of Ganesh inside her knapsack. The supervisor looked at her through glasses which made her eyes seem enormous. They had seen the scratches on the backs of her hands: sleep made her face pink and flushed. They were being kind, but she was profoundly suspicious of any sort of kindness and simply felt a sickening sense of repetition. First they were kind, then they sent you away.

'Sorry,' she repeated, scrabbling for dignity.

'No worries, love. Get your head down. Don't forget your parcel.' Ravi went back to his desk. The supervisor took her to the door. She carried a gift-wrapped package under her arm and felt as if she were running the gauntlet of eyes, although nobody here took any notice of anyone else: that was the whole point of it. Outside, she stood alone, waiting for the taxi, absent-mindedly ripping at the parcel. Two layers of brightly coloured, much-Sellotaped paper encased a polythene envelope, which had a slight, indefinable smell. With nothing to do but wait, she persisted. Inside the polythene, inside two layers of white tissue, was a dead bird with a red bow round the neck. A very small bird, long dead, desiccated rather than putrefying. The note, folded alongside, was on dry paper, cool to the touch.

Are not sparrows five for tuppence? And yet not one of them is overlooked by God. More than that, even the hairs of your head have all been counted. Have no fear: you are worth more than any number of sparrows. Luke 11.

She was stuffing it back inside the paper when the taxi arrived. Put the thing in the haversack, wiped her hands on her jeans before opening the door.

'Where to, sweetheart?'

'Westminster.'

'Going up in the world, are you?'

She was shaking and looking for the wisecrack when Ravi opened the door and jumped in beside her.

'Walk you home?' he said.

Barbara did not apologise. Kim went home as soon as the midday meal was cleared away and Therese watched her go with regret, waving from the kitchen door as if she would never see her again. Barbara, the indefatigable chairwoman of three local charities and also due a meeting with the Bishop's bursar, nodded curtly to Agnes on the door and strode away for the bus with noticeable relief. The convent car, with its respectable pedigree and low mileage, had sold with such ridiculous speed, she wondered if they had asked enough. The light in the kitchen was grey. The sisters dispersed to their various pursuits: a posse of three went into the parlour and knitted for a cause. Matilda came into the kitchen to find Therese setting up the ironing board.

'Has Anna been?'

'No, Sister. Not yet. She has a job. She comes in when she can.' Her throat felt tight and the words emerged tersely.

'Will she come in today, I wonder?'

'I don't know, Sister, I never know.'

'But she'll be in soon? Surely she'll be allowed . . . we need her . . .'

'Sometime soon, I expect. Oh, Sister, will you wait a minute?' She fished into the pocket of her tunic and brought out the knife she had rescued from the laundry bag, wrapped in a bag and not immediately obvious for what it was, except to someone who already knew. Matilda's eyes opened wide: she grabbed the knife furtively and transferred it to the depths of her gown with a mumble of thanks.

'Might I ask why you keep it, Sister?'

Matilda hesitated, studying Therese's pale face anxiously and then shaking her head.

'It's all to do with what I need to discuss with your sister, child.'

'Perhaps I could help.'

Matilda shook her head. 'No, dear. I need to talk to Anna . . . because she is not one of us.'

'She certainly isn't one of us,' Therese said bitterly, continuing in a rush of words she could not control. 'She broke the chapel window.'

'Who told you that?'

'Sister Barbara.'

Matilda felt for her beads, fingered them nervously, struggling with the uncritical, ingrained behaviour of fifty-five years.

'I can assure you, child, Barbara was . . . misinformed. Anna did no such thing.' She reached out and stroked Therese's hot cheek with a bent finger. Therese tried not to flinch. She was so often petted and stroked like a furry mascot and today she hated it in particular. Matilda smiled her beatific smile and continued the futile fingering of her

200

rosary. The click, click, click of the beads made Therese twitch.

'And as for the knife, my dear. Let's say I use it for fruit in my room. Edmund used to sharpen it for me. You know what a greedy old thing I am.'

The afternoon yawned. Therese finished the ironing. Sick of the smell of it, she moved to the chapel for a prescribed hour of reading. Scripture of her own choice, so she always went back to favourite passages, or let the New Testament fall open wherever it would. Luke 12,22:

I bid you put away anxious thoughts about food to keep you alive and clothes to cover your body. Life is worth more than food, the body more than clothes. Think of the ravens: they neither sow nor reap: they have no storehouse or barn; yet God feeds them. You are worth far more than the birds. Is there a man among you who by anxious thought can add a foot to his height? If then, you cannot do even a very little thing, why are you anxious about the rest?

The last two lines were the perfect tract for her sister, who had always tried to grow, and after that, Therese could read no more. Silly Anna, who practised smiling in front of the mirror and always wanted to be taller. She could think of nothing else but Anna and what Barbara had said. Not only what Barbara had said, but her own, complete silence in the face of that barrage, a silence provoked by shock, but disloyally maintained. It was one thing to be angry with her own sister, but another to have someone else insult her, and when she had first come in here to pray to God and the departed soul of her mother, there had been the ominous silence of disapproval. Therese went up to her room to fetch her coat.

There was no rule forbidding her to go out: she was not encouraged to hide away from the world beyond the walls; she was not incarcerated. She could walk in the park and gaze into shop windows like any other free agent. She had been told in no uncertain terms that the Order did not want someone who was a refugee from an ordinary, secular life purely because they were afraid of it. At the point when she would be sent out to learn to pay her way, she was not to be frightened of crossing the road, but it had not happened yet and she had become not only indispensable indoors, but increasingly reluctant to go out. It was a progression no one had forced. Her tasks complete, she was unfettered, free as a bird, with nothing to stop her going and finding Anna, or anyone else. She came back down the stairs. Agnes opened the door without comment or enthusiasm and Therese stood in the street for the first time in weeks. Free as a bird with a broken wing. Freedom required practice and equipment. She had no handbag, no money, none of the armoury of the urban foot soldier. It took so short a time to forget what it was like, the noise, the petrol smell, the slight dampness of the pavement and the light. The light, blinding even on a grey day, a whole expanse of it, weighing her down, making her lose direction. Left and left again, hugging the perimeter of the garden wall until she reached the junction, where the noise was greater. She passed the naked door in the back wall, looked at it longingly, went on to the block of flats where Anna lived and rang the bell, buoying herself up with what she would say, trying to control it, plan it, make it a strategy of calm questions. There was a niggling thought in the back of her mind that she also wanted Jude's missal.

Barbara had hinted that Anna must have stolen it, and still, she had not said a word.

Standing by the panel of names on the door, each with its own buzzer, she felt conspicuous and alien, and then when there was no reply, no crackling voice from the old entryphone system, she felt entirely bereft. Therese leant towards the panel in case she had missed the response. The lack of it was total rejection. Instead of making the logical assumption that Anna was out, all Therese could imagine was Anna upstairs, listening to the sound of her breath through the machine and laughing at her. Anna had never laughed at her, but the image of Anna grinning and jeering remained. Therese turned and walked briskly back. Agnes took a long time to open the door and by the time she did, Therese had begun to chew her nails. The day was greyer than ever: the sound of the door closing behind her was a leaden relief.

She was tired, that was all. Tired and overwrought and hungry, as her mother used to say. *There will be tears before bedtime if we don't pull ourselves together and realise what's good for us.* She would have liked to have been scolded: she would like to be given a set of rules far more rigid than those that bound her. She wanted order, predictability and work, and as soon as the door was closed, she missed the sky.

In a little while, the lull of the afternoon would be over. Still with her coat on, Therese slipped past the three dozing sisters in the parlour, asleep over their knitting, and went into the garden to find Francis. Fail in one task, find another. He was nowhere to be seen. Halfway down the path, level with the statue of St Michael, she saw the ginger cat, sitting where Matilda normally sat, washing itself. She reached out a hand to touch it. It sprang away and slunk down the path with an indignant backwards glance. Feeling like Alice in Wonderland, she followed.

This church was a million miles from the chapel, nearer in spirit and magnificence to the Hindu temple Ravi had shown her with such pride and although he had scarcely spoken a word, apart from agreeing to be taken wherever she went, she was glad he was there. Strange, to feel ever so slightly competitive about the artefacts and decorations displayed by the religion into which she had been born and did not believe, as if it was part of a birthright, to be shown off in all its splendid glory, like the kind of rich and famous celebrity relative who gave a girl status and credibility at school, even if she hardly knew him. Really, she thought, nothing beat the Church of Rome for showing off. This temple glittered with gold. She liked best the smaller chapels to the sides and the soft light of the iron candle stalls, ten pence each, minimum, small night lights, aching to be lit, irresistible whatever the price, as if the small act of lighting one from another was all that illuminated the darkness. It felt as if ten pence would save a soul. The side chapel she liked the most was St Paul's, with a small, domed ceiling of brilliant blue, lit with golden stars, flanked in front by a ceiling of green mosaic, inset with three stern heads of haloed saints, more symbolic than human, looking for all the world like three gentlemen suffering from dyspepsia. It seemed from all the other evidence that it was impossible to create a smiling face from small pieces of stone. Anna said to Ravi that the cathedral, with its huge collection of recumbent cardinals, laid on top of stone coffins in vast dark corners, was made not to the greater glory of God, whose depiction was rare, but to the greater glory of men, especially those who worked in marble, because there was every shade and variety of this cold stone. He nodded. The pulpit for the high priest of the day was like a huge, white version of one of the coffins, standing on eight pillars beribboned with twists of contrasting colours, the body of it heavily inlaid with mosaic and big enough to hold thirty. A single cardinal, even with a hat, would be dwarfed in there.

Halfway down the nave, a huge crucifix hung from the ceiling. Far beyond, in the fraction of the vast space used for services, a crowd, three hundred strong, sat facing the newly gathered choristers as they filed into their designated rows flanking the altar. Anna sat, too, Ravi beside her, nearer the door for a quick escape, watching the long black robes and broad red sashes of the clergy, deftly dividing the wandering tourists from the devotional seeking entry to the service. She wondered what kind of feast day this was. The devotional would know; the tourist neither knew nor cared. Anna found it a foreign place, made smaller by memory, and peculiarly unholy by the riotous lack of harmony of the interior. Ravi's temple did it better, she decided. In a whisper, she told him so and he nodded again.

She fixed her eyes on the huge crucifix suspended on chains. Perhaps it was freakish to be so consistently drawn to so cruel an image and she wondered when it had started. Ten years old or something like that when Daddy had pointed out how comfortable a particular Jesus had looked on a particular cross. Seeing Jesus as an object was probably the death to faith. Father had always been subversive and she had never missed him more. She pointed out the crucifix to Ravi. He did not like it.

This was not a comfortable crucifix, but it had the familiar effect of concentrating her mind, and it was, in its

205

own way, as hideous as any she had ever seen. The cadaverous figure, with a long-haired, haloed head and a crown of thorns well off the forehead, was looking to the left, supported on emaciated arms extended at rigid right angles. The long, bloodless torso of a starved man twisted into a knee-length wrap, from which slender legs led down to feet which looked as if they were agonised by shyness. The wood against which he rested was brilliant red, edged with green and gold decoration and finished above his head and at each end of his extended limbs with symbolic pictures she could not discern from her distance, also edged in gold. All the same, this was a Jesus who inspired the reverse version of wonder and the scorn she needed. There were things to ask, scolding to be done. Ravi sensed her preoccupation, moved away to the side chapel of St Paul with a signal that he would be back. She sat, refusing to kneel, began, silently, another version of a conversation.

'You know what you are, Lord, you're a little bleeder. Spoiled rotten. It's no good for people like you to be adored. You were too young.'

The organ music began, rolling down the nave. The three hundred devotees gathered for the service sat unfussily, waiting for a command. Anna ignored them and continued her own address.

'Too much attention too young, maybe that's why your judgements aren't always sound. And Dad's theory was probably right. Your old man sent you on a mission to the men of the world, and look what they did to you. Reviled, tortured and humiliated you, and then made you look as undressed as this. So what does Papa God do? Spends the next few centuries taking revenge on the world. That's what a normal father would do. Stuff forgiveness.'

The choir began to sing, an exultant blast of sound.

'Is that why you treat your devoted servants so badly? You've got a bunch of impoverished old women, headed up by Attila the Nun, threatened by hobos at the back door and the Bishop at the front, and what do you do for fun? You send them someone who looks like a saint and put him in control. What are you trying to do? Oh, for God's sake, *why*?'

In a single movement, the crowd in front of her stood. The noise of their movement had a greater resonance than the music or the singing. It was wave upon wave of shuffling vibration, the movement of coats, the clearing of throats, the motion of the bodies creating a living sound and sensation like the beating of wings, sending a draught rolling down the aisle and fluttering echoes into the rafters. It struck her that the movement of people was the most powerful of sounds. Then she heard it, back inside the frontal lobes of her brain, Sister Jude's favourite poem:

> Still with unhurried chase,
> And unperturbed pace,
> Deliberate speed, majestic instancy,
> Came on the following feet.
> And a Voice above their beat –
> 'Naught shelters thee who will not shelter Me.'

'What do you want me to do?' she whispered.

Honour thy Father. Seek the truth.

She was as cold as ice when Ravi came back. He put his arm round her shoulders, the first time he had touched her. Warmth flooded into her veins; she could smell cloves.

'It's a beautiful place,' he whispered in her ear. 'As good as ours, I think. And now I know why you are so sad.'

'Because my mother tried to kill me,' she said evenly.

He laid his head against hers. 'Because you never knew your father and you speak to him all the time. And most of all, because your Gods are so unhappy.'

The crowd in front of them sat with the same great wave of quiet sound.

CHAPTER TEN

Think of the lilies: they neither spin nor weave

Gardens had always been mysterious places to Therese and although they too were built to the greater glory of God, buildings always seemed a better reflection of his ingenuity. Anna and herself had been turned out into this garden when they had visited the convent the very first time as children. It was Anna who had climbed the trees and come back inside dirty. She could have sworn Edmund's old shed was there, even then. The dim memory of that had nothing to do with the fact that Therese had rarely ventured this far into the depths of it, and she felt ashamed of the fact that although it was an exceptionally long garden, it was only a matter of yards rather than miles, but it had never presented itself to her as a peaceful wilderness. In the spring, she had been dive-bombed by tiny fledglings, deafened by the sound of them and always shy of the presence of slow-moving Edmund with his tacitly discouraging manners. Besides, there was nowhere to sit or even to lean except for his bench, which was so clearly shared with the birds, festooned with the droppings that clung to his clothes. It was a litter-filled, unsavoury place, made more so by his dying in it. Coming round the last bend in the path, aware of the shushing sounds of the trees behind, she half expected to see him there on the dirty bench, outside his malodorous shed with the broken door, as dead as he was when she had covered him with a blanket only two weeks ago.

Instead, the area was swept clean, old paving stones emerging as if by magic from the beaten earth that had been there before. The bench had been scrubbed, revealing a seat of graceful proportions in pale wood with black, wrought iron legs. As she drew closer, there was a smell of creosote, which she was slow to recognise as anything other than a smell both faint and cloying. To the left of the shed, there was a small bundle of rubbish and a selection of tools, and from the side of it, the sound of singing.

> Praise Father, Son and Holy Ghost
> Whose gift is faith that never dies:
> A light in darkness now, until
> The day star in our heart arise.

A hymn for the morning, rather than the afternoon, but still a hymn, sung in a robust, unselfconscious baritone. Therese called out, hesitantly. The singing stopped abruptly. Francis emerged with a paint pot in one hand and a brush in the other, perfectly unsurprised to see her. She noticed that the door of the shed no longer hung askew, but stood open, revealing a clean, whitewashed interior. He was indeed a miracle worker. He had even silenced the raucous birds of spring and his grin was infectious.

'Sister Therese!' He flourished a bow and she could only laugh, nervously, remembering what Kim had said: *Gay men know how to be nice to women.*

210

'Try the spring-cleaned bench,' he said. 'And be the first to admire my work. Even Barbara doesn't know. Sit, please, it's perfectly dry.'

She sat, tentatively. The wood felt warm against her back. He sat at the other end of the bench, a body's width away, and placed the paint pot at his feet. Then he leaned forward. The movement startled her, but he kept the distance between them.

'Don't tell anyone.'

'There are no secrets here, Francis,' she said severely, and even in saying it realised how far from the truth she was. 'What exactly is it you're doing?'

'I'm making an *arbour*.' He swept his arm expansively. 'Well, an *arbour* might be a bit of an exaggeration. What I'm doing is *creating a space*, like they do in those gardening programmes on the TV. Do you ever watch them?'

'I'm afraid not.'

'I didn't think you would.' He grinned at her. The day was suddenly less grey.

'Although I'm not actually creating anything,' he went on. 'We never do, do we? That's God's privilege. I'm just digging out what there was before. A clean place to sit and think, for a start. Then I can cut back the ivy, plant things round the edges, and lo and behold, it will be an area for use rather than disuse. And I don't want you to tell, because I would like it to be a treat in store.'

He had a slight accent; London, overlaid with somewhere else.

'How kind,' she murmured, meaning it. For a moment, she had quite forgotten the purpose of her expedition. His enthusiasm was as warming as the wooden seat on which she sat.

'And I'm afraid Matilda disapproves. She thinks it

211

should stay the way it was, but old people don't like change, do they? Would you like tea, Sister?'

The invitation surprised her. How would even someone as innovative as Francis create tea at the bottom of the garden? Without waiting for a reply, he leapt from the bench and into the shed, where she could see the flame of a camping gas stove and hear the rattle of spoons. There was a rough-built bunk bed against the far wall. He poked his golden head out and seemed to bring the sun with him, reminding her of a small boy she had once met, displaying a new conjuring trick with all the aplomb of a performer anxious to impress. The shed had taken on the appearance of a summer house, bigger than she remembered, large enough for a person to sleep and quaintly romantic.

'We have water, and I provide the rest.' He arrived back with a mug of strong, orange brew. 'When I can get some lights down here, it'll be a fine place for a summer evening.'

'Yes.'

'So, you won't tell yet?'

'No.'

He placed the mug into her hands and pressed his own around hers so briefly, she would scarcely have noticed, except that she did not flinch from such a careful gesture, so far removed from the grasping demands of elderly, quavering hands. She was half aware that she was committed to yet another secret, but it did not seem to matter much. The tea was strong, the way she liked it, unlike the pallid brew dictated by convent economy, and it was too comfortable for words. The cat sprang on to the bench between them and settled itself close to Francis, startling her, until she thought, Why should it? St Francis was the saint of animals and birds; it was natural this creature would go to his namesake and the intrusion reminded her of some of the things she had come to say.

'Francis, were you the one who found my sister in the garden last night?'

There was no evasion.

'Yes, I'm sorry. I was.'

'Barbara just told me *someone* apprehended her. What on earth was she doing?'

'I wish I could tell you. Something about *praying*. I don't know. I just followed her over the wall, thinking she was a burglar ... I'm sorry, but she was drunk and foul-mouthed. And she has long nails.'

He turned his perfect profile to exhibit the worst of the linear scratches and then bowed his head. Dear God. Anna had always cherished her nails, an odd vanity for a tomboy.

'Did you hurt her?'

'No, *no*, I promise you, no. She's so small, there was no need to hurt her. Spitting angry at first, that was all, but harmless and calm by the time I saw her home safely.'

She was suddenly, enormously grateful to him for that, because Barbara's assurance that Anna had been unscathed was no longer reliable and it mattered.

'I was sorry for her,' Francis said, softly. 'And I rather admired her. She fought like a cat and I like cats. There's a way of handling them, you see.'

Therese did not want to discuss it further. She could feel nothing but Anna's humiliation and an angry help-lessness, and if anyone was protecting Anna, she would rather it was either the Lord or herself.

'And were you sorry for Sister Joseph, too?' she demanded. 'That you take her money and buy her drink when she asks you?'

He hung his head, the golden curls falling over his face as

he sighed, and she thought, irrelevantly, how odd that such hair should look effeminate on one man, yet not on another.

'Joseph was desperate, Sister. I thought it would do more harm than good, she twisted my arm and I was wrong, I suppose. I shan't do it again, but I'm new to all this, Therese, I have to learn. I didn't know the effect of the stuff, and I thought it would make her happy. She's a powerful woman. How are we going to make Joseph happy?'

The use of her name without the prefix of 'Sister', the use of 'we', as if they were allies, made Therese feel warmer, a pleasant feeling of a burden shared and thus lifted, and a mission partly achieved. Pleasant feelings were to be resisted. She finished the tea, put the mug carefully on the bench and rose to go. Francis rose too, with the alacrity of an old-fashioned gentleman.

'You must be the first to discover the *arbour*,' he said, with another of his bows. 'And come here whenever you need.'

She turned back as she reached the first bend in the path. Her last sight of Francis, just as it began to spit with rain, was that of a golden-haired, bare-armed man, cradling an orange cat.

She knew she would come back. She would come back before anyone else discovered it, at a time when Francis, with his disturbing, charming presence, had gone home, because although the convent was really too big for them all, there was absolutely nowhere else where she could be sure of being alone and she thought she had better get used to it. And the shed reminded her of another place, another garden in her first home.

It was an almost soundless rain, a damp, persistent drizzle.
'You mean,' Anna said slowly to Ravi, 'that all the time

I argue with God, I'm really talking to my own father?'

'It's an idea.'

'Which could be psychobabble bullshit.'

'That could be true, also. It would be natural. If your father is in heaven, why not?'

'I think he's more likely in hell.'

They were sitting in the wooden shelter near the gates to the park, the last customers of the ice cream van, which had done a bad day's business, and although it seemed less than appropriate to talk of God and the tricks of the soul while eating ice cream sprinkled with chocolate, Ravi had no problem with that. 'In my religion,' he told her, 'food is a source of joy. We offer it to the Gods and then we eat it in celebration. Food is often sacred and never profane.'

'Do you think if we fed our saints they would be less miserable?' she asked.

He nodded agreement, unwilling to speak as he ate. There was such delicacy in him, she wanted to study the way he made each movement of hand to mouth and resisted the temptation to stare at him rudely.

'Perhaps. But I do not think food would appease them. They are all so thin. They all look hungry and they would still be unhappy. These saints, these Gods of yours . . . such unfulfilled lives, it seems. Such agonies, and it is the agonies they show on their faces. Never the joy of the holy state. Always they show the punishment, never the reward.'

She thought of the doll-like Gods in the temple, beautifully dressed, bedecked with jewels, missions accomplished and tranquil in their prosperity.

'And do yours have rivalries?' she asked politely, as if they were discussing relatives.

'No.'

'How do you know?'

215

'They would tell me, and anyway, why should they? They have given their examples and now they live in peace. They look after us and we look after them. They are not there to punish; we do that to ourselves, by not listening. Did you ever listen to your real father?'

She thought about that. 'Oh yes. He made me laugh.'

'Ganesh makes you laugh, too, but he does not mind.'

'Ravi, do you have holy pictures like these?'

She flicked open Jude's tired old missal. The spine of it was cracked with the weight of the picture cards inserted between the wafer-thin pages. Single card pictures of saints, Matthew, Mark, Ignatius, Bernadette, the Sacred Heart, but mostly of Mary, the virgin mother. Little pictures, sold by the gross, used as birthday cards, message cards, note cards, one side blank for messages and the other printed with pictures or prayers, symbols or faces, variously decorative or garish, sentimental or simple, part of the currency of Catholic devotion. Each of these had notes scrawled on the back, in Jude's spidery hand.

Take care of my niece's soul, Lord. I know what evil she does in your name. She has made those children invalids, brainwashed and poisoned them because she cannot bear the thought that they will grow and leave her. Help them, Lord. I am powerless in their service.

'We have the holy pictures, yes,' Ravi said. 'But I don't understand this prayer.'

'It's difficult.'

He looked at his watch, apologetically, glanced at her out of the corner of his eye, checking. 'I'm sorry, I have to go home now. My parents . . .'

'I know you must,' she said, gently. 'Thank you for this. It's going to rain in a minute. You'd better run, or you'll get wet.'

And then there was nothing to do but go home herself and let the anxieties rumble quietly on the bus, watching the faces and comparing them all to theirs. Two masculine faces, Ravi's and her father's, wildly different but strangely interchangeable. Ravi, dark and inscrutable, her father, weathered and pugnacious, both of them blurring into the post-rush-hour faces of the top deck. Tired faces, lively faces, a preponderance of middle-aged faces going home before the other generation came out to play. A pretty face on the other side of the aisle, reminiscent of her mother, but the reminder was as vague and distorted as her mother's face. She must remember not to stare, and if caught in the act of staring, smile to show no offence was intended.

It was pointless to stare as hungrily as she did. There were few enough clues to the universe to be found in faces. An artist could paint the devil as handsome as a Jesus; a mad mullah could look like an angel and Golden Boy could look like a saint, and he was wicked. She transferred her gaze out of the window and imagined she could see him, walking in the street, waiting to cross the road, and all the tenuous calm of the park and Ravi fled as soon as she was in the vicinity of her home. She ran for her own front door although there was as yet scarcely a hint of dusk, and as she flung herself inside, she thought, that's what he has done: he had made her afraid of the dark and she had never been afraid of it before. And then she thought it was not he who made her afraid. *The Gods do not punish us, we punish ourselves*. She scrambled up the ladder on to the roof before the light should begin its slow, autumn eclipse.

An ungenerous light, because of the now persistent drizzle, which slicked the dry roads and made them slippier than a cloudburst. She thought of the damp paths leading beyond St Michael in the convent garden, moss covered even in summer, thought of the damp foliage around Edmund's bench, and thought finally of Golden Boy, and what the hell it was he wanted. Perhaps, like the devil, he demanded a sacrifice. The rain made the lead-covered valleys of the roof slippery too, but it was a warm wet on her bare feet. She brought the knapsack with her, and in the remaining light detached the dead bird from its wrapping, stuffed the note in her pocket, and threw the corpse into the garden, aiming left for the trees and away from the bench with a good strong overarm throw, watching where it went until she saw it land in a bush. That was where it belonged and where it might continue to decay in peace because that was where it had died. No one else but Francis could have sent it. Unless, in some perverted attempt to give a message, Therese had done so, and that was the worst thought, which persisted eerily.

The rain brought mist in the wake of itself, but she could still see through the trees, towards the new semi-circle created out of chaos around Edmund's bench. Golden Boy Francis should have gone home by now, via the front door, like everyone else. She looked at her watch: supper-time in there; still warm, if damp, outside. She could see the clean bench, the painted shed, the decimated shrubs, the fresh-swept ground and a light from inside the shed.

You are even prettier than your sister.

He is making a trap for her. He was inside the garden last night. He does not go home.

Oh, nonsense.

She chewed a fingernail, tried to scold herself for being so dramatic. *Nothing* happens in that convent, that was the point of it. Who needs *you*, Anna, and what was poxy little Francis anyway? Some supped-up, odd-job man, their

218

self-appointed, self-important guardian, the wanker: a boy with nowhere else to go for all his looks and an itty bitty morsel of power gone to his silly little golden head. She looked at her watch again. Definitely eating time in there. She could taste the remnants of chocolate and ice cream, like a moustache around her lips. By the whitish stone of St Michael, she could see the black-clad figure of Matilda, invisible to anyone else, vainly waving. She blinked and the figure was gone. Anna scrambled down the steps and shoved the ladder back. Searched her mind for the convent number, dialled it. Agnes would have instructions not to let her in through the door, but they could not stop her dialling. The phone rang and rang and rang, the way it did during meals. She paced the floor. Redialled. Same response.

Drizzly rain soaking the cassock he wore for visiting the sick, as if this uniform gave him credibility, and as if it had been worth it, Father Goodwin hung on the doorbell, muttering beneath his breath, 'Bugger, bugger, bugger.' His shoes did not keep out the damp, the sick had been comatose and all that was left was the urgency of duty. He rang again, before consulting the time on the watch he could scarcely see without the spectacles he could never find. Damn, damn, damn and buggery. The convent door opened to Barbara. She was still chewing and it did not add to her attraction. She would have shut the door if he had not barged past, straight down the black and white corridor, into the parlour. Barbara followed in the high temper which had been so much a feature of the day that interrupted food could only make it worse. The room was chillingly cold. She put on a single light and sat a long distance away from him.

'This *will*, Sister. Didn't you see it for what it was? It's a dangerous document, it surely is . . . It's a time bomb . . . it's *blackmail*. Did you not understand what he was trying to do?'

She sat, as frozen as a statue, looking like a basilisk on an Egyptian temple.

'He's wishing his children to the devil, Sister. Can't you read?'

She got up and turned the key in the central door that led from the parlour to the garden. The bolt at each side of the window, a grille pulled across, a padlock to secure the grille would be the final precaution for the night, as early as she chose. Then she skirted around the back of his chair, as if reluctant to come closer, sat in her own, a dozen feet away. She may as well have addressed him through a megaphone. Noise passed softly here. There was no hint of the presence of a chapel where people sang on Sundays, even less of a crowd of old women eating at the other end of the corridor.

'You think yourself so very clever, Christopher Goodwin, but why should I pay any attention to a nervous breakdown priest?'

'I beg your pardon?'

'You went mad, didn't you, Father?'

He laughed, uncertainly. Who had been talking to whom? He remembered that Barbara had only been here four years, long enough surely.

'Unfortunately not. I had a nervous breakdown, yes, which was common knowledge. Before your time here, Sister, and a matter for sympathy rather than concern, especially since you seem to be heading for one yourself.'

'Well, whatever, but I won't be breaking down on account of sexual interference with little boys, shall I? Not like you. Not like you at all.'

He gasped as if she had struck him, and then started to

smile, because of all the things of which he had been accused, including the things of which he accused himself, this was so far from truth, it was risible. Wee football-playing boys? That really was rich. He thought of Kay McQuaid and the agony of her proximity, of his necessarily understated and nevertheless passionate love of women and the hell it had given him, and laughed and laughed, even while knowing that laughing was the worst thing to do, and only when she did not laugh with him, stopped.

'Jesus, woman, there's a lot more reasons for a nervous breakdown than that. Have you no imagination at all? It was faith and failure that bothered me, not little boys.'

'That's not what Francis says,' she intoned, stubbornly. 'Not what he told me this morning after you'd gone.'

Francis, Francis, Francis. What was this boy? The new Messiah? His temper rose and exploded.

'And how the hell would Francis know? The vain little beast. Is a priest supposed to have fallen upon him, like all you stupid women? Has he been reading to you from a newspaper? Is he better than the official record? For God's sake, you treat him as if you fuck him. How the hell could he know anything about me?'

He was advancing towards her, wagging his finger, eyes blazing, a picture of unbalanced craziness. She stood her ground.

'He knows because he's afraid of you. He knows because he was a tiny little boy in this parish when his mother used to clean for you. He was a teenager when you were removed and he knows exactly why.'

He had raised an arm, almost ready to hit her. Instead, a shock of realisation hit him like a tidal wave. He put both his hands over his face and groaned, the very picture of shame. Yes, he remembered the boy.

'Was he one of the victims, Father? Don't say there were so many of them you can't count. A nervous breakdown, was it? What rubbish. I know how the Bishop deals with these things. The way bishops do. The way *men* do. They hide it.'

The clock ticked in the silence.

He was about to say that she had an accurate understanding of the higher clergy, but that even the most recalcitrant bishop from the bogs of somewhere would not send a paedophile back to the parish of his sins within a mere two years of their commission, would at least send him somewhere else. But he knew if he spoke at all he would scream and spit and whatever he said would be futile. The rage had subsided to a furious indigestion, and still it choked him.

'You will regret this, you dumb bitch.'

'Don't threaten me.'

'Where is this bastard Francis?'

'Don't you *dare* call him that, you pervert.'

'At home, I presume.'

'You don't even *know*, do you?'

There was a look of uncertainty, and if he stayed for a moment longer, he really would hit her. He left her standing in the middle of the parlour and slammed the door shut behind him, hoping she would have followed and got it full in that plain face. The noise of the slamming door reverberated in a building where doors were never slammed and his own footsteps sounded angry. And then ahead of him in the poor lighting of the black and white corridor, he saw the unmistakable figure of Therese, hurrying away, back towards the refectory. He roared after her, 'Therese!' but she broke into a run and disappeared.

He could see her, standing on the other side of the half-open parlour door, a minute ago, waiting to knock and ask

222

if the visitor required coffee or tea, listening to it all, and saw, again and again, the death of trust.

The rain settled around him like a cloak as he stood with his back to the door, breathing heavily. The lintel above sent drips on to his thinning hair, shockingly cold. The mist of the drizzle blurred the street lights, so that they looked as if they were wearing haloes. Bring Barbara, or dear old Agnes out here, and they might well fall down in worship. He crossed to the other side of the road and looked at the building, handsome from the outside with its mellow red brick and mullioned windows, giving that oh-so-deceptive impression of calm solidity, a haven of peace in an urban landscape, isolated by that very impression and the height of the walls, and yet they were besieged, from within and without, poor devils. If he left them now and refused to come back, he would be their last link. He counted on his trembling fingers. They had lost the reasoning voice of Sister Jude, who, from her sickbed, had been a surreptitious influence, a quiet counsellor to all of them, the keeper of secrets and reason. And then there was Edmund, with his obdurate independence, the man who listened to no one. And then there was Anna, with her far-seeing eyes and uncanny intelligence, a vital link between their world and her own. And now himself, not banned as yet, but his role made untenable by rumour. He would miss the chapel. Compared to the modern box church where he otherwise officiated, it had a magic charm, and it was the only place he knew where God was not silent.

As He was now, even in the holy glow of the street lights. Easy enough to defect, go home, turn on the television, tuck himself up with his spartan comforts and hope no one would call, but the anger had done him good. He wanted to

223

throttle someone and was briefly, ironically aware that all the targets he would like to murder were of his favourite sex. Kay McQuaid, Sister Barbara, his own dead mother and even silly Therese for running away. And if he stood here any longer in his cassock, with his fists clenching and unclenching and the rain on the back of his neck, looking ready to howl at a non-existent moon, someone would arrest him. Christ, it would almost be a relief. Urgency made his throat dry. There was nowhere to go, except to another person in disgrace. If Anna would not let him in, he would sit on the doorstep and wait.

'Calvert' on the bell, he knew exactly where, although he had never been inside, only glancing up sometimes, as he passed unnecessarily often. He should have visited and told what he knew of the truth, a long time ago. Should have, should have, should have.

'Recrimination,' he said loudly into the entryphone, 'is the death to all endeavour.'

'What's that, Father?' she said, her voice so disembodied it made him leap with shock. There was jarring background noise.

'Can I come up?'

'Of course.'

Even a man could hear the disappointment in that voice. He began the long march up the interminable flights of ill-lit stairs and thought, At least she is safe here.

Music, of a kind, poured from the top flat as he panted up the last flight of stairs. The wailing of sitars and beating of drums almost stopped him. He had forgotten how young she was: with music like that, they had not a cat in hell's chance of understanding one another, but then again, maybe it was not understanding they needed.

The scale of the place was almost that of a dolls' house,

to his mind, bigger when he looked from the small living room to the kitchenette beyond, but still too small for all the sound. By now he was so hot inside the damp cassock and anorak, he could not imagine breathing in such a place, even while he noticed it was not as he imagined. It was not strewn with clothes and youthful detritus, but merely functional, two chairs, two pictures, the stereo on the bookshelf, and that was all, as if the space was always needed for something else. Anna turned off the music, for which God be praised, but in the sudden silence, he did not know what to say.

'Have you come to tell me off?'

'No. I've come to build a wax model of Barbara and that bastard boy Francis, and stick pins in them.'

'In which case, you're welcome.'

He sat, presuming he was asked.

'Did the old bitch throw you out?'

'In a manner of speaking, yes. I'd like to think I left.'

'Did you climb over the wall, or something?'

'No, she thinks I'm a paedophile.'

'Bless her,' said Anna, smiling, and then it was all right. 'Would you like a drink?'

'Water,' he said. 'Whiskey by the pint would be better, but I've somewhere else to go.'

A long journey to the sea. He thought of it as she brought the water, with dread, running the train timetable through his mind. Every hour on the hour. Yes, he would get there before midnight. The dark was deceiving; it was early yet. If any parishioner died tonight, they would have to die alone. She was watching him drink the water with a motherly concern at odds with her tiny size.

'A man who interferes with children? I can't see it, myself.'

'A similar accusation to the one applied to your father, as I recall. His own children. At least I'm supposed to have gone for other people's.'

She stood completely still. 'That is utterly and completely untrue,' she said, slowly. Then she shook herself. 'Can you manage a few more steps, Father?'

Without waiting for a reply, she pulled the ladder from the wall from behind its curtain, climbed up and pushed the trapdoor at the top. A draught of delicious air descended. He followed her, awkwardly. She pulled him on to the parapet with a grip of surprising strength and before he could begin to wonder how on earth he would get down, he was seeing the stars and realising exactly why she would live in a flat as claustrophobically small as this. He found his footing on the slippery lead, followed her a couple of steps, leant as she leant, with arms folded on the stone wall, safe as houses and quite at home. He had always liked heights. The difference was that even leaning like this, his torso protruded over the parapet a whole foot more than hers. He stood and leant back for balance, a giant next to a midget.

'So what did you come to say, Father?'

'I quite forget. Only that God really will forgive you, whatever you do.'

'I don't care about that. I care about Therese.'

'All right, I came because I felt the corrosive effect of disgrace, which I thought you would understand. And because I feel a great sense of danger hanging over you and Therese. Nothing can begin to cure it other than the brutal truth. Your father's will—'

'Never mind that. Therese hid it from me, I knew she did and I didn't care. What was he like, my father? I mean as man to man. You knew him, a little.'

He fished for the cigarettes. None.

'Knew him a little and liked him a lot. He had great love in him and he adored you both. But love made him naive and he was no match for your mother.'

'No sane person can be a match for somebody *insane*,' she said, slowly. 'No one can match that kind of will power. Especially not when it wears the armour of angels and the great shield of righteousness.'

Father Goodwin caught his breath and found himself suddenly close to tears. It was the lack of bitterness in her voice that moved him more, the dry absence of reproach, and the release of tension in himself which made him stagger and grasp the parapet firmly with both hands, noticing even then how she had flung out her arm to stop him falling. A child with a protective instinct stronger than anything else, which may have come, in a purer form, from her mother.

'When did you realise this?' he whispered.

'I don't know. I don't *know*. Not in the beginning, not for the first year when we were ill. I think that might have been real and he was wrong. There was shouting in the background, all the time. Then my father went; then he tried to kidnap us; then I tried to run away, and oh so many things, all blurred. No strength, you see; no strength to do anything at all, or think a single thought. I could read, but I couldn't think, or rather I couldn't think and carry anything through to a conclusion, and we were *accomplices*, you see. We agreed with her, we had to, there was no one else, but somewhere, sometime, I knew what she did. Munchausen something, isn't it? But she made us believe we were ill and we believed. It became fact. For Therese, it still is fact, but believe me, Father, there was no need for either Sister Jude or your good self to hint to me that those four, dead years were anything other than my mad mother's fixation that she would rather we died than left her to go to the devil. She was terrified for herself and for us. I used to think that it was me who started it, by being naughty. Giving her the hint of how bad it could get.'

'Nonsense.'

She stretched her arms in front of her, palms locked outwards, and he could hear the click of her fingers.

'But it took a long time to *know*, even longer to *admit*. I was a better reader than Therese. I could read the books of symptoms better than her, but it was only later that I queried the drugs. Common stuff. Valium she got for herself, Benylin can knock you out, and every variety of mildly poisonous food. She was a dietician and she did the reverse. You can make a person very ill with food combinations and herbal remedies. Especially if you never let them get well. Paint fumes, she was always painting, and joss sticks. I can understand why my father went. I should be grateful he set his lawyers on her. But I wish he had written.'

The anger was coming back; quiet, but useful.

'And how, dear child, would you ever have received his communications? Who opened the door to the postman? Who answered the phone? Was there email?'

'He could have sent someone.'

'He was forbidden by law. He was accused of molesting you, and the law moves slowly. He was arrested six times outside your door. A mother has the real power. He sent me, slender reed that I am; he sent Sister Jude . . . the door was barred, and we, of course, were weak.'

'As frail as all flesh,' she said. 'Never mind. I wish I had known, but there it is. And the irony of it all is that Therese

228

has tried to protect me from any hint of him, while I have tried never to sully her abiding memory of our mother. It would be nice if she could keep that. Even if it did give her the infection of faith and her bloody vocation.'

'Theodore's last will and testament—' he began.

'Not now, Father, it doesn't matter. I can't take it and you have somewhere else to go.'

She stood up straight, grasping the parapet as firmly as he had. In this proximity, her shoulders were the height of his chest and yet he knew which of them was the stronger. The urge to weep remained.

'Tell me what you can see,' she said.

He did not look down, he looked across. 'I think I can see the whole of the park. I can see Knightsbridge. I can see an aeroplane, oh Lord, I can see lights. It's marvellous, I can see—'

'I should have realised before,' she said in that dry, matter-of-fact tone, 'that a tall man sees such very different things.'

She smiled with that dreadful wryness he hoped would never become permanent.

'My father, you see, was a giant. As tall as you. Or at least, that's how I remember him.'

He ran down the stairs feeling the weight of the bundle of documents inside the anorak pocket, cooler now, just as wet, racing for that damn train. There was enough money for a taxi to the station, no cigarettes, no food and just enough of the anger to get him there. Inside the station, the dog collar got him a discount, and as he waited on the platform, a sad old geezer offered him a cigarette. God forgive him, he took one for later as well.

★

Sister Barbara looked up from the bookwork in the office next to the parlour, disturbed by footsteps. They padded by her door, but the direction they took before beginning to fade was uncertain, backwards or forwards, she did not know: towards the front door, or away, she did not know. Her nerves, as she told herself, were frayed and there was something askew with the conscience she did not want to consider just at the moment and never in the middle of arithmetic at any time. *Pitter, pitter, pitter,* quiet as a cat, skirting round the light of her door on the black and white corridor, and then, she was sure she was right, going back as if nervous to go on. Barbara knocked her heavy ledger on to the floor where it fell with a bang. An indication she had heard and whoever it was risked displeasure.

She waited for a minute. Too late to do anything more useful here, anyway. Young men in offices worked after ten at night, but she was not one of those, and even if sleepless, she was past her best at least three hours earlier. A good thing, too.

Because of conscience, or something related to it, she opened her office door carefully and looked to left and right. Nothing. In her stockinged feet, she walked into the parlour. She pulled the grilles and checked the bolts and put the keys back in her office. Good. Then she went in the other direction to the chapel.

The moon rose behind the huge windows, enhanced by the bare, still branches of the trees. She looked upwards towards it, remembered how long it was since she had last prayed in here, and hurried away. Safe for the night.

CHAPTER ELEVEN

Do not fear those who kill the body and after that,
have nothing more they can do

Matilda saw Father Goodwin striding down the black and white corridor after supper and tried to stop him, but he did not notice. Before that unmemorable meal, she had seen Francis leave via the front door, and although she could not quite hear the fond farewells and suggestions he eat something sensible for his own supper which she was sure would come from Agnes, she could imagine the sentiments. It filled her with angry misery. Delusions were the stock in trade of the devil. All that she could remember after a sojourn in the chapel was that the rain had stopped and it would be safe to linger in the garden for more than a few minutes alongside St Michael.

The parlour was deserted as she crept through, turned the key and went out with a feeling of relief, bearing her gifts. For the last days, she had been afraid to spend any time in her favourite place, confining her visits to quick, furtive forays, never staying for long, waving her arms towards the sky, in the hope that the little person who sometimes watched from that roof over there would see her. But Anna had been forbidden: perhaps little Anna would never come, and Matilda, with an endless capacity

231

for forgiveness, could quite understand why she should not. She was a rash, brave child, who might have seen what she herself had seen, since she had tried to wound Francis after all and scratched his face in that futile process, poor child, but no one could be brave all the time. So, there was nothing for it but prayer, and even in the relative cold and dark, which made her mourn the blessed warmth of a kindly spring, she was pleased to see St Michael and sit in a familiar place. The benefit of small mercies was something she had learned in a long life. Each moment of peace counted; regret was as futile as the endless questions, which were a constant source of indigestible pain.

Such as, why did God engineer life in such a way that those whom you loved were always the victims of pride and held their sufferings from you in case you should understand them all too well? Why had Joseph, her closest friend, turned away from her in such bitterness, as if she had not already accepted her frailties entirely? Perhaps because of the deafness, which inhibited their once endless conversations. And why did the God of forgiveness and understanding make those very same virtues so difficult for proud people to accept? Shame was a foreign concept to Matilda. You did what you did, felt sorry and puzzled about it, since to err was human and forgiveness just as natural. Pain was pain, to be offered comfort and the promise it would be better tomorrow, that was all. She sat heavily on the stone bench at Michael's feet with her back to him, hating the need to ask questions at all without relying on plain, simple acceptance, which was the real virtuous state. Doubt was sin and questions were anathema.

Such as, could she have prevented Edmund's death? To that particular question, the answer was no, because death was the will of God and a matter entirely of His timing, and she doubted, in all honesty, if she could have done much about the method. Francis had been the instrument, first by the simple expedient of finding a way to Edmund's heart and then breaking it by killing the birds. Heart first, spirit second, and the fragile body last. On the evening of the decimation of the chapel window, she had heard the *pop* of the air rifle, clear against the blur of other sounds, which her incipient deafness selected with a random choice that still amazed her, and quite apart from that, she had seen the young devil with his weapon and his artfulness, passing her by as she sat as quiet as the statue of St Michael, amused at first by this young man's arrogant assumption that someone as old as herself would be blind as well as hard of hearing, concluding that, in the way of the young, he simply did not *see* her at all. But, then, most people didn't. And she had refrained from insisting to Edmund that it was Francis who killed the birds, because that would have broken his heart sooner, at a time when he wanted love from the boy, and hoped for it. He would not have listened, and no one would listen now.

Except Anna, who must know exactly what he was like, because Anna lived in a world full of evil persons just like that, and Anna watched, from her roof. But Anna was in disgrace, and might not come back, and Joseph, dear Joseph, as well as Barbara, had made herself blind to the boy. Oh dear, oh dear.

Supper had been bad tonight. Cold meats and bread, leaden and inadequate, leaving an unsatisfying lining to the stomach. Therese had eaten nothing and she worried about that, too. Matilda had taken extra fruit from the plate and a lump of cheese in the same way she had when Edmund was alive and they would share her fruit in exchange for his biscuits. Grapes were his favourite, but

233

they rarely had grapes unless they were given. Instead, there were endless apples with slightly wrinkled skin, better eaten peeled with Edmund's fruit knife, which she had taken from where he had left it last, and kept to ward off the devil. Which was Francis, no doubt it was Francis, and she was so afraid of him she kept the knife in her pocket with her handkerchief. Sighing, she took out the lump of cheese from the wrapping of another handkerchief, the best-looking apple from the bowl plus two chocolates, which she really wanted, and laid them on the seat beside her. There were times when nothing else but sacrifice would do.

'Help us, dear Michael, there's a love. I brought them specially for you. If I leave them and don't eat them, will you ask the Lord to take note of my hunger and make something good from it? Such as get rid of that boy, before he murders us all?'

She sat forward, resolutely ignoring the sight of her own, tempting offerings, wanting them to be snatched away, before she could retrieve them. She watched the darkening sky and stood to greet it, moving two steps down the path so that she could see if the back bathroom window of Anna's place was lit at all. The girl was prodigal with electricity, like the young, and she herself was a silly old woman, and it was late to be out, mourning unchangeable things, feeling herself swell with fury when she thought of that boy. Because he *knew* she knew his wickedness: she had seen it in a single, frightened glance of his and in his conspicuous failure to approach her at all, the only one of them who was not eating out of his hand. It took God years to win a heart, but the devil could do it in five minutes.

'Eat it up, Michael dear, or give it away. There's no telling what else you might get in heaven.'

She sat, puzzling it all, elbows on knees, refusing to rest against the stone of the feet, which had once seemed so warm, trying to resist the feeling of great, helpless sadness, which her own blithe optimism kept at bay most of the time, whatever happened, even when Joseph turned her back. Then she stood and wandered the few steps further to the bend in the path, which had always delineated the beginning of Edmund's domain and that of the birds, listening. In the height of spring, she could hear them in the morning; at this time of last year, she could hear only the shrill sounds of alarm and now there was nothing. Another few steps led on to the best view of the back bathroom window of Anna's place. The path was slippery with the rain which still hung in the air with the promise of more. Matilda put out her hand to feel the way she knew better than the way to her own room: always wished her sight had gone sooner than the refinements of her hearing, if there had been any choice about either. Her hand felt the wire across the path. There was a rustling behind her.

In the best of worlds, it would be St Michael, eating his food, but she knew it was the cat. She clutched the waist-height wire, which was thin, cold and moist. Which saint was it, killed by the garotte? St Agnes. She pulled at the wire; it was a further trap for the birds, as if he had not already massacred them all, the bastard. It was a warning, a keep out sign, it was abominable, and held fast. The rustling behind continued. Dear God, the wire should be around the neck of that murderous cat. Matilda yanked the wire. It loosened suddenly, so that she stumbled on her own weight, falling backwards as her feet skidded from beneath her, and stayed half upright by still holding the wire and pulling it free, as if it were bindweed. She was breathless with the effort, shaken with the overbalance.

Thin, harmless wire, which would not have impeded anything other than a midget running at it full pelt. She flung it to one side, aware of her terrible weariness, the darkness, the futility of waving at that distant light, and retraced her steps, unsteadily. The statue of St Michael had its own familiar outline and she felt as if she were wading towards it. Sat, once she was there, and then turned to place her hands on his feet. There were countless times she had done that; her hands on his lichen-covered toes, dozing in good company, peacefully. She rested like that for a minute, trying to recapture the peace of summer. Then she noticed the damp between her fingers, raised her head and examined the strange sensation of soap that oozed between them.

She could just about see that the feet of St Michael were covered in a foamy substance, reaching up to his manly calves. She withdrew her hands with muttered disgust and looked for somewhere to wipe them, finding nothing but the handkerchief she had left with her offerings. She worked with that, until her palms began to tingle, then to burn, and then she began to brush them against her habit frantically, until they stuck to the cloth and still burned as if they were on fire. She wiped them on her breast, spat on them, wiped again, and then, trembling, stumbled towards the patio with its light and promise of water. Fell on the slippery path, found the cool of the stone a benison to the burning skin and after that, crawled. She crawled towards the parlour door, with the cold, damp stone of the patio giving the only relief, and when she reached it, unable to bear the thought of taking her hands off the ground, raised her feet and kicked at the door. There was no response. The security light showed the closed grille and the drawn curtains.

Matilda crawled to the planter at the side, and dug her hands into the damp soil, and even in the extremes of this dull pain cursed at the irony of a regime of obedience and silence, which in making such efforts to keep people out forgot the importance of letting them in. And as she tried to stand, feeling her feet slip from under her and her head hit the side of the pot with a thud, wondered what she had done for St Michael to reject her so much he covered his own feet with acid. Remembering asking Edmund to clean the moss away, wishing against any other wish that she had not done that, calling softly for Joseph to come and help her, hearing nothing.

Anna needed sleep, more than anything else in the world, but pyjama-clad and restless, she climbed back on to the roof. On the busy side of the view, traffic passed and the Oppo Bar thrived, far from closing time, with a few brave customers sitting outside beneath the awning to celebrate the end of the rain and the end of the summer. On the convent side, the garden was black, until she stared down into it, and the familiar shapes began to emerge, clearer through the leafless trees. The contrast between this side of the building and the other was almost bizarre, live music and traffic visible from one angle, and from the other a place disused because everyone went ridiculously early to bed. It was not so much their style of life that isolated the dear Sisters, she thought, but the way they kept to a sleeping and eating timetable suitable for children younger than eight. What did they do with all those wasted hours? Could you dedicate sleep to God?

The peace of the garden and the darkness of the house infuriated her: they did not deserve it.

The new bareness of the trees allowed her to see as far

as the patio, faintly illuminated by the security light, which, only a week before, had twinkled with dim insignificance behind leaves. She was too far away to observe detail, wished she had Father Goodwin's height, which would enable her to see more, but she could see enough to notice that the patio had changed, very slightly, from when she had last looked, with him, an hour or so before. No major change, simply the addition of a big black bag in front of the door.

Which meant, in her exhausted estimation, that someone had put it there. That someone had, perhaps, been working in the garden at an hour which was late by their standards of lateness, and the thought induced panic, because the obvious person was Francis, coming and going as he pleased, plotting whatever sabotage he meant for their lives. The panic succeeded the anger at their stupid somnolence and the anger succeeded the panic. Why should Barbara not answer her phone and why should she be allowed to sleep? Anna slithered downstairs, picked up the phone and dialled 999. She remembered to withhold the number and was the model of succinctness in her speech. She was a neighbour of the Blessed Sacrament Convent in Selwyn Road, she told the calm voice that asked her which emergency service she required: she had seen three people climb over the wall at the back and knew that everyone in the building would be dead to the world. They were old and vulnerable. Would they send someone quick? They would need to bang long and hard on the front door to get a response; the old dears never knew their danger, and no, she would not give her name.

That done, she put the roof ladder back against the wall and drew the curtain around it, which made it look like a makeshift student's wardrobe, and put out the bathroom light. Perhaps this piece of mischief would allow her to sleep, but oh God, she had done it again, stupid, so she was not going to watch what happened. It would invite disclosure and compound the childishness, but she hoped they caught him. Duvet over the head, willing herself into the cure of sleep, she regretted the 999 call, because it was what she did all the time, react without thinking and then regret it. Other people thought before acting, while she lived with the gaps in her life and fought with the conclusions like a mud wrestler, making futile gestures as she slithered around, and she was sick of simply reacting, rather than planning, but she did not know what else to do, except cry, for her mother, her father and Therese, not necessarily in that order, and then try to sleep, because whatever else, there was work the next day and that was the only certainty. Tomorrow, there would be a metamorphosis. She would wake up wiser, and begin to plan . . . And in the midst of this, the entryphone buzzer went on buzzing.

It was like a wasp, trapped in the room, and for all the time she had lived there, with visitors as scarce as friends, it was still an unfamiliar sound to be buzzing without the normal backdrop of the music she turned up loud as soon as she came inside. Against the silence, it was commanding and offered no alternative. It went against every instinct she had *not* to respond to the sound and fail to let someone in, because it could always be Therese; it might be Father Goodwin again. But that tiny bit of logic said, shit and damnation, it would be the police, because that was the consequence and she'd better face the music. Wearily, she pressed the button on the console: a simple, automatic reaction, followed by the single thought that maybe this was a foolish thing to do.

Foolish, at eleven o'clock at night, when she was crazy

tired, mixed up, bound to make every explanation for every stupid action sound sillier than it was. She had enough time to consider that if it was a copper asking why the hell she had called them out, she would have the option to shrug and say Who? and act like some dumb child they would be reluctant to arrest. She *had* to get to work the next day, *had* to: it was the only fixed thing in her life and she needed it. And then she thought, no, she would not behave like a child, taking advantage of her own size; she had done enough of that. She would behave like a truthful adult, tell it like it was.

Music came from the flat below hers, a comforting reminder of close humanity and another reminder of how she had never attempted to make friends with any of them. She held the door half open, composing herself for the portentous footsteps of a policeman making enquiries. They were swifter steps, coming upwards from the well of stairs, until she saw him bounding up the last flight with his yellow hair and she was suddenly completely paralysed, until Francis was there, with an enormous boot, jamming the door open. Golden Boy, with his shining, saintly eyes.

'I've come to apologise,' he said.

In the distance, she could hear sirens. Nothing was ever going to happen in the right sequence. He was supposed to be in the garden, waiting for them. And now he was here, smiling to the *thump, thump, thump* of the music downstairs, which would never protect her, from anything.

Christopher Goodwin knew his way from the railway station in Kay's town, the way he told people he knew the inside of his own pocket, a comparison he repeated to himself now while knowing it was daft, because he was always so unsure of exactly what his pockets contained. Items collected in there with the ease of dust but greater bulk, such as biros and pieces of paper, receipts for purchases, an umbrella, the crumbled remnants of cigarettes, un-answered letters and a pair of useless nail scissors, which his fingers clutched in the search for cash. The pocket of a cassock and the capacious pockets of his anorak were probably the equivalent of a handbag for a woman and, getting out at the right station and setting off at a good speed, he had a vision of himself with one of those, instead of the routine, design accessory of an ugly old polythene bag.

He walked by the sea, which was nothing at first but a cold, dark backdrop, calling Kay McQuaid all the names under the moon. If she were not in her house, he would bomb the place, and the very thought of that made him pause with the thought of his own impotence. All right, he would pick up pebbles from the shore where Theodore Calvert had drowned and break all her windows. Oddly enough, the anger had been easy to sustain over an hour and a half's journey in a cold train. All he had to do was to think of that poisonous document of a will and the sad draft that accompanied it, the posse of drunken youths at the far end of the carriage, Sister Barbara and that boy, Francis, to make him hyperventilate to screaming point, cross his arms over his chest and rock back and forth. Understandably, no one bothered him on the train and no one was going to bother him on this road by the sea, a kind of small esplanade where the street lights illuminated the wet concrete and the curl of the waves breaking into foam on the shingle below mocked him with their patient consistency. What's it like to do the same thing every day? he asked the waves, pausing for a moment to watch a piece of flotsam move sluggishly on the current, floating inwards and sideways towards the foam, trying to guess how far it would travel before it hit the shore. In the brief time he watched, considering how his own St Christopher would have waded into the waves and rescued it, it moved far to the right, almost out of sight, edging closer and moving back in a coy dance. Even a broken crate could move with grace, fighting the strength of the current. He shuddered at the thought of Theo Calvert's body, deposited here with far less care. The man Anna referred to as her giant of a father.

Kay McQuaid was not a person who went early to bed, or one to be alarmed in her somnolent, ultra-respectable road, to have someone knock at her door on the right side of midnight. He went to the back of the house, where light shone through the glazed kitchen door, and knocked thunderously. Timid knocking made people ever more nervous. There was a new lock, a big brute of a seven-lever Banham, of the kind favoured by his rich parishioners, although perversely, it was the poor who were burgled most. He could see a bright-coloured dressing gown hovering behind the door.

'Open up!' he roared. 'For God's sake, woman, it's only the priest.'

She opened it slowly, to show a tired face, in which relief was notable for its presence and the lack of cosmetics for their absence. A different gown to any he had seen, with a stain down the front of its satin texture, and not a hint of surprise in her whole bearing, only a degree of resignation. Christopher Goodwin realised that his old friend Kay was moderately drunk. Good.

'Hello, Kay. Surprise, surprise.'

'Not really,' she said dully, letting him past her with all the enthusiasm she may have offered someone who had come to read the gas meter, following him through the

242

kitchen into the living room, still fashioned around the donkey cart of drinks and the Buddha squatting in the fireplace, looking ready to burp. He noticed how the doors to her garden were curtained, shutting it out, making an announcement that life had moved indoors and summer was now officially finished until next year. She always had been a bit of a control freak, trying to influence the weather and then shutting it out if she didn't like it, changing her face to overcome her mood, changing her clothes, latterly, to control the time of day. She was a one, that Kay McQuaid, but even in the electric light, he could see that her eyes were pink, her eyebrows unattended, so that they looked fierce, and the room subtly disorganised. It was not the living room of someone at the end of their tether, but the room of someone who had not moved very much or very far for more than a day.

'Help yourself,' she said, sinking back into an armchair, which had obviously borne her weight for several hours without any of the obsessive plumping of cushions that was her custom. He went for the Jameson's, relieved to find it pristine, fussing over it with umming and ahing, going out for a clean glass, to give her time to compose herself, hide the stain on the gown and whatever she needed. He found a piece of stale bread, sitting on a crumb-filled bread board, and ate it. Once settled in the opposite chair, with a glass in hand, he put the damp parcel of documents on to the smeared glass table between them both.

'Don't,' she said. 'I've never been much good with the written word.'

'What a liar you are, Kay,' he said, agreeably, easing himself down and wishing he was not so hungry, thinking he might go back into the kitchen to find that open packet of peanuts he had also seen, spilling on to the floor. 'You were always good with a letter. You were granted a primary education, somewhere. Always wrote well. Good signatures.'

She grunted and smiled at him, vacantly, a fatuous smile spreading across her face, and then two parallel sets of tears coursed down her cheeks. Plump cheeks, like the rest of her, hidden bones in a pulpy face he had always found so vivid before. Beauty was ever in the eye of the beholder.

A scar, ticking away beneath the disorganised eyebrow, otherwise disguised.

'I've something to tell you,' he said. 'Your boy Jack is working in the convent garden, the convent itself, more like, and had them all in various states of sublime adoration. Francis, he calls himself now. Blond and beautiful and poisonous. Have you any idea of what it is he might be trying to do?'

She shook her head and moaned.

'Of course you do,' he continued evenly, although it was an effort. 'Theodore's will says that it all goes to his daughters, provided they do not *sin*. Should they be *seduced* away from the paths of virtue he had come to loathe, he would rather leave his inheritance to the devil. Otherwise known as Jack McQuaid, bypassing the middleman, so to speak. Who the hell persuaded him to write such a thing, darling? You?'

She roused herself.

'*No.*'

'But you knew. You signed it.'

'I signed whatever Theo wanted me to sign.'

'Ah, yes. As one does. And you have a copy in the house?'

'Yes.'

'And you have the draft with the notes?'

'No. I never had that.'

He waited. She pulled herself further up the chair and used her index finger to stroke her eyebrows straight. Alas, he thought, drunk, but no drunker. Pity. He preferred confessions from those of the slurred voice, Help me Father for I have sinned, with enough of the drug- or alcohol-induced inebriation aboard to tell some approximation of truth or at least as much as the confessional ever offered. He drummed his heels on the floor. The vibration seemed to echo in her chair. The closed-in room reminded him of the convent parlour and he was, to his own relief, as angry as ever.

'*Francis,*' she pronounced it with the emphatic care of someone unused to the syllables and adding a lisp on the S, 'stayed here for three years. Theodore treated him as a son. But long before that, ever since he was ever so small, he was convinced he was Theo's son. He started to believe it when I left you and went to work for the Calverts. Remains convinced.'

'On what grounds, darling? Why the devil would he think that?'

She squirmed in the armchair, looked at her gin. Empty. He got up, swifter-footed than he would ever have thought, and poured, into a fresh glass. The one from which she drank had done service far too long and there was no shortage of glasses. She gulped at it. Christopher Goodwin felt slightly ashamed of himself.

'I don't know quite why. He'd always asked. I never said. Drove us both mad, those questions. I took him to meet the girls when I worked for the Calverts. They fascinated him, they were so pretty and so small. *Petite,*' she snapped. 'Tiny little overprivileged things, like dolls. With a mother who chucked him out, the bitch. Couldn't stand a raw-blooded male, even one with a crucifix round his neck, even if he was only twelve at the time. Ha, ha, ha.'

'A crucifix?'

'I put one round his neck when he was small. To ward off the evil eye. He always liked it.'

She got up, steadily, and went to the bathroom. He heard her footsteps trailing away and, after an interval, coming back. Bathroom on every floor in this house, all luxurious, equipped with toothbrushes, soap, talcum powder, flowers, in case anyone should ever arrive, the points in the compass of this big house where she still did everything Theo had suggested. Christopher did not prompt her as she sat back in her armchair, where he had rearranged the cushions in her absence, for comfort. It made him feel ever so slightly offended that she did not notice. Women should appreciate such small attentions, even if the intention was subversive. Maybe he was just another unreconstructed male after all.

'And?'

'I suppose I let him think it.'

'Think what?'

'That Theodore was his long-lost father and the girls were his younger sisters. I let him think it by refusing to tell him who his father was. I had always refused to tell him that, *always*. He created the myth of Theo as his daddy out of his own mind. I don't know when it took root. When I sneaked him into the Calverts' house? Later, when I moved here, bringing him with me? It must have looked like Theo coming into his own as a parent at long last. Offering his boy a home and a start in life, to make up for what had gone before. And Theo had this huge, bitter gap in his life. He wanted a young thing to make a fuss of. A substitute daughter. He was *very* kind to Jack. Spoiled him. I never

246

had, never could. It must have been like coming in from the cold.'

The whiskey was warm and acrid. Kay had washed her face in the bathroom, making it pink and herself more fluent. Christopher did not know if this was good or bad. The fluency was an effort. She lapsed into silence.

'Surely you told him it was all nonsense? That he was just a lucky boy, to have found a place like this to live, someone who would take care of him . . .'

'Jack, I mean *Francis*,' she spat, 'didn't want *luck*. He wanted a birthright. He wanted the *right* to live in a big house with no worries. Always wanted to go to a posh school when he was a kid and be like the sort who came home in a uniform with a mobile phone in each pocket in case Daddy got worried. *Francis* wanted everything. I told him Theo was not his father. He wouldn't have it. He hated me.'

'But he left. You told me. Ditched the idea of college and went for a job in London. If he liked it so much, why did he go?'

She got up again, sloshed more gin into her glass, added tonic, spilling some. She produced her cigarettes from the pocket of the gown, lit one and threw the packet towards him. Old friendships die hard.

'Whatever gave you the idea he simply went? Oh, I see, *I* did. Well, he was bound to be the one who bit the hand that fed him. Jack was corrupt from the moment he was born. By that time, I couldn't have shifted him from the notion that Theodore was his father even if I'd tried, but Jack would always want an insurance policy. And he could see Theo going demented, trying to get his daughters away from their mother. Distancing himself from everything else . . . killing himself with love and anxiety, although, God

247

help him, he never went for the drink again. Saving himself to be a father.'

'Oh, for heaven's sake, woman. Didn't Francis ever demand proof that Theo was his father? Something simple? One of those DNA tests? People in the parish do it all the time. Or at least, I don't know if they do it, but they ask me how it's done.'

Kay gazed at him with disdain. He was being slow. 'You don't ask for proof if you have no doubt. Would you ask for proof of your own paternity?'

He thought of his mild father, and his quiet mother, who had always wanted more children and brought up their own with a rod of iron, their vocations all decided for them.

'No, I wouldn't have dreamed of it.'

'No more did he. But in case his father should reject him first, he thought of another angle to keep him loyal. Sex. I told you he was corrupt. Lost his cherry to some old man when he was about ten, I think. He traded in sex before we left London. He could see poor Theo was starved of it, even at his age, so he tried to seduce him.'

The spiral of smoke from the cigarette in Christopher's hand shook. He took a long drag on it, trying to suppress shock. Get a grip, man: you've heard worse, and she may be lying again, but he did not think she was.

'It's an odd thing to try with your daddy,' he said, conversationally.

'Not at all,' she said in the same tone. 'Daddies do it with babies all the time, so what's the difference the other way round? So Theo's unhappy and half asleep, Francis crawls in beside him and gets to work. Mistake. Didn't get far. He was gone next day, with a bit of money, to be sure, but gone.'

248

Father Goodwin stubbed out the cigarette, somewhat at a loss for words. Then he sighed.

'Well, at least the boy knows which sex he likes. He has an orientation—'

'Oh, is that what you call it? Don't kid yourself. Francis would have fucked his own mother if he thought it would help. Anything goes with Francis. Women, men, dogs for all I know. You must have known boys like that.'

He did, feral creatures, from an early parish somewhere else: orphan predators.

'Would it not have helped if you had told him who his father was? Would it not have given him some pride?'

She laughed. Laughed until she choked and he moved to her side to pat her on the back. It did him good to slap her between the shoulder blades, belting out some of his own tension and bugger the bruises. Tears seeped down her face. He could see, with the ice chip in his soul, the wisdom of not wearing face powder to be streaked and ruined by such tears, tried not to let them distract him as he sat back in his own chair, away from her. They had some distance to go yet.

'You don't tell a child that he's the product of a gang rape in an Irish garage shed. That you don't know who his father is, except that he might come from a mixture of all the bad blood in a small place. That he would have been aborted if his mother's parents hadn't listened to the priest. He was born with me screaming hatred, Father. What else is there to tell? Do you wonder I never loved him?'

He was determined to avoid pity. There was no time for it. It was late, he had got her on the run and there was no telling what she would be like in the morning. Pity was for another time. A good priest, even an indifferent priest, learns to ration compassion. He made coffee in the kitchen, leaving her to stare blankly towards the pattern of the curtains, which shut out the night, brought it back, pulled his chair closer and spread a copy of the Calvert will on the table between them.

'I take it you knew that *Francis* was working for the convent?'

'I didn't know, I promise you. But I do now.'

'And he's seen this will of Theodore's?'

'He could have done. I wrote to him after Theo . . . died. Told him to expect nothing. He wouldn't have believed me.'

'But he's seen *this*.' He stabbed his finger at the official-looking will, rather than the other document festooned with notes.

'Yes. He's probably been back here . . . many times.'

'Which means he has.'

He took another of her cigarettes. Lit it on the third attempt with trembling fingers. She was shrinking back into her chair.

'So he knows that if he manages to make Theo's daughters stray from the path of virtue, if he makes them *sin*, in a very obvious way, he stands to inherit.'

'Yes.'

'What better *sin* could the boy imagine than, say, to make a girl commit incest? He believes these girls are his blood sisters. Surely it would be a *sin* to be seduced by a *brother*? To be tempted into wickedness by him? What worse *sin* could he imagine? Or does he imagine that he could drive them to sin another way? Drive them into some outer darkness, like his own?'

She shrank back further, muttering under her breath.

'What?'

'I said, Francis would do it just because he hated them.

250

That would be reason enough. They had everything he thought should be his.'

Christopher Goodwin leaned forward, picked up the copy of the will and tore it in half. The sound of tearing paper seemed abnormally loud.

'This thing is a piece of useless rubbish. It might be signed, but it's only a draft. It's no more valid than a piece of toilet paper. You can't put conditions like this in a will. You signed it as a witness, too. A beneficiary can't be a witness. The whole thing's crap.'

'And Jack's belief that Theo was his father is also *CRAP*!' she shouted. 'But the point is, he *believes*.'

Christopher imagined someone looking at this will and finding its legal verbiage entirely convincing. The mention of trustees thereof and devising and bequeathing would lend credibility at first and even second sight. It would be easy to credit.

She let her cigarette fall and ground it into the carpet with a slippered foot.

'So what's so odd about him believing all that? For Chrissakes, *Father*, you should know all about that. You're an expert in believing the unbelievable. The more incredible it is, the more you believe. The Resurrection? The Virgin Mary. Belief without doubt? Hope? It's what you bastards call having *FAITH*. Francis has his own version.'

Chapter Twelve

Thou shalt not bear false witness

She knew that she was mortally afraid of him, more afraid than she had ever been. The top of her head was somewhere level with his chest and looking up at him, she fixed her eyes on the golden crucifix round his neck. Edmund's crucifix with a mended chain. A crucifix rather than a simple cross, because of the tiny figure resting on it. The cross was too small to be ornamental and the chain too fine for the breadth of Francis's neck, and yet they belonged as if he had always worn them. It transfixed her as he came into the room diffidently and sat in one of her two, facing chairs. She fell into the one opposite. When he leaned forward with his elbows on his knees, their eyes were almost level, but she kept hers fixed on that miniature figure visible in the gap at the neck of his shirt.

'Do you remember me?' he asked, earnestly, somehow taking command, but anxious to appease. She was forced to look at him, one brief look into his eyes, and then back to the golden cross. The symbol of sacrifice.

'Remember me, I mean, from a long time ago?'

'No.'

'No? But we look like one another. The same hair. Surely you noticed that?'

'No.'

'Perhaps it's my imagination then. We are all brothers and sisters in Christ.'

'Yuk.'

He sat back. She looked at his feet, ankles, knees, waist. Good shoes, soft chinos, clothes that made him all the more intimidating, although it was the ease with which he sat that was worse; the way he made no effort to keep her in place, because there was no need. She tried to remember if the door behind was shut, if he had kicked it closed, glanced sideways. The last time she had hated him rather than been afraid of him. Now, he seemed able to read her mind.

'Please don't think of running away. I don't want you running away from me. It wouldn't be right. It's your own home. And I thought you invited me in.'

'No, I didn't.'

'You didn't? Oh, I'm sorry. Did someone else open the door and wait for me? I'll go, if you like. It's a pretty place you have here, you've made it nice. I'm always looking for a place. What's it like to have a place of your own? Is it expensive? Please don't look at me all frightened like that. I think I like it better when you pull faces.'

She could feel the blush rise. To her dying day, she would regret that puerile gesture to Barbara, and yet had the absurd desire to repeat it now and the desire loosened her tongue. She held the fabric of her pyjama jacket with both hands and spoke clearly. She was vulnerable to anyone who admired her room: it flattered her. She focused on his neck. An elegant neck, the only vulnerable thing about him.

'Where did you get that crucifix?'

'This?' he said, surprised, touching it. 'My mother gave it to me. Why do you ask?'

His mother gave it to him.

'What do you want?'

'I want to be friends.'

The *thump, thump, thump* of the music downstairs ceased abruptly, making his voice sound louder, so that the words echoed like an announcement.

'You *what*?'

'I want to be friends.'

'Oh, very funny.'

She did up the button of her pyjamas for something to do, glad that her bedtime clothes were the same as they had always been. Modest and unsexy, little-boy striped pyjamas to which she had always been devoted. She was suddenly cold and her teeth chattered. It was a different crucifix he wore. His mother gave it to him. He had grown into it and it was still too small.

'Friends? Don't be bloody silly. You beat me up, you *lie* about me . . . Go and stuff yourself.'

'I didn't lie,' he said with soft indignation. 'I did think you were a burglar and I had to say it was you who broke the window. And when I said it, I thought it was true. I'd seen you before, but I didn't know who it was in the dark and I'd no idea how small you were. And if I've done you wrong, I want to put it right, I really do.'

Looking up at him, meeting the eyes, she noticed the brilliant blue and, to her amazement, the sheen of unshed tears. Again, she fixed her own eyes on the cross around his neck. The tears were embarrassing: she never knew what to do, except pity them, and the memory of him throwing her to the floor with that mixture of casual strength and the

254

careful reining back of it, which saved her from serious harm, suddenly became confused, the details blurred as if it were all in her imagination. He could have broken her neck, but he had not. The omission seemed kind. She put her hands on her knees, felt the grazes beneath the cloth of her pyjamas to remind herself, refusing to look at the scratches on his face.

'I suppose,' Francis said, hurrying as if he wanted to get a shameful confession out of the way, 'that I wanted to impress Sister Barbara. I can't tell you how much I *need* this job. It's my lifeline and she could fire me any time. I wanted to look like a hero. I really need this job. I don't know if you can understand that. It's the first time I've ever felt safe.'

She watched him lace his fingers together, head bowed, so that she could see the curly thatch of his blond hair, smelling clean and fresh, like the rest of him, and making her feel faintly dirty.

'It makes me feel wanted, and I'm not used to that. They're good to me. It went to my head a bit, if you see what I mean. I really wanted to protect them. I want them to admire me. I went overboard.'

She looked at the cross, glinting round his neck. The presence of it teased at the back of her brain; it puzzled her and yet helped her focus. She looked steadily at the symbol of sacrifice, the aid to contemplation, the tiny figure of the crucified Christ. She looked at it and willed the chain to swell in size and choke him, watched it intently, imagining in miniature the ornate crucifix of Westminster Abbey and that brilliant shushing sound of hundreds of people moving to kneel and then to stand, feeling in the air, the breath of their movement, making her calm.

255

'Yes,' she said, reluctantly. 'I can understand that.'

He was nodding eagerly, boyish, foolish, apologetic.

'Look, I know you don't want the story of my life, but it hasn't been lucky. I was brought up to think I was bad all the way through. Then I met Edmund and knew I wasn't. And then I meet a whole lot of other people who don't think so either. It takes some getting used to.'

'Who broke the window?' she interrupted.

He hung his head further, so that she could scarcely hear the mumble.

'It was Edmund. He was shooting at a magpie, but I couldn't tell anyone that, could I? It's not fair now he's dead. I don't think he really knew he'd done it. I only just found the air rifle in his shed, yesterday. I'm spring cleaning for the autumn, you see.'

She thought again of the cathedral sounds, and heard in her mind the smashing of the glass in the window, finding it easier to listen to him if she kept removing herself. He was pulling at her heartstrings and she wanted it to stop, because in this humble state, she could feel the lure of his beauty and see why the dear Sisters would eat out of his hand, like the garden birds with Edmund. There was something else, too: a slippage of facts, an incomplete equation, an unfinished crossword puzzle, which his sheer presence made her unable to complete. She was listening, yes, but there was something she could not hear. She always wanted forgiveness to be freely given and received; she wanted it now.

'And I came tonight,' he said, 'because Therese told me I must. She could see I was worried, and so was she. She sent me to the place where you work with that present for you.'

Her head spun. There was a flash of uncontrollable

jealousy, a spurt of protective fury. The juxtaposition of this man, this *boy*, alongside her sister was intolerable, and yet at the mention of Therese, all her defences slid and her heart began to beat with slow anxiety, so loud she was sure he could hear it. *Therese* sent her the dead bird? Or Therese sent her the scripture? That was the worst fear; Therese unbalanced by something fearful, like her mother. Therese was losing her mind. Or she was losing hers. She *must* see Therese, before it was too late. His voice reached her from a distance.

'She and I talk, you see, we always did from the first day I got there. I suppose because we're the only young ones, apart from the girl in the kitchen.' He took a deep breath. 'Therese wants to see you, but she says the only way that can happen is if Barbara allows it. She asks that you understand the rules of obedience. And look, I know this seems arrogant, but I reckon I can bring Barbara round to that, if anyone can, if I say that you and I are friends, now. Therese sends you her love, by the way. She's a lovely girl, isn't she? She knows you miss the chapel. Sweetest person I ever met. I wish she was my sister. She's teaching me not to tell lies.'

Anna was speechless.

'So I told her that I'd kissed you on the way home. Which was a bad thing to do, but I couldn't help it, because you're so pretty. I'd noticed you before, you know, sooner than you did me, and then at Mass, even if I wouldn't have known you in the dark.'

'And what did Therese say about that?'

'She said it was insulting and I needed my head straightening out.' He paused. 'But she also said it was time you found a nice Catholic boy. And that please, could you and I forgive and forget and be *amiable* for her sake?'

It sounded so like Therese, she could only laugh, and as if to copy Francis, felt tears pricking at her eyelids. She rubbed her nose on her pyjama sleeve.

'We've got a lot in common, you and I,' he said. 'All the Sisters, and what to do for the best for them all. We could do so much, you know. They won't survive without people like us. They have no mirrors. They cannot see themselves. Anyway, Therese says, will you try?'

She sat, silently, resenting *people like us* and yet suddenly buoyed up with hope. Therese thought of her. Therese spoke of her. Therese might go mad without her. Therese needed her.

He rose, awkward and concerned. 'I'm sorry. It's late and I've stayed too long. I'd have phoned . . . she gave me the number, but I thought you'd put the phone down. So I took the risk. Thanks for listening.'

'Wait.' He waited.

'What sort of friends do you want us to be?'

He had a complicated smile. He could have sold it for a million. A devastating mix of the smile of a saint, the grin of an innocent boy looking for trust, and a hopeful suitor with the lips and teeth of a pop star sportsman.

'Any kind you like. How about doing something tomorrow night? Seven? After work. I could bring you flowers, start over, properly.'

'That kind of friend?'

His eyes swept down the length of her body, back again to her face. They were knowing eyes.

'Oh yes, that kind. I'll see Therese in the morning. If two people meet in the wrong way and then get it right, I think that's romantic, don't you?'

She cringed and then tried to smile. He couldn't help being clumsy, could he? He liked Therese, he wanted to like her, he was only another lost soul who made mistakes. If only he didn't wear that crucifix.

'Yes. All right, whatever you like. Give her my love.'

His footsteps echoed away down the stairs. The sound of his whistling lingered behind him. Something about the whistling disturbed her. It had a note of triumph. Anna brushed her teeth, and after half an hour of frantic activity wrote a few words in the notebook and then, in a fury of confusion, cried herself to sleep. He made her feel, above all, ungrateful.

Christopher Goodwin made Kay McQuaid brush her teeth before he tucked her up in her own bed and told her everything was going to be all right, knowing that a statement as optimistic as that made him as much a liar as she was herself. Because, even as unstrung as she was, Kay could still hide, by which he meant she would answer the questions he uttered, but not the ones he did not know to ask. He ignored the small spare room where he was normally placed on the rare occasions he missed the last train and went and lay down in Theodore's room because he liked the sight of the moon through the balconied window. It was a restful moon and he needed something to stare at while he willed his eyes to close.

Composing himself for sleep was difficult enough and harder still in a room devoted to the use of another. It was a strange sensation and made him feel as if he were not alone. He opened the door of a handsome wardrobe to hang his jacket and found it was still full of Theodore's clothes, old-fashioned tweed jackets, well-worn, neatly pressed shirts and a heavy winter coat. No need for any of these in the other world and he wondered briefly which way Theodore had travelled after death, heaven, hell, or

259

purgatory? One thing was certain and that was that he would not have asked for forgiveness for his sins, not even at the end. There were blankets but no sheets on the bed. Christopher crawled beneath them in his underwear, wishing he could remember the man better, or that he had known him well enough to read the complications of his mind. A man who played with power and loved games, but unlike himself, who only enjoyed them as a spectator.

It was a good bed. Everything in this house, apart from Kay's additions, reeked of solid quality. Good, soft, clean-smelling blankets, too. She was an excellent housekeeper, whatever else she was. Judge not that you may not be judged. It was always assumed, he was telling himself, that a celibate cleric like himself could have little understanding of that peculiar love of parent towards child, which could turn a quiet woman into a virago and a father into a murderous protector, the love that made every other commandment and consideration entirely irrelevant. He could hear the common cry from a desperate mother in his parish, shouting at him that he did not understand, but he thought he did, however incompletely. The accusation always felt like an insult to his imagination, which could *feel* the sensation of a child in his arms and know, like his own St Christopher, that he would carry it until he dropped or drowned rather than let it go. Oh Lord, I would have loved a child, he thought, and on that anguished note, he slept.

And woke, disorientated by the strangeness of the cool room, with dawn pressing against the windows and prodding him awake through the half-closed curtains. He washed in the bathroom, fretted about the problem of being without a razor or toothbrush, until he saw everything he needed on the shelf above the basin, which he used in a guilty fashion, feeling as if he were, in a strange way, standing in another man's shadow, benefiting from the failure of that man's housekeeper to clear away the effects of the deceased. Either she was not equal to the task or disqualified herself from it and his only complaint about the arrangement was the mirror being set too low, so that he had to stoop to see his own chin, all of which distracted him sufficiently to allow him to complete his ablutions without cutting himself. The anger lay curled in his abdomen, like indigestion waiting to strike as soon as he was fully free of the drug of sleep. He would walk for the early train and clear his head by the sea. In the living room, he collected the documents he had brought with him, wondered how many more of them Kay had and where she had put them, decided not to wake her and ask. He had more than he needed. Instead, he left her a note, it was kinder to let her sleep, and let himself out through the back door.

He could see Theodore Calvert's point in living so near the sea on a morning like this, when it moved and heaved with a cheerful sluggishness and almost invited the full baptism John the Evangelist gave to the new followers of the Messiah in the River Jordan. This sea looked more like a river, easily crossed. It was water to walk upon, glinting with light and disappearing into a misty horizon. Father Goodwin stood and watched, praying that it would calm his soul and inspire a course of action, because in between sleeping and waking, he knew no better what he should do, or what he *could* do on his return to his neglected parish, other than commit murder. He was unsure of the preferred order of the homicides, Barbara or Francis first. He could discuss things with the Bishop's emissary, insist on an interview with Therese, if he could insist, but the rights and duties of a priest were ever vague. He may have been an accidental parental substitute for two orphans, with enough love for the task, an appalling responsibility, but no rights whatsoever. It was perplexing, to say the least, even without consideration of the unpredictability of Satan. In the name of God, what had Theodore Calvert thought he was doing, making a pact with the devil, or had he been drunk when he drafted that will, the last delirium of a man who wanted to die, with no idea of the effect? Christopher Goodwin watched the sea, imagined it parting into two towering walls to let through the tribes of Israel, led by Moses. It was the most convincing image he had ever retained from the Old Testament and the only one to impress him as a boy. The single scene that convinced him of the power of the good God, together with the rendering of the next scene by Cecil B. De Mille, where the waters fell back and killed the army of Egyptians. Why did he wait to do it until they were in the middle? Why not hold them back on the other bank? The God of the Israelites was a murderer, after all, simply selective in genocide. And that was the trouble with religious knowledge. It created a superstructure of images, which got in the way of every view and prevented one from looking simply at what there was.

As he looked, trying to concentrate on what there was, noticing the dark gathering of clouds and delighting in the sharp light on the water, Christopher noticed another piece of flotsam, at first sight similar to the one he had seen dancing on the waves in almost the same place the night before. On second sight, squinting at it and wishing he possessed such a thing as a pair of sunglasses, he could see it was different, a green barrel, or something of the kind, rounded and heavier looking, bobbing along sweetly and moving fast. He walked along level with it, feeling like a dog playing a game and about to bark at a stick, trying to

262

match the casual speed of his steps with its floating pace and finding he had to move faster to keep up. Despite his foul mood and the underlying indigestible distress that weighed him down, he enjoyed the game until the road turned towards the station away from the sea and he had to leave it. Regret made him pause, then he stopped altogether.

Such strong currents on this stretch of coast. If Theodore Calvert had gone swimming on the piece of shore nearest his home and drowned, he would never in a million years have come floating back to the same place. And if Theodore Calvert had left a bogus decoy of a will, where was the real one?

The green barrel passed out of sight. He watched it until it disappeared, the light blinding his eyes. He hesitated, blinking furiously. Then he turned round and went back towards the house. He would wake her and shake her until she rattled. He would not be welcome. He slunk past the kitchen window, angry and uncertain, ready to hammer on the door, saw her inside in another dressing gown, talking on the phone.

Dawn yelled like a curse and she was naked in her own bed, light and floating on a tide of sleeplessness. *My name is Anna Calvert*, she had written in the notebook, *I am an orphan and I must go to work*. The eight in the morning through until two in the afternoon shift, and that was all that counted. Cling to certainties. *I need this job*. She crawled down to the bottom of the bed and held on to her own feet, hoping that the light of dawn would make sense. The scribbling in the notebook, learned from her father, to make the words clear. *Do you hate that boy at school?* her father would say. *If you do, write down, I hate him, and see*

263

what happens. You might not hate him quite so much. You write to clarify your emotions.

The room was tidy and cold. A chair was jammed beneath the door knob, a futile precaution against trespass. A breeze rattled the window left open wide to dispel the smell. The other chair on which he had sat was pushed into a corner out of sight with the cushion from the seat removed, cut in half and stuffed into the kitchen bin along with the torn pyjamas. There was damp on the carpet where she had scrubbed the area he had trodden. She looked at the room, sanitised by her own mysterious hyper-activity in the middle of the night, and was struck by the awful thought that when he came back, Francis would think she had done all this for him. He was going to come back and she was going to let him in. Probably. Almost certainly. She had gone over in her mind everything he had said and revisited the scenes in which he had so completely and effortlessly overwhelmed her, not once, but twice. Made her stand in her shower after the first time, scrubbing away the touch of him, cutting her long nails in case they should hide traces of his skin. And then, this second time, when she had been disarmed by him equally effectively and then gone on to such frantic lengths in a haze of exhaustion to fumigate the room as if he carried an infectious disease.

Francis, the Golden Boy, knew everything that went on in the convent. He was the only acceptable outsider, now the only link between herself and Therese, which gave him power. He was the key to the garden, and in some strange way, he wanted her, because that was the message in his eyes. Well, if he was the link, so be it. And if it was her use-less, undersized body he wanted, well, he could have that, too. Listen to yourself, she told herself, someone offers you

264

friendship and all you can do is suspect. But most of all, she wanted to stop fighting. She was sick of it. But she did not want to stop fighting when she felt so powerless, as if there was no single other card in her hand, at a time when her brain felt as if it had turned to sludge.

At six-thirty in the morning, she pulled out the ladder and went up. If she were to look up from the convent garden, all that she or anyone else would see of her apartment block was the blank back wall of it, punctuated with the small, opaque bathroom windows, which were oblongs of light after dark. The most one could ever see from below was a silhouette through frosted glass. Francis did not know what she could see from here and the thought gave her a kind of comfort. It balanced out the power a little, this extra, useless eye. The uneven parapet was her own chest height at this vantage point. Francis would not need to lean forward in order to admire the view. Like Father Goodwin, the parapet, which guarded her completely, would provide less protection for a man of his height. She could see him toppling over, turning in mid-air without a sound, before he disappeared. *What was wrong with her?* He wanted to be friends, and she was continuing in the same old way, looking for enemies.

Still looking down, she remembered Matilda, and the way she no longer sat outside since Edmund's death. Matilda with her finger on her lips, the other watcher. She scrambled back down the ladder, put it away, turned on the music for one long blast before she ran downstairs and slammed the door. She would have one more try at the convent door, borrowing his phrase, *I've come to apologise.* A bright, rational smile, a request to come back later and make her peace, that should work fine. The sunshine really did make all the difference. Monsters were fostered by the dark: they only grew in the culture of night-time dreams. Early in the morning, they shrank. Until she banged on the convent door, checking the time, almost breakfast, make this quick, can't be late for work, compose the smile, checking the clothes while she waited, jeans and clean training shoes, polo neck because it was not warm, hair fresh with shampoo, who could resist her? Agnes, standing behind the door like a concrete post, opened it partially and then, immediately, tried to close it until Anna pitched her whole weight against it, only succeeding in delaying the momentum and keeping the heavy thing open only by a big enough crack for Agnes to shout through, '*Go away.*'

'Could I come in, Sister? I want to see Matilda . . .'

'Oh, in God's name, *go away.*' And the door pushed shut.

She stood away from it, imagining all the other doors inside, the black and white corridor, the chapel, the smell of food, and as she stood, the ambulance arrived.

Anna moved further down the quiet street and watched from the recessed door of the next house. They were quick; someone inside was ready. She saw the wheelchair, which went in folded and came out, rapidly, fully burdened. There were sounds of argument, a discussion on the appropriateness of a stretcher, Barbara's voice saying, fine, fine, fine, yes, yes, no, no, no, and a man pushing Matilda in the chair up the ramp, making soothing sounds into her ear. She was recognisably Matilda, with large, red-raw hands twitching in her lap, her eyes closed, her face as slack as her body, dressed in her habit, but without the veil, which was, instead of its natural decorum, wrapped round her head like a towel over wet hair. The sounds of argument increased. Barbara was on the step. The chair went into the ambulance. Sister Joseph, fully dressed,

266

knocked everyone aside and followed, her face purple with rage and wet with tears.

Matilda, kind Matilda. The only other one who watched over the garden. Anna's feet were rooted to the spot. Until she uprooted them and ran to work. Mind still like sludge, optimism fading and the sunlight with it. Inside Compucabs, there was the same buzz of noise, which stabilised her again, but once she was in the safest of places, it was as if the delayed intellect started to kick against her skull, making the inside of her head thump. Matilda with her blistered hands dominated her vision, and Ravi, over there, with a face like the moon and a smile as wide as the sea, fading slowly when she made a grimace and put on the headphones, ignoring him.

'Compucabs, how can I help you? Account number? Thanks. Your job number is . . .'

'Feeling better, are we?' The supervisor, standing by the desk.

'Great. Thanks, I'm fine.'

'Great.'

The phones did not stop for three whole hours. There was always a busiest day of the week and on balance, she would rather tap out the keys and repeat the same words again and again than do anything else. It was as calming in its own fashion as the telling of rosary beads to others. Ravi hovered by the desk, raising his eyebrows in an invitation to adjourn somewhere else, either outside for the air or for tea or water and the desultory chat of the back room. She followed him outside. Somewhere in the course of the last three hours, looking at his serene face from time to time between the screens and headphones, she had come to realise that she could not tell him anything about Golden Boy. It would somehow wreck whatever it was they had;

some precious little thing, like a fragile gemstone, easily lost. They sat on the step and she sipped at the tea he had made for her in the kitchen, the way he imagined she would like it, laced with sugar, which she did not like, but drank gratefully, keeping her distance.

'Walk you home?' he asked.

'Not today, Ravi, I've got to go somewhere else. Can I ask you something?'

'Of course.'

'Something I asked you before, only I can't remember what you said. I know. Praying. What exactly do you do it for?'

'And I told you I don't pray to get things.'

'Why ever not? What's wrong with asking?'

'Nothing is *wrong*, but you can't demand. You can't make bargains. You can't say, look, if you do this for me, I'll do that for you. What have you got to offer that the Gods don't already have? Nothing.' He hesitated. 'You pray to give honour and praise. You pray for guidance. You don't say, give me that thing, God. You say, please give me the wisdom to see if this is the thing I should find for myself. You pray for the wisdom and strength to do it. You pray to give praise and all you can ask is the ability to *see*, for yourself.'

'Ah,' she said, 'that's where I'm going wrong.'

'What are you staring at me for?'

'Because I like to. I like looking at you.'

He smiled and cuffed her arm, and that was the point when a whole number of impressions began to slip into place, and all because of Ravi's peculiar, lopsided, spontaneous smile, which felt like a benediction, a ray of sunshine through the chapel window, and made her think how she was in the presence of someone who was, for want of a better description, *good*. Which did not mean flawless, but possessed of a kind of purity, which was not the same as innocence. She looked at him and, without intending to, made a comparison between him and Golden Boy, which went far deeper than their colouring and disparate size. If Ravi were put into a fighting ring with Francis, Ravi would not stand a chance. He would have all the inhibitions of decency while Francis would have none. In Ravi's kind, inquisitive face there was a spirit entirely absent from that of Francis.

The contrast shocked her. She smiled at him.

'I like looking at you,' she repeated. 'So just let me, OK?'

There, she was being stupid again, seeing phantoms. They returned to work.

Back at her desk, the phone rang.

'Good afternoon, Compucabs.'

'Ah, *there* you are. Thank goodness.'

'Hello, sir. How are you? Are you going out to lunch?'

Despite herself, she was grinning. That old, familiar voice, talking over hers.

'. . . very worried. I keep getting someone else when I wanted to speak to you. Are you all right?'

There was something about that old, tired voice that made it impossible to lie.

'No. Not firing on all cylinders today. Confused and worried.'

'You can come to me. Drop everything and come here. At once.'

'I can't do that.'

'I wish you would. Here's the address. Write it down.'

She wrote it down in a meaningless scrawl.

'But you won't, will you? I know you won't. Listen, I phoned to warn you. I had a premonition. Don't believe

269

anything that boy says. You can't trade with the wicked. When did the devil ever honour a bargain? Evil has no inhibitions and always the advantage of surprise because the good don't know what it is and don't see it coming. The uncunning cannot see the cunning. You know where I am.'

The phone went dead. She dialled 1471. She looked at her writing on the scribble pad and found she could not read it. The phone rang again. The screen blinked the time, three in the afternoon.

'Compusoddingcabs.'

'No need to swear, love. It's cab number 110. Got a call from one of you lot to pick up a Sister Joseph from Paddington Community Hospital, only I can't find her.'

'Sorry, you're on the wrong line for queries. I just do bookings, try 291.'

Shaking slightly, wanting to scream. The phone rang again. Somebody wanted to go to an airport. It seemed like the most desirable place on earth.

A jet plane sped through the sky, way above her gaze, crossing the blue and passing into the clouds like a distant exotic bird leaving a trail of plumage. Therese rose from the pristine white feet of St Michael and stood idly, watching the sky in the middle of the afternoon. What a terrible day, beginning with the evening before, when Barbara had been so peculiarly watchful. Watchful and guilty, dismissively kind in her approach and her words – *you're tired, child, and we all need an early night, off to bed with you, plenty to do tomorrow* – almost as if it were an apology and a promise of more, or was it just wanting everyone out of the way and the place secure. Therese did not know, only aware she was watched as she passed the phone by the door, in case she should try to use it; watched until she was up the stairs and probably checked for the sound of her washing. Watched, not trusted, as if her unintentional eavesdropping had been noticed; as if she was like her sister. Which she wanted to be, but the proof she was not must lie in her own actions of quiet obedience. Agnes cried in her sleep, the way she did, and Matilda did not respond, until there were anxious sounds along the corridor and Agnes left her room. Therese waited to be called, but no one did. And then, in the morning, when she went downstairs, earlier than ever, yearning for something to do and long past the point of even attempting to pray, there was a secretive bustle around the parlour, as if everyone but herself was there.

She could not work it out. Someone had knocked at the door in the night and said Matilda was in the garden. Someone had brought her in and made her comfortable in the night down there, because that was what she wanted and it was important not to disturb anyone else, and even that Therese only knew later from the conversation at breakfast, which was not directed at her, and where someone had suggested that, knowing Matilda, it was because of something she ate and surely she would be fine. But she had not been fine when Therese had seen her being wheeled down the black and white corridor. Whatever it was that had blistered and purpled her hands seemed to have also been smeared on her face. Her eyes stared wide, seeing nothing, not even Joseph battling for possession of the chair; she was not hearing the tide of argument that followed her. It was an awful, suffering face, etched on her memory now, so that she preferred to look at the sky whilst trying to make her makeshift prayers in what had been Matilda's favourite place in the hope that the very action of sitting here would bring her back, with the hopeless

271

conviction that it would not, wanting to apologise to her for her own resentment of that patting and clutching. There seemed little purpose in prayer; it was achieving nothing.

No one knew what had happened, and if Barbara knew, she was not about to explain. Looking at the smooth feet of St Michael, completely free of lichens so that the stone was unnaturally white, she touched them gingerly. However infrequently she passed anywhere, she always noticed change. What would it take to remove moss? Some form of caustic, like oven cleaner, and that was perhaps what Matilda was doing. An act of devotion to her saint, like Mary Magdalene washing the feet of Christ with her tears and drying them with her hair. Clumsy, undomesticated Matilda who dropped things and hid them, expressing her devotion. Suddenly all such acts of piety seemed revolting.

It had been a day of fitful weather, bursts of sunshine drying out the lethal slipperiness of the ground, temporary dark clouds, which threatened rain and then desisted, mirroring the fractious mood indoors. Even Kim was surly, pleading a sick child to leave early, allowed by Barbara with her strange watchfulness, looking at them all, Therese in particular, as if to see which of them was the interloper who had brought them misfortune, and daring anyone to criticise. Even Kim had been hurtfully shrill, when Therese had tried to sympathise about the child. *Oh, shuttit, you wouldn't understand,* she said. *You don't know what it's like.*

A dull luncheon, with stilted conversation, punctuated by Joan and Agnes discussing among themselves how Joseph and Matilda had been inseparable once and whatever had happened. Was it the fact that Matilda had gone so deaf and Joseph so lacking in patience and wasn't it grand they were together now? The empty places left by

272

them both looked like the spaces of missing teeth in a mouth. They talked about Matilda as if she had already died, and it was all the will of God, no less, a mere rite of passage. It made Therese sick and took away any hint of appetite. It made her sick with the knowledge that she did not want the kind of faith that made them accept the unacceptable.

The aeroplane passed out of sight, and the prospect of going back indoors to the uneasy somnolence of a typical late afternoon inside was . . . bad. How long was it since she had eaten anything of substance? Not today, nor yesterday either. Bread pellets, an apple. She was queasy with the lack of food and repelled by the thought of it. She could have stepped outside and run to Anna, but she knew she was afraid to do that after the last time and equally afraid that if she did, there would be another rejection. She had, after all, taken sides by silence. She patted the clean white foot of St Michael and asked him if men in brotherhood were different. Do brothers have this problem? Because sisterhood, whether of blood or affinity of purpose, like Joseph and Matilda, or the sisterhood of Anna and herself, posed huge problems. It was as if she and Anna had a hypodermic syringe permanently parked in the vein of the other, ready to trigger into the opposite bloodstream a fine cocktail of uncomfortable mutual knowledge, love, anxiety, DNA and need, with a percentage of irritation. There was no antidote, no pill to take to offset the effect of that sometimes destructive bond. Absence, in times of distress, did not make the heart grow fonder; it broke it into little bits, sharp crystals of loneliness. Everybody said that she and Anna had been too close. At breakfast and lunch, the same thing had been said about Joseph and Matilda.

Sunlight again, the traitor, while perversely, she wanted

the flavour of the dark and the aspect of her own, prayer-less room, rather than the dread of Joseph's return from a long vigil at hospital with news she could foretell even now. Anything rather than her own conclusion that Sister Barbara should have called the ambulance far, far sooner, instead of trying to keep what was laughingly known as 'the peace'. Oh, Lord, who was there to trust?

It was chilly in the shade. Therese hesitated – forward or back? – and then went further down the garden, pretending to herself she was only looking for the lonely cat and knowing it was a pretence, because she was really looking for sanctuary, and there it was.

The clean oak bench, utterly devoid of Edmund's ghost, the area around it wonderfully silent and colourful. A riot of busy lizzies in pink and white framed the semi-circle, which widened inside the compass to the new table in front of the bench, so scrubbed it was fit to eat food straight from the surface, standing on ground swept to reveal the contours of the paving stones. Off to the side was the shed, which now looked like a tiny house, fit for a small, not very useful person, with no other purpose in life, to look inside. There was a small bed against the back wall, covered with chintz. Warmth seemed to waft from the doorway. A gingerbread house, with a kettle on a camping stove, a smell. A person could pray in here. She had been looking for a place to pray.

In the background, Francis was singing.

He came round from behind the structure, still humming, the most cheerful sound of the day, stopped and smiled, the only smile of the day. He was so wholesome, so very far away from death. Even the scratches on his face had faded to nothing and there was a smudge of dirt on his nose.

'Hello, I was just making tea. Do you want some?'

Tea, the palliative for all ills. Good tea, she remembered, outdoor tea, but she shook her head.

'No, thank you.'

'Are you all right? You look tired. Not much fun indoors today, I suppose. Any news of Sister Matilda?'

There was a colossal lump in her throat, announcing the imminence of tears. It was always thus. She could hold them back, repress any display of emotion, until something insignificant triggered it, such as a kind enquiry, or the sight of something that appealed to her, like the cat, slinking away into the undergrowth, or the sight of the chintz on the little bed. The cat was probably on some murderous mission, but that did not matter, it was a beautiful creature governed entirely by its own rules.

'No news,' she said.

'I'm keeping out of the way, too,' he said, softly. 'It was me made Barbara call the ambulance, you know. She should have done it sooner. She hasn't needed me since.'

'Nor me. They don't need me, either. I wonder if anyone does.'

And then she was inside the circle of his arms and he was hugging her gently. Her head was pressed into his chest and his body shielded hers. She stood, unable to move, arms at her sides, unresisting, unshocked, but warmed by the feeling of him and provoked into intense curiosity by the smell of him, which was earthy and sweet, and she only knew that when he withdrew, with a brief, friendly pat on her shoulder, she did not want him to leave her and it was a touching she could not resent. The embrace had brought them closer to the door of the gingerbread shed. They had moved a couple of paces and she had not noticed. The desire to weep had gone; she felt oddly relieved and shakily tired.

'You must always remember you have a brother in me,' Francis said. 'And do you like what I've done with this rotten old shed?'

She peered inside. The warmth of the interior seemed to spill outside and surround her. Therese wrinkled her nose at the smell of burning joss sticks.

'For the bugs,' he said.

It was a smell reminiscent of the room she had shared with Anna in the days when they were ill, scented sometimes with joss sticks to mask medicinal smells, a heavy scent, which had come to be associated in her mind with safety, lassitude and a pleasant sleepiness.

'I had a little room like this once,' she said. 'I used to want to live in a cupboard under the stairs.'

He laughed, standing away from her, just when she preferred his closeness.

'Your size rather than mine. Why don't you stay here and rest? Get away from it all?' He looked at his watch. 'No one'll know and I'm going home in a minute. You can have some peace, away from the kitchen.'

Therese stepped inside, drawn to it, and sat on the chintz-covered bed, which looked and felt like a hard bed for a child. There was little else in the interior, apart from the large paint can, which formed the table for the camping stove, and a set of shelves on the wall to the left, containing smaller, jaunty paint cans, matches and a box of candles. Francis plucked his coat from the back of the door.

'All right?' he asked.

'Yes.'

'I'll leave you to it, then.'

She heard his footsteps go away. It began to patter with rain, an almost comic, whispering sound at first, becoming soporific as the drops hit the roof of the shed with a quiet, musical tempo. Therese closed her eyes. The wooden wall of the shed seemed to hold the warmth of summer and refused to let it go. The rain grew louder. So peaceful, sitting still in a small space of warmth with an open door, and the dizzying smell of man, and joss sticks stuck in a paint can, adding to the heat.

Then she opened her eyes to a different sound. The door, swinging shut, quietly.

Francis met Barbara standing in front of the parlour door, looking for him, scanning the garden anxiously.

'Are you away home, dear?'

'Yes, unless there's anything I can do?'

'Do? There's nothing anyone can do.' The voice was tinged with hysteria, muffled by sadness. 'Matilda was getting better, chatting away, and then she had a heart attack this afternoon at the hospital, so there's another one gone, and we seem to have lost Joseph. No, there's nothing anyone can do. Have you seen Therese?'

'I'm so sorry, Sister. I'll pray for Matilda. Therese? The little one? I thought I heard Agnes say that she'd gone out to help Kim with a sick child or something. An errand of mercy.'

'Well, mercy be damned. We'll need her here. She's no right to run off.'

She was tapping her foot in agitation, then braced herself.

'Off you go, Francis, dear. There'll be plenty to do tomorrow when they bring back the body. I don't suppose there's anyone lingering out there in the rain?'

He shook his head.

'Bless you, what would we do without you?'

The phone rang and she shot back into her office. Francis proceeded over the tiles to the front door, where Agnes sat, red-eyed and waiting for him. He embraced her and detached her with an audible kiss and the whispered words, *Goodnight, Mother,* and closed the door behind him.

CHAPTER THIRTEEN

Thou shalt not kill

There was no doubt about the door being jammed shut and about it being darker inside here. The small window in the door was the only source of light, a square of grey on which Therese kept her eyes fixed when she returned to the chintz couch after feeling for the presence of a handle in the rough wood of the door and finding there was none. Therese could visualise the shiny new latch on the outside of the door. If that was all keeping her inside, she was quite sure she could press it open with her own strength, and one thing she had learned after more than a year in the convent was how to deal with doors and windows warped and stuck by damp. She would be strong enough to get out, but there seemed little point in trying, right this minute, when she was more puzzled than anxious and still suffused with that pleasant laziness. What did it matter if she stayed for a while? Feeling around on the wood of the door had only resulted in a sharp splinter in her palm.

She sat on the bed and looked up at the square of light which was the window in the door, realising as she looked that the relative absence of light changed the contours of her abode. She could see all she needed to see, the outlines of the paint cans on the shelves with their colours more vivid in the half-light, and found herself wondering about the contents. Then she dozed a little. She was simply fulfilling the purpose of a garden, even a small, locked-in corner of a garden like the one she inhabited, and turning it into a place of peace. The long-lasting joss sticks still burned; she stared at the stems of them, sticking out of a paint can on the shelf, rose and took two steps to the door. The window was high and only by standing on tiptoe could she see outside, where the busy lizzies glowed in the grey light and the rain fell.

She went back and sat with her back to the wall, grasping her knees. The wall was warm and seemed to become warmer as the square of light began to fade and the rain made its music on the roof.

There was a nun she had read about who lived in a caravan in the grounds of her own convent, along with volumes of books illustrating the medieval painting which was her passion and her aid to prayer. This sister had featured in a television programme years before and evoked a whole way of life. Therese realised that she had never really had any passions at all, other than the desire not to be touched, prodded, pulled at, and the thought of going on living just like this, on the fringes of sisterhood rather than within it, seemed the best of all options, if she could deal with hunger, thirst and hygiene. Small spaces, spartan surroundings, had their own appeal. They encouraged a degree of acceptance. They were consistent with small ambitions.

A clever person, with different ambitions, like Anna, would have made a greater effort and worked out how to get out by now, Therese thought, but for herself, she would simply wait for whoever had made the mistake of locking her in to rectify it and come along to let her out, and in the meantime, consider the fate of poor Matilda. The Sisters could get their own supper. There was a satisfaction in that.

No need to bother about hygiene, yet. Her bladder seemed to have shrivelled over the last days, and while hunger had begun to gnaw, it did so with small, soft teeth. It was not unpleasant to be timeless and beyond the call of regime, almost weightless and beyond responsibility, lulled into sleep by the warmth and the smells she could now detect. The lingering fumes of paint and creosote, masked by the joss sticks, a hint of cat and, in her nostrils from that brief contact, the smell of Francis himself, making her wonder briefly what it was that made a man smell like that, what her own smell was like, what material covered the roof to make the rain echo the way it did, and then she noticed the small mirror propped on the shelves next to the paint pots, and rose to look at herself. The light was too dim to see anything more than a very pale face, which seemed to consist mainly of eyes, and she was disturbed to see her own reflection, which seemed to have so little to do with herself. The only mirror in the convent was by the front door, where few of them ever looked and only then to check their own dignities before making an exit into the outside world. Otherwise, if the appearance of one of the Sisters was ever defective, a habit hitched up in a belt, a veil not quite straight, another Sister simply adjusted it, discreetly, to murmured thanks. They could all of them dress themselves in the dark and mutely relied on one another to correct the missed details of rudimentary grooming. It reminded her of primates considerately ridding one another of fleas. The mirror reminded her that the light, such as it was, was fading, and she should use it to find the

281

candles she had noticed earlier. Cheap candles, not like the beeswax candles of the chapel, stickier to touch, and when she found one, struck a match and melted the base before sticking it on the shelf, a fresh smell entered the chorus of the others. There, now she could pray. The candle flame, slow and steady without any draught to give it flickering life, was the best aid of all to prayer.

Oh, dear Lord, why are you doing this to me?

Lord, have I sinned, and if so, how? How can I know if I've sinned, unless it's perfectly obvious, or you tell me? Be reasonable, I'm only human.

I don't know if this is punishment . . . And then, thumping the bed impatiently, *Why the hell don't you talk to me? I'm your child.*

She tried the rosary, without benefit of rosary beads, because the rosary was such a useful prayer. The one that allowed daydreaming and prayer at the same time, one Our Father, ten Hail Marys, one Glory Be to the Father, and then begin again. She tried not to daydream, but think of the mysteries, which were the prescribed accompaniment to the stanzas, but found she could only think of the sorrowful ones – Jesus in the garden of Gethsemane, the scourging, Calvary, with the niggling background thought, Oh why, sweet Jesus, why did you let yourself in for that? Why did you think we were worth it and why didn't you escape? What difference did it make? She gave up. The rain stopped.

It was only in the following silence, which seemed to mushroom around her, creating a sensation of stuffy fog, that Therese began to feel the rising of panic. There was no air in here. What little there was was subsumed by the still-glowing joss sticks and the candle flame. She was afraid of staying still, got up and pushed at the door, then banged at it with her fists, but it did not yield, only vibrated with sound. She wanted to tear at her own hair and scream, but was controlled enough to realise that that would make everything worse. This was not a sanctuary, it was a prison cell. She tried to think of a saint in captivity, any saint, and what he or she might do if they were her. Contemplate, offer the indignities to God for the benefit of another soul in purgatory, wait in faith to be released, be patient and still? No. *No.*

Moving lengthways, rather than towards the door, there was a maximum of four small steps between one side of the cell and the other. Therese tried to imagine she was either in the kitchen with Kim, or back inside her bedroom at home, with Anna, long ago, whiling away the hours of illness on a relatively good day. Both of them playing around and teaching themselves the model walk, copying one another in the exaggerated gyration of hips and the silly, one hip forward, head flung back, stroll they had learned from pictures in magazines and a TV programme of ballroom dancing, which they had watched with the sound turned down until they laughed themselves sick and Mother had to take control. The tango-influenced catwalk-model walk looked effortless, but was full of effort. It had exhausted them, and she did it again and again, now. Two steps forward, two back, flung herself on the bed, posed, got up, did it again. In the tenth circuit, dizzy and over-heated, she stripped off her clothes. She would do this until she was beyond doing anything. Something had bitten her: something scratched. Her skin scorched.

It was late afternoon when Christopher Goodwin arrived back in the city. He breathed the air in the underpass which linked the station to the Underground, noting the various flavours of humanity and dirt, artificial light, organised chaos, noticed a couple of homeless boys who had already given up on the day, and wondered if Francis McQuaid had ever been one of those. An unwashed head stuck out of a dirty sleeping bag and he was ashamed of having no money to give, but on balance, he thought he preferred this inhuman, human bustle to the relentless pull of the tide and all that heartless sky. Kay McQuaid should come back: this was home. Although he knew it was irresponsible and he would pay later in conscience for the further neglect of his parish, he detoured via the park. On this Wednesday afternoon, the feast day of St Matthew, apostle, evangelist, symbolised as a man with wings, but once a tax collector, the boys' football team was finishing a game. He stood and watched the sheer energy and grace of their movements, listening with delight to the innocent savagery of their yelling, until he sensed he was watched himself as he stood apart, wondering again if Francis, born simple Jack bastard McQuaid, had ever been one of these, playing football in the drizzle with the express purpose of learning how to break the rules.

On the last regretful circuit of this end of the park, Christopher saw a nun, sitting on a bench, and had a distinct temptation to change route and avoid her. He resisted and, as he drew level, watched to see if she was familiar, hoping she was a complete stranger until he saw with a shock that she was one of what he had sourly come to consider as Barbara's bunch. He could recognise them individually, but never quite remember all of their names, except for the one or two of whom he was fond and the ones who had taken the masculine names, and he remembered Sister Joseph all the more as the one who was frequently mentioned in Sister Barbara's catalogues of trouble, as well as being the one who was drunk, but admirably controlled, at the last meeting. A similar condition seemed to apply to her now. She was not drunk, but under the influence; on the way to being drunk and weeping copiously to add to the dampness of her habit, which was muddy at the hem. Pedestrians crossed the path to avoid her and as he sat down beside her, with the old, familiar irritation that accompanied so many a Christian act, especially one that interrupted progress to more important things when he was hungry and tired, he could see why she was being shunned. Even without the frightening accoutrements of a nun's soiled habit, Sister Joseph was eminently resistible.

'It's Joseph, isn't it?' he asked, with his practised gentleness, which so often emerged as more bracing than sensitive and did so now. 'What ails you, Sister? Can I help? Can I walk you home?'

'Piss off.'

This startled him, to the point of laughter. He was used to the deferential smile, the oh no, Father, it's nothing at all response, which typified their stoic reactions to their own distress, even on a deathbed. It was a deference that had often annoyed him, but he found he did not want the opposite either.

'What's the matter, Sister?'

An inane question, but he had to persist.

'What's the *matter*, you fool of a *man*? What's the *matter*?' Her voice was only slightly slurred and rising, so that he could not gauge the level of her inebriation, although experience of others made him guess it had some way to go before violence or oblivion, whichever took hold first. She was a strong old woman. He had often thought that the residual physical strength of the old must be as

285

frustrating as their weaknesses, a formless, useless energy, and he did not look forward to it. She looked up at him with bleary eyes, identifying him for the first time.

'Christ, it's the bloody priest. Where are you when you're needed? No one could rouse you this morning. Just think, you could have sat with me and Matilda. Sat and listened to her telling me how the devil himself had murdered Edmund and the birds and put poison on her hands. She was in such pain. The devil himself, she told me. And then . . . she died, Father. She died without you.' The voice moved from a hiss to a mumble.

He crossed himself, depressed with guilt. 'Matilda's dead?'

'Matilda's *killed*,' she spat. 'And I loved her. We were *real* sisters. She's the only one who ever loved me.'

Tears flowed. He hesitated, then touched her sleeve gingerly. It was smeared with mucus and tears. She slapped at the hand.

'You must go back, Sister, you'll make yourself ill.'

'Get your hands off me,' Joseph said with deliberate venom. 'Save your worry. I've got money in my pocket and a will of my own. I don't need your *blessing*, I need my anger, so *piss off*. Is there anything about that phrase you don't understand?'

It was, he admitted, perfectly clear and did not allow alternatives. She was an adult woman of God, not a child.

'What did she mean, the devil himself?'

'Piss *off*.'

'If you're sure?'

She nodded emphatically. There was a clear glass bottle sticking out of a cloth bag, which looked like a laundry bag or the shoe bag he had carried to school, on the bench beside her. The bag was bulky, probably with Matilda's things, he thought sadly, and not proof against the rain. He felt in the left pocket of his anorak for the small umbrella that always lived there and he never remembered to use, handed it to her. Joseph looked at it in disdain, took it all the same and stuffed it in the bag.

'Not much of a weapon, is it, Father? I can do better than that. Piss off.'

He knew he would have to come back later and see if she was still there, as well as digest what she had said, but he hurried home. Oh, good God, not another death or another fantasy. The papers crackled inside his jacket, he was no lighter without the umbrella, and for all the strangeness of the meeting, the ghastliness of the last twenty-four hours, he was nursing a small nugget of exhilaration and he had a sense of resolution and purpose, which did not usually come from having too much to do. There was always either too much or too little, with the whole of life revolving around the juggling of priorities, obligations, duties, so that indoors there were messages from Barbara, the office of the Bishop, and twelve others, including the last from the carer of the old, brave invalid whose company he had so often kept in front of the football replay videos, offering no more than mute admiration for bravery and the consolation of another, like-minded presence. They had the same way of praying. The message was a plea for the administration of Extreme Unction. A man wanted blessing for the last rite of passage and there was no choice. Christopher Goodwin changed his trousers, seized his paraphernalia and set out for the other end of his parish.

Ravi was wrong. Anna shunned the park and longed instead for the chapel. Now, look here, Lord. Prayer was an instinctive activity in anyone who had ever become

287

accustomed to it, even if they no longer knew to whom, or what, they prayed. A bad habit, acquired with ease and training, difficult to break, an affliction, a pain-in-the-neck need, which never went away and could never be shared with anyone who had no idea of what you were talking about. Ravi had a religion, so he knew, although he did not know what it was like to pray to Gods who had already abandoned you, and he was wrong about a person being able to do it anywhere. Perhaps he meant anywhere there was a shrine. She meant anywhere it worked well enough to quell the furies, and the places were limited. It had to be a place she loved, the convent chapel, sometimes the park, and otherwise the roof. Other people were probably the same in choosing a place to have an argument. There had to be something to look up at, something to look down on, or something to look across and preserve the idea there was something beyond that and something beyond even that. Anna thought that an aeroplane would be a good place for prayer, provided she could sit near a window.

She was very, very shaken and feeling in a way she could only describe to herself as odd, although that was an understatement, since oddness was her middle name and anyway, there was plenty about which to feel odd and it only created another phrase, *oddgod*, which she was repeating in the same way she once said bother. And then, *How odd of God, To choose Hindus*, a couplet distorted from something else. Oh, oddgod, odgod, doggod, dogged, dogged, dogged. The flat was pristine. She was waiting and knowing in her heart of hearts, as well as in her churning stomach, that Francis, the Golden Boy, was making her wait. He was not late yet, but he would be late soon. The ladder was out, up to the roof. There was time.

She was dressed like a girl, like a miniature tart, in a

288

dress. Floral thingummy, with little roses printed in the lightweight cloth, buttoning up the front from mid-calf to neck and a touch of lace, for oddgod's sake, at the neck. She hated it all but her bare feet, climbing the ladder stack and getting them dirty in the gunwales of the roof, who cared? The thought of the wine in the fridge made her sick.

Better, up on the parapet, with sultry city air cleansed by the rain, which only threatened to resume, but not yet, please oddgod, not yet. She propped her elbows on the parapet, so that they were level with her shoulders, and put her feet inside the shelf she had created between the lead flashing and the brick, to give her a better view. Saw a clear evening, prematurely dark, and the garden further darkened by the lights from the chapel window, although, as yet, she could see the details. There was a breeze, teasing at her long, clean hair, washed again for the occasion.

'Oh Lord, help me. Am I to be a sacrifice? Am I going to have to let him have me in order to get to Therese? Help me to see in the dark.'

Edmund's bench began to fade. She thought she could hear from the chapel the sounds of the singing of the Misericordia. *O clemens, O pia, O dulcis Virgo Maria*, sung in those voices by Jude's graveside, followed by the voice of the hound of heaven. *I fled Him, down the nights and down the days, I fled Him down the arches of the years; I hid from Him* . . . She yelled into the darkening sky, *Just leave me alone*. Let me see. Make me concentrate and make me see all that my fogged-up mind is missing. I am not old, I'm not wise.

First she looked at the sky, which was a blank, bumpy landscape, turning dark, but not dark enough for stars. There was nothing on which to focus the eyes, no nice arrangement of clouds, no inspirational moon. She watched the branches of the trees, daring them to move, and then she looked at the window of the chapel, so brightly lit that the shape of it, upturned boat or bishop's hat, was appealingly clear and the desire to be on the other side as sharp as homesickness. To the left of this beacon, lower down, there was a visible light from the parlour windows and from the rooms on the floors above. The place seemed lit for a celebration, indicating crisis, visitors, or a death. This was the way it had looked on the night Sister Jude died, as if the death of a Sister created the need to bustle and spring-clean, to fix everything so that the gap was obscured. They were busy.

There was no birdsong, not a single cry of alarm.

Anna concentrated on the smaller details, the shape of the flower tubs, the shiny damp path into the shrubbery, the point where St Michael stood, currently visible, and then let her eyes follow the path to the point further down where the bushes obscured it and where she had been when Francis had intercepted her. She could not pinpoint the exact spot, but focusing on the likely place made her begin to think of everything she knew about the Golden Boy and place it in the context of what he had said. She knew nothing, but looking at the garden, she could see what he had done.

There were no birds any more.

There was Edmund's bench, with the light, scrubbed wood of it still visible in the clear area surrounding it. Francis had obliterated any sign of his predecessor and mentor so that it was difficult to remember that Edmund had ever existed at all. Edmund, whom she had watched neglecting the garden and feeding the birds with whom he shared that filthy bench. Ironic that Edmund was the gardener who should have been called Francis, after the saint who could magic the birds from the skies. Now there were dead birds in the garden, she had trodden on one; dead birds and a killing cat. The wrongly named Francis had lied last night. Edmund would never have shot at a bird, any bird, and he would never have broken the window. Francis would have done that as part of his ruthless cleansing operation and his preliminary step to the gaining of power. She thought of how he would have achieved that power, first by breaking Edmund's hold on the place, then by becoming indispensable and always by being beautiful. His saintly beauty and his sex, powerful passwords. Agnes would let him to and fro whenever he pleased; Barbara adored him. There was no place sacrosanct, nothing he could not contradict. And then, although she had played a part in her own banishment through her stupidity, it was he who had achieved it. She stroked her fingers down the side of her face, remembered his hand holding her claw and raking it down his own face. The scratches had made him even more beautiful. Why, when she had faced him the night before, had that memory faded, melted by that self-same, humble charm? Why had she believed him? She clenched her own hand into a fist and looked at it. A small, puny weapon.

And as for Therese sending the bird . . . Therese would never have touched a dead bird, except, perhaps, to bury it. She would have been afraid; she was fastidious. *Look at what Francis has done to the birds*.

Then she remembered Edmund's fist, his arm outstretched on the bench, with the gold crucifix and broken chain lying next to it, which she had thought was his and preserved for Matilda until Francis had reclaimed it. A thing he had worn since childhood, almost outgrown. Too small by far for Edmund's fleshy neck. A hypocritical adornment, a badge of solidarity, an indication of faith. She thought of it being inside her pocket alongside the statue of Ganesh, and, staring at the bench now, imagined Edmund in the throes of dying, ripping the crucifix from the neck of the man who might have helped him. Or murdered him. The scene enacted itself in front of her eyes with hideous clarity. Matilda was the only one who might have known. Matilda with her bright eyes, and burned hands. He would have seen to that, too.

Craning over the parapet, she could just see the back door to the garden. That was how he came and went. He did not even need the complicity of Agnes. Most of all, she remembered her frantic scouring of the place the night before, the instinct to eradicate traces of him, although as he had sat there, she had believed everything he said and the mist of credulity had descended. She had been sorry for him; she had wanted to be liked. *Oh, Lord*, she said. *We believe what we want to believe.* And disbelieve what does not suit. Was it you who phoned with the warning? *Good people do not see evil. Evil has no inhibitions.*

She looked at the luminous dial on her watch. She could hear the door buzzer from here. Francis had not arrived and what was more, she could see now that he had never intended to arrive on this particular night. That promise was yet another lie. Perhaps he enjoyed the idea of her waiting for him, a piece of control, designed to humble her and make her long for him next time. Or perhaps it was something else. Perhaps he simply needed her to be captive in her own flat, waiting as he could guess she would wait for the very mention of Therese, or out of the pathetic desire for love or friendship; she would wait, poor, lonely, powerless thing. And then she remembered the other words, *You are even prettier than your sister,* and retched over the wall. He had never wanted her. He wanted her out of the way, and with that settled conviction came another, namely that Therese was suffering.

When they had been ill, their symptoms were originally different, but had come to coincide as if they cross-infected one another, and then it was more than that. It had turned into a physical empathy with how the other felt, an instinctive knowledge, which lessened with health and absence, but still persisted. In the friendlier conversations, the normal ones that followed the confrontational ones after Therese joined the convent, they had laughed about it. Thought of you yesterday, Therese would say. Did you have toothache, because I did. And period pain? Yes. Now, on the parapet, her empty stomach was churning. She felt for her sister an almighty fear, as if Therese was up alongside her and about to jump, and she felt for Francis the Golden Boy a hatred so intense it would have poisoned the moon. He was a monstrous corruption. Instinct said it all. Instinct knew best. He killed the birds. He would hurt and corrupt and never know conscience.

She could not bear to look at the bench, which now blurred into nothing as the last light died and she vainly tried to concentrate on what little she could see, willing it to expand into clarity. The outline of the shed was just visible. There was a light inside.

A tiny, flickering light, so small she could have imagined it. A signal, the arc light of the chapel window pointing the way to the tiny light in Edmund's store.

Lamb of God who takest away the sins of the world, have mercy on us . . . Agnes was muttering, grumbling and frantic and confused and hungry and . . . *Agnus Dei, qui tollis peccata mundi.* Joseph had come home and God bless them all. This was no way to respect the dead, no way at all, coming home from the care of dear Matilda, stinking of the drink and shouting like a banshee, all over the black and white corridor, half sick, half demented, the colour of a bruised plum and yelling, *Where is he, where is he?* not even able to remember if it was day or night. *Where's who, Sister? Who do you mean?* and only getting back, *Where is she, where is she, the bitch?* In the name of the blessed virgin, they couldn't call the police to one of their own, and if only Francis would come back, her darling son, and instead of him, there was Anna running down the road in a pretty frock and those ugly training shoes she wore and which she herself privately craved. Agnes was not going to let in anyone else who made trouble and the only person she wanted to gain entry was her own darling boy. Or maybe the priest. Heaven help her, she was sick of the sight of women. After she slammed the door shut, and returned to her cubicle, waiting against hope for either the food to which they had not been called, or the return to order, which Barbara would surely restore, she put the phone under her chair where it had rested all evening with the receiver detached. She had taken the unilateral decision that they had enough to cope with, and from the depths of the black and white corridor, she could hear Joseph, shouting, tried to close her ears to what Joseph said and could not. Joseph had a way with words.

Fuelled by fear, it was even easier for Anna to get up to the top of the wall than it had been the last time. Bugger who watched, let them. She could kick, she could scream, she could yell, and the extra power came from thinking, if they close that door on me one more time . . . Ripping the dress while straddling the wall did not matter either; she tore a strip off the hem when she paused at the top, wrapped the material round her wrist like a bracelet, and then slithered down the other side with sickening speed, because the ivy was wet and slippery as oil, so that she clutched enough to impede freefall and landed with a silent thud that winded her and shook her into where she was. It was the time of the evening when sounds from outside penetrated as far as they ever would in here. The jarring of the final landing made her breathless, squatting where she landed, suddenly as careful as a cat. And there *was* the cat, eyeball to eyeball. She hissed at it, watched it scurry away, scared of her.

You are even prettier than your sister. Stronger, too. Anna tiptoed from the back door towards the area of the bench, looking for the clutter which had been visible from the window only three weeks before and was now startling for its absence. The scent of autumn flowers arrested her, but the flickering light from the shed drew her into the circle outside it. She could hear whimpering from the half-open door, felt the waft of body heat and sweat. Whimpering from the body beneath the other body on the patterned fabric she could see through the door, in tune with the voice of the Golden Boy, who half knelt, glisteningly naked, with his long legs too long for the couch, above the body of her sister, who lay face down with her hands clutched in her hair, saying no, Mother, no, trying to prise together the legs he had forced apart with his knees, so that her forelegs thrashed without purpose, and as she watched, he bent his whole torso towards her and bit her ear. You know you want this. You waited for me, naked. I am your brother. We do it this way so you don't have to watch, trust me.

Anna hesitated. Then she took in the detail of the way he massaged his enormous prick and smeared it with spit

295

while his other, big, brown hand, held down Therese by the neck. Therese might want this, but Therese was held by the neck. Passion did not whimper, did it? And then Therese screamed, bucked, used all her tiny weight to shrug him away. Anna felt around for a stone. His voice reverberated. *Shush, no one'll hear, sister.*

She was going to kill him, smash in his head, now. To the mind's echo, *Thou shalt not kill, or suffer the death of thine own soul.*

Golden Boy had left a pile of jagged lumps of concrete. She found one at her feet. She was going to kill him.

And then she was knocked sideways. A figure in black superseded her, yanked open the door, and punched repeatedly at that naked back as if she was trying to revive it, making repetitive, unrepeatable sounds, *hmuph, hmumph, humph,* then *humph, humph, humph,* as if she was digging into his neck. The screams grew into a symphony, his like an electrified pig, hers the sound of fury, and the body beneath adding a whimpering chorus. Then Sister Joseph of Aragon yanked back Francis's head and plunged her small-bladed knife into his throat. She did it with a degree of determined attachment, seven times, and even in the frenzy of the attack avoided his eyes. The candle fell with the vibration of movement, caught at the damp hem of her gown, flared and went out. After that, it was all darkness and voices.

Anna dropped her lethal piece of concrete. She ran to the shed and dragged Therese from beneath a warm and twitching body. She heard only the sound of the incessant sobbing, which came from Joseph. Then there was a flurry of Sisters surrounding Therese, shushing her, covering her, leading her gently back to the house, three of them, masking the bloody nakedness and saying there, there, there. Someone else took Joseph, equally gently. Barbara remained, scuffing the earth with her shoe, addressing the sky with her authoritative voice, shining her torch into the open doorway. The Golden Boy closely resembled Sebastian, with his multiple wounds. She stepped inside and felt for a pulse, stepped back, with blood on her hands.

'Fed Joseph drink, did he? Burned Matilda's hands, did he? Did you think I was a total fool, Francis? Well, so I was, you devil. You try to rape a bride of Christ and you're as dead as I've been blind.'

Her anger was shimmering hot, the voice colder than ice.

Anna stood behind her. Agnes and Margaret stood either side. Anna wanted to go to Therese, soon she would go to Therese, and even now, in the midst of everything else, she felt an overpowering relief that it was not her who had done this. Three reedy voices rose into the air, chanting. *To you we cry, poor banished children of Eve, to you do we send up our sighs, mourning and weeping in this vale of tears . . . Turn then your eyes of mercy towards us. O clemens, O pia, O dulcis Virgo Maria . . .*

They faltered on the notes. Then there was a long silence. Barbara's torchlight did not waver. Her bosom heaved.

'Right,' she said. 'Do we bury him or burn him?'

She turned to the others.

A small voice, coming from nowhere, said that perhaps they should call for the priest.

CHAPTER FOURTEEN

In the second week of the month, Kay McQuaid busied herself in the middle of a rainy day by dragging the golden Buddha out of the house and down to the back fence, where she could see it from the kitchen window. It tarnished to a fuller sheen almost overnight. For something else to do the next day, she surrounded it with small evergreen shrubs of the kind she had been told would attract the birds. She buried a small gold crucifix on a chain amongst them. Standing with gin in hand and sweat on her brow, she decided she needed more work of the same kind and went back into town for dozens of bulbs to plant for the spring. The statue had already melded into the right place, and sat there, contentedly, surrounded by fertile attention. It was the best she could do to create a shrine and it gave her peace of a kind. Next year, she would really get to work out here, now that she knew she was not going anywhere else. Make something of it. Scrap those neat borders and fill it with shaggy shapes and colours. She muttered a guilty prayer of thanks, for feeling safe. The garden would help her make amends. It would be a labour of love. Someone Up There, whoever it was, would approve.

The third week of October, and by some miracle, there was a fire lit in the parlour.

'I don't have much belief in the existence of the devil, myself,' Father Goodwin was saying to Anna. 'I find him far too convenient a concept. Evil, yes, the devil, no. Not a devil with horns and a tail. Maybe a fallen angel. That's the way Satan started, after all. The angel separated from God in a messy divorce.'

They were sitting in the back of the chapel, talking in normal voices as if the crucifix did not loom over them. The place smelled clean and chilly with the side windows open. Not a trace of incense or added decoration. There had been no recent funerals; those four in the four weeks behind that, Sister Jude, Edmund, Matilda, Jack McQuaid, had all been conducted with the fullest of honours and amounted to a record and now there had been none for a month. It often happened like that, Christopher Goodwin had stated, firmly. A cycle of disasters do not amount to a permanent pattern, like the corridor floor. Nothing is predictable, other than seasons, and now we have the welcome hint of winter, with the promise of dark, protective nights, things on toast and the blessing of sleep. Think of that and other small mercies.

'Thank you for that, Christopher, but I do not think it is an idea I could share with Therese. It is easier for her to believe in simple miracles. Such as the devil in disguise taking on a human form, just as Christ is supposed to have done, although with the opposite purpose. It's more picturesque to believe in two superhuman men slugging it out, with the devil as the force for evil, which only God can recognise and destroy. It makes it easier to rely on God.'

He thrust his hands under his armpits in order to warm them.

'Well, then, she is not equipped for the Christian life, or any religious life, for that matter. If she clings to such concepts, particularly if she trusts in the ultimate reliability of God, she denies herself essential knowledge. As soon as a God takes on human form, which all Gods do, they take on frailty, also. And they are frail. They can only work in co-operation with us. Likewise the so-called devil, and Francis was not the devil incarnate, whatever Therese wants to believe. Although he may have evolved into something dev-ilish, with plenty of human help.'

'But he was *evil*, wasn't he? Not born, but made, I con-cede that, but he must have been already fully evolved when he came here. Beyond redemption. Perhaps it's better to say he was cursed . . .'

'I prefer that,' Father Goodwin interrupted, adjusting himself to the uncomfortable rush seat. 'Cursed, rather than innately evil. Cursed in a way to which many other people contributed. Including his abandoned mother, his friends he may not have chosen, and the way he came to look for recognition. A cursed man will take revenge for the absence of an identity.'

'He was a rent boy . . . once?'

Christopher sighed. 'Yes, I'm told so. From time to time. Which is why the police are disposed to believe that he was a sexual deviant, caught in the act and killed in vicarious self-defence, as he richly deserved, by a woman not in command of her right mind.'

'And all that's true, too. In a manner of speaking.'

He thought of Kay McQuaid and the annotated version

of events he had tried to give her, until he saw how she preferred the truth.

'In a manner of *convenient* speaking, although I might
not take the risk of setting it in stone. I am afflicted by the
idea that after he came here, there may have been moments
when he could have been redeemed if he had not been so
positively misjudged. You cannot know for certain sure if
he killed Edmund or merely watched him die. Or if, when
he delivered you to Barbara to the tune of lies, he was
merely trying to consolidate a position he knew was precarious, because it always was, you know. Nor do we know
if he *intended* Matilda's fate, or if his jealous washing of St
Michael's feet was intended as a favour to her. Or a favour
to the saint, or a response to a request. He was a *tidy* and
domesticated man, like his mother. And how strange it was
that he *signalled* what he had done, and what he was going
to do, at every turn, as if he wanted to be stopped . . . He let
his mother know he was there, he wore the crucifix . . . We
don't know what moved him. We do not know, either, if he
actually locked Therese in her cell, or if the door jammed.'

'It was him who came back, nobody else.'

'And found a naked girl, waiting for him.'

'He came back. He orchestrated it. You can't suggest
otherwise.'

'No, I don't suggest otherwise. But the nakedness was a
contributory factor, and that *is* my point entirely. Therese
had no idea of what she had aroused by being what she was
and where she was, but she still contributed, even with
innocence, just as she did otherwise. The point, my dear, is
that devils, if they exist, thrive on circumstance. They grad-
uate because of ignorance. They are not clever enough to
invent the culture that lets them thrive and cannot, should
not, be blamed for everything.'

'And you are the devil's advocate.' She sat down in the aisle. 'Making the opposite point that virtue cannot afford to be blind or it isn't real virtue. And also that anyone can do a wicked deed by default, since neither God nor the devil know what the hell they're doing. She won't find that particularly helpful. I don't find it nearly as useful as my own intelligence.'

'Exactly, my dear. You've arrived where we began.'

She stood, physically restless, but otherwise calm. The long hair was cropped: she looked like an adolescent boy with feminine curves. His heart ached for her survival, by which he meant survival with honours, so that she might become the extraordinary woman he knew she could be. Someone who could love and be loved and act on that furious intellect, perhaps with a belief to sustain her, any positive belief. He had hopes for her, such hopes, they made him determined to stay alive and do what he was good at. Nurture. Debate. Talk. They had been debating and discussing every known fact every day. The chapel was the place for it. She paced forward and then back, sat down again.

'You don't think I haven't thought of any of that, or imagined alternative explanations to the poor old devil, do you? I've had no choice about that. After all, I might have killed Francis myself, on no better basis than what I thought I could *see*, and while I believe my impulse was right, and he was cursed, I sincerely wish he was not dead, whatever he was. I can't see the justice in that. It was my family that added a crucial contribution to the evolution of Francis. And it was my father who set the whole thing running by inventing that wretched, meaningless will. That was what started the last chapter, and then there was *us*, continuing it by not reading his letters. We contributed too.'

302

'You were very young.' *Us*, he noticed. *We*. Not Therese. Anna was still taking responsibility for Therese. She still wanted that burden.

'Let's go out in the garden for a cigarette.'

'No. It's cold. The Lord won't mind if we smoke in here. The Apostles probably smoked dope at the Last Supper, for God's sake. Here, have one of mine. When can I meet Kay McQuaid?'

'When she's ready. Do you know, I think you're perverse enough to actually *like* her.'

'Unless she's changed, I always did. She was kind to me. How else do you judge?'

'Anyway,' Christopher said, looking at his watch, 'you were starting on the last chapter, but the story began with the first. It started with a rape. It started with a child no one wanted, but no one could destroy. It started with Jack McQuaid's isolation. It continued, after a few intervening chapters, with your father's grief and bitterness on a cold wet night when he drafted a will. Probably after a few drinks. You know what an influence that can be.'

She thought of herself pulling faces at Barbara, that abiding shame which somehow persisted.

'Tell me again what Francis said to you when you arrived in time for the last Sacrament. When he wasn't quite dead.'

'He said, *Tell them their father was a good man.*'

'It sounds like an act of contrition. And highly ambiguous. *Which* father? Forgive me, Christopher, I'm not entirely sure I believe you.'

'You know very well that I cannot influence what you believe.'

'I believe that God, some God, some hound of heaven, helped me to see, and helps me still. I no longer have the

303

arrogance to deny the existence of Gods, nor do I want to, but I couldn't just believe in one. Monotheism is what makes for wars. Anyway, not one of them can make me see clearly enough why my father did it. I don't mean write the will, but write it that way and send it.'

This was old ground.

'Pay attention, that's all, and then you can see. Use your intelligence. He wanted to attract your attention. He wanted you to think. He wanted you to know what moved him to write such a document. He wanted you to be curious, at least. He wanted to upset and surprise you into thinking and discovering. He wanted you to know what he was like. He was terrified that you would be perverted by your mother's religious mania, and he was furious with you, and of course, he never intended this result either. Never in a million years. No one could ever have planned this. He merely wanted to provoke.'

She puffed at the cigarette and watched sacrilegious smoke spiral into the air in the direction of the side window. The bare branches of the trees beyond the big, curved window they faced moved gently. It was these they addressed when they avoided the eyes of each other.

'Christopher, I think it's a bit much to expect me to forgive Francis for what he was and did, or my father, for that matter. I loathe that old cliché, to understand all is to forgive all, blah, blah, blah. It denies the right to be angry, which is often more constructive.'

'Oh, blah, blah, blah, it happens to be true, and I expect no such thing, but invite you to consider. The impact of the works of the so-called devil is not always entirely negative, I think. Look at what Francis has done by accident. Made your sister re-evaluate her vocation, sooner rather than later. Made her remember the hand of your mother pressing against her neck? Jolted her into an existence based on truth? Made you and she recognise the murderous potential of love and lies . . .'

'Also of good intentions. And made me grateful for Joseph. For doing what I might have done. From which I would not have recovered my heart, my soul or anything. I owe her my life.'

'That is her sole consolation. Apart from the fact that she killed him in revenge for Matilda and does not really regret it, she is comforted by the fact that she saved another from the same deed. I was merely hoping that you might have been able to forgive your father, in the same, exceptionally generous way you seem to have been able to forgive your mother.'

'Now, wait a minute . . . What is this? This imposition of virtue? Christopher, we've talked so much, I'm beginning to talk like an old cleric like you. Make no mistake, I don't *forgive* her. To use your *vernacular*, I've simply done her the courtesy of trying to understand what dreadful fear she felt for us, what dreadful madness in herself it was that made her imprison us, what fear of abandonment she had, and her only saving grace is the fact I know it was not hatred. I think she was stupid, beyond self-analysis, full of self-loathing. What she did was a perversion of love, but I'm a long way from forgiving, you better believe. I blame *Him*.' She jerked her thumb in the direction of the crucifix. 'Blessing her every action. Good boy, Jesus.'

This moved him to anger, so that he almost shouted. One of the Sisters was at the door and went away, rapidly. What had this child done to him, apart from renew his faith? He could not have Christ impugned and insulted.

'*No*, He did not! She reinvented the God who would do that. People reinvent God all the time. To whom do you

305

think the terrorist prays? The God of his Bible, or the God of his own invention?'

She grinned at him and he groaned. He was always taking the bait.

'I knew that would get you going. Let's go in the garden, after all. It's wrong to smoke in here.'

'Yes, let's.'

He shuffled nervously out of the chapel, through the parlour, looking round as if pursued. How odd of God to make it warmer out here than in that chilly, elegant space. They finished the cigarettes by the statue of St Michael. Christopher seemed anxious and she felt protective about his persistence and what it cost him, but also cautious. She didn't wish anyone else messing with her mind. She had had enough of that. It didn't want messing with, it wanted all the education it had missed, exercise. It wanted to learn.

'What about your father?' he asked, sweeping the ash from St Michael's foot. If she wanted him to go further into this garden, he would not, could not: it haunted him as the place where he would always arrive too late. She took a deep breath. Nothing else in the last month had made her tearful. Not even telling Ravi it was better they did not see each other until she was a little further down some path or other, maybe then, when she was fit.

'What about my father? I wish, wish, wish I had known him. I wish it had been allowed. I wish it wasn't the reason for not being able to forgive my mother, because that was the worst she did. She taught us to hate him, because she did. I suppose we *contributed*. I suppose he did. How lonely he must have been, lonelier than me, and all I can remember is the laughter in church. The questions. He was like me, he's as angry as me. I'd have liked the chance for a row.

I've had no one to learn from and only religion to rebel against. I'd have liked the chance to make reparation. The chance to put it right, as far as it could be. To take back misjudgement and all that bloody ignorance.'

Christopher Goodwin felt himself beginning to sweat.

'Even if he was manipulative, a player of games? Occasionally untruthful?'

'So are the best of people, when they need to be. I might be all of those things, you certainly are, so was Sister Jude. It depends on the motive. You can be all of those things in a vain attempt to be good. Or be listened to. Or avoid causing hurt. They're not incompatible.'

She let out a long, regretful sigh.

'So, I've only got one problem, Christopher, and it's the one I can't handle. One great big area of sheer self-pity. And it's all because I'm just too young to be an orphan. I wish I wasn't. It's the gap I can't cure with my mind. It puts me at risk of creating something unreal, to fill the gap. I feel *cheated*. And so was my father.'

He tried to breathe deeply, speak slowly and carefully, and still choked on the words.

'I think he should be waiting in the parlour, by now. Twelve o'clock, he said.'

'*What?*'

'Your father. You might recognise his voice. Although he's quite good at disguising it.'

She stood up and wiped a trace of grime from the back of her jeans. Then slapped her own face, lightly, to stop herself trembling. He blanched, as if he could feel the imprint of her hand. Then she laughed uncertainly.

'Is this a miracle? You liar. I thought we agreed you would never lie to me.'

'And I never have,' he said, crossing his fingers behind

307

his back. 'Not about your father's grief or his motives or why he found his life so unbearable he made a will and disappeared. Or about what he hoped to achieve by dying. The attention of his daughters' souls. An elaborate, stupid, selfish, wicked conspiracy, because he did not die. He simply waited. And as we discussed, the devil himself is rarely worse than a man with good intentions.'

'You talk too much. He phoned me. It was *him*. I used to dream it was him. Oh Christ, you bastard. What on earth shall I say? Where did you say he was?'

'You heard me the first time. In the parlour. Why else would Barbara light a fire?'

She ran. Christopher sat by the feet of St Michael and marvelled how clean they were. Then turned his eyes to the sky and the comforting presence of buildings. For a minute or more, before he failed to resist the temptation to spy. They would not notice.

He could see Theodore Calvert. A very small man, the way he had always imagined Christ and St Christopher to be, small and determined, perhaps a touch aggressive. A little like a rude Italian restaurant owner who knew his food was better than anyone else's.

Anna stood a few feet away from her father. They examined each other, warily. She was not going to be fooled by the tears, which almost made her speechless. Almost. He could not speak. She spoke first.

'So where have you been, all this time?'

'Somewhere like hell,' he said.

'And what's that like?'

He sighed, stumbled on words.

'I think you know. I think you've been there. You carry it with you. A crown of thorns.'

She crossed the room to him then, a small, almost ugly man, instantly familiar with his dome of a forehead and a face as creased and vibrant as an old hound and tears on his chin. She grabbed at his jacket and tugged his hair to prove he was real, and then held on, tightly. They swayed in a clumsy embrace, holding each other upright.

'I'm sorry,' he muttered into her shoulder. 'I'm so sorry. I shouldn't have . . . shouldn't . . .'

'Stop saying that. We're neither of us going to say that. Don't, don't, *don't*.'

He had a deep, broken voice.

'Oh, thank God. Thank God.'

They stood in silence. The fire crackled. Barbara had spared no expense.

Her own voice sounded small from the depths of his jacket.

'Did you really say that?'

'What did I say? Oh, thank God you're alive . . . Thank God.'

'Did you hear yourself, Dad? Did you hear yourself say that? Will you listen to yourself? Shame on you. You never thanked God for anything.'

He had a fine-tuned laugh, remarkably like her own. The sound of their gulping laughter reached the roof, until Anna detached herself from him, still holding his hands at arm's length, to look at him again from head to toe, still crying.

'Oh, Dad, what am I going to do with you?' she wailed. 'I've told everyone you were a big man. A giant. How am I going to take you anywhere?'

He had a wide smile, like hers.

'I'll just stay sitting down.'

★

309

Christopher Goodwin thought he had never heard anything more beautiful than laughter. Except, perhaps, the roar of a crowd. In a minute, the two of them might be arguing and that would be fine, too, entirely natural, in fact. He had told Theodore Calvert not to have any illusions about reclaiming his daughters' lives. Or imagining he could tell them what to do.

He blew his nose and considered the next problem. It would be a little harder to persuade Kay McQuaid that her boy had done some good. Because, as rumour had it, when you did good, you were supposed to mean it.

The Nature of the Beast

To Hilary Hale;
absolutely.

ACKNOWLEDGEMENTS

Novels are written in isolation, but inspired by human contact. (E-mail does not do the trick.) Thanks to Charles Cook, veterinary surgeon, for his help on the subject of dogs. Thanks also to Carolyne Osborn, creator of fantastic follies in miniature and whose book, *Small Scale Modelling*, informs many of these pages. My knowledge of libel law was supplied by Robert O'Sullivan, an honest barrister-at-law and handsome with it. (For appointments, phone his clerk.) All mistakes and misinterpretations are my own, not all of them deliberate. Last but not least, my thanks to Brian Thorpe, for his ability to describe a building so well that the place enters the imagination and becomes entirely real.

FOREWORD

Letter to Helen West from Elisabeth Manser
August 8th

Dear Helen,

Here I am, sitting and chewing the varnish off my fingernails, when I should be writing a report, as you ordered. You've been very kind and supportive, but you always were bossy. *Write your version of this case in numbered paragraphs, beginning with your name and your role in the proceedings*, that's what you said. Only a real lawyer like you could make a request like that.

I can't do it. It isn't a *case*, it's an episode in a series of lives including my own and I want to be outside in the garden. I may well be a lawyer, too; this story is littered with lawyers, but I never really liked the law. Too dry and clever for me. *You* told me to write it down in a way to round it off and make sense of it, which is the

sort of activity which suits you down to the ground, but
not me. You think I know all the facts, and it's facts you
want. Rubbish. Of course I don't know all the facts.
Nobody ever does. To start with, I know bugger all
about *love*.

Anyway, I can't write this report. Quite apart from
the other problems about being truthful, I've no experience of rich people, which is one of the reasons which
make this *reporting* so difficult. I've never known the
sort of people who are so rich that they don't have to go
to work, and have the houses and pastimes to go with
all that. Which is why I didn't understand that Douglas
and Amy Petty were different and therefore irritating to
his nearest and dearest, for not being content with
beautifying their house and showing off. If I was rich,
I'd want to show off; what's the point, otherwise?
Neither do I understand people who are dotty about
dogs, and I only have the sketchy background I had for
the case.

Numbered paragraphs, you said, as if that would make
all the difference to my lack of discipline. The sun is shining and all I can hear is the sound of someone lecturing
me. Your voice, or John's voice, so, I shall obey.

*1) All right. My name is Elisabeth Manser. I am a
non-senior barrister, although hardly junior in years,
only in status. In the spring of this year, I was
employed in the case of Petty v Associated Press, as the
carrier of bags, researcher, gofer and dogsbody for John
Box, QC, who is the man to hire in a libel case, on*

account of him having brains and a flair for tactics
and a rather fine face. Juries love him, even when he
sniffs. Douglas Petty was our client. He had been
libelled and he wanted to fight his corner to preserve
his reputation.

2) What reputation? Well, our client was once a glamorous bachelor with a notable career as a criminal
barrister, before he disgraced himself ten times over. He
has an amazing, mellifluous voice. Should have bot-
tled it and sold it; there was nothing else to recommend
him. He was a lesser celebrity of sorts, slightly famous
for colourfully amateur charity stunts. He was
bankrolled in his youth by an eccentric and rich, self-
made father, who spoiled him rotten and finally left
him a house with a lot of money, hedged in with a lot
of conditions. The conditions included the care of a
stepmother and stepsister who had nursed him as a
child through a freak attack of polio, which might
explain a lot about his attitude to them. The other condition of his inheritance was the carrying on of a dog
sanctuary.

3) The dog sanctuary was started by his father in the
stables of the house and it was/is weird. Weird, because
it was more of a hospice for old, sick dogs ready to be
put down. Douglas had this passionate belief that dogs
should be allowed to live out their natural span unless
they were in pain, and he was very outspoken about
it. He married late, forty-fiveish, surprising everyone

*because he did not marry the dark, slim, slightly
aristocratic kind of model he usually courted, but a
proper size fourteen blonde nonentity with big knock-
ers! A part-time beautician/aromatherapist, got picked
up in a nightclub, got lucky and Douglas got a wife to
bully.*

*4) The wedding hit the gossip pages on a dull day.
Newspapers always liked Douglas. He was rich,
charismatic, evil-tempered, with a wonderful house
and a loud moral agenda. He was absolutely ideal for
defamation. Such a silly, tinpot libel at a time when
there was a dearth of other news, or no national paper
would have run it. Who cared? Libel is a rich man's
hobby.*

*5) Douglas and silly Amy Petty had been living in the
house along with his stepmother and the dog sanctuary
he was planning to extend. Amy was helped and advised
by her stepsister-in-law, Caterina, a frequent visitor …*

Oh, sod it, I can't write this. I haven't, as John Box
would say, the *objectivity*, or as you would say, the *concentration* to be other than lazy and careless. Besides, how
can I write a report when I was part of the saga? I can't
think in straight lines. I can only jot down a few separate
scenes from what I saw and imagined and from what
Rob, the trolley man, told me. I can only begin it with the
first day, the first day when it began to *matter* to me, and
then I can only let the whole thing follow a route of

its own, like a train on defective rails, running on to somewhere. I think in scenes, because I played a part. An accidental part in the manner of an understudy who wandered into the role by mistake. That's all I can do for now, Helen. Set it rolling with the first scenes. I'll write the report another day.

Elisabeth Manser

Scene One

As the train sped through a slice of darkness and on into the sudden brightness of the spring day, she remembered being teased. *The trouble with you, Amy, is that when you say you see a light at the end of the tunnel, you mean a train coming in the opposite direction.* But she had never earned a reputation for pessimism. It was only the nervousness which was habitual.

No; she was a blithe spirit, rocking slightly in her seat in the svelte, half empty InterCity train, going from a small Kent town to London. The train gave the impression of condescension. It was too big for their suburban station and seemed to sigh to a halt there as if it was too much trouble to stop in such an insignificant place. It flowed towards cities like a snake on invisible wheels, utterly confident of its destination, and as she sat inside, near the back, she wished it would go on and on, so that she did not have to get off.

What if I told him? I'll ruin everything. I can't. I'll make everyone unhappy.

A lounge lizard of a train; a clumsy, elongated lizard, rather than a snake. Something on invisible rollers, slithering towards a city to hide under buildings instead of a rock. Amy was alarmed by her ever-increasing tendency to find some equivalent in the animal world in everything she saw. The process of making the comparisons had been confined to familiar human beings at first; thus Douglas was a Rottweiler with blunt ears, carrying the paper in a soft mouth, and Caterina was a kitten. The woman in the local shop was a horse, baring her teeth and flicking her tail, while the man on the checkout at the Cash and Carry was a pig. So obvious. The ticket collector on this train was a ferret with invisible teeth, his hair brushed into a spike of aggression; a ferret or a weasel, and the trolley man, Rob, was a mournful labrador. It worried her that the comparisons went beyond that and extended themselves to objects, so that here she was, sitting inside a lounge lizard on an upholstered seat which felt like a sheep. She lived in a house which was a big, sharp crystal. It had reached the point of absurdity. She was either living in a farmyard or a jungle, on the run from humankind. What would it be like in a courtroom? She would react as if she was in a zoo: she might laugh like a hyena and point.

There were a couple sitting diametrically opposite, arguing in the semi-silent way of circling cats who have not yet begun to fight, snarling quietly at one another.

The light at the end of the tunnel is only a train coming in the opposite direction. A shift of direction, the lizard turning east and the sun piercing through the gaps in buildings like a laser, straight into her eyes through the glass of her spectacles. She closed her eyes briefly, ready to bask in it, at home in this carriage, with her overstuffed handbag (which was like a puppy, fast asleep) nuzzled by her side and the man in the seat opposite shouting into his mobile phone. He resembled a small elephant speaking into its own trunk. 'Hallo Sylvie? Yah, yah, yah. I'm on the train. Just coming in now. Should be with you in fifteen . . .' Why on earth did anyone need to know that? Amy believed that mobile phone users simply spoke into them on trains to prove they had someone to listen. There was no Sylvie; she was an invention and he merely used the phone to stop himself sucking his thumb.

Amy bent her face to her magazine in case he should sense her observation, but he had caught her glance and smiled at her. *Smug elephant leers at grey squirrel.* He probably leered at someone every morning. Being leered at was supposed to be preferable to being ignored. She was wondering about that proposition and deciding she did not agree. She was wishing she was the sort of person strong enough to hit him.

Then the spectacles flew off her face. In that split second, she thought he had leaned forward and grabbed them away in some bizarre revenge for being viewed as an elephant. She saw the raw tentacles of a metal octopus whip against the windows in outrageous fury; she gripped hold of the puppy handbag and the whole world tilted sideways. A flying object hit the side of her head, hard. The elephant man bellowed with rage. *Will they miss me? No, they won't.*

Scene Two

Two men, one stocky and wolfish-looking, casually dressed; the other thin and dressed in a suit. A woman in her thirties, too plump for fashion, also dressed in a suit. She was asking the questions.

'Is it true, Mr Petty, that your wife used to be a model?'

'What's that got to do with anything? I thought you wanted to talk about the dogs.'

'I only asked.'

'Well, unask. Irrelevant.'

'But if she used to be a model and a beautician, mightn't that influence her judgement? Her taste, I mean. You know, party girl and all that, and she was, wasn't she?'

He leaned forward, intimidating, his eyes shining with irritation, not so much infuriated as simply impatient.

'I repeat, what has this to do with anything?'

'Genes, Mr Petty . . . I think . . .'

'Jeans? She never modelled jeans, for God's sake. She modelled underwear for some catalogue, once, I think. Brassieres for Middle England. Before she gained weight or lost it, did something with it. She was never really a model. She was a beautician who did massage, ask her for God's sake. I'm far more interested in the fact that over fifty thousand unwanted dogs are put down every year. I don't know what she did before we were married. It's none of my business. I don't care. I never did.'

'Surely you must understand that your wife's previous occupations may affect her credibility?'

'Surely what? Oh for Chrissakes, you're as idiotically

oversensitive as she is. You mean *surely* some dumb underwear model/masseuse could not have become a perfectly satisfactory housewife in a house like this? Well she did. Without genetic modification. She's perfectly competent, although in one way, I take your point. Einstein she isn't, thank God. She doesn't need to be and she certainly wouldn't be with me if she was. Is that all?'

'Well, er, no. I was hoping to elicit some information about your life together. It is important for the jury to know, Mr Petty, just how dependent she is on you and how much she would lie for you, if necessary. I suppose she's busy at the moment, massaging someone. Doing a facial, if she still works.'

'No she doesn't. She's gone to London, Mzzz whatever your name is.'

'Elisabeth Manser, as you know. And don't lose your rag, Mr Petty. This is only a dress rehearsal for the sort of questions you might be asked in court, possibly by a woman like myself, only worse. Why do you always keep your wife in the dark, Mr Petty? Are you ashamed of her? Why has she never been available for comment?'

'Why? Because most people have the sense not to ask. She's never been a subject of interest. Besides, I couldn't keep her in the dark, she's frightened of it. And look here, you stupid cow, we might live in an age of equality, but marriage is still a very good way for a woman to get a bloody life. Have you ever thought of trying it?'

He was looming above her, voracious in his contempt.

'Sorry,' he said. 'What a bloody stupid, *irrelevant* thing to say.'

The interview ended. Elisabeth Manser sighed and left her seat.

Scene Three

Shake rattle and roll. He could see the Lloyds tower as he went through the carriages for the last time, collecting rubbish. Gave him a sense of achievement, as if he were the first person to see it. There were certain customers on this train for whom he had a soft spot. A serious soft spot, in her case, which meant a hole right in the middle of his solar plexus through which the wind blew in a gasp, as if he was hollow. Stupid really, for a hard man like himself, a thorn in the side of authority, temporarily slouching over this sodding trolley which had a life of its own. It was worse than a hyperactive baby in a pram or a wilful supermarket trolley; it lurched like a drunk, careered like a lunatic, danced like a teenager on Ecstasy and aimed for his shins like some renegade terrorist on a random mission to disable. It was crippling; it was vicious; it deserved to be shot. One of these days it would burp boiling water all over his blue, synthetic uniform and the shameful matching tie which he always ripped off before he went home. The water would make him melt, wane away, dissolve into a sludge of royal blue with yellow stripes, but not with the same immediacy as the way he wilted when she smiled at him in Compartment B.

The nicest compartment in this motley selection of carriages; nicer than first class, which was not worth the extra. It had regular passengers, including the man who looked like a rhino with a suit too small, the fashion girl who looked like a drowned rat, complained about the price of the tea every time, but drank it loudly, disgusting though it was. Then there was the morose doctor, the fidget who looked like a marmoset, the men with the laptops and the mobiles who never looked up, and then there was her. Pretty and slightly motherly and artificially blonde and just fucking gorgeous. *Woof!* Nice, really nice, as if she was waiting for him, ready to smile and listen and prepared to buy all his sandwiches if that helped. With a Marilyn Monroe type of sweet vacuousness, she always had the right change; none of this rendering a twenty-pound note for a single coffee. It was only two hours at most any of them spent on this train; what dumb prick could fail to arm himself with a quid or two in change if he wanted a drink? That was the way he judged people, unless they wore uniforms, in which case he hated them on sight. It was whether they had coins or whether they did not; those who washed their hair and those who did not. Nobody else based personal judgement on that.

There was the couple he had seen before, bickering quietly over the aisle from her. They radiated poison. When he thought about it, these idiots, repressed wage slaves, wives/assistants of wage slaves, metropolitan cannon fodder, were all a bunch of tossers and the air they breathed should have made him choke, but he just couldn't work out why, with those two exceptions today, they were so much nicer in here, near the back of the train, and why even the sodding trolley behaved better. It went smoothish among the sticking-out legs and the briefcases. They were careless about belongings, stuff all over the place, but that was not a problem. Did he like them? Too strong a sentiment. He just liked them better than most, even if they did resent giving up their seats and clogged the aisles when the train filled.

It was not that *she* was particularly talkative, and she was only on the train once a week if that. Somebody's personal assistant, wife or girlfriend, sent on errands. Yes, a wife – she had that family look. Well dressed, but a few pale hairs clinging to her skirt. Ten years older than him maybe, but still, *whooomph!* – the air blowing a hole through his ribs as if he'd been hit with a large ball.

She was smiling at him, clutching that big, soft bag she held beneath her arm like a puppy, anxious to please and pleased to see him, once a week, sometimes more, often as not, pretending to read. She would always chat. Her husband might have been a bully and she his pet. He could tell these things. He doesn't deserve you, he would say to her one day. He's an upper-class git with a house near Staplehurst who doesn't give a shit for you, that's what he is and you're not from the same drawer, and if that rhino in the opposite seat yells down his sodding mobile one more time, I'll brain the bastard, OK?

You are *gorgeous*.

He turned to check the carriage. Saw that the man of the bickering couple had placed his hands round her neck and her hands were grasping at his wrists in a peculiar kind of game.

Then the trolley wrenched at his arms and suddenly

disappeared. Whisked out of sight. Then it came back like a flying bomb, spitting fury and revenge and hot water. Knocked him almost senseless and then veered away as everything tilted sideways and he felt he was flying through a window. And at last, he was in her arms, her hair in his mouth. Separated again, dragged away, rolling, someone kicking his head and someone else whipping him until he rolled back.

He shouldn't have touched her. Shouldn't have fantasised, not with commuters in second class.

Should've controlled himself.

CHAPTER ONE

There was silence after Elisabeth Manser resumed her seat.

'I don't think that was a good idea,' John Box said quietly. 'Never a good idea to speak briskly in front of a jury. They want you to look at them straight in the eye, keep your temper and smile. I thought you were used to dealing with impertinent questions and insults from the press. I wasn't sure. I had to see how you might react. Just as well we had a rehearsal. Not good, I fear. You'll have to learn.'

'When I think of my father's humble origins,' Douglas said, 'it's a wonder these bloody journalists treat me with the contempt usually reserved for the landed gentry. I'm not a bloody politician. And I didn't expect cross-examination from a woman. Oh God, I *hate* women.'

'Not, if I may say so, a sentiment you should repeat, in the circumstances. And it's as well for you to appreciate the sort of questions and innuendos you will hear in the High

Court. Possibly issuing from the delicate lips of a sweet young blonde, primed for the purpose of winding you up.'

Douglas looked at Elisabeth Manser, whose face he liked, but whose name he could never remember, to see if she was resenting his remarks, but she remained entirely expressionless. He rose from the straight-backed chair he had designated for himself, by mistake. It was the least comfortable in the room and he had sat in it for the rehearsal in deference to the guests, John Box, Queen's Counsel, and the woman, Elisabeth, laughingly referred to as his junior, as if either of them were other than sexless, ageless lawyers, seated in a rough semi-circle round the fireplace, with the empty chair at the outer edge. Even in the absence of Elisabeth, the chair looked angry. Douglas noticed that the seat was covered in fine hair, left by the cat, and he smiled with a brief satisfaction at the thought of what that might have done to the woman's black trousers. The chair occupied by Mr Box was far more commodious, wasted on such a skinny runt. A disgusting little prick, actually, far too tall, sitting so still, as if he was never tempted to move, fart, eat too much, laugh too loud, take his clothes off in a hurry and yell. From his own side of the room, Douglas wanted to shout himself, crossed his arms over his barrel of a chest and sighed loudly instead. A man in his position, with his own experience of the law, had to remember that the older man had other ways of kicking the shit out of people. Silence was one of his weapons.

'But I'm supposed to let you lead me,' Douglas said. 'Rely on your protection. I might have been a barrister once, but now, I'm the bloody client.'

'So you will know how lonely and vulnerable a *client* is as soon as he takes the witness stand. Nobody can protect him then. You, of all people, should know how brutal cross-examination can be. You know how a witness can be made to *writhe*. And the decision about who will do it is not mine to make. It will *not* be someone who wishes to accentuate a picture of domestic bliss in a beautiful family house. It will be someone who wishes to undermine you as cunningly as they may. And *you* must not let them do it, since I shall not be able to prevent it, except through constant interruptions which will make you look ever more foolish. Hence a rehearsal, to be continued.' He gazed down at his hands, linked on the papers in his fleshless lap. 'And as to all other decisions on the conduct of this case, you must continue to trust me. Absolutely. As you no doubt would once have insisted that your clients did you.'

'Is there any chance of some coffee?' the woman asked. Elisabeth whatever her surname was managed to be deferential and demanding at the same time. She was the diplomat who knew when to interrupt. 'I could get it . . .'

Douglas sprang to his feet. 'Of course. Over there. In the thermos. Amy left it ready. Help yourself. I'm going for a walk.'

They were left in the room. Spring sunlight filtered through large windows; a draught swirled from the chimney and the trees in the garden swayed. In common accord, John Box and Elisabeth Manser moved without haste towards the tray containing coffee and biscuits, helped themselves and retreated to the same seats. In the distance, there was the sound of a door banging, a piercing whistle, a shouted command, another door. Looking through the windows, they could see Douglas, striding out of sight. He was the client who had convened a meeting at 8.30 in the morning and he was not a predictable person, but he was paying. John watched him, relieved by his absence since being in his presence was like sharing a room with a volcano unless his wife was there with him and by God, they would need her in court to vouch for his virtue.

'There is something fascinating,' John said, 'about a man who masquerades as a hero and is really a beast. To think of it.'

'I'd rather not think of it,' Elisabeth said. 'I'd rather he remained in the hinterland of minor, philanthropic celebrities, untouched. And I'd remind you, John, that that is exactly where he belongs as far as we're concerned. In a herd of semi-extinct wildebeest, revered for being handsome, if you like that sort of thing, contentious and fleet of foot. He's innocent, of course. All you have to know is that we have an innocent man, severely traduced by enemies.'

'Spell that for me.'

'What? Enemies? E – en—'

'No, *traduced*. If you ever use such a word in front of a jury, we've had it. Too much like Latin, too archaic. If you have to spell a word to a jury or explain what it means, you've lost the buggers. Speaking of which . . . oh shit . . .'

'Don't mention shit. Oh please, don't mention shit, please.'

They both dissolved into childish giggles. John sniggered into his handkerchief with a series of haw-haw-haw

noises, like the muted braying of a donkey. He was a long
and dapper man, wearing a faded but excellent suit, and it
was his cadaverous face which lent him dignity. He haw-
haw-hawed into a capacious piece of paper napkin which
bore the legend of something or other. Pizza Express,
Connex South; tissues he collected as he went around too
absent-minded to equip himself with handkerchiefs. He
had impressive, deep-set eyes, and his sense of humour, as
Elisabeth resolutely refused to notice, was often reserved
for the suffering of others. Tell him a cunning joke and he
was puzzled; watch a man slip on a tiled floor and he was
beside himself. His glee was always short-lived, but it
made Elisabeth feel faintly guilty for her own laughter
when they so rarely laughed at the same things. Affection,
love, whatever she called it, was a random force, quite
beyond rational judgement; chalk often adored cheese and
besides, all the same, it was *bloody* funny.

Bloody, used in this context, was so far removed from
anything to do with real blood, it did not impinge on the
joke.

'Under our existing laws on privacy, such as they are,'
John said, recovering himself and wiping half the smile off
his face with the napkin, 'these photos are entirely admis-
sible as evidence in any court of law. They were taken
from outside a man's private property, from the safety of
a tree' – here he began to snigger again – 'whilst looking
into the garden. Oh dear. And in the others, the ones in
the stable, they are stills from a security video which our
plaintiff threw out with his rubbish. There is no property
in abandoned goods. How can he have been so stupid?

And why is it, my darling junior, that we give ourselves such licence to spy on one another?'

He was returning to an oft-repeated theme and it seemed artless to comment that without such licence to spy, he would not be in a position to earn his living and her own modest stipend would be severely diminished. He might still have owned houses and cars, but items of a different, smaller kind, and even if the licence to spy had not afforded him luxury, it would have made no difference to what he did, since he was addicted to it.

A parasite in the gut, his wife had remarked in her dry, committee voice, and the memory of that smothered his laughter temporarily. John Box, QC, specialist in libel, would not have dared to ask his own wife to take the stand in his defence, which is what *this* client would be doing. He felt some sympathy for Mrs Amy Petty, which nevertheless dissolved in merriment again as he picked up the nearest photograph from the pile which scattered across the surface of the desk. The photos were slightly sticky to the touch and bearing the shameful traces of a thousand fingerprints. Everyone who had seen them had laughed.

The photo, enlarged to an obscene degree, had the blurry outlines of a badly executed video still. It was part of a series of markedly worse quality than the photos of dull-eyed dogs lying in straw or strolling with the listlessness of ill health. This photo showed a man, running across a lawn, pursuing a large, yellow dog. Both were of powerful build, oddly similar in the paleness of their colouring and halos of blond hair. In comparison to the man, the dog was a masterpiece of elegance, fluid in flight, tail held aloft like a flag of courage. The man was naked from the waist down. His torso was dressed in a garment resembling a striped pyjama top, held together over a barrel chest by a button or two, a substantially firm and large belly exposed. He had what appeared to be a stick in his hand – it could have been a whip – and his face was contorted, again in contrast to the calmer profile of the dog. Also exposed on the man was a prominent penis, caught on camera as a piece of body furniture held at about fifty degrees. There were heavy shoes on his otherwise bare feet. He looked monstrous. A view improved in the next frame in the sequence, when the angle of either the shot or the subjects had changed and he had caught the big dog, grasped it, fallen on it, the pale moons of his buttocks exposed and . . .

'Fucked it,' John said, sadly. 'Oh dear. And him with such a lovely wife, too.'

The coffee was fine and strong, the cream thick and the biscuits rich and crumbling on the tongue, a good replacement for breakfast for her while filling the ever yawning gap of John's appetite. She had a memory of another occasion, when the delectable Amy had provided them with lunch, on the basis of which Mr John Box, QC, had decided, with good reason, that she was exactly the woman to put straight her husband's injured reputation at the now imminent libel trial. Such a sweetheart, nicely warm and flustered; the perfect spouse to swear to the contentment and normality of her husband. Even if he did keep a menagerie.

'Of course he has no need to beat his animals,' John

said. 'Or to attempt to fuck his dog. No need at all. Not with a wife like that.'

'Star witness,' Elisabeth agreed. 'Absolutely vital. Good woman. She'll stand by. Like good women do.'

They sipped, like decorous schoolmarms, not quite waiting for Douglas to come back, because that was not an event they could anticipate. Douglas was volatile. Neither counsel had ventured an opinion as to his sanity, even in private, but each treated him with the firm deference given to someone who was mentally unstable. Elisabeth touched John's hand, briefly, a gesture reserved for private moments, or occasionally the train, where no one noticed.

'I sometimes wish,' she said, 'that we had never volunteered for this case.'

'Nonsense. It's unique.'

In the distance they could hear the sound of dogs barking furiously and both shuddered imperceptibly. John gazed around the room, a familiar place through three similar meetings over the last month. It was an extraordinary house, not really designed as a house at all. It had been some rich man's foible in the last century, when the creator of it had used this valley as a setting to build a folly, consisting at first of a large, circular room, which was where they sat now. The room, with an ornately moulded ceiling and featuring a geometric frieze and large French doors looking out over a lawn, had been designed to ape the style of a gentlemen's club, the Reform, perhaps. It had the look of a louche library, a place to be used for elaborate picnics at the far end of an estate. Then there were the additions which made it into a house, the large rectangular extension which was added to the back two generations later to provide kitchen and scullery connected by a flagged passageway, with stairs from there to bedrooms and bathrooms. The result was odd to say the least. There was no real entrance, apart from the French doors on the lawn or through the kitchen, where the extra addition of a porch did little for the symmetry at the rear. Seen from the front lawn and the willow tree, the line of the gently domed roof of the round room was broken by the addition of a chimney. The whole of the exterior, front, back and sides, was painted bright, reflective white to make it seem more uniform than it was. The original room was the only magnificence, used, so history had it, as a palatial summer house for the ladies of the family, but also, it was rumoured, as a sort of hellfire drinking club for the men, for the conduct of debauchery away from the public eye. Stables had been built for their horses. Subsequent to that, by the time the place began to look from the air as if a bite had been taken out of a circular structure and a huge box stuck on the back, some family eccentric had been dumped here, again out of the public eye, to keep a menagerie of animals collected from foreign parts. The stables had then served a different purpose. Now both those pieces of its history would make it suitable for a man like Douglas Petty and his father before him. It was rather a man's house. Women were irrelevant.

The room in which they sat was undoubtedly elegant in proportion and quite magnificent enough to attract journalistic attention, although the decor left something to be desired. The circular contours created difficulties with furniture. The fireplace was custom built. The moulded ceilings had been white once, now an antique cream, with darker corners where the residue of cigar smoke stuck, like in the ceilings of an old pub. The main feature was the stretch of curved, ceiling-height windows covering most of the outfacing wall, with the huge French doors in the centre. They brought into the room all the blinding light of a late spring morning and the view of the gracious willow tree, vibrant with fresh leaves. Saggy damson-coloured drapes were pushed to the side of the windows, trailing to the floor and obviously never disturbed. The faded cream of the walls and the semi-circle of armchairs, dwarfed by the size of the room itself, were in various states of repair.

'What a nice day,' Elisabeth remarked, letting the place charm her.

It would be exceedingly cold in winter, with or without the fire. The impression given was that the room was occupied by animals as much as by human beings. Visitors in dark clothing would leave covered in visible fur. The carpet was clean, but looked as if the struggle with animal presence had proved unequal. The large kitchen beyond, which Elisabeth had seen on a previous visit, was a better-kept place, where the war against the muck of the garden was waged if not won. All that effort, and the frilly cleanliness of the upstairs rooms, was probably down to the fragrant Mrs Amy Petty. What a treasure. She certainly needed domestic help in the face of a husband who entered and left like a gale-force wind, all the dogs in the stables and a mother-in-law. There was also a Petty sister, Elisabeth remembered, not yet seen, but still a point of reference as a frequent visitor. If John and she should ever live together, she thought idly, she would inherit far more hideous complications than that.

'We have to concentrate on the main points of the case,' John said, looking at his watch, suddenly busy. 'What was it about those articles and these pictures which offended him most? What harm does he want undone? Is it the ridicule he resents, the allegation of sexual perversion, or is it the accusation of cruelty?'

'Oh, the cruelty, I think. Don't you? I doubt he'd mind what anyone thought about his sexual habits, not with his reputation. Cruelty to a woman might be fine, but to a dog? Insupportable.'

They began to gather their papers, as if something had been achieved.

From the hallway beyond, they heard the click-click of a metal-tipped walking stick on the stone tiles. Moving slowly, pausing, hesitantly. Without further discussion they began to stuff papers, more particularly the photographs, into their bags with increased, silent efficiency. The footsteps turned away, and the sound of the stick tap-tapped towards the kitchen. They breathed out in mutual relief.

'I don't know why he persists,' Elisabeth hissed. 'He's lucky he isn't in prison. He should have been prosecuted.'

'I thought *you* might have influenced his reprieve,' John hissed back.

'Don't overestimate me. How could I influence any-thing? I only said I knew the lawyer who's been looking at the criminal side. Helen West. She's an old friend. We were at university together.'

'How terribly useful,' John murmured, 'to have a friend at the criminal end of the Civil Service.' He had an unshakeable belief in the power of contacts, unaware of how much she neglected her friends and how few the favours she had to bestow.

Elisabeth did not share his faith in friends. She looked at him blowing his nose and wondered why she adored him. It must be his profile and his eyes, deep blue in the light. Good looks, good brain, seductive.

A big room, full of desks, screens, people; the poorer end of the law.

'Mr Douglas Petty is a lucky man,' Redwood intoned. 'He evades the fury of the criminal statutes, or so you say. Briefly.' There was the minimum of paper in Helen West's file. Paper was discouraged for lack of space and all he considered was the first line of her written note on the merits of prosecution, or not.

It is impossible to estimate just how much buggery with animals takes place, the note read. *After all, the recipients of attention, unless they are talking parrots with a large vocab-ulary, are not really in a position to complain.* She was being flippant, as usual.

'Was that a nice change for you, Helen? You always complain of being bored.'

'I'm never bored. But it did make a change, yes.'

'Albeit another version of the same thing. Another contemptible male, doing the wrong thing with the favourite part of his anatomy.'

'A variation, yes. I meant it makes a change to deal with a crime which the Bible takes far more seriously than the law ever has,' she said crisply. '*If a man lies with a beast, he shall be put to death and you shall kill the beast.* It does seem unfair on the beast. Anyway, the issue is cruelty rather than bestiality, reputation above anything else. What else do you need to know? Douglas Petty was an infamous barrister with radical views of no known persuasion. Great success, but no sense of decorum. Got rich by inheritance from a colourful father, got sacked from the bar for the famous stunt of streaking through the High Court, remember? He's faintly famous for being famous. Whooped it up at all the right London parties, where he was rude to everyone, string of broken hearts. Would have been sued for breach of promise, let alone libel, if that had been possible. Remarked of one mistress, "She's a silly little tart, give me a straightforward bitch any day." Very quotable, always referring to bitches, viz, "There's nothing you can do with a bitch on heat; they don't care what happens to them." He was talking about vulnerable dogs at the time, to be fair. Married late, lives with sweet old mother and current wife. He keeps an inherited small sanctuary for dogs, on the basis, I quote, "Animals are so much nicer than people." Becomes more famous for this commonly held sentiment.' She coughed to attract his attention. 'Now, as you know, the law brackets bestiality with gross indecency . . .'

'Yes, I know all that. Get on with it.'

'Well, the newspaper in question say they received a set of photographs and a video, anonymously, which probably means they commissioned them. Having published them with a couple of inflammatory, hugely libellous articles, they then turned them over to the police with the righteous demand that Douglas be prosecuted for what they consider to be incontrovertible evidence of cruelty to his animals and buggery. Consistent cruelty, shots of animals with marks of beatings, etcetera. Well you know the way it is. Any evidence gathered by a newspaper is generally useless for a prosecution. They can't prove who took the video from which they distilled their incriminating pics; they can't prove the dates; they can't prove the tape hasn't been interfered with. The problem is that the pics definitely include him, doing strange things with dogs. Well, ambiguous things with dogs, while he was wearing his pyjamas.' She began to smile. 'Half his pyjamas.' She turned the page. 'He must have been keen, it was cold. You can pinpoint the time of year and his identity without much difficulty.'

'The bastard.'

'Probably, but the pictures aren't the surefire evidence the careless local newspaper thought they were. Might be enough to defend the libel action he's brought against the national paper which repeated the libel, but not enough by a long stretch for us to indict him. Civil lawyers are not like us; they don't deal with all this nonsense about the burden of proof beyond reasonable doubt. As for the pictures of animals – dogs, I mean – in distress, there are several of those, but no one knows when they were taken. He runs his dog sanctuary on strict lines. You deliver your sick or maltreated animal to the back door, absolutely no questions asked. Makes the RSPCA mad as hell. They've accused him of sympathising with animal beaters by guaranteeing their anonymity. Anyway, there's not one of these donors who's going to come forward and say "my dog wasn't like that when I gave it to him". So, pictures of injured beasts, which may have been abused by him or by their previous owners, don't say much.'

'Staff?'

She delved into the file, frowning, her glasses precariously balanced on her nose. 'No one at the time, temporary help, sometimes. A man he sacked just before, who won't say anything. Then, in the house, there's the mother, and his wife. Who seems a nice kind of floozie who will stand by her man and his income, and say he wouldn't harm a fly and anyway, was so busy in bed with her he didn't need dogs. Or the thrill of hitting dumb animals when he'd got her for the purpose, I don't doubt. No sign of any other abused creatures on the premises when they searched, but that was a whole month after the publication of the so-called evidence. I'm sorry, that's a lot to absorb, am I talking too much?' Her voice was louder, a hint in his direction to make him concentrate.

'You don't seem to like him much,' he said.

She looked surprised. 'No, but we don't prosecute people for being unreconstructed male chauvinist pigs. Or for being nasty and brutish.'

'Is that why the newspapers gun for him?'

She rose from her seat, placing a copy of her note in front of him. Her hair was untidy, the rest of her neat, clean and inscrutable. 'Don't be silly. It's simply because he's rich. A lawyer who once laid down the law, rich by inheritance and sometimes talks about morals. This is England, Redwood. Get real. He's everything we hate.'

She turned away, looked beyond the glass cubicle he occupied at the end of the open-plan floor, littered with desks, machinery and boxes. No one could think clearly in such a place. She was looking away to hide her impatience. At the far end of the room, a crowd of people was gathering, talking urgently.

'Is there anything which would influence your decision? Anything which would make you review it?' She turned to face him again, reluctantly.

'Yes.'

His face fell. 'Oh?'

She leant her elbows on his desk. He hated it when she got close like that. 'New evidence. A repetition. His wife turning on him. I'll be keeping an eye on this libel nonsense, if my friend Elisabeth Manser will deign to talk to me. What on earth's going on down there?'

The crowd at the other end had swelled and moved to the space by the windows which flanked the room. Prime position for the luckier ones was facing the light; secondrate citizens were lined against the back wall in darkness. Someone broke ranks and came towards them. 'Excuse me, has anyone seen Paul? Only we were worried about him.'

'Paul? Why?'

'Because he isn't here yet. He was on that train. Haven't you heard the news?'

Elisabeth Manser and John Box waited, both wanting to catch the train, read newspapers, touch hands, and both hoping they might be out of the way before Mrs Petty, Senior, hove into view. She did not have the same, slightly ditzy desire to please of her comely daughter-in-law, nor was she as easy on the eye. She had no potential as a witness in her son's cause because she rarely left the house, not even to go as far as the stables, was professionally infirm and would say nothing about him except to declare him a saint. For present purposes, she was a social obligation they could do without. The only mystery about the elder Mrs Petty was the way Douglas deferred to her.

Elisabeth stared through the windows, half lost in admiration of the view until with some relief she saw the client, striding back across the lawn in their direction. There was a dog at his heels. John wiped at the ginger cat hairs which stuck to his trousers below the knee. They had a stickiness which made them impossible to dislodge. The sound of Mrs Petty's walking stick came towards them down the corridor, unusually hurried. 'Douglas?' she was calling in her quavering voice. 'Douglas?' The back door slammed, forcefully. 'Douglas?' she called again as her head appeared around the door of the grand living room. Why did she repeat herself so? Elisabeth found the plaintiveness so irritating, it made her want to knock her over. As the dog might do at any minute, and then they would never get away.

In the event, son and mother coincided in the doorway. She clutched at his arm. 'Ah, *there* you are,' she said, breathlessly and unnecessarily. Her hair was the colour of pewter, beautifully styled. Her tweed ensemble matched her shoes.

'What is it, Mother?' The mildness of his tone when he spoke to her was always surprising. It was as if he risked punishment by speaking any other way, but then the threat of reprisal never seemed to stop him otherwise. Elisabeth suppressed a frisson of dislike. He was rude and crude and his wife had *bruises*, real *bruises* . . . She had seen them.

Mother paused, with dramatic effect. 'Amy did catch the 8.15 up to London, didn't she, darling?'

'I suppose so, unless she missed it.'

Her hold on the sleeve of his sweater increased into a clawlike grip. Her nails were manicured. Not a woman who attended to animals. 'I heard it on the radio. There's been the most awful, monumental crash. Headlong collision. Her train ran into the 125, or something, and she always goes to the front, doesn't she?'

Douglas detached her hand from his arm, walked the length of the room from the door to the French windows. Then he threw back his head and howled. The enraged, mournful, animal sound of it seemed to go on for ever.

Later, Elisabeth tried to tell herself it was the dog beside him which had made that inhuman noise.

CHAPTER TWO

The glance between Amy and the man with the trolley had been like an electric shock. Not for the mutual recognition of one another as allies, because they were already friends of a kind, but for what they had both seen, over the aisle, the man with his hands round the woman's neck, a piece of hatred in miniature. Then came the huge vibration. Whatever it was. Something which felt initially irritating and downright insulting, like being tripped up, or pushed and otherwise treated with outrageous rudeness. They sat, a little dazed, tangled with one another, breathless and winded for several minutes. The trolley man was in the seat next to her, without any apparent reason for him to be there, a puzzling state of affairs. All she could hear was heavy breathing.

They sat like dummies, awaiting orders. There were sighs of irritation, a few murmurs of disjointed talking, a chorus of *Oh, fuck this, what the hell*, nothing much. She had the irreverent thought as she saw that the luggage rack above the elephant man appeared to have emptied itself all over him, so that he was buried beneath two coats and a briefcase, that it served them right for carrying so much, messing with mobiles, laptops and being sulky when asked to move them. Elephant man's lack of protest was peculiar. He did not even try to move the coats which covered him. Amy tried to move her hand so that she could tidy him up, but her hands did not want to function, and the trolley man was pinning her against the window. There was a peculiar smell. They waited, dumbly, for announcements, obedient to authority, grumbling rather than waving fists and shouting.

Then there was a communal awareness, an increase in the level of unease, as they heard the sound of distant voices. Someone screaming from the next carriage, *Get outta here, it's getting hot, hot, hot*, and a vibration of movement. The sound of banging. An increase in the alien smell, people coughing. Without discussion beyond the repetition of the grumbling, they began to get up and form a disorderly queue for the nearest door. Amy was close to it, one of the last to move. The trolley man and the elephant man seemed afflicted with the same ability to delay.

The queue became rougher, more vocal. *C'mon, get out, for God's sake, get a move on.* Not panic, quite, but unpleasant. A woman began to cry. There was loud, insistent banging. The nearest door was behind her and would not open. She felt for the handbag and could not find it. The trolley man's pale face stirred against her shoulder as he braced himself against the arms of the seat and propped his chin on her shoulder. 'Did you see that?' he asked her, almost conversationally. 'Did you see that?'

'Yes.' The absence of the handbag distressed her. Others were pushing past while she looked for it. Vision was blurred. It seemed important to stand and follow, the urgency growing along with the heat. She noticed how others left their strewn belongings as they climbed over the wreckage of the trolley and pushed towards the door. Someone, somehow had opened it and smoke filtered into the carriage. There was pushing and shouting alongside her and she saw the man of the bickering couple with his woman slung over his shoulder, making room for their exit by pushing hard. Then the trolley man hauled her to her feet and they shuffled, almost the last, to the space between their carriage and the one in front. Facing the door, Amy wanted to go back. It was a steep drop to the track and she did not trust herself to jump. It was as if she was being told to jump from a plane without a parachute and the relative safety of the train seemed preferable, but she was pushed and she jumped.

Smoke, everywhere. People, looming up out of the smoke, standing disconsolately. By some common momentum, they began to move down the track in the direction of the station. The carriage in front lay on its side, windows smashed, figures in a fog emerging clumsily like a series of drunks trying to get over fences. Bloody faces, a number of bloody hands, weeping noises, moans, and in the distance, the wailing of sirens. They kept moving forwards, clutching at one another, some element of humanity making them offer support to the slowest, while all the time wanting to run.

The enormity of the damage occurred to her when she saw the figure of a man, almost surely dead, hanging out of a window, too high to reach, abandoned. 'Shouldn't we?' she said to the trolley man.

'No,' he said, roughly, 'he'll have to wait for the experts. We'd never get up there.'

'We must,' she said, pulling away. There was a yawing, creaking sound and the carriage shifted ominously. The crackle of fire. Someone pushed her on. She had lost the trolley man. There was nothing to do but go forward, get out of the way. There were more people now. Strange to see so many people carrying nothing; it looked unnatural. It was safer to look down than look up; she kept her eyes fixed to the track; she could watch her own feet and believe in her own progress. The pall of smoke was thicker, with great, gobby flecks of sticky black ash floating round like snow.

Her eyes caught the flash of something bright on the track, and she stopped. She was wondering how she and the trolley man had become detached; had he gone into the dangerous carriage or were there simply others who needed him more than she? A stray shaft of sunshine penetrating the smoke, quickly obscured, reflected the glint of something solid and gold. She could make out a gold ring on the track. Amy stopped and stared at it, bent towards it. Then noticed that the ring was attached to a hand, the hand protruding from the sleeve of a blouse, the arm outflung away from the body of a woman who

lay quietly on the ground, the position of her head so distorted it appeared as if she was staring backwards. Eyes at
the back of her head, open and fixed. Amy recognised the
blouse of the bickering woman, with the man who had
lifted her out of their carriage squatted beside her. 'Piss
off,' he said to Amy, as if it were a natural thing to say and
this a normal greeting. 'Just piss off.' Obediently, she
stumbled on, beginning to cry. Kept on moving in the
same direction.

Past another wrecked carriage, then another, the sound
of sirens louder and the stench almost unbearable, a mixture of indefinable smells, none bearing close analysis,
the combination worse than anything she had ever
smelled with her nose so finely tuned to the nuances of
perfumes and animal smells. The smell of singeing, vomit,
blood was overpowered by the acrid smell of diesel fuel.
Then there was an order. Go back. The unruly column,
obedient again, turned round and began to retrace their
steps. From the carriages there came the eerie, disembodied ringing of mobile phones.

It was worse, now, even though they were being led.
Men in yellow jackets, herding them without being able to
shield their eyes. She tripped and fell over a greasy pile of
clothing, which was warm and wet, but not recognisably
human. The crying was uncontrollable. The plodding
onwards seemed endless, more hazardous. Please don't
stop, the order came down, keep moving, make space for
the ambulance men. There were more obstacles to avoid,
bodies, pieces of bodies, cases, polythene bags, cables,
and the sound of dripping fluid. She forgot how many

carriages. Perhaps they were going to put them back on the train again and take them all away.

Then she saw the woman again, that yellow blouse half-covering the outstretched arm, but by this time a man in an orange jacket was hurrying her on while he shielded the body, his legs astride the arm. She tried to tell him about the woman, but he said, *not now, you can't help*. She looked back at the hand, haunted by its helplessness and complete abandonment. Someone had taken the ring.

Behind the last carriage, the one in which she had travelled, they were herded across the track and told to walk down the other side. She could see a pylon, balanced across the train's roof, dripping with wires. This side of the train was fire-damaged; by the time they reached the next carriage along, the stench was appalling. The faces she saw were blackened, the clothes filthy and the presence of the orange and yellow jackets greater, moving among recumbent forms, shouting orders. Amy felt horribly self-conscious of the ability to walk and, because she was blessed with it, made herself walk as straight as she could without falling over. Among all the other sounds, there was again the intermittent bleating of mobile phones, a background chorus of pathetic pleas for attention, lessening as they scrambled down a bank, across a road and into a car park.

The presence of cars seemed odd, as if they had no place in this alternative world. A few shiny, clean cars, standing in rows, a reminder of another life. Dirty people leaned against them, leaving black marks and bloody handprints. People sat on the ground, stood, lay down. A sense of organisation grew imperceptibly. She found herself moving round, automatically, touching people, asking if they were all right, knowing she was less damaged, quicker to spot the sources of first aid and hear the voices giving instructions. The surface of the car park was sticky with blood. *You do what you can, what more can you do?* A distant memory of Douglas's voice, barking at her, and a woman whose shoulder she embraced, reminding her of a soft, sick rabbit she had rescued from the jaws of a dog, the blackened, ravaged faces of the people becoming those of poorly animals, a doe, a terrier, and that thin man over there, a giraffe. There was nothing she could do, nothing. She knew how to reassure a frightened animal; she had once possessed other skills, but all of her talents seemed facile and pathetic now. Even in hell, she was redundant.

She heard, with one ear, the discussions among the able-bodied about how many were dead. An idea had been forming, shocking in its clarity, born out of this familiar sensation of being useless, heavy, stupid. It was time to leave, was all. She had no contribution to make; she was as useless here as everywhere else; she should have gone. An idea which came full circle when a policeman approached with his pale face and trembling hands, trying to obey orders in the face of his own, profound shock. He asked for her name and address, and instead of the usual obedience, she murmured politely that she had given it already, to that woman over there, pointing to another uniform equipped with an identical clipboard.

The boy looked relieved. His ability to write was impaired and he told her if she moved to the left of the place, that was where she could make phone calls and get help with getting home, as long as she was sure she didn't need a doctor. Amy thanked him; politeness was second nature. She remembered the mobile phone in her lost handbag and she was suddenly very cold, crossed her arms over her lightweight jacket and moved in the direction he had indicated. The word *home* had a hollow sound.

Home. She was not going home. There was no such thing.

That smell; that sickening smell. Burnt clothes, wet wool, the stench of carcase, blood, old food, urine. She tried to equate like with like in her sensory memory, but there had never been smells like this. Not even in the burying of a dog which had died and been mourned so long the digging of the grave was delayed to find the right place. A sweet, bad breath smell it had, for all the stiff, soft fur, a scent about it which made it easier to consign to the earth.

An hour and a half had passed, endless and timeless. She followed others down a side road, the ones who were particularised, finished with, ambulant, allowed to go, following one another like a line of hobbling lambs. They would have moved faster on all fours. The loop of road took them past more flak jackets. Human beings like sheepdogs, brindled yellow and white, urging them on with awkward gestures which wanted to be kind and turned out to be officious. Like lollipop men waving children over a zebra crossing. She felt like a refugee, not even wanting to be recognised. The lambs, walking away from slaughter, slower than they had approached it.

There was a conviction in her mind that none of this was in the present and all of them were extras on the set of a film made about war. Soldiers covered in fake blood, aiming for breakfast. The loop of side road took them back across another, unrecognisable service road over a set of hastily laid planks and into the station. A long walk. Then they were ushered across the station concourse. It looked so normal. Burger King, the Upper Crust, Cafe Select, all open and waiting for business, their operatives jabbering in diverse tongues, waiting, offering tea, anything, most of them crying. Kids. Apart from that, the concourse was eerie. White tiles, smutty with the smoky dirt of footsteps, destination and arrival boards, empty, silent as the ragged band shuffled past, eyes straight ahead, looking for whom they might meet on the other side of the exit. Some stopped and accepted drinks. Some were able to laugh.

She saw ahead of her the bickering man, the one who told her to piss off. She recognised the coat; she was used to noticing details. Beigey, dirt slicks down the back, no blood, walking with his hands clenched behind his back. As they reached the exit to the station, he paused and looked back, without undoing his hands.

She only smiled at him because she was puzzled; he should not have been there, but she could not remember why and because it was necessary to smile. *Excuse me*, she wanted to say, *but haven't you left something behind?* It was a good luck smile, as automatic as most of her smiles recently, a paper smile. They were faced by a phalanx of meeters and greeters who had come to collect. It was the meeting place for the survivors. If you wanted to go home, there was home to greet you in the form of a person waving a handwritten notice attached to a stick. *Paul! Sandy! Sis! Jack! Sally! Clara, Joe . . . Over here! Home.* The word made her sick.

The time on the station clock was midmorning; enough time to create this anxious crowd of lovers, friends and family, none for her. Eleven now, 8.15 when she set out. The smile which the man returned with a stare and a nod was a grimace of recognition, no more, and then they passed through the crowd like a pair of unrelated strangers, she hating him for a nameless reason, both of them ungreeted. The lonely ones, suddenly efficient, walking through traffic as if they belonged. Facing a road full of cars with no idea how to cross.

She was stopped at the entrance, asked if she wanted help. 'No thank you,' she said. 'I'm being met.' And she waved towards someone in the crowd, as if it was true.

Amy was dirty, conscious of the fact only as she became aware of the occasional glance in her direction, but she was in an area of dirty people. Around the station on this side of the river, grime was commonplace and no one cared to notice the quality of her grubby clothes. Sticky dirt, black, oily marks on quality fabrics. She had the idea that if she smiled some more, they would leave her alone. It worked. Hers was not a smile to attract; it was manic.

She was walking aimlessly and slowly and it took her

some time to realise that she was, in her way, following a prescribed route. Away from the station and over the bridge. She felt lost without a handbag; it made her feel disembodied, panic-stricken. She stopped for a moment and patted her pockets. Her hands were filthy.

Amy Petty, petty Amy, *silly* thing. *Pretty Petty . . . the light at the end of the tunnel . . .*

There was the sound of her own footsteps, hard against the metal walkway of the bridge. The pall of smoke was now behind her and she did not look back. The sun on the water of the river was blinding. There was a dearth of people, abnormal silence. A breeze which made it seem as if the bridge was moving, instead of herself, staggering. The only imperative was to get to the other side. She did not like the south side of the bridge. It was ugly. There, now she knew where she was. Walking towards Blackfriars, a little steadier now, a plan emerging as if pre-formed.

Go to the flat. Not far now. She could see the dome of St Paul's. The traffic was jammed solid, tailed far back from the blocked roads around the stations. Cars, glimmering in the sunlight, and herself frightened that once she started to move across, the whole mass of them would move too. She crossed slowly, leaving the landmark of the river with regret. Down Blackfriars Road, towards Clerkenwell, getting a few more sideways glances once she was beyond the area of dirty faces and mucky hands. She walked resolutely, relieved it was not yet lunchtime when these pavements would be dense with people, troubled by the sly thought that it might be better that way.

No one was noticed in a crowd; crowds were secret places and this was not quite crowded enough. She reached the side street and the door to the block. The keypad was inside a box in the recess of the wall, the numbers as grubby as her hands. The numbers to press were embedded in memory.

It was the pied-à-terre of a handsome couple who lived in the country but occasionally needed the convenience of somewhere in town, and it was intended to be as quiet and anonymous as it was. Two flights up from the door, tucked in this back street. Douglas had owned it for years. A bachelor hole, once full of kitchen machinery, a stupendous supply of booze, rudimentary crockery and an overlarge bed. This was where he had first brought her, seven years before. Into a scrapheap of a place where discarded clothing from the last visit remained thrown into a corner of a kitchen where there was nothing to eat. Amy paused at the door. There had been no pretence and no blandishments. He had been a man who had missed his last train, went to a nightclub out of sheer boredom, and picked up a body for bed. She had danced with him because she was mesmerised by his voice. It was like dancing with a bear who neither listened to the music nor knew the steps. He had smelt of dog and his clothes were wrong and when he said, 'Let's go, shall we?' they got into a taxi and went the short distance to . . . here. 'Do you take drugs?' he had barked at her as the only attempt at conversation on the way. 'No.' 'Good.' They were both more than a little drunk, but in her case, not drunk enough for the clear purpose of the exercise.

She was not really made for this cruising lark. She had
stood at the door to this small apartment and seen the
expensive squalor, litter and furniture jumbled together
with no attempt to please or impress, touched with the
aroma of neglect. She could smell garlic on his breath; she
was impressed by him and afraid of him, but above all
weary, suddenly sober and utterly depressed by the
prospect of fucking someone who would never remember
her name, for nothing more than the saving of a taxi fare
home and being warm.

She stood unsteadily at the door and tried to remember what she had done. Waited for him to go to the
lavatory and then left, closing the door behind her, while
he was probably searching for a condom in the mess of
his bathroom as a token gesture towards courtesy. No
one had promised anyone the best of all honourable
intentions. She had left this little flat out of an instinct for
safety and a belated desire to preserve a shred of dignity.
He had become, in a space of minutes, as repellent as she
felt herself. A bloated shark with big, white teeth. A long
time ago.

Her eyes felt as if the grit of the train along with burnt
pieces of skin had formed into sand beneath the lids,
scoring her eyeballs pink each time she blinked. She
blinked now. This room, the living room, was awful after
Caterina's makeover. Pastel shades, no mess. Green curtains and matching carpet still bearing the brushmarks of
a hoover, no dust, no personality, like a hotel room maintained in a state of neutrality. Ready for human
occupation and somehow resentful of it. Fitted wardrobes

in the bedroom, his and hers. The sight of these pristine
clean walls made her want to scrawl graffiti. The clock in
the small vestibule where she stood with her view of the
whole place announced that it was 11.45. The mirror on
her left showed a woman with a grubby pleated skirt,
shirt, jacket and no handbag, a wild gleam in the bloodshot eyes. A sluttish woman. Behind that image lurked the
picture of how she had looked on the first occasion.
Cheap black dress reaching an inch or two below the
crotch and corseted to push up her bosom into twin
melons, an excess of mascara making soot on her cheeks,
a ladder in the tights. His estimation of her had been
entirely right and probably still was. She had been lonely
then, but not as lonely as now.

She needed a wash: shower, bubbles of soap, a scrubbing brush. She paused. The telephone was ringing and
she suppressed the automatic move to answer it, took off
her shoes, carefully, instead. Tiptoed over the small area
of mown carpet as if the phone could hear her and
washed her face and hands in the bathroom with all the
nervous reluctance of a small boy who hated water. Dried
her skin on a hank of toilet paper, sat on the lavatory gingerly and flushed all the traces away. Dabbed at the jacket
ineffectually with more toilet paper, flushed that away,
too. Began to hurry. The phone rang again, accusingly.
They would be looking for her by now; it followed from
that that someone would arrive. She could only take from
here what no one would notice, and while she knew that
Douglas was normally oblivious to the contents of the
bathroom cabinet, she was not taking chances. She looked

at the cosmetics with longing, her favourite things. From the Nescafé jar in the top kitchen cupboard she took the stash of banknotes, about five hundred pounds, she guessed without counting. Douglas never cared where cash went; there was always a reserve.

Back the way she had come, this time with her hair brushed and held back in an elastic band, the lunchtime crowds beginning to swell the view. Passing a restaurant window, she was acutely conscious of the dirtiness of the jacket. The dark print of the skirt absorbed more; dirt had become part of the design, but the jacket was different and her cleaning attempts had made it worse. On an impulse, she backtracked to the window, saw a small, smart, dark city watering hole, the sort of place she disliked. A place where a man brought a mistress and the sort of place she had been inside often enough, wearing the sort of clothes she was not wearing now. The window glass was smoked and the door stood open. She could hear a distant murmur of voices and smell beef and spices.

Inside the door was a full coat rack which Amy examined with two things in mind, the length of the garment and the sex of the owner. A man's coat would be no good, but she did want something which kept out the rain. There it was, olive green, lightweight, soft to the touch as she slipped it on. A little on the big side, covering her top to toe. She adjusted the collar and put her hands inside the pockets, making it her own. There was another kind of conspicuousness about the coat, though, as she walked along. The day had grown warm and the coats worn or carried to work had been abandoned now. She was over-dressed and still cold. Again, never mind. She smiled to herself, briefly. After all, taking the *best* coat in the rack instead of her own was something she had always sneak-ingly wanted to do. One of those exciting, forbidden things, like pulling the communication cord in a train.

When she was back by the side of the river, she was glad of the coat because the wind whipped up off the water and the parapet of Blackfriars Bridge was inade-quate shelter. The sun was bright again, the traffic still gridlocked, the air dense with fumes. She stopped and stood on tiptoe to look at the water, winded by memory.

This was where he had caught up with her on the night they had met. She, hiding down by the parapet and wishing she had a coat, and he, heralded by panting foot-steps, coming into view in an ungainly jog, his face pink in the streetlight, seen in a moment of fear when she believed he would simply pick her up and hoist her over the wall and into the river; he was strong enough for that. When they had danced to that unmemorable music, her bosom had bobbed somewhere higher than his thick waist and the top of her head was level with his enormous shoulders. Squatting down beside her, breathless in his shirtsleeves, all he said was . . . nothing until he recovered his breath. Pulled a battered cigarette packet out of his top pocket and offered her one. 'Oh, for God's sake, you silly bitch. You'll catch your death. Have you got a light?' And at that point she realised she had left her handbag in his flat. He sat down beside her and began patting trouser pockets, extending large feet as he sat – feet, she noticed, which wore socks, but not shoes. 'And I,' he said, 'seem to have forgotten my sodding keys. We may have to stay here all night.'

Three attempts to light a match, and his face was illuminated as he cradled the light and bent towards her. A broad face, widely spaced eyes, huge forehead, like a high-bred, cruel hound. A limping pigeon had nestled next to her, hopped into her lap and then across to his. He did not shoo it away.

So much for fairy tales. Amy flung herself away from the parapet as if it were that which made her cold, and walked back. She could no longer look at the river. In the distance, she could see that the pall of smoke had died into a kind of smog on the further side of that other bridge. She felt sick with sadness and at the same time buoyant with a sensation of freedom as she walked on, the overlong coat gathering dust behind her heels.

'She doesn't answer her phone,' Douglas said flatly.

His stepmother stirred in her chair.

'She's always hated the mobile, Douglas, you know that.'

'She knows what it's for,' he said shortly. 'She doesn't have to love it to use it. She might have lost it. She's always losing it.'

'Yes, dear, she does. Did you try the flat again?'

'Yes of course.'

'The police liaison, whatever it's called, they said they'd call as soon as they've located her, didn't they?'

'Yes.'

'So all we have to do is wait.'

'I don't want to *wait*. Not wait and watch *that*.' The television murmured in front of them with a running commentary on the disaster. *It will take several hours to establish the extent of the casualties. The number to phone is . . .* 'And THAT!' he shouted, staring at the silent telephone. 'I should be *doing* something.'

'What can you do, darling? You wouldn't be allowed near, even if you could get there. The roads will be blocked and—'

'SHE CAN'T DO THIS TO ME!' Douglas shouted. 'She CAN'T, SHE CAN'T, SHE CAN'T!'

The dog ambled across the room and put a large head on his knee, gazing at him soulfully. He fondled her yellow ears. They resembled each other.

'Caterina will be here soon,' his stepmother said kindly. 'Just go out for a while, Douglas, dear. It might calm you.'

Rob, the trolley man, sat in the line outside the Accident and Emergency department. He had left the queue inside and come outside to sit on the steps in the sunshine, although he was not quite sure how he had arrived there. Maybe he had been led outside by the man who was questioning him, clipboard in hand and Biro poised, both out of their depth and Rob weeping quietly and incessantly throughout, impeding the repetitions of his replies. Roughly how many people in that second to last carriage, Rob? Can you remember? No. Lots. Did they all get out? Yes, I was the last, I think. I don't know. Did any of them go through to the next carriage? I don't know.

His hands were grazed, his chest hurt more. Christ, it hurt, and the crying made it worse. I shouldn't have left her, he kept on saying. I shouldn't have let her go. I should have looked after somebody, at least.

Who? I mean why?

That woman. The blonde. None of your business.

But she might have wanted to die.

CHAPTER THREE

Libel. A defamatory publication which holds up the plaintiff to hatred, ridicule, or contempt. At worst. Otherwise, published words or pictures which lower the plaintiff's character in the estimation of right-thinking members of society generally.

In the evening of the day, Douglas returned three dogs to the stables. He walked slowly; the dogs, sensing his mood, were equally listless. An odd mix of creatures, so far removed from pedigree stock that their antecedents and their ages were difficult to guess. Hermione had one eye instead of the two, Viglen was missing half a leg and Buster had a weird kink to his feathery tail. They lived in a communal kennel, formed out of one of the stables. The stables themselves formed three corners of a square round a paved yard where Amy had established tubs of greenery, offset by the herbs which grew between the cracks of the stones, smelling sweetly now and stronger in the summer. In contrast to the whiteness of the house, the stables were of mellow red brick.

There was a hierarchy in the living accommodation. These three dogs lived together, harmoniously, in one room, as befitted their disabilities and sociable tendencies. Tonto and Lone lived in another, tolerating no other canine company. They had been guard dogs together, he guessed; delivered to the door only when neglect had failed to kill them. What spark of humanity in a man made it impossible for him to kill his servant when he had already effectively destroyed it, Douglas had wondered. It takes far more guts to kill a thing than to neglect it, and no person would ever get close to these two now, except for Amy. In the third stable, left unlocked at night, two yellow retrievers called Sally and Josh, for no reason he could remember, slept reluctantly. They did not know about neglect; they had simply outgrown their elderly owner when the bitch was accidentally pregnant and the dog began to wander; they were all beauty and muscle and slaver, without a brain cell between them, and could be relied upon to bark and run for the house at the first sign of trouble, out of duty or cowardice.

The trouble with dogs, the vet explained, is that they confuse their loyalties. They are the only species of animal which can change tribal allegiance. Give a dog to a man and he will want to adopt that man as the leader of his pack, regardless of his weaknesses, inadequacies and lack of a tail. He will associate with man more closely than any other animal and forswear all kinship to his own kind. To the extent that if he is taken away from mother and siblings too early, he will not recognise them at all, will snarl at them with suspicion for ever after and cling to the human like baby to mother. On the other hand, if the dog should reach adulthood without human contact, he will revert to being a wolf. The two retrievers had reached the ideal compromise of pets. They were friendly with other dogs, but given the choice, preferred humans and raced towards them with fickle speed at the first opportunity.

Douglas knew he should refer to a dog as an 'it'; to do otherwise made him sound as if he was talking about people, but he could not refer to any of them as an 'it'. They were always 'he' or 'she'.

He bedded the two retrievers in the third stable with Dilly, an arthritic greyhound, who regarded them with vague contempt, as if she did not really enjoy the company. Dilly was peacefully ill, her tenure of life a daily uncertainty, but her complicated infirmities did not yet interfere with the desire to live, in particular to bask in the sun. She could die any time. Douglas patted her head with gruff tenderness. She had never wanted fuss, only recognition, did not stoop to crave affection and he admired her all the more for her dignified indifference even though this patient acceptance of disabilities was alien to him. He was dog-tired himself, a gnawing pain of anger settled in his throat.

The house was out of sight of the stables, on the corner of the drive which dipped at the gate and turned uphill to the back door. It would be better when the new quarters were built and attached to the house. The stables were not quite out of earshot on a still night, but a step too far for emergencies. Which was why at the back of the fourth, small stable there was a room of sorts, with a bunk bed for a human occupant. The mellow brick buildings, older by far than the house, were a relic of the grander times of horse, carriage and sweeping acres. Dogs loved the fields. Douglas attended to the dogs with fastidious, concentrated care. In his mind's eye, a map unfurled. Dogs, here; the car in front of the house, the road to the station car park, the hourly London train. A clear route of migration he never wanted to take. He coughed to clear his throat of what felt like a hairball of prickly fur.

Food, water, washing, bedding, guardianship and attention. There was another dog, a sick, undersized mongrel, residing back at the house and there was too much to do. There had always been too much to do. He concentrated on tasks, whispering, 'Sit down, you silly, go there, come here, eat this . . .' mindful of their diets, talking like a teacher in charge of a nursery, making his voice heard. He tidied up the fourth stable, the one with the bed, the map of the route to London still in his mind, not wanting to think about it. Amy had an attachment to the city which he no longer shared, some bit of her which was exclusively metropolitan, perhaps, but she would be back, walking through the door, anytime soon. No point waiting on her. She would be back.

He bent down to stuff the bedding into the industrial-sized washing machine which occupied the same room as a ton of dry feed. Felt a touch to his shoulder, hot breath on his neck. Flung out his arm to push away whatever had got too close. Felt the man gasp as if he had been hit, instead of merely slapped across a skinny thigh.

Douglas turned, winced as his knees creaked and stood. He was getting too heavy; anger made him weightier. A wizened face, half obscured by a cap, yellow in the light, was scowling at him. It was the face of a pixie, looking older by far than his thirty-eight years. An ageless goblin. Douglas bunched his hands into fists. The man stepped back and sat on the bed; Douglas unclenched his fists.

'What the *fuck* do you think you're doing here, Jummy, you . . . *cunt*?'

Jimmy winced, as much at the mispronunciation of his name. Glasgow *Jummy*, a walking cliché, with his battered, ageless face, thick accent, wasted frame, roll-up cigarette hanging lifelessly from the side of his mouth until he grabbed it and stuffed it into his pocket. He was like a diminutive street fighter, pickled by alcohol and weather, far from home and beyond repentance. A randy little bastard.

'Aw, leave it out, Dougie, will ya? I scarcely touched you. Just saying hello. She hasnae come back, has she? I heard . . .'

Douglas sat down heavily on the bed beside him. The difference in their sizes became less significant. Upright, Douglas towered over him, looked as if he could have felled wee Jummy with a single punch. Sitting level with each other, it was more apparent that anyone who had a go at Jimmy would not go away unscathed. His agility was obvious; he sat still, but twitching; he would bite at the ankles or stab at the groin and go down fighting. He would scratch like a cat, Amy said.

'No,' Douglas said heavily. 'She hasn't come back.'

Jimmy scuffed his boots on the worn lino of the floor, nodded. 'I thought not. Heard about it. Thought to myself, Tuesday it is. Went to the car park at the station just now and there was her car, still. A few of them, poor buggers. In the hospital, is she?'

'No.'

'Ah, *shit*.'

Jimmy leant back against the wall behind the bed and blew out a sigh of disgust.

'Don't make yourself at home, you *cunt*,' Douglas snapped. 'You'll dirty the bedding.'

Jimmy was unmoved. 'So where is she, then?' he asked, hopefully, sitting up again and feeling for the roll-up in the pocket of his trousers. He had a lot of pockets; pockets were his favourite thing. Deep pockets in which things were lost, constantly.

'I don't know. We wait, and hope.'

'There's many dead. Burnt.'

'Thank you for telling me that, Jimmy. I really needed to know. She may be one of them.'

They were silent for a full minute while Jimmy found the cigarette. Once it was established between his blackened fingers, Douglas snatched it away and ground it beneath his heel. There was no protest. Silence resumed, punctuated by shuffling from the stable beyond and the sigh of a dog, dreaming.

'Well, I couldn't stand to think of it,' Jimmy said. 'I saw the car and I came to see. If she'd been here, I'd have gone away. Then I thought you might need some help.'

'Help? From *you*? You must be fucking joking. After all

the harm you did, I'd as soon have help from a rat.' It was calmly said in that commanding voice of his.

Jimmy knew better. 'Help from anyone,' he suggested softly, bending down, picking up the mess of tobacco with deft fingers, putting it into another pocket. 'You'll need it, maybe.'

Bad enough with only two of them, latterly, attending to eight canine cripples and the dogs up at the house. If Amy did not come back, it was going to be impossible. Money bought food, not help. There was so little money could actually buy, such as trust, reliability. Money was an over-rated commodity.

'You know I love them,' Jimmy whined. 'I'm just daft. Wee bit of a problem, maybe.'

'A wee bit of a problem? You were supposed to be looking after that poor sick bitch with her whelps, and what did you do? You fuck that girl, both of you drunk as skunks. Set this bed on fire. Sal nearly lost those pups. Help? From *you*? You daft sod.'

'I was good enough before, I can be good,' Jimmy said. 'You can hit me if you like,' he added helpfully.

Douglas stood up and punched him on the jaw. The blow wavered at the moment of impact, not full force, enough to make Jimmy's head rock back against the wall and tears start in the eyes. He blinked, shook his head slowly, eyes watering.

'You're a useless, two-faced, ugly bastard,' Douglas said. 'Come up to the house.'

Dusk was fallen, in the slow way of spring dusk within a

month of the changing of the clocks. All bad things happened after dark. Countryside dark, not town dark, always more noticeable. A short walk if they had gone the straight route via the drive with the worn holes where the intermittent repairs with wheelbarrowfuls of gravel failed to stop the rot for more than six months. Rain found the weak spots, sluiced away the grit and left the hole deeper than before. Strangers like John Box and Elisabeth Manser would have stumbled, as indeed they had, oh dear, while habitual foot passengers moved unerringly. One minute was all between point A and point B. Not long enough for Jimmy. He did not want to reach the house and hear unwelcome news. Nor did he want to see wee Dougie's mam in the kitchen, wearing her rubber gloves and saying, 'Good evening, Jummy,' whilst she stirred some piece of poison in a pot which could have contained her painted nails for seasoning. Pure imagination, Jimmy, my lad. She just made him feel like shit, was all. Not her fault. Never said a cross word, never a real one either. He could see her now as they rounded the bend, a slender silhouette against the kitchen window. He knew who he wanted to see in there, out here, anywhere; the thought made him wince with grief and want to blub like a bairn. He put a hand to his cheek and felt it was already wet; his jaw hurt; he wanted a drink. Wanting a drink was constant; he was born lacking just the three double measures which made him feel right. Being sober and facing the elder Mrs Petty while his jaw throbbed and he wanted to cry was not a combination he could handle. His feet sidestepped the holes in the track and he could hear himself thinking, I'll go now;

bad idea, this. Then, to his relief, Douglas detoured away to the side and led them down the path which skirted the house to the front where the living-room windows mirrored the lawn and the bench was rooted beneath the willow. He was not the only man here who did not want to go inside.

A curtain of dark was pulled on the day as they sat on the bench and Jimmy began his erratic search of his pockets for the remnants of tobacco and other bits he needed. Ten pockets in all, a great deal of fiddling. Douglas was halfway down his own cigarillo before Jummy took the first draw on his own. He could blow smoke circles into the still air, could Douglas, a trick Jimmy greatly admired. He was not blowing pretty patterns now though. He was fingering the mobile phone clipped to his belt and smoking as if the small cigar was a substitute for breath and his life depended on it. 'You're a shit, Jummy,' he murmured. 'An absolute shit.'

'And so what are you, faceache? Some fucking saint or what? You're a *cunt*.'

'*Bastard*.'

'You're the bastard. Makes two of us. *Cunt*. Aah'm just a drunk. You're just a turd with money, you. You're just bollocks, you. You wouldn't give me a chance. Not you.'

They smoked furiously. Jimmy's jaw ached less; Douglas's huge left hand fingered the phone as if willing it to speak.

'Not *yew*,' Jimmy continued. 'Not great big yew, Muster Big Guy, yer fucker. I fuck up, fuck yew, you say. But she's a good woman, her. She'd have give me the chance.' He dragged the last gasp from the charred Rizla paper and started again about the exploration of his pockets. The task exhausted him and he began to cry. 'I canna bear it. She's never *dead*, Mr Petty. Is she?'

'Possibly.'

'You fucking great *shithole*. She never is?'

'I don't know.'

They went to the back door. Of common accord and long habit, both took off their boots and threw them into the porch with all the other boots. Douglas shed his coat: Jimmy never had a coat except for three days a year. A coat impeded him; he wore instead several layers of thin, decrepit sweaters, which, in the days when he had worked at the stables, had gone into the washing machine along with the dogs' bedding from time to time and smelt roughly the same. The kitchen was empty, with the look of recent abandonment, as if Mrs Petty, Senior, had become exhausted by the peeling of potatoes which lay, half done, on the draining board.

'I expect she's gone to call in the cavalry,' Jimmy said.

Douglas nodded; their eyes met in a moment of understanding as they sat heavily at the kitchen table. A cat peeled itself out of a box by the Rayburn, stretched and moved to sit on Jimmy's lap, as if he belonged and had not been missing for two months. Douglas could not understand the attraction of Jummy's body either to cats or to females. Must be the smell of him; the succession of sweaters with holes.

'She'll be calling up your sister, maybe.'

'Already has.'

Jimmy remembered not to let out a sigh of relief to be inside this kitchen again. Too soon for that. He liked the daft, white doll's house which perched next to the sink; he liked the uneven red tiles on the floor, the constant warmth of the Rayburn, the battery of equipment he did not understand, the heavy wooden chairs, the clutter of paperwork which always had to be moved off the table and the sense of being in an engine room. There was always a litter of yellow Post-its, containing Amy's lists. They were her particular hallmark, stuck to the fridge, the table, everywhere. It was the only room in the house which counted and he rarely went any further. The sight of a pot of drooping tulips on the window ledge above the sink renewed the threat of tears. Amy always had to have flowers in here and she always kept them long after they were dead.

'Och, Dougie,' he wept. 'What are we going to do?'

'Oh for God's sake, stop grizzling, man. Helps nothing. And yes, I could do with you back. I fucking wouldn't if I had a choice. I must be mad. That poor bitch might have died.'

'But she didn't die, Douglas, did she? Amy got her right. And you know damn fine it wasn't me talking to newspapers . . . could've been Dell, digging the dirt on you.'

'Have you got rid of that scrubber?'

'Oh yes. Far away, gone.'

A bottle of whisky appeared out of the kitchen-table drawer. Douglas slopped two generous measures into small tumblers. Jimmy refrained from grabbing the glass with both hands. The gesture of the whisky meant, OK, start work tomorrow. He nodded, the closest he could get to saying thank you. Thanks and apologies were not on his agenda. Then he caught sight of an apron hanging over a chair and his eyes filled again.

'And when my sister comes, you stay well clear of her. No closer than a bloody mile, you hear? You can be as rude to her as you always were to Amy.'

'Oh, for sure,' Jimmy said. He always had been rude to Amy; his affection for her a well-kept secret. 'I canna believe it, Douglas. She'll walk in that door any minute. She's just having you on.'

'That's not what Amy does, Jummy. Not in this house.'

'No, I suppose not. What about her family, Douglas? Someone you should tell?'

'No,' Douglas said. 'Apart from us, absolutely none.'

'Was she an orphan, then, or what? No brothers or sisters?'

'No,' Douglas repeated. 'She came without family.'

They fell silent and listened for the sound of Mrs Petty's cane. A man did not say fuck or cunt in her company.

It echoed in her mind, the sound of the stick. When the evening closed in, Amy was glad of the coat because the fickle heat died with the sun and it was only spring yet, not summer at all; she began to panic. The choices which existed in the middle of the day no longer seemed viable. Euphoria had died and something else had replaced it. The component parts of shock and guilt, hunger as well, although the thought of food was sickening. She sat in two cafes and one burger bar, faced with coffee, microwaved apple pie or cheese roll, unable to eat the food, only drink the coffee and find herself shaking. Now she tried tea instead, in another burger bar where she was the only one nursing a single Styrofoam cup rather than eating out of cardboard containers the mess of food which looked worse than what she spooned out of tins for the cat. Life has spoiled me, she thought. I have learned to cook and resent crowds: taught myself to live in a way I once found alien and impossibly difficult and now I can't adapt. I have got used to an entirely different set of sounds. I need not have bothered coming back once a week to keep myself acclimatised; the therapy did not work. I am homesick. But this is my new home.

Trafalgar Square was home to no one. A magnet for tourists and pigeons, a gathering place for strangers. Before midnight, the police would clear the benches and in the early hours of the morning, someone would tidy up the litter and it would all start again. The evenings longer now; time shorter. She could find a hotel, but she did not want a hotel, because the money would be gone in two days and she did not have a cash card to put in a hole in the wall, even if she could have used it. She was dead. She had seen the *Evening Standard* posters – TRAIN CRASH! FORTY DEAD! – and here she was, sitting here, one of them. Her thoughts were less of the dead than the disabled. She thought, briefly, of the trolley man and wondered how he was. It was better not to think. Thinking, like food, made her nauseous.

How silly to imagine that there ever had been any doubt about where to go. Amy clambered off her stool, searched for her handbag and felt foolish for forgetting she did not have one. There was not enough to do with her hands without it, except stuff them in the pockets of the coat and pretend she did not want to keep stuffing them in her mouth to bite the nails. Short, square nails, neatly trimmed, not like her mother-in-law's nails, painted a different colour every week. A vanity of hers. Sitting on the bus, she found herself looking at hands, concentrating on the fingers which curled round a newspaper or a book lying dormant in a lap.

It began to rain. The bus edged round the square and then broke free of the clog of the traffic, escaping up the broad road to Westminster. Ran free from Pimlico into the hinterland of the metropolis where tourists did not go. Going south. She could almost imagine she was going home. The place where you put your heart, and left it there. Not the housing estate where she had grown up, surrounded by rigorous hygiene, where curtains were pulled at the first sign of dark. A goldfish bowl, where the fish inside swam around in relative safety provided no one could see.

The bus journey was endless; stop, start, welcoming on board a different population. More hands, laced together on the bench seat opposite, guarding a bag, a stomach, an umbrella, or propped on the side to rest the head, or poised to dive inside a bag of crisps. Thumbs crept into mouths as darkness fell, a little nibble of a forefinger as someone remembered the thing they had forgotten on the way home. The territory ran out of useful shops but never out of buildings. Smaller streets, mock town centres with lights coming on now. The bus emptied. She sat on the bench seat almost alone, linking her own hands and trying to look relaxed.

Get off here. The roar of traffic from the ring road, an urban motorway which sounded like hell. Down this road to the shop on the corner. The Paki newsagents, as he referred to them, where she looked in the window, shielding her eyes the better to concentrate, and examined the advertisements. ROOM TO LET, a tired postcard among all the others explaining the existence of an e-mail expert, a plumber without qualifications, a three-piece suite and several tarts. No point going in here and asking about the room. He would tell her what he had told her before. No one ever takes it, darling. He only puts the card in there to make sure he gets fifteen visitors a week, which he does, regular. Likes company, turns them all down. The card was still there, folded innocuously inside its plastic folder on the display with all the others, innocent among the sly invitations to sex, but quite at home. She passed by. The centre of London was far away. The fifty-year-old semi-detached streets were too ugly to suffer the lure of a fashion makeover. They had never been tempted to gentrification. Amy turned off the main thoroughfare into a narrow road where the cars were crowded on to the pavements, bumper to bumper, shiny wet with the drizzle. Some looked as if they belonged to no one and had landed where they were by mistake. Three men crowded round the bonnet of another, staring at the engine and arguing about it. The litter was damp and flattened into doorways. She passed a house which reverberated with the *boom, boom, boom* of stereo sound. The next house bore the gallant signs of effort, with fresh painted window frames and net curtains behind the double glazing, while the next looked dark and empty, the windows thick with dust and a cracked glass panel in the front door.

From the outside of the houses, it was impossible to gauge how many people lived within. Successive property booms had passed this area by and moved north to places served by more than the erratic bus service and the far distant station. Bayview Road, it was laughingly called, summoning some vision of the sea instead of the contrasting sound of the railway line running behind the back gardens. A local wag had altered the sign on the wall, changing the Y to a T and the B to R. Ratview.

The house she had reached was not the worst in the row since it did not have an air of neglect and the cars immediately outside possessed all of their wheels. Their bulk blocked most of the light to the ground-floor windows but it did not seem as if the occupants would mind. The curtains dragged untidily across the front window, with their dun-coloured lining facing the world, looked as if they were never drawn back; the bunching of material on the window ledge had the look of undisturbed permanence. Amy stood on the step and rang the bell. A car cruised slowly down the street, filling the valley with the echo of more loud music. She turned to watch it. When she turned back, the door was already open with a figure retreating down the hall in a mute invitation to her to follow. She went inside.

'I suppose you've come about the room,' his voice floated back in neutral tones. 'Come in, do. Close the door.'

She did as she was told, noticing the smooth, almost noiseless click of the latch, and followed his right turn into the room with the curtains. Heavy curtains, which allowed no chink of light either out or in. The room was so bright, it hurt her eyes. There was a distinct set of chemical smells – paint, glue, white spirit – clean smells which she liked. They were sharp scents which cleared her nostrils of the other smells which had lingered since the train – blood, diesel fumes, burning.

He was a bright little bird of a man, about sixty-five and nimble, standing with his hands in the pockets of an old cardigan which stretched to his knees with the wool of it bobbled and flecked with different colours of paint and dried clay. He was pale with apple pink cheeks, big eyebrows which moved when he smiled and no more than a dusting of white hair on his head. She was taller than he, but not tall enough to see his skull. He was so clean-shaven that his chin shone and the smile on his wide mouth creased his whole face into a look of delighted curiosity. He usually minded his manners.

Almost always. His manners, she noticed, were all about being careful and precise in everything he did and wanting to preserve his environment. She was not the person, or even the category of person, he was expecting and it seemed to confuse him. She did not know if his turning away, back to the task in hand, was deliberate or just something he did to hide indifference or disappointment. Or maybe the task was more important. He had picked up the thing he was mending and held it together with his two thumbs and first fingers. It was a tiny chair, made from balsawood, high-backed and almost as tall as a matchstick, the seat as broad as his thumbnail. He was pressing one of the tiny legs into the seat from which it had become detached. It required a certain kind of glue.

'Broke,' he explained. 'Some person sat on it too long. Too heavy. Bit like you.'

Amy tried to smile. He concentrated on the chair, staring at it as if willing it to stick. She looked round the room. The drawn curtains hid treasure. There were shelves on three sides with tables in front, crowding the room. On each of the tables was a doll's house. The frontage of the one he faced opened like a door, revealing the rooms and stairs and inmates otherwise visible only by peering through the windows. Each house had a theme; she knew that already. One was a gentlemen's club, with a library upstairs, where tiny old men in waistcoats sat in armchairs with newspapers, while in the main room below more of them sat around a fireplace. One younger gentleman stood with his back to the fire, raising the tails of his frock coat to warm his behind on the coals created by shredded red and gold foil paper in the grate. A butler hovered with a tray.

The doll's house with the opened front, from which the broken chair came, was different altogether. This was a brothel with pretensions to Victorian grandeur, with flock wallpaper on the walls, genteel and delicate furniture painted gold and gaudy furnishings of net and plush velvet. Painted ladies lay in deshabille on three chaise longues in the living room, attended by a demure maid in black and white. Upstairs, another miniature woman lay in a hip bath with her clothes, including a corset, strewn over a painted screen. It was the brothel on a Sunday, with no customers in sight. The ladies were bored by their own elegance. She did not look closely; he did not encourage it, but she still admired. Amy was too big for the limited space left in the room. The tiny figures she could see through the windows made her feel even more enormous. She stumbled against the edge of the table with the open doll's house, making it rock. The young man with the raised coat-tails fell over. She reached inside and righted him carefully.

'I've almost got enough for my big exhibition. And my book. Isn't that nice?' he said, checking to see that the miniature had been returned to the right place.

'Hallo, Daddy,' she said. 'I can see you're busy. But I've got to stay a while.'

'How long?'

'I don't know,' she said. They did not embrace; they never did. She thought of the vast space of the circular living room at home and the willow tree outside and began to cry.

'You told me I could come here. I can't go back and I could look after you.'

'My darling child,' he said, without moving towards her. 'You're so defenceless. I wonder how different you would have been if you had the slightest capacity for retaliation. Where did you get that coat?'

'I found it.'

'And I found you. This is your home now.'

CHAPTER FOUR

Elisabeth Manser always wanted to go home. Or outside, where spring was having a debate with summer about which of them was winning. Inside here, it made precious little difference. She and John Box sat on the stone benches which lined the vast hall of the High Courts, five steps up from the tiled floor, facing the dun-coloured stone of the archways opposite. The archways led to curved stone stairs, disappearing to the floor above. High above them, the leaded windows of the east wall let in a colourless light, offsetting the dramatic stained glass of the windows at the far end. The building had the dimensions of a cathedral. The tiles of the floor, set in huge mosaic patterns of warm colours, made it less like a cloister and more like a vast railway station, built as a temple to the steam train, with the height of the roof more suitable to absorbing the sound of machinery than echoing the music of worship. The presence of gigantic stone in the huge pillars, balustrades, vaunted ceiling, archways, steps and multiple decorative motifs made it feel as enclosed as if they all sat, stood and moved in an underground cave. Voices echoed; a shout became a whisper; ordinary conversation became a mumble, the place too large for eavesdropping and perfect for secrets. The whole, huge space lent itself to privacy and defied hysteria.

There were no rules against cigarettes. Cylindrical ashtrays stood here and there against the walls, tiny against the scale of the rest and as unnoticeable as smoke. The size and the stone reduced the human element, their bad habits, bad breath, peculiar costumes and everyday clothes, to complete insignificance. A millionaire would have less presence than a gargoyle.

'So much easier to think about one's client when one hasn't seen him for a week,' John said, ready to return to his theme. 'Easier to sympathise from a distance. The law's an ass, you know. We have no real right to privacy and yet we persist with our strong concern to protect the rights of reputation. Shutting the stable door after the horse has bolted.'

'Yes,' Elisabeth agreed. 'No offence to focus your telephoto lens on a bedroom window and record how little a woman wears in bed, but publish and be damned. Rather like giving your scavenging journalist access to all the tasty scraps and then telling him he cannot digest them into words.'

'Poetic, my dear, but scarcely accurate. Who cares about privacy, anyway? Provided your life is as dull and ordinary as most lives are, you attract no interest. You're entirely safe, and you can beat your wife or your dog with complete impunity. You need no law to assist you. If you have courted the limelight, well, a different matter. I do so dislike the kind of client who beckons attention for her cleavage, but is furious when she is snapped being sick at the party. Which is a difference with our Douglas Petty. He doesn't seek attention, never did, but somehow, he incurred it and it remains consistent. There's many a public relations expert who would like to know the secret.'

'But it is tantamount to dislike,' she said. 'The one we love to hate. No public relations company would want to emulate it.'

John blew his nose on a large red paper napkin, rescued from somewhere, speaking simultaneously. 'The grieving widower. Poor woman. What an awful way to die. I hope she wasn't frightened.'

An odd hope, she thought. It was the lunch hour and therefore a time of relative calm. How Dickensian they must look in this setting. The High Court enclave was almost obscenely opulent in its decor and at the same time severely uncomfortable. The stone seat, inset into the wall, had the gradual effect of stiffening the spine. Both of them leant forward, resisting the chill of prolonged contact with the unyielding wall. Neither of them had chosen it as the ideal place for conversation. They had been passing through, using the front entrance in the Strand and aiming to exit through the back as a short cut into Carey Street. There was nothing awkward in this sudden sitting down.

She fancied they resembled two garden gnomes, turning to stone, as if the daily apparel of wig, gown and suit had stunted their development, petrified them into something quasi-permanent and definitely old. Elisabeth suspected that John might like the place *because* it was uncomfortable as well as vast and anonymous in its vastness. Or he might like the opportunity to sit here and watch the women pass, walking quickly and peculiarly framed against the tiles. He had a way of observing women in particular, the brief, frank examination of someone looking for something to admire, like a hurried visitor to an art gallery who was curious but had no intention of buying. It was so objective, she found it impossible to resent.

There were two ways of walking in the High Courts, the brisk walk of someone who knew where they were going, or the pretended brisk walk of the majority who did not. The staircases on the left led to an impenetrable warren of impregnable doors, the maze of nightmares.

'But highly convenient, in one sense,' John remarked. 'By Amy Petty's death, Douglas gains sympathy, surely? Even if she isn't there to add to his credibility, she's a force *in absentia*. An absent piece of virtue who cannot be cross-examined.'

'And no risk she'd break down in public and say he was a bully. No risk that the defence could find some murkiness in her background to make her look . . . dishonest. A person prone to lies. A gold digger.'

'Oh, come now, we could have objected to that. Entirely inadmissible. And what could they have found? There's nothing.'

'Which is odd, don't you think? I'm not suggesting they could have raised whatever they found at trial, only used it, threatened to publish it, to get him to back off. You can always find something.' Elisabeth felt nervous. It was always present, beneath the surface, when she was with him. He was so analytical he intimidated her as he always had and that had nothing to do with love.

'No, I disagree. She might have been a scrubber, how I hate that word. An opportunist, maybe, but she wasn't important enough for notoriety. The cloak of ordinariness is a good enough armour. Even if she did indeed model underwear and work as a mortician.'

'*Beautician*,' she corrected, standing up briskly. 'But Douglas won't stop on her account, will he? Wouldn't that be nice?'

'How can you say that? I do hope not,' John said fervently. 'My practice is half what it was a few years ago. I mean, look at the lists.' He waved in the general direction of the freestanding noticeboard near the entrance. 'One hundred and fifty judges in here, and not one of their eminences trying a libel case at the moment. We've priced ourselves out of the market. Scarcely anyone takes the risk of libelling anyone any more. But that stupid local paper did and the national compounded it. Then they enter a defence; they don't even get themselves off the hook by making an offer of amends. So rare, alas, to have opponents as ill-advised and careless as this. I *need* this case. There are other reasons too, of course. *We* need this case. I shall advise him that widowed or not, his reputation is still sacred and any settlement they suggest is inadequate. I want a *fight*.'

His voice cut into silence. An excellent speaking voice, like Douglas Petty's, but without the latter's peculiar resonance. Elisabeth thought of the courtrooms upstairs, where the relentlessness of stone gave way to equally relentless wood panelling and the creaking oak of the floors. She thought of the crackling tension of the mornings and the sleepiness of the airless afternoons in those rooms, and wondered if he needed anything of the kind. Without Mrs Petty to decorate the occasion, the scenery would be monumentally dull. And there was something behind this case which made it more disconcerting than its originality. A slipstream of malice, rare in its irrationality and indifference to money. Surely there was nothing else worth an argument but money; in real life, yes, but in litigation, no. Why care about reputation if you were rich enough to survive the loss of it?

Elisabeth shivered. They walked across the tiles towards the rear entrance, John blowing his nose again. The sound was infinitesimal; even the loudest of farts would not attract attention.

'This was where Douglas did his naked run,' she began.

'Where did she come from?'

'Who?'

'*Her.*'

A girl tripped down the steps in front of them, illuminated from behind by the light streaming through the stained glass. It turned her into a silhouette with a cloud of hair, her neat black suit invisible, a figure with legs, a thing of beauty. Once she was out of the light and they turned to regard her, they could see what she was, of indeterminate age, high heels, good legs, plain face.

'Do you know,' John said, 'everyone has moments of beauty? If only they knew and if only it were enough.'

She smiled. Their footsteps up the steps were louder here than on the tiles. They could turn left or right at this point, take one of the side exits, quicker, if either of them had wanted to hurry. He became indecisive at moments like these.

She thought of Douglas Petty, running naked through here for a bet, his big body spotlit by the windows.

'Just as well Petty was the wrong kind of advocate. Only ever did crime. If he worked in here, they'd have to call the Tipstaff and get him arrested.'

'He *was* arrested, just outside the doors, remember?'

'Ah yes, of course. An amazing disgrace. He did a streak from the back to the front, didn't he? Then got disbarred. What an absolute ass.'

Elisabeth hesitated. 'John, this libel . . . I know who printed it, but who started it? We don't know, do we?'

'The rival animal sanctuary? One of the many people he's offended? An old lover? Who cares? It doesn't matter who started it. Money in the bank, this one.'

They took the exit to the left with the windows above. Kissed by the doors, briefly but not furtively, and went separate ways.

Elisabeth went via Chancery Lane, past Ede and Ravenscroft with its display of formal clothes. The dummies on which the costumes sat reminded her of overgrown dolls, like the models displayed inside the High Courts. The High Court models were encased in glass, at the foot of the first set of stone steps which led to the left, just behind the entrance. They stood in their gloomy passageway, displaying the traditional finery of the Judges of Europe, as if to reassure the litigants who passed that the apparel of the judiciary upstairs was no more elaborate than anywhere else. The items in the Ede and Ravenscroft window were also uniforms; suits of stiff wool gaberdine and evening dresses like armour. Elisabeth disliked costume. She disliked the wearing of her wig, even though she believed in it. It made her into an advocate, defined her role in judicial proceedings, encouraged the person she was beneath the gown to behave accordingly and it was the very antidote to vanity. Not that vanity was one of her sins; she could not concentrate long enough for grooming and there was nothing to be vain about. There was instead a yawning gap of insecurity, indecisiveness and the constant belief that her world was as tenuous as her career, and that she herself was nothing but a fraud.

She did not want to go back to chambers, she wanted to go home and start again tomorrow. There was plenty of work to do at home. Better to go there in the early afternoon when the trains were less crowded and the detours to the line less irritating. It shamed her slightly that she was able to shrug off the horror of that train crash, still prominent in the daily headlines, and catch her train on the parallel route without a second thought except for impatience about having to go to an alternative

station and the whole business taking longer. She should
have been more hesitant and less practical, she thought;
she should be boycotting all trains, in deference to the
memory of Amy Petty, whom she had liked. But people
died and life continued, that was that, and since she had
neither the money nor the inclination for a flat in central
London, she was a commuter and a second-class citizen,
in a way. Second-class barrister also, hanging on the coat-
tails of a lover. Who did she think she was? A fish out of
water who should have gasped for mercy long since. A
woman without grooming who needed a wig to cover her
hair, working a career for which she did not feel remotely
competent, although John always said otherwise and
sometimes she believed him, and if she was as serenely
confident and ambitious as she appeared, she would not
be living where she lived, and she would not be in the
fourth year of her affair with a married man, whom she
loved to desperation without even being able to approve
of him. It was an odd way to live on the brink like this,
feeling constantly not up to it, whatever it was, waiting for
it all to crash. With the knowledge that, if it did, the pieces
of her wreckage would be remarkably small.

She was halfway to the regular station before she
remembered it was still closed, due to open again next
week once they had removed the remnants of the crashed
trains to allow life to continue as if the accident had never
happened – beyond the recriminations which would
reverberate for a year or three and the civil actions which
would provide lucrative work for three dozen lawyers.
Now that would be the perfect symbiosis, acting for a

victim of negligence, behaving like an indignant human-
itarian whilst earning high fees at the same time. There
was nothing like well-rewarded altruism, but she would
not have been up to that, either. She got quality work
because of John's blatant favouritism. It was a subject of
comment, Elisabeth's practice being better than she
deserved. Occasional sex in return for patronage.
Sometimes she believed it was true. Usually she knew it
was not. She loved him and she was afraid of him. Even
more afraid of admitting defeat.

Detouring into the Tube for the creaky Northern Line
service to London Bridge, she had a sudden fellow feeling
for Amy Petty, based on nothing but her own sense of
inadequacy. That was what Amy had been like, all the time
giving the impression of trembling on the brink in a way
not obvious to John, only to herself. Call it feminine intuition, a phrase she loathed even though she did not doubt
the existence of such a thing. It was a mistake to have
meetings in the house of a client; you learned too much
from a house and a client should remain a stranger. You
should not be sent off into the kitchen to make tea with the
client's wife, to watch her fuss and apologise about the dirt
on the floor. Elisabeth did not despise those who made a
career of housewifery; she envied them. It was a daunting
task in its own way and a noble calling. Amy had taken her
to see the dogs. That was where she was competent, but
she did not think she was, any more than Elisabeth considered herself a natural lawyer or a star anything, for
that matter. She was a thirty-five-year-old, unkept and

sometimes unkempt mistress with a very small house and garden far outside the walls of a big exciting city which she had never quite grasped or enjoyed.

The roof over the platforms of London Bridge station was probably a little taller than the roof of the High Courts, she decided, but there wasn't much in it. She was thinking of the size of the Petty household in comparison to her own, which she kept with indifferent care, apart from the garden. She was thinking that if she had been Amy Petty she would not have been up to her job, either, not if it entailed keeping a man like Douglas Petty happy and getting beaten up by him, to say nothing of his mother, and she was wondering at the same time exactly when the moment was that Amy and she had fallen into liking with one another, however briefly. As she sat in the train, fishing in her bag for the packet of mints she usually carried, all dusty at the bottom, she suddenly remembered Amy remarking in the kitchen, 'He's nice, your man. Do you know, he looks just like a *whippet*?' And then, before Elisabeth could interrupt and state in her best icy tones that John was not her *man*, she was simply his assistant, Amy put her hand over her mouth and murmured a flurried apology. 'Oh, I'm so sorry, what an awful thing to say, but I like whippets. They're fragile-looking, you see, but ever so tough. Sorry.' Busying herself with tea things like a nervous waitress, so that Elisabeth had laughed out loud and not bothered with any denial. The woman had a sixth sense about her relationship with John, but like feminine intuition, it would be easily ignored. 'So what do I look like then?' she had

asked to prove that she did not really mind anything the
mere wife of a client might say. The question had startled
Amy and given her pause for thought, but so short a
pause, she had obviously thought about it already. 'You?
Overgrown cocker spaniel mixed with terrier, nice
colouring.' 'And yourself?' Elisabeth had asked, still smiling and oddly flattered, eyeing the Post-its on the
mantelpiece, covered with neat handwriting. Amy had
shaken her head and lifted the tray, her long sleeves falling
back from her wrists. 'Battersea Dogs' Home special
issue,' was all she said. 'Although Douglas says I'm more
like an Afghan. They haven't got much brain.'

When the sleeves fell back from Amy's arms, Elisabeth
noticed the bruises. Old, pink and yellow bruises. Nothing
was said about them. Remembering that, Elisabeth shed
a tear for Amy Petty and chewed on a dusty mint. Three
meetings in that house and on each occasion, it had presented itself in various states. It had not been a quiet
house, or one where a single room was left undisturbed
for long, despite the number of rooms. All that livestock.
On that second occasion, they had all thanked her for
the coffee except that bastard husband of hers. He hit
her; how else did she get bruises? *Mongrel with good taste.
Grizzled grey bulldog, several owners.* Elisabeth fumed.

The journey to her outpost was forty-five minutes, but
this train went two hours further than that, right as far as
the coast. Sometimes a man, woman or hermaphrodite,
Elisabeth never noticed which, pushed a trolley through
so fast there was scarcely a chance to stop the damn thing
and ask for a tea bag in boiled water. She preferred to get

on her train clasping good coffee purchased at the station, fussy about that, trying to forget her hunger which was more of a thirst and remember the fact that a brief, dry kiss in parting from a man who looked like a *whippet* was, nevertheless, worth having.

But the words of the article which had defamed Douglas Petty echoed in her head. *Why does this one-time defender of law and order take in his waifs and strays? Is it so that he can sentence them to this?* And alongside that the picture of the defrocked Douglas with the raised stick, chasing the dog across the lawn, with the caption *Dougie frolics with doggies, but why in the dark?* And *why*, if it were not true, would anyone seek to reveal Douglas Petty as a man not only cruel but perverted? All right, there was a rival animal sanctuary run by some woman, but where was the *money*? Who could possibly stand to gain? And, most importantly, why, if he was such a monstrous, reactionary bully, did a woman like Amy stay with him? Money, the root of all loyalty. Not a bad motive either; there were certainly worse. A bargain was a bargain. The kiss lingered, as if her cheek had been pinched.

Douglas kissed his stepsister in the perfunctory way of a brother with greater things on his mind. He put his hands on her shoulders and placed the kiss in the general direction of her left ear, followed up by a gentle slap between her shoulderblades, as if his giant hand was looking for a place to land without encountering anything sharp. Caterina had an angular shape, with the kind of spiky hair which looked permanently arranged above a long, slender neck and the sort of physique designed for elegance. She was made for flowing drapery and large chunks of interesting, metal jewellery. As she was now, recently out of bed, she looked more like an overgrown waif who could fold herself piece by piece into a chair. The loose jumper, tight jeans and bare feet suited her forty-year-old face, which was youthful with skin stretched tight over high cheekbones and enormous brown eyes. She took hold of his hand before he moved away, pressed it lightly to the side of her almost beautiful face, and then released it. She watched his progress to the other side of the table with a look of concerned devotion, as if he might slip before he reached his chair. He reached for the packet of cornflakes.

'You were up late last night,' she said in her high, singsong voice which surprised people. An almost childish contrast to the voice of her stepbrother, which was deep and carrying, even when he swore beneath his breath.

'I usually am.' He was not encouraging conversation. Caterina sighed, unfolded herself from the easy chair and came to sit opposite him. Douglas poured milk on the cereal and munched solidly without any sign of enjoyment. Bacon, eggs and all the accompaniments were not available under the regime Caterina imposed out of preference for the muesli and yoghurt type of sustenance. Cornflakes and toast were a compromise arrived at without discussion after a week. She did not think Amy would have achieved this, but did not say so. She knew when to limit her remarks.

'Locking yourself away,' she teased. 'Not good. Oh my poor Douglas, I do feel for you.'

'I know you do,' he said between mouthfuls, 'only I wish you wouldn't say it.'

There was a silence. She shrugged to suggest she was not really hurt and smiled. Caterina had a wide mouth and her smile had a devastating charm. He smiled back. They were, in their way, a handsome pair of step-siblings. When he was a barrister and she a twenty-year-old student, he had been proud to be seen with her and announce the relationship to jealous male friends. Did he have friends in those days? Yes, he remembered them; hard-drinking bachelors, quite unsuitable for his status in life even then and all disappeared now. They either took up the domestic mantle or abandoned him when he was disbarred. It was only Douglas who had been able to sustain bachelor behaviour into the age when it was less than dignified. Right up until the time he met Amy and made his late marriage at forty-five. A man with money does as he pleases.

'Yes, yes, dear,' she said. 'I know you don't like *emoting*. But do remember that it is allowed in others . . .'

'Cat, don't think I'm ungrateful for all you're doing. I am grateful, very. You've been a terrific buffer zone these last few days. I may as well have been guarded by a Rottweiler. It's allowed me to . . . well, come to terms in my own way. Get on with things.'

Get on with *dogs*, he might have said. Walking the dogs, feeding the dogs, comforting the dogs in their loss and leaving her to deal with Mother and the police and all the

rest which she had done with great efficiency. Years of
intermittent work in public relations had developed that
singsong, listening voice with overtones of authority. She
was a good listener. Officials of all kinds respected her
voice.

'The police are still puzzled, you know,' she said carefully. 'As well as embarrassed, for lack of a better word, at
their failure to find a body. There's a nice officer deputed
to talk to me who seems to take it personally. He also
takes it personally that he's not allowed to talk to *you*, so
perhaps you'd better, next time. It's just that . . . well,
there was only one fatality from her carriage, which was
near the back, a woman who fell and broke her neck getting out of the train. Tragic. They know which carriage
Amy was in because they recovered her handbag—'

'The puppy,' he murmured.

'The what?'

'Nothing, go on.'

'And they think she either walked through to the front
of the train, before it crashed, forgetting her handbag. Or
she was in the loo and went in the wrong direction once
the crash happened. It's so easy to get disorientated on a
train, I've often done it, now, where *was* my seat, especially if I'm thinking of what I'm going to do next. She
might have gone forward by mistake. Into the carriage
which burned.'

'Amy would forget her own arm,' he said shortly. 'Did
anyone see her?'

'They haven't quite got round to all of them yet.
Besides, he reckons people will remember the crash and

nothing else. They asked me to ask you, what was she wearing?'

Douglas was listening intently, drumming his fingers on the table. Then he was silent for a full minute as the clock ticked on the wall, the cat sighed in the basket by the Rayburn and she grew impatient.

'Ask Mother,' he said finally.

'Mother was still in bed when Amy left.' There was another long pause.

'I don't remember what she was wearing. I never do.'

She rose from the table, gracefully, removed his cereal bowl and took it to the sink. He stared at the toast rack, thoughtfully. There was such a contrast in their movements, Amy's and hers. Where Amy was noisy and frequently clumsy – she could make a row, even laying a table – Caterina was silent and deft. She could eat without a sound.

'I'm sorry I can't help with the dogs,' she said quietly. 'I wish I wasn't allergic to them at close quarters. Someone else keeps ringing. A woman from a sanctuary, you've mentioned her before . . . is she the one you said can't decide whether she's totally New Age or a born-again virgin? Oh and that lawyer, Box, whatever his name is, wants you to call. When you can. I told him you probably didn't need him any more. Nonsense to go on with that silly case in the circumstances, isn't it?'

'I don't know about that. I'll speak to him.' There was a warning note in his voice she was careful to heed. He was not about to abdicate all decisions.

'Are you sure you can't remember what she was wearing?'

'No. I told you, I never notice.'

Caterina smiled. 'Never *did* notice,' she corrected automatically.

He had an overpowering desire for the company of dogs. When she looked up from the loading of the dishwasher, he had gone.

Practising the deep breathing learned in yoga class, designed for concentration and useful for the creation of a soothing persona, Caterina left the domestic chores for which she was exquisitely well trained, and went in search of her mother. She was as yet not entirely sure where she might find her, since Mama had the habit of varying her routine, especially in the mornings. At least, it may have been a habit; or it may have been the result of such a dreadfully *upsetting* week, if not an upsetting year. Caterina was a frequent enough visitor in this house to know the regimes, but she was not entirely familiar with how the morning bit worked. At the moment Mother was inclined to wander. Not, thank heaven, in the physical sense, but simply in conversation when her son was around, perhaps because she did not know quite what to say, or so Caterina had advised him. She isn't really being indifferent, she had explained to her darling brother, but you do have to realise, my love, that at that age, they've been to a lot of funerals already and take bereavement rather more for granted. A slight exaggeration, she had to concede, since Isabel Petty had not attended a burial service in many years. Appearances did more than justice to her years. Her porcelain skin belied it; she had the figure of one of those frail, stooped angels in the graveyard, built on wire and able to withstand the foulest storms.

The rain outside was dwindling, the grey day beginning to show promise. Mother might have stayed in her room with her tea tray or she might have come downstairs to sit in the same chair of the living room, to look towards the garden where she would not walk until it was warmer and even then with small footsteps, for fear the heels of her shoes would catch in the dampness of the lawn.

And there she was. Like a Tibetan spaniel, Amy had once said in the days when she and Caterina had been friendly. She's like one of them because the head is small in relation to the body and the muzzle is fairly short and blunt without being flattened or wrinkled, and Caterina had been amused by the comparison until she began to wonder what breed of dog she herself might be taken to resemble; a Saluki, she hoped (lithe and graceful with the head of an aristocrat), but there was a faint feeling of unease that Amy might make a different comparison altogether and think of her as a cat, or worse. This pretence of mourning was really a bit of a strain.

Isabel Petty had a way of sitting which made her seem so still she was almost invisible. An unfamiliar person might walk in and out of the room without noticing her presence, as if she was a permanent fixture in the chair she always occupied in here. If she were not acknowledged, she remained silent. Perhaps the fact that so much of her life had been spent married to an autocratic man and, after that, alongside a son of similar disposition made her wary of initiating conversation. Perhaps it was laziness or disinterest.

'Would you like some coffee, sweetheart?'

'Oh, is it that time already?' Her head peered out from behind the newspaper which she always managed to read without rustling, a feat Douglas had remarked upon as impossible. Midmorning coffee was not appropriate until she had devoured every item of the national and international news and begun on the crossword. Her mood would be ebullient if she had finished it by lunchtime. She lowered the newspaper soundlessly and smiled sweetly at her daughter.

'Oh dear,' she went on. 'How time flies when one tries to distract oneself. I should be doing something useful, shouldn't I?'

Mother's usefulness was limited by her appearance. Her hair was piled on to her head and pinned into a neat French roll, in a labour-intensive style of the 1950s. She wore a skirt which was heather-coloured, a cashmere sweater in cream and her stockings and shoes matched the skirt. They were colours in which her daughter would not be seen dead, but they suited her mother's style. The clothes were unsuitable for work; they were the clothes of someone who had once dreamed of owning such clothes when she was taking down shorthand in another era. She had worn different clothes in her working days, which had captured the attention of her boss, who had announced his intention of making her a lady instead of a deserted mother. A challenge to which she had agreed, although the transition was more in his mind. She had always been a lady who insisted upon ladylike behaviour in her presence. She had been a fine cook; she had always wanted a son and adored his son. They all three adored his son. Isabel Petty never raised her voice.

'Oh, no, don't worry about anything,' Caterina said. 'All under control. Well, more or less.'

Nothing could be further from the truth, but both took comfort in the idea. The priorities were to keep Douglas as content and stable as possible, offer him the succour of a pleasant environment and emotional support should he require it. He showed few signs of needing it, and he was, as always, conspicuously polite to them both, something they seemed to copy in their own conversation, always aware of not letting the side down. It was far too soon to remind Douglas of how much the food had improved.

'If we had a memorial service of some kind for Amy, I wonder who would come?' Isabel Petty asked, more to herself than her daughter.

'I don't know, Mummy.'

'Well, we shall have to think of something. In due course. He won't be up to it. He was in his study, last night, writing away. Well, I mean, I don't know if he was writing or not, one is never allowed in there, but he stayed there ever so late. I do wish I could sleep. Makes me feel so sluggish. Yes, coffee would be lovely. In here, shall we? The sun'll be out in a minute.'

The room had grown cleaner and freer of dog hair over the last few days. For lack of anything better to do, Caterina had had a go at the windows, inside and out,

taking a morning over it, with a stepladder sinking into
the flowerbed as she cleaned away rain marks from the
outside and the grease of cigar smoke from within. Clean
windows made everything cleaner, encouraged dust to
fling itself into the hoover and the colour of the rugs to
emerge. Caterina itched to do something with the curtains and knew that within a few more days the
temptation would be overpowering. Douglas would
hardly notice and once this death was confirmed, she
could make a start on Amy's clothes. Somebody had to
do it.

There was a series of photographs in now clean but
usually tarnished silver frames on the oak table by
Isabel's chair. Three in colour of Douglas and Amy's
wedding, where the sheer volume of Amy's dress
seemed to obscure everything else like a barrage bal-
loon in the sky, and three more, older by far, black and
whites. Douglas's father, dead these many years, but
laughing uproariously every time he tried to avoid
posing for the camera. Petty Senior, wearing his son's
judicial wig and looking a fool, always having the last
word. A man with a firm belief in primogeniture as well
as responsibility for the fairer sex, so that he left to his
wife a small stipend, to his daughter a gift of cash and to
his son a fortune and a collection of convalescent dogs,
along with the instructions that he should look after the
women until hell froze over, or be damned for eternity.
Damien Petty had made the last of his fortunes in lawn
mowers, never used one once, took his attitudes from
prehistory and his language from Dickens. Except

among friends, when he told them that the sun shone
out of his son's arse.

'So she's dead, then, Douglas.'

'Yes, Jimmy, I know. Do you always have to state the
obvious?'

'Where will we bury her?'

'There's no more room for burials, Jimmy. You know
we stopped that a while since. Call the vet and get her
taken to the crematorium.'

Together they lifted Dilly the arthritic greyhound,
wrapped in her blanket, took her out of the stables and
laid her on the paving stones.

'Let her keep the blanket and rest in the sun for a bit,'
Douglas suggested. 'I don't like leaving her in the dark.'
He uncovered the black and white head, closed her eyes
and tucked the blanket round her neck. 'If that poor bitch
had ever known kindness before now, she could have
lived another three years,' he said. 'Let her get a bit of sun.
She loved to sit out here.'

Jimmy nodded, suspicious of sentiment. The blanket
looked incongruous in the neatness of the yard. Jimmy
doubted the vet would treat the corpse with so much
respect, probably would not even come himself. People
were staying away from Douglas at the moment, probably
because he was able to mention words like 'crematorium'
and 'burial' without flinching. He seemed savagely indifferent to the death of a wife, although moved by the
demise of gentle Dilly and her shorter span of days.

They went into Dilly's stable and began the task of

clearing it out. A scrubbing from top to bottom, clean bedding. From inside the thick walls, where warmth lingered as if trapped from season to season, they heard the sound of a van pulling to a halt. Jimmy looked out of the door, hesitated and groaned; Douglas went on working, deliberately deaf to sound, the way he was in the last week when anyone called his name or the telephone rang. The engine stopped and footsteps moved towards them. Then there was a scream of outrage.

'Bastard!'

'She's asking for you, Douglas,' Jimmy said calmly. 'Take your pitchfork, I would.'

It was a reminder of an old discussion; would it be better to bed the animals with old-fashioned straw so that they could behave like ancient farmhands, wielding pitchforks to clear it and burn it cleanly, or was this too much trouble for words? Straw pricked and rubbed and harboured insect life, could scratch an arm raw, whatever its cleansing qualities. So it was wool and cotton and washing-machine-durable blankets, better than they had in most houses, Jimmy said. Should have sewed ribbons on them. Douglas took his sunglasses from the breast pocket of his shirt and put them on, winking at Jimmy, which was a sight Jimmy had longed to see, before picking his cap off the floor of the stable and pulling it low over his forehead. The headgear and the dark shades effected a strange and sinister transformation, completed by the small cigar he lit quickly and carefully, changing him into a vision of a louche racehorse trainer at the races, a city bandit disguised by nothing but his baggy jeans, a bit of a wide-boy, with muscle. Pity he was clean-shaven, Jimmy thought. A beard would have made him look like an assassin.

'*Bastard! Bastard! Bastard!*' the voice outside shrieked, then lowered to a keening wail. 'Ahhh, you poor thing, ahhhhhh. *Bastards!*'

'You've gained a plural,' Jimmy suggested. 'Better get out there, before there's more of yous.'

Douglas patted his chest and strode to the door, one hand in his pocket, the other controlling the cigar. The sun shone on to the paved yard of the courtyard, fickle as all hell, as if it had been there all the time. Half in and half out of the sunlit corner where they had laid Dilly to rest, the shrieker stood, her hand poised in benediction over the black and white head with its collar of yellow blanket. It was a large, fat hand, with rings on the fingers, and the body behind it dressed in a long, open-weave coat the colour and texture of hessian with various dun-coloured layers beneath trailing over boots, the whole of her trembling with rage like a motor engine at traffic lights. Douglas was looking at the crown of her bent head, long hair, white at the roots, variegating between dull brown and chestnut before it touched the ground as she bent over the bulk of her own body. '*Bastard!*' she yelled again. Her hand did not quite touch Dilly's muzzle.

'You do repeat yourself,' Douglas said, standing close, so that when she unbent she was at risk of collision. 'Can I help you?'

She turned her head, flicking at his face with a flurry of hair and lethal earrings which dangled to her shoulders, then took a step back. She smelled of lemons, hay and the unwashed creases of a sagging body overlain with sharper perfume worn specially. There was brief, unspoken recognition of the fact that each found the other acutely distasteful.

'I've come for the dogs,' she said. Her voice was deep, vibrant with indignation. 'I've got the van, so let's make it easy. They can't stay here, can they? They'll all die and get slung in a corner, like this one. Let me look at her. I want to make sure she wasn't beaten to death.'

Douglas blew a thin stream of cigar smoke straight down into her eyes. 'Hallo, Delilah. Nice day for it. Been shaving with a blowtorch again, have you?'

She took a step backwards and almost tripped over the recumbent form of Dilly. Douglas grabbed her arm with unnecessary force to keep her upright. On her bosom, a large ceramic badge reading 'DELL THE ANIMAL SANCTUARY THAT CARES' clanked against a silver chain necklace. The same words were emblazoned in red on the van, parked askew at the entrance to the stable yard.

'Don't touch me, you beast!' she yelled, shrugging him off.

'Don't fall over the poor animal then,' Douglas said calmly. 'Didn't nurse her to have her crushed post mortem by a heavyweight.'

'You *pig*!'

'Oh stop being such a lout, Dell. What do you want?'

She could not stare him down through his reflective glasses. All she could see was a distorted reflection of herself. She put her large red hands on her ample hips. 'I told you, I've come to take away the dogs. You aren't fit to look after them. They might have had a chance before, and now they haven't any at all. Dying like flies, obviously. Probably starving without a woman to feed them. *Bastard.*'

'Come on, Delilah. You've always wanted these dogs, because you haven't got enough animals in that place of yours to justify the money you wheedle out of the public. Not much of an empire for you, is it? Perhaps that's why you want mine. People'll start asking about why you need two Volvos. Even if you have got God on your side.'

'Oh, isn't that just typical, Mr Petty? Contempt for poor people as well as poor animals. All you wanted was power and what do you do when you've got it? Kill the poor buggers. How can I let these poor things stay here with you? My conscience would kill me. You, you can't even grieve for a wife, can you? What was she to you? Just another *bitch*—'

'Watch it, Delilah.'

'*Me* watch it? What have I got to watch? Just give me the damn dogs. And may God have mercy on your wife, she must be glad to be dead.'

Douglas caught hold of the sleeves of her long coat and yanked it down over her shoulders, pinning her arms to her sides. There was the sound of ripping material; she whimpered in protest as he turned her round, fingers pressing into the lardiness of her shoulders. She whimpered louder as he spun her round to face the door of the stable and walked her towards it.

'Rape!' she screamed.

'Yeah, serial rape,' Douglas said.

She felt his grip tighten and then she screamed in earnest, just as he let her go. Framed in the stable doorway there was a pair of protruding buttocks, skinny, white and moving, Jimmy bent over with his trousers round his ankles, bare bottom exposed, waggling his hips. Mooning.

'Let me go!'

'Nobody's stopping you,' Douglas said. 'Just go.'

She adjusted the coat and looked at him, ready to spit. Then she smiled. Too late he saw the girl on the other side of the van, with the camera, catching it all. The dead dog in the corner, with her head in the sun, himself with the shades over his eyes and his hands on the woman, and wee Jummy's rump, wagging a tune.

Delilah posed, displaying her torn coat to the camera. Tottered towards the van like a martyr running from a lion and collapsed into the passenger seat. The van sped away.

'Aw, *shite*,' Jimmy muttered, fastening his trousers and fumbling for a cigarette. 'That's fucking done it. Am I sacked again, Douglas?'

Douglas threw his sunglasses on to the stones and ground them underfoot, then smiled for the first time in a week.

'Keep that up, you'll get fucking promoted,' he said.

The cleaning woman let herself into the Pettys' London flat by fortnightly arrangement. It was one of her favourite jobs because all she had to do was make a mark on the place to show she had been there, like dragging the hoover across the carpet, rearranging the odd item, dusting the dust and leaving the odd, tasteful fingerprint to show she had tried. Sometimes, if someone had been in residence, there might be a humble note on a Post-it, pointing out a particular task, *Can you have a go at the stain in the sink, thanks, and take out the rubbish?*

She always knew when someone had been, even without the note. The velvet pile of the carpet reacted to the lightest footprint and a bathroom used was a giveaway. So she cleaned more than usual, buffing the enamel on the cream bathroom suite to a state of shine, although it was hardly marked, and looking into the cupboard above the basin. Such a lovely range of unaffordable lotions and creams. Seen *that* one advertised, and *that* was a favourite of her daughter. With a fingerful brushed over her face, she could see why.

In the living room, there was an answerphone on a table with a light blinking to show messages waiting. It was a bit old-fashioned, she thought; a silly expense when a mobile would do, but she had never seen the light winking before so she pressed PLAY. A disembodied voice crept into the room.

'*Amy Petty, answer, why don't you? I hope you're there. Don't worry, I shan't come looking. Not yet.*' Click, whirr.

'*Amy, you know I'll wait.*' Click.

'*Amy, there's no point in freedom without comfort. You must need money. For God's sake speak to me.*' Click.

'*Message for Mrs PITTY . . . we have your drycleaning ready for six weeks, OK?*' A voice in the background interrupting, saying, shushh, not that one. '*Oh, sorry, Mrs Pitty. Didn't know you was dead.*' Click.

'*Amy? Amy? Don't go away. I'll find you. Stay where you are.*' Click.

She was rather shaken by these brief recitations and could not work out if the voices other than the drycleaner's were the same person's. The machine was older than any she recognised, without instructions to save/delete/repeat. She unplugged it from the wall and dusted it thoroughly. Drifted back into the bathroom, took out all the almost full jars and put them in her bag. Dead was dead.

CHAPTER FIVE

Amy Petty missed her fine face creams. She had taken, in the last few days, to smoothing her empty hands over her dry face compulsively, as if her empty hands could feed her skin. It stopped her feeling so woozy. *He'll find me. I know he will find me. Someone will find me . . . Stop it.* The sun would be shining on the white house; the kitchen at home would be catching the light from the side window. There would be a breeze in the trees, mud on the floor, not this dust. She could see the willow tree, bursting into leaf . . . Amy stirred from her daydream. She was not going to take any more of the calming pills he gave her. It was kind of him, but she felt better without them.

'It's not so clean in here, Dad, does it have to be like this?'

'Are you saying it's dirty?'

'I didn't say it was dirty, just that it wasn't exactly clean.'

'It isn't a laboratory, Amy. And I don't want you clearing it up. That's what you do at home, but you don't do it here. Prison used to drive me mad like that. Cleanliness next to godliness, all that rubbish.'

She put the tasteless yellow spread which was not butter on to her toast and ate, slowly. At *home* there would be butter. How childish to long for butter, but to all intents and purposes she was a child for the moment. She had been a child for over a fortnight.

'I thought you quite liked it in prison.'

'I never said I *liked* it,' he said crossly. 'You are stupid. Years of hell, apart from the workshop. Arts and crafts to clean our dirty little minds.' He wagged a finger at her. 'It gave me a hobby and a sort of living, so I should be grateful. Everything comes in by post and goes out by post. I love the post, live for it, did that in prison, too, although I never got a letter from you. Pass the jam, will you?'

She touched the pot, detaching her fingers from the stickiness. 'But you didn't learn about doll's houses in prison. You always made them.'

'Yes, I suppose,' he said absently. 'Only not all the time.'

He always sat a distance away from her, not always in the same place at the kitchen table, but as far away as space allowed. The table where they ate acted as a staging post between the outside world and the rest of the house. For each meal, the items that had gathered in the meantime were moved to one side to allow room. If she sat at the narrow end, he would move the pile of magazines, pipecleaners, paperclips and small postal packets so that it lay between them. She passed the jam jar over the heap, lifting herself out of her chair to do so. Today, he looked like a chicken, or more like a small cockerel, with his white hair stuck up in a comb. He was in a talkative mood.

'So what would you have been doing if you had been at *home*, then?' he asked.

'Oh, probably cleaning,' she said with a smile.

'There you are then,' he said comfortably, and then as an afterthought, 'You look so much better than you did.'

She knew this was not true, but appreciated the kind intention. Her hair had been turned from blonde to dull brown with a rudimentary dye he had provided and her own efforts with scissors had reduced its unruly volume to a passable bob, not quite the same length on both sides of her face. Her skin had grown paler and her cheeks were pink from the constant heat of the kitchen, a look he seemed to prefer to the weathered flush which had not survived the first ten days. She had a touch of pallor, like his own. A newspaper rustled, folded by his plate; she wished she could open the window, but if she did, she would not like what she could hear; no trees, no mewing of the cat. She shook her head to clear the fumes of sleep. She had slept so much.

He was an inveterate reader of newspapers, which collected on the front doorstep early in the morning along with a selection of magazines and catalogues. The delivery of the wrong newspapers was a source of loud complaint, although he conceded that his was a difficult order, what with a different paper every day, a rabid tabloid one day, *The Times* the day after, the *Guardian* the day after that and this local Kent paper every week, the one he flourished towards her now. She did not think he could ever be the sort of old man who could fall down in his house and be ignored for days. The papers on the doorstep would tell the tale of a man with eclectic tastes, seriously indisposed. She looked at him with desperate fondness. *This* was home.

'Looks like your stupid spouse is in trouble again. I only take this thing because I can get it by post, sent for it after I saw your wedding picture. Long time ago, eh? "Beauty and the Beast", or was it "Pretty Woman marries Playboy"? Some page four headline like that, and a picture of you with that great big frock. I always wonder who chose that dress for you.'

'His stepsister helped me.'

'Ah, she would have been the one standing by the side and looking like a model. You call it *help*; I'd call it sabotage. Dear, dear Amy Fisher, if it weren't for newspapers, I'd never have known where you'd gone. Once I had some idea of where you were going to live, I started getting this paper, still do. It's such a *bad* paper. Anyway, your widowed husband has lost his rag again.'

It shocked her. *Husband; widowed.*

'Let me see it, Dad, please.'

He held it playfully, between finger and thumb, as if it was contaminated. 'Only if you promise not to get upset. I don't like to see you upset. You were screaming in your sleep.'

'I promise.'

'You've a good pair of hands,' he said, washing his own under the tap and bouncing out of the room, whistling.

She had been making an effort to be like him, but she did not share his addiction to newspapers – in fact, had come to regard them as the very bane of existence. They were the intruders into homesteads, the harbingers of doom; they destroyed harmony and stopped more conversations than they ever began. They were something she read with caution, except the magazine sections with the features on lives which she could enjoy reading about while doubting they were true, and the cookery and household and cosmetics sections which she devoured with interest while others argued the toss about politics. Amy could never allow herself to get angry about things she could not change and did not think she could change anything much, except, perhaps, her clothes, her face creams, or the colour of the walls, and even the latter had proved difficult. What a silly person she was. She looked around the room. How soon this way of life had become normal in its simplicity. Her father ate bland food in small quantities, variations on a grilled chop with vegetables, and he insisted on cooking it. That was the evening meal; daytime food was toast, beans, cereal and fruit, which hung around the kitchen always slightly past its best. Food was not important and that was a relief. Nor was the shabby decor. Her father could have decorated his small house from top to bottom; he was fit enough and artistic enough, but he never bothered. This room, like all the rest, teetered on the brink of unsavoury ugliness, but saved itself from complete condemnation by his cursory efforts to keep dirt at bay. The only thing she found particularly hard to tolerate, even in her befuddled state, was a fridge littered with inedible leftovers. She could demand their removal or throw them away herself; but she was a guest, a child, and it was not his fault that he was so frugal, it was a necessary part of his existence, she told herself, just as the careless over-provisioning of her own home had been part of hers. And she supposed that her adapting to this other existence had been made easier by the fact that she had always known how little you needed to survive, never quite at ease with affluence, but she had also come to realise that she had arrived here on a tidal wave of shock, a state which made her more docile than normal. The passive state was receding now she had got used to the sound of the trains running through her head every hour of the day. It wasn't home, though.

Home. She made an hourly effort not to think of it, but thought of it now, trying to push back the wave of misery that threatened to drown her. There was an image of the willow tree in the garden on the day she had seen it first, the sound of a barking dog, and early-morning black-birds which would be at their rowdiest now. The back door open to the draught of spring, the fields in the distance and the solace of endless space. All she had ever wanted, she had known that as soon as she saw it. That house was quite imperfect enough for her; it could never make up its mind what it was supposed to be: the two of them were alike in that way and fell for each other easily. Come to think of it, that home had something in common with this mean little house in terms of what it was like to live in it, insofar as she was still the visitor, never the mistress, and the sphere of her influence was small. Amy Petty Nobody. *Stop it*. She reached for the newspaper.

There was a feel to it she did not like: it felt as if it would disintegrate into the soggy pulp it was made from at any minute; the harm it could do out of all proportion to the rough flimsiness of its texture. Nothing on the first page, plenty on the second. A violent photograph. Douglas Petty, cigar in mouth, partially disguised as he pulled the coat off an older woman whose face to camera was twisted in a scream, with two other photos continuing the narrative, one of them of a swaddled dog, lying neatly, another of a bare bottom. *GRIEVING WIDOWER GREETS GUEST! I was terrified, said Delilah Hall, owner of Dell Animal Sanctuary; I only went to offer help. Petty can't bring himself to say a single thing about his wife's tragic death – is he human? So I worried about his dogs* . . . A close-up of the bruises on her arms. *And what did I find? Brutality.*

Amy smiled. She smiled a lot. That stupid Dell was really silly. What did a few bruises matter? Then she picked up the magnifying glass her father used for small print and focused on the swaddled dog. She drew the glass further away to improve the image of the head, touched it with the tip of her little finger and began to cry. Rollie Fisher, the bantamweight father who did not resemble her, came back into the room, stopped whistling and spoke quietly, pointing at the paper.

'Look, you knew what he's like. A pig of a man. That's why you took the chance to leave, because of him.'

'Is it?' she said. 'Did I ever say that? You know I don't

talk about it.' And then, under her breath, so that he could scarcely hear, her finger still stroking the head in the photograph, 'Poor Dilly.'

'Poor who?'

'Nothing.'

Rollie Fisher sat down unwillingly at the other end of the table, trying to hide the slight impatience of a busy man who kept to a routine and found it difficult to interrupt his daily regime. She felt she had no right to monopolise him and disturb the order of things, even though he loved her. Love, the anchor of the soul, as necessary as food. A man's habits were difficult to break. He wanted to be in his workroom and was making a big effort to readjust the day in order to help her. Father and daughter quality-time. She brushed away the tears.

'You've done the right thing, my darling, even if not in the right way. The right thing was to get away from him, by whatever means. Do you know, I shall always feel responsible for you marrying him. If I had been a proper father to you, instead of an absent father, an *imprisoned* father, you might have found a different kind of partner altogether. You were looking for the father figure because you hadn't got one. That's my theory, anyway.'

'You mean people marry the person who makes up a gap in their lives?' she said, with difficulty.

'Possibly.'

'Well, if that's what I did, it's hardly your fault, Dad.'

'No,' he said furiously. 'It isn't my fault. It isn't my fault that I ended up in prison because of your mother's lies and the gross incompetence of the law. It isn't my fault that I was denied any access to you, but I still feel responsible for not being there. You might have done entirely different things with your life if I had been. Still, at least I'm here now, eh?' He straightened the items on the table into a neat pile of paper and got up, slightly embarrassed by his outburst and not knowing what to say next.

She was quite prepared to agree that her mother told lies. It was the feature about her which she could remember best, Mother's penchant for fantasy which amounted to lies, her pretence that Amy's father, her first husband, had not only *died* but gone to heaven, a fiction so often repeated that it ought to have become suspicious, although for an eleven-year-old girl subsumed in her own misery, it was not. The abrupt moving of house, school, the new man, produced with miraculous speed as if by a conjuring trick, were more than enough to fill the waking hours and provide the stuff of nightmares, while Amy's mother elaborated on the nature of Daddy's heaven. She described it fulsomely as a large house, surrounded by fields, with a stream at the bottom of the garden. It took Amy a long time to realise that the fiction of Daddy's heavenly house was simply a scaled-up version of the doll's house he had left for her, with dogs by the fire in the kitchen and, out of the back windows, a vision of green trees and lawn painted on to the inside of the window panes. The back of the house was covered in painted ivy. Amy kept it in her room and took it with her when she left that home.

He touched her lightly on the shoulder and withdrew

his hand quickly. She would have liked to have held on to it for a while, but somehow knew she should not.

'Poor girl,' he said. 'Look. Go out and walk, or shop or something. No one's going to haul you off the street or anything like that, you know. I do hate to mention it, but you are dead, to all intents and purposes, and nobody seems to think otherwise. I've scoured the papers. They've been full of train-crash horror and all that, but I'm afraid the first mention I've seen of you was an oblique reference to that non-grieving husband. No one's going to point the finger at you.'

. . . Dead. It is now presumed that the fireball which followed the impact was caused by up to 2,000 gallons of fuel spilled from the trains. One coach of the high-speed train and the middle carriage of the turbo were burnt-out shells.

'Poor Dilly,' Amy said absently.

He was standing with his hands on the back of her chair, jiggling it and giving the impression he was about to pull it out from under her if she did not move of her own volition. 'I think the sun's shining. And you've always got your mac in case it rains.'

There was the terrifying feeling, once she was out on the street, that the door behind her would remain permanently closed and either she would have to scream and shout to be let back inside or she would be forced to wander for ever and a day, descending from pavement to gutter, from room to cardboard box. Think what you've got used to already, she marvelled at herself; you've already worn the same clothes for days, even though you wash your underwear and shirt every day and put them on creased and crumpled the next. What would it be like if she could not even do that? And the money – dear God, she had left most of the money indoors too; she could not last longer than a day, but then she remembered that this was not the first time she had been out, and he had let her inside as soon as she returned. Why would he not? On the third day, he had treated her like a brisk surgeon, desperate to get the patient up and walking, pushing her out of the door and telling her to go to the shop. This was the third time and the first when it had not been raining. The sun was a revelation, so bright it winded her, making her pause on the doorstep of the house with the drawn curtains where light, however grey, was slow to penetrate. He had muslin tacked over his windows to let in diffused light upstairs and the first time she had seen it, three years before, the sight of it had unnerved her. It was unnatural for someone to turn their own presence into a shadow in case anyone should observe the detail from the street, although over the last week she had been grateful for that flimsy barrier between the outside world and herself. She hated curtains, but she could understand his paranoia now. It came from the fear that at any moment, someone would look in and say, *there he is, get him*, making him vulnerable in the privacy of home, without any chance of running away, and she knew what he meant, felt it herself. It was not a new sensation; it seemed to her to be something familiar, revived from a long time ago. Perhaps the net curtains of childhood, rigidly installed in the new house after Daddy had died and gone to his heaven, had something to do with it. Hiding was second nature.

And it was an inconsistent fear, because it did not stop her father from leaving his council-owned terraced property to walk down the street like anyone else, shop at the newsagent and the more distant Spar shop which was the source of most of their bland food, with the only difference in his demeanour being the fact that once he had left the house, he ceased to whistle. Nor did the covered windows make him reluctant to ask indoors the visitors who came in pursuit of the room to rent, only to be told after a brief chat and a cup of tea that it was already let. If they seemed the right kind of person, he might show them the doll's houses. Daddy was not afraid of encounters, only those he could not control. It was as if he wanted to inspect the human race, in his own time and on his own terms. Only when she reached the end of the road did she realise how hungry she was for the presence of human life and what a benediction there was in the fingers of sunlight which touched her pale face, kindly.

There were not many human beings. There were only cars. First the variegated, crowded-on-to-pavement cars which lined both sides of the street and sat sulking in the sunlight. Cars which were as much the subject of argument as noise, for ending up outside the wrong door, taking up personal space, blocking light from windows, looking ungainly. Cars and vans which colonised the road and squashed people into their houses, as if it was the cars that owned the place. Like cockroaches, she thought irrelevantly; dead cockroaches, waiting for an order to march. She could get into one of those cars and drive away. The thought of being inside some moving object was disturbing; she would not be able to control it.

At the end of the road, she turned left and walked again. The road itself had been quiet and now the noise was thunderous. Two lanes of vehicles rumbling by in each direction, slowing to a halt at the traffic lights fifty yards away. There was a metal barrier in the middle, separating one column from another, in case they should quarrel. To cross the road and find the multi-purpose shop was a long walk across the junction at the lights. Standing in the island in the middle, waiting for the green man, she felt peculiarly exposed and faint among a sea of cars. Here, the motor was king and the pedestrian an awkward freak, easily flattened. *Moving cockroaches eat beetles*. The feeling of exposure was the white light of anonymity; she could not have been less significant in this landscape of metal. The green man appeared and she crossed. The red light was the invitation to death. Wait for the light to turn and the engines to rev, then jump.

But she had never wanted to be *squashed*, not even when she had been so loaded with secrets and divided loyalties that the burden had been intolerable. She had only wanted that impossible dream, a life of quiet industry with dogs all around and that version of heaven which was attributed to her father and might also have been a lie. *Daddy gave me a dog*.

There were no trees; sunlight bounced off metal, with

nothing to feed. What would she be doing by the time this spring heat turned into real heat and the road burned under her feet and her own death was history? She could not think of that. She tightened her sweaty grip on the polythene bag which held two ten-pound notes. She needed new, cooler clothes and could not think of that either. Her feet ached; she did not want to be out, and she did not want to be in. The bullying cars made her furious with their arrogant dominance. The air was poison.

Further away from the main road, there was still a dearth of people on foot. A block of flats on the right provided shade; there was scrubland and a few stunted bushes between that and a sister block, a mere twenty floors high and modest in comparison to others which loomed behind them. She made a note of the shrubs. At least her father did not live in one of those flats. He had his own garden, tiny and neglected and blighted by the railway line, but his own.

It was on the corner of the road facing the minimarket and the garage alongside that the idea came to her of what she would do with the time, now she was *better*. Dig his garden, listen to the trains, make something out of nothing and wait for a plan. A poorly row of bedding plants standing outside the garage shop made her think of that. They were the bravest things she had seen all week, pansies and pelargoniums, waiting for someone buying petrol and fags on his way out of here to remember the window box waiting at home. She could not remember if she had come out with any specific errand; she had simply come out, but now there was only one thing to buy in this wilderness. Even at these inflated prices, twenty pounds would buy a lot of plants. She could come back for the compost. It could take the whole morning. Amy forgot her promise to help her father in his front-room workshop because she was overjoyed with her own distraction and, at the back of her mind, she knew that he was not telling the truth when he said she had a good pair of hands. Not for his kind of work, she didn't – her hands were like flattened hams, big, spatulate, with blunt finger ends. When she spread them wide, they could cover a back, and she had the well-developed shoulders of a masseuse.

That was the part of her beautician training she had liked most, even though she had embarked on it straight after school purely because it was a course her mother had advocated since it meant you could probably ensure having work for the rest of your life, which was a consideration for a big, raw-boned girl with a sweet smile and not much upstairs. *Should have been a gardener; should have been a kennel maid, even then.*

She could feel her fingers twitching as she approached the garage, eyes fixed on the wilting plants which were in worse condition than they appeared from the distance of the other side of the road, making her anxious to get them away. How silly to feel like that, especially as Dad's garden was hardly a better haven at the moment, but this kind of anxiety was almost a pleasure. She had not felt as purposeful since leaving home. *Home.*

There were a few brown leaves around the edges of the pansies and the petals of the purple flowers looked faded and dry, but there were also buds and emerging shoots. She passed from these to the verbena, which looked spindly and unpromising, with the little flowers still a distant promise, sly things, which could quadruple in size and poke their way almost through brickwork. There were smaller bags of compost with handles, so that she could heft two at a time going home, and surely there was some soil under the debris of Daddy's garden. There were parts of his dream he had neglected, but then Mother was a liar to suggest he had ever craved garden and trees, unless they were painted on the inside windows of a doll's house. Daddy never looked at his garden.

She was feeling and touching the plants with her big hands when she became aware of the noise of argument from inside the garage. There was no immediate cause for a row like this at a quiet time of morning with one customer busy at the pumps, no other noise but the not-so-distant roar of traffic and the hum of the pump as the salesman stood by his Ford, waiting impatiently as he held the nozzle inside the tank of his car and watched the price tick away on the dial. The surface of the forecourt around the pumps was slick with grease and water, as if someone had been out with a hose to wash away petrol spills. There was a removal van parked alongside the wall, next to the air pump, looking as if it had been left for another day. By the third of seven pumps, a deserted minibus was parked with an air of resignation.

The petrol meter stopped and the salesman with the Ford remained where he was, with the curved nozzle stuck into his car, dreaming for a minute as the sun crept under the canopy and warmed his forehead, thinking of the next destination and also of the same argumentative noises from inside the kiosk which was big enough to be a shop, where everyone went to pay in these bright daylight hours. At night, money and cards were received through a grille thick enough to stop a bullet and all the frivolous things – plants, barbecue bricks, flowers – hid inside.

There was always a story at the back of an argument. Amy went into the shop, followed by the customer who had relinquished the hose and finally remembered that he had fed his starving car at pump six, both of them curious about what was going on. There was a tenor to the raised voices which made them safe rather than threatening. It was not a fight, only a row.

'Listen, what'm I supposed to do?'

'Dunno, man, get the fucking thing outta my place. I dunno what to do. Get it outta here. Was you knocked it down.'

'I never, it was there, and I never run it down. Just come out sideways and biffed the wheel and now look at him, poor sod, not dead or nothing, looks like it might be, but it ain't my fault and the sod's on your premises. I'm not waiting for no police.'

'Get it outta here.'

'What, like it was me brought it in, it was fucking here, I tell ya, just fucking appeared, it did, what'm I supposed to fucking do—'

'Drive slowly, mate, is all, steaming in here, like you own it, I dunno.'

'Half dead, anyway. Sling it out the back.'

'Nah, leave it alone.

'Scarcely touched it, honest, it just bounced off the wheel when I turned in here, never saw it. I didn't go *over* it, honest, never felt it . . . and there it was howling, it *came* in here, I never brought it . . . Tried to bite me, so it can't be dead.'

'Well it can't stay here, can it? Doesn't look like it's going anywhere now.'

'Call the police, I say.'

'Is it a he or a she?'

'Fucking thing damn near bit me . . .'

Against the back wall of the shop, furthest from the door, was a fridge containing cold supplies of milk and soft drinks, freshly stocked. The customer from pump six stood in front of it, uncertainly. ''Scuse me,' he said. 'I wanted a Coke.' Then he looked at her and blenched. She quite understood; she did look odd. From his feet came a low growling sound and he stepped back hurriedly, giving Amy a view. A large mottled dog, part greyhound, maybe even three-quarters, lay against the fridge door. It was a vaguely brown colour with grey round the muzzle, a white star on the chest and a white stripe up the middle of a long nose; the coat was smooth and it had a thin leather collar. Somebody's old dog or an old dog which was once somebody's. It looked exhausted but the growl was intimidating. One back leg lay flat against the ground; the other, held slightly off the ground and unnaturally angled, quivered.

'Do you remember that story last year?' the man at the

checkout said. 'About that greyhound which ran out straight off the track at the end of a race at Walthamstow stadium and just kept on running? Perhaps this is it and it never stopped.'

There was the muffled laughter of confusion. They were not really angry; they did not know what to do. Indecision made them callous. 'What about my Coke?' pump number six asked plaintively. He was in a hurry, wanted out of here.

Amy did not notice. She squatted down near the dog, drawn to it like a magnet to metal. She may have pushed him aside to get so close, she didn't know. The fridge hummed and the lorry driver, the one with the loudest voice, shouted at her.

'Don't you go near him, he's nearly had my hand off! Dangerous, *don't.*'

'He's a *she*,' Amy said.

'It's dying.'

The animal looked at her through a single wary eye, not moving its head from the shiny floor. Not so old, she thought, feeling for the collar and turning it gently, but no spring chicken either. The sex, from the splayed back legs, was obvious enough. No head wound, no obvious wound at all, simply that wavering back leg and the dull eye of pain and fear. There was no tag on the collar, but marks on the neck where the leather had worn at the fur, one notch too tight for comfort, the beginnings of a sore. She found the buckle and loosened the collar, making soothing noises; she stroked it behind the ear and the eye closed for a second. The group in the shop fell silent. Amy took her hand down the bitch's back, feeling the spine, touching the quivering leg; there was a growl and an intake of breath from the audience. 'Shhhh,' she murmured. The dog shushed. Then she got one arm between the dog and the fridge door, hauled her up and stood bent over her, holding her beneath the chest with her own arms forming a sling. The dog turned her long nose, Dilly to the life, with that long white stripe, but not Dilly at all, another dog, because Dilly was dead and this one was not due to die, not yet. She was only hurt. Amy removed her arms and kept a light hold on the collar. The dog stood uncertainly, but unaided, on three legs, the last still shaking, dipping to the floor, touching and curling back. Amy took a couple of steps backwards; the dog limped towards her.

'Does it want water?' someone asked.

'Give it a Coke.'

The man from pump number six sidled behind the dog and got his Coke can from inside the fridge, letting the door clunk into the renewed silence. He paid with a credit card, accepted sullenly apart from the click and whirr of the machine. He left quickly. The rest watched, to see what else Amy would do with the dog.

'If it walks out like that,' the lorry driver said, 'on three bloody legs, it'll only get killed.'

'No, it won't,' Amy said, stroking the ears again. 'I'll take it home.'

There was a sigh of relief, without any alternative suggestions, except when the cashier said, 'What if someone comes for it?' doubtfully, not wanting to be caught in the wrong or accused of theft.

'I'll be back tomorrow,' Amy said.

'You haven't got a lead.'

'She doesn't need a lead.'

'Shall I take you in the bus?' She could see the minibus driver, wishing he had not said that.

'Please.'

She sat in the seat behind him in the minibus, holding the dog which trembled and did not like cars. It took longer to go round an elaborate one-way system than it had to walk, and by the time they got to the top of Amy's father's street, the driver was regretting his generosity even more, because she could not tell him the way by road. No sense of direction.

'Got a way with animals, have you?'

'Yes,' Amy said. 'I suppose I have.'

Which is more than I have with human beings. Just a thought as she lifted the animal out of the vehicle, listening to his comment about how strong she was and wasn't it heavy, then she waved goodbye, and thought as she stood with a reassuring hand on the dog's collar how this might make her father very angry indeed. The bitch licked her hand and quivered from head to thin, dilapidated tail. Amy did not care who might be angry. This animal was going to get well. And she hadn't been an idiot, either. Two trays of plants and a sack of compost came too.

Rollie Fisher stood at his bedroom window with the lit cigarette he would never smoke in the workroom downstairs. Too much inflammable stuff down there. Should not smoke at all. Would never drink again; drink had almost done for him, once. Here, he let the smoke float against the muslin pinned against the window frame, thought of the exhibition, and looked hungrily into the street, disappointed to find it so empty. It was the wrong time of day again; he tended to forget time or only acknowledge his favourite time of the afternoon, when he waited and watched, winter and summer. There were few enough children in this street and such as there were meandered down the road at about four o'clock, shrieking abuse at one another. There were three little Asian girls, who managed to be tidy and subdued even at the end of the school day, and he waited for them, often in vain. They were busy children, not always allowed to walk home alone, and when they did, and he saw them, he smiled. Now Amy was here, he might get her to ask them in.

He stubbed out the cigarette, hating the habit and loathing the smell, looked at his own, spatulate fingers, the shape of which his daughter had inherited, and concentrated on the planning of the next project. He took a pill from the cornucopia of medicines in his bedside drawer. Doctors were generous with old men who said they could not sleep. His exhibition, when it happened, must contain rare and unusual ideas, a *new* version of the doll's house. He was a model-maker, an artist or inventor, not someone who simply played with the thing and sold traditional, gimcrack furniture through magazines. Model houses did not have to be cottages, Victorian dwellings, cosy shops, places with lace curtains. They could be fairytale palaces, visions of heaven or hell, whatever he wanted them to be, creations upon which the imagination could fasten in order to stop itself going mad. This morning he had fashioned on a pipecleaner base a particularly bent figure, and this afternoon, he would add to the gentlemen's club, or maybe the brothel, some image of a judge, with a full wig and his trousers down . . . One day, he would create a Garden of Eden out of modelling clay. All the same, he wanted to make something conventional next. A sweet shop with a red roof, looking as edible as a cake.

What was that, coming down the road in his direction? Oh God, his big clumsy daughter, followed by a *dog*. The longer she stayed, the better, but he hated dogs.

Elisabeth Manser stood in her kitchen and looked out at the garden she had made. She was five minutes from the station and she was going to miss the train, dammit, but it was too nice to leave and she was furious, also gripped by an unreasonable anxiety that the bedding plants – verbena, lobelia, names like gracious women – which she had planted out the weekend before, might die before she got home late in the evening. A parallel anxiety about how they might drown after being so liberally doused with water at dawn, and how they might be affected by her own anxiety. She leant against the phone on the wall, angry that it was affixed and she could not pick it up and throw it.

Good news, good news, John had said. Douglas Petty's going to go on with his case. He's so bloody angry with the latest report, he's absolutely determined. Determined about what? she had asked, and hoped she had not yelled, spoken the quiet way he preferred. Determined to not let them get away with it, John said, pleased. Mr Petty says the original libel affected his marriage and made his wife unhappy. He wants his revenge for that. He has to do it to protect *her* reputation.

What? Did this vainglorious brute have the nerve to say that he was going to continue with a futile libel suit against a couple of newspapers in order to honour his *wife*? Had he actually explained to John that the latest newspaper report, albeit only local, made him even more anxious to exonerate himself from the original allegations of cruelty and bestiality, because these reflected on his *wife*? Because, he said, if he were to look as if he was ignoring it, it would also look as if his wife had been turning a blind eye to all this stuff, and that, in turn, made *her* look as if she condoned it, deliberately failed to notice if animals were being abused, or something like that. That might have been what Douglas Petty had said, or it might have been John Box paraphrasing it to make it sound even more hypocritical, i.e. first the client had wanted to protect his own reputation and now he wanted to protect the reputation of a dead spouse. Really.

He probably wanted something to do, Elisabeth thought. Something to fill the gaps left by a death and the fury which follows death in the same way that it follows defection. Douglas Petty had always been a restless man, but it took that restlessness to the limit for him to continue waving his stick in the direction of a national newspaper, in memory of his wife. She looked at the paperwork on her kitchen table. There was a study in her house, equipped with e-mail, fax, paper, books, but she still ended up in the kitchen with a view of the garden, because it was the nicest place and there was always food at hand. A place where she could survey her cooking pans. If John ever left his wife and lived with her, he would surely be fatter than he was. The paperwork on the table was what he called her homework; her vital task of researching all things known about the client. He was, after all, almost the only sodding client. She had to get her head round it. Her head was feeling over-large with her newly washed hair; should have used a conditioner. She had dirty hands, too long in the garden, not enough reading.

She should act like the intellectual she was not, *think*. The newspaper could plead justification for what they had printed if what they had implied was *true*, i.e. Douglas Petty was cruel to animals, guilty of unnatural practices with a certain golden retriever, guilty of hypocrisy and cruelty to dumb beasts, *at the time* the photographs were taken. If they could not prove current guilt, then they had a second chance of defending themselves if they could show that he had done something similar in the past. Something which meant that he had a tendency to the current actions, could easily have done them, was that way inclined, so that what they were saying about him in the present was far more likely to be true than not. What he did after the damn libel did not count unless it was literally a duplication. Beating up a rival dog lover was not a duplication. Elisabeth found a bar of chocolate hidden at the back of the fridge and eased her left hand round the tight waistband of her skirt while she ate it, guiltily, with her right.

Was there something she had missed? The homework was the dredging of press cuttings far and wide, the exploration of any mention of Petty, damn his eyes and his silly name, to see if there *was* anything in the past to support the likelihood of the present innuendos being true. She had also explored the reasons for his relative celebrity. After all, the man had done nothing but raise the roof with certain boorish pursuits. The charitable bit had always been there, in the form of some venture like running the London Marathon in sky pink Lycra while smoking cigarettes, all in aid of lung cancer. That was in his thirties and an odd thing to do for a man with a figure like a squat chimney stack, but nothing special. She eased the waistband again, pondered briefly the subject of vanity and comfort food, ate the rest of the chocolate because it was there. There were other sightings, less philanthropic, such as dunking the head of a parish priest into his own font when he had refused baptism to the child of a heathen friend, drunkenness, broken relationships with bimbettes quite inappropriate for his career as a barrister and only possible because of money; drunkenness, knocking the helmet off a policeman; kidnapping a police horse and then a police dog. Fame was not based on achievement, she had to conclude; it was based on flimsy incidents where a person stood out from a crowd either by accident or design. Then there were too many women of B-list anorexic celebrity status, criticism from his peers, a picture emerging of a party animal who was frequently crass and never apologetic, and only accused of hypocrisy because by day he donned a suit, conducted his hangover to court and looked the solid embodiment of the Establishment, as keen on law and order as he was to break it. The real fame, though, was the streak through the High Courts.

Elisabeth sat and sighed at this point, turning over pages and wishing John had read her copied pages with greater interest. The public had taken Douglas Petty to heart for that *streak*. Probably a late-night bet, that he would shed the pinstripe in Carey Street by the railings there and run, stark bollock naked, from the back entrance of the High Courts of Justice, down the stairs and all the way across the vaulted hall with the mosaic floor, dodge the guards and run through the swing doors at the front where he would get a taxi in the Strand. That was the bet which he almost won; he was the only man led away with a copper's helmet held over his gonads, captured by the cameras on the far side waiting for the appearance of a film star and her cheating husband. The tank of his body was wrestled to the ground; he was disbarred for disrespectful conduct and stayed a wee bit celebrated ever since.

There was nothing in this which allowed the defendant in the case to plead *justification*. Douglas Petty was simply a silly willy.

'Who beat his wife,' she said out loud. 'And probably a bore in bed, too. Had a better chance with a dog.'

If she had her own way, she would never leave home.

CHAPTER SIX

There were a number of irritating things that went with
the commuter existence, some of which Elisabeth secretly
liked. She lived a quick walk from the station, without
any of the complications of trying to start a car and
manoeuvre it into the car park, which was worse, to her
mind, than walking in the rain. She could watch other
commuters jockeying for space with their shiny vehicles
and pity them for it when she travelled early, or admire
the serried rows of useless cars when she walked across
the space midmorning to wait on a virtually empty platform, feeling superior in the knowledge that her day was
not nine to five. The major irritant was the train timetable,
varying in predictability in a way that bemused staff as
much as anyone, but again, she liked that. This little station, smaller than its car park, was on a loop where
mainline trains detoured at peak times to provide services
ancillary to the small train she awaited now. Despite fine

blue livery, the three-carriage trains were prone to delay and the signals on the branch line seemed to have a mind of their own, although things worked, most of the time, on good days. There was a delay of ten minutes which might stretch to more and it would make her late for the meeting with John and another client, but never mind. All a good commuter could do was put herself into the hands of fate on bad days, and be grateful that she was not on the line from London to the coast carrying the trains which had crashed over two weeks before. This may have been a shorter, less significant line, but all the cars in the car park belonged to people who were alive.

She sat beneath the canopy which covered the platform for half its length, content to wait. Train time was thinking time. The second shower of rain drummed on the roof and the sparrows protested loudly, an interesting noise and all the better for thinking. She never craved perfect silence; it filled the head with buzzing.

She looked up at the rowdy sparrows; two other waiting passengers stared at the weeds on the track. That was what Douglas Petty was, a rowdy man who stormed about making a noise. The sort of young man first made infamous by the death of his father and always up for a dare. A man who raised money for charity in the manner of a famous disc jockey, gaining notoriety for being willing to make a fool of himself. There was nothing in those newspaper reports of old that allowed the defamers to plead *justification*, except, well, the underlying *violence* of the man. The way he had lashed out when arrested after the streak, taking three of them to hold him down; the way he had kicked a car in another incident; the way he clenched his hands when he spoke; the sudden shouting, springing up, ready to attack; the aggressive energy of him. The bruises on his wife which she had seen; the plain talking which was almost violent; the dismissal of an enemy with the words 'He's a cunt' and a chopping movement of the arm which made it clear he would knock that person's head off if that person was in the room. The way, when the tribunal of his peers had met to decide that he was not a fit person to practise law at the English Bar, he had roared at them about being silly old farts and been forcibly dragged from the room. Uncomfortable at close quarters.

The rain stopped and the racket of the birds grew more subdued as they flew from their nests on foraging expeditions. Rich pickings in the spring. They were busy, busy, busy.

But there was nothing cruel about the man, surely. They would be able to plead justification for allegations of hot temper and even ungovernable rage, but there was nothing he had ever been reported to have done which smacked of the coldness of cruelty. But cruelty, she thought, watching the other, quiet passengers, does not have to be cold any more than it has to be systematic, and it might not even involve any enjoyment in the inflicting of pain. It was just as cruel to beat an animal or a person because they got in your way or would not do what you wanted as it was to beat them in cold blood. The effect was just the same. Bruises, wounds, shock, and, worst of all, the fear of fear. Amy Petty had been sorely afraid.

The train arrived, grumpily. Three-quarters of an hour for a short distance as the crow flew, but probably longer today as the train limped down another branch line to take in an extra station the last one might have forgotten. Elisabeth got out the Kent newspaper from the day before and gazed at the photo of Douglas Petty in violent confrontation with Delilah Hall from the animal sanctuary. Smiled at it and then grimaced, realising she should not smile, even in private, when faced with a depiction of a valued client behaving in an ugly way and looking like a bandit. But the persistent fact that she could not ignore was the fact that in looking at this picture, she herself found Delilah Hall to be a more frightening specimen than her assailant. Now there was prejudice for you: one woman disliking another on sight of her photograph, and purely on the analysis of her coat and her dreadful hair and the obsessive look of her. Elisabeth did not believe that anyone, male or female, could be genuinely engaged in any practical purpose if they wore sodding great earrings like that. Delilah Hall looked as if she had dressed up for the occasion. What lies there were in pictures, but all the same, the fear of the woman might not have been feigned. Petty was undoubtedly violent. Rich, spoiled, violent. He would even put his feet up on the seat in a train.

She was tempted to put her feet up on the seat opposite. Bad manners, but irresistible in a totally empty carriage midmorning with no one to say 'don't'. So she did and caught sight of the shoes she wore to do the garden, nasty canvas lace-ups, once white, now stained brown. *Shit*. They were a problem she had not contemplated; maybe there would be time to buy replacements at the other end; they looked ridiculous, like some awful reverse fashion statement, and they were dirty. Elisabeth curled her feet beneath the seat and decided not to think about them, yet. There was time for that. Concentrate on Douglas Petty, so that she might have something useful to contribute when next he was discussed, perhaps this afternoon, after the other client.

John did not care about this recent little scandal, he said; it was merely local newspaper stuff. Mr Petty did not mind accusations like that; it was only the implication of cruelty to his rescued dogs that made him want to play the Russian roulette of the law. And now he wanted to gamble on behalf of a dead wife, who might have been frightened of him too. *Crap*.

Elisabeth was pondering that uncomfortable thought in the luxury of her empty carriage, enjoying the view of the same bank of primroses for some minutes before she realised that the train had actually stopped. Damn. The coffee drunk in her kitchen was a long time ago; she was thirsty and restless, wanted something to do with her hands; wanted to throw her disgraceful shoes out of the window, and now she would be really late. She looked down at her fingers and saw soil beneath her nails. She was not at her best. John would be annoyed.

Then there was a rattling crash and her blood ran cold. No, surely, nothing to cause alarm, but no one with whom to share the sudden fear. Trains did not crash every day of the week; they crashed every few years and it was not her turn. The door connecting this carriage to the next was flung open and the trolley came through, battering against the wall and then back again, rattling its contents. She breathed out slowly and then shrank back against the window. The man and the trolley were not getting on well; it was heavily overloaded and not entirely within his control because he was shaking so hard she could imagine his teeth were rattling in between the strangled words that came out of his mouth. His face was the colour of chalk, like someone about to be sick.

'Fucking bastard, fucking thing, bugger, bugger, bugger . . . *shit.*' He kicked the trolley and then noticed her. 'Sorry,' he muttered. 'Did you want something?'

'Tea, please.'

He held the plastic cup beneath the water spout level with his chest, but his hand shook so much the water slopped over the edge and on to his wrist and he yelped loudly. Then he tried again and managed to fill it half full, although the coordination of holding the cup and pressing the button for the hot water seemed to take every ounce of strength and even then, some of the water went on the floor. Perspiration exploded on his forehead; he staggered wildly.

'Stop it!' she yelled. 'Stop it! Stop it and sit down.'

He did as he was told, feeling for the armrest of the seat as if he could not quite see it, and flopped into the seat opposite hers, his colour alarming. She looked at him for a second, then stood up beside the trolley, found the packets of sugar, emptied two into the half-full cup, teased the teabag which floated unattractively and put the cup down on the shelf beside him. 'Careful, it's hot. Where's the milk?' He pointed. Elisabeth found three cartons the size of tiny egg cups, tore off the tops and poured them in the yellow-looking tea. Disgusting. The teabag floated like a corpse. After a minute, he grabbed the drink in both hands and sipped it unsteadily. Colour returned to his face in the form of two spots of red in his cheeks.

'Sorry,' he gabbled. 'I'm really sorry. I shouldn't have come back to work, stupid really. They said are you all right, you can stay off for weeks, but I said no. Stupid.'

The same clump of primroses stared back through the window.

'S'funny,' he said. 'I'm fine when the bugger's moving, but when it stops and I don't know why it stops, I come over all strange. For two pins, I'd jump out, I fucking would, really, but it's best to keep going.'

She was as confused by his verbal diarrhoea as she had been by her own instinctive reaction to sit him down and give him tea from his own trolley. She did not usually act with such spontaneity, always felt she would be the last to pull a communication cord while she thought about whether it was the right thing to do. The hectic colour of his cheeks, spreading now to the tip of his nose, told her she had done something right and she took a sideways look at the trolley to see if she could improve upon it by offering something more medicinal than tea, such as brandy. Perhaps not; she leaned forward across him to open the top part of the window, heaving on it to pull it down, one of those stiff windows in this old train. They were nearly all old trains, the sort she liked, and she wondered if she would be behaving like this if there had been anyone else to witness. He went on talking, but the trembling was less. He could manage the cup with one hand. There was an empty hole in one ear, she noticed, as if he had forgotten an earring he had worn for years. As she watched, his spare hand went to fondle his ear lobe, as if thinking the same thing. He was talking more to himself than to her, wrapped in a sick and shaky world of his own.

'Lost it in the crash, don't know how. Only I wanted to go to work. No point sitting at home, not where I live, does my head in, that does. Put me on a different route, though. I was all right yesterday when there was someone else and plenty of people, even though I did throw up, once. It's not when it's pissing along all right, it's when the bugger stops. And you can still see the tower from this line. I wish they'd get moving.'

'Maybe you should go up front and tell them,' she suggested, light dawning on her confusion.

'Oh yeah, yeah. A lot of difference that'd make. There's probably a mouse on the line.' He cackled at his own wit.

'Leaves,' Elisabeth said. 'Snow.'

'Blossom, fucking blossom, that's it . . .'

'Good weather. Newspaper on the track, rogue rabbits . . .'

'Wrong kind of rain, more like.' He paused and gulped the tea. She did not envy him the taste.

'Shall I get you some more?'

'No, thanks but no thanks.' He smiled unsteadily; a nerve jumped beneath his eye. '*She* offered, you know, one day when I was poorly. Said she'd go down the train for me. We had a laugh. Well, not poorly, not like yesterday. I had a fucking great hangover that day, to be honest. Did my head in.'

'Whoa,' Elisabeth laughed. 'You've lost me there. Am I right in thinking you were on one of those trains that crashed?' She sounded pompous to her own ears, but he nodded vigorously, gazing at her, dying to talk away the symptoms of panic. She had the impression that once the train started again, he would move and she did not want that. Her laughter was artificial, but he did not seem to notice. He had the vulnerable figure of a lanky lad and a face far older; he fingered the vacant ear with more irritation than fondness. 'But I don't know who you mean,' she said, 'when you talk about "*she*".'

The train creaked and he listened to the sound, startled, then gazed out at the primroses. She found herself checking the bank to gauge how difficult it would be to jump out, waiting, oddly, for the train to tilt and almost bracing herself to counteract, sitting up straight as if she really was a sensible person. He grinned, waved the almost empty cup, put it down and continued rubbing his ear. She felt like a teacher, itching to tell him to stop. Stopping was not an option for him; the empty carriage and the creaking stillness of the train had the same effect as a confessional. *Cross-examination consists of never seeming to ask the questions*, and she sat here now, as if she was indifferent to the answers.

'Funny you should mention that,' the trolley man said as if they had been talking for hours, 'only when I come through that door, I thought you were her. You'd got your handbag on your lap, see? She always used to carry hers as if it needed looking after. And she sat at this end of the carriage, usually, when she could, I mean. And she always had tea, never coffee. Staplehurst, she got on. Waved to me when she got off. I sometimes got on at Ashford. I used to say, are you going to have a nice day then, and she'd wrinkle her nose, like that' – he wrinkled his own, which was now scarlet – 'and say, not really, how about you? And I'd say, I'd say . . . I'd say . . . something. She'd say something like, that ticket collector we've got today, he looks just like a ferret. He did, you know, he really did.' He laughed.

'And was she in the crash, too?' There was the sudden, intrusive image of Amy Petty, sitting as she sat now, hugging her handbag. Elisabeth tried to dismiss it as nonsense and felt light-headed with strange excitement. The trolley man scarcely listened.

'She always dressed nice,' he continued, 'but always a bit wrinkled, if you see what I mean, looked as if she'd had a cat on her lap, and yes, now you mention it, she was in the crash. I helped her off and she helped me, and they want me to look at videos to see if she walked back through the station, 'cos she shouldn't have died, she really shouldn't, not in our carriage, only I dunno where she went. I keep telling myself that she just walked off somewhere. Running away. Not getting in that carriage that went up in smoke. I don't believe it.'

'Couldn't she have just walked away?'

Her voice seemed to penetrate, at last. He leant forward, earnestly, elbows on thin knees, head supported by fists, foot tapping the floor. They were scuffed shoes, brown once, with his navy trousers creased at the knee, the rubber soles of the shoes making a small noise.

'Well, that's what I thought, but it wasn't that easy to do, I mean, I wanted to walk away, but I couldn't, I just followed the band all over the fucking place. You did as you was told. So I reckoned if she walked, she wanted to walk, really wanted to. And I was trying to work out if I saw her on the videos, this afternoon, what should I say?'

Again, the excitement which made her impertinent. 'Why don't you start at the beginning?' Elisabeth said. 'You'll have to remember what she was wearing. Did she always wear the same things?'

He saw nothing odd in the questions; he was too far gone for that. There was a crackled announcement mentioning signals. The trolley man shook his head.

'That's the trouble, see? They stop at every bloody signal now, black, white, green, you name it, get out, check it, phone for advice. Ah yes, a patterned skirt that day, wool stuff, bit warm, I would have said. Lovely skin, nice hair, bouncy, bit like yours really.'

So that was what Amy and she had in common: the big hair of slightly blowsy blondes. The image of Amy Petty with her slightly tanned skin and floppy blonde curls grew into sharper focus.

'And her name?'

'Never knew that. She knew mine, though.' He pointed to the name tag on his lapel. 'Rob. Probably remembered it too, knowing her. Yes she did. She said thank you, Rob, when we got out the train.'

'She got out of the train after the crash?'

'Yeah, course she did. We all got out. It wasn't a train like this, though. These ones you can open the doors. Then I lost her. She might just have got back in.'

'Why?'

'To help. You can't explain what it was like, you just can't. It was terrible . . .' He began to shake until the sunlight invading the carriage in kind contrast to the rain calmed him. She had no idea how long they had been stationary: she was mesmerised by his voice and his pale hands round the cup.

'And now *they* want you to look at video footage to see if you could see her, is that right?'

'Yeah, that's right. Not just her, though, there's a few they just can't explain. But if she did walk off and got as far as the station, and Christ, I bloody hope she did, she had a reason to do that, didn't she? I'm not going to say, yeah, that's her, there she is, if I do see her. Get them looking for her, why should I? She must have a reason . . .'

'When do you have to look at the videos?'

''Safternoon. Ah, shit, here we go.'

The train sighed, moved uneasily; the primroses disappeared, replaced by the backs of houses, a station platform for Grove Park. Rob stood up, tested his legs by pressing his hands against his knees and stamping his feet in turn, looked at his watch, embarrassed.

'I think it's cruel to make you do that,' Elisabeth said loudly over the creak of the train. 'Making you do that. Brings it all back.'

He shrugged, beginning to tremble again. 'What makes you think it goes away? Look at the state of me.' He held out his hands, shaking wrists, bloodless fingers.

'Who's going to go with you?'

He shrugged again, surprised at the question. 'No one. Who'd fucking go with me? My mother?'

It was the day for silliness and recklessness. She looked at her watch, realising the meeting was almost missed and she had not even apologised; she could see her disliked mobile phone sitting on the kitchen counter from which she was always forgetting to retrieve it, but the trolley man, Rob, was somehow uncannily likeable, shambling, vulnerable, brave and none of that stiff upper lip; she felt maternally defensive of him and so curious she was watching herself turn into the kind of officious busybody she would otherwise despise.

'I'll go with you, if you like,' she suggested casually, picking up the newspaper and documents which had leaked out of her case on to the seat, stuffing them back. 'I'm a lawyer. Do this kind of thing all the time.' She handed him a card.

'I'd never have known,' he scoffed, recovering now and taking in the grey suit and the almost uniform neatness of her, marred by a crumpled collar, the mud in her finger-nails and the hideous shoes. 'And I can't afford it.'

'Sure you can, when it's free.'

His face, now pink, split into a wide smile. It was such a smile, like a light switched on inside his skull, to illuminate an expression of sheer good nature, that she could immediately see why Amy Petty might be pleased to see him. It would be easy to let him brighten the day, plain stranger though he was, and she felt slightly, hysterically mad.

'OK, you're on. Four o'clock, platform six. It's in an office. I'll take you.' He paused, both of them regretting the making of a commitment, yet still wanting to make it. 'You won't make me *do* anything, will you?'

She tried to sound careless and authoritative. 'The whole idea is that you aren't forced to do anything. I'll be there.'

He pushed the trolley against the door. 'I don't see why you should,' he said. 'And you probably won't.'

The Lloyds tower was visible on the right and the scenery was brick. There were hoardings either side of the track, hiding everything to the left. The station was open for business again for the first time today, trains sloping in and out, slowly, queueing for a platform. The clock above the ticket booths had stopped. Hurrying across the concourse in the direction of the Underground, Elisabeth felt nothing but foolish and who did she think she was? *You probably won't be there.* No, she probably would not. She was out of her mind, buzzing with excitement.

She walked up from the Embankment, crossed Fleet Street and deliberately wasted more time by cutting through the High Courts. The shoes were entirely forgotten until she paused at the back entrance, trying to conjure the image of Douglas Petty stripping himself of his pinstriped suit and brogues, then shedding his underwear, leaving not a stitch before he began to run, and wondered who had taken the photos then of his pile of discarded garments and who was supposed to collect him, afflicted with a nagging memory of a refinement to the whole act which might have been her imagination. Afflicted, too, with the memory of that barrel chest, the swinging prick. Did he wear nothing but a wig? She must look it up again, later, and think clearly now. Forget about the trolley man, put him away.

She no longer cared enough about the meeting to hurry; John did not need her for this conference. It was only another case, a defamed businessman who thought he was better known than he was, attending to be told in gentle terms that the pursuit of a libel action against a magazine was likely to be as counter-productive as it was costly and although the suggestion of an adulterous affair on some minor gossip page was probably untrue, the allusion to it had been phrased in such a way that it was merely a suggestion that this married man was at it again; hardly a dent in his unimportant reputation to imply he was indulging in a lifetime hobby and no effect whatever on his company's credit ratings. No case. He was angry because he had almost lost a wife.

Useful things, wives, Elisabeth thought as she sidled into the room with an apologetic nod, finding the corner desk which hid her feet, met John's steely glance and noted the pristine state of his shirt and tie, so fresh they could have come straight out of the packet. They had been better off on their own, he and the client, who was similarly dressed, perhaps by a similar spouse, the two of them talking man to man, with John telling the other how much better it was not to open the can of worms which was his life. John hated to give negative advice. The client paid for it, but not nearly as much as he would pay for a trial. His room overlooked the square of Lincoln's Inn Fields, where the new leaves on the trees glistened after the rain and the blossom had been blown into a carpet on the ground. Now that was luxury.

The client was in the stage halfway between blustering anger and acceptance. She could feel the displeasure of Mr Box, QC, settle around her like a pall and she resisted the urge to ease her grubby shoes off her feet in case her toes revealed themselves as even worse.

Amy Petty may be alive, she wanted to shout, but then the coldness of his expression lowered the temperature and dulled the need to say anything. There was no middle way with an affair like this. The balm of his approval, like the praise of a father on an insecure child, was everything she had lived for at first and still craved. Almost as much as the touch of his hands on her skin which was never often enough to be familiar; still had an almost alien strangeness after all this time. But the pleasure she took in making that thin face crease into laughter bore no comparison to the agony of misery he could cause in her without even trying. She made it easy for him to wound her by being so vulnerable to criticism before it was even spoken, began to react to the edge in his voice and the expression in his eyes even before she had any right to guess that she was the cause. Only with him, not with anyone else. The weariness in his tone might have nothing to do with her lateness: it might be the result of a bad night and an irritating interview, but it felt already as if it was for her. How odd that she could survive the most scathing remarks of a judge and the choice insults of an opponent without turning a hair, and still quail at the prospect of a brief and probably kindly admonition from him. She wanted him to reach into a pocket for a piece of red paper napkin to blow his nose and make him human, but he was rising from his seat, smoothing back the thick grey hair, extending his hand to the client, who took it, reluctantly. Elisabeth shook hands too, enough for a brief introduction and this polite and meaningless farewell. There was not only dirt in her fingernails, but a streaked stain of spilt tea on the back of her hand. She showed the man out, down the stairs and into the square, her only contribution to his case, apart from the backroom research which informed his chances. No reason for him to know about that. She paused for a chat with the clerks before going back upstairs, determined to ignore the shoes as the client had. The conversation with the trolley man and the urge to tell John about it became more distant by the minute.

John stood by the window, looking at the blossom driven down from the trees by the rain, tapping his fingers against the pane.

'Where were you?'

'The train was ridiculously late and then it stopped . . .' She stopped too.

'I'm sorry I interrupted you at your housework this morning. But it seemed important at the time. And I did have the illusion that if I spoke to you at nine, you might manage to catch a train at eleven for a prearranged meeting at twelve. A little challenge for you. Silly me.'

The reference to *housework* stung. Why did she devote time to home and garden if not to be proud of it whenever he saw it? To watch him sink into a chair, say this is nice, or where did you get that?

'Signal trouble,' she said. 'They're being extra careful. Blossom on the line.'

He did not laugh. 'Only an idiot uses the excuse that every two-bit criminal uses when he's late for court. Trots it out without thinking, how come everyone else manages public transport without getting mugged by it? *I needed* you.'

She stood in front of his desk, looking down at two enormous feet. 'No you didn't. It doesn't take two people to give advice. It was you he consulted, not me.'

'Just as well then, isn't it? Always better to go to someone who's capable of catching a train, I find.' He blew his nose, discreetly, a regular handkerchief this time, all of him laundered and fresh today, as if he had been put through the cleaners. 'And of course I needed you or I wouldn't have asked you to inconvenience yourself. You have such great placatory powers, you women. He's such an irritating man, I almost hit him.'

'Well I'm very sorry I wasn't there to *almost* stop you. I could have made the tea.'

'Coffee,' he corrected gravely, without irony. 'He wanted coffee. And we both needed a woman in the room.'

Like a male doctor with a female patient. She was realising too late that she was wrong-footed, and that she had been uneasy about acting as semi-silent witness to two men of the world, talking about the best way to limit public awareness of the consistent infidelity of one of them. She had not wanted to watch him acting as an embodiment of virtue, discussing adultery as if it were any old subject, like cricket or football, just another fact of life, only important if it was discovered. Did not want to hear her own lover debating the best way to minimise the hurt which might be felt by a wife, or the prospect of expensive revenge. It made her uncomfortably guilty; it had influenced her dawdling this morning easily as much as thoughts of Douglas Petty and it made her silent now. She did not want to rock the boat; she would drown. She pushed her fingers through her hair, to hide the silence.

'Don't do that,' he said mildly.

She blushed, stopped doing that and remained silent, although her hands itched to do something, such as fiddle with her necklace, smooth down the collar, check her tights for runs, remove the shoes. Amy Petty with her similar hair also blushed easily, turning her smooth skin an unbecoming shade of brick: Amy Petty and she, they were both in awe of their men. The trolley man turned pink in patches, beginning with his nose. She had never monitored the progress of her own blushing and she was not going to mention either of them, not now.

'Don't do what?'

'Make yourself look ridiculous. Any more than you have. You look like you've walked through a hedge.' And then he smiled, but it was already too late. She felt like a dog whipped soundly for a trifling offence when a mild cuff round the ear would have done. She thought of the trolley man's empty ear lobe and shook her head. John was folding up the Skoyle papers and tying them neatly with tape. Downstairs, the computer ruled; upstairs, there were still old-fashioned habits. She had lost her tongue. He unbent from this minor task and talked to her with face averted.

'Maria's going to be away tomorrow night, I said I'd stay up here, but I could come and stay with you. Could I?'

'Yes,' she said. 'Yes of course.' She was glad she had planted the plants and pruned the apple tree in that tiny space and she always said yes, even though he did not need her. He came to her side and smoothed her hair, briefly, always cautious about touching her in the public arena of his room; so often, like now, anxious to shoo her out before the clerks downstairs began to comment as if they did not already. He was as particular about her as he might have been in his own home. The smoothing of her hair felt as if he had put a torch to it and still she said yes. Even though he was going to drive from his large place to her small one and park his car a hundred yards away, she still said yes.

In his diary, yes. An appointment.

She was on ground level, kicking the blossom beneath the trees and trying to pretend the movement of her feet was accidental rather than whatever it was. Sad, the release of a woman of thirty-three, who, with the onset of summer, slept with a man once a fortnight, did not have enough work and spent Saturday evenings tending her garden and an awful lot of time on trains, without even having the sense to want it otherwise.

She followed the throng on the narrow pavements of Fleet Street. She cut down Fetter Lane and went into the church. She went to her own chambers and talked about the lack of work. She took forever to buy a pair of shoes and find the right rubbish bin for the ceremonial disposal of her own. She bought socks in the Sock Shop, a cheap silk T-shirt against her better judgement and a sandwich which she took down to the river where she could lean on the parapet and consider the Blackfriars Bridge without the faintest idea of who the black friars were, as well as looking at the railway bridge which ran from this side to the bunkers of the South Bank. All to pass time. Then she hitched the strap of her soft leather briefcase over her shoulder and walked back to the station, far too soon, passed more of the time with a good cappuccino, the 20p lavatory and a newspaper which she tried to pretend engrossed her with vital information as she lingered in the vicinity of platform six, pretending not to wait. She felt dirty; her hair looked like a burning bush of artificial blonde curls; one day she would train it to be smooth. Useless to eye the clock; the clock was closed.

''Allo.'

'Hello there. Where do we have to go?'

There was no more conversation than that, no indication that Rob was pleased to see her as he turned on his heel and led the way across the concourse to the side entrance and then down the street and into a room. So normal the room it was almost discomforting, with the look of occupants who spent their lives inside it. Smoke-free, businesslike, three men with desks and a TV screen.

She had expected a cinema. So had Rob. He began to giggle and held on to her.

'Who's this?'

Elisabeth did not let him answer. 'His legal representative, OK?'

She was used to obstruction after introductions of a similar kind, but here it was sweetness and light, no names, no pack drill. Might take an hour, OK? You want tea? Coffee, she corrected and then changed her mind and accepted tea, because of her bladder.

It did not take an hour. Rob, the trolley man, who did not know her from Eve but had a nice face anyway, clutched at her arm in their plastic chairs. She patted him consolingly, as if they were friends of long standing.

They were watching a black and white tape of the walking wounded as they paraded across the concourse and out to the front. Some upright and brisk, some impatient, some dazed. Tell us where you want to stop, Rob was told. Some of the people on the video did stop. They looked at the clock, as if for redemption, they wavered and turned, they tried to deviate out of line and go to the exit they normally used and they were shepherded back, all to go out through the same arch, into the same light, to be captured on video. It seemed a final insult to their dignity to herd them all in one direction purely to be recorded on tape in states of shock. It was cruel.

Singed hair, dirty faces, weeping eyes, people without belongings. What would she feel if the only person on the other side had been a John Box lookalike telling her to straighten up her act and smooth her hair? Would she have fallen at his feet, grateful for recognition? At the end of ten minutes she forgot what she might have done or felt and was weeping. They looked like a tribe of lost souls, landing on an alien planet.

See anyone? the voice said, someone nudging the trolley man. Like I said, we freeze the frame, make a picture whenever you want. Elisabeth could feel the dampness of his palm, placed flatly over her knuckles on the arm of the chair.

Then, from the left, came a tall strider in no doubt about where he wanted to go, but appearing to notice something on his coat at the elbow which bothered him and made him shrug his shoulders and rotate his arms as if warming up in desultory fashion for exercise, and then going back to holding one arm in another and looking at the damn elbow, like someone consulting a watch in the wrong place. Stretching his arms over his head, next, then putting his hands in the pockets of his raincoat.

'I remember him,' Rob murmured into her ear.

'What?'

'Nothing. Fuck, nothing. Bastard.' He shivered violently and then said, louder, to the listening audience, 'That man, the guy flailing his arms, he was in my carriage.' The tape was taken back, then forward, frozen, resumed when Rob nodded. So that they could see, a few uneven paces behind the tall man, Amy Petty, with plentiful yellow hair, walking slow and determined with her arms crossed across her chest, turning to look at the clock until she got near the exit where she wavered, uncertainly. She was not significant among these others, but Elisabeth knew her immediately. So did the trolley man. He gripped her arm and let the tape run on for a whole minute. He waited another three with every sign of indifferent calm, and then he was violently sick. His undigested hamburger and coffee formed a pool by her shoes, but he did not say anything, except to apologise.

Someone mopped up and they resumed, less heartless than efficient. Watched to the end as the last stragglers straggled through.

Occasionally, he asked for the tape to be stopped again, but he did not say anything.

Neither did she.

In the circumstances, it seemed hypocritical to accept thanks for their cooperation, but Rob did it gracefully although with ill-concealed anxiety to be out of there. Smiles all round and she followed meekly, as if he had been John and she the carrier of his bag. He loped back round the corner while Elisabeth struggled to keep up with him, until they stood at the side entrance to the concourse. There he stopped.

'I could buy you a drink at the bar,' he said, jubilation trembling in his voice. 'To fucking celebrate.'

'Celebrate?'

'She's *alive*,' he hissed. 'She's fucking *alive*.'

'Yes,' she said. 'Yes, yes, yes, a drink, but not *here*.'

It was not the rush-hour crowds which inhibited her – their frantic zigzagging towards platforms with their burdens of luggage, shopping, business bags, coffee, tea, chocolate eaten on the run, while others waited, open-mouthed, staring at the departure boards as if they were the clue to life – but the presence of Douglas Petty, solid as rock in the midst of them, refusing to be budged with his size and presence forcing even the most hurried to detour and avoid contact. He was scanning the crowd, glancing at the faces as they swept around him. He looked like a father waiting for a child, covering all the angles, unsure of the direction from which his child might come. He managed to be both lonely and threatening. The child, when it got there, would be in for a bollocking. He was carrying a small purple bag, a feminine article which looked as if it might contain a gift.

'We're going somewhere else,' she said, snatching Rob by the arm. 'I've just seen someone I don't want to meet.'

The crowds thinned out to busy trickles of people. Douglas moved to Cafe Select further away from the trains and stood with a double espresso. A pigeon paddled round his feet. They were rats on wings, intrusive vermin, but he did not shoo it away and dropped crumbs of his cake for it to gobble. He did not want the cake and he was fond of pigeons.

He ticked off the list he had made on a Post-it stuck on the back of his diary. Lists were necessary; they focused the mind. The ticking-off of tasks gave him a sense of achievement.

Tuesday 4th May
Go to ghastly flat, check it out
Cash and Carry

Phone vet, query bill
Letters
Train 2.33
Home

Not an impressive list of achievements, nor even an impressive list of duties. He had done the most important. Douglas turned for the journey home. He hated trains.

CHAPTER SEVEN

Douglas sat in the station car park at Staplehurst, waited for the next train to come in, and counted the days. Fifteen since the crash and the cars of the four dead who had departed from here long since collected, along with the tributes of flowers he had seen from a distance but never approached. It was prematurely dark when he set off through the small centre, round the one-way system and away from the town. The distance was less than two miles but he had already entered a different zone and the city he had left might have been on a separate planet. His eyes ached from the artificial light of the carriage. The small town slumbered, bereft of amusements after eight in the evening apart from two pubs, a restaurant and the window-shopping of the single, select street.

The headlights of the old hatchback strafed the banks of the narrow country road which deviated from the main highway towards his house, picking out primroses, bluebells and blossom. In contrast with the quiet self-containment of the town, the woods which flanked his route teemed with nightlife which he could sense without ever seeing the secret rituals. He disliked the hazards of an early morning drive in summer, when rabbits and birds came out to bask on the relative warmth of the tarmacadam and lost all instinct for survival, so that however slowly he crawled through the lanes to avoid them, there was always some bloody corpse in evidence, flattened by a vehicle in the headlong rush to the station. The commuters were like the Gadarene swine driven by a curse. He did not suffer from a similar impatience at that time of day, but then did not have to go to work, and that privilege alone should be enough to make him tolerant.

It did not have that effect, although he knew his situation was enviable and he had taken great joy in his freedoms. Douglas considered that not going to work should be the height of any sane person's ambition. Why else scrimp and save and get and spend, if it were not for the privilege of being able to stop and consider the lily? There was never any difficulty in filling the days, which seemed, in winter, to be unmercifully short, although the prospect of the endless light of summer was not the delight which other years had promised. He shifted in his seat, changed gear to slow down on the bend with the overhanging hawthorn bush where last week he had seen a fox flitting across the road like a cunning shadow. He could have sworn it had winked at him.

He turned left into the small valley which contained the house, sheltered from the Downs beyond, less than half a mile to go without any of the usual lifting of spirit. Fifteen days, he repeated, only fifteen. He accelerated angrily for the final, straight stretch. Then his headlights caught the golden dog, trotting towards him in the middle of the road, nose to ground, tail aloft like a flag, raising its head at the last minute, so that its eyes caught the reflection of the headlights and shone back, blindingly, like a pair of brilliant torches aimed at his windscreen. Douglas slammed on the brakes; the dog stopped, transfixed, and the car screeched to a halt with a couple of yards to spare and he sprang out, swearing. The dog moved as he approached only to wag its tail and then let it droop in anticipation of disapproval. Douglas felt for the distinctive collar, a thin leather band in red with name, address and phone number on a plastic disc hanging from the buckle. Then he held the dog by the collar, felt briefly for a warm, wet nose and led him to the back of the car.

'Josh,' he scolded. 'If you were a girl, you'd be a whore. So who's a randy hound, eh? You.'

The dog clambered obediently into the back and settled down with a big soft head placed on the back seat, regarding him mournfully through the driving mirror. 'I don't know,' he told it. 'You're all over the place looking for a bitch in heat and you don't even charge them. Shame on you.'

He drove on into the hollow by the stables and parked by the entrance, leaving the lights on full beam to catch the colour of the mellow brick, and the dog began to whine. Jimmy was outside, hurrying towards them, the worry etched on his face turning to relief.

'Oh Christ, you got him. I'd my back turned for a minute, I'm sorry, I shouldn't have . . .' His breath through the open window was minty fresh. 'Sorry,' he repeated, the words difficult to say, stepping back as Douglas swung himself out and stretched.

'Never bother, Jimmy. Can't be helped. This dog could get out of Alcatraz if he had the right scent. I don't give a damn if he mounts every bitch in the county, but he's got no road sense. He can die on the job, but not under a car. I'll take him up to the house. Everything all right?'

'Fine.'

'No intruders with poison arrows?'

'Nope.'

'Get off to the pub then, I would. Listen out for gossip. We can't keep guarding the place like a fortress. None of them's on the critical list.'

'I can come back here and sleep.'

'Could you? Even assuming the enemy's not gunning for us this evening. It'll be easier when I build the new place.'

'Are you still going to do that?'

'Of course. I'll leave the car here. 'Night.'

His footsteps crunched away into the dark with the golden dog sulking at his heels. Jimmy shook his head. Leaving the car as an indicator that someone was with the dogs every single minute of the day and night would not fool anyone with an ounce of intelligence, or even the cub reporter from the local press who had been there again today, but Douglas was right. If the alarms they had installed meant that neither of them could ever be absent, there was little enough point in installing them at all. They had to pretend that life was normal. Jimmy looked at the house, where lights twinkled welcomingly, shook his head. Someone was trying to ruin this man and he was not sure who. It was too much to ask of a man to guard his women as well as his dogs.

'There,' Caterina said to her mother in the living room. 'What do you think?'

Mother sat in her regular chair and peered at the windows. The heavy curtains, which were usually thrust to one side and rarely pulled, so that they spent most of their lives bunched against the wall on either side of the curved window with dust gathered in the folds, had been taken down and shaken out, the dead flies of last year removed and the fabric rearranged so that it draped the window from the centre, looped into grand theatrical folds at the side with huge tassels hooking the weight to the wall. Almost a day's strenuous, back-breaking work; Caterina was proud of it.

'Makes the window look like a stage,' Mother said indifferently.

'Exactly.'

'Douglas would prefer not to have curtains at all.'

'Exactly.'

Mother smiled. 'I didn't know you had the strength, dearest, they must weigh a ton. It does make the room look grand. A place fit for a party. What a waste this house has been. I may as well have moved out to the kennels and let the dogs live here. I can't wait to move.'

Caterina touched the tassel at one side, straightening it up, stood back again to admire. 'He'll sell, in time. You just have to be patient. If no one brings any more dogs and he loses his reason for being, he'll sell. If he persists with that libel action and loses, he'll sell. That's what you had in mind, isn't it?'

'Or he'll stay and see reason. Give up gracefully and take to a life with a bit of style. Not a house annexed to an animal hospital. Ridiculous.'

'You didn't mind so much before dear Amy arrived.'

Mother let her sewing fall into her lap. 'No, but at least one had a chance,' she said petulantly. '*We* had a chance to rid him of his obsessions and make something more of himself. This place could be so beautiful. It *will* be beautiful. So inconvenient of Amy to die like this. Gives her a status she hardly deserved.' The venom in her voice was all the more resonant because she spoke so quietly. Caterina wondered if her mother was really insane and smothered the thought; look at her, a piece of perfection, mending her own lace blouse with her uncannily good eyesight. Caterina looked at the white hands which took up the needlework again so gently and had a moment of realisation about how other people might see them if they knew how rotten they were to their elegant backbones with sheer envy and yet she could not feel any shame about it. They loved Douglas; they had always loved Douglas. They were entitled to be as they were; they were only what they were made to be. Everyone was entitled to fight for the birthright which had been given and then taken away and anyone would scheme to save something precious that was being spoiled. They were the only ones who knew what was good for him.

'I'm sorry all the same that Amy had to go quite like this,' Mother went on calmly, redeeming herself slightly with this expression of regret. 'What an awful way to die.' She paused tragically and then smiled with an awful serenity. 'But at least it saves alimony. Do they still call it that? She'd have been gone within the year, probably; she was working up to it.'

'You were very nice to her, Mummy.'

'We *both* were,' Isabel corrected.

Even in private, they talked in a careful code as if they could be overheard. The effect of the restyled curtains on the room was undoubtedly dramatic, especially after dark. They blocked out the uncomfortable expanse of the sky and reminded Caterina of a plush restaurant in a country-house hotel, designed for opulent candlelit dining, but perhaps a little sombre at breakfast. The other thing it reminded her of, less comfortably, was the stagey curtains at a crematorium, behind which the coffin slid quietly to oblivion. Still, they emphasised the curve of the room and gave it the grandeur it deserved.

'Whoever chose damson curtains had a lot to answer for,' she remarked.

'Nobody chose them, they were *there*,' Mother said. 'Nobody but me thought there was any point getting new ones after Daddy died. Douglas said they would do, he always says that.'

'Did you hear the car?'

'No, did you?'

Caterina hated the silence, willed herself to hear vehicles and voices, anything but the hooting of an owl, the dawn and evening chorus, or the barking of dogs, which was worst of all. She disliked being in a house surrounded by this blackness where the kitchen door was not locked at night. The kitchen door stuck; it was another irritating thing waiting to be fixed and that was the sound she heard in the distance now. She sank into the chair nearest that of her mother and took up the newspaper. 'We'll really have to plan this memorial service, you know. People will think it so odd if we don't,' she said demurely.

'What people?' Mother asked, hearing the same sounds. 'She didn't have any friends. She only talked to the dogs.'

The kitchen smelt of savoury casserole, probably ready for him to eat. The cat had been mewling outside, running down the path to meet him and weaving in and out of his legs as he opened the door, so impatient to be on the inside and close to food that it forgot it might defeat its own purpose by barring his progress. He kicked the door open wide and let it through first; the mewling increased in proportion to the smell. The cat was a lazy scavenger, addicted to anything cooked for human consumption rather than the blander alternative that came out of a tin. Douglas lifted the casserole out of the oven and spooned some of it into a bowl, which he left on the counter to cool for the cat while it continued rubbing his ankles in an orgy of cupboard love. Exactly the kind of company he needed, selfish but undemanding provided he understood what was expected of him, quite unlike the women in the room beyond, whom he did not understand at all. The cat should have been fed sooner than this. He spooned a little more into the bowl, indifferent to the rich smell of a bourgignon flavoured with herbs, onions, wine. Bloody filth. Waiting for the cat's dinner to cool, he wandered over to the doll's house, which stood by the sink, taking up space that would have been useful to a dedicated and practical cook, something Amy had never managed to be. The doll's house attracted dust and grease and required meticulous cleaning from time to time, one of those activities for the proverbial wet afternoon when there was absolutely nothing to do but attend to details and there were not many afternoons like that. Douglas looked at it curiously, the one thing Amy had brought into this house apart from a selection of clothing, lotions, potions and creams and a few pairs of shoes she treated with reverence. She had acquired nothing else but this strangely accurate facsimile of the house in which she had come to live. See? She had told him, see? This is our house, I mean your house, and in a way she was right. There was a living room, with the garden painted on to the windows and damson-coloured curtains, where the master sat in a chair with two dogs at his feet. In the kitchen, a woman worked at an antiquated black range, with another dog in a basket and a cat sleeping alongside. Upstairs, there were two frilly bedrooms, with another dog adorning a counterpane.

Douglas picked out the figure of the master, noticed the poor state of his rather decayed clothing, admired the frayed tweed of the jacket and wondered how it might be repaired. He had never been curious about the manufacture of the doll and it only made him think of weary afternoons at primary school where they had made things out of Plasticine instead of playing and where the idea had been *not* to pulp the different coloured strips of malleable stuff into one multicoloured ball to stick in the ear of some other boy. The project had been to make something nice, mould figures or at least a cat composed of two round shapes, one for the head and one for the body, not forgetting ears and tail. All he could do was disrupt the class.

The figure in his hand remained as it was when removed, sitting in the same position as it occupied in its wing chair, with both arms at right angles and one leg crossed over the other. Inside the chair, the doll looked impressively life-like, but in the palm of Douglas's large hand, it seemed curiously deformed, like a dead lizard. If he held his finger and thumb apart so that they were parallel, that was the height of the figure if the figure had been able to stand. He got out his glasses to examine it more closely. The leg would move within limits and the clothes were constructed like real clothes, made to be placed on a standing figure during an appointment with his tailor and squashed now into permanent creases from having sat down all these years. A clumsy seam at the back of the trousers had split, revealing a substructure of tape. Looking at the feet below the trousers showed him that they consisted of small lumps of clay, painted grey for socks and black for shoes and the calves were made from twisted wire. The ingenuity of it suddenly delighted him, but then the modelled head, which he had handled roughly, fell off into his palm, revealing a pipecleaner neck. He easily put the head back on to the stem of the body and sighed with relief, but the head was at the wrong angle, with a tiny porcelain face looking upwards, making the body seem distraught. He adjusted it as much as he could and put it back inside the house, where it sat less easily in the chair. 'Arseholes!' he yelled.

The cat was up on the counter, sniffing the too hot stew and Josh was whining to go out in pursuit of lust. Should have had that dog seen to, but he hated to emasculate a dog. He sat at the table, tempted to put his head in his hands and feel his temples in case his brain was bursting, but instead he bellowed at the cat, 'Get down, you stupid twat!' and the cat obeyed. Something was often achieved by shouting; it invariably made him feel calmer. He put the cat dish in the fridge to cool for a minute while he washed his hands and put the casserole back in the oven. Then he put the cat's portion on the floor and watched her eat with delicate greed.

Caterina sidled into the room. 'Hallo, didn't hear you!' The first untruth of the evening. 'Are you hungry?'

'Sorry, no.' He stood shielding the cat on the floor so that his sister would not see what it ate. Josh resumed his irritating whining. 'You go out on a lead, or not at all,' Douglas said, turning to his sister as the cat finished. 'I caught him out on the road. Off hunting.'

'As you men do,' she said.

Douglas felt in his pocket for the small cigars, spoke

quietly. 'Cat, tell me something. Why did I ever marry anyone as silly as Amy?'

'What a strange question! I can't answer it. She had fine qualities and you were running out of options,' she said carefully.

'Where did she get the doll's house?'

'I've no idea. Awful thing.' She paused, not quite sure what to do in here to occupy her hands. Everything was clean, every dish washed or out of sight. He hated it like that, felt he should walk about on tiptoe in socked feet for fear of making marks.

'. . . But there was something, Douglas . . . I don't know how to say this, but she was hiding something. I mean, it isn't only men who go out hunting, is it? Those regular trips to London when she never seemed quite able to explain what she'd done or where she'd been . . . do you think there might have been . . . ? Did it occur to you?'

'How discreet you are, Caterina. And yes, it did occur to me that there might be a lover lurking somewhere since I'm not oblivious of the fact that she is fifteen years younger than me, but it only occurred to me after Mother raised the possibility. Then I considered it and dismissed it.'

'Why?'

'Because I would have known. I didn't ask her what she did or why she wanted to go because she didn't want to elaborate and that was entirely up to her. Not much of a life for her here.'

'Douglas, she had everything she could possibly want. Adored the dogs, too, absolutely mad about them.'

'She worked hard. She was entitled to stop.'

'About once a week for three years,' Caterina said flatly. 'Enough to keep a lover happy, especially if he was also married.'

'Oh, shut up, please. For all I know, she might have been going to see a doctor, in the time-honoured fashion of Edwardian ladies who find themselves unable to conceive. She might have gone up once a week to spend the whole day on the Ferris wheel. She might have gone to get away from dogs, or me. I don't *care* where she went. As long as she came back.'

'I think that's called knowing what side your bread is buttered,' Caterina said.

'I'm amazed at you. What are you trying to do?'

'I'm trying to make you accept human frailty, including your own. That bloody newspaper was right. It isn't natural to behave as you do. If you could accept her as a human being, you might be able to mourn. Come and have a drink at least.'

He lit the cigar, suddenly weary in the way he was if he spent a day with only a small ration of physical exercise. It was as if he had to expend the energy in order to acquire more. The smell of the tobacco leaf was reassuring, mollified him, and he allowed Caterina to lead the way down the flagged passageway to the front room where he went to her chair and kissed his mother lightly on the cheek and waited for the full-bodied smile of welcome which always pleased him. She tugged his hair and tutted at the cigar he was waving in front of him. 'Shouldn't do that, dear,' she said sweetly, without really meaning it, the words only another form of greeting. It was only a mother who could speak to a son with a rebuke and make it sound like a welcome. He sat in the opposite chair, crossed his legs and waited for Caterina to bring him the whisky. The master of the house, like the doll in the doll's house, lord of all he surveyed. Then he looked up and saw the damson curtains, ruched into ornamental swags, hiding the moon.

'What the fuck . . . ?'

He ignored the glass which Caterina presented to him and strode to the French doors almost concealed in the middle, battled with the cloth to find the handle and flung the window wide.

The alarm sounded from the stables, like a sore-throated siren. The dog that had followed him into the room galloped for freedom. Douglas followed.

He ran over the lawn, which was spongy beneath his feet, brushed his way through the willow tree with the drooping branches snatching at his face, cursing the wrong kind of shoes and the lack of a torch. His feet hit the track to the stables and pounded on, stumbled once, gathered speed. A minute, no more than that, but still too far. He splashed through a puddle and went on, the breath rasping in his chest, punishing him for the cigar which he threw in front of himself as he ran and watched the small spot of light land on the ground. The alarm grew louder, accompanied by a cacophony of barking, the dogs' voices joined in a chorus ranging from basso profundo to shrill yelping. The gate to the stable court-yard was open. The barking ceased unevenly as if his presence was sensed, except for the small dog which went on after all the others and then stopped abruptly. He checked each stable, talking to them; nothing wrong, went into the stable with the bed and the control switches to reset the alarm. The nightlights lit the yard with a serene glow and as he went to close the gate, he saw the new dog, heard its breathing before he saw it. He switched on the spotlights.

The head of the thing was half out of the sack used to transport it. He could hear the weak, scrabbling sound of claws scraping at the canvas of an old post office bag, mercifully loose at the neck. It looked as if the whole parcel had been flung over the wall; he hoped whoever it was had at least opened the gate and carried it inside. The dog stared at him with frightened, bloodshot eyes and bared teeth. There was a fresh wound by the ear: someone had struck it to keep it quiet. Probably safer to keep it in the sack.

It was not the first time that a new charge had arrived this way. Douglas sighed and wished he had not sent Jimmy to the pub. He gently picked up the animal, sack and all, found it lighter than he expected and wondered why he was surprised. Animals arriving here rarely had much flesh on their bones and he hoped no bones were broken. He began the slower trudge back to the house. That clean kitchen was the best place for this and if he were going to be called out at night, the vet preferred to be close to the whisky.

He could see the tyre tracks in the mud by the gate and paused to look down with the dog still light in his arms.

The night was deliciously clear with the moon showing up the stucco of the house and making it glow white beneath the scudding clouds. The scent of the courtyard herbs after the rain lingered in his nostrils while the dog smelled rancid and sick. Breeze rustled the friendly trees and despite the anger, he felt completely at home. It's a lovely place, he told the dog; you'll like it here; the forecast for tomorrow is healing sunlight; what do you like to eat? The animal was beyond protest, shocked almost to death, and he was afraid it might indeed die without Amy to weave her magic. Amy, come home. The bluebells have begun and the May blossom will be out. You can walk this dog on the Downs.

Elisabeth had the wide-awakeness of the not entirely sober and her face as seen by herself in the train window during the journey home was one she would rather not share, with a puffiness round the eyes and the jaw made slack by the unkind reflection in the black glass which distorted her into something freakish. It made the crumpled collar grey, smeared her mouth into bulbous lips and her hair as if it was a clutch of nesting snakes turned over by a spade. Her throat felt like cactus. There was no such thing as a nice place to drink in the vicinity of a rush-hour station; there were only bars full of screaming spenders, shedding the day like a second skin. Thin girls and thick men, separating themselves from both work and home, challenging each other to drink the fastest. Or there were the clandestine meetings, not always hurried assignations in the quieter corners with a furtive holding of hands, women who looked like she might have looked when she met John sometimes, not hiding, but not shining either with the sparkling shimmer of the skinny unattached, waiting only for summer to bare the flesh from ankle to thigh, hip to bosom and announce they were there to be caught. She wished she had ever been like them, but instead, she was the one in the corner, wrecking an evening for the prospect of half an hour with a man before he caught his train.

And such lies they all told each other in the bars, about who they were and what they did; she could hear them, low-decibel lies, loud lies, lies by evasion. In a different sense, she had also lied, or at least been economical with the truth, to use a phrase overworked in the law, and Rob the trolley man deserved the truth, even though, in defence of her present feeling of shabbiness, she told herself it would be almost impossible to explain, especially when he thought he had found an entirely spontaneous friend. And so he had, but the other agenda she carried, like a weighted knapsack by now, was not easy to explain to someone like Rob with his instinctive dislike of persons in suits, whatever their sex; he might not have spoken to her at all if she had not looked like the pretender to status which she was. He had a chip on his shoulder a mile high, which did not prevent his fierce affection once any individual had struck him to the heart; he was an odd mix of cynical and naïve, a hater of authority, and if she had once announced that she had a vested interest in the identity of his missing pal, well, she did not know what he would do. Divorce her after a day on the basis of their incompatibility. Elisabeth found herself giggling, whoops; not good, try again; she had drunk one overpriced, gassy lager too many. No, several too many.

She almost missed her stop and then strode out of the station with the fixed determination of someone pretending they could walk as soon as the anaesthetic had worn off. Sped through the route to her dull terrace, reflecting upon the idiocy of time. The journey this morning had felt like the equivalent of a whole day and the travelling home seemed like five minutes. There was no such thing as time, only a perception of it. God had rained water on her new plants; she could forget about them for the time being. The wine in the wine rack was a more tempting prospect than food. Blotto was an excellent idea.

She turned into her street and as soon as she was near the front step, the security light came on with a comforting glow. There was no sound of TVs or loud music; the neighbours were all far too discreet until barbecue time in high summer, supposing it ever showed, when oily vapours would waft across her clematis along with the sound of parties to which she would not be asked. Elisabeth did not really want to know her neighbours any more than she wanted to examine the psychology of the trolley man, and it was only her lack of curiosity in that regard that made her feel guilty. His loneliness was like a clarion call to her own; she should respect it, but she did not want to do that. She wanted to find Amy Petty, all by herself, and that was all she wanted to do.

Key in lock, light goes out once inside. Mobile phone in same place, proper phone in bracket on wall, with a light to signal messages, good. Wine in fridge, home forever in need of cleaning, cat had peed in sheer disgust, bad. She dumped her bags and kicked off her new shoes. Found pad of paper and pen and started to make notes:

How find Amy P? Look, you pillock. All you do, looking. You aren't a lawyer at all, you're a backroom person who knows about finding press cuttings, et al. You know where you go for birth certificates. Is the Fisher I had down as her maiden name her real name? Might be.

If you were on the run, where would you go? Mum and Dad. She hasn't got any. Who says? Hubby says! Everybody's got one or other, even me, only I wouldn't go there at the point of gun, cos they think I'm a success. Why shouldn't she have them? The sort not fit to introduce? Everybody's got someone, somewhere . . .

A pause for a gulp of wine and an effort to make the hand with the pen more businesslike. It was a nice pen, some special make of fountain pen John had got for her, perhaps to lend some dignity to her shambolic signature and cryptic notes. Real ink looks nicer on the page. Cold-blooded bastard, ink in his veins. Her giggling shook the crockery; she became more businesslike.

Obvious, innit? Birth certificate and work back. Not as if you had anything better to do. Look up fishy Fishers. Any mention in press? No need police computer (if only), try bad debtors and stuff.

Oh shit. She staggered out into the garden and managed to aim the vomit on to the paving where she could hose it down. Jesus, the garden cost more than any room in the house and she was a lousy drinker, not an expensive drunk since a little on a big stomach seemed to go a long, long way. She came back inside, remembered the answer-phone message.

Darling Elisabeth, I'm a crabby old devil and I'm sorry if I was rude, however late you were. The trouble is that I am incredibly lonely without you. Everything goes wrong without you, my talisman. Hope you understand and know you do. I love you.

She put down the phone, suddenly sober. How could she be afraid of John and also love him?

Amy Petty did not notice the state of other people's houses. She was the one who went inside and wondered why anyone ever apologised about their mess. When she looked at a room, she saw the shape of it and registered it on a scale of one to ten for comfort. When she looked at a garden, she looked for space and colour, the more vivid, the better. No taste, Caterina said.

The back garden of her father's house looked, by the light of the moon, as if all colour had been leached from it. There were a few valiant shrubs around the edges of a cracked concrete yard which sprouted tough dandelions. A buddleia hung precariously from the back wall, the only thing she would want to preserve; she had seen these often on the brick escarpments flanking railway lines; they seemed to like the height and flowered in the face of misfortune. She longed for the sound of the owl that lived in the garden at home and she would have sold her soul for the murmur of wind in the trees. Instead, she heard a train go by in the cutting and, when it had passed, the background hum of cars.

She had cleared up all the cardboard boxes he had thrown out here, torn them apart, pressed them down, bagged them, then set about turning the old coal bunker into something else. It was a square, concrete box, open at the front, designed to keep fuel dry, and it was now a kennel with a clean interior which still smelled of coal. Amy was very tired.

Her anticipation of her father's anger when she came home accompanied by a crippled dog was entirely accurate, but she had underestimated the scale of his displeasure. She may not have known him very well, but the reaction surprised her all the same. Stupid of her to forget that not everyone shared her defensive devotion to dogs. After the outburst, he had retreated to his work-room and stayed there apart from a few forays out for tea and sandwiches. TAKE IT AWAY! he had shouted. But where would I take it, she had asked. The police? The RSPCA, who would keep it a little while and then destroy it, humanely of course, but still before its time? They destroy thousands of dogs every year, Daddy; dogs have no rights as soon as they are abandoned. Only for a few days, Dad, please, until I can make it better. He was so angry, it crossed her mind to wonder if it was safe to leave the dog in residence while she went back to the shop for supplies, in case it reacted to his resentment, but she knew he would not harm it and there was no alternative. She was right about his decency, of course. Somewhere in the late afternoon when she was clearing the yard, he had placed some food in an old pan on the floor for the dog, which chose to ignore the leftover chopped-up sausages and portion of rice from the fridge and slept instead. Water was its only requirement; gallons of water, which cost nothing. It settled into the kennel she had made, bedded down on the old eiderdown from her bed, with the extra padding of a moth-eaten blanket she had found. Daddy had nothing new.

Amy looked at the space she had created with extreme satisfaction. A good day's work, even if her father was still refusing to speak a word and was unlikely to come out of the doll's house room, even to say good night. She knelt by the kennel, fondled the dog's head and heard the thump of a tail. If the dog lived out here or in her room, it need never bother him at all and once he·saw it sleek and well, he would be proud of their acquaintance.

Amy fetched the pan of food which the dog had ignored, intending to place it by the kennel. There would be better food tomorrow when the beast was hungry. Then, as she carried it from the kitchen into the relative darkness of the yard, something in the pan caught the light. She shook the container and looked again.

Beneath the rice, there were shards of glass.

CHAPTER EIGHT

Amy Petty nee Fisher looked hard at the pan with the glass shards only clumsily concealed beneath the pallid boiled rice and wondered where he might have laid hands on them. It was against her father's nature to break things; she was the clumsy one, he had remarked the day before when she dropped a tumbler and he had hastened to sweep it up, spiriting away the remains into his work-room. There was a use for everything in there.

She closed her eyes and tried first to imagine the pos-sibility of mistake and then to think of why he had taken it away and for what use. As she prodded the shards, she could feel the sensation of glass in her own mouth, imagine her teeth crunching on that alien texture, thought how long it would take her to attempt to spit it out. Such a sensitive thing, the mouth, the way it tested food for sweet and sour, dry and moist, welcome, unwelcome, and all inside a split second of instinct, but hunger deadened instinct and a dog chewed less, especially a starving dog. A dog would eat what a cat would disdain, but the dog out there in the back yard had been too traumatised for this unappetising mess. She wrapped the lethal food in newspaper and made a dish of bread soaked in milk, which it sniffed first, then ate when she made to take the dish away, sighed, as if the effort was great and it did the world a favour by being so obliging. It was not the kind of cunning dog that courted love by showing gratitude in a semblance of human manners; it pretended to ignore her. Amy sat by the kennel and watched as it settled again, one eye open, watching. A train ran by in the escarpment beyond the yard and the damp ground vibrated gently. She had an overpowering need to say something; a sense of profound shock made her want to speak in order to make sure she could control her own voice without screaming.

'You're OK here,' she told the dog, 'because I should have been a vet, or perhaps not because I've never met a vet who wasn't impatient. My father, would you believe' – she nodded her head in the direction of indoors – 'bought me a dog, once; stole me a dog for all I know, but it was still mine, and because it was mine I read every book going about dogs so that I could take care of it. It was *mine*, but when my father *died*, as they say, and we moved, the dog disappeared. I've been replacing it ever since, I reckon. How's that for psychology?' She adjusted her too heavy, severely dirty skirt over her knees and leant against the barbecue. 'My mother didn't tell me to kiss it goodbye, someone just got rid of it and told me it had gone to heaven with him. How old are you, buster? Sixteen going on seventy? What was it like to be young? A lot of fun, I bet. Do you want any more?'

The animal closed its single, watchful eye and let her stroke its head.

'As for that man in there,' she whispered to it, 'I am his only child and he was a teacher in a primary school. He taught them reading and writing and how to play with Play-Doh. He didn't go to heaven; he went to prison for seducing the girls. Long stretch. I never knew that until much, much later. Framed, he says, at a time when people were hysterical about such things. Is that true? I never stopped loving him. He gave me a doll's house and a dog after all, what more can a girl want? I still love him. That's the way it goes.'

The light came on behind her, far up against the back wall, in the bathroom. That had been his vantage point to watch what she had done in the afternoon. The dog whimpered.

'Shhh,' she said. 'Shhh. Let him listen.'

Speaking out loud in this even tone of voice so as not to alarm the dog had an oddly calming effect on herself. She was so silent in this house, lived here like an inconvenient lodger on sufferance.

'He found out where I was after I married Douglas,' Amy continued. 'And sent me an article he had written about doll's houses so that I would know it was really him. Don't tell anyone, he said, so I didn't. I'm excellent at keeping secrets, like my mother. I came and saw him, I was sorry for him and I've always wanted him to love me. That's part of the reason why I ran away. All those lawyers and newspapers would have found out, wouldn't they? They find everything out and what would his life be like then? I've read about people like him being lynched, almost. Driven away, and this is all he's got, his doll's houses, his miniatures, and me. And then, I wouldn't have been much of a witness for Douglas, would I? Amy, the pervert's daughter. What would Douglas think about not being told?'

She could feel her voice rising and did not care. 'But that was only part of it, not even the biggest part. The worst thing is . . . what do you think? Not being loved? No, you can get used to that, *you* should know; I *was* used to that already. It's being undermined, being hated in a way that isn't even personal . . . And not being able to say . . .'

'Not being able to say what?'

Amy did not jump, she had half-expected to attract his attention and lure him down. Nobody spoke out loud without wanting an audience. Rollie Fisher stood at the kitchen door in a pool of light, looking sad, dishevelled and tired. She glanced at him over her shoulder, folded her arms and looked up at the sky. Never quite dark here, not like home, where the dark was like a soft blanket she could pull over her head without suffocating.

'Not being able to say to your husband that the two people he loves best in the world are his greatest enemies. And knowing that if you suggested such a thing, he would think you were mad.'

She turned on him and laughed without humour. 'I

never thought that talking to a dog was a way to get people to listen,' she said. 'Perhaps I should have tried it before. Why did you try and kill this poor dog, you stinking, *sadistic, inadequate BASTARD*?' She clamped her hand over her mouth, frightened by the words and wanting to swallow them back. They tasted like glass.

He shuffled. 'I didn't . . . I didn't think it would actually *eat* it. I thought they knew better. I just wanted you to know how angry I was.' He slumped against the door frame, trembling with the effort of standing so still. There were tears in his eyes. 'I'm so sorry. So sorry. I don't know what possessed me. It was in the pan, I just put the stuff on top by *mistake*. I'm sorry.'

'That's what my mother said when she told me you hadn't died. Or gone to heaven,' she added. 'She had to wait until *she* was dying and no one knew where you were. I've heard quite a few sorrys. I can't distinguish between the real ones and the other kind. *Sorry*.'

He rallied, stood straighter. 'Your mother was having an affair and she wanted OUT,' he hissed at her. '*She* spread the rumours and put the police on me. I was *innocent*. All for her freedom, not mine. It was a *mistake*, do you hear me? I'm SORRY.'

He began to cough, guttural spasms racking his chest and turning his face purple. The phlegmy cough went on and on until she moved towards him and patted him on the back but he retreated from her, waving his hand as if to say, don't, it'll go in a minute, and hacked loudly until it ended, leaving him stooped and painfully old. An old man who fumbled and made mistakes.

'Go to bed, Father,' she said. 'I'll lock up, just let me. Go to bed and I'll bring you some milk.'

He nodded and tottered through the kitchen, out of sight, footsteps receding on the worn carpet of the stairs as she followed him inside. She could hear the sound of running water and the flush of the toilet. The sound of next door's music penetrated into the room and for once she was grateful for the irritation and listened until the end of a half-heard song. After a while, she went upstairs, knocked and entered his room, placed the milk and a saucer full of the plain biscuits he liked on the rickety table by his bed, not quite caring if he was really asleep. Streetlight seeped through the tightly closed window with the view up the road and made his skin look yellow. It was a small room, everything in it looking as if it had always been old, just as he did. She knew that he sat on this old counterpane on his carefully made bed for an hour in the afternoon, unaware that she registered his habits and movements. She was trying to work out how they resembled one another and found nothing at all, although in other lights, they had the same eyes, the same large hands. Then she went downstairs and double-locked the front door. His workroom was still brilliantly lit; distress or whatever it was had made him forgetful of switching off the light and of his reluctance for her to enter his lair unless he was there, too. Inside, there were fourteen doll's houses, a workbench, several one-room tableaux, innumerable catalogues and magazines, carspray paints, acrylic paints, poster paints and the smell of glue and turpentine which distinguished the place. There was an old typewriter in the clean corner where he recorded what he did for the book he was writing, *Modelling in ¹⁄₁₂ scale,* and where he conducted an acrimonious correspondence with other model-makers and enthusiasts. *Dear Madam, Your letter to* Miniature Model Making Monthly *on the use of cold porcelain was entirely misleading . . . Dear Sir, The house you described in your article as an original model supplied by Hamleys in 1929 is clearly NOT. The windows do not match with . . .*

She turned to the pages of his notes. *Building miniatures from scratch is the greatest challenge. Almost everything is useful. (My wife has a system of filing spare bits and pieces in the large yoghurt pots we get for the grandchildren, which are useful themselves! All numbered, of course.) Preliminary models can be made from all kinds of packaging. The boards at the back of school notebooks are particularly useful. The lack of wooden punnets for fruit is a shame, these days, but chocolate boxes, egg trays, canes for plants and tinfoil wrappings are invaluable, and takeaway meals often have useful containers. Christmas decorations can be used to resemble table decorations or the trimming on a fancy garment (a piece of tinsel can be a boa, for instance), tinfoil can be used for mirrors and special effects. A piece of broken glass, say from a mirror, or any object with a flat surface, can be used to make a miniature lake. Cardboard absorbs moisture from the atmosphere, though, so it will warp in time unless you coat it with varnish . . .*

All written in the same enthusiastic style of the letters pages of the magazines devoted to the making of tiny dolls and their abodes which Amy had read during the nervous distraction of her first week inside this house. There had been a mixture of motives for her reading in those first days, initially to distract herself during the waking hours when she had been listless with nightmares and second, with the thought that if she learned, she would be able to help her father in his endless endeavour to create the miniature masterpiece. She had read the magazines in the kitchen, secretly puzzled by the obsession of those who devoted lives to the making of *toys* with the same passion an architect might bring to the building of a cathedral, and she had listened to him talking about the writing of a book, but nothing here could explain why ever he would want shards of glass from a cheap, broken tumbler, and why, in the writing of this chapter, he would claim a wife and suggest a style of living which belonged not to himself, but to someone else. Writing as if his house were full of the detritus of a normal family life. There were no takeaways, chocolate boxes or celebrations of Christmas here.

There was only a dump of a house, in which he made his alternative worlds, out of romance or competition. Preparing for an exhibition which would stun the world and make it accept him. She had no idea why he should lie and wanted to dismiss the disquieting thought that he lied with automatic flair, all the time. Then she considered his life; of course he was bound to lie. No one was going to read a letter or a book about wholesome pastimes if the author of it confessed he was a convicted paedophile who had refined his hobby into an art form whilst serving at Her Majesty's pleasure. They would draw the simple parallel between doll's houses and children. Poor man; it was necessary for him to lie. But the inventive, quarrel-some adults who read the magazines, bought the kits and swapped notes like trainspotters through the columns of the several publications did not create these tableaux for the touch of sticky fingers and the witnessing of childish delight; they did it for their own amusement, in the same way that it used to be grandfathers who spent afternoons with the Hornby train set rather than the grandsons. They probably did it to escape from a daily life that lacked the necessary romance. Or they had a hidden agenda.

She still could not see why he had wanted to preserve the broken tumbler, or why, even in private, he should elaborate upon the lies surrounding his existence. When he had said *sorry* for the accident with the glass in the bowl, he had been entirely sincere. A deliberate act of frightful sabotage had already been translated in his mind into a *mistake*, and that was what he would believe tomor-row, by which time there would be no other suggestion. It was a rapid conversion of fiction into unshakeable truth and he probably did it all the time. As natural as breath-ing, the same type of liar as her mother-in-law. But surely such instinctive. rapidly formed lies did not surround the central facts of his life. Amy found that idea impossible to contemplate. You could tell a lie, but you could not live one. She could not even tell a fib; they stuck in her throat like a piece of gristle and refused to budge until she choked, making silence preferable.

Her skin was sticky and dry. She longed irrelevantly and frivolously for a scented bath, a delicious face scrub and a thick creamy moisturiser of the kind her face could drink in through the pores and leave her feeling pampered and relaxed. The pleasures in life were the small ones; the evening bath at home a reward for the achievement of the day. There was no alcohol in this house; otherwise she might have attached it to her arm via a drip and anaesthetised herself. She would remedy that tomorrow. Buy some wine as a luxury for herself and her father, look after him, remind herself that they loved one another, because that, of course, was the essential truth. He loved her and needed her, which was why she was encouraged to be here. He was a man treated abominably by life; he had been falsely accused; his life, like hers, had been wrecked by the presence of other liars far worse and that was the real truth, and if she repeated it often enough, it would become truer.

Amy went back to the kitchen and out to the back yard to check on the sleeping dog. It had been grossly unreasonable of her to bring it home; she must have forgotten for a moment where she was. Not at home with Douglas, where the collection of an injured stray was a matter only for congratulation and debate, but here, where she was needed.

He doesn't love you, you silly little clot. The words, whispered out of the darkness, remembered from another time, struck a chill to her bones. *He doesn't even admire you; you aren't the sort of person he could ever admire. And that's what you wanted, Amy, isn't it? To be admired, not ignored.* Poisonous words from somewhere else, intolerable echoes from another place, carrying in their wake an inconsistent homesickness. Words that had been said beneath the gentle shade of the willow tree, which she could see in her mind's eye now, and still the longing for home was so strong that she could imagine herself scrambling down the bank to the railway line and running east, just to get closer. She would go; she could go; she could brave it when the dog was better; she could walk it, like a hobo. She could stand in this pathetic space she had created, keeping company with a dog that did not really like her, and weep the night away.

Instead, she went back inside and began to clean the kitchen. If she looked up at the ceiling, she could see cobwebs gummed into corners and drifting down the walls. If they had been live cobwebs, she might not have been able to remove them and kill the busy spiders, but they were abandoned homes, ruined by grease and overburdened by dust. She would take down whatever she could reach with an old stick duster and a chair; she would clean each surface to within an inch of its life and she would scrub the wooden table so that she could see it was wood, all to forget the sound of the trees at home and the existence of liars. And she would buy her own newspapers tomorrow, instead of reading the pages he fed to her. That was what she would do.

The cutlery drawer had the musty smell of the hurriedly washed; it was cheap stuff and she would polish it to a shine, but she had days and days to do that. After she had found somewhere to walk the dog and practise talking out loud. It clarified the mind.

'It was your sister's suggestion,' John Box said gently to Douglas, two days later, 'that I might represent you in the first place, and she further suggested that I might extend that to covering your wider interests and not just the interests of your libel case against the whistleblower. Excuse the nickname. I never mention real newspapers in conversation because it makes me so angry. Call it a kind of discretion, if you like. Childish. You could have someone far cheaper than I to shield you in your dealings with the police *et al*, not quite the strength of this side of the profession, but your sister suggested you might appreciate someone already familiar. Is she right?'

'She's always right. Just get on with it.'

John blew his nose. Elisabeth noticed the blue handkerchief that had rested by the side of the bed, distracted by the fact that he had just said something which seemed important although she had missed it. How sweet and needy he had been the night before. The handkerchief disappeared into his pocket before she could guess at its origin. She thought she knew them all.

'I only wanted to mention,' John went on with equal gentleness, 'that a QC is rather expensive as an alternative to a postbox. You might be better off relying on your solicitor.'

'The man's a greedy little shit,' Douglas said with no acrimony in his splendid, musical voice. 'And silly as arseholes.'

The man in question did not seem to notice his dismissal. Nothing could have added to his discomfort and he did not know where to put his legs. Caterina laughed a sisterly laugh and patted her brother's knee with one hand, then leant across the distance of two feet to touch

the elbow of the fourth person at the meeting, the solicitor who was readjusting his skinny body into a new twist,
so that she had to reach further as he slouched to the
opposite side and almost overbalanced. There was nothing else he could do that could gain him the attention he
was obviously seeking to avoid, but he could not stop
twitching in his desire to be out of here. Insults went over
his head, but the small flies and the sudden heat got right
up his nose.

Douglas nodded in the direction of Elisabeth, who
managed the discomfort of her deck chair by sitting back
and remaining still in case any movement of her shapely
but heavy frame should drive the wooden legs further
into the damp ground.

'Well, that's frightfully considerate of you, old man,' he
drawled. 'And you're quite right to mention it, but since
Caterina *is* always right, you may as well be the liaison
officer. Unless, of course, you want to pass it over to your
deputy here.' He pointed rudely and obviously to
Elisabeth. 'I mean, she must be cheaper. Even if she is
half-asleep."

'Only half,' she murmured, straightening up as much
as possible. 'I was just admiring the tree. It's so beautiful.'

They were sitting in the circle formed by the weeping
willow, all of them on assorted oddments of chairs which
had the appearance of being recently hauled out of cellar
or attic for the first airing of summer. The deck chair in
which she sat had a canvas speckled with mould and she
sat in it regardless. What all of those present envied about
her was her ability to relax like a cat and forget where she

was. A dog sat at her feet, adopting her. Caterina was the
only one who looked in command of her own posture,
but she had the benefit of sitting on the wooden bench
which always stood beneath the tree, next to her brother,
whose suggestion it was they should convene in the open
air. Most unbusinesslike, reminding Elisabeth of school
lessons al fresco, where nothing was learned. She had
never been able to work out of doors. Caterina had disapproved of the suggestion, but Douglas had insisted.
The chairs were there already and the decision was a *fait
accompli*. Caterina's quickly suppressed annoyance had
given Elisabeth unexpected pleasure. It was the first time
she had met the woman and her immediate reaction was
dislike. It might have been the height of her, the slim perfection of her perfectly creased linen trousers and the
artful top with the cap sleeves that did it, but Elisabeth
doubted that since she always admired the well-dressed.
Nor was it the fact that John and she appeared to be
acquaintances at least of long standing; she kissed him on
the cheek, for God's sake, and what was Douglas Petty
doing letting her choose his legal counsel? Caterina had
his air of command with none of his redeeming features,
although Elisabeth was surprised to find herself thinking
that he had any of these. Strange, how you had to see
someone as dislikable as he was in the company of someone worse in order to see anything remotely admirable in
them. Such as the accuracy of his rudeness. That solicitor
twisted on his stool really was a greedy little shit.
Adequate to formulate planning permissions for the new
kennels, useless for anything else. Elisabeth knew what he

charged, for which he did very little. But the day was hot; a blissful, insect-buzzing heat rare for early in the year, and it felt like they were being given a treat.

The willow tree, fed with rain and now blessed by the sun, was at its best. Elisabeth would have lived here for the willow tree alone. The tree had grown tall but crooked, so that its graceful branches, weighted with pale green leaves of amazing delicacy, drooped in an uneven circle away from the slender, speckled trunk. The longest branches swept the ground; it gave the perfect degree of incomplete shade, so that the sunlight twinkled through the leaves, dappling the ground and all their faces. And it created the perfect degree of background noise, a mild and musical rustling sound, like the swish of long evening gowns. A very feminine tree, beneath which Douglas sat, looking like a satyr, making him far preferable to his sister, who looked like a *snake*. She must stop this. Elisabeth felt that the identity of Amy Petty had taken up residence in her brain, although John looked less like a whippet today. The white façade of the house glimmered through the leaves, glowing in the full sun of the afternoon.

'I tell you what,' Douglas said. 'John can deal with the libel side of things. Elisabeth deals with my wife's affairs. She didn't make a will and she didn't have anything to leave; should be easy.'

He spoke with such brutal casualness that Elisabeth forgot the redeeming features. 'I don't know anything about probate,' she said. 'That really is a job for a solicitor.'

'Well, hoity-toity,' Douglas said, 'I'm sure you can learn. I didn't think you people ever turned work away. No job too small and all that. Not like when I was at the Bar. Work oozing out of every pore, however bad you were. You shut the door on them and they crawled through the window trying to get at you. I reckon I had the best of it. It can't be much fun now.'

She leant forward to retrieve the teacup she had placed on the ground for lack of anywhere else to rest it, took a sip and placed it back down. Looking up, she saw Caterina nod imperceptibly in John's direction. Quite the old friends. She could not think why the recent knowledge that it was Caterina who had chosen him to represent her brother should be so infuriating. Not that the choice was bad; John was the best, after all, but Douglas should have chosen for himself. Ah well, that was the way of it, she thought ruefully. We all want our men to take advice from women, have the sense to abdicate control and be led by us, and yet despise them when they do.

'It isn't so much the probate aspect of things,' Caterina said in her singsong voice. 'It's finding out when her death can be declared official, that sort of thing. Difficult,' she added, with a reverential lowering of the voice, 'without a body. I don't know what you do. It's a question of research. We have no *closure*, you see. Poor Douglas can't make appropriate decisions until we get that.'

'Including appropriate decisions about continuing with the case?' John prompted gently.

'There's no decision to be made about that,' Douglas

said sharply. 'We have to go on with it. I told you why. If I let a sodding newspaper make me out to be an animal who beats and buggers other animals and I don't fight it, then how does that reflect on my wife? She'll simply be remembered as someone who conspired to make me into that animal. Encouraged me, stood humbly by and let me do my worst. Amy would kill anyone who was cruel to a dog. I can't have anyone think that of her.'

Elisabeth noticed his use of the present tense, wondered if it was accidental.

'Douglas,' Caterina said with a deadly gentility he did not seem to notice. 'What does it matter?'

'It matters to me.'

The branches of the willow tree stirred in a sudden breeze, covering the silence. Elisabeth reached for the teacup again, even though all it contained by now was a brackish brew the colour of rust which had left circles on the inside of the china to mark her sips. It tasted like real Ceylon tea, the kind she liked least, and it scarcely quenched her thirst, but it was not to be ignored. Douglas had made the tea and it was Douglas who dragged them out here beyond the cool of the living room. You sneaky bastard, she thought with a venomous admiration; you have organised all this to get us at a disadvantage and you've done this before. It worked on all of them, John included, except herself, because she was hugging a secret and she loved the sun and the tree, which put everything else into the realms of nonbeing, or almost did. The sun made her an indolent dreamer; it was the most sensual of comforts; whatever vexed her mind or if she had been told that hell would freeze over the next day, she could always sit in it at the faintest excuse and treat herself as a piece of bread ready for toasting. The sun turned her into an idiot; a deck chair was heaven and even though this was not the day for the smart-heeled shoes she longed to kick off her feet, or the tights, or the long-sleeved blouse she wanted to rip off, and even though she was a worried and guilty woman, it still felt great. She struggled to sit upright and overturned the teacup with her foot.

'I'll do whatever you want me to do, Mr Petty. I don't know the answer to your questions at this moment in time' (God she hated herself for talking like that, so pompous) 'but I'm only junior counsel to Mr Box and I can only act under his aegis. Otherwise, I'm unemployable.' (Christ, that came out wrong, she wanted to take off her shoe and throw it at the branches.) 'I mean, I'm only his assistant and I can only take orders from him, not from you.' Even worse; she sounded like Miss Whiplash with an addiction to bondage, looked towards John for approval and saw him nod, even though his face was blurred with sun and she could not be sure what the gesture meant – go on; don't go on, or shut up. She went on. 'Certainly I could find out anything you want to know. Research is my strong point.'

Yeah, all you needed was an accidental meeting with a trolley man and the habit of silence which came from sheer uncertainty. And twenty-four hours' research into the mystery of a living woman who was supposed to be dead, resulting in not a lot, yet, apart from thinking about her all the time and not being able to say so. There was nobody she trusted with this virgin knowledge; no one, and anyway, Amy Petty might have weaved her way out of that damn station to do nothing other than become a suicide statistic in a rented room, or another body in the river, the sort that drifted from bank to bank until unrecognisable. The sun dived behind a cloud and she was shivering, smiling brightly and shivering. 'Do you mind if I get some water and would anyone else like some?' she asked. They all shook their heads no. 'While you discuss this with Mr Box? Don't worry, I know my way.'

Getting out of the deck chair was easy, moving aside the branches of the willow tree with a semblance of dignity was harder on the spongy ground with the heeled shoes. She walked as fast as she could to the French windows of the crazy room, fought with the curtains which blocked the light from outside and swore. There was the older Mrs Petty, sitting like a monument to patience by the side of the fire as if waiting for it to be lit, while peering over her half-moon spectacles at a newspaper, her sewing in her lap, the very soul of calm. She looked just like a potted plant. A favourite aspidistra which has stood in the hall for a long time, or maybe a peace lily no longer in flower but demanding attention, and she bestowed on Elisabeth a smile of distracted sweetness. Elisabeth hurried down the flagstone corridor, into the kitchen, aiming for the sink and the tap. *Does my head in*, the trolley man said when he had phoned the night before. Well, yes, she said, I suppose it does, and now she knew what it meant, but all she wanted was water.

A man sat at the table, slurping a mug of tea. He had begun to stand up at the sound of her footsteps and then when he saw who it was, sat down again, nodded. 'Afternoon.'

'Hello. Do you know where they keep glasses?'

He grinned. 'Do you mean the *good* glasses or the everyday glasses?'

'The chipped ones, I'm only the hired help.'

'Use a mug then, there's a couple in the sink.'

She rinsed one out, filled it with cold water and drank it down.

'Tea's the best thing for thirst, I find,' Jimmy remarked.

'Depends on the tea.'

'Can't stand that poncy Earl Grey stuff,' he said conversationally. 'Real mouse-piss. Are you one of those fucking lawyers poncing about on the lawn and wasting his money?'

''Fraid so. Who are you?'

'Jimmy, hired help, like yourself. Only with the dogs, though. Which makes me useful at least, which is probably more than you are.'

She refilled the mug and drank again, slower, and put the mug down with a bang. 'Why is *everyone* in this household so fucking rude?' she asked. 'Is it in the water or do you take lessons?'

'No, it just comes natural.'

Elisabeth laughed, refreshed by the water and the rudeness which was oddly liberating. He laughed too, his face creased like an old leather shoe.

'I've heard about you,' she said. 'You're the one who

got sacked before Mr Petty got into trouble with the newspapers, so you were a fat lot of good to him. And I've seen a photograph of your bum, the other week. I rather enjoyed that, I must say, but I don't think you're entitled to call me useless when you don't even know what I do.'

He inclined his head. 'Point taken,' he said.

She sat down beside him, carrying the empty mug. 'Any more of that tea?'

He poured from the pot into the mug and slopped milk on top, accepting her company. His hands were dirty and he smelled of dog and nicotine. The cat which was curled in his lap stretched and jumped off, resenting the intrusion.

'Will they be long out there?' Jimmy asked. 'Only I'd like a word with the master.'

'You're having me on. You don't really call him the master?'

He grinned again. 'Sometimes. It was a joke I had with Mrs Petty. We both used to call him the master when he was out of sorts.'

'Were they happy?' she asked recklessly.

He showed no signs of resenting the question. 'Sure, to begin with. Everyone is, aren't they, to begin with. Completely fucking mad about each other. Loved the same things. No, I mean they really were, before . . . Oh, fuck it. Only don't ask me to talk about her, it makes me cry.'

'Well, alleluia,' Elisabeth said. 'At least there's someone willing to cry for her. *The master* seems remarkably dry-eyed.'

'Well, he would be, wouldn't he? He doesn't believe she's dead.'

'What!'

'He doesn't believe . . . He *can't* believe. He'd go to pieces, else. Uh-oh, that's enough.'

A loud greeting echoed down the corridor and Jimmy got to his feet hurriedly. 'That's Caterina. I'm off. You want to watch out for that one, she's worse than she looks. Eats fried balls for breakfast.'

He was out of the back door before Caterina appeared, flowing into the kitchen like silk. 'Ah, there you are,' she said, as if it was not entirely obvious. 'Wondered where you'd got to. They've changed their minds. They all want water.' She moved deftly, found a tray, crystal tumblers from a cupboard and a tall jug which she filled with mineral water from the fridge. Elisabeth looked round the kitchen. It was far more streamlined than she remembered from the time she had come in here with Amy and admired the homeliness. Furniture had been moved; there was less clutter on surfaces and the doll's house which had got in the way was relegated to a corner. The kitchen had never been tidy, but now it was aggressively clean.

'Here, let me carry that.' She took the tray from Caterina.

'Thanks. Watch out for the flagstones. They're a bit uneven.'

Caterina said this as she swept out of the kitchen, leading the way. Elisabeth followed, cross with herself for volunteering to help and feeling rebuked, admiring the other woman's carriage and the way she walked as if she had been taught to dance. The passageway between the rooms was comparatively dark for the distance between the door and the hall where the stairway began and the light poured down, reminding her of the heat outside. The tray was heavy and she trod carefully, remembering the warning about the unevenness. She turned into the living room, feeling the thick carpet beneath her feet. The new arrangement of the curtains framed the room and darkened it; she was looking up as she stepped through the open French doors, tripped on the step and let go of the tray. Two of the glasses flew through the air and bounced on the lawn; the rest crashed on the steps as she rolled on to the grass, still holding one handle of the tray.

Caterina stood over her, hands on hips, looking down at her with exasperation rather than downright anger, amazed at her clumsiness. Then she thrust out a hand which Elisabeth took reluctantly to haul herself back to her feet. Caterina was strong, for all her slenderness; her arm was sinewy and her palm cool and dry; Elisabeth relinquished it, looked at the damage. Broken glass littered the steps.

'I'm so sorry . . .'

The other woman folded her arms and stared at her. 'Do you know, you're just like Amy. Sort of thing she'd do. Excuse me while I find a brush. We can't have the precious dogs getting this in their paws.'

Elisabeth rubbed at the grass stains on her knees, wondered if it was true and she was just like Amy. She was certainly no longer herself.

She stumbled back to the shelter of the willow tree, mortified.

'I thought I heard the sound of breaking glass,' John said.

'Yes, I'm sorry.' Elisabeth turned to face Douglas, who still sat on the bench. 'I just dropped a tray . . .'

He was not listening. He was looking at the object he held in his hands, an item which had just been presented to him by the solicitor. A clear polythene bag with a plastic seal, containing what seemed to be a handbag. Tan-coloured, like one she had at home.

A bag, anyway, but scarcely gift-wrapped. A bag belonging to a dead person and sent home, in lieu of herself, to be buried. It looked like a laboratory specimen sealed in an airtight plastic cover in case it might contaminate, not to be touched in case of germs. A last souvenir, a confirmation of finality. The greedy shit of a solicitor had got his revenge, delivering to Douglas what had been officially delivered to him. Douglas was the colour of chalk; his bare arms rigid by his sides and his hands hovering above the ugly package. Then, in the manner of someone horrified by a snake which had landed in his lap, he picked up the thing and hurled it at Elisabeth. The aim was accurate and the bundle bounced against her chest, soft and heavy, winding her. She fell back into the deck chair and held it to her chest. The feel of the polythene was peculiarly unattractive.

'You can begin with that,' he said, wiping his hands down his trousers. 'Just get it out of here.'

Elisabeth cradled the handbag as if it were alive. A sleeping puppy.

From the distance there came the sound of Caterina moving across the lawn, humming to herself, carrying the fresh supply of water.

CHAPTER NINE

This time they went back together on the train, although to different destinations. They were driven to the station by Jimmy in a beaten-up hatchback with suspicious stains of long standing on the upholstery and so old that everything about it creaked ominously. Another attempt to discommode them, Elisabeth thought as she sat in the front with Jimmy who stared ahead and flung the car around bends as if both he and it hated the road. John and the solicitor sat in the back and clutched at the handles, talking to one another. She pulled the seatbelt across herself, clipped it, then used the time to push the exhibit bag into her own empty briefcase. The case was the wrong shape, but the bag could not be carried around naked and the arranging of it made a chorus of polythene creaking sounds. Jimmy had the windows shut; he wanted them to be hotter and stickier than they were, eyed her sideways and went faster. The ten minutes seemed longer. She looked across and down, marvelled at the skinniness of his thighs, like a jockey's, nothing but muscle and bone held together with threads of thin fuse wire beneath the frayed cotton of his trousers as he changed gear with the same aggression as a man whipping a horse to win. There was something about that tan-coloured bag he wanted to devour: once it was out of sight and they reached the outskirts of the town, he went slower. In the back, they continued talking, tight-lipped.

At the station, Jimmy leapt out and opened the back doors officiously, saluting like a chauffeur without a hat, a parody of insolence. Out of sight of the others as they parted in the car park, Elisabeth slapped him on the shoulder, her hand meeting a sharp ridge of bone.

'Thanks,' she said pointedly. 'That was fun.'

'Fuck off,' he muttered under his breath. 'Fuck *off.*'

The heat persisted. John and herself waited on the platform for the train which would take them to Tonbridge where he would leave and she would change for the branch line.

'The train's not for fifteen minutes, time for a drink?'

'Where?'

'Nowhere.'

'It's not long. Home soon.'

'Yes.'

The late afternoon was airless and listless, infecting them both. Meeting with the Pettys had left them shaken. It was not as useful as it might have been for her to live fairly close to John as the crow flew. They were on a different part of the commuter belt, scarcely connected. She had seen photographs of his house, the sort of house that ate money; a mock-Tudor thing with acres of space for a privately educated family to leave, one of these years. She was not a convenient lover. The relationship might have flourished better if she had lived in the City in a flat accessible during working hours.

They waited together but separate on the functional station, built to withstand wind, prettied up with tubs of geraniums still in bud to add a touch of class.

'I wonder if that dreadful man knows more about the libelling of Douglas Petty than Douglas thinks he does,' John said, referring to Jimmy. 'And why on earth does Douglas employ someone like that?'

Elisabeth pretended to consider. Her mind was on other things, relieved all the same to find his mood so equable after an uncomfortable and largely wasted afternoon that had not featured deference from anyone, even herself.

'Considering what it must be like to work for him, I don't suppose he has a lot of choice. I rather like Jimmy.'

'Anyone with money has a choice,' John said with a trace of resigned envy, speaking as one who never had enough. 'Still,' he added, 'Caterina might manage to get rid of him.'

Elisabeth cleared her throat of dust and looked down-line, shielding her eyes from the sun and suddenly back in the here and now. 'Where did you meet her?' she asked casually. 'You never told me you knew her so well.'

'I don't, really. Met her years ago. She worked for a magazine I defended, successfully, as it happens.'

'What does she do now?'

'Corporate publishing. You know, in-house magazines for banks, that sort of thing. She's a very able woman, *when* she works.'

For someone who did not know her well, he seemed remarkably well-informed and Elisabeth felt the brief thud of jealousy, overcome by curiosity. 'So, she's a bossy bitch with contacts in newspapers,' she said. 'Well, well, well. What I don't understand is why Douglas is letting her rule his roost.'

He did not rush to Caterina's defence and there was a small comfort in that. He looked at her, interested in her opinion, choosing his words carefully in his endearing way. 'Guilt, I expect. He has it all, she has nothing. The terms of his father's will insisted upon unfairness. They're beholden to him and he is beholden to them. Papa didn't believe women could make their own decisions. I believe our Douglas was ordered to revere the womenfolk, at least *these* women. Not others, obviously. Rather like Mafia fathers and sons – Mama and sisters are sacred, but you can shoot the others if they get out of line.'

'It would have put the cat among the pigeons if Amy had produced babies, wouldn't it?'

'I don't know,' he said, bored with it. 'But she didn't in five years, poor soul. She had dogs instead. Perhaps she and Douglas didn't copulate, who knows?' He paused to squint at the sky, spoke sadly. 'The greatest secret of all time is the true state of anyone's marriage. No one on the outside can ever really know. Even those close to it don't know. For God's sake, even the parties to it often don't know.'

'He hit her,' Elisabeth said.

'You've suggested that before,' he said, a touch impatiently. 'And I think you're wrong. You don't know much about men, do you?'

The platform alongside them was suddenly filled with raucous children turned out of school to go one stop down the line, home to tea. Three boys tussled with one another and threatened to fall over the edge while two more shouted encouragement and a posse of girls watched, scornfully. John watched the girls and she watched his profile, admiring and resenting his ability to reduce her to silence.

'My children will be off our hands in a year or so,' John said. 'Not like those. Then I'll be free. To be with you, if you still want me.'

It startled her, this intimate pronouncement, coinciding with the slight vibration which signalled the imminence of the train. It made her uncomfortable; it was out of context when they should have been talking of anything else. Did he mind the fact that Douglas had instructed her in the matter of his wife's death, for instance? It was as if he knew that she was being pulled away from him and had to say something to reclaim her attention. She smiled at him and touched his hand, to let him know he had succeeded.

'You don't mind this division of tasks, do you?' she said as they sat in the corner of the carriage furthest away from the marauding children, who settled down to the serious chewing and swapping of sweeties produced from pockets, all pretension to adulthood forgotten.

'No, why should I? I know no more about the finalisation of death than you do, and I don't want to know. The solicitor should do it, but never mind. All our roles are up for grabs these days. How odd of Douglas to throw that handbag at you like that.' He did not, she noticed, criticise the client either then or now for outrageous rudeness to his junior. It was up to her to tolerate that kind of behaviour and meet it with equanimity, just as he did.

'I don't think he could bear to touch it,' she said. 'Was that on account of hate or love, do you think?'

John shrugged. 'Who knows? Fury, that her death was confirmed by the return of her property? Angry that it meant no one was looking for her any more? I don't pretend to understand him. There was never any real doubt about her death. She somehow got into the wrong carriage where thirteen people were incinerated into ashes. Even if he had precious little feeling for her, the bag was a pretty callous reminder. They could hardly send it back in pretty paper.'

The train gathered speed.

'They're a pretty callous pair, those siblings,' she said.

'Nobody's that callous. Not even Caterina Petty.'

'How do you know?'

He shrugged, irritated and cagey. 'As I said, I don't. She's put me in the way of work, that's all. But I do know enough to find her quite impossible to like, however handsome she is.' He sighed and stretched his long legs, crossing one over the other, elegantly. He was one of the old school who hitched up the knees of his trousers before he sat; she found it endearing. It showed prudence and consideration; she could see him being taught to do it as a child at the same time he was taught to hang his shirt over a chair.

'She is rather beautiful, isn't she?'

'If I were a woman,' John said, 'a *beautiful* woman, I think I would be perfectly content. Utterly satisfied that the very presence of me was enough to give such pleasure. I would feel it entitled me to everything. Why isn't it enough simply to be admired? Why do you all want so much?'

He was not demanding an answer. The train stopped and all the children piled off, screaming. Elisabeth was not listening to him any more; she could see a corner of polythene sticking out of her briefcase and she itched to tear it apart and there was another part of her which was furious with him for not sharing that avid curiosity. Why should he? The woman was dead; she was no longer beautiful and he had ceased to be interested and she herself had an unreasonable fear that Rob might be working on this line today; glanced around, hoping not. When they got down from the train, she felt guilty to feel so relieved to be saying goodbye.

It added to the other guilt, which ranged from anything to everything, apart from her clumsiness in breaking the Petty crystal, which was, in retrospect, faintly enjoyable. She could hear the sound of it now, a shocking little echo; a tale on which to dine out, if she had friends with whom to dine on a regular. basis, but John and their affair had isolated her without her noticing, and that fact intruded now into a conscience already riddled with regret. She never saw Helen West any more; she never saw anyone. Friends drifted and she had let them drift once she could no longer explain who it was she saw or why she invented excuses; she could not trust herself to trust gossip. *Careless talk costs lives*, an old adage which applied to her and marooned her even more than all those evenings of waiting for the phone, afraid to miss the chance of speaking to him.

She could not open the ugly exhibit bag with its heartless appearance and vicious seal while waiting in the public eye of a busier station than the one from which they had embarked. They were reaching rush-hour time; she could not tear at the seal with her teeth, so she had to think of something else. Such as what was John doing, mentioning a future so specifically, was he saying, wait for me, please, or what? She would not have continued with this, however besotted, if he had been one of those whingeing men who claimed their wives did not understand them, all that crap. Or a man who blamed his spouse, or criticised her to excuse his own infidelity. John never did that; he adored his two children and agonised, in his cool way, about the conduct of his life. He would not like ridicule and contempt. Please do not betray me, he had said; I offer you nothing but myself from time to time and that is all I offer, there is nothing else to be had. And now he was altering the dimensions of the goal posts and introducing a hope she had never entertained, although it had always been there. *I'll be with you if you want me to.* Elisabeth shivered. She had never tried to take him away; she did not want the responsibility of another woman hating her.

Her train came in, packed. She guarded the briefcase as if it contained a gold ingot and it felt heavy enough for that, weightier by the minute, and she handled it with the guilty care she might have given to smuggled goods as she stood in the aisle, keeping balance with one hand on the pommel of a seat and the right side of her body dragged down by the case which she could not bring herself to put down on the floor because of the absurd fear she would forget it. See her own stop with such relief that she would push her way out of the carriage with her own handbag, leaving the case behind, as if she would. There was no space for dipping into the newspaper which was also in the case; no real inclination, either.

Another twenty minutes of crowding without the relative silence of rustling newspapers. She marvelled at the way the phones came out and passengers chatted, issuing instructions towards home, planning meals, finishing business or pretending to be busy in a series of pointless conversations which made her sigh for being so lacking in a certain something, something that made her leave her mobile in the kitchen because it was just another thing to carry and forget and she hated, hated, hated the dreadful challenge of saying anything important in public. The case grew heavier. Nobody noticed.

The train made her angry, as it often did when she was

granted uncomfortable, claustrophobic thinking time. She pushed her way out as rudely as she dared; her own, small house beckoned like a beacon. It was still warm on the way back from the station to her door, where the security light came on regardless of the daylight. One month before the longest day in the year, and the light and heat seemed endless. The cat yowled. She fed it, opened the kitchen door on to the area at the back she referred to as the garden. A small back yard, ready to burst into bloom, made possible by a ridiculous mortage, kept on a promise. She loved it.

The answerphone blinked; so did the insulting mobile. Elisabeth got the polythene sack out of the briefcase and tried to tear it open, but it was strong and unyielding. She could not find the scissors. Nothing for it but the serrated carving knife, the sharpest in the block, but approaching the parcel with a lethal weapon in her hand seemed hideous; she felt as if she was about to murder it, standing there with the blade poised like Lady Macbeth. It was so stupidly dramatic, so she sat instead, pulled the bag towards her and made a small, tentative hole with the tip of the knife, tore it larger, and took out the tan-coloured handbag as gingerly as if it was alive.

It felt alive. Slightly warm to the touch, with a circular base and a drawstring top, pulled tightly closed, and the leather strap handle dark with dirt. It smelled of cinders and good soft leather, worn softer by constant use, comfortable slung over a shoulder. It had an expandable shape, into which anything could be stuffed, not the kind of bag Elisabeth favoured, because it was the sort in which a woman would spend half her life, scratting around inside its depth, looking for things, but a good bag for the purpose. A person could carry a life around in a bag like this.

The contents were disorganised, jumbled together in a mess which made Elisabeth decide to upend the thing on the table and look at it all in total rather than item by item, although it seemed a horribly impertinent thing to do and she was not sure if it was more intrusive because of her belief that Amy was alive. A bag like this was sacrosanct, an area of privacy rarely shared; if she were to put her hand inside another woman's handbag without permission, it would be a form of assault if not theft. She was always faintly ashamed of her own and would never want it examined, because the endless mess of it revealed all her deficiencies, so she made a mental apology to Amy Petty and told herself that this particular bag had already been neutralised by the touch of others. Someone must have gone through it.

Some nameless police official, who would replace all the contents and fix the exhibit seal. Exhibit A, a life, returned to next of kin. Why the fuss? The contents were only typical and smelled sweet. A waterproof makeup bag, full of cosmetics. Foundation, mascara, lipstick, eyeshadow, brushes, excellent quality. A small tub of exquisite moisturiser, Floris perfume which had leaked, hence the smell. Amy Petty liked her cosmetics and probably never travelled without them. There was another cloth bag, with a sachet of shampoo, toothbrush and paste, a miniature tub of cleansing lotion, all of which surprised Elisabeth. Did Amy know she was going away for longer than a day, or was this a precaution she always took? A diary, stained by perfume, a brush, comb, endless paper tissues, house keys and a bulging purse which was the same colour as the bag.

A hundred pounds in cash, a lot in these days of payment by card, but there was nothing odd in liking cash, useful stuff. A full array of credit cards and numerous bits of paper. Amy was the type of person who only cleared the many compartments of her purse once a year when it became so full it split the seams. Receipts by the dozen, for groceries, household stuffs; she favoured Tesco, Waitrose, Brown's Pet Supplies, and a local high-street chemist which kindly itemised what she purchased. Clarins creams. And then spread through these was a clutch of small receipts for a newsagent's with a blurred print address in SE23. Small expenditures of four or five pounds featured in these. Elisabeth tried to guess what. Cigarettes? Amy did not smoke, as far as she knew. A box of chocolates to take to a friend?

At the back of the purse there were appointment cards. Dentist in Wimpole Street; that would explain some of the London visits, but not every week and none recently. Facials at a local beauty shop, next one due last week. A massage therapist for aromatherapy. Amy took care of her face and teeth. She did not buy books and spent nothing on clothes, if this collection of receipts was a true indicator of habit, but she did like a bit of pampering and Elisabeth was faintly disappointed in her. She laid the appointment cards in a neat row and turned them over, absentmindedly, as if she was playing patience. On the back of the dentist's appointment card was a tiny, printed sticker. *Rollie Fisher, Miniaturist and model-maker, 12 Ratview Road SE23*. Not *Ratview*, on closer inspection; *Bayview*. Someone had playfully written over the B and the Y. It was a very small sticker, like the kind used on apples.

Slowly, Elisabeth flexed her fingers, counted to ten and left the table. SE23. Same as the newsagent's with the remaining numbers of the postcode blurred on the receipt. What the hell was she doing in SE23? SE23 had absolutely nothing to do with the rest of her life. Had anyone else looked at these? And if they had, what would they be looking for? They would simply be establishing that this purse belonged to this woman, nothing else. But there was far more. Elisabeth poured a large glass of wine and pulled the other papers out of her briefcase. All she had got so far on the search for Amy Petty. Her birth certificate, easy to get once you knew her date of birth, which she had known since first taking instructions from Douglas. John always insisted on taking full particulars from clients. *Amy Fisher, born 1965. Father Roland Fisher, schoolteacher. Mother Ursula, nee Jones*. Deceased in '93, that much she also knew.

In the initial stages of a libel case, John wanted to know the identity of anyone who might be affected by the libel. When a man comes to be held in contempt, the ripples spread wide; it affects his family, his cousins, his relatives by marriage and the extent of the effect could be reflected in the amount of compensation. Was there anyone else apart from yourselves who was distressed by this publication, he had asked. Caterina and my mother, of course, Douglas had barked. Amy's lot are conveniently dead and she was an only child, that's right, isn't it? Amy sitting quiet and nodding agreement.

The phone rang, horribly shrill in her quiet kitchen. For a moment she was confused; the silence of the place and her own concentration made any sound alien, and at first she did not know which phone, picked up the mobile and put it down, touched the other one. Let it go on to answering service; no, it was too insistent, but she had an awful dread of answering it, as if everything she was piecing together would disappear in the sheer effort of conversation. As if Amy would dissolve into mist as soon as she was talked about, something she had felt for days. Amy the illusion, dispelled by word of mouth.

She whispered into the phone, waiting to hear her, with the ridiculous impression that the voice would be Amy's, admitting her existence and wanting to speak. Amy had once possessed her card and her number. Both she and Douglas had. They were credentials presented on first meeting, like badges of identity, something given to prove you were real, like the identification badge shown at the door by the man who came to read the electricity meter. *Amy does not have your card any longer, you fool; she is not thinking of you just because you are thinking of her and rifling her handbag.*

'Hallo? Elisabeth Manser here.'

'Oh it is, is it? What took you so long?' There was a choking sound at the end, and she could imagine him reining himself back from saying *you silly bitch*, his deep voice instantly recognisable.

'Good evening, Mr Petty,' she said, louder and more formal.

'What's *good* about it? S'fucking raining, or didn't you notice? An' I'm a bloody fool. Fucking hell—' There was the sound of a stumbling crash. 'S'cuse me, lost the fucking glass. Again!' Then he laughed, a full-throated sound which reverberated around her kitchen and was oddly comforting. She had never heard him laugh, always imagined, if she had thought about it at all, that it would be abrasive. She sat up straighter, looked at the wine bottle on the table full of papers. Only half-gone; she was better than he, obviously.

'Bit pissed,' he was saying unnecessarily. 'Jus' a *bit*.'

'Good for you,' she said, reaching for the glass. 'I'm still working on it. What do you want?'

He terrified her; he beat his wife; this was what was meant by Dutch courage. No, that came from gin. Courage, in her case, came from impatience and irritation and the fact he was not in the same room.

'D'you know,' he slurred, 'Jummy says you're OK? Okey-cokey. Never noticed myself. Always wearing daft shoes, you. Daft shoes and big hips. We like that. *Biiig* women, *yesss*!'

'What do you want?'

'Wha' do I *want*? Oh for Chrissakes . . .' His voice tailed away into laborious breathing, interrupted by the slurp of a drink and the sound of swallowing, then a long silence. 'I wan', I wan' . . . You gotta send me back that bag . . . That fucking bag, why did I throw it at ya? I dunno. I was stooopid. I wannit. Bring it back. Now.'

'Now?' she said, politely incredulous, consulting her watch. There were sounds of laboured breathing and another swallow of drink.

'Now.' She could see that big head, nodding. 'Now would be fine.'

'You gave it to me. You gave me *a fucking* job to do and I'm doing it. You threw it at me.'

More laborious breathing. 'Yeah. I did.'

She waited, like she waited in asking questions, distancing herself and letting the silence do the work.

'Hated that bag,' he said. 'Never did like that colour with her. All those country *browns*. Only woman I ever knew suited blue. Lace and pretty things. Like you and the Queen Mother.' He sighed. 'Wen' to the flat, I thought . . . *she* went to the flat and took away her face creams, she *took* them, yes she did, she was *there* . . . I can't force her, just got to wait . . .' Then he seemed to rally into the silence which she did not fill and compose himself. 'Bring it back,' he muttered. 'Bring the fucker back. Shouldn've los' it. Is all I got. I need it. I *want* it.'

'Why? So you can eat it? Throw it to the dog?' She could almost smell the breath.

'You bring it back. Shouldn' have given it you.'

She remained silent, listening to his breathing.

'You come back here, Big Lizzie. Need you, too. Come and break a few more things, will you? Never could stand those fucking glasses. Too heavy for drinking. Come back . . . I'm the master of the house, or at least, I've got him with me.'

She let him take another drink. Whisky was the drink he would suit. Her hand held the receiver tightly.

'The dog died, darling,' he said wearily. 'The new one. Someone had tried to cut its fucking throat. Think tha' might have been Dell, don't know though. Come back.'

The phone went dead, leaving what was to her mind the saddest sound in history. That buzzing sound of abandonment, being cut off, ignored, finished.

She would have to give back the bag, but not yet. He had the tone in his voice of someone who had been crying. Not only a pig, but a drunk, sentimental pig. Elisabeth had the temptation to cry herself, but went to find the *A–Z*.

SE23. A life in a handbag; fragments thereof.

Jimmy turned on the new mattress in the stable, felt the scratches on his arms from where the destructive Alsatian crossbreed had kicked with his legs as he held it for the vet. He liked that dog, it was his favourite. He liked the ones that bit and tore up blankets and destroyed everything they could reach, because the poor bastards had been pushed from pillar to post, shifted from house to house and never fed – snarled and snapped and swore as if to hide the broken heart and ravenous hunger. When no one looked, he sat with them and told them stories and fed them stuff. Never for as long as Amy had done. She would croon and feed for weeks until they stopped tearing the bedding to shreds; she groomed them into trust as if her life depended upon it. Never talked as much as when she was talking to dogs.

He was drowsy when he heard the footsteps, and heard too, through his heart rather than his head, the shuffling of the three dogs occupying the room next to his own. Maybe Douglas coming back, but he was gone, two hours since. Jimmy swung his feet off the bed, glad of his boots and his status as fully clothed, and began to whistle. There was a variety of sounds which wakened the dogs. They were impervious to fucking and whistling – cocked an ear at that and went back to sleep. *Natural* sounds made no impact. Not the sound of the grey owl, or the squeak of prey, or the quiet footsteps of a familiar. They were wise fools, dogs were. He listened with their ears. Not Douglas, but another member of the pack.

Caterina was carrying a flashlight, because she was not attuned to the ruts in the track like her brother was to the extent that he could walk it three sheets to the wind and sideways. She was careful and delicate, and a familiar scent because she came here often enough and far too often for Jimmy's taste. All big eyes and no hips, noiseless until she sneezed, quietly, but somehow ostentatiously, as if to prove she was there and did not like it because of this allergy of hers which prevented her from close contact with dogs. Nor did he like that quiet sneeze and her soft footfall over the stable yard. He turned on the radio by the bed. That never disturbed the dogs, either; they knew what it was, a soothing sound of mumbled voices or music.

He was standing and ostensibly busy with the door

wide open for escape by the time she was over the yard. He was trying not to look shifty as he straightened the bed on which he had been lying, feeling in his pockets for a smoke and knowing she did not like that. Her perfume came before her, like a noxious cloud to which he was not immune, because he loved all the smells of women.

'Hi there, is there a problem, or what?' he said cheerily, as if she was welcome, biting his teeth on his own reaction. *Skinny bitch, boneache, spaghetti legs, too clever by half.*

She smiled and he noticed she had donned her lipstick as well as her flashlight for this simple trip down the drive so well on the right side of midnight you could hardly call it late for a townie like her. Good God, rumour had it they ate at ten at night, while he would have called himself hollow three hours before that. She was shaking her head. A well-groomed bob of black hair swung across her cheeks, obedient to her every move, and her brown eyes were like pools of shitty muck. She always turned her head when she smiled, as she did now, presenting the better profile, and in this thick, electric light, which sent deep shadows over her features, he could see not the slightest resemblance to her thickset, blue-eyed brother. Stepbrother, he corrected. Not the same kind of blood.

'I came to see if you were all right,' she said softly, as if she was some sodding spy on a foreign mission and taught to speak in code. 'I'm afraid Douglas is a touch *hors de combat*, if you see what I mean. Might have left you in a pickle. I wasn't sure if you were here.'

'Of course I am.' *Horse de whatsit* was not his vernacular; why didn't she just say *drunk*, he would have got the picture anyway. *She's a bit like a fish, all smooth and shiny with muscles all round her middle.* Muscles on her eyelids, too, fluttering in an attempt to express concern, or maybe a reaction to the light as she eyed the bed where they had slept, Amy, Douglas and he, on separate occasions.

She nodded. 'Are you sure?'

'Of course, *ma'am*. I do this all the time.'

'I know,' she said. 'How cosy you make it. I only wondered . . .' she hesitated prettily, 'if Douglas had been all right to you. Such a mood, you see. He does tend to *lash* out when he's like this.'

'Has he hit me, do you mean? Not recently.'

She had no conception of irony. 'There's really no need for you to stay here at night, you know, not when it's so much warmer; it really isn't fair of him to insist. I think you ought to stop.'

'He doesnae insist. And it's not every night, only when . . .'

'Don't do it, then.'

'Could I not see you home?' Jimmy said evenly. 'So kind of you to come out. All this way.'

The smile did not falter. She smelled sharp and clean. 'I was also wondering if you might help me with the garden tomorrow. If you've time, that is. It's all getting out of control.' She spread her hands in a gesture of helplessness. They did not look too dirty to him. Jimmy had watched her out there; all she had done so far was spread poison to kill the slugs which had eaten their way through a clump of hostas and left silvery trails over the French window steps.

'If I've time. I'm no gardener, mind.'

'That would be awfully kind of you. Oh excuse me!' She sneezed again, loudly, and found a handkerchief with her left hand, while the right still held the flashlight, pointing to the ground in a pool of light and illuminating her feet. Neat black shoes, suitable for a funeral.

'Bless you,' he said automatically, and was rewarded with the full smile.

'Good night.'

Her footsteps receded towards the house, with the flashlight dancing before them. Jimmy stood in the yard and lit a cigarette. So that was the way of it, then. She was not going to fight with him; she was going to befriend him. Save him from her big, powerful brother. Make civilised creatures of them both. In the way Amy never tried.

And she had not come here to enquire after his health. That was out of the question.

Aw, Douglas, man. Wake up, will you?

It was the night-time reminded Amy most, even when the traffic on the main road waned and there were moments of comparative but never complete silence and the area was a depressing reminder of all that it was not. Today she had remembered the date, felt the stealthy encroachment of summer and noticed how, even at this hour of the evening, the light was slow to fade. The long hours of daylight were nothing but a waste. It was the second evening that she had walked in the darkness with the dog loosely attached by a piece of rope looped round her hand and attached to a bandana of softer cloth round the animal's neck. It would look bizarre by daylight, but anything went by night. She followed the familiar route to the garage where she went every day and the man in the shop was a kind of friend. Faced with a barrage of cars, the dog quivered. No one had claimed her; no one would. She limped painlessly and was improving, without enjoying the exercise that was the ostensible purpose of the nocturnal stroll. Like Amy, the dog belonged somewhere else, but it was important to get them both out of the house and remind them they had working limbs. When she was out, she talked to the dog. There was a different man locked into his box in the garage at night, so she did not wave as she passed and walked further up the road, thinking she was rather like the dog, a creature in search of interesting smells. Jasmine, syringa, wet grass, finding instead the cloying scent of cars and the elusive smell of food. A bus rumbled by; it was only because she had left the money behind that she did not race to the bus stop further up the road and raise her hand to arrest it. Get on, pay, go to the station on the route she knew, get the train, go HOME. Amy turned back, and although the big road was empty, she did not trust herself to cross, and waited in the eerie emptiness for the little green man to give her permission.

She still felt naked without the bag and mourned it, but without the bag there was nothing to steal or stalk, and besides, she did not care. She was so consumed with longing to be walking down the path from the back door of the white house to the stables, where she could smell the herbs she had planted and hear the real sounds of the night, that someone walking behind at the same erratically slow speed was not a problem. There was nothing to be afraid of any more; there was no fear worse than the thought that she might never see that place again. When she turned into the car-strewn road where her father lived and felt for the keys on a string round her neck, she was afraid of nothing but that, kept her eyes ahead, her hand on the rope. As she stood by her father's door, the footsteps went on by.

She closed the door behind her, quietly. Equally quietly, she settled the dog and went to bed. The homesickness was always better in the morning, when there was so much more to do. She would not swallow the pills he left for her. By this time, she had learned to close off part of her conscious mind, but not to sleep without dreaming.

CHAPTER TEN

In the morning there were fewer silvery trails on the broken concrete of the yard in the early sunlight. They had seemed almost pretty yesterday until Amy saw how the snails had eaten away at the verbena plants from the garage, still in their plastic pots for lack of anything else, their promise diminished by the ravages of the night. Silvery trails on the foliage too, hopeful shoots snapped before their prime. Slugs or snails, she could never tell which; greedy monsters and the only creatures in the natural kingdom of snakes and rodents, insects and other pests that she despised with a thoroughness bordering on hatred. They had no moral code, these molluscs; they consumed the freshest of greenery regardless of its innocence; they thrived in the damp and the dark of walls, operated by stealth and would even eat one another. They had blind faces and bloated slimy bodies beneath those smooth shells and they thrived on destruction.

Any desire to be organic or vaguely environmentally friendly went in the face of this kind of enemy. She had decided she would kill them with the bright turquoise slug pellets also available in the increasingly useful emporium of the garage, but once she had got this lethal material home and looked at the warnings on the label, the plan changed. By now, the daft dog ate anything it could find, regardless of shape, size, colour and smell; nothing could be left in the vicinity of its appetite. Salt killed snails too; they could be induced to drown in a dish of beer and she could protect the base of the pots with impassable material, like tree bark, sawdust, broken eggshells, none of which things were easily to hand. Or there was the simpler expedient of waiting in ambush, picking them up, putting them in a bag and walking somewhere to throw them away, but she had balked at that and scattered salt, with partial success. Salt was also cheap; in the first two weeks here, she had spent nothing; in the last, one hundred and fifty pounds. Even dog litter and redundant slug pellets were expensive. There was another kind of problem in the offing. She tried not to worry about that and made herself count the compensations of her current existence on a bright morning after a restless sleep which refreshed her only enough to convert the homesickness into a sub-acute pain. It remained a chronic condition; she carried it round like an illness, but there were consolations and at least she and her father were on speaking terms. He had demanded an inventory of yesterday's shopping expedition, expressed interest in the yard, accepted the improvements and seemed to mellow with the sunshine although he retreated back to his curtained room as much as ever and hurried in from the daylight as if it might damage his skin. Rollie Fisher had recovered from the sulk, although not from the racking cough; he had regarded the clean kitchen without comment but at least without disdain, and approved the new neatness of the garden with particular reference to the pathetic showing of flowers. Nice, he said, very nice, in the manner of someone patting her on the head and giving her permission to proceed. Neither the dog nor the broken glass were mentioned. This morning, he had gone shopping. He was still in charge of food.

'Do you know,' Amy told the dog, 'that he and I might have had one of the easiest conversations we have ever had? I don't mean just recently, but ever. He might feel easier with me around when I'm doing something rather than nothing. Everybody likes me better when I'm busy, even you. I'm best tolerated when *they* think I'm not listening. Stupid and over-industrious, Caterina said that about me, but I like working, it's as simple as that, and there's only one person in the world who does not think me stupid. There is no such thing as *too much work*. Do you know, in my wild days, I almost became a tart? That wouldn't have been very good, I'd never have managed the money. Are you comfortable, dear? We'll go for a walk later, not in the dark.' She examined the inside of the kennel. 'You'd do me a great favour if you would stop ripping the bedding, although I know why you do. And I'm sorry I can't feed you as much as you want, but, my dear, I do know best.'

The dog was not sociable; it was wary, ravenously hungry and destructive, but its eyes were bright, its leg was mending and even after a few days of proprietary food, the coat was thicker. This one was a neurotic animal, requiring food and stability more than affection; the old blanket was torn to shreds and fouled. It would consent to be stroked over and around the left ear, but not the right because of something painful there. Amy wished she was a vet with a dispensary, rather than a self-taught, instinctive nurse. The dog liked conversation, provided she never turned her back as she talked. It did not care what she said.

'As far as my father is concerned,' Amy was saying, 'don't expect *love*. Tolerance does just as well, I promise you, we can live with that.' She was busy removing the torn bedding; the kennel needed insulation from the cold of the floor. 'Easier for you than for me,' she added. 'He isn't your father and I would really be a fool if I hadn't already noticed that he finds me entirely repellent, in the physical sense, I mean. I think he always did. Are you all right?'

The dog closed one eye. It was half in, half out of the kennel, torso stretched languidly to feel the sun, the one ear cocked to hear threat. Then it scuttled back into the bunker, curled into the furthest corner. Amy turned to the sight of a head poking over the bowed wall at the furthest end of the yard. A train rumbled by in the cutting, chilling her slightly with its sound. The head was the head of a girl, eight years old or thereabouts, with a perfectly spherical face of brown skin, lit by enormous dark eyes

and crowned by black curls, offset with a single gold stud
in one ear. Amy recognised the face; she had seen it from
the window among a posse of girls en route to school,
early in the morning. It was one of the faces her father
waited to see, coming back down the road in the afternoon.

'Hallo,' Amy said.

The head grew into a head with shoulders as the child
heaved herself further over the wall and leant on it with
her elbows. She was wearing a yellow sweater.

'You've got a dog,' the child announced.

'Yes, so we have. Why aren't you going to school?'

'I've got spots.'

'That's a shame.'

'*You* look funny,' the child said, releasing an arm and
adjusting her precarious balance to point.

Amy looked at her skirt, fashioned from the endless
supply of old curtains of garish colours her father kept,
and felt the collar of her shirt, which even after washing
still smelt of him. 'I suppose I do. Do I?'

'Yes.'

There was a conversational impasse. Amy scattered
more salt.

'Are you his girlfriend?' the child hissed, suddenly confidential.

'Whose girlfriend? Do you mean my father?'

'Oh.' There was palpable relief, and then a rush of
whispered words. 'Your *dad*. He's got lots of *dolls*, hasn't
he, with *houses* for them . . . has he?'

'Who told you that?' Amy asked, coming nearer as the

child became self-important, bursting with superior knowledge.

'Our lodger told us. He went to your house first. And your daddy said there was no spare room any more, but he showed our student the dollies' houses. Our student plays football. My mummy says your daddy makes the doll's houses to get little girls to come in.'

'No, he doesn't,' Amy interrupted. 'It's his hobby. He likes to make things.'

'Can I come and see? Can I, can I, can I? It'd be all right if you were there . . .' The child stopped, conscious of Amy's silence. It was not a feigned silence; she simply did not know what to say.

As if on cue, the dog emerged from the kennel, issued a single indignant bark and went back. Immediately there was a babble of instruction from the other side of the wall, and the head disappeared unceremoniously. Then there was the sound of scolding and the back door of the house next door banging shut. Amy was shaken. Daddy's secret life was not as secret as he assumed it was, but surely he *must* know that, even if no one came any more to view the room he never let. *I was keeping it for you*, he had told her; *I never meant to let it*. The presence of a woman in the house did not go unnoticed, even in a street as sublimely antisocial as this. Still shaken, she went inside to look for alternative bedding for the dog. Rollie Fisher never, ever threw anything away. There must have been an extremely acquisitive phase in the early stages of his occupation resulting in the stockpiles kept inside the ugly wardrobe in her room, the contents of which had the look of a charity shop. His subsequent collecting was as eclectic as his newspapers and it was futile to attempt to determine what he had in mind. He often explained to her, with evident pride, how it was that almost anything could be recycled into a doll's house. Small pieces of curtain material for wallpaper; tissue paper for frilly frocks; the material from an old shirt, of which there were many and one of which she wore, for miniature sheets on miniature beds or the apron on a parlourmaid. The copious old curtains looked as if they had been donated by someone who had realised they did not deserve a place in anyone's home. Amy had turned one of these into the skirt she was wearing which did not fit particularly well and added so much to the oddity of her appearance that even the child remarked on it. Orange flowers down to the knees; blue and white striped shirt on top; no wonder the man in the garage embraced her as a simple eccentric; no one could look as discordant as this and have any capacity for harm.

Your daddy makes doll's houses to get little girls to come in. It'd be all right to come in if you were there ...

Was that why he had welcomed her? As an alibi? With a frivolous irrelevance which embarrassed her, Amy longed for a large sample of Clarins *multi-régénérante* night cream, a long bath in herbal foam and the touch of lace. She sat on her small bed in the drab imprisonment of her room at the back which was scarcely improved by the removal of the muslin from the window, wishing that the sun would not shine, a selfish wish, she knew, since it shone on everyone else and was welcome. It made the dog better, her father more amenable and the house brighter, but against all expectation it also increased the intensity of the homesickness to such an extent that she moved in a daze and could not think beyond the next task. Take now, for instance; what was it she had come into this room to find? Her handbag; she was always looking for the nonexistent handbag; that was a constant preoccupation; there was always something she wanted from her bag; it was part of herself. She was looking for something dispensable to use as bedding for the dog, because it would be a while before the creature learned not to tear everything to pieces. She was looking for displacement activity, so that she did not have to think of the child. She *must* think of the child and how to protect them all.

Instead she sat on the bed and dreamed. Took herself back home to the shade of the willow tree, saw herself on the bench beneath, looking towards the dazzling white façade of the house, surveying the garden through the veil of leaves, and wondering again what to do about the snails which would have eaten the hostas by now if no one was guarding them. She had been a clumsy, wait-and-see gardener, even with the help of books on *How to Create a Wilderness*, but there would still be harebells and campanulas, bluebells in the shade, speedwell in the grass, all the blues. Hardy annuals in the flowerbeds around the steps which led to and from the room she loved best, the minimum of lawn and the maximum of meadow; dreams of a pond where the half acre of land sloped downhill and became marshy in the dip. Five glorious summers in which she had never noticed the weather and made her best attempts to be *busy*, to justify this miraculous existence she had been given and ignore the rest . . . until it was too late.

Sitting here in the airless room, she knew with the slow-burning certainty which had increased by the hour that she would have to go back before she could resolve anything here. Go back, once. Once, just the once, before the money ran out. Once, before she could reconcile herself to *this*. There were crucial things she had to do before the money ran out. She counted on her fingers, like the child in the next garden probably did, reminding herself of what she had come to find.

Newspaper; Rollie Fisher had newspaper stacked, piled and stuffed all over the place. There were newspapers twisted for use as draught excluders in the bathroom; newspapers bundled and kept for various purposes; there was newsprint wrapped with string in untidy piles. The base of the wardrobe, which leaned to one side, was welded to the floor by the solid weight of newspapers. Maybe he kept it against nuclear fallout – people did that once, in the days when they built underground bunkers against the end of the world. She tried to understand, even as she sat where she was and thought of the newest newspapers which had arrived that morning. They did not have the musty smell of these. The dog would like them better. Some days, Daddy scarcely read the things. She stared at the open wardrobe with the wobbly hinges. There was just enough space for a few folded clothes before the heap would touch the unused hanging rail at the top. He would never have meant to let the room. The room was a decoy. You would have to be desperate to take this room. He did not need rent, he lived on benefits and financed his hobby by making dolls for doll's houses. He made shuffling runs somewhere with dolls in bubble wrap, little corpses in polythene . . . might have got the postman to collect them from the newsagent's. *My mummy says he makes dollies' houses to get little girls in . . . I can come in if you live here too, can't I?*

Sometimes the homesick sensation was akin to a heart attack, because it felt as if it must be fatal, this time. Better to move, but in the darkness of the stairwell it was worse. She steadied herself, clutching at the rail, and then went back. *Go home, go home, go home. No, CAN'T.* Not yet, not now. It was worse than his coughing. *Ughome, ughome, ughhooome,* echoing at night.

Downstairs, the front door banged: she could hear him whistling on his way through to the kitchen while she remained as she was, sitting on the stairs, fighting for breath. Then she went down, loathing the texture of the synthetic carpet beneath her feet. How could he live in this near squalor and create, by contrast, the exquisite interiors of the doll's houses? Why this passion for ugliness?

The new newspapers were spread over the kitchen table. Amy had forgotten her plan to get to them first before he selected what she should read and spirited away the rest. There now, she was being ridiculous to read anything into this. Here was a white-haired old man, reading his daily intake of news and getting ready to rant about the state of the world he otherwise ignored. He looked like a sheep today, baa-ing at her by way of midmorning greeting as he looked up from the page. Amy put the kettle on, comforting herself with ritual.

'Look at this,' he said quietly, flattening out page two of *The Times*. There was a montage of photographs, each of them passport-sized, some clearer than others, and each with a brief description of the person portrayed. *The Final Roll Call of the Train-Crash Dead . . . None of these people should have died.* Amy sat next to her father; he moved further away and left her to examine the page. She scanned the photographs, looking for herself and finding her own face in a blurry image of a head dressed in a wedding veil, thought briefly of who might have supplied the photograph, and then scanned the rest. Thirty-three; so many it made her angry, the murderous wastage of it all. What had any of them done to deserve this? She found herself looking for a familiar face, looking at the men first and thinking of the trolley man, hoping against hope that she would not see him there. But why should she? They had all got out of the carriage, even the smug elephant man with his phone; it was not their carriage that had burned.

The dead were mostly men. Amy looked at the photos of the other women, and as she looked, stopped. There, at the beginning of the third row, was a particularly clear photo which struck a chord. The woman who had sat opposite, with the hands of the man round her neck in the split second before the crash. The woman who had been carried off and left by the track with her arm outflung and the ring on her finger which someone had removed.

A memory suppressed and now outrageously, brutally clear.

'Why did she die?' Amy said out loud, incredulous and furious. 'They were having a fight; he'd lost his temper, lost it completely, didn't care who saw . . . but we saw. She didn't *die*. He *killed* her. Either he strangled her or he threw her on the track and broke her neck. Then he walked away. Like . . . I did.' She could feel nothing but a sense of excoriating shame. 'Me and Rob, we *saw* him. He wanted her *dead*. He *used* that crash to do it! *She should not be DEAD*.' Amy realised she was shouting.

Rollie was listening closely and seemed to understand. 'Shouldn't be dead?' he asked. 'Neither should you. What do you propose to do about it?'

'*Tell* someone.'

He began to laugh. A giggle which turned into a guffaw, became longer and louder before interrupting itself to cough. He laughed and he laughed and he laughed.

It was then that she began to realise that whatever he had felt towards her, it was not love.

She had played herself into everyone's hands. If he had *loved* her, he would never have taken her in. He would have sent her home. He thought of her in the same way she thought of snails. With loathing, hatred, contempt. Amy went into the back yard and stood trembling next to the dog. Go *home. No, not yet.* Go OUT.

It was perfectly simple. Go to Bayview Road and ring the bell. Or knock on the door. Elisabeth squinted at the *A–Z*

mapbook of London and tried to visualise what the area
was like. Densely built, criss-crossed by trunk roads, foreign territory to her, like most of the hinterland which
spread from the centre. Rather a box in the suburban
loop touching the ever smaller green belt than a house in
the other kind of suburbia that had nothing. There was
a vast superstore labelled at the northern end of SE23, as
if it were an ancient landmark, and a sportsground. The
map would not tell her if there were trees. There was a
railway line marked in black, but the local station was two
squares away on the map. Buses and cars, then. Buses
had always been a mystery to Elisabeth; she recognised
no form of transport other than the train, the
Underground and her own two feet, all of which got her
around the small compass of the places where she needed
to be. South of the Thames was the foreign territory she
glimpsed from the train. What a snob she was to dismiss
what she simply did not know. There were probably a
million contented people in SE23, loving every minute
and fantastically fit from walking everywhere, bargain
properties and leafy cul-de-sacs she had never seen.
Elisabeth got out the bus map, admitting that she was
secretly afraid of the whole adventure and disliked the
idea of the bus most of all.

But there it was; it had to be done and here was a
bright sunny day to be doing it in before she had to consider the returning of the handbag. She would have to do
what the client said and he was quite right, he should
never have thrown it at her. It was all they had to bury or
cremate; she could see it, ceremoniously consigned to

flames in a bonfire in that glorious garden of theirs in front of that glorious room, with the Petty family watching the smoke. Perhaps she should take the handbag with her to Bayview Road, but she might lose it and it was not hers to lose and besides, a woman with two handbags would look lopsided. Elisabeth realised she was postponing an expedition she did not wish to undertake. Half the day was already gone and she had only got as far as Charing Cross.

A glance at her bank statement, the most unwelcome thing to arrive with the morning post, was not an incentive to spend time on non-fee-earning pursuits. Whatever the fate of Douglas Petty's libel case, it was not going to earn anything for anybody in the short term. Whereas prompt legal advice about how to deal with this death would pay something, for sure, a consideration which made her wince. Earning money by research into a death which she knew had not occurred was really biting the bullet of hypocrisy. So even if she had imagined there was a choice about finding this damn bus and going to godforsaken SE23, there really was no choice at all. Already she had delayed. The bank balance made the easier option of taxi travel a bad idea and there were other reasons for that, too.

Amy Petty had left the station with *nothing*, sweet fuck all, *nothing*. Elisabeth wanted to do the same. Her unused credit cards were in her wallet. Unless her knickers were stuffed with cash and she had planned the whole bloody crash, she would have left that place as a pauper. She must have had somewhere to go, or nowhere. Perhaps there was a man, a knight errant, with prospects. If she closed her eyes and made a wish for Amy, she would invent for her a lover of gentle habit and no complications who was content with an afternoon a week, while saying come live with me and be my love and I shall hide you. Someone who could transport her to a garden in the South of France and let her live without bruises. Fat chance. It would be nice if such a person existed but Elisabeth did not believe it. If Amy had gone anywhere, she had gone by bus with the coins left in her pockets, unless they let her ride free.

The one-man-operated double decker which she took from Trafalgar Square presented a granite-faced driver behind a Perspex screen and a phalanx of machinery. No one got inside this damn bus without money. Flat fares, so she paid the maximum, went upstairs and consulted her map. She felt surreptitious and found maps more difficult than words.

Wise of Amy to choose this time of year to disappear. The central city bloomed and the Thames, traversed briefly by the bus, glimmered like a gold-embossed invitation to extravagant pleasures. Then the bus turned east, away from the riches of it all, and Elisabeth was lost. She had the sad realisation that she would have felt braver and more confident in far more ramshackle transport in some hot, Third World destination, where her relatively pale skin would have made her a stranger to be helped, while here she was the only one who did not know where she was. Somewhere along the convoluted route she began to follow it, and all the same, forty minutes later, found herself reluctant to get off.

It was her constant bad conscience rather than the view that made her doze for some of the journey. She was a sleepy animal, easily lulled, constantly lured into closing her eyes when the sun beamed even through the prism of glass. She woke, knowing it was minutes rather than hours, consulted the map, recognised the name of a street. Thundered down the bus stairs and was out of the doors half a mile too soon. Walked. Practitioners of the law always protested that they knew how the other half lived. It was not true. She knew nothing about crime except for theft; she knew about bad blood and reputation, but she did not know what it was like to live here. The bald instructions of the *A–Z* were accurate. No trees, only roads, which meant when you followed the map, which suggested you could cross the big road *here* in order to find the small street *there*, the map told a downright lie about the relative size of everything. She faced a thunderous highway with a garage on her left; three crossings later, she found the turning to Bayview Road and turned away, because she did not quite know what to do now. The alterations on the street sign, *Ratview*, made a great deal of sense; she would have laughed at it if she had any sense of humour left. Once that went, she was in deep, murky shit, left with nothing but the realisation that she should have eaten something more than dead cereal before she set out. Food was the fuel for bravery. Anything was possible on a good stomach.

Amy, she remembered, walked easily in her hour-glass shape, propelled with a certain elegance via powerful hips, big bum, small waist tapered into narrow torso below a generous bosom which bounced. Not a million miles from herself, apart from that uncannily gorgeous face which haunted her now and was, as she realised in her seconds of hesitation, the reason for her being here at all. It was not only man who was seduced by female beauty: Amy had a face which mesmerised. A face lit with artless kindness and a complete absence of malice. Elisabeth passed the window of the newsagent, where her own reflection was marred by the advertisements in the window. You're not so bad yourself, girl, get on with it.

The newsagent's was an island which attracted single swimmers from the anonymous streets and squat tower blocks that surrounded it. They sneaked into this mini-centre for humanity in pursuit of fags, milk, newspapers, sweets and computer magazines together with a selection of videos. It gave the impression of the sort of place where the kind of magazines and videos not supplied by Disney might be available from the recesses of the counter, behind which an old man sat in a pall of boredom, looking as if a robbery might be just about sufficient light entertainment to keep him awake. Not that it was the kind of area where such violent criminal activity seemed imminent unless someone commandeered a truck for the purpose. It felt unthreatening to Elisabeth, merely sinister for the lack of people moving around on two legs instead of inside vehicles. In the middle of the morning, a display of Jellytots, mini Smarties and lollies on sticks was the only sign that children existed.

Senselessly, she looked at the display and selected two

packets of fruit pastilles for the bottom of her handbag, plus a packet of cigarettes for emergencies. She paid and he handed her change from the ten-pound note, with a receipt, remembering what the law said about receipts. They should always be given, or at least available on demand; the receipt must enable the purchaser to identify the seller, which meant in practice that a receipt in a shop like this was usually neither given nor required and would be as anonymous as a bus ticket unless the seller had developed the punctilious habits of *Oza's, Hurst Lane, SE23*. Lane? This was at the junction of a virtual motorway, guarded by railings to stop the deaf, dumb and blind from straying into the road. She nodded thanks and went outside.

The private detective of fiction would have purloined a photograph of Amy Fisher and said, *Have you seen this woman?* Yeah. And the man behind the counter with his heavy glasses would have said, *No.* Elisabeth was no detective and she had not rehearsed; she was a refugee from logic on alien territory and she walked down Bayview Road for the second time without any idea of what to say but knowing that she felt such a fool to herself that she would have to knock on the door even if she was hoping that no one would answer and she could go home.

In the event, there was a perfectly ordinary bell and insufficient delay before it was answered for her to phrase an innocuous question or fix a smile. The door opened quietly to reveal a sweet old man who stood there with his white hair standing up in a coxcomb and an apron over his clothes, looking as if he had been interrupted.

'Mr Fisher?' Her voice sounded to her own ears like a ghastly stage whisper which the whole street could have heard.

'Who says so?' he replied playfully.

'Oh . . . er . . .' It was on the tip of her tongue to say something daft, like *I've come about the room*, so that he would know immediately that she was an impostor and he would slam the door in her face and she could run away, but then inspiration struck in the form of her memory of that tatty little sticker, fixed to the back of a card, and she stumbled on. Such a small sticker, for a small object.

'I'm *so* sorry to bother you, but are you *the* Mr Fisher, the miniaturist?'

Something about the question appealed to him; he stood straighter, as if he had been saluted. 'I could be.'

'Oh good, wasn't at all sure, you see, but my name is Elisabeth Jonathan and the thing is my daughter's crazy for all that kind of thing . . .' (Oh Jesus, *what* kind of thing?) '. . . and she's ill and . . .'

'Do come in.' She followed him into the hallway and immediately saw what looked like an old curtain slung over the newel post of the facing stairs, catching her eye only because of the garish combination of black and orange and the fact that it was the only thing to notice apart from a pile of newspapers and colourless Artex paper on the walls, staying in her mind as the door closed and the hallway was plunged into darkness. Her eyes adjusted to the gloom soon enough for her to follow him left into the front room. It was stiflingly warm from the heat created by the spotlights which lit the series of miniature buildings ranged against the closed curtains and on the workbench at the rear. Somehow the view from the door was orchestrated to make the houses leap straight at the eye and after the brightness of the day outside it was like entering a theatre. She gasped.

'Your daughter, you said?'

'Yes, Maria, collects *little* things. Dying for a doll's house,' Elisabeth gabbled.

'I *have* been known to make doll's houses to order,' he was saying, 'but really I prefer to buy the shells and concentrate on the interiors. Furniture and figures are *really* me. More a miniaturist than an architect, how clever of you to know. How old is your daughter and how did you get my address?'

'Oh *gosh*,' Elisabeth gushed, all trepidation gone and invention flying high. 'She would *love* this. She's ten and she's had meningitis. I don't know *how* she got the address. I think it was stuck on the bottom of something, I don't *know*. Oh, this is *wonderful*.'

The last part was not feigned. Conscious though she was of the necessity to give this suddenly created child a name and, possibly, a personality, Elisabeth was genuine in her jaw-gaping surprise and her pleasure pleased him too, inspiring him to a level of almost boyish confidence. She had the feeling that both would burst into spontaneous laughter, any minute now. New best friends.

'This is what I'm working on at the moment,' he said, gesturing towards the workbench. 'Not a proper house, as such, more like a tableau. It's my haunted house, papier-mâché, moulded rather than built. Gives a nice texture, don't you think?' It was a wonky, off-centre model, more like a tall cottage lilting to the left. 'I shall paint it a nice sludgy colour with lots of ivy up the side walls. Rats in the basement and rather traditional ghosts.' He giggled. 'But when I have my exhibition, *this* will be the centrepiece.' Without actually touching her, he seemed to drag her across the room to the house with the Victorian façade which stood in the centre of the other seven ranged across the front of the curtains. Deftly he lifted a hinge to the right of the façade and opened the front to reveal the complicated interior on three floors. 'My brothel,' he said, giggling again. '*That'll* show them. All *they* ever make is silly shops and cottages. Mind you, I'm also making a shop.'

'They?'

'Miniature-makers. They get together at fairs, purely to squabble. They don't like the avant-garde. I'm above all that.'

'Oh.'

It was not the house he showed her now which had drawn her first, but the cabinet house to the left of it, with a stunning façade, reminiscent of something her father had once taken her to see. A closed house which would open to dreams and many rooms of splendour. That was what drew her eyes, but obediently she looked at the one he wanted her to admire. It was a beautiful, witty construction, reaching from the waist height of the table where it stood to her shoulder, so that she scarcely

had to stoop to see a lady in her bath upstairs, a gentleman lounging downstairs, two whores, wearing corsets
and little else, busy about their ironing in the kitchen, one
with a cigarette hanging out of the corner of her mouth.
She laughed with delight, looked closer, stopped laughing
and then began again with a falsity she hoped he would
not detect. All these little inch-high tarts were prepubes-
cent girls. Not a bosom in sight. Except for the fat lady in
the bath with her grotesquely painted face and she was
the ugliest of them all.

'Fantastic,' Elisabeth said. 'My husband would *love* it,
but my daughter prefers animals. You see, I wanted to
get her a *stable*, no I didn't, I wanted to get her anything
she could add to, something where she could go on collecting pieces to fill it. Do you *have* any daughters, Mr
Fisher? They're a pain in the neck. *Oooh*, look at this!' She
deliberately moved away to stand and gaze at the cabinet
house. 'That's what I'd like her to have. And I promise
she'd take care of it. Do you have any children, Mr
Fisher?'

He was standing alongside her, carefully shutting the
door of the brothel, only as much on his guard as he
might have been with a big woman who looked as if she
might be better at riding a horse than fingering delicate
objects.

'The best thing you could do is bring your daughter
along and let her see,' he suggested mildly. 'I expect she's
very pretty, looking at you.'

'Not *yet*,' Elisabeth said, beginning to enjoy her own
creation and imagining herself at ten. 'She's plump and

she's shy and she has to wear specs. Do you have children, Mr Fisher? I'm so sorry, I asked you that before.'

She noticed then, before he stepped back from her, how those blue eyes were almost translucent, at the same time that she realised he was propelling her out of the room and striding ahead to open the door.

'Children, Mrs Jonathan, at *my* age? Grandsons, *yes*, courtesy of my son, and I must say, I'm glad they don't visit very often. It is absolutely *vital*, I find, for an artist to live alone.'

'Granddaughters would appreciate this more than sons, I suppose.'

'I wouldn't know, Mrs Jonathan. I used to teach little girls and most of them preferred games. There's no telling what they like.'

He had suddenly had enough of her. There was not going to be the offer of a cup of tea and a prolonged chat, which was disappointing in one way and a relief in another. She was blundering; she would not be able to keep this up; sweat trickled down the back of her neck and she wanted out, badly.

'I see what you mean. If I asked you to make something for her, I'd get it wrong, wouldn't I? I usually do.' She laughed heartily and slapped her thigh. If she did not look as stupid as she felt then Roland Fisher was blind. 'Perhaps I could get her to write to you?'

'Yes, of course. Get her some of the magazines and books. Bring her to see.'

He was not actually pushing her, but the movement forwards was inexorable. She was being ushered out into the gloomy hall, past the curtains and the newspapers, looking forward to the opening of the door, standing back to let him go first. *Click*, and a chink of daylight. Then, as the door opened, she felt something warm pressing against her calves, a large, hairy presence inserting itself between them, pushing towards the light. Elisabeth screamed. The door slammed shut. '*SHIT, DAMN, you BASTARD!*' His voice thick with fury. She heard the sound of a kick, then a yelp, felt the dog twist against her legs and try first to fling itself against the door, then turn back, twisting to avoid the kicks. Not her kicks; she was frozen to the spot and all movement ceased. Then the panting of breath and the dog scuttling away.

Suddenly she was alone in the gloom. In the near distance, from the doll's house room, she could hear a crash and a scream of rage and the only thing she wanted to do was run. Instead she stumbled back in the same direction, following the sound. The warmth of the room hit her, brought tears to her eyes.

The dog was trying to get away. It had leapt up at the workbench and knocked down the papier-mâché house which lay on the floor with the animal crouching behind it, trying to seek refuge beneath the bench, unable to get in there because of the piles of newspaper. Roland Fisher was advancing, hammer in hand, the dog whimpering, the man growling.

'*No!*' Elisabeth yelled at full volume. '*No!*'

He stood in the middle of the spotlit room, with the claw hammer in his raised right hand. The hand remained as it was for a full second, then faltered. His shoulders

slumped and he turned to face her. The dog had frightened her first; now it was the venom of the man. The dog
became still, waiting to be beaten to pulp.

'Oh my word,' Elisabeth trilled. 'What a nuisance. Oh
do put that thing down. You might damage something
valuable.' She moved past him, picked up the haunted
house and set it back on the bench. 'No harm done. You
naughty dog.' The hairy thing slid by her and out of the
room. She smiled brightly and adjusted her handbag.
'*Awful* things, dogs, aren't they. Why on earth do you
keep it?'

'I don't, it's my—' He checked himself and was
abruptly fully in control. '—friend's.'

The hammer was replaced quietly on the workbench.
This time, he saw her out without incident. Elisabeth
gulped at the air like a fish coming to the surface, remembered to wave gaily at the door closing behind her in case
he waited to see if she would, and set off up the street at
a canter. Her steps were unsteady; as soon as she was
three doors down, she stopped, looking for somewhere to
sit. There was nowhere, so she moved on slowly. Nothing
in her mind was able to compute. She was trying to
remember the location of the bus stop. Turn right, one
hundred yards down on the other side of the road. For
once, the roar of the traffic was comforting. She began to
walk quickly towards the crossing. Not a soul walked
ahead or behind.

Then, in front of her, waiting to cross, she saw the
woman. Elisabeth was moving quickly towards her at first
simply because it was another human being and she

wanted to be near one, any one. She was watching a white woman with heavy carrier bags dangling each side, no handbag, dark hair. The lights changed; the woman walked over the road to the island in the middle across two lines of grunting, fuming traffic.

The most significant thing about her was the awful colours of her skirt.

Elisabeth began to run.

The dog ran faster.

CHAPTER ELEVEN

She was almost at the traffic lights when the dog overtook her; the sight of it skittering past and up to the traffic lights made Elisabeth stop suddenly. She could see the figure of the woman in the patterned skirt over the top of the railings which bordered the road, standing in the middle. Then the realisation that that *bastard* had let out the dog to follow her and run into the road; sent it to chase her, bite her, but the thing was suicidal; she made a grab for it, too late.

The figure in the skirt was waiting for the next green light, while the northbound traffic in the section of road Elisabeth faced grunted into ominous life and began to shudder. She made a futile wave at it, as if to say, *stop, stop*, the gesture only resulting in her stumbling forward towards the railing, and as the cars began to move, the dog darted into the road without hesitation, prancing ahead as though it was deaf and blind. She could not look. There was the howl of a horn as an articulated truck reapplied the air brakes and the cab juddered to a halt with a squeal and a delayed *thump* as the car behind collided with the rear. The cab was halfway across the lights, the towed container slewed sideways across two lanes. Elisabeth could see neither the traffic lights themselves nor the central reservation, heard the crunch of car metal, no deathly squeal of pain. A motorcycle manoeuvred around the locked vehicles with callous speed and roared away on the offside. The truck remained in place; she began to cross in front of it, nervously, putting up a hand to ward off danger, just as the lights changed to green again and the driver of the lorry opened the door of the cab to wave his fist. He seemed a long way off the ground, shouting at her *bloody*, *fucking* dog, but the man from the car behind was running the length of the lorry, yelling even louder. Elisabeth jogged for the small island which separated the carriageways, feeling marginally safer as soon as she reached it, shielded by the bulk of the traffic.

The woman in the skirt was bending over while two heavy tins rolled away from the bag she had dropped in order to clutch the dog by the scruff of the neck. The traffic travelling west stopped, the first two drivers staring left at the stationary lorry with curiosity. There but for the grace of God go I.

The silly bitch was embracing the dog and the sight of it made Elisabeth want to puke. One glimpse of her face as Amy turned briefly with a vacant smile and Elisabeth knew who she was. She poked the stooped figure in the

shoulder, waited the split second for her to turn again
and then made rapid, shooing motions to the far side of
the road. *Go, go*. Amy nodded; the three of them scuttled
across like guilty children. It was not mutual recognition:
Amy was responding only to the urgency of getting away
from trouble and the instinct to run. The one shopping
bag she still held bit into her wrist while her right hand
gripped the fur on the back of the dog's neck, making her
run at a crouch with her back bent, irritatingly determined all the same, never letting go of either. The
deafening traffic alongside them began to move again in
a succession of high-sided vehicles which blocked them
from view of the lights and argument. In this fashion they
moved about fifty yards, Amy leading, Elisabeth following, Amy scolding the dog and Elisabeth wanting to hit it.
They turned left, into a side road flanked by empty
ground on one side, a block of flats straight ahead with
parked cars in front. A patch of green appeared at the
side with a single, stubby tree entirely out of scale with the
surroundings, the first tree Elisabeth had seen. Once
closer, she could also see that the patch of grass was more
earth than green and the tree not large enough to offer
shade, but Amy seemed to regard it as a destination. She
let go of the dog, growling an order. Then she tipped out
the contents of the polythene bag, twisted it and tied it
round the dog's neck in a makeshift collar, unselfconsciously absorbed in the task as if nothing else was
important. Only when she was finished tying a knot did
she look at Elisabeth directly for the first time. Closely,
but not with any great interest.

What colour were those eyes of hers? Blue? Elisabeth could not remember. They seemed to have changed, or maybe it was the pallor of her skin, or the ghastly hair, brown with a hint of pale yellow roots, the opposite of the norm.

'Amy . . .' Elisabeth said weakly.

Amy shook her head, vigorously, nodded. Shrugged in resignation and wrapped her arms protectively over her chest. 'Shall we sit down, Elisabeth?' she said. 'My legs have gone wobbly. And I'm not even sure what we're running from. It gets to be a habit.'

They sat on the uninviting grass, Elisabeth out of breath with an unaccountable desire to scream. Amy adjusted her skirt, to save it from the dust in a superfluous gesture for such a hideous garment. She was not out of breath. Her pale calves, protruding from the skirt, had the firm muscles of regular exercise.

'Thank you for helping with the dog,' she said formally. 'Not everyone would have done that. It may be extremely ungrateful, but I'm not. I think it has a death wish.'

That makes two of you. Elisabeth was silent. She wanted to ask, *what the hell do you think you're doing*, but she could not find the words. 'Oh *fuck*,' was what she said. 'What a mess.'

Amy nodded agreement. She was recovered and her sang-froid was exasperating, especially since she did not seem to feel an immediate need to say anything more. The silence was filled by the panting of the dog in tune with Elisabeth's laboured breathing; she moved away from where it sat obediently, apparently pleased with itself. It was a disgusting dog and it was this sour observation which finally provoked her to speak.

'I think you're supposed to be wondering what the hell I'm doing finding you in the middle of the road in this godforsaken area when you're supposed to be fucking dead,' Elisabeth said furiously. 'And nearly getting myself killed in the process. How can you just *sit* there?'

Amy plucked at a blade of grass, held it up to the light and examined it. She seemed so relatively relaxed that Elisabeth's exasperation grew, but instead of slapping that delicately large hand, she was arrested by the sight of chewed and grubby fingernails which filled her with a sudden empathy and pity. They were peculiarly similar to her own.

'You said I was like a cocker spaniel,' Elisabeth said. 'Perhaps that's why you remember me.'

Amy nodded again and Elisabeth wondered which of them was the least insane. Amy seemed to read her mind. She smiled an incongruous smile which was nevertheless as Elisabeth remembered it, enchanting.

'Yes, you are. The unusual-coloured variety. You may think I'm entirely mad.' She chewed at the grass root. 'And you may be right. Forgive me, but I've quite lost sight of how other people might see me. It doesn't seem relevant and I haven't really had time to think of it. And, for some reason I really can't explain, I was sort of expecting you. You, or someone.' She hesitated. 'Not at the edge of the road, you understand, but somewhere. Perhaps I was just expecting a face to appear in a window.

So I'm very glad to see you, really. I scarcely knew you, but I rather liked you when I was alive. A trustworthy person, I thought, like a spaniel. I suppose you've been to see my father. I should have thought about him pushing the dog out. Quickest way to kill it, after all. Anyway, I'm glad to see you because I've got to tell someone about the man on the train.'

The tree offered a fraction of shade after all, but the heat Elisabeth felt was not on account of the sun. Perspiration oozed from her hair down the back of her neck. She pushed damp curls back off her forehead. The ground was hard. She thought of the willow tree in the garden of the Petty house and what a pitiful imitation this one was. The calm authority of Amy's tone made her stammer.

'I've got your handbag,' she began. 'There was a sticker . . .'

Amy clapped her hands; the dog leapt to its feet. 'You've got my handbag! How wonderful. You've no idea how much I've missed it.'

Again, Elisabeth wanted to scream. She began to scramble to her feet and found it surprisingly difficult. From a position on her knees with her knuckles supporting her weight, she spoke firmly. The face of the dog was level with hers and its breath was sour.

'Listen, Amy, I'm going to go and find a taxi out of here, go home and tell the police and your bloody husband where you are. You've caused mayhem. How selfish can you get? How *dare* you just disappear and leave everyone mourning you . . .' She was choking with anger, furious to find herself shouting in clichés.

Amy frowned, waved her hand dismissively. 'Don't be silly. Nobody will have shown the slightest sign of mourning me. At least I don't think so. *Please* sit down,' she said humbly.

Elisabeth sat. There was such palpable truth in the statement about not being mourned that it quite took her breath away. It was not the pathos of the sentiment and her own inability to contradict it, but the cool sadness with which it was made.

'I'll try to be helpful, shall I?' Amy said. 'Oh God, I'm hungry.' She hunted amongst the shopping strewn on the ground, found nothing. Elisabeth dug into her own handbag and found the pastilles she had bought in the shop, broke the tube and handed Amy half.

'Thank you.' The dog, which had been sitting indifferently between them, sniffed. 'Not for you,' Amy said. 'Your teeth are bad enough as it is. Where was I?'

'The beginning.'

'The beginning? Oh no, I can't do that. The beginning's all too long ago. Excuse me, it's difficult to talk to a human being. I'm better talking to dogs. I should have said how nice to see you. My manners have gone completely, you see. It's amazing how quickly it happens.'

Elisabeth tried to breathe regularly. *Remember this woman was legendary in her own household for being* thick. *And she was beaten. There may be precious little difference between being terminally stupid, abused and downright bonkers.* Whatever it was, it was infectious.

'Yes I do see, Amy. Are you all right? I mean, not ill?'

'Of course I'm not all right. I'm dead. And you're quite

entitled to consider me mad, but please don't join all the others in thinking me stupid. My logic might be warped from time to time, but it does exist, even if I'm more inclined to act in response to instinct. Don't you? I can't imagine it was purely logical deduction from the contents of my handbag that brought you to this wasteland. Wouldn't be my first choice. Instinct must have played a part.'

Elisabeth was dumbfounded. She kept her eyes down and sucked on a fruit pastille, felt Amy's hand touch her arm.

'It was kind of you, Elisabeth, as well as silly, to make this expedition, for whatever reason you've done it. I'm grateful. And I'm sorry to burden you with this, but unless I know that you *aren't* going to go straight back to Douglas, I shall go and lie down in the middle of that road, is that clear? I don't see why you should care if I do, but please understand I'm perfectly capable of doing it.'

Elisabeth nodded.

'Besides, you owe me something. No, that's wrong, you owe me nothing. Perhaps Mr Box does. Douglas should never have been encouraged to start off that libel action. That was the catalyst. I might have been able to stick it out if it wasn't for that. But I had a secret, you see, and I really thought the libel action would smoke it out. My father.' She plucked at the grass. 'He taught art and crafts to schoolgirls. He was convicted of trying to have sex with them. He served twelve years in prison, disappeared and remained disappeared long after I found out. Then he got in touch with me after I married Douglas.

He was ill, he said. Wanted to meet me in secret. So I did. So secretive, you wouldn't believe. Worse than meeting a married lover.'

Elisabeth found herself blushing.

'I couldn't risk anyone finding out about him. You know what people do to paedophiles. Stoning, for starters, newspaper exposure, house burnt down. I believed my father when he said he was innocent. I believed him because he built me a doll's house and gave me a dog and because my mother was such a liar. I believed him because I never stopped loving him. You don't, you know. I believed him when he said the libel action would smoke him out and set the hounds of hell on him. I believed that it would be all my fault. The only thing I didn't believe was when he said he was only in prison because of Douglas. He only says that in his sleep. Then he wakes up coughing.'

The fruit pastille was in the soggy state where it stuck against teeth. Elisabeth was all aches, pains and information-overload. 'You've lost me.'

'Douglas has something to do with this,' Amy said, looking at her as if she expected her to know and this was a piece of obvious, universal knowledge. 'But I don't know what. I don't know what to believe any longer. We'd grown fond of one another, Dad and I. He's very persuasive and I'm very weak. He said he would be my secret refuge for ever. He said the only unconditional love you ever get is from your father. He said I would need a refuge one day, and I did.'

There was a long, bewildered silence. Elisabeth peeled

back the foil on the half-packet of pastilles and ate the last two. Her stomach rumbled and bile rose in her throat. She could only recall the man with his doll's houses and the venom in his eyes and believe him capable of anything; she was reeling from indigestible facts and now the sweat had dried, chills crept between her shoulderblades and made her want to scratch. Staring ahead, she could see the route they had come and hear the murmur of traffic. Somewhere over there was a sportsground and a school, according to that lying, monosyllabic map which never mentioned the lack of trees and the real dimensions of the lethal roads.

'I want you to find something out for me, and I want you to do something for me,' Amy was saying. Her authority and the rapidity of her speech were nothing short of miraculous. 'Get today's *Times* for a start. Third left in the second row of photos of people killed in my train crash is a woman. Can't remember her name because I never knew it. She was in my carriage. She didn't die by accident. She had a man with her who was so furious with her he was ready to throttle her in public. Tell somebody. That man killed her. There was no reason for her to die. And he took her ring. Nobody should get away with that. I can live with a lot of things, but I can't live with that.'

Elisabeth got to her feet, head dizzy. She clutched at the branches of the tree which was more of a shrub, felt the brittleness of twigs.

'That's the most important thing,' Amy continued, dry and businesslike. 'And then, if you don't mind, I would

like you to find out what it was my father was supposed to
have done. I've always believed most of what he says and
I can't any more. I can pay you, but not much. And you
don't have to keep quiet about me for ever and ever. Just
until I know. Give me a phone number. He hasn't got a
phone.'

'Here's a card. Got my number and address. Phone the
mobile. Where are you going to put it? Oh for God's sake,
this is crazy.' The image of the fortunate, docile Stepford
wife with so little to say and no will of her own had
receded into a red mist and left nothing but dithering
confusion. She watched her take the card and stuff it into
her bra without thanks. 'And *why*,' Elisabeth spluttered
with a return of the fury which rose to hide her own feeling of being the stupid one and the one entirely out of
control, 'do you imagine I'll do any of this? Why the hell
should I?'

'I don't know why. Because you've got this far. Because
I might well die if you don't.'

'Of what this time?' Elisabeth snapped. 'Insomnia? A
dog with bad breath? A broken heart?'

Amy smiled her enchanting smile. 'Oh, that happened
some time ago. It's lasted well, all things considered. You
can have bad teeth and still manage to eat. There's not
much of my heart left and I'm so sorry. I've no right to
expect anything at all. You'd better go home and do
exactly what you think best. I'd like it if you'd give me a
couple of days' grace, though.'

They were both on their feet. Amy looked at the
strewn shopping, perplexed by it until she found among

it a roll of pedal bin liners, put everything in one, including the rest of the roll. They began to walk, slowly, Amy holding the dog by the polythene loop she had made.

'What I don't understand,' Elisabeth said, adopting Amy's dry tone, 'is why all this stuff with your father made you take this overdramatic turn. Awkward, yes, but surely not the end of the world. You could have told Douglas.' She had a momentary, vivid memory, not only of that willow tree, but of the bruises on Amy's arms in the coldness of spring. Perhaps telling Douglas was not an option.

'I should have told Douglas,' Amy said. 'Right at the beginning when my father first wrote, I should have told him and trusted him. But I didn't. I listened to my father instead; I was overjoyed to see him. I was biding my time, but secrets get to be habits, don't they? They become elaborate and impossible to explain.'

Again, Elisabeth blushed.

'But it wasn't because of my father that I walked away from the crash. That wouldn't have been nearly enough. There was far more to it than that. I'm sorry,' Amy repeated. 'Because I explain things to dogs, I forget I haven't explained them to human beings.'

'I thought you ran away,' Elisabeth said, speaking louder as the infernal traffic noise increased, 'because he beat you up.'

Amy stopped so suddenly they collided with the dog sandwiched between them. How Elisabeth loathed that dog, even though she was glad it was alive. Amy's face was pink; tears welled in her eyes and spilled down her cheeks. 'But that's *ridiculous*,' she said. 'Beat *me*? I didn't go *because* of Douglas. I went *for* Douglas. I went because they were too strong for me. I went because I thought he really would be better off without me. Can't you see that?'

They were proceeding down the main road now, with the traffic roaring, *yeeow, yeeow*, alongside. No wonder nobody ever came out. Elisabeth had an unshakeable conviction that if she did not do exactly as she was told, then Amy would do exactly as she said, go and lie down in the middle of it, until she was like a squashed hedgehog on a country road.

They reached a bus shelter where the flimsy walls, made only for protection from rain, failed to baffle the vibrating noise.

'What else?' Elisabeth yelled.

'Give me two days,' Amy yelled back. 'I'll phone you.'

'What?'

'Two days . . . PROMISE?'

'OK, I PROMISE.'

'This is your BUS. You will be all right, won't you?'

That was the last Elisabeth remembered. A look of genuine concern from a woman with nothing to lose. Concern for *her*. The bus emerged out of a distant line and drew into the layby created for it and nothing else, with a desultory efficiency. The doors slammed open, *whump*, and then as soon as she was on the first step, propelled there by a shove, the doors *whumped* shut behind her and the whole edifice was moving before she fumbled for the fare. Handbag, purse inside handbag,

coins inside purse, dammit, coins were useless, fingers
were useless. A tin of dog food had found its way in there;
she hated dogs. Swaying on her feet, she found the purse
and some pound coins. The machine spat a receipt;
Elisabeth was propelled to the back as the bus gathered
speed, sat with her handbag on her knees. It weighed a
ton and seemed to grow before her eyes.

Get home. Phone . . . *who*? Who would believe this?
Who could be trusted with this? No one.

Amy slammed into the house and went straight through
to put on the kettle, looking for him, hoping she would
not find him, trying to stop the furious tears. *How DARE
she?* She took the polythene-bag collar off the dog and
pointed it at the garden. Mid-afternoon; he would be
keeping station upstairs, waiting for the children to come
home, so he could watch. The door to his workroom was
shut; the house was quiet, the door out the back open. By
the dog's kennel she could see the dog's bowl, half full of
food she had not left. The dog strained towards it. She
went out into the yard, looked at it, brought it back inside
and threw it in the bin. She fed the animal from one of
the remaining tins. Went upstairs past his silent door, into
her room.

The money she had left in the wardrobe was gone. The
other half under the mattress was still there. It was only a
matter of time before he found it. She took a hundred
pounds, picked up the rope for the dog, went downstairs
and made herself eat. Bread, butter and mousetrap cheese
in large quantities, unpalatable, workmanlike food to line

the stomach and give her ballast. At the table she wrote a note for her father.

I am taking the dog to a safe home and may be back late . . .

There was more to say than that, surely. It might be better if they communicated in writing. Questions, such as why do you hate me? Is it me you hate, or is it Douglas? Was it me you wanted to destroy, or is it him? She waited at the table for the afternoon to wane, drumming her fingers and crying fat, useless tears. Heard him cough his way down the stairs, as if deliberately alerting her to his presence before he went into the doll's house room and shut the door. She *could* be calm; she had proved it. She had to plan the journey.

The bus took forty-five minutes, depending on its timetable and the traffic. The trains went from Charing Cross on the hour. The journey was an hour. The walk home across the fields would be half an hour. She wanted to arrive so long after darkness that everyone would be asleep.

Going home now, she told the dog. Running short of time. She won't tell anyone tonight, I'm sure of that. Amy fetched the coat from where it hung neatly on the back of her bedroom door, slipped it on and there was another person. The olive green coat lent her a respectability which would not bear the close inspection it was not going to get. Accompanied by a dog on a rope lead, she could pass as a country eccentric of the kind who had no time for makeup or vanity, even to do credit to her dog. She had seen far worse.

Quick, quick, the bus . . .

The mirror image of herself reflected in the doors of the bus told a different story, but not so different that it worried her. An accurate depiction of a poor, drab woman, prematurely aged from thirty-five to fifty, with badly scuffed shoes and an inconsistently good coat only slightly too warm for the time of year, sitting in a half-empty bus at the time of day when all the mysterious occupants of the hinterland were travelling back from the centre rather than towards it. She stroked the fabric of the coat, which was soft, with satisfyingly deep pockets for the house keys, the wodge of toilet roll, and the small proportion of the money which was not tucked into her bra with Elisabeth's card. A person travelled lighter without a handbag, armed with nothing but a bottle of water and a plastic dish in the standard-issue polythene carrier, without which life was untenable. Who needed a handbag?

The excitement grew; she let herself dream. The house would be empty; she would be able to range freely, touch everything. No one would see her or guess her presence; it would be easy to explore, take pictures of it with an imaginary camera in order to make a volume of memory she could keep. Each night away from it, she climbed the stairs and tried to remember what lay behind each door; she lived in the garden, looked into the round room and lingered beneath the tree. She knew every inch of that house better than anyone else. Whoever was there, she would be able to hide from them; there were so many nooks and crannies for a ghost, and that was what she was. A light, lithe spectre, able to slip in and out of windows, the invisible woman. She might even be able to purloin her favourite pair of shoes from their room; she might raid the bathroom for the night cream, collect fresh underwear . . . Dream on. The dead were allowed to dream. *Home*. See home, just *once*, please, please, be as you are and let me in just this final once.

Let me see Douglas, once. Hear his voice.

The dream diminished at Trafalgar Square. Crossing through the sheer density of the crowds seemed impossible, although the details of their appearance were reassuring and made her realise she was the soul of nondescript in comparison. In the window of McDonald's she could see dreadlocks and pierced noses, black battledress and torn leather, ancient denim and shimmering pink, crowded together as if marshalling for a riot. They had nothing to do with her; she had never been one of them; she had never drunk her coffee alongside creatures such as these, even before she died. It was only the dog that made her feel substantial, straining at the rope leash in pursuit of another dog crouched in a shop doorway with an owner already clad in a sleeping bag, ready for the night. Amy dropped a five-pound note in the begging bowl, more for the dog than the man, and dragged her own beast across the road into the station. Sanity returned. It was past rush hour, shops closed, concourse still busy. A crowd gathered beneath the board which showed the destinations of the trains, waiting for information and ready to canter in the direction ordered, a small queue for tickets. She stood in line with the dog, listening to the snippets of conversation, watching the others, finding herself looking out for a familiar face and not sure if she was relieved to find none, realising with a sickening dread how difficult this was.

It was the sound of the trains, not the disembodied, anonymous engines she had been hearing every day, but real trains, close. The sound of her own voice, which requested the return ticket in a perfectly normal tone and said thank you when it appeared on her side of the glass, was as alien as her own ability to pick it up and move away from the queue towards the right platform, walking steadily with the sulking dog. The homesickness still burned like acid indigestion; there was no choice about this journey, none at all; it was absolutely inevitable, only there was something she had failed to anticipate. The train.

The train was enormous. It sat there at the platform, making its rumbling, whirring, ready-to-depart noises. She stopped at an open door, one hand in her pocket, crushing the ticket, fingers mobile, the rest of her paralysed. It was a monster and she was supposed to get inside its belly; once she was inside it, it was going to *crash*. She could feel the vibration of jarring impact, feel the weight of her handbag pressing into her chest, smell the burning and the stink of diesel. See the elephant man with his phone, covered with stuff from the rack, hear the screams and taste the blood in her mouth from where she had bitten her lip so hard it had bled down the back of her throat. *Oh Christ*, she could not get on this train.

But the dog knew. Shivering on the bus, hating every mile, trying to make itself smaller and smaller beneath the seat, and here, it strained at the rope leash, panting to board and whining with joy. Eyes wide open, refusing to focus, Amy let it lead her, almost pull her up the steep step into the second-last carriage and into the seat nearest the door where she sat, trembling uncontrollably. The dog settled under the table at her feet, as if it travelled by train every day and knew all the rules about how dogs should make themselves inconspicuous. She could feel the warm body of it against her legs and kid herself that it was offering protection. Jolt; movement. They were close to the lavatory, convenient for vomiting. She was in there, heaving up the bread and cheese as soon as the train began to move. The face in this mirror was full of terror; she was frightened at the sight of it.

The dusk outside was a blessing; she made herself look out of the window and fix her eyes on the lights as the train rumbled over the bridge. When the beast gathered speed, and the lights became a blur, she closed her eyes. With eyes shut, she could feel safer, even with her hands clutched into white fists on the arms of the seat, waiting for the crash. Then she opened them again, because if she could not see, she could hear more and the sound of the train was painfully loud. Deliberately, she made herself stare at the other passengers she could see if she leaned sideways and looked down the aisle. *Got to get you home, dog, too, quick, before you get murdered.*

The man in the next seat opposite looked like a monkey, with a small wizened face. The woman next to him looked a marmoset. The ticket collector coming down the aisle was a ferret. Once this was established, she would breathe. She pressed her eyes open. The home station was small enough to miss in the dark; she must not miss it. The watch told her there was time to worry about that and she did not believe it. She looked again at the passengers as they emptied out. A twitching grasshopper, a girl with legs like a newborn colt, a fat woman with widely spaced brown eyes over an enormous bridge of nose, a good-natured cow. It was not insulting to be called a cow. Cows were nice. Breathe in, breathe out, slowly. The weakness would have made her slow to get off, but the dog was having no argument. Out from under the seat, discreetly at first then dragging her by the rope lead. Then over the bridge to the exit with a few others, not that late. The darkness had the fresh look of novelty. She could remember the other kind of relief she used to recognise when she had got as far as this on the route back from London. Relief, first, and the dread coming second as an aftertaste as she looked for her car. She could never remember where she had put her car, because the configuration and number of cars always changed between the time she parked and the hours later when she collected. She looked for it now, surprised not to find it. Puzzled to see the dead remnants of flowers in a pile by the exit in a normally tidy place. A couple of doors slammed as the late-working commuters hurried away.

Her car would be long gone. Someone efficient like Caterina would have collected it. Caterina would be at the house and Amy did not like that. Somehow, it took some of the urgency out of the mission. So far, all means of transport to get her this far had seemed excruciatingly slow; now she had lost the impatience.

She wandered down the High Street unselfconsciously. She knew how people failed to recognise someone they did not expect to see and she was aware of looking markedly different from her normal appearance. The dog itself was a disguise; there had never been the need to bring a dog into town. Nor had her hair ever been this colour, or her face this thin or her body clad in non-descript green. Amy preferred whites, blues, creams; it was Caterina who suggested the beige linens and brown silks which suited her own sallowness.

All the same, if she skulked in shadows someone might notice her in this place which reeked of neighbourhood watch and good citizenship; if she moved like a person living in one of the neat town houses that ran off the High Road, out with a dog for an evening stroll before the rain, no one would turn a hair. The dog was as well-behaved as if it had come from one of those houses and never been anywhere off the leash. Neither of them behaved like runaways. She did not linger by the windows of the smart pub, even though no one ever looked out of these mullioned windows; people only looked in. That was where she had seen Caterina having a drink with Dell from the Animal Sanctuary and the other man. She got to the end of the street and set off down the road out of town, keeping to the pavement until that ran out and the streetlights stopped. Then she walked along the verge. Two miles was not far to a person used to long walks. A couple of cars passed. She walked on without turning, facing the oncoming traffic. The air smelt of rain.

'Rain would not be suitable,' she told the dog. 'Rain would make us wet and miserable and heavy. I hope it doesn't rain.' That would be the only thing she would care about; the prospect of rain and its effect on her shoes. Her mood fluctuated between weariness and exhilaration; nothing mattered apart from seeing home. Not going home; seeing it, just *seeing* it. The willow tree would shelter her from the rain; the rain would muffle sound. Rain was not such a bad idea. Amy hummed as she walked along, looking ahead, swinging the lead and enjoying the sound of the dog's paws on the tarmac as it trotted beside her. They were both proud of the mended leg.

At the next bend, where the may blossom was covering the road when last she had seen it, she turned into the fields. The fields were riddled with footpaths and dark or light she knew them all, had walked too many dogs to ignore any of the routes. Including dogs that were best walked at night, because they were so ugly and scarred they would frighten the other walkers. And Dilly; poor Dilly, who preferred to walk at night. The smell was intoxicating, peaty, acrid, sweet, dispelling the memory of other smells. There was nothing to fear in this kind of night and she had never been afraid of it. It was hers to command. She entered a copse of trees and shivered with sheer pleasure at the sound of the branches, like the sound of waves on a seashore. Perhaps that would be the only way to dispel all memory of this place; live somewhere else with equally soothing sounds, like the sea. The screech of a bird of prey cut across the whispering of the trees. It did not alarm her. Something always had to die in order for something else to live. Death was so often for the greater good of the living, including her own.

I couldn't save you, Douglas, not without making you hate me. I couldn't expose you to the wreckage of all you hold dear ... those others were there long before me. Stop thinking of him. Put him entirely out of mind. 'Listen,' she said to the dog. 'Listen, isn't it lovely? When we get home, you have to be very, very quiet. No barking.'

Walking up the valley, she could see the outline of the stables and veered to the right, keeping her distance. If Jimmy was there, his ears were sharp. She knew how the alarm system worked and she knew how to evade it, just as she knew how not to set the dogs barking, if she was careful. Supposing she had lost the knack? That was for later. Amy cut across the dip at the back of the garden and slipped between the branches of the willow tree. There was the house, glowing white. There were scudding clouds racing across the moon which glowed like a huge oil lamp swathed in muslin, the forgiving light of it changing the aspect and shape of the building and never revealing it as less than beautiful.

It's only a house. No it isn't. It's my house and a special house. Mine ... why did you drive me out?

She sat on the grass, next to the obedient dog. Sometimes dogs needed a big shock to make them obedient; they needed that bit of fear. *Like a woman.* Who said that? Douglas, are you there? Amy whispered to the dog, 'Let me tell you about this house. *He* liked it because it was never finished. Because it's half a house with one magnificent room. See that? The way the front there comes out in one great big, sexy curve of windows that no one else sees? There should be a drive sweeping up to this, but there isn't. They built a dome, but it isn't a dome any more. It's half a dome. A folly, they call it, with all sorts of bits added on.' She fondled the underneath of the dog's chin where the hair was grey, the only other place it liked to be touched. Jimmy would sort out the ear infection, one day soon. 'It has *historical importance*,' she whispered. 'Like any hellfire club, dowager house, yeah, yeah, yeah. Some lord kept his llamas here, and his *snakes*, would you believe? It was always a menagerie surrounding that room. See the lights at the back? Someone upstairs. A new addition, *darling*, circa 1950. *Ruined* it.'

In the hushed mimic of her mother-in-law's voice, Amy realised that something was terribly wrong. Light was supposed to come out of the big, curved window, shine on to the steps and reveal what was within, but the steps down to the garden were dark. She had never once closed those curtains in the whole of her tenure, never wanted to do anything other than rip them down or, failing that, finally regard their presence with indifference as long as they slumped to one side and did not interfere. That room was supposed to be lit with sunlight or moonlight, so that you could see the fox slink across the garden, the grey owl as it cruised away, the mole as it made a hole, the willow tree as it grew and bent, as if vexed by concern, under the weight of snow. You should be able to see all your friends at once and hear their noises, scuttling, preying, fighting, growing, dying, creaking, barking. The windows of the grand room looked back at her like big, dead eyes, reflecting nothing but the oil-lamp moon and her own, uncomprehending stare.

'Shhhh, *siiit*.'

This to the dog, who sensed the acuteness of her distress. Then there was a light. The French doors opened and two people stepped out, one smaller and stockier, the other, taller than he, supporting him by the elbow and shrieking '*Whoopsadaisy*' in a high voice as he stumbled. The fraction of light framed them nicely. They were backlit like sculptures in a museum as they kissed.

CHAPTER TWELVE

Her first reaction on seeing the black wall of curtains hiding the room was one of outrage. It was as if someone had put a filthy old blanket over the whole house and shrouded it. The whole point of this odd house was the light released through those vast windows, streaming in from the outside during the day and returning the compliment by filtering out from the room and over the steps more gently at night, so that the house and the land were all part of a whole, reflecting each other. To blacken the windows at night was to make the house small and mean and the people inside it shameful prisoners. To close those curtains was to despise it.

The reflection of the hazy moon in the dark windows mattered more than the sight of her husband and Caterina letting themselves out of the French windows like a pair of conspirators, only to embrace, like lovers. *Like lovers*; the phrase had resonance. Was it possible to be *like* lovers without actually *being* lovers? There were newspaper reports which suggested it was perfectly feasible and frequently desirable. It was sometimes politic to act like a lover. They looked so good together, these two, like ideally paired celebrities posed for the camera. Seen from the distance of a hundred feet, backlit by that mean little fraction of light escaping from behind, it was not so much a kiss as a hug in which his body was awkwardly stooped and each rested a chin on the other's shoulder in a brief contact from which he pulled away, quickly. She knew every nuance of his movements; an embrace from Douglas was an all-enveloping, wholehearted, arms and legs, rib-crushing exercise with nothing perfunctory about it. When he stood away from his stepsister, he staggered slightly, as if he was drunk or exhausted. Yes, he was a little drunk; there was a certain way he muddled his feet when he was like that, and all the same, Amy was breathless with hurt. It did not make any difference if he was influenced by whisky and resisting the affection he was being offered; the fact remained, he had still entered the circle of Caterina's graceful arms and stayed there, however briefly. She seemed to be scolding him now; she pointed him back into the room as she might have directed a disobedient pet. Amy was too far away to hear the words; only watched as he went back inside, followed after an interval by her. The curtain was drawn back again, leaving the blank wall of glass, dutifully reflecting the moon. Drawing those curtains and shutting out the sky was sacrilege. The room was an observatory. And he had let it happen; allowed her room to be transformed into a giant grave, in the same callous way he refused to mourn her. What *was* it she had wanted? Comfort? Amy looked at the luminous dial on her watch, a present from him. She was early, like a guest arriving an hour too soon and embarrassing a host still in the throes of preparation. She sat on the bench and fondled the left ear of the dog, remembering not to touch the right. Douglas was like that, too, bits of him where he did not wish to be explored, ticklish bits where the touching was agony even if it was accompanied by the giggles of the tormented which sounded almost like laughter.

'Sit. Stay still.' The dog leaned against the bench, content to be stroked. Amy had invented a history for the animal, based on observation and imagination. A country dog, unused to roads or leads, strong in bone and sinew from a well-nurtured youth and only neglected in later life, it would learn to trust again once it was settled here. It was a curable dog and a good listener. Hidden behind the curtains, the house was still busy. It was not bedtime yet. They would have to wait.

'Do you know, I once thought that woman was my friend,' she told the dog. 'She seemed to be, at first. Probably when she thought I was just a flash in the pan. Better be nice to stepbrother's new woman; she won't last, they never do. But he married me. They took their time, she and her mother. They are the people he loves best in the world. They were his boyhood; they were the ones who nursed him through sickness and forgave him everything; they can do no wrong in his eyes. He wouldn't hear ill of them. He simply couldn't.'

The dog leaned closer, warming her legs. The hair of it would grow thick in winter.

'I can't remember when they started. They hate the dogs, you see. They hated his passion for dirty, hairy, four-legged things. They thought he would stop, see sense and start to live a gracious life. Something like that. They were sick to death of dogs. His father started the sanctuary; his stepmother must have hoped that it would end when he died, but it didn't. She might have thought it would end when he married me, but it didn't. It got worse because of me. I should feel sorry for her. She married a man who cared only for his son, his dogs and his first wife, in that order, and then she finds she's stuck as the dependant of a stepson who still cares more about dogs than anything else and is planning to spend money she thinks should be hers on new stables and a charitable foundation. All that. She's a brilliant actress. Where was I? I know, I was saying, I can't remember when it started.'

The rain began, soft and gentle, pattering against the leaves of the willow tree in a benign, musical drizzle. It was a sound that reminded her of small feet running away, and it was enough to convince anyone of the existence of fairies and elves coming out to play. How could they sit inside that room and hear the rain without wanting to watch it sparkle on the glass? What strange, foreign creatures they were.

'First there was his mother, looking at me with her big, sad eyes. *What a shame*, she would say. You were so pretty when you first came here and now you aren't. Look at you, covered in dog hair. That isn't the way you should

look if you want to keep a man. Can't you cook something better than this, instead of spending all the time in
the garden or with the dogs? I laughed and tried to tell
him, but he said don't criticise her, darling, she's had
enough of that. Standard mother-in-law stuff. But it
wasn't. Then, when he was away once, it changed. *He
doesn't love you*, she'd say. There's only one person he's
ever loved, you're useful, that's all. Because you love dogs
and a man has to have a nice, solid wife for the good of
his image. Can't have people thinking he fancies little
boys. Or his sister.'

The rain stayed soft and the tree shielded them both.
The curve of the white house glowed. Upstairs, a light
showed. When Douglas was drunk, he took himself to
bed, alone. She shuddered, crossed her arms across her
chest.

'So I asked Caterina, what does your mother mean?
Caterina only came at weekends, not always then, so I
was slow to notice the malice in her. I don't know what on
earth my mother means, she said at first. I knew about my
father by then; I had plenty of secrets to carry around. I
had his voice in my ears, telling me how much Douglas
would despise him and me for belonging to him and I
knew Douglas cannot bear people who hurt others.'

The dog sat closer.

'It was then Caterina told me that she and Douglas
were lovers. Told me how he had seduced her when she
was little more than a child. Said, in her polite way, not to
worry, that was what men did, but she had often wondered since why it was that all the women he fucked,

before me, should be her size, her shape, her colouring. She told me this as if she was reciting a recipe for beef stew and it didn't matter at all.'

The rain penetrated the leaves after a while. Amy felt a single, cold drop hit the top of her head and roll down her face like an isolated tear. She caught the drop in her mouth. It felt sweet.

'Oh, I knew they loved him. I just didn't realise what *kind* of love, how strong it was; how essential to him. So what would you have done? These were the risks, dog. If I confronted him with *that* confession, either he would say it was true and he never loved me, which would be the worst. Or he would think that silly little me had made it up to get attention and Caterina would gasp and stretch her eyes and say what a wicked liar I was, she never said any such thing. Or he would believe me and send both of them packing, which would break his heart. They are his life; I was the recent addition. The interloper. So I said nothing. Then someone started sabotaging the dogs. It's no wonder, is it, that when all that nonsense came up in the newspapers about Douglas buggering dogs and being cruel to them, I could hardly take it seriously. It wasn't like the Caterina stuff, because there was absolutely no prospect of it being true. And I think I know who started it, but I couldn't say that, either. I behaved as normal, only quieter. Then I began to think, if I went away, everything would be better. Everything would go back to normal without me. I think we've sat here long enough, don't you?'

She got up and stood behind the bench, holding on to

the warm wood, stretching her calves and looking at the watch. Another light went out upstairs to the far left. Mother-in-law's room; she slept like a log. Amy attached the dog's rope to the bench and sidled through the branches of the tree. It was all their fault. If they had not blackened out the room, she might have been content to look through the windows, check from that safe distance that everything was the same. Now she had to get inside. There was a problem with the raincoat, which rustled louder than the rain when she moved, so she took it off and left it with the dog. That way it would know she was coming back.

'*Stayyy* . . .'

The one advantage to those viciously blind windows was the certainty that no one would see her walk across the lawn of wet grass. It was springy beneath her feet; she wanted to dawdle and take off her shoes to feel the damp. The night was hers before the five a.m. train, all the time in the world. So she held the shoes and walked the short distance to the steps, disapproving of the short cut of the lawn. It looked as if it had been taken to the barber's and she preferred the grass long and shaggy with clover. Near the steps she trod on something sharp and stifled a scream, sat down on the step and cradled her foot, brushing away the glass. No visible damage. She put the shoes back on and winced with pain. It concentrated the mind. This was *her* house; she could enter at will. Passing by the curtains to get round the side, she could see no trace of light from the room.

The back door would be locked. Caterina or her

mother would have seen to that; they disliked her preference for an open door and a house where there was
nothing to steal. The spare keys Amy never declared and
kept entirely for herself were underneath the flowerpot
halfway down the side of the house, hidden by an evergreen azalea which did not mind the shade. She felt her
way in the pitch dark with cautious ease. The pitter-patter
of the rain was louder than her own footfall.

Were they right, Douglas? Did you ever want silly me?

In a way, she did not care in the least if she was heard,
and she had the firm conviction that she was invisible.
People *were* invisible inside their own houses; latterly she
had crept from place to place inside this house and they
had ceased to notice her existence. Had he been concerned by her self-effacement? Yes, of course he had.
Concerned, inquisitive, and finally impatient. A wounded
bear, blundering around, hurt, unable to ask explanations
for the inexplicable. Angry at the persistence of her nervous quietness, furious at the accusations of cruelty.

Amy turned on the kitchen light inside the porch.
There was none of the usual mess of boots and shoes;
instead there was a neat rack of carefully arranged walking sticks, like something out of a magazine. If Caterina
had been in residence for any length of time, there would
be no dogs, in deference to her allergies, but all the same,
the lack of them surprised her. It was as if a large piece of
furniture had been removed, leaving a gap. Or as if the
walls had been painted a different colour. She gazed
round the kitchen. It was the same room and it was no
longer hers. There were no flowers dying gracefully in the

jug on the sill, no Post-its by the sink with her shopping lists; the table was clear of litter; there were no pots, pans, plates waiting to be put away, but never put away because she would need them again soon. Nothing lingered in the sink; every surface was clear and the doll's house was relegated to the furthest corner, the roof of it bent as if it had been dropped. She looked inside; all the figures had been removed. A new clock ticked on the wall, replacing the other which had never functioned but stayed because it belonged. Amy's sense of outrage grew; she wanted to cry, bit her lip instead. She turned off the light and went down the corridor to the living room, careless of the sound she made. A single lamp glowed in the furthest corner of the room. Someone had forgotten to turn it off. It was enough to show the differences. The room was smaller with the curtains drawn; it smelled of Douglas's cigars, with an underlying, chemical smell of strong cleansing fluid. The chairs and the sofa were more formally arranged; the carpet was straight. An ornate mirror had been placed over the fireplace instead of the picture which had hung there. A second-rate painting Douglas approved for its sheer size and sentimental depiction of a pack of hounds streaming across a field in pursuit of a long-escaped fox. He had liked these dappled dogs, however amateur and highly coloured their depiction. They had appealed to him. There were other additions – a shawl over a chair, ornaments on the mantelpiece. It was like an elegant museum.

Amy went upstairs. She held the banister and walked carefully at the edge, knowing how some of the stairs would creak like pistol shots if she walked in the centre, but still not much caring if anyone heard. She was dead; they were not expecting her; they were wiping away all traces of her occupation; she hated them. Her foot hurt and felt sticky inside her shoe. It would be nice to find alternative shoes.

The spare room which Caterina habitually used was at the furthest end of a long corridor opposite Mother's room. Facing her was the bathroom she and Douglas used, with the door standing ajar. From the room next to it, she could hear him snoring rhythmically. It was a test of love to sleep with a man who snored. There were the three doors in a row – bathroom, bedroom and his study in this corner of the odd, rectangular extension, all with a view over the garden and the willow tree.

Bathroom first. How he teased her about what he called the lotions and potions and marvelled how she needed so many. Look at my side of the cabinet, he said. Shaving brush, razor and soap, that's all and there soon won't be room for that. Now there was nothing but the shaving stuff. All her night creams, day creams, eye creams, acquired for the sheer pleasure of their exquisite smells and textures, her grown-up playthings in an otherwise non-indulgent life, all gone. It felt like theft. There was a small airing cupboard in this room, where she kept her underwear; Amy looked: empty. She wanted to shriek *thief, thief*, but that temptation passed and she felt utterly bereft. There was no anger in her wondering how soon after her disappearance it had been before the eradication of her presence, her taste, her methods of doing things, her garments, her toiletries and probably all her clothes. They might have begun the process within hours of the news, probably had. It wouldn't have taken long. The items were not so numerous, however precious they were, and the traces of herself so easily dispelled it was laughable. Useless to think she would find shoes in the hallway cupboard. She backed out of the room into the corridor, quietly, ignoring the opposite door into their bedroom, from where she could still hear the sound of his noisy sleep. He was not always a snorer, only after too much whisky and never when an animal was ill and he was on duty. He had two types of sleep: the solid kind, where he would rest undisturbed by thunder and lightning, and the normal kind where the slightest sound would rouse him, violently. They had never had a night-time prowler foolish enough to ignore the dogs, for which Amy had been grateful. On a night of normal sleep, no intruder who woke Douglas would stand a chance. But on a night of snoring sleep, she could enter that room with impunity, playing a drum. She did not wish to do so, in case she should see herself in that bed, curled away from him in the silence of the worst days. Silence in bed was the worst punishment; she had not meant it as such when she did not know what to say, but that was what it must have felt like. Nor did she want to see her ghost in that bed in the other days when it was she who had made the greatest, unghostlike noise. Also, it was her turn for anger again, of the dull, sad variety. It was he who had let this happen; he who had allowed the women to wipe away her presence with the same ease they might have wiped a basin clean of

scum and then run water over it to make sure it was all
gone. He was the overseer. She might kill him in his sleep.
Mourn her? No; he drank and he snored and regarded his
empty bathroom cabinet with satisfaction, that was what
he did.

She went into his study instead, pausing at the door.
This small corner of the house was sacrosanct. Not even
his mother would venture here. By some unspoken rule,
no one did and no one ever had unless it was her, bringing coffee or tea, or the accountant twice a year. The
study required no lock upon the door to preserve its privacy as his domain; custom established it. If he closed the
door behind himself, he was not to be disturbed unless he
asked; if he closed the same door as he left the room, no
one would open it again until he came back. Nor would
there be any need for the women to go in there now with
their fretful fingers itching to change things, because
there were no traces of anyone else to be scrubbed away
and nothing that could be altered. There was only a handsome, two-tier desk, a phone fax, hidden beneath a deluge
of paper, a filing cabinet and a swivel chair. No curtains
to close. The moon swam blearily into view. She had put
flowers on top of the filing cabinet, sometimes; he liked
that, but the addition of anything permanent and decorative was taboo. The small space was organised chaos; he
did not want anyone else to understand it. There was a
laptop on the floor, ignored; he preferred pen and paper.
Plenty of paper. There were the plans for the new stables
and surgery, kept separate on the floor. *Her* plans.

The area of the desk looked as if a bomb had struck.

Yellow Post-its were stuck on to letters and bills and on to the edges of the desk, all bearing his scrawl. She switched on the lamp, alarmed for a second at the unfamiliar loudness of the *click* which made her start. The Post-its were the first thing she noticed, but then her eye was caught by the model figure, acting as a lightweight paperweight to a pile of letters in the centre of the desk. It was the little man in his armchair, rescued from the doll's house downstairs, sitting proud and dust-free with a Post-it attached to the back. Amy sat down in the swivel chair and took the little man in her hands. She peeled away the Post-it and saw his writing on it. He always used a fountain pen and black ink. She bent her head to read it. *The master of the house, ha, ha!* Amy put the figure back, hurriedly. Slowly she looked at the rest of the desk without touching anything, sitting on her hands to keep them safe, her eyes taking in the messages on the Post-its. She had never known him use them before, he found them fiddly; it was she who used the things.

There were messages on the Post-its, senseless scrawls, ready to be scrunched up and replaced with other senseless scrawls.

Where is Amy? Amy is here; Amy will go back to the flat again. Must get back handbag, why, why, why? Amy is not dead, I know she isn't.

Amy, how am I going to find you?

Then, in block capitals on a bigger piece of paper, level with her eyes, dead centre on the top tier of the desk so that she could not miss it: *AMY, MY DARLING, ALL YOUR CREAMS ARE IN THE FRIDGE.* Where did he mean? Fridge downstairs, stables, the flat? She gasped. Felt as if two huge hands were pressing into her shoulders, forcing her down into the seat. The sound of his snoring calmed her. Then she counted these strange notes, as much to stop herself crying as for any other reason. Twenty-five of them, all featuring her name. As if, in the midst of doing something else, he distracted himself by writing it again and again, all of them rehearsing in one way or another the same theme – that she . . . *was not dead*, or rather his own refusal to believe it. *If Amy was dead, I would be dying; I would KNOW . . . Amy is not DEAD she went to the flat, she wiped the messages.* This was his grief, this was the reason for the stoic *lack* of mourning to which the newspaper had alluded. He had never been a reasonable man; he would go on believing black was white until the black consented to change colour. It was the way he achieved things as well as avoided them. Bloody stubborn. She wanted to crawl into the bed beside him; she had always wanted to do that. Get in there with him so they could hug each other silly for hours and hours.

She pushed the chair back from the desk. She must not weep on the paperwork or the black ink would run. And if she were to do any such thing as crawl into the bed next door, what would happen? They would be back to square one, with more to explain and forgive than ever. She would be crawling into bed like a sickly, infectious bitch, pleading forgiveness for her own disease.

She found the last Post-it. *Amy, love you better than life; come home.*

Time was passing; the moon was peering through the window accusingly as she found clean paper and pen and worked out in her mind where she could leave her messages. In the filing cabinet, at the back where he would find them, not tomorrow, but sometime; where he would not be able to guess when she had left them, but know for sure that she had. Five written messages, to be littered through the old paperwork, written with a shaky hand.

AFGHAN LOVES ROTTWEILER. ALWAYS SHALL.

Her foot throbbed painfully, a reminder of reality. She tried to ease it out of the ruined shoe, but it stuck as a punishment for doing as she did now and the pain of it reminded her she was not a ghost. Made her turn off the light with another loud *click*, and close the door behind her before she went back down the stairs. Her foot felt sticky as she crossed the clean kitchen floor and let herself out. Went halfway down the side of the house before she remembered to go back and lock the door.

FACE CREAMS ARE IN THE FRIDGE. The fridge in the stables where medicine and specialist diet food was stored, where she was bound with the dog. She did not care about face creams when she felt like a leper and she began to know she was not invisible and be afraid of her own substance.

She was a leprous blob, crossing the barbered lawn, hobbling slightly under her own weight, spotlit by the moon, jeered by the trees and made heavier by her own tears. Most of all, she wanted to hide beneath the willow tree and cry herself into a stupor. She wanted to cry for not being able to turn back the clock a couple of years in order that she could act and react then with the knowledge she had now; she wanted to remember what it was like to be loved and treasured and respected by a tyke of an awkward, difficult, clumsy, passionate man who would have listened to her if she had believed she had the strength to make him listen; a man who detested lies, told the truth and would recognise it finally, however brutal it was. A man with a short fuse and blinkered faith in those who purported to love him, a terrible vulnerability on that account, an inability to express his emotions, more blind spots than a travelling tortoise and more bloody-minded integrity than anyone should possess, even with shoulders that broad. For God's sake, if he had screwed his stepsister, he would probably be proud of it. Why had she listened? She stopped by the side of the house. One last look at the windows, tears blurring her vision. She had never even been afraid of him, unlike so many others. She shook her head in the darkness. That wasn't quite true. There had been that moment, when he found her in that daft dress, sitting on Blackfriars Bridge with the pigeon in her lap, when she had been absolutely terrified, and that was the only time, the fear tempered by something he said that same first night. *No need to run away. I'm only an ugly old dog.*

The dog sat, tethered to the bench. She sat beside it. It was easier to stay alive as a dog; they had shorter memories and a greater ability to have trust restored, even if they were cursed with a different capacity, on a shorter time-scale, to have it destroyed. And they could equally die of a broken heart and had to be kept, unless they were wolves living in a different landscape. She had an irrelevant memory of another dog they had taken in after it had been living wild for a year and starving and still it bit the hand that fed. Maybe human beings were not so different. That dog had lived in the remoter corner of the stables, refusing succour for a long time. Plenty of pride, and him such an ugly dog too. She had cried when it died and she cried now, but crying upset the animal beside her which was learning trust at a fast rate and had got her on and off the train, and distress was contagious, so she stopped crying. You could not turn clocks back, any more than you were allowed to dwell in British summertime, or command the rain to stop, so she exited the sacred shelter of the tree from the opposite side without looking back and took the back way towards the stables, carrying the coat. *Going home*, she told the dog softly, *this is home*.

There was a point on the left wall where she could approach and not activate the alarm; she would tether the dog there after it had drunk from the fresh puddle-water. Not so long before dawn, I promise you, sweetheart, not so long, I promise you and I have never ever reneged on a promise I have made to a dog. Only to a man.

How quiet it was; how loud each teeny sound they made, each footstep sinking with a splishy whisper as if they trod on cymbals. Closer to the gate of the stables, she could imagine the smell of herbs and the sweet, sour scent of animals, let her thoughts wander. Dell of Dell's Animal Sanctuary was a stupid, egotistical *bitch*. She never took the ugly ones, not Dell, she never took the nearly dead, and she wanted what Douglas had, power, authority, reputation. Dell hated men. She could be behind the sabotage, but never without an ally. Ahhh; the gate was to Amy's left as she sidled along the wall. Wait. The lights were all wrong. Jimmy was drunk again.

Amy stopped. Douglas would have got Jimmy back; it was only ever a matter of time before he got Jimmy back. And he would not have drowned his sorrows and gone to bed without someone being here, not with Dell on the loose; not with *whoever* it was on the loose, some spirit of malice, dancing in the shadows. There was a mere hint of damp dawn in the sky, promising warmth. The gate to the yard stood open. Amy slung her raincoat over it, tied the dog's rope to the post, patted the grizzled head. Douglas would find her in the morning. Mission accomplished. Goodbye. But the gate should not have been open. Something was wrong. She could smell the herbs, vividly, as she stepped across the threshold.

The stable used as living accommodation was firmly shut; wrong. The storeroom to the left of it was open, with the light from within seeping into the yard, along with noises of movement too slight to disturb the sleeping dogs, *wrong*. Amy stood to the side of the door and peered round. Someone was busy about the sacks of dry food which were the staple of the diet for the canine residents, bought in bulk, one sack finished before the next was opened, each sack sufficient for three days. There was an open sack, two-thirds full, with which the busy person fiddled industriously, stirring something into the sack, bending over it with her arm inside, elbow-deep, mixing the contents. On top of the adjacent fridge, Amy saw a familiar sight. Three tubs of slug pellets with a familiar logo, unsealed, one lying on its side and ready to roll away, empty.

The bitch, the stinking mad bitch.

Such nice hair, her mother-in-law had, always elegantly coiffed at the expense of a wasted hour every morning. Making duty visits to the stables like a visiting royal often enough to be familiar to the animals, not an intruder, not really. Mixing up a nice mess of poison for the dear little doggies which would make them sick enough to kill the more vulnerable and have these clean stables awash with filthy liquid shit from the rest. That could get them closed down, as it almost had before. *That* would break his heart and make him biddable. That would stop building. Frail mother-in-law, with the elegant, silver-handled stick she scarcely needed propped against the door.

He's never loved you, you know. It's only us he loves. We want all of him. And all of his money.

The moment of shocked objectivity which made her so still melted into incandescent rage. A desire to leap on the woman, scratch her eyes out, claw at her porcelain skin. Hold her by the skinny neck and shove slug pellets down her throat, like stuffing a goose before eating its liver. Amy picked up the stick and lifted it high. Heavier than it looked, the momentum of the downward arc carried her with it into the room and the silver handle thumped into the side of the grey head with a sickening thud. Delicate Mrs Petty screamed and slumped forward into the bag of meal, clutching at it, sliding to the floor, crumbs of dried meal cascading over her clothes in a flurry of dusty movement until everything was still. In the next stable, a dog began to bark, then another, then all of them. Their noise was deafening after the silence. Amy kept hold of the stick and backed out of the door. Kept walking backwards until she collided with the gate, felt for the raincoat as if it would save her. The dog she had left there snarled and joined in the cacophony of barking. The row increased and went on and on, echoing round the walls with the sound of a baying mob, yelling for blood. She ran.

She ran out of earshot of the dogs as fast as she could, so that she could lose the illusion of all of them following her, snapping at her heels, bringing her down to earth in recrimination, making a bloody hole and burying her. She ran through the woods and into the path across the fields, slowed to an unsteady walk and then to a full stop. If she were to run any further she would fall. Somewhere in the initial flight, she lost the stick. Leaning against a fence, she vomited again, stomach heaving painfully to produce a thin stream of bile dribbling into the grass. As the spasms passed, leaving her as weak as a kitten, so did the trembling and breathlessness. Sickness took the last of her energy, leaving nothing but weakness. The sky was growing lighter and the hem of the raincoat was damp with dew. There was mist hanging over the field and she could hear the raucous overture to the dawn chorus. The best time of the day. Too empty for anger or regret, she wet her hands in the dewy grass and wiped them over her face. In the growing light of the day, with the hopeful racket of the birds, she felt the freedom of someone with nothing else to lose. There were no broken bridges behind her; they were burned. She found herself giggling hysterically. *Eat dirt, Mother.* Choking on her laughter until she stopped. The birdsong grew louder, the blackbirds loudest, indifferent to competition. The mist was thinning into parallel strips of floating whiteness. Go back to being dead.

There was a shrouded street with a milk float. The station was conspicuously empty, a noticeboard inviting ticket holders to use the side entrance before seven a.m. Litter drifted the empty platform; with no more than a frisson of disgust, she found some almost unused tissues under a bench and used them to clean her hands with the lubricant of spit. She shook out the coat, checked the pockets. Put it back on.

She hesitated as the train grunted to a halt, on time; it was still a monster, waiting to devour her, and it was only the empty horror of being left behind that cancelled out the fear of getting aboard. The train somehow gulped her in. She glanced at the sprinkling of passengers; none of them looked back. She did not look as murderous as she felt. Strange how one gravitated to the same seat, sat down in the same way with a quick look round before settling, like a dog patting the bed. There was a man sitting in the seat opposite, staring at her. She only noticed him when he got up and moved. A faintly familiar face she forgot as soon as it was gone.

Jimmy trudged over the field, head hurting, mind hurting, hands in pockets, one looking for his cigs, the other scratching his balls. A long time since they'd seen action. What a fool to bring back that wee girl to the stables after a night in the pub, playing tonsil hockey outside up the alley, and then getting into the banger, a good idea at the time, even if it had been winter. Only that was the night that poor pregnant bitch decided to go premature with her pups and her bad hips and he'd been too pissed to notice, lying in a stupor after a wee bit of the other and the postcoital fag burning a hole in the mattress while he contemplated the fact that he was such an irresistible personality, to say nothing of his prodigious cock, that the girl was gone long before he woke in his own stink. Maybe it was the dogs spooked her, or one whimpering bitch, to be precise. Funny he should think of it now, all these months later when he was back with the job from which he knew he had well deserved the fucking sack. Must be on account of thinking of bitches in general and that one in particular. 'S'cuse me, Caterina fucking Petty, you can come down the stables like lady bitch of the manor at nine in the evening and order me home, but you can't stop me walking back at five in the morning if I please. Couldn't sleep, you see, as if you fucking cared. It must take fourteen hours of insomnia-free kip a day to keep the lines off that face of hers, so there was fat chance she would notice anything in the middle of her beauty sleep. Who the fuck did she think she was anyway? And why had he been daft enough to obey?

He grumbled his way across the field to disguise the fact that while early rising was second nature, it was not usually quite as early as this and it was a weird premonition that had jolted him awake in his room on the edge of town and got him so far. Something wrong, daft images whirring round in his head, not far away from the dread of waking up and finding Douglas standing over him alive and well and wanting to bludgeon him to death. Daft. Then he saw the stick, sticking out of a bush with the silver handle uppermost, which he would never have noticed if he had not almost collided with it. Old Mother Petty's stick, not that she was so fucking old, still looked at her son as if she wanted to eat him . . . wait a wee minute. Something wrong here. He plucked the stick and broke into a run. Nearer the stables he could hear the barking, one or two of the noisy ones sustaining a chorus which the others had dropped, all punctuated by the howl of the one tied to the gate. Dilly to the life, shockingly similar, apart from the howling, because poor Dilly never said a word, just listened all the time.

Still carrying the stick, he found the storeroom with Mrs Petty on the floor, lying there covered in dog meal, the sack of it dragged down with her and all over the place on her moaning face and her skirt which had ridden up to show knickers, *knickers*, on that one, who'd have thought it? She lay in profile with a purple contusion spreading from her grey hair into her forehead, above the left eyebrow, one hand outflung, the other clawed to her chest and her breathing unhealthily audible. Jimmy was still holding the stick, grasped in the middle, as if he was the leader of the majorettes and about to twirl the thing. He twisted his fist and looked at his watch, 5.45, Jesus help him. First things first. He took the stick to the sink, ran it under the tap, wiped it all over with paper towel and propped it by the door. The rain, which was probably the only thing that had woken him after all with its intermittent, indecisive pattering, began again. Even as he washed the stick and noticed how the imprint of the fresh bruise on her ladyship's fucking forehead bore a surprising resemblance in scale to the handle, and long before he had connected the slug pellets to the meal and the spillage and the bod on the floor, his own motives for cleansing the thing were perfectly clear. He was getting rid of the traces mainly on account of the fact that who-ever had clonked the woman deserved a break. They deserved a fucking medal.

And now, at long bloody last, the shit could hit the fan.

CHAPTER THIRTEEN

Amy Petty limped across the almost empty station concourse, taking the same route to the left she had taken with all the others after the crash. There were video cameras discreetly placed above the exit. A man followed, keeping his head down and his hands in his pockets; she did not notice him or anyone else.

Everything was clean in the morning. The view from the top deck of the bus was crystal-clear; the river had been lit with gold and even the endless cars of the hinterland gleamed. The bus covered the distance efficiently, filling and emptying with quiet, morning workers. Amy told herself that one day soon, she would get one of those jobs where a person worked at night and came home in the early hours like this, at the only time of the day when it was possible for her to admire this present world without making comparisons to another. She was built for work and made herself think about nothing but work all the way back, until, two stops before the regular stop, she saw a sign for a supermarket, neon-lit. Asda Superstore, so near to home and yet so far, it made her feel ashamed for not noticing it before. The omission pointed to a kind of blind laziness. She would go there, later. Buy a bottle of whisky, keep it as a memento. She wanted the smell of it. There was nothing else she could buy here to remind her of home.

Back in the treeless zone, the traffic was lighter as she walked past the newsagent's and down Bayview Road, her steps growing slower and slower. Not even the cool morning of almost eight o'clock could redeem Ratview from ugliness. There were footsteps behind her own which slowed with hers. She kicked a lump of polystyrene into the road, looked at the closed doors. There was something she had seen in a magazine about the Far East, where houses turned in on themselves, presenting drab, dark walls to the outside world in order to misrepresent the riches within.

Photographs of beautiful, hidden courtyards came to mind, vistas of plants and stone fountains and cool, welcoming rooms. The whole façade of this street might hide scenery like that, where every family kept its aspirations indoors. That was what she would make herself believe. It was one way to live. Her father did it. He had placed his real houses inside his own makeshift house and lived in fantasy. Dwelling among the work of a lifetime, the prince of a kingdom. The doll's houses were his real passion and without them he would be nothing. Each to his own deficiency. Amy had no judgement to make of herself, yet, and none she could honestly make of him. The sound of the blow in the bright light of the stable echoed in her mind with a strange liberating effect and yet she was heavy with grief. She could not judge anyone.

She unlocked the front door to the smell of white spirit in the hall, and in the middle of the kitchen table there was a pair of shoes in her size, standing on a piece of paper on which her father had written, *My dear daughter, I hope you are home safe. Please don't wake me early, I haven't been well. I thought you needed these. PS From Asda, they also have clothes.*

He was not well, she remembered. He had grown more feeble in the weeks of her residence, a visible decay evident in his growing indifference to food. The shoes on the table were cheap and ugly canvas ones, but their very existence made her tearful. There was nothing she needed more. She stared at them, her mouth forming the words, '*he does care for me, after all*', then sat at the table, picked up a Biro and wrote on the border of a newspaper the word '*DISLIKE*'. There was a boy who had once come to the stables for a job, with the word '*H.A.T.E.*' tattooed on his knuckles; there was a difference between the two and how you lived with them. You could dislike your daughter and still buy shoes for her, she thought earnestly, but surely you could not buy the shoes at the same time as *hating*. You could not do a single kind thing for someone you hated. She missed the dog. She would think more clearly if there was a dog.

In the fridge, alongside a loaf of the kind of everlasting bread her father preferred, there was a surprise cache of

sweets, pushed to the back. Three tubes of fruit gums
and two bars of nut and raisin chocolate, next to pink and
yellow jelly babies, the colourful packets bright against the
other, bland contents. He never ate sweets. Amy stuffed
the bread back inside and went out into the back yard.
The persistent sun was hard on her eyes, a reminder of
the exhaustion which made her wired for sound, unable
to remain still, weary and yet not able to crawl into the
ugly little room upstairs in the hope of sleep because she
was afraid of crying and waiting for the ghosts of regret to
come haunting. Better to stay awake, even moving like a
drunk with all of a drunk's awareness of time and space.
The flowers in the plastic pots were wilting; she noticed
that the homemade kennel for the dog had been tidily
demolished. Raising her face to the sun, she tried to think
of the implications of her father keeping sweets in the
fridge. The desire to weep was almost overpowering.
There was movement from a corner of the yard. The dark
head of the child ducked down, almost out of sight, showing only the top of her sleek hair.

Amy shouted at her. 'Go away! Go away or I'll hit you.
I'll hit you hard, I can do it.'

There was a scuttling sound, followed by silence and
the slamming of a door. Amy went back inside, made tea
and sat at the table. *My father is not a bad man*, she
repeated to herself, *only a sad one*. There was nothing
wrong in buying sweets in the hope of small visitors, provided they came openly, through the front door, not by
the back in response to the crudest of temptation. But she
knew he was neither innocent nor harmless, even if he

had never been guilty as charged so long ago. She had seen him staring at the children when they came home from school with that hopeless look of longing in his eyes, as if he would reel them in with hoops of wire if he dared. And how could he change, how did anyone change? How could he, even old as he was, redefine desire, emasculate, lobotomise himself, cut chunks out of his own heart and soul to make himself different? Wanting what you could not, should not have, she knew all about that. She was his daughter. She had none of his tidy dimensions, but she had his nose, his eyes, the same obstinacy. She was angry with him, but along with the anger there was a furious pity. He could not help what he was.

Amy sat for a long time, trying to fathom if there was any good in either of them. She needed to do that for the sake of her sanity. The shoes stood centre stage on top of his note and yesterday's unread newspapers, while the new ones dropped through the front door. Amy was consumed with trembling weariness until she heard him in the bathroom, stirring, her alter ego, her daddy. She could not face him yet, not now. She might shout at him, curse him and, whatever else, he had been kind. He had left her the shoes, he had let her in; he had no life, wanted what he must not have and the act of kindness was more than she could bear. She thought of the anonymous hiding place of the supermarket she had passed, full of space and people. Hurriedly she peeled off her wrecked shoes and put on the new ones. They fitted loosely and again she felt a rush of gratitude. She left a note for her father, *Thank you, back soon*, picked up the keys and hurried from the house.

The morning was still kind, the air still fresh. Mr Oza in the newsagent's smiled as she bought a bar of chocolate. He only smiled when he forgot to stare at her clothes – she had left the coat behind. She smiled back and walked to the bus stop. Going to Asda had a purpose. She was a freak, an ungrateful child, possibly a murderess, and dressed as she was in the hideous skirt, she was not even in disguise. Waiting for the bus, wondering why it was her father had never mentioned the existence of the supermarket before, she thought of Elisabeth in her careless, good-quality clothes, rather like her own used to be and then, reminded by the bus driver, thought fleetingly of Rob the trolley man, and his lighter blue uniform. A uniform would be good. She wondered, with an ache of longing, where they were, and was glad that neither of them could see her now.

There had been footsteps behind her on the way. In canvas shoes, her own footsteps were silent.

The sun shone through the stained-glass windows of the High Court, adding a discordant note of cheerfulness to the gloom.

'*Rob? Look, someone has told me that there was a man in your carriage who tried to kill the woman next to him . . . before the crash . . .*'

'*You've found her, haven't you? No one else saw that.*'

'*Well . . .*'

'*Did she ask about me? No, no, no, doesn't matter. She's OK, is she?*'

'*About the man . . .*'

'*Yes, he threw her off the train. She didn't die in the crash, none of us did. But if you think I'm ever going to say anything about that, you're off your fucking trolley! Don't want no bogeyman after me. Is she hiding?*'

'*Yes.*'

'*Give her my love. She didn't ask about me, did she?*'

Repeating to herself this conversation of the night before, Elisabeth sat and watched the passersby. There was the clicking of a stick on the mosaic of the tiles which sounded louder than anything else. It *tap-tapped* from left to right slowly, the man with the stick taking his time, attracting no attention except her own. The sound of the stick reminded Elisabeth of something she could not grasp and she watched the slow movement with scepticism. No one who really required the solid support of a stick used one with a silver tip. It needed a ferrule.

Inside these august halls there was an officer, formally known as the Tipstaff, with a duty to parade on ceremonial occasions in nineteenth-century clothes and also to arrest those malefactors who evaded the jurisdiction of the High Court or were violent within it. Rather than a stick, the Tipstaff carried a short staff, decorated with a crown and hollow in the middle to hold his official warrant. The staff was a fourteenth-century invention, also useful as a weapon and an early model for the police truncheon both in size and weight, all of which Elisabeth remembered from a history lesson personally delivered by John Box inside these very walls, which lesson included the fact that what a modern Tipstaff did more often than not was to take into custody children who had been made wards of court.

Could *one*, she wondered, make a *wife* a ward of court? Have a judge declare on the application of a husband that his lawfully wedded spouse be returned by her abductor, in the way that a father could be ordered to return a kidnapped child? Alas, not. The man with the stick exited stage left up the stairs, where someone held open a door for him, the old fraud. *Tap, tap, tap.*

Today, the High Court was gloomy, gothic and quiet. Sitting where she was, Elisabeth was overwhelmingly conscious of the thousand rooms and three and a half miles of corridor squatting oppressively above, alongside and below where she sat. It was late lunchtime and the place was beginning to buzz, like a railway concourse, with the difference that most of the movers were soberly dressed and heavily laden. There was little enough of the early summer frippery in evidence here. Long sleeves and dark suits.

In evidence . . . If she ceased to be a lawyer, would she stop using this terminology, or was it so ingrained that she would talk like a legal parrot until the day she died, and think like one too, as if the law was branded on her brain. She was stuck with the vernacular and she was distracting herself with *irrelevancies* because she was bursting with speech and, if she had not arranged this meeting, might have found herself burbling at the bus stop or on the train to any stranger who was prepared to listen, like one of the poor nutters who lurked on the Circle Line, looking for someone to abuse. She really needed a friend. A more confidential friend than she was herself, because although she could keep secrets perfectly well, they burned holes in her pockets like money waiting to be spent. A friend. There were few enough of those and all the same, when she saw Helen West standing by the noticeboard, dwarfed by the scale of the place, looking around as if she expected a reception committee, Elisabeth wanted to shrink. A friend she had neglected over the years but one with all the right legal knowledge, a friend she was *using*. When Helen cantered over to where Elisabeth sat by the wall she had all the elegance of a dancer. This was not a woman who had difficulty finding clothes to fit. She dumped her bag and lit a cigarette in one fluid movement. At least there were some bad habits.

'So what's all this about then?'

No accusations, such as why do you only keep in touch when you want something and why should I interrupt my day to walk up Fleet Street and meet you here? None of that. Simply a brief, once-over inspection, followed by a critical nod.

'Elisabeth Manser, you're in a pickle and you haven't brushed your hair this morning. So tell me what you want me to do about it. Smoke?'

Elisabeth shook her head. She could feel dust shaking itself out of her brain, like dandruff. Helen never prevaricated and it was best to respond in the same way, taking a deep breath first.

'I need to find out about a case twenty-five years ago, in which a man called Rollie Fisher was convicted for indecent assaults on little girls. I don't know how to get them, but I need to know the facts.'

'Why?'

'Because it connects to a libel case. Fisher is Amy Petty's father . . .'

'And she's married to that *bugger* Douglas Petty. Got it. That was the reason for the last time you phoned. You wanted to know if he was going to be prosecuted. Likes dogs. Amy's the dead one. Train crash.' There was no sentiment about Helen, whom Elisabeth remembered as reading every page of every newspaper like someone addicted to newsprint. She had a prodigious memory, pursued information like a beggar after coins and would have been the better libel lawyer. A better lawyer full stop, but it didn't prevent her from being a human being. Or from styling her long dark hair into a clever knot at the nape of her neck from which only the minimum escaped.

'Amy Petty might not be dead,' Elisabeth muttered, wishing it did not sound so melodramatic.

'Well you're either dead or you aren't. There's no middle way.' Helen gave a rude chuckle, loud only because it was an unfamiliar sound in here. It had a perversely calming effect.

'What offence do you commit if you fake your own death?'

A spiral of cigarette smoke escaped towards the ceiling. 'Depends if you actually *fake* it. I mean if you actually hatch a deliberate plot to make people think you're dead. Or if you did it to facilitate a theft. Instead of just buggering off and letting everyone assume you're dead. I can't think there's any offence quite covers that. Is that what you wanted to know?'

'Supposing that's what she did – the latter, not the former – but before she disappeared from the train crash, she saw something which would indicate that someone was killed, non-accidentally. Murdered, and the train crash used to cover it. Supposing she has a conscience about that . . .'

'Yes. The woman you mentioned when you phoned. In *The Times*.' At least Helen did not react as if she was off her head. She had always been like that, paying close attention without responding until the end. You could sit down with Helen and announce an ambition to have a sex change and she would not bat an eyelid.

'And she wants someone to know,' Elisabeth ended lamely, watching Helen considering the problem as if contemplating a chess move.

'Well I know what I'd do. I'd write a series of anonymous letters to the police, my MP, the DPP and a couple of newspapers, suggesting the death be reinvestigated. If I didn't want anyone to know my identity, that is. It would do the trick, without achieving much. A witness can't be clandestine and effective. And if she did come forward, she might not be believed either. She's hardly showing signs of reliability and credibility at the moment, is she? Why do you want to find out about the father?'

'Because . . .'

'Let me guess. Douglas Petty might abandon his libel case if that particular skeleton crawled out of the cupboard. Wouldn't do much for his *reputation*. And you and your learned leader would lose the chance to make all that lovely money.'

'I'm not like that,' Elisabeth protested. 'Honestly I'm not.'

Helen nodded. A little of the shining hair escaped from the knot on the back of her neck. Interesting earrings, like small, curled flowers.

'I know you aren't. Which is why you're probably in the wrong line of work.' She puffed contemplatively, brushed away the smoke with a wave. 'You know the one thing which always struck me about libel? How easy it would be to orchestrate. You only need a bent journalist – plenty of those – in cahoots with the victim or someone close. The so-called victim and the journo create the libel and the journo gets it published. There's no real defence to it, so the newspaper has to pay out. If they have to pay out at the end of a trial, so much the better, because juries hate newspapers and give ridiculous awards. The journo doesn't suffer, only the newspaper. Then he and the victim can split the proceeds. A bit like an insurance scam.'

Elisabeth thought about this, not for the first time. 'The victim himself wouldn't need to be involved, would he?' she said. 'It could be somebody wanting to ruin him. Or achieve another purpose.'

'You've surely been long enough in this game to know that every law made to protect the weak or the innocent is infinitely exploitable by those who are anything but. The right to silence, the right to privacy, they're all exploitable. What I want to know is who's exploiting you? Are you in the grip of some mad dead woman or is it still John Box?'

Elisabeth was silent. They both watched as the foyer began to clear, the busy to-ers and fro-ers crossing the floor as in some ritual dance, before disappearing into the corridors and rooms. There was a sprinkling of robes and wigs, looking entirely natural in the setting, as if their wearers had emerged like that from the stonework.

'OK, you don't know,' Helen was saying evenly, gathering up her bag. 'And you want me to go and look at the Crown Prosecution Service archives from before the days of computer records, as if I had nothing better to do, so that I can tell you what this Rollie Fisher was accused of doing. All in such complete breach of the rules about the rehabilitation of offenders, I'll likely get sacked. Fisher won't be on some convenient register for paedophiles, you know. That's only for the recent ones. It's as hard for me to get this information as it would be for you.'

Elisabeth was stricken with remorse. 'Oh, Helen, I'm sorry, I didn't think . . . of course you mustn't . . . it was only . . .'

'You didn't know who else to ask? Story of my life.' She was standing and patting Elisabeth reassuringly on the shoulder. No need for her to say that none of this was ever to be repeated. That was a given. Even when they were students, Helen was famous for gathering gossip without ever repeating it.

'Shame on you, Elisabeth,' she said, grinning. 'I was only teasing. If you remembered any criminal law at all, you'd know that R v Fisher is in all the casebooks, if it's the same Fisher. You can't keep your anonymity if you make a point of law. He was one of the first to establish the principle that the evidence of a child can be accepted without corroboration. And it was in the bad old days when a wife couldn't give evidence against her husband, even if she wanted to, so there was some point made about that. I'll find it and fax you a transcript this afternoon. I've still got your home number, even though you seem to have lost mine. Bless you, all this cloak-and-dagger stuff for something you might have found out easily yourself.'

She was laughing.

Elisabeth felt monumentally ashamed. 'I am in the wrong job, aren't I?'

'Yes, you are,' Helen said. 'Why didn't we do something sensible and marry rich men?'

'You mean like Amy Petty?'

'Perhaps not.'

They had reached the doors of the Court and emerged into the grey daylight of the Strand. Elisabeth watched her go and wanted to call her back. It was suddenly lonely without her.

Lonely, *amen.* Everyone needed friends. A lover was no replacement, especially if he was not also a friend.

She took the mobile phone out of her handbag and stared at it, willing it to ring. Please, Amy, *ring.* Even if there is nothing to say, please ring. POETS day: Push Off Early Tomorrow's Saturday. John was firmly in the bosom of his family for the weekend that stretched ahead without promise. A two-day interlude of keeping company with the cat and trying not to drive herself mad. Feeling guilty all the time, as if she had done nothing and nothing had been learned. But it had. And it was not as if there was nothing to do but wait and wonder. She could write anonymous letters for Amy; she could tend her garden, all three inches of it, and if Helen was true to her word, read about Rollie Fisher. It would not be the same Fisher, life was never as simple as that, and of course, if she were the private detective of fiction, she would have had a grizzled police contact to assist with vital information, unearthed from illegal sources and freely given for the price of a drink in a grubby bar in Soho. Recasting herself as another kind of woman altogether, fleet of foot and as fearless in enterprise as an avenging angel, amused her somewhat on the way home, but not for long. Helen's blithe remarks about how profitable it could be to orchestrate a libel were only an echo of what had already entered her mind and stayed there like indigestion. Who *had* started the Petty libel which seemed so unimportant now? That aspect of the thing had never been touched; nor had John been assiduous in trying to find out. *Like an insurance scam.*

Supposing Douglas was short of dosh, and he had set the whole thing up as a gamble, and hadn't he been a bit of a gambling man? Nobody set up a libel which made them look such a fool. Not a vain man, anyway. Her handbag remained silent on the way home. With the mobile phone inside it, it gave her the impression of being alive, a small animal in its own right, ready to squawk. POETS day afternoon was dull and cloudy. The flowers in the tiny garden did not need her. Amy Petty needed her and Amy did not ring. Amy's tan handbag sat on the kitchen table, squatting there in mute imitation of a cat. There were three bottles of wine in the rack, pushing their necks to her, temptingly.

Slowly, without thinking about it in advance, Elisabeth rummaged in the *Petty v Associated Press* folder which stood by her bed and found the video the newspaper had supplied, declining to name the source or the camera-man. The photos came from that. She slotted it into the video.

It could have been any wintry lawn. There was the golden dog, lolloping across the grass in the direction of the woods, the road and freedom. Followed by the ungainly figure of Douglas Petty, with his bare legs and barrel chest half-covered in the striped pyjama jacket, brandishing a piece of wood. Elisabeth froze the frame. The wood looked heavy enough to hurt. She shivered. The man with his naked genitalia and fierce expression launched himself on the animal, bringing it down. They squirmed together on the ground, for all the world like lovers locked in the combat of copulation. She could see the steps leading into the house, the white of the stucco faintly visible as a backdrop to the thrashing couple, before the picture flickered into a blur of branches, then nothing. Elisabeth went back to the beginning. She did not laugh as she and John had done when they first saw it; instead she felt squeamish, felt it was she herself pointing a camera through the bare branches of the willow tree to catch a man being a beast, salivating at the sight of naked-ness and an act of bestial madness. Maybe they were both growling. Something was. There was a thunderous knocking at her front door.

It was only a small house; the application of a fist on the door was enough to make it shake, or so it felt, and interrupted in this voyeuristic viewing which was already making her feel ashamed, Elisabeth was annoyed. Why not ring the dinky little bell which gave delicate warning of visitors? The thumping resumed after a pause and she had the unpleasant image of a burly policeman outside, ready with a warrant of arrest, flanked by a posse of curious neighbours. Guilt made her think like that. She ran to the door. There was a peephole she never used and did not use now. The thundering on the door indicated emergency. What the . . . ?

'What the *fuck* do you want?' she shouted. Christ, her language was getting worse.

There was no time for words. Little Jimmy, the Pettys' factotum, stood on the other side, his fist raised to knock again. A large fist, she noticed, for such a small man. The battered estate car was parked in the street, dirtier than any other vehicle. Greetings were not in order.

'What fucking kept you?' he said and pushed her inside.

Pushed, pulled, could have been either. They half stumbled into the living room where she had been watching the video, the freeze-framed picture glowing on the screen, Douglas locked on the bucking dog. Close, like this, Jimmy smelt of dog hair and sweat, a smell she remembered from the front seat of the car with the closed windows.

'Get your *fucking* hands off me!'

'Oh, don't be a silly bitch. I've been sent to fetch you.'

'You *what*?'

'*You what?*' he mimicked. 'Are you deaf? S'pose you must be if you don't hear the fucking door. You're to come over for a drink, he says. Since you won't bring the fucking handbag back. I been sent to fetch it and you alongside. If you'd be so kind. Won't take long. Same fucking county.'

His slightly squint eyes were taking in the details of the room in a way that made her feel peculiarly self-conscious about it, as if he was a prospective buyer for her house and she should be hurling herself over the cracks, the rude bastard. She was not afraid of him, merely angry and desperately wanting to hide the television, with the frozen frame of Douglas Petty. Possibly that frame on the screen said more about her taste than the whole house put together and she moved to stand in front of it. He pushed her aside. She heard the phone in the kitchen which she had turned on to fax bleeping the receipt of a paper message.

'Fuck you, lady . . . is that the kind of thing you watch, is it? Well bugger me. I seen that one, too. It's himself, isn't it? Nice arse, for his age. A wee bit more photogenic than my own.'

'Wouldn't be difficult,' she snapped.

He looked at her and laughed. There was something primeval about him, like a goblin lately arrived from a swamp, dried-off and scaly, pleased with himself, utterly confident in this alternative world of fucking suburbia.

'Nooo. He's plenty of backside, that one. Like yourself. Needs to lose a wee bitty weight, maybe. Here, go back to the start. It's a good one, this. People'd pay good money to see this. Turn it back to the start.'

She picked up the remote and did exactly as she was told, rewinding the tape to the beginning of its two-minute stretch, amazed, at one remove, at her own complicity. It did not seem surprising that Jimmy slumped into a chair as if he had been invited and she had offered to slip out to the kitchen for a cold beer.

'This is good, this is,' he repeated. Somehow the remote was in his hands. She could feel the imprint of his fingers on her arm where he had grabbed her, sat in the seat opposite and listened while he used the same hand to stab towards the screen, explaining his commentary.

'See this dog here? That's Josh. He's a wanderer, he. Came tae us with his sillybitch sister, too big for the old woman who kept them. Only handsome hound we have. The bitch is pregnant, see, with bad hips and all, retrievers, they have that, overbred bitches, wee hips, big pups, no good. Got me sacked, that sillybitch. Didn't realise she'd whelp so soon, had to be watched, pups might kill her. I get drunk, he sacks me. This is later.'

She was lost and he was entirely at home, beginning to chuckle. Bring on the ice creams.

'Well, there's a man over the way who'd shoot Josh if he comes near their bitch. Douglas won't take the bollocks off a dog. Stupid bastard. Plus Dell wanted to kidnap him, to prove some fucking point – she likes the good-looking ones. Fucking pedigree. Dougie would have been down there to look after the bitch and her pups, that time of year, anyways. He'd have made Amy stay in bed. That Josh is a wily bastard. Look at the great daftie! Did you ever see any such thing?' He roared with laughter. Douglas was romping over the screen.

Elisabeth could not work out what Jimmy was laughing at. Maybe he just laughed, the way hyenas did; he had the same pointy face and funny eyes. The golden dog moved. Jimmy was fumbling in his pockets with one hand, fetching out cigarettes and crumbs of tobacco. She wished she could open the window, but she did nothing of the kind. The car stood dirtily in front of her house, darkening the room, and then the cat, the treacherous cat, crept into the room and stole into his lap as if it knew that warm, smelly space was there and she hated it for that.

'See this? He'll have been sleeping down there, gone out for a pee and let the damn dog out. It runs, he chases, that bloody dog loves a game. Retriever? Won't swim, won't *retrieve* a fucking thing, except a stick. See how he throws the stick to one side? Makes him veer a bit. Gives Dougie a chance to bring him down. Yesss! Goal! Fucking dog always stops for a piece of wood to chew. Never fucking brings it back. Look at the daft bastard. That Josh, silly as arseholes.'

'He looks like he's fucking it,' Elisabeth said.

'You *what*?'

'*Fucking* fucking it. Douglas fucking it.'

Jimmy looked gobsmacked. His mouth hung slack and then he giggled. '*Douglas,* fucking it? But it's a fucking *dog*. Fucking impossible. Give us a break.'

'So what's he doing then?'

'Look, sunshine, he's chasing a wandering dog to save it getting shot. Or give Dell a chance. He's been out for a pee in the cold and lost his trousers when he sees him go. He's thrown a stick and got it to go sideways, then he grabs the sodding dog any way he can, right? What do you think a dog would do if a man tried to bugger it, for God's sake? Bite his fucking head off, for God's fucking sake, that's what it would do. Get him in the leg, at least. Dogs might trust you, yeah, but not that much. Fucking hell. Don't you know *anything*? Josh'd take your arm off. Didn't you see him throw the stick?'

The film blurred to the end. Jimmy shook his fist at the screen and drew a deep gasp of his fag before grinding the stub beneath his heel on her carpet. It was an oatmeal carpet, easily scarred. Maybe tomorrow it would matter, or next week, when John would notice. *Shit.*

'They're strong, retrievers,' Jimmy said admiringly, as the video blurred into branches. 'Muscular dogs. Couldn't be buggered, oh no. Never a dog, they know when they're being hurt. A bitch in heat, though, that's another matter. Take anything. Tried it myself, but I was only an ignorant lad then. Only the once. I think she liked it. Come on, we gotta go.'

'I'm not going anywhere.'

'The fuck you are. All that pissing about with trains you do. Same fucking county, what's wrong with a car? Shall I switch this off? Good one, this was. Come on.'

The cat fled off his lap as he rose.

'You can fucking wait, Jummy!' she shouted. 'I'm going to wash my face and comb my hair and—'

'Why? Fancy our Douglas, do you? You've got no fucking chance. He's in love already—'

'SHUT UP! What does he want?'

He grinned, showing brown teeth. It was a slow smile of satisfaction. 'He wants a fucking referee. Stop him doing murder, mebbe. OK, I'll wait.'

What to look like? A fucking lawyer? She went upstairs and put on jeans and a long shirt. Brushed her hair with a trembling hand, thought of shinning down the drain-pipe outside the back window, went back to the kitchen instead, collected Amy's handbag, stowed it in her brief-case with a notebook. This way, she could pretend that the expedition was official. Jimmy did not disturb these preparations. He was watching the television, roaring with laughter at some cartoons, not a care in the world, listen-ing out for her all the same. There was a brief temptation to open the back door and attempt to escape over the garden wall, but embarrassment made her hesitate. The thought of hauling herself over the prickly roses onto next door's minute lawn was a deterrent. The TV fell silent.

'I think you've had time enough,' Jimmy said from the doorway. 'Anyway, it's a nice evening for a drive.'

'It's your bloody driving I'm worried about.'

'What d'you mean? What's wrong with it?' He was hurt. Pretending to be hurt, while being at the same time manically cheerful, steering her out of the house and opening the car door for her like an assiduous cab driver working towards a large tip, grinning at her as if she was his favourite fare. She settled into the seat obediently. Surprised to find that she did not really mind the bullying; it was almost pleasant to relinquish control. Then she was afraid; she knew he would black her eye and break her nose without a second thought; there was a challenge in behaving as if it was almost normal. A rural ride on a late Friday afternoon. Ha ha.

And it was a novelty, almost, to travel by car. Other people lived in them, treated them as an extension of their homes and themselves in a way she could not imagine.

'Clean this car often, do you, Jimmy? Smells nice.'

'Aw, shut your face, woman. What's the point in cleaning a car? It only gets dirty again.'

He drove slower than she remembered, perhaps in deference to her presence, or perhaps to the traffic, it was difficult to tell. She could not visualise the route in her mind; train travel ruined her sense of geography; she followed the logic of train lines rather than roads. He might be taking her to a different destination than the one promised, a deserted quarry, a railway siding, a rubbish tip for a ritual homicidal dispatching, but reason predominated; she had done nothing to deserve that and besides, she no longer cared. The weather was muggily warm; black-fly weather, pleasant with the window open. At a set of traffic lights, Jimmy shrugged off his jacket, revealing a grubby singlet and releasing his underarm smell. Not as bad as she feared. Like his legs, Jimmy's arms had slender, well-defined muscles. He would be a good subject for a life-drawing class. Then, as he indicated left and hauled at the wheel, she noticed how both forearms were purpled with bruises, some old, some new.

'Where'd you get the bruises, Jimmy? Fighting?'

He laughed. 'Naa, I'm too fucking old. Bruises are just something you get if you hang around dogs. Occupational hazard.'

'How's that?'

'Don't you know anything? They knock you over. They play; they nip.'

'Oh.'

The car lurched on to a stretch of motorway. There was an ominous knocking sound as it gained speed. She saw a sign for London and felt slightly reassured.

'What *is* all this about, Jimmy?'

'He said not to tell you, just bring you.'

'Those puppies, Jimmy, the ones that got you fired, what happened to them?'

'They went to good homes. Easy to find good homes for pups with a touch of *pedigree*,' he added scathingly. 'Old, sick dogs, not the same. You keep those until they die.'

The knocking in the engine stopped as if it was tired of making the noise. They left the motorway and turned through a recognisable town. The conversation was between bouts of gazing at the green fields, listening to Jimmy whistling. The briefcase looked incongruous in this car. Only twenty-six hours since she had promised Amy Petty she would keep silent; she must remember that.

It was the most beautiful time of the day when they turned into the valley which held the white house hidden discreetly in a fold. The sun was low in a rosy sky; the colours of the trees so vibrant they hurt the eyes. Look at me, they seemed to say; look how fine I am. The curve of the bright white house disappeared as they went round the back. A house without an entrance; a secret house. *Everyone who deals with dogs has a few bruises.* Now, there was a context to that, and she was struggling with it, even while mesmerised by the light and clutching her briefcase as if it contained state secrets. Amy Petty bruised by contact with dogs rather than a husband. Douglas not a rude *bugger*, but the soul of sweet nature, merely addicted to the protection of animals . . . For reasons he did not explain, Jimmy parked the car by the stables and led her up the rutted track round the side of the house and over the lawn. The willow tree breathed appreciation of the day; there were brilliant green hostas by the steps. The great semi-circle of windows basked in the sun. Surely this house civilised all who lived within it, the master included. There was no need to be afraid. An echo of Amy's voice . . . *Douglas? Beat ME?* She followed Jimmy into the room, via those glorious windows, ready to be cool, calm, collected, forgiving and discreet, whatever Mr Petty, the master of this house, wanted, her eyes adjusting to the indoor light. He was the client. She had the handbag; she was in control. The curtains confused her; the room was different, dark and dramatic with the windows shrouded. She stumbled over the step, saw the interior and screamed, short and sharp, before Jimmy put his hand over her mouth.

Caterina Petty was sitting on a stool, fetched from the kitchen, with her legs twisted round the legs of the stool and her feet bare. Her back was supported by the pillar of the fireplace surround. With her legs parted and her feet shoeless, she looked inelegant and her once pristine white linen shirt was creased and stained with a slick of brown down the front. Her face was pale. Mrs Isabel Petty lolled in the armchair to the left of the fireplace, both of them facing outwards towards the windows. There was a large pressure bandage on the left side of her head, which she held with her left hand. The other hand was taped with Elastoplast to the arm of the chair. Her face was pink, and she moaned softly. Her feet were also bare. The lack of shoes and the dirtiness of their clothes seemed to strip them of dignity. It was as if they were prisoners. To Elisabeth's eyes, the scene was barbaric.

'Don't worry,' Jimmy said in her ear, pointing rudely at Mrs Petty, 'we've had the vet out to her.'

Douglas was standing between the women in front of the fireplace. The mirror above him reflected the light which entered, almost like a spotlight, from the French doors. The room was muffled. Each woman had a small side table to her left with a glass on it. He held a bottle of whisky. Another empty bottle was on the floor. The smell of cigar smoke lingered.

'Took your time, Jimmy, didn't you?' Douglas said mildly, nodding at Elisabeth. She sat in an armchair as bidden, facing the ghastly tableau of sickly women. Caterina glared at her, then she tried a conspiratorial smile. Elisabeth churned with sudden pity for her, mixed with fear.

'So what've you been doing that's so fucking useful?' Jimmy snapped back at Douglas.

'Language, Jimmy, please, not in front of the ladies. I've been keeping them comfortable and making sure they have enough to drink Take another sip, Mother, please do. It's good for you.'

He took the glass from the table and, with one hand round her shoulder, guided the half-full whisky glass to her lips. She drank obediently, but weakly and slowly as if beyond protest. He wiped her chin with a clean handkerchief and patted her arm gently. 'Mustn't have *too* much with the paracetamol, must we? But enough. And you mustn't keep scratching yourself.' He turned to Caterina. 'And now you, my dear,' placing the other glass in her grubby hands. His solicitude was appalling.

'No.'

'Yes. All of it.' She drank.

Elisabeth smelt the liquor and felt sick. 'Mr Petty,' she said loudly. 'This is bloody monstrous. They're ill, both of them. You can't do this . . . If you don't—'

'Thank you for coming,' he interrupted her, with the same dreadful mildness. 'Very kind of you. I wanted you to take notes, if you wouldn't mind. And they aren't ill. They're intoxicated with my sole company, perhaps. And all *girls* get a little demoralised, I suppose, if someone discourages them from washing or changing their clothes.

Or wearing their shoes. They love their shoes. Jimmy, get the lady a drink. I think she'd prefer wine. White or red?'

'I . . . white.'

'Good. Did you bring the handbag?'

She took it out of the briefcase.

'Thank you so much.' He had a lovely voice.

He cradled the handbag briefly in his arms and then put it gently on the floor. Jimmy shuffled back with a wineglass so full, the liquid slopped over the sides as he put it down beside her. She hunted in the bottom of the briefcase for a notebook and pen. Douglas beamed approval. His geniality was utterly intimidating, compelling obedience.

'I'd better bring you up to speed, Miss Manser. I'm afraid my dearest relatives – although, of course, we don't share any blood apart from the bad kind – have been a bit naughty. Something I've suspected for a while, although my lovely stepsister, Caterina, has been very good at deflecting suspicion. Do you know, she had the nerve to tell me that she thought Amy might be the one behind the sabotaging of the dogs? Amy, I ask you. Suggesting a touch of mental instability, perhaps, in poor, silly Amy, who was longing for city life and maybe, just maybe, a lover, although to be fair she didn't suggest that until recently. Where was I? Ah, there you are, Dilly, come in.'

The dog slunk into the room from the kitchen. Elisabeth looked at it. A brindled half greyhound of some age and startling familiarity. Amy's sillybitch, the one without road sense, which came and sat at Douglas's feet between the two women, facing her. The shock paralysed her. No, of course it was not the same animal; it was just another old dog.

Douglas addressed his sister. 'This is a new dog, sis. Just to let you know. She's only here to put things in perspective, make us behave, and she needs to feel at home. Now where was I?'

'Bringing the lady up to speed,' Jimmy murmured.

'Ah yes.' Douglas turned to Elisabeth. 'This morning, very early, my frail stepmother was found mixing slug poison into the dogs' food. Would have made some of them sick, and maybe some of them die. This has happened before, but we never knew who. Then I suppose she might have phoned the local newspaper. Luckily, someone stopped her by hitting her on the head. Jimmy found her. Caterina was next on the scene, I wonder why, and came rushing up to tell me Jimmy had done it. He's hit my mother, sack him. He's hit my stepmother and poisoned the animals, she says. Well, once I saw, I knew it wasn't Jimmy. He'd have made a better job of it, he'd have killed her. And he might be a sad bastard, but he does love dogs. There was a bit of a contretemps. Are you taking this down?'

Elisabeth nodded.

'Right. Question time. Now Mother, why did you do that?' His tone was wheedlingly sweet.

Hers, in reply, was embarrassingly childlike, anxious to please and definitely tipsy. 'I hate those dogs, Dougie dear. All my married life I've lived with them. No one ever put me first. I *hate* those *fucking* dogs. You used to love us best when you were a little boy. We were your world then. We had nice furniture and beautiful things. Then it's dogs, dogs, dogs. Just like your father. Then, with Amy, there was going to be more dogs. No money or comfort for me. I wanted you back. *I HATE DOGS*.'

It was a rapid, breathless delivery. Elisabeth almost admired it.

'Is that why you hated Amy?'

Mrs Petty seemed to consider the question and gave a deep sigh. 'I didn't hate Amy,' she slurred. 'How could anyone hate Amy? There's nothing to hate. I sometimes hate you, though. For what you did to Caterina. Funny how I can hate you and love you at the same time.'

There was a pause. Douglas put his hands on his hips. 'What did I do to Caterina? Apart from squire her round and introduce her to suitable males, bail her out, put her up here between jobs, support her so-called, non-existent career, act as a prop to all those insecurities . . . pick her up and dust her down, try and make her *work* for a living and stop exploiting men . . . What did I *do*?'

Isabel Petty sighed dramatically. Her voice descended to a whisper. 'You know very well. You screwed her, Douglas dear, when she was only twelve and made sure she could never have anyone else but you. She *can't*, you see. And why should she work? *You* don't. You screwed her. Then you screwed her again.'

There was a deathly silence. Douglas leant against the mantelpiece, heavily, his head bowed. The silence continued. The sitting dog got to its feet, the only movement in the room.

'My God, how I get people wrong,' Douglas murmured. 'Tell them it isn't true, Cat. Tell them.'

Caterina smiled glassily. 'Of course it's true.'

She threw back her head and laughed. A shrill, drunken laugh which went on and on. The dog did not like the laughter. It moved next to her stool and growled. Then, in a curious change of mood, began to lick her bare feet with a long, wet tongue.

Caterina screamed.

CHAPTER FOURTEEN

Elisabeth stared at Caterina's toes in disgust. So did Caterina, cringing away from her own feet and then kicking out at the dog. There was a dull thump as the heel of one foot struck the dog's head. The dog lay down without protest, as if this was normal and the best thing to do was to stay quiet. It smelt as if it had been rolling in manure. Only Isabel Petty did not seem to notice what had become an overpowering smell, although her delicate nose wrinkled. Somehow, Elisabeth was not perturbed by the behaviour of the dog and yet shocked by the realisation that yes, it was the same animal and no more surprising that it should recline on an Indian carpet within reach of a dirty, vicious foot than that it should try to kill itself on a busy road. It seemed to have no sense of self-preservation. Nobody said anything until she spoke.

'Well,' she said brightly, 'do I record that as a comment?'

Nobody heard. Caterina, closest to the smell of the dog, pursed her mouth and turned her head away, clenching her fists and presenting a fine profile to the audience. The dog began to whine and paw at the carpet, conscious of wrongdoing, raising a muzzle to regard Caterina's sticky feet. Douglas shushed it. All the time he stared at Caterina, willing her to turn her head. Elisabeth gazed at Douglas. His face was as sad as a bloodhound; he looked every day of his fifty years.

'That's some allergy you have, Miss Petty,' Jimmy ventured, finding the silence unbearable. 'You should be out in fucking hives by now. It'll crap in a minute. Does it all the time.'

'Shut up, Jimmy.' Douglas moved to Caterina's side and touched her shoulder. She flinched, her head still averted. 'Come on, Cat. Can you look at me and say it's all true? I'm afraid the animal's attention was quite misguided, not really affection at all, but don't kick her, she might bite.' He was still terrifyingly mild.

'Any confession obtained under duress is not worth the paper used to write it down,' Elisabeth said loudly. 'It means fuck all, Mr Petty, as you know.'

"Thank you, *Miss* Manser, for that reminder of why I needed a lawyer present, and one of such integrity, too. You're quite right. But this isn't a court of law and no one is going to get hanged. *Yet.* Speak to us, Cat, please.' He ruffled her hair. Finally she turned and let her head rest on his chest. She was very drunk.

'Always loved you,' she said.

'Needed me, Cat.'

'Yeah. That's it. And you needed someone like *her*.' She pointed her tied-up hands at Elisabeth, one holding the other with a single finger extended from her two fists, mimicking a gun. 'Silly cunt.' She let out a deep sigh. 'You never even touched me. Nope, I tell a lie. You slapped me on the leg once. Shame, really. Certainly got her attention, though, didn't it? Stupid Amy.' She turned the gun salute on her mother. 'Bloody tough it is, too. When your mother loves her stepson so much, she won't even challenge him for raping you. Worships the ground he walks on. Jus' like I did. So whadya think it's like, brother? After all those years of trying, all those years of *helping* you, you have everything. Me, nothing. A mother with a conscience, at last.'

She let out a dry sob and clutched at the whisky glass he had already refilled.

'I think you're rewriting history, Cat,' Douglas said wearily. 'A rich stepdaddy who didn't like you much, that was your disease. Amy tried to tell me that before she stopped talking and I stopped listening. And I never counted the money I gave you, Cat, you know that. I simply trusted you and I felt guilty. I thought you respected me.'

She giggled. 'Respect? When you fuck up a career by fooling round and taking your clothes off when you might have loved me? Oh, you *ARSE* . . . When you could have had me for the taking. *Adored* you,' she said dreamily.

He let go of her gently, so that her long back remained supported by the fireplace pillar. He seemed uncertain of what to do next. Elisabeth intervened. Cross-examination came naturally, after all, and she could not resist it. Both women looked ghastly. She could not get over her impression that they were somehow stripped and bound, had to remind herself they were not. The dog and the whisky were the only incentives to tell the truth.

'Did you discuss this with Amy, at all? I mean, is there any chance you did that? Told her how much Douglas had loved you for so long?' *Always address the witness in a manner which encourages them to believe you respect them.*

Caterina turned her bleary eyes in the direction of the windows, squinted at the last of the light coming through, nodded and raised the hands to shield her eyes from the single shaft of the sun. 'Course I did. She had to know he was my love and I was his.'

It seemed as if Douglas might punch her, so tightly were his fists clenched; Jimmy moved across and took hold of his arm. There was a muttered exchange while Douglas shrugged him off, during which Elisabeth sat impassively, shivering. It felt cold, suddenly; not full-scale summer yet and the house had cooled. With the curtains covering the windows in their dramatic folds, the room could not store up the fragile heat of May. Then they were all back in their places.

'And she trusted you,' Elisabeth continued. 'Because you were a good friend to her and helped her with everything. After all, she didn't know anything about any of you, did she?'

'Stupid cow.' The last slug of drink made Caterina more sober by the second. She straightened up and looked smug, just at the point when Elisabeth began to feel sorry for her. 'She didn't know what *he* was like. He'll fuck anything. Except me.'

'You're a fine one to talk,' Jimmy said angrily. 'You've even made a fucking pass in my direction. And that lawyer fella.'

'Which lawyer?' Elisabeth asked.

'Don't be silly,' Caterina said with disdain, looking towards Jimmy. 'When you saw me and Mr Box in The Wheatsheaf, we were merely discussing business. And as for you, you don't even count as *anything*. I'd rather be fucked by a pig. A fucking pig!' Her laughter was shrill.

Jimmy got up and took two steps towards her. 'If that dog craps,' he said, 'it would make a lovely wee face mask.'

'Stop it!' Elisabeth yelled. The dog leapt to its feet. Jimmy retreated and sat down. He fumbled in his pocket for fags. 'Mr Petty, I really do think you should untie your mother.'

'Are you all right, Mummy?' he crooned at her, mimicking her childish voice. She inclined her head, weakly. 'She says she's fine as she is. Jimmy, please do not mention crap.'

Elisabeth leant forward, grasped her wineglass and took a long pull, as if it was beer, conscious as it hit the back of her throat that it was too good for gulping. In the pause, Douglas lit a small cigar. The smell of it was sweet relief. He seemed to be abdicating control of the proceedings to her, like a ringmaster at a circus introducing the clowns. Elisabeth sipped the wine this time, took up her pen and scribbled in the notebook. So far, the page was pristine clean.

'Perhaps Miss Petty can cast some light on the libel which got everyone so upset,' she suggested soothingly. Silence from Caterina. Jimmy nudged a roll in the carpet with his foot. It was Mrs Petty who rallied and spoke, trillingly, from the depths of her chair.

'Such fun,' she said. '*Such* fun. Catty thought of it. Get someone to take some pics. Maybe have Jimmy swearing at the bloody dogs, he does it ever so nicely. Or pics of Amy *talking* to the bloody things, she did it all the time. We could have her declared mad. But then *you*, Douglas dear, you turned up trumps, running about with a stick like that . . . In your jim-jams.'

'Who took the video?' Elisabeth asked.

Isabel Petty waved the hand with the dressing in it, impatient with detail. 'Someone Dell knows. We like Dell, don't we, Cat, even though she is such a *vulgar* woman.' Caterina kept her head turned away. 'Dell would have taken all the dogs away. And Dell's got a cousin in the local paper as vulgar as she is. And we thought it would stop people bringing more dogs, but then the big newspaper took it up and you got furious, didn't you, Douglas dear? No sense of humour.' Her girlish giggle was embarrassing. It made her speak faster so that she could get out the words before the uproarious funniness of the situation quite overcame her. Whilst scribbling doodles in the notebook, Elisabeth was trying to imagine her stirring poison into the animal feed and found it all too easy.

'So, whoopsadaisy, all these lawyers. Well, that was all right. Nice to have visitors and Amy so upset too. Cat wanted it to go on, because Douglas might get lots of

money at the end and give her some. Or lose Amy somewhere along the line, something like that . . . Give me a
drinkipoos, darling.'

Douglas obliged. Her polished nails clinked on the
glass as she drank like a hungry bird.

'Where was I? Oh yes. It all went too far. Once Amy
was gone and we had Douglas to ourselves, it was all
going to be all right, you see. But Douglas was still going
to go on with it, that lawyer *insisted* . . .'

'Which lawyer?' Elisabeth asked, sharply this time.

Isabel Petty squinted at her. 'Not *you*, dear, the other
one. That thin man who sniffed. Lovely face, like a statue.'

Elisabeth wrote in her notebook, *Box the Fox*, and kept
silent.

Isabel fixed her with a radiant smile. 'So I thought,' she
said, with amazing clarity, 'it was time for another disaster. Only someone hit me.'

'Who hit you, Mummy?' Caterina crooned.

The smile receded and the question confused her.
With the wavering hand, she pointed at Elisabeth. '*She*
did. I think.'

'It was Jimmy,' Caterina said through gritted teeth.
Jimmy picked a clump of fur from the carpet, moulded it
into a neat lump and lobbed it into her lap. She screamed
and squirmed until it fell on to the floor. Then she began
to cry, slumped against the support of the fireplace pillar,
tilting dangerously.

'What exactly did you tell Amy?' Douglas asked quietly.

'I think we can guess the rest,' Elisabeth interrupted. 'I

think she would have manipulated Amy's sense of inferiority into believing she was neither valued nor loved. And I think that's enough, Mr Petty. I really do. There are limits and you're going way beyond them.'

He nodded. There was a weariness in the nod which did not correspond with the deftness of his movements. He reached a piece of damp towel from the mantelpiece and, for a split second, Elisabeth thought he would wrap it round his stepsister's throat. Instead he simply wiped her feet, gently, and caught her as she fell sideways. Then he hoiked her over his shoulder and carried her in a fireman's lift towards the door. He patted her on the back like someone burping a baby. 'Bedtime,' he stated. His heavy footsteps sounded in the stone corridor and, more distantly, up the stairs. Jimmy went across to Mrs Petty and removed the Elastoplast which held her wrist to the arm of her chair. He chafed her wrist.

'She would keep scratching,' he said. 'Wee bit of arnica for this bruise on the head, maybe,' he murmured briskly. 'Works a treat.' Mrs P did not respond. Her head settled comfortably against the leather of her seat and she began to snore, softly. Jimmy shook his head in amazement. 'Don't know how you can sleep with a conscience like that,' he said admiringly. 'And that son of yours can take you to bed, 'cos I'm not going to carry you.'

Douglas came back into the room and repeated the fireman's lift with his mother, disappearing again in the direction of upstairs. The atmosphere was suddenly lighter.

'More wine?' Jimmy asked. Her glass was empty. The image of the women as captives suddenly faded.

'I'd kill for another glass of wine.' She could have drunk the whole cellar, felt mildly hysterical. Jimmy left and came back with the wine. He seemed to be able to traverse the passageway between kitchen and here with remarkable speed and presented a clean glass, again over-flowing, with the cool, pale liquid spilling over his grubby brown hand. The same hand which dealt with dirty dogs. She tried not to think of that, slumped back against her own chair, looked round the room and took several deep breaths. The feeling of hysterical relief faded. She tried to focus, took refuge in looking around.

'It's different in here, Jimmy. Why the hell have the curtains gone up? It's so gloomy.'

' 'Cos it's supposed to be elegant. Fucking art.'

'Wouldn't take long to pull them down.'

'Dead right it wouldn't.'

There was a brief silence, with noises in the distance. 'Did you know about any of this before, Jimmy?'

He shuffled, uncomfortably, not uncomfortable enough to hide a gleeful gaiety. 'Aye, I did, I suppose. Some of it. Sometimes I heard Amy chatting to the dogs. I saw the way those bitches treated her and watched her change. I never knew about the fucking libel, though, I really never. Is there really money in that rubbish?'

She thought of John Box and his need of money. 'Yes, there is.'

'Well I never. One fool born, two to take him. What's keeping the man? Can't take so long to bed down a couple of drunks. Come here, you daft creature, you've not done badly.'

The dog ambled across, put a head on his knee and wagged its tail.

'She's nice enough but she's got no road sense, though,' Elisabeth said, and then corrected herself hastily. 'I *bet* she has no road sense. Not much by way of domestic manners, either. She smells and she goes towards the person who hates her.'

'Manners? In that case, we'll get along fine. There's no point having manners if you live here.'

Mrs Petty's slender stick still rested by her chair. It looked as if the silver had been polished to a shine. A useless stick, except as a weapon. The assailant had not drawn blood. Elisabeth tried not to think of Amy Petty wielding that stick. The woman she had met the day before did not seem capable of getting on a bus, let alone driving a car. How had she done it? Of course she had not done it. But if it had been Amy wielding the stick which struck her mother-in-law, surely that exonerated Elisabeth herself from her promise of silence? Was that the reason Amy had been borrowing time? To cause mayhem? No, it was impossible; the dog was a different dog, and a promise was a promise, regardless. Douglas came back, sat in his mother's place, recharged his glass and raised it to her. He took a sip, reached for his wife's handbag and put it in his lap.

'They'll sleep like babies and no harm done, Miss Manser. Does that reassure you?'

She sipped and considered her reply. 'It might, Mr Petty, if you could give me a guarantee of good behaviour towards them in the morning. Steady on the threats of dogshit and the booze, if you see what I mean. Whatever they've done.'

He sipped his whisky. 'It may be far too old-fashioned to say I give you my word on that, but I do. For what it's worth.' He sipped again. 'Besides, they'll be busy packing their bags. They can both go and live in Cat's cottage. Don't worry, they won't starve. Even though they have a daft notion of how much I'm worth and it'll never be enough.'

'It was love that they wanted,' she said quietly.

He smiled at her, not the ferocious smile she had seen him bestow on John Box, but a real smile. Then he sighed. 'That's as maybe. But mine was spoken for.'

'Dogs,' she said flatly, eyeing the beast with its muzzle in Jimmy's lap. 'Spoken for by dogs.'

'Not entirely. The animals and the two women were a sacred trust given to me by Father. I love the dogs because I can make a difference, and I love them more because Amy does. Amy herself is another matter. I didn't choose Amy because she shared my passions. I chose her because she is the greatest of them. Do you know where she is, Elisabeth?'

The use of the present tense for Amy and the question, delivered like a lethal bullet at the end, shook her new-found composure and she spilled the wine. Scrubbed at the mark of it on her jeans with the sleeve of her shirt, ineffectually, affected by his voice. So smooth, almost without inflection, almost hypnotic. No wonder John Box envied him.

'I beg your pardon? Amy's *dead*, Douglas.' Saying his

name out loud sounded odd, as if she had never referred to him as such in private.

'*Afghan loves Rottweiler*,' Douglas said dreamily. His voice had a mesmeric quality when he spoke as softly as this. 'And now at least, I know how my darling wife came by the extraordinary notion that I neither needed nor adored her. Post-its, bloody footprints on the kitchen floor. Clarins creams gone from flat, my own conviction. A dog like Dilly. I was so relieved to be right, I could have wagged my fucking tail.'

'I haven't got the faintest idea what you're talking about,' Elisabeth said with complete conviction.

He sighed again. 'Probably not. Did you find anything in the handbag?'

'Plenty.'

'And?'

'And nothing. I met a man on the train who thought the world of her. He served the tea.'

Douglas shouted with laughter. 'That figures. Probably small, perfectly formed and rude to her. Like Jimmy. She has the knack of liking the unlikable.'

HAS. Jimmy grinned, manifestly unoffended.

'I should like to go home now,' Elisabeth said. She sounded to her own ears like a child wanting to be taken away early from the party, pompous and petulant.

'Of course,' Douglas said quickly. 'Don't you like the wine?'

'I like it far too much. It bears no comparison to what I usually drink. In other circumstances, I would enjoy it hugely; but if you'll excuse my prudishness, I'm in a state of shock. What on earth possessed you to cover the windows?' They were talking in non sequiturs. She could not help it. She wanted neither to go nor to stay. She felt like an alien recently landed on the wrong planet where the air did not allow for quiet breathing.

'Caterina did them,' Douglas said. 'She said it lent style to the room. It probably does. Jimmy, for God's sake have a drink and call the taxi. Luscious Lizzie's had enough alarms without being driven home by you. Besides, I don't want to ruin her reputation and I'm worried about the suspension. Sorry, I do mean the car.'

Jimmy poured what looked like a quarter pint of whisky into a glass and exited again, to the kitchen. The dog followed. Elisabeth was relieved about that. The dog puzzled her to death. Jimmy came back in his jaunty, jack-in-the-box style with another glass of wine for her.

'Ten minutes, petal. Time for you to drink it.'

'You'd be a good butler, Jimmy,' she said. They all sipped in unison. It felt ridiculously easy, although the curtains shrouding the room from the dusk outside made it seem as if they were all talking underwater. She had been here four times before and missed the view from here to beyond as if she belonged.

'There is this funny business about *trust*,' Douglas said to her. 'I don't know what it is. Or how it's formed, I really don't. Sometimes it takes an age to acquire, sometimes a second. I haven't the faintest idea why I trust you, but I do. I learned it from my father. Blind trust, sometimes, but always worth repeating. Amy didn't have that chance. She didn't have the chance to learn it and I managed to deny her the chance to acquire it. I don't trust that leader of yours, I'm afraid. It's a strange phenomenon, isn't it, *trust*? Something akin to respect. Acknowledgement, mutual recognition. The bare bones of love, but not the same. Dogs trust Amy. There's a kind of power in her innocence. I hope I never lose the habit of trusting to instinct. It works far more often than not.'

Elisabeth bowed her head, humiliated for no reason she had time to analyse. She knew she had been trusted, even if she had been bullied into it. She did not trust him, any more than she could have thrown him, which was a matter of inches, but she knew the accolade of being trusted and she knew she liked Jimmy. Probably because of his poetic influence on her language and all the *fuckings* he employed in his own. She pulled herself together with a visible effort. Pushing up the sleeves of her shirt, squashing the useless briefcase shut, which was easy with only the notebook inside it. A notebook of the type widely used in the profession, blue on the outside, serrated and lined pages within, slimline and harmless. The sound of a car horn sounded from the back. She finished the wine and stood up, slightly unsteady, put the handbag over her shoulder. Douglas extended his hand. It was warm and dry.

'Goodbye, Elisabeth. Thank you for bringing back the handbag.' He hesitated. 'I do know that trust isn't recip-rocal, but if you do happen to know where my wife is and trust me enough to tell me, please do.'

'I think she's dead at the moment, Douglas.'

He shook her hand. The grip was so strong she had the suspicion the forearm would fall off at the elbow.

'Thinking's a far fucking cry from believing.' That was Jimmy, grumbling at her side as they went through to the back door, crossing the alien kitchen, where the new dog skulked, luxuriously, beside a Rayburn oven which looked as if it had been born in the last millennium.

'Know any good jokes, Jimmy?' she said.

'Don't know no fucking jokes.'

'Well there's one about ovens. Do you know the correct way to refer to a middle-class pregnancy? You can't say she's got a bun in the oven. You have to say she's got a fucking ciabatta in the Aga. Oh, forget it.'

He was ushering her into a new-looking Ford with polished interior, a swinging deodoriser over the back window and a woman driver winking at him from behind the wheel.

'What are you going to do now?' she shouted at him from the back seat as he shooed her into it in the same way he had shooed the dog out of the room.

'Pull down those fucking curtains,' he yelled back. 'It's the only way I'll get the bastard to mourn. He can't do it with the windaes shut.'

The car slid away, bumping down the track with cautious ease. She looked back towards the house, seeing the white curve of the half-dome with no idea of whether she would ever see it again and, as soon as it was out of view, missing the sight of it like a mild indigestion, all the way home.

A short way home, quicker than arrival, the roads emptier now. Not black night, but dusk night, dark without being entirely dark, fumbling on the brink of night. Rain out there, somewhere, fucking up the view. A nice car, three colossal glasses of wine, the equivalent of a bottle, and fuck this, did she have the fare? Life was an empty briefcase. *Luscious Lizzie*; the bastard, how dare he?

The car cruised neatly between country and town, across motorway and centre and side road and finally into the terrace where she lived. She played cat's cradle with her fingers. Laced them one over another and turned them inside out. It was a nice car, without bumps and crumps, with a silent, efficient driver. The sight of her own door was a shock on account of it being so small, she felt she should stoop to open it. Jimmy's fistprints were in the dust, lit by the useless security light, the imprints of his knuckles lit above the central handle. All paid, the driver said; must've cost a fortune. She fumbled with the key and opened her own little door as if she was a stranger.

Stored heat. A yowling cat, as well it might. Food for it. The winking answerphone, the mobile phone she had left behind. *Shit*. The fax machine, attached to the phone, last heard whirring as she went out, a year ago.

She wanted to bury her head in a piece of nice warm sand somewhere. Or lie in a hot bath and think, but she also wanted something to do. The relative harmlessness of paper was easier to deal with than the accusing sound of voices, so Elisabeth began with the fax, postponing the messages. Coffee in one hand, chocolate in the other as the proper way to read. She would never have thought that the sight of neat handwriting attached to several sheets of legal prose would be soothing. Her friend Helen was always legible, probably thought in legal prose, or at least formal prose, infected with the sometimes sonorous language of judges. No effing and blinding – neat, unadorned work. Helen would never call her Lizzie. Helen was as sleek as an otter.

Dear Elisabeth,

Here's an extract from the judgement in R v Fisher. He was forty years old at the time, in 1975; would that make the ages correspond to indicate it's the same Fisher?

The judgement deals with points of law, of course, and there's only a short precis of the facts, so I'm allowing myself to read between the lines. Apart from the legal points, the case had some notoriety at the time, because he was an art teacher and it was early days for the 'outing' of 'respectable' sex offenders in positions of authority. What he actually DID was not so bad; if you put activity short of penile penetration or fellation in that category. It must have been more titillation and gratification for him than release. (Put another way, he kept his tackle inside his trousers, but liked copping a feel.) The worst aspects were his isolation of each little girl in turn, his penchant for what he sweetly called 'duskies', and his chosen method of keeping them quiet. Which was to introduce them to glue-sniffing (I suppose you may as well use what comes to hand). They were all about ten years old. A very persuasive man, but, unfortunately for him, the aberrant behaviour caused by fun and games with glue was what brought the thing to light, although it dented the credibility of the witnesses and confused their memories. (One had also been encouraged to 'taste' lead paint. I think they have less poisonous materials in schools these days.)

Two interesting facts (why do I do this for you, the way I used to write your essays? Why don't I let you read it for yourself?):

ONE: Fisher's daughter was to have been his alibi for the occasion of the most serious assault, but denied being with him at the time.

TWO: THE PROSECUTOR WAS ONE DOUGLAS PETTY. An old hand here says he was a real tough one in his youth and did a lot of deviancy cases. Perhaps it infected him? Turned him into an animal?

More importantly, my dear, I spoke to Superintendent Bailey, who is working on the train crash. The victim with the broken neck you mentioned is down on record as travelling alone. However, the partner to whom the death was reported at home later that day is a travelling salesman 'not unknown to police'. (I can't say more than that.)

And FINALLY, I have to tell you that I can't let your cryptic remarks about Amy Petty rest there. It just isn't on. Why should conscientious people spend days investigating these terrible deaths only to have the facts distorted by someone pretending to be dead or hurt? It isn't right and it isn't fair. I know you meant it to be confidential but some things just cannot be that. There's such a thing as public duty, you know. So Bailey will be coming to see you tomorrow and if there's anything to tell, I advise you to be frank.

Yours, whenever you need me,
Helen

Oh why oh why did she always get people so wrong? Underestimate them, overestimate them; inflate them, deflate them, but consistently misjudge? And what price promises? The coffee burned her mouth, the chocolate furred her teeth and the cat twined round her ankles. 'Bugger off,' she told it. Oh Christ, and now she was talking to animals, too. She threw the coffee down the sink and resisted the impulse to smash the mug against the wall. Faced with a police interrogator tomorrow, she would blab, of course she would; she was not an investigative journalist insured to protect her sources. Her and her own big mouth and fuck Helen, what about trust? She put down the fax with shaking hands. The paper had an unpleasant texture which stuck to her fingers. Should have done the phone first, maybe it was easier after all.

There were two messages on the mobile phone, the first echoing with desperation.

'Elisabeth, where are you? Oh I wish you were there. It's Amy. Can you come back tomorrow, soon? Now? *PLEASE?* Save me . . . from myself . . .'

Elisabeth phoned back the number shown on the mobile's screen. Heard the lonely, continuous ring and imagined the deserted callbox with the traffic thundering by.

CHAPTER FIFTEEN

The bright lights of the Asda superstore were very bright.
It was an alternative world, all by itself. When she entered
the place that Friday morning on her flight from Bayview
Road, Amy concluded that this was where everyone went.
Into the equivalent of the parish church, built on a larger
scale. They came here from the deserted pavements as
soon as they had discovered where it was. They got into
their cars and came here to pay homage. A pedestrian like
herself, approaching a side door, felt like a pilgrim,
entirely different to the imperfect country housewife she
had been before, dumping the car, grabbing the family-
sized trolley, safe in the knowledge of the credit card and
the large, affordable order. Without people and dogs to
feed, she felt strange, limped through the aisles, distracted
by the music, unenchanted by the place but busy, concentrating. It was another kind of normality. She wished
she had found it sooner; it was a hopeful hive of activity.

She selected one cheap tracksuit, the same dun green of the canvas shoes, carefully chosen for price and lack of pattern. She did not like patterns. The clothes section looked as if it had been picked over by a million hands, feeling for bargains, but the presence of *new* things was thrilling. She put the suit into her basket, turned to tour the other aisles. Two pairs of socks, two of knickers, one tube of E45 moisturising cream, which she clutched like a talisman. She wandered through the two dozen aisles of food, unable to focus, but planning all the time. There was everything here; even on a budget her father did not need to eat in the way he did. She would come back, get food to whet his appetite, make him think of food rather than anything else. A well-nourished body would make for a quieter soul. For the moment, all she selected was a litre bottle of whisky and a packet of cigarillos, because she wanted the smell of both, all of which went into the basket along with a packet of bright hair slides. She paid carefully and found the ladies' lavatory by the exit. In the safety of a cubicle, she changed into the tracksuit. The sleeves of the top and the legs of the bottom were too long; the fabric was harsh and mostly synthetic, but the freshness of it was delicious. She bound back her hair with a purple hairgrip and saw in the mirror a renewed, almost respectable person, less alien than the one who had arrived, and felt an enormous sense of achievement, exaggerated into pride as she stuffed the skirt into a rubbish bin.

At the checkout, she had watched someone slide a packet of sweets into his pocket and wondered if her father might have done that. Perhaps she could be a thief, Amy thought as she waited at the bus stop with the whisky in a bag bumping against her thigh, feeling almost competent. She could be a thief who simply sat in one of those parked cars and drove it away: she could live on stolen food. But a thief required sleight of hand rather than clumsiness, and what would happen when she was arrested? What would they do to her if she simply smiled and smiled, saying nothing, with nothing to identify her? They would have to put her somewhere, if not a safe place, safer than this. Suddenly there seemed to be choices; she would find work, begin again. She felt a surge of optimism; she had new clothes and moisturising cream; her father had bought her shoes. She would get back her money from him and buy good food; she would plan their lives for a week and make a difference. She would protect him.

She should have bought something for him today, as a start, a reminder to him of how they could go on. She remembered that as she opened the front door to see the door of his workroom locked with him busy inside, and despite the determination to somehow begin afresh with him on an honest basis, she was secretly relieved to postpone a conversation again. The fatigue hit her like a brick. She wanted him to see her with all the authority of her new clothes, notice her, ask where she had been, talk to her openly, but she needed above all to close her eyes. She was monstrously tired; she had tricked her grief into submission for a few hours but now her need for sleep was as relentless as toothache.

The new newspapers were on the kitchen table, still folded. Amy placed the whisky by the sink and crept upstairs. When she had slept, she would find the right words to speak to him clearly. He had bought her the shoes. They would sort out a way of living with dignity, protecting each other for a while. In the bathroom, she scrubbed herself in cold water. The habits of cleanliness died hardest. It felt as if a decade had passed since last she slept. She took off the new tracksuit and folded it carefully; it had to last. The sheets on her bed were grey . . . must wash . . . must scrub teeth . . . must sleep . . . must . . . avoid grief. Not cry. A dream-filled sleep. Nonsense dreams, when she was cleaning a house belonging to someone else, rubbing at stains which would not go away on an oatmeal-coloured carpet which was as hairy to touch as the coat of a dog. Elisabeth Manser asking her, why do you bother? The question ballooning out of her fine-featured, expressive face which became as large as the moon. Bother with what? Coarse, chauvinistic, bullying men and old, sick dogs. Her face was nose-down into the pillow. Someone was pressing the back of her head so that it was difficult to breathe; a hand touched her hair. She brushed it away, but still the question had to be answered. *I have always loved dogs ever since I had one and it was taken away. I love them because I am never clumsy with them. I know what to do. I am never afraid of them as I am of almost everything else; they are never afraid of me. I am deft and clever with dogs . . . I make a difference. I have always wanted to make a difference. And Douglas? He was just love.* She could feel Caterina's manicured fingers next, pretending to massage her shoulder, her long nails biting into the flesh, a voice telling her, *Sleep, darling, don't worry about a thing*. Voices drifted from downstairs, entering the room like fog. A door slammed.

Amy woke, breathless. The curtains of the room were stretched shut. Light filtering through the thin fabric showed the contours of the room. The wardrobe stood still, like an empty coffin. There was a sharp smell of whisky in her nostrils and the sound of quiet, cackling laughter. Then a tuneless singing.

Rollie Fisher sat on a chair in the middle of the room, as far away as he could get from the bed, always keeping his distance. '*Rock-a-bye baby, on the tree top, When the wind blows the cradle will rock, When the bough breaks, the cradle will fall, Down will come baby, cradle and all . . .*' He crooned the rhyme in a cracked voice and then laughed some more until she closed her eyes against the sound. Opened them again to see that he was nursing a tumbler of whisky. There was a teacup on the rickety table at the side of the bed, half full of liquid.

'My dear silly daughter, WAKE UP, pet.'

She raised her head.

'Ah, that's better. Isn't it nice to see you? Such a popular woman you are. A man called to see you just now. Said he knew you from the train, you tart, and followed you home. I told him there was no woman here. A *nasty* man.'

'No one's looking for me,' she murmured, groggy with sleep, but still enraged by the lie and the irrational hope it created.

The whisky smell grew stronger. Rollie Fisher reeked of it as he shook with mirth. He was drunk, something she had never seen. He hated drink; said it had almost killed him; she remembered the whisky, left by the sink, her silly, sentimental purchase, made for the smell. Rollie was wicked drunk, uninhibited, talkative, manic. Gleeful.

'I told the man you weren't here so that you would have time to *leave*,' he said with heavy emphasis. 'Soon, sooner, *soonest*. I don't want you here any more, never wanted you at all. You've stayed quite long enough. Tee-hee-hee. I won, didn't I? I won! Don't want you here. I want you to go. I mean go, just bugger off. Those shoes were made for walking.'

'Go?' she said stupidly.

He slurped at the whisky. The pouch of skin beneath his chin trembled; he seemed to be brimming with triumph. He put down the drink, clapped his hands loudly, picked it up again. Part of him was entirely in control.

'You went home, didn't you? I knew you did. And when you went you knew you could never go back. He'd *hate* you if you did. A man like that loathes to be fooled. They dish it out but they can't take it. Too late to go back now, isn't it? You've blown up your own home, ha ha ha.'

She could see that his face was scarlet, his eyes peculiarly bright, like the glass eyes of some of his dolls.

'So you can get out now, Go, go, go. I'm finished with you. Besides, I need the room.'

Amy struggled for words. 'You said I could stay. As long as I wanted.' She knew she was plaintive and frightened, hating it in herself. Panic rose in her throat. She could not imagine how she had ever craved the smell of whisky.

'Listen, dear, I got you the little shoes so that you could walk away. As soon as you can, dearest, before it gets dark, anyway.' Again, the giggle. 'Otherwise I don't know how I shall feed you. Turpentine in the tea, perhaps, please don't tempt me. I can resist anything but.'

Amy sat up, pulling the sheet to cover her shoulders.

'Ugh,' he said, sipping more of the whisky, grimacing at the sight of her.

'Why do I have to go?' she said slowly. 'Where would I go?'

He waved his empty hand. 'Oh, I don't know. Anywhere. I've finished with you really. Even before you frightened away that lovely child next door and invited a strange man to the house. Rock-a-bye baby, great big lump.'

She folded her arms across her knees, watching him.

'Do you know, when I was in prison, I dreamed of this,' Rollie said, tapping the glass. 'All the time. And then when I was out, it made me ill. But it took my mind off his voice, the bastard. Do you know, when you were ten years old, you were as much a conniving little bitch as any of them?'

'I don't know what you mean, Father. Which voice?'

'*His* voice, of course,' he scoffed. 'As if you didn't know it. You probably think of it all the time, too. That lovely, *manly* voice. Making me squirm and cry with his questions. In court, in front of everyone. For years I could hear his voice . . . He made me out to be a leper, made me admit . . . Bastard DOUGLAS PETTY. Handsome Petty once, with a fucking fortune . . .' He transferred the glass from right hand to left and wagged his finger at her. '"Such a *gifted* teacher you were, Mr Fisher,"' he mimicked. '"An *artist*. A trustworthy man. They adored you, those children, did they not? And all you could do was *lust*." He made me admit . . . he made me cry. He made me say . . . He damns with faint praise, assents with civil leer, and without sneering, taught the rest to sneer . . . He *diminished* me into *nothing* . . .' His voice was rising to a scream.

Amy hugged herself tighter. Rollie Fisher went into a paroxysm of coughing, still holding the glass steady.

'That hypocrite, with his *voice*,' he choked. 'Your *spouse*. Was him I wanted, not you. I followed what he did. How could he talk about *lust* when he had all those women? How could he brand ME a *pervert* for loving innocence? And then I saw you,' he went on dreamily, his voice subsiding into a chant. 'In a newspaper. You in that frock, looking ridiculous. He must have loved you to be so blind. He'd forgive you anything if he could forgive that frock. It must have been real *lurve*. Must have loved you to *death*. He had what he wanted, poor fool. He *trusted* you with his happiness. So I thought I would take you away. Leave him with dreams, like me. Mr *Petty* wrecks my life; I wreck his. Simple.'

The outburst exhausted him. His voice became a triumphant whine. 'And then you came to see me and *pitied* me, Mrs *Petty*. *My* daughter who marries my *persecutor*. And you let yourself believe you were my precious, important little thing, even after that treachery! I could never have planned it as good as this. You helped . . . you believed, you *pitied* . . . You *let* yourself be taken away. You came willing. You preferred me to him. How he'd *detest* you if he knew what a credulous fool you are. You can't go back. You can only go to the gutter. And he won't die wondering, because one day I'll tell him and make him squirm. I'll tell him what you became because you believed me, not him. I won, I won, I won. Do you understand, you big lump?'

She did understand, perfectly. She had never mattered at all. *Hatred; dislike; indifference; contempt.* She had never even merited any of these. Amy got out of bed, naked. There was a small ration of space in the room. Her clothes were over the chair in which he sat and she needed the armour of clothes. Kicking her way out of the blanket, she knocked over the teacup he had left; the sharp stench of white spirit was sickening. He leapt from the chair and backed towards the window; stood there gazing at her. The laughter died. His face was contorted with disgust.

'Look what Douglas can never have. Christ. And you thought I cared about *you*? You were only a means to an end. You aren't even an *enemy*. You're *nothing*.'

'What about my money?'

'*Your* money? I deserve that for keeping you.'

She loomed above him, trembling, feeling for the clothes and staring him in the eyes. Rollie put his hand over his mouth and stumbled from the room. She heard his clumsy thumping down the stairs, the chanting voice drifting back, '*I won, I won, I won . . .*'

She yanked back the curtains with such force they tore in her hands. Later afternoon daylight, diffused with clouds. The sounds of a street full of hidden eyes. Music through the wall from next door. She did not want daylight; she wanted darkness.

The shoes were on the floor where he had left them. Her left foot slipped inside easily; the other was swollen. She could not wear his shoes. She dressed slowly in the new clothes, waited a while and followed him downstairs, barefoot. The door to his workroom stood open, presenting his theatre, ready for admirers, clean and swept and spotlit, the heavier curtains left partially open, so that the interior could be glimpsed from the outside. Houses and dolls built as honey traps a modern child could resist. He would be better to have lined his lair with computer games. On his workbench there was the almost finished shell of a new building, $\frac{1}{2}$ scale, balsawood, bigger than the others, the paint of its red roof still gleaming wet. Amy laced the fingers of both hands together into a single fist and brought the fist down like a hammer. The red roof crumpled. Such large, strong, capable hands she had. Her face burnt in the warmth of the spotlights; her mind registered the fantastical shapes of the houses and the years it had taken to make them.

She left the room.

In the kitchen, Rollie was slumped back in his habitual place, sleeping an unhealthy, noisy sleep with long, ragged breaths. Drink was a dangerous, unpredictable novelty. The whisky bottle stood where she had left it, empty. His arms were crossed over his slight tummy, his neck bent back and his throat exposed. He was like the one of his dolls she knew best, the defenceless master of the house, lolling in his chair. She could pull him apart in a minute. Her hands hovered above his thin throat, touched his paper skin. Not a real man; it would be a painless death; she could do it, it would be easy. She leant forward and whispered into his ear.

'What kind of man strangles love out of people, Daddy? Douglas didn't deserve you. He didn't make you guilty; you were guilty. You aren't fit to lick his shoes. All he does is tell the truth. He always does that. You can do what you like to me, but I'll kill you for hating him.' Her fingers tightened on his throat, her thumbs pressing into the flaccid flesh of the neck, harder, tightening around bone. She could shake him until he was dead, dead, dead. Douglas deserved enemies he could see and fight, not these cunning shadows. The touch of her father's skin repelled her; her paint-sticky hands smeared crimson against his chin; there was the reek of whisky-sour breath, bringing sanity. Then his eyes opened wide and looked straight into her own. Clouded eyes, widening in terror, closing again as she backed away, retreating until her hip collided with the sink. The empty bottle fell to the floor with a thud.

Amy washed her hands, repeatedly and compulsively. The red paint stuck. Real blood would be a different colour, almost brown. It was dark outside, the day gone. Nothing changed nature. She breathed deeply. Nothing changed what she was. If she killed him, she would murder herself. Then he would have won; that might be what he wanted. Part of the game, the bequest to Douglas

of a murderous wife, even better revenge than a desert-
ing, deceitful wife. Revenge was not hers, not now;
violence was unnatural to her, but she hated him, hated
him, hated him. She made herself breathe steadily and
look down at his smeared throat for a long time. Until,
through long concentration and an effort of will, all she
could see lying in the chair was an old, sick dog with
incurable diseases, a pathetic piece of existence. He was
also still a man she desperately wanted to hurt. He stirred,
opened his eyes again. 'Don't leave me,' he murmured.

'No,' she said.

His eyes closed; the ragged breathing resumed.

Amy went back to the room of the doll's houses. She
closed the curtains tight and shut the door behind her.

Now she was at the phone box. The phone stood by the
edge of the road, near the bus stop, defying anyone to
enter the bubble surrounding it to make themselves heard
over the traffic. A midnight phone for using when all the
lorries had gone to bed. She had lost all notion of time.
Amy dialled the number she knew by heart and heard the
neutral voice of a recording, speaking in clipped, elec-
tronic English, *please speak after the tone*. She heard herself
shouting back, 'Elisabeth, is that you?' Yelling into the
foul-smelling phone. *'Are you there, Elisabeth? Speak to
me, please. Can you come?'* Then a male voice, cutting
across her own. Jimmy's voice, shouting back, *'Amy! Amy!
Hallo, hallo, hallooooo!'* Slammed back the phone as she
realised what she had done. Dialled home. Silly, silly, silly.

She paused for a deep breath and dialled the other

number she had learned by heart and meant to dial the first time. Slightly calmer, she heard the same, neutral voice and left a message. '*Elisabeth, please come. Come and save me from myself. Please.*'

There was a man outside the bubble, waiting. He seemed to be waiting for her. He stared at her bright red hands, tear-streaked face, wild eyes and bare feet and backed away.

The traffic was lighter and faster. Cars whined into sight and whined away, speeding into the night. They moved faster, this time of night. Amy paused at the edge of the kerb, listening to the murderous hum of engines. It would be so easy, so simple to run amongst them. Better than going *home*. If she went home and her father taunted her with his triumph over Douglas, she might still stab him. She was feverish with rage; she could do anything.

Amy walked barefoot, parallel with the traffic. Red paint smeared the front of the new tracksuit. The trousers were covered with multicoloured dust and fragments, and she did not know from where they came. The Asda sign she had never noticed winked in the distance and she suddenly remembered her father's phrase. '. . . *must have loved you to death . . . he'd forgive you anything.*'

She opened the palm of her hand and saw that she was clutching a single pound coin, nothing else.

The lights of the cars tantalised her.

The light at the end of the tunnel is the train coming in the other direction.

CHAPTER SIXTEEN

Elisabeth hated the watery light of early morning 'C'mon, c'mon . . .' she fretted. *Come and save me.* That was what Amy said. What could she have done at midnight but wait for morning? Nothing.

There was a *tick, tick, ticky* sound. *Tick, tick, tick.* This was a sick train, sulking while a few of them stood on the platform, waiting for permission to board. *Tick, tick, SHIT.* There was something wrong with it. The ticking mimicked the racing of her heart.

Elisabeth sat on a bench with her hands pressed between the backs of her legs and the metal, all the better to resist chewing her fingernails. The metal was early-morning moist and scaldingly cold. It was the wrong time for a train to break down, although there was a kind of relief in the delay. Better to travel hopefully. *Tick, tick . . . sigh*; a human, scolding sound, mocking anxiety.

Six-thirty a.m., in time for the first train in the

doubtful light. Elisabeth removed her hands to the pockets of her jacket. There was a Saturday-morning sprinkling of people, nothing like the weekday commuter crowd, all of these hell-bent on innocent pleasures. She should have set off the night before, only she had not. *Should have, should have . . . shoodav, shoodav*, a pointless recrimination sounding like the train, but the darkness had taken away courage. *Should* have been at home when Amy rang. Should *not* have phoned John at home and heard the icy voice of his wife saying, 'Do you know what time this is, Miss Manser? Of course you can't speak to him.' Exercising the inalienable rights of a protective spouse.

The train fell silent, then stuttered into life with a show of vigour, became a lazy animal recovering from a dawn chill, responding to the weak heat of the sun on the carriage roofs, deciding that movement was preferable. Orders were shouted; everyone got on and settled down, none of them, except a mother and daughter, sitting together. The carriage gathered speed in the interludes of countryside between stations, too fast for her uncertain digestion, although the movement was better than staying still. It meant progress, a sense of purpose, as if she was driving the thing herself, a lulling of the gnawing anxiety, and it meant having to do nothing for a little while. Which presented the fact that she did not know what she was doing anyway. Running in the direction of Amy's danger, like a headless chicken; running away from a severe policeman, responding without planning. Typical. She chewed her nails. Why the hell hadn't she just called them first? The one thing she could do was use a phone. But there was that bloody promise of two days' silence, which seemed insane in daylight, even though it made sense the night before. Fear, that was all it was, fear and cowardice that made her wait. What the hell she was going to do when she got to Bayview Road she had no idea. Drag Amy away by the scruff of her neck, as if she was a fighting cat? Take her home? Find a way to deliver this piece of property back into the hands of its rightful owner, like a lost dog which might well be beaten by its master for the crime of its defection? She would be sick with relief if she found Amy feeding some old dog. That would be fine, but she would be too late and it would be her own fault. Rollie Fisher might have killed her. Elisabeth yearned for coffee while knowing it would only make her shake; it always had that effect the morning after the night before, even if the hangover was purely emotional. *Do you know what time this is, Miss Manser? Can't it wait until morning?* This journey was unbearably lonely.

She thought of other journeys on this train, to and from, always on her own, and knew this was the loneliest of all. She had not asked Helen for help; she was disgusted with Helen. She had wanted John's help, forgotten it was never really there. So she had tried sleep instead and regretted it now.

The Lloyds tower was visible in a blue sky, giving the illusion of closeness to a city signposted by similar obelisks. More passengers had joined at the intermediate stops, a tribe of men going north for a football match, girls with sportsbags, team players all. With her gaze fixed outside the window, Elisabeth nursed the handbag on her knee, half waiting for a crash, until someone occupied the seat beside her. She angled both body and handbag further towards the window. A hand poked her arm; she turned her head, ready to glare.

'Oh *fuck.*'

There was Jimmy, with his crumpled brown face like a paper bag, his finger on his lips, saying, 'Shhhhh.' The evening before was a distant dream, far further away than a matter of hours. His face was remote enough to surprise her; it was out of context. It did not belong on a train; it belonged on a planet where trains and cities did not exist. She felt shocked at the sight of him. Jimmy belonged somewhere else, and all the same, she was numb with relief.

'I've seen you looking better, Liz. Not used to getting up early in the morning, are we?'

She clenched her hands around the handbag and turned her head back to the window. A blush was spreading over her face and she was furious, the pulse pounding again. The fury sank into a flutter of irritation, followed by resignation. No one could keep secrets; they were infectious, with the hidden life of a virus, spread by the sheer act of breathing, and she was glad not to be alone. So pleased, she could have screamed and hugged him. There was *someone*. Even a rude, aggressive bundle of skinny muscle and bone like Jimmy was someone.

'You look like a piece of shit yourself,' she said.

'Ah, but that's normal.'

She frowned and stayed silent, lost for words. The train

stopped at London Bridge at a side platform flanked by dark and sinister brickwork, a platform to avoid at night. There was an exodus of the football party, the train moved off again, moaning and groaning in a slow crawl over complicated tracks. Jimmy clutched her arm fiercely, so that his fingers dug through the fabric of her sleeve.

'I never go on trains,' he said. 'Fucking things scare me to death.'

'Shame.'

'She phoned last night,' Jimmy said tremulously, still clutching her arm. 'By mistake. Asking for you. Always was dysfuckinglexic with numbers, Amy. Know that voice anywhere. I didn't tell him, I just came over to follow you.'

She suppressed the joyous relief that he had. There seemed no point in explanation or denial. 'Why didn't you tell him?'

'He might fucking murder you for not saying you knew where she was. Though God knows why, he guessed you did. I fucking didn't, not until she called by mistake. I knew then he was right. Oh, Jesus Christ, look at that,' he said, still holding her arm with one hand and pointing out of the window with the other. 'Will you just look at that?'

The Millennium Wheel rose above the river as if it owned the landscape, including the gleaming, moving expanse of the river below. The train slid into the darkness of the station. Jimmy dragged at the strap of her handbag like a dog on a lead.

'You're going to see her, aren't you, I know you are. I've been waiting outside your house. We need to bring

her back, he'll have those two out by this afternoon.'
Jimmy spoke like a spluttering firework.

'Because of Amy?'

'Aye, because of Amy.'

'That might not be the problem, Jimmy. She's got this
father who's an ex-con . . . paedophile. That's where she is.'

'So what fucking difference will that make to
Douglas?' Jimmy shouted, missing the point entirely. 'It'll
be the same bastard been writing him hate-mail for years.
Besides, his own father was a fucking crook.' He tugged at
the window, slamming it down, ready to jump, poised on
the step, ready to run.

'Her father hates her, Jimmy. He's filled her with lies.
She's coming apart . . . he might be dangerous.' To her
horror, she could feel tears welling in her eyes.

Jimmy stood on the platform, hands on hips, a bantamweight man with the physique of a terrier. 'Don't even
think of fucking *crying*. Why didn't you say so, for God's
sake? Just take us.'

She was fumbling in her handbag for her purse,
unconsciously mimicking the way he was feeling in his
pockets for tobacco. 'I need cash for the taxi.'

His brown hand produced a wad of notes, bunched in
his fist.

Taxis did not want to go to SE23. Jimmy kept the notes
visible until one of them did. The morning was fine, clear,
calm, the population harmless. Cruising through the City,
she was struck by the irrelevant wish that Jimmy had
brought one of the dogs. The cityscape rolled by; the

details went unnoticed. He was entirely unmoved by the Westminster spires and the density of buildings.

'Her father might try to poison her,' Elisabeth said wildly. 'He might have tried to kill her.'

Jimmy turned his head from the window. 'You don't know Amy, do you?' he said.

Elisabeth shook her head. 'No, I don't know her at all.'

It was a quiet street when they reached it. Not as ugly as she remembered. Just another street where people lived and breathed and nothing much happened.

There was a figure in the doorway of number twelve. A crumpled heap of dirty clothes, sleeping. Emerging on touch into a woman. The overlong trouser bottoms covered her feet. She uncurled and stood upright, unsteadily, revealing cold, bare feet. Squinting at them. Smiling that deceptively vacuous smile, which embraced them both and gave no indication that she had expected to see them, only hoped.

'Hallo,' Amy said. 'I forgot my keys. Aren't you glad I forgot my keys? It means I haven't killed him.'

'. . . *The house was so dark*,' Elisabeth wrote to John at the very end of the day. '*Darker than I remembered. It faced east, I think; a dark, cold house. It would have killed your spirit to live in it the way it was. There was so much newspaper in it. Thank God for Jimmy. It was him who broke down the door and went upstairs and found Rollie Fisher in his bed. Not dead, the bastard. Not even dying. He kept saying SHE'S DONE FOR ME, SHE'S DONE FOR ME. He was sleeping with his*

*bedroom door barricaded and a range of broken miniature dolls
by his bed. He was gibbering. Jimmy cleaned him up and got an
ambulance on his mobile. They said, who'll be here when we
bring him back? I said no one, none of us were relatives, only
passing strangers. I can be heartless, sometimes.*

'*The doll's house room (see above, if you haven't been following) was a pile of rubble. Everything smashed to
smithereens. Who did this, I asked Amy. She was frozen, not
monosyllabic, but oddly composed, as if something was settled.
"It will take him a long time to put them together," she told
me. Looking at the carnage was the only time I felt regret for
him. I told her they were beautiful creations as I remembered
them, and she said that all depended on why they were made.
I didn't understand. She kept on saying how glad she was she
had forgotten to take the keys when she went to phone. There
was red paint on his neck. He screamed when he saw her, I
don't know why. She said thank you to him. Thank you for
what you said about some people loving each other to death.*

'*I said we would take her home. When I said that, she
trembled so much, I thought she would shake to pieces, but
there was not much choice. And I knew I had to go with her.
Protect her, and I can't tell you how much I dreaded that. She
wanted to wash and borrow makeup, fretted about her
shoes . . . Ah, I can hear you say, the priorities of women.*

'*I wondered why her father was suddenly so afraid of her.
Gentleness, thy name is Amy. I thought the danger came from
him, but it was him who was afraid . . .*'

Cash talks and cash hires cars. There was piercing, dappled sunshine through the trees, the beginning of a

brilliant June before the rain as they emerged from the town and into the valley. All three of them were in the back of another car with Elisabeth in the middle. They were going home. Amy was dozing, with her head leaning against the window, eyes closed, like a person dreaming for courage. Jimmy was calm and whistling.

'Is this really the right thing to do?' Elisabeth whispered.

'What else to do?'

'She could come and stay with me.'

He stopped whistling. 'Nope. My job is to bring her home. She wants to go.'

'Does she? What are you Jimmy, a bounty hunter?'

He looked at her scornfully. 'You know what, Miss fucking Manser, I reckon that somewhere in between yesterday and today, Amy got to understand something, which is more than you ever seem to do.'

'Understand what?'

'The nature of the beast,' he said. 'The one who goes by scent and instinct, just like she does. You don't know anything.'

Elisabeth subsided into her seat. 'He could have come and fetched her,' she said.

'I told him, no. He would have crashed the car.'

The whistling resumed.

The car stopped by the side of the house. All three of them crossed the lawn, their figures casting shadows. Elisabeth stayed close to Amy, looking up at the white façade of the house, noticing that the windows of the big room were bare. Douglas shambled out of the French

doors like a bear, moving at a run. Elisabeth put her hand
on Amy's arm, pulling her back. Amy pushed her aside,
gently, and went towards him, unconscious of anyone
else. Not Jimmy or the dogs keeping a distance. The two
of them collided, slowly, as if conscious of their fragility.
Then they were hugging, Douglas crying like a helpless
child and murmuring over and over, *Oh, you silly bitch,
you sillybitch, my dearest sillybitch, my darling* . . . They
could have been surrounded by fire and never noticed.
With the peculiar, intoxicated walk of addicted lovers,
arms entwined, they disappeared inside the house, leaving
the swishing salutation of the willow tree.

Jimmy had turned away, shuffling in his pockets for the
fags.

Elisabeth tried to stay cool, like a fucking lawyer. 'The
nature of the beast?' she asked, voice quavering.

'Yeah, tha's it,' he sniffed. 'It's not what you fucking say
that counts. It's what you do. Who needs fucking discussions? Animals don't need them.'

She could hear the sound of barking in the distance.

Jimmy adjusted the cigarette. 'I'll have to feed the dogs.
C'mon with me. Nobody needs us here.'

She felt peculiarly light-headed, followed down the
path to the stables, turning back to look at the house.

Much later, going home on the train, she cried and
cried and cried and tried to compose the words she
should use to tell all this to John Box, while knowing she
could never explain to him the nature of the beast.

CHAPTER SEVENTEEN

Rain, relentless rain, persisting through Saturday night and all of Sunday. Appropriate rain; rain was her background for writing and reading and confessing, sitting in her tiny kitchen with Helen West's policeman, an uncritical confessor, better than a priest and far more sympathetic. A discursive man with a surreptitious notebook; a person who forced her to analyse. To the tune of the rain, Elisabeth Manser found it all too easy to cry. Sundays, he told her, were always sad days.

There were phone calls. Many.

It still rained on the Tuesday morning, when John Box and Elisabeth Manser met inside the portico of the High Court entrance.

'You're late,' he said.

'The train was late. Weather.'

He looked at the grey clouds and felt for his

handkerchief. Today's was a paper napkin from Starbucks. He looked as he felt, uncertain and exposed.

'I got your letter,' he said. 'One from Douglas, too.' His face was haggard; for a moment, Elisabeth pitied him. They walked inside, beyond the phalanx of security desks, and sat beneath the vaulted ceilings on the cold stone bench which ran along the side. The rain dulled the light from the stained-glass windows.

'You mustn't send letters to home,' he said, putting the handkerchief back into his pocket. 'And you should have told me sooner.'

She could feel the hardening of her heart, looked at him and wondered what it was she had so found to admire. It was his cleverness most of all, the presence of a fine brain behind a noble forehead, an articulate mind and a seductive voice. She always remembered voices. She had expected to be nervous, but she was nerveless.

'I suppose I should have done. But you were never there to be told. And I couldn't communicate on a Sunday, could I? So I wrote you the letter. I've got into the habit of writing. The news will break tomorrow. Newspapers will have a field day. You needed to know.'

He nodded. 'There'll be an uproar, I suppose. No doubt the Pettys will retain you to help with the fallout.'

There was a trace of bitterness in his voice; a touch of jealousy. She had stolen the client.

'So they say, but I doubt if I'm diplomatic enough. Besides, they don't need help. They have each other. They won't care about being libelled or scorned. They just don't care. They know what they are . . .' Her voice broke.

She coughed and recovered, kept her voice light and her hands stuffed in her pockets, still wanting to touch him. 'Listen, my dearest dear, am I wrong or am I right? Nod once, or twice for the latter. You set up the whole libel, didn't you? No, *you* didn't. Caterina came to you with it all tied up neatly in a package. Video and photos ready to roll, friends in the trade ready to grab. Outraged victim, encouraged by his sister, everything ready primed and big damages a safe enough gamble. An anonymous journalist gets it all past the night lawyer for a share. You knew none of it was true before we started.'

'That wasn't quite how she put it . . .'

'*Fuck* the way she put it. You followed a lie for the money.'

He winced. He was a handsome man, in his slender, aesthetic way, generous sometimes, a skilful, patient lover. She would miss him. 'It could have been a lot of money, Elisabeth. It could have been freedom.'

She looked at him as she might a stranger on a train, with dispassionate curiosity.

'Freedom to be with you,' he said. 'We make a good team.'

Elisabeth shook her head, hoisted her handbag and walked away. Her footsteps were loud on the mosaic floor, moving smartly towards the rain. Endings were best kept brief.

ENDPIECE

September

Dear Helen,

I still can't write this report. Not even with numbered paragraphs. Rescue me.

I hope you preferred the way I told it to you, in chapters, with scenes. How many bottles of wine went into the telling? I've lost count. And you still think I should write an official report, for the sake of my legal intellect, to say nothing of my reputation.

But I keep getting sidetracked by REPUTATION. What a flimsy construction it is. A cardboard edifice, built on only the most obvious impressions. Such as being blonde and shy, short-tempered and loud, well-dressed and calm, rough or smooth, old and harmless. All made of paper. Take Douglas. I always assumed he was capable of beastliness, without a scintilla of evidence that he had ever done anyone harm. Rather the opposite; he always did what he said he would do, a strange sort of weakness. I can understand him better than Amy.

Because she did kill her father in the end. Effectively. She smashed the doll's houses. I know in my bones that she did that; it was woman's work. She could not have killed a living thing; she did worse. She took his lures and his real reason for living, left him with the wreckage. She emasculated him and rendered him harmless. I can see her in that room, destroying everything bit by bit. I don't know if she locked herself out before or after, but she did it and left him with nothing. There's more violence in that, to my mind, than a straightforward throttling. She had her revenge; she may be the strongest of them all, and if I were her enemy, I would watch my step.

I don't think she did it for herself. She did it out of anger for Douglas. And it was her father's perception of how much Douglas loved her which made her know she could go home. So he did something for her after all. I'm guessing that part. Maybe she simply came to understand that he could love her as much as she loved him, and if she found there was nothing to forgive, then so would he.

I can't write this fucking cathartic report for other reasons. I've got better things to do. I'm aware that you and your peers, you wise ones whose voices form the choir of authority, have made your decisions about the murder on the train. NO CASE, you say, on account of a dearth of reliable witnesses, the chief of whom is an attention-seeking blonde with big tits and a fevered imagination, who might well have been in the throes of a nervous breakdown at the time, corroborated only

by a bolshie trolley man who hates uniforms and won't say
nothing. Not to the likes of you, anyway. You also take the
view that the victim of the murder was no better than she
should be because she was obviously having an affair. I may
be a lousy lawyer, but this officious, defeatist, hypocritical attitude completely enrages me. I'm going to find the truth, if it
kills me. Nobody should get away with wanton murder. Not
even a lover. Not even on a train. Watch this space.

I don't know much about love, any more than I did when
I started, only to have the vain imagination that I might now
recognise it when I see it. What about you?

Anyway, must rush. This fellow, Jimmy, is driving round
with a bottle. The cat adores him. I find I rather like politically
incorrect endearments, and I've always had a thing about
skinny men. Besides, I no longer give a shit where a man
keeps his brains.

Love,
Elisabeth.